# HISTORY OF HOLLAND

Copyright © 2007 BiblioBazaar
All rights reserved
ISBN: 978-1-4346-2512-0

Original copyright: 1922

GEORGE EDMUNDSON

SOMETIME FELLOW OF BRASENOSE COLLEGE,
OXFORD HON. MEMBER OF THE DUTCH
HISTORICAL SOCIETY, UTRECHT FOREIGN
MEMBER OF THE NETHERLAND SOCIETY OF
LITERATURE, LEYDEN

# HISTORY OF HOLLAND

**BIBLIO**BAZAAR

# HISTORY OF HOLLAND

# GENERAL PREFACE

*The aim of this series is to sketch the history of Modern Europe, with that of its chief colonies and conquests, from about the end of the fifteenth century down to the present time. In one or two cases the story commences at an earlier date; in the case of the colonies it generally begins later. The histories of the different countries are described, as a rule, separately; for it is believed that, except in epochs like that of the French Revolution and Napoleon I, the connection of events will thus be better understood and the continuity of historical development more clearly displayed.*

*The series is intended for the use of all persons anxious to understand the nature of existing political conditions. 'The roots of the present lie deep in the past'; and the real significance of contemporary events cannot be grasped unless the historical causes which have led to them are known. The plan adopted makes it possible to treat the history of the last four centuries in considerable detail, and to embody the most important results of modern research. It is hoped therefore that the series will be useful not only to beginners but to students who have already acquired some general knowledge of European History. For those who wish to carry their studies further, the bibliography appended to each volume will act as a guide to original sources of information and works of a more special character.*

*Considerable attention is paid to political geography; and each volume is furnished with such maps and plans as may be requisite for the illustration of the text.*

G.W. PROTHERO.

# PROLOGUE

The title, "History of Holland," given to this volume is fully justified by the predominant part which the great maritime province of Holland took in the War of Independence and throughout the whole of the subsequent history of the Dutch state and people. In every language the country, comprising the provinces of Holland, Zeeland, Utrecht, Friesland, Gelderland, Overyssel and Groningen, has, from the close of the sixteenth century to our own day, been currently spoken of as Holland, and the people (with the solitary exception of ourselves) as 'Hollanders[1].' It is only rarely that the terms the Republic of the United Provinces, or of the United Netherlands, and in later times the Kingdom of the Netherlands, are found outside official documents. Just as the title "History of England" gradually includes the histories of Wales, of Scotland, of Ireland, and finally of the widespread British Empire, so is it in a smaller way with the history that is told in the following pages. That history, to be really complete, should begin with an account of mediaeval Holland in the feudal times which preceded the Burgundian period; and such an account was indeed actually written, but the plan of this work, which forms one of the volumes of a series, precluded its publication.

The character, however, of the people of the province of Holland, and of its sister and closely allied province of Zeeland, its qualities of toughness, of endurance, of seamanship and maritime enterprise, spring from the peculiar amphibious nature of the country, which differs from that of any other country in the world. The age-long struggle against the ocean and the river floods, which has converted the marshes, that lay around the mouths of the Rhine, the Meuse and the Scheldt, by toilsome labour and skill into fertile and productive soil, has left its impress on the whole history of this people. Nor must it be forgotten how largely this building up of the elaborate system of dykes, dams and canals by which this water-logged land was transformed into the Holland of the closing decades of the sixteenth century, enabled her people to offer such obstinate and successful resistance to the mighty power of Philip II.

The earliest dynasty of the Counts of Holland—Dirks, Floris, and Williams—was a very remarkable one. Not only did it rule for an unusually long period, 922 to 1299, but in this long period without exception all the Counts of Holland were strong and capable rulers. The fiefs of the first two Dirks lay in what is now known as North Holland, in the district called Kennemerland. It was Dirk III who seized from the bishops of Utrecht some swampy land amidst the channels forming the mouth of the Meuse, which, from the bush which covered it, was named Holt-land (Holland or Wood-land). Here he erected, in 1015, a stronghold to collect tolls from passing ships. This stronghold was the beginning of the town of Dordrecht, and from here a little later the name Holland was gradually applied to the whole county. Of his successors the most illustrious was William II (1234 to 1256) who was crowned King of the Romans at Aachen, and would have received from Pope Innocent IV the imperial crown at Rome, had he not been unfortunately drowned while attempting to cross on horseback an ice-bound marsh.

In 1299 the male line of this dynasty became extinct; and John of Avennes, Count of Hainault, nephew of William II, succeeded. His son, William III, after a long struggle with the Counts of Flanders, conquered Zeeland and became Count henceforth of Holland, Zeeland and Hainault. His son, William IV, died childless; and the succession then passed to his sister Margaret, the wife of the Emperor Lewis of Bavaria. It was contested by her second son William, who, after a long drawn-out strife with his mother, became, in 1354, Count of Holland and Zeeland with the title William V, Margaret retaining the county of Hainault. Becoming insane, his brother Albert in 1358 took over the reins of government. In his time the two factions, known by the nicknames of "the Hooks" and "the Cods," kept the land in a continual state of disorder and practically of civil war. They had already been active for many years. The Hooks were supported by the nobles, by the peasantry and by that large part of the poorer townsfolk that was excluded from all share in the municipal government. The Cods represented the interests of the powerful burgher corporations. In later times these same principles and interests divided the Orangist and the States parties, and were inherited from the Hooks and Cods of mediaeval Holland. The marriages of Albert's son, William, with Margaret the sister of John the Fearless, Duke of Burgundy, and of John the Fearless with Albert's daughter, Margaret, were to have momentous consequences. Albert died in 1404 and was succeeded by William VI, who before his death in 1417 caused the nobles and towns to take the oath of allegiance to his daughter and only child, Jacoba or Jacqueline.[2]

Jacoba, brave, beautiful and gifted, for eleven years maintained her rights against many adversaries, chief among them her powerful and ambitious cousin, Philip the Good, Duke of Burgundy. Her courage and many adventures transformed her into a veritable heroine of romance. By her three marriages with John, Duke of Brabant, with Humphry, Duke of Gloucester, and, finally, with Frans van Borselen, she had no children. Her hopeless fight with Philip of Burgundy's superior resources ended at last in the so-called "Reconciliation of Delft" in 1428, by which, while retaining the title of countess, she handed over the government to Philip and acknowledged his right of succession to the Countship upon her death, which took place in 1436.

G.E.<br>
*November*, 1921

# CONTENTS

   I  THE BURGUNDIAN NETHERLANDS............ 17
  II  HABSBURG RULE IN THE NETHERLANDS ... 28
 III  THE PRELUDE TO THE REVOLT ..................... 43
  IV  THE REVOLT OF THE NETHERLANDS ....... 63
   V  WILLIAM THE SILENT ......................................... 86
  VI  THE BEGINNINGS OF THE DUTCH
      REPUBLIC ................................................................. 99
 VII  THE SYSTEM OF GOVERNMENT.................. 127
VIII  THE TWELVE YEARS' TRUCE.......................... 136
  IX  MAURICE AND OLDENBARNEVELDT....... 144
   X  FROM THE END OF THE TWELVE YEARS'
      TRUCE TO THE PEACE OF MUENSTER
      (1621-48). THE STADHOLDERATE OF
      FREDERICK HENRY OF ORANGE ................ 156
  XI  THE EAST AND WEST INDIA COMPANIES.
      COMMERCIAL AND ECONOMIC
      EXPANSION ............................................................ 176
 XII  LETTERS, SCIENCE AND ART ........................ 203
XIII  THE STADHOLDERATE OF WILLIAM II............
      THE GREAT ASSEMBLY..................................... 220
 XIV  THE RISE OF JOHN DE WITT.
      THE FIRST ENGLISH WAR................................ 230
  XV  THE ADMINISTRATION OF
      JOHN DE WITT 1654-1665
      FROM THE PEACE OF WESTMINSTER
      TO THE OUT-BREAK OF THE SECOND
      ENGLISH WAR ....................................................... 244

| XVI | THE LAST YEARS OF DE WITT'S ADMINISTRATION, 1665-1672. THE SECOND ENGLISH WAR. THE TRIPLE ALLIANCE. THE FRENCH INVASION .......... 255 |
|---|---|
| XVII | WAR WITH FRANCE AND ENGLAND. WILLIAM III, STADHOLDER. MURDER OF THE BROTHERS DE WITT, 1672 ..................... 270 |
| XVIII | THE STADHOLDERATE OF WILLIAM III, 1672-1688 ................................................................ 277 |
| XIX | THE KING-STADHOLDER, 1688-1702 ........... 293 |
| XX | THE WAR OF THE SPANISH SUCCESSION AND THE TREATIES OF UTRECHT, 1702-1715 ................................................................ 304 |
| XXI | THE STADHOLDERLESS REPUBLIC, 1715-1740 ................................................................ 318 |
| XXII | THE AUSTRIAN SUCCESSION WAR. WILLIAM IV, 1740-1751 ......................................... 326 |
| XXIII | THE REGENCY OF ANNE AND OF BRUNSWICK. 1751-1766 ......................................... 337 |
| XXIV | WILLIAM V. FIRST PERIOD, 1766-1780 .......... 342 |
| XXV | STADHOLDERATE OF WILLIAM V, *continued*, 1780-1788 ..................................................... 348 |
| XXVI | THE ORANGE RESTORATION. DOWNFALL OF THE REPUBLIC, 1788-1795 ........................... 359 |
| XXVII | THE BATAVIAN REPUBLIC, 1795-1806 .......... 366 |
| XXVIII | THE KINGDOM OF HOLLAND AND THE FRENCH ANNEXATION, 1806-1814 ..... 379 |
| XXIX | THE FORMATION OF THE KINGDOM OF THE NETHERLANDS, 1814-1815 ............... 390 |
| XXX | THE KINGDOM OF THE NETHERLANDS— UNION OF HOLLAND AND BELGIUM, 1815-1830 ................................................................ 399 |
| XXXI | THE BELGIAN REVOLUTION, 1830-1842 .... 413 |
| XXXII | WILLIAM II. REVISION OF THE CONSTITUTION. 1842-1849 ................................ 429 |
| XXXIII | REIGN OF WILLIAM III TO THE DEATH OF THORBECKE, 1849-1872 ..................... 435 |

| XXXIV | THE LATER REIGN OF WILLIAM III, AND THE REGENCY OF QUEEN EMMA, 1872-1898 | 443 |
| XXXV | THE REIGN OF QUEEN WILHELMINA, 1898-1917 | 451 |

EPILOGUE ............................................................................... 455
FOOTNOTES: ......................................................................... 461
BIBLIOGRAPHY ..................................................................... 463
MAPS
    THE NETHERLANDS, about 1550 ............................. 479
    THE NETHERLANDS, after 1648

# CHAPTER I

# THE BURGUNDIAN NETHERLANDS

The last duke of the ancient Capetian house of Burgundy dying in 1361 without heirs male, the duchy fell into the possession of the French crown, and was by King John II bestowed upon his youngest son, Philip the Hardy, Duke of Touraine, as a reward, it is said, for the valour he displayed in the battle of Poictiers. The county of Burgundy, generally known as Franche-Comté, was not included in this donation, for it was an imperial fief; and it fell by inheritance in the female line to Margaret, dowager Countess of Flanders, widow of Count Louis II, who was killed at Crécy. The duchy and the county were soon, however, to be re-united, for Philip married Margaret, daughter and heiress of Louis de Male, Count of Flanders, and granddaughter of the above-named Margaret. In right of his wife he became, on the death of Louis de Male in 1384, the ruler of Flanders, Mechlin, Artois, Nevers and Franche-Comté. Thus the foundation was laid of a great territorial domain between France and Germany, and Philip the Hardy seems from the first to have been possessed by the ambitious design of working for the restoration of a powerful middle kingdom, which should embrace the territories assigned to Lothaire in the tripartite division of the Carolingian empire by the treaty of Verdun (843). For this he worked ceaselessly during his long reign of forty years, and with singular ability and courage. Before his death he had by the splendour of his court, his wealth and his successes in arms and diplomacy, come to be recognised as a sovereign of great weight and influence, in all but name a king. The Burgundian policy and tradition, which he established, found in his successors John the Fearless (murdered in 1419) and John's son, Philip the Good, men of like character and filled with the same ambitions as himself. The double marriage of John with Margaret, the sister of William VI of Holland, and of William VI with Margaret of Burgundy, largely helped forward their projects of aggrandisement. Philip the Good was, however, a much abler ruler than his father, a far-seeing statesman, who pursued his plans with a patient and unscrupulous pertinacity, of which a conspicuous example is to be found in his long protracted struggle with his cousin Jacoba, the only child and heiress of William of Holland, whose misfortunes and courage have made her one of the most romantic figures of history. By a mixture of force and intrigue Philip, in 1433, at last compelled Jacoba to abdicate, and he became Count of Holland, Zeeland and Hainault. Nor was this by any means the end of his acquisitions. Joanna, Duchess of Brabant (1355-1404) in her own right, was aunt on the mother's side to Margaret of Flanders, wife of Philip the Hardy. Dying without heirs, she bequeathed Brabant, Limburg and Antwerp to her great-nephew, Anthony of Burgundy, younger brother of John the Fearless. Anthony was killed at Agincourt and was succeeded first by his son John IV, the husband of Jacoba of Holland, and on his death without an heir in 1427, by his second son, Philip of St Pol, who also died childless in 1430. From him his cousin Philip the Good inherited the duchies of Brabant and Limburg and the marquisate of Antwerp. Already he had purchased in 1421 the territory of Namur from the last Count John III, who had fallen into heavy debt; and in 1443 he likewise purchased the duchy of Luxemburg from the Duchess Elizabeth of Görlitz, who had married in second wedlock Anthony, Duke of Brabant, and afterwards John of Bavaria, but who had no children by either of her marriages. Thus in 1443 Philip had become by one means or another sovereign under various titles of the largest and most important part of the Netherlands, and he increased his influence by securing in 1456 the election of his illegitimate son David, as Bishop of Utrecht. Thus a great step forward had been taken for the restoration of the middle kingdom, which had been the dream of Philip the Hardy, and which now seemed to be well-nigh on the point of accomplishment.

The year 1433, the date of the incorporation of Holland and Zeeland in the Burgundian dominion, is therefore a convenient starting-point for a consideration of the character of the Burgundian rule in the Netherlands, and of the changes which the concentration of sovereign power in the hands of a single ruler brought into the relations of the various provinces with one another and into their internal administration. The Netherlands become now for the first time something more than a geographical expression for a number of petty feudal states, practically independent and almost always at strife. Henceforward there was peace; and throughout the whole of this northern part of his domains it was the constant policy of Philip gradually to abolish provincialism and to establish a centralised government. He was far too wise a statesman to attempt to abolish suddenly or arbitrarily the various rights and privileges, which the Flemings, Brabanters and Hollanders had wrung from their sovereigns, and to which they were deeply attached; but, while respecting these, he endeavoured to restrict them as far as possible to local usage, and to centralise the general administration of the whole of the "pays de par deçà" (as the Burgundian dukes were accustomed to name their Netherland dominions) by the summoning of representatives of the Provincial States to an assembly styled the States-General, and by the creation of a common Court of Appeal.

The first time the States-General were called together by Philip was in 1465 for the purpose of obtaining a loan for the war with France and the recognition of his son Charles as his successor; and from this time forward at irregular intervals, but with increasing frequency, the practice of summoning this body went on. The States-General (in a sense) represented the Netherlands as a whole; and it was a matter of great convenience for the sovereign, especially when large levies of money had to be raised, to be enabled thus to bring his proposals before a single assembly, instead of before a number of separate and independent provincial states. Nevertheless, it must be borne in mind that the States-General had, as such, no authority to act on behalf of these several provincial states. Each of these sent their deputies to the General Assembly, but these deputies had to refer all matters to their principals before they could give their assent, and each body of deputies gave this assent separately, and without regard to the others. It was thus but a first provisional step towards unity of administration, but it did tend to promote a feeling of community of interests between the provinces and to lead to the deputies having intercourse with one another and interchanging their views upon the various important subjects that were brought before their consideration. The period of disturbance and the weakening of the authority of the sovereign, which followed the death of Charles the Bold, led to the States-General obtaining a position of increased importance; and they may from that time be regarded as forming a regular and necessary part of the machinery of government in the Burgundian Netherlands. The States-General however, like the Provincial States, could only meet when summoned by the sovereign or his stadholder; and the causes for which they were summoned were such special occasions as the accession of a new sovereign or the appointment of a new stadholder, or more usually for sanctioning the requests for levies of money, which were required for the maintenance of splendid courts and the cost of frequent wars. For not only the Burgundian princes properly so-called, but even Charles V, had mainly to depend upon the wealth of the Netherlands for their financial needs. And here a distinction must be drawn. For solemn occasions, such as the accession of a new sovereign, or the acceptance of a newly appointed governor, representatives of all the provinces (eventually seventeen) were summoned, but for ordinary meetings for the purpose of money levies only those of the so-called patrimonial or old Burgundian provinces came together. The demands for tribute on the provinces acquired later, such as Gelderland, Groningen, Friesland and Overyssel, were made to each of these provinces separately, and they jealously claimed their right to be thus separately dealt with. In the case of the other provinces the States-General, as has been already stated, could only grant the money after obtaining from each province represented, severally, its assent; and this was often not gained until after considerable delay and much bargaining. Once granted, however, the assessment regulating the quota, which the different provinces had to contribute, was determined on the basis of the so-called *quotisatie* or *settinge* drawn up in 1462 on the occasion of a tribute for 10 years, which Charles the Bold, as his father's stadholder in the "pays de par deçà," then demanded. The relative wealth of the provinces may be judged from the fact that at this date Flanders and Brabant each paid a quarter of the whole levy, Holland one sixth, Zeeland one quarter of Holland's share.

As regards the provincial government the Burgundian princes left undisturbed the local and historical customs and usages, and each province had its individual characteristics. At the head of each provincial government (with the exception of Brabant, at whose capital, Brussels, the sovereign himself or his regent resided) was placed a governor, with the title of Stadholder, who was the representative of the sovereign and had large patronage. It was his duty to enforce edicts, preserve order, and keep a watchful eye over the administration of justice. He nominated to many municipal offices, but had little or no control over finance. The raising of troops and their command in the field was entrusted to a captain-general, who might not be the same person as the stadholder, though the offices were sometimes united. In the northern Netherlands there was but one stadholder for the three provinces of Holland, Zeeland and Utrecht, and one (at a somewhat later date) for Friesland, Groningen, Drente and Overyssel.

The desire of the Burgundian princes to consolidate their dominions into a unified sovereignty found itself thwarted by many obstacles and especially by the lack of any supreme tribunal of appeal. It was galling to them that the *Parlement* of Paris should still exercise appellate jurisdiction in Crown-Flanders and Artois, and the Imperial Diet in some of the other provinces. Already in 1428 Philip had erected the Court of Holland at the Hague to exercise large powers of jurisdiction and financial control in the provinces of Holland and Zeeland; and in 1473 Charles the Bold set up at Mechlin the body known as the Great Council, to act as a court of appeal from the provincial courts. It was to be, in the Netherlands, what the *Parlement* of Paris was in France. The Great Council, which had grown out of the Privy Council attached to the person of the prince, and which under the direction of the Chancellor of Burgundy administered the affairs of the government, more particularly justice and finance, was in 1473, as stated above, reconstituted as a Court of Appeal in legal matters, a new Chamber of Accounts being at the same time created to deal with finance. These efforts at centralisation of authority were undoubtedly for the good of the country as a whole, but such was the intensity of provincial jealousy and particularism that they were bitterly resented and opposed.

In order to strengthen the sovereign's influence in the towns, and to lessen the power of the Gilds, Philip established in Holland, and so far as he could elsewhere, what were called "vaste Colleges" or fixed committees of notables, to which were entrusted the election of the town officials and the municipal administration. These bodies were composed of a number of the richest and most influential burghers, who were styled the Twenty-four, the Forty, the Sixty or the Eighty, according to the number fixed for any particular town. These men were appointed for life and their successors were chosen by co-option, so that the town corporations gradually became closed hereditary aristocracies, and the mass of the citizens were deprived of all voice in their own affairs. The *Schout* or chief judge was chosen directly by the sovereign or his stadholder, who also nominated the *Schepens* or sheriffs from a list containing a double number, which was submitted to him.

The reign of Philip the Good was marked by a great advance in the material prosperity of the land. Bruges, Ghent, Ypres and Antwerp were among the most flourishing commercial and industrial cities in the world, and when, through the silting up of the waterway, Bruges ceased to be a seaport, Antwerp rapidly rose to pre-eminence in her place, so that a few decades later her wharves were crowded with shipping, and her warehouses with goods from every part of Europe. In fact during the whole of the Burgundian period the southern Netherlands were the richest domain in Christendom, and continued to be so until the disastrous times of Philip II of Spain. Meanwhile Holland and Zeeland, though unable to compete with Brabant and Flanders in the populousness of their towns and the extent of their trade, were provinces of growing importance. Their strength lay in their sturdy and enterprising seafaring population. The Hollanders had for many years been the rivals of the Hanse Towns for the Baltic trade. War broke out in 1438 and hostilities continued for three years with the result that the Hanse League was beaten, and henceforth the Hollanders were able without further let or hindrance more and more to become the chief carriers of the "Eastland" traffic. Amsterdam was already a flourishing port, though as yet it could make no pretension of competing with Antwerp. The herring fisheries were, however, the staple industry of Holland and Zeeland. The discovery of the art of curing herrings by William Beukelsz of Biervliet (died 1447) had converted a perishable article of food into a marketable commodity; and not only did the fisheries give lucrative employment to many thousands of the inhabitants of these maritime provinces, but they also became the foundation on which was to be built their future commercial supremacy.

The Burgundian dukes were among the most powerful rulers of their time—the equals of kings in all but name—and they far surpassed all contemporary sovereigns in their lavish display and the splendour of their court. The festival at Bruges in 1430 in celebration of the marriage of Philip the Good and Isabel of Portugal, at which the Order of the Golden Fleece was instituted, excited universal wonder; while his successor, Charles the Bold, contrived to surpass even his father in the splendour of his espousals with Margaret of York in 1468, and at his conference with the Emperor Frederick III at Trier in 1473. On this last occasion he wore a mantle encrusted all over with diamonds.

The foundation of the Order of the Golden Fleece in 1430 was an event of great importance, as marking a step forward on the part of Philip in its assumption of quasi-regal attributes. The title was very appropriate, for it pointed to the wool and cloth trade as being the source of the wealth of Flanders. The Order comprised thirty-one knights, chosen from the flower of the Burgundian nobles and the chief councillors of the sovereign. The statutes of the Order set forth in detail the privileges of the members, and their duties and obligations to their prince. They had a prescriptive claim to be consulted on all matters of importance, to be selected for the chief government posts, and to serve on military councils. The knights were exempt from the jurisdiction of all courts, save that of their own chapter.

Philip died in 1467 and was succeeded by his son, Charles, who had already exercised for some years authority in the Netherlands as his father's deputy. Charles, as his surname *le Téméraire* witnesses, was a man of impulsive and autocratic temperament, but at the same time a hard worker, a great organiser, and a brilliant soldier. Consumed with ambition to realise that restoration of a great middle Lotharingian kingdom stretching from the North Sea to the Mediterranean, for which his father had been working during his long and successful reign, he threw himself with almost passionate energy into the accomplishment of his task. With this object he was the first sovereign to depart from feudal usages and to maintain a standing army. He appeared at one time to be on the point of accomplishing his aim. Lorraine, which divided his southern from his northern possessions, was for a short time in his possession. Intervening in Gelderland between the Duke Arnold of Egmont and his son Adolf, he took the latter prisoner and obtained the duchy in pledge from the former. Uprisings in the Flemish towns against heavy taxation and arbitrary rule were put down with a strong hand. In September, 1474, the duke, accompanied by a splendid suite, met the emperor Frederick III at Trier to receive the coveted crown from the imperial hands. It was arranged that Charles' only daughter and heiress should be betrothed to Maximilian of Austria, the emperor's eldest son, and the very day and hour for the coronation were fixed. But the Burgundian had an enemy in Louis XI of France, who was as prudent and far-seeing as his rival was rash and impetuous, and who was far more than his match in political craft and cunning. French secret agents stirred up Frederick's suspicions against Charles' designs, and the emperor suddenly left Trier, where he had felt humiliated by the splendour of his powerful vassal.

The duke was furious at his disappointment, but was only the more obstinately bent on carrying out his plans. But Louis had been meanwhile forming a strong league (League of Constance, March 1474) of various states threatened by Charles' ambitious projects. Duke Sigismund of Austria, Baden, Basel, Elsass, and the Swiss Cantons united under the leadership of France to resist them. Charles led an army of 60,000 men to aid the Archbishop of Cologne against his subjects, but spent eleven months in a fruitless attempt to take a small fortified town, Neuss, in which a considerable portion of his army perished. He was compelled to raise large sums of money from his unwilling subjects in the Netherlands to repair his losses, and in 1475 he attacked Duke Réné of Lorraine, captured Nancy and conquered the duchy, which had hitherto separated his Netherland from his French possessions. It was the first step in the accomplishment of his scheme for the restoration of the Lotharingian kingdom. In Elsass, however, the populace had risen in insurrection against the tyranny of the Burgundian governor, Peter van Hagenbach, and had tried and executed him. Finding that the Swiss had aided the rebels, Charles now, without waiting to consolidate his conquest of Lorraine, determined to lead his army into Switzerland. At the head of a splendidly equipped force he encountered the Confederates near Granson (March 2, 1476) and was utterly routed, his own seal and order of the Golden Fleece, with vast booty, falling into the hands of the victors. A few months later, having recruited and reorganised his beaten army, he again led them against the Swiss. The encounter took place (June 21, 1476) at Morat and once more the chivalry of Burgundy suffered complete defeat. Charles fled from the field, half insane with rage and disappointment, when the news that Duke Réné had reconquered Lorraine roused him from his torpor. He hastily gathered together a fresh army and laid siege to Nancy. But in siege operations he had no skill, and in the depth of winter (January 5, 1477) he was attacked by the Swiss and Lorrainers outside the walls of the town. A panic seized the Burgundians; Charles in person in vain strove to stem their flight, and he perished by an unknown hand. His body was found later, stripped naked, lying frozen in a pool.

Charles left an only child, Mary, not yet twenty years of age. Mary found herself in a most difficult and trying situation. Louis XI, the hereditary enemy of her house, at once took possession of the duchy of Burgundy, which by failure of heirs-male had reverted to its liege-lord. The sovereignty of the county of Burgundy (Franche-Comté), being an imperial fief descending in the female line, she retained; but, before her authority had been established, Louis had succeeded in persuading the states of the county to place themselves under a French protectorate. French armies overran Artois, Hainault and Picardy, and were threatening Flanders, where there was in every city a party of French sympathisers. Gelderland welcomed the exiled duke, Adolf, as their sovereign. Everywhere throughout the provinces the despotic rule of Duke Charles and his heavy exactions had aroused seething discontent. Mary was virtually a prisoner in the hands of her Flemish subjects; and, before they consented to support her cause, there was a universal demand for a redress of grievances. But Mary showed herself possessed of courage and statesmanship beyond her years, and she had at this critical moment in her step-mother, Margaret of York, an experienced and capable adviser at her side. A meeting of the States-General was at once summoned to Ghent. It met on February 3, 1477, Mary's 20th birthday. Representatives came from Flanders, Brabant, Artois and Namur, in the southern, and from Holland and Zeeland in the northern Netherlands. Mary saw there was no course open to her but to accede to their demands.

Only eight days after the Assembly met, the charter of Netherland liberties, called The Great Privilege, was agreed to and signed. By this Act all previous ordinances conflicting with ancient privileges were abolished. The newly-established Court of Appeal at Mechlin was replaced by a Great Council of twenty-four members chosen by the sovereign from the various states, which should advise and assist in the administration of government. Mary undertook not to marry or to declare war without the assent of the States-General. The States-General and the Provincial States were to meet as often as they wished, without the summons of the sovereign. All officials were to be native-born; no Netherlander was to be tried by foreign judges; there were to be no forced loans, no alterations in the coinage. All edicts or ordinances infringing provincial rights were to be *ipso facto* null and void. By placing her seal to this document Mary virtually abdicated the absolute sovereign power which had been exercised by her predecessors, and undid at a stroke the results of their really statesmanlike efforts to create out of a number of semi-autonomous provinces a unified State. Many of their acts and methods had been harsh and autocratic, especially those of Charles the Bold, but who can doubt that on the whole their policy was wise and salutary? In Holland and Zeeland a Council was erected consisting of a Stadholder and eight councillors (six Hollanders and two Zeelanders) of whom two were to be nobles, the others jurists. Wolferd van Borselen, lord of Veere, was appointed Stadholder.

The Great Privilege granted, the States willingly raised a force of 34,000 men to resist the French invasion, and adequate means for carrying on the war. But the troubles of the youthful Mary were not yet over. The hand of the heiress of so many rich domains was eagerly sought for (1) by Louis of France for the dauphin, a youth of 17 years; (2) by Maximilian of Austria to whom she had been promised in marriage; (3) by Adolf, Duke of Gelderland, who was favoured by the States-General. Adolf, however, was killed in battle. In Flanders there was a party who favoured the French and actually engaged in intrigues with Louis, but the mass of the people were intensely averse to French domination. To such an extent was this the case that two influential officials, the lords Hugonet and Humbercourt, on whom suspicion fell of treacherous correspondence with the French king, were seized, tried by a special tribunal, and, despite the tears and entreaties of the duchess, were condemned and beheaded in the market-place of Ghent. Maximilian became therefore the accepted suitor; and on August 19, 1477, his marriage with Mary took place at Bruges. This marriage was to have momentous consequences, not only for the Netherlands, but for Europe. The union was a happy one, but, unfortunately, of brief duration. On March 29, 1482, Mary died from the effects of a fall from her horse, leaving two children, Philip and Margaret.

# CHAPTER II

# HABSBURG RULE IN THE NETHERLANDS

Maximilian, on the death of Mary, found himself in a very difficult position. The archduke was a man of high-soaring ideas, chivalrous, brave even to the point of audacity, full of expedients and never daunted by failure, but he was deficient in stability of character, and always hampered throughout his life by lack of funds. He had in 1477 set himself to the task of defending Flanders and the southern provinces of the Netherlands against French attack, and not without considerable success. In 1482, as guardian of his four-year old son Philip, the heir to the domains of the house of Burgundy, he became regent of the Netherlands. His authority however was little recognised. Gelderland and Utrecht fell away altogether. Liège acknowledged William de la Marck as its ruler. Holland and Zeeland were torn by contending factions. Flanders, the centre of the Burgundian power, was specially hostile to its new governor. The burghers of Ghent refused to surrender to him his children, Philip and Margaret, who were held as hostages to secure themselves against any attempted infringement of their liberties. The Flemings even entered into negotiations with Louis XI; and the archduke found himself compelled to sign a treaty with France (December 23, 1482), one of the conditions being the betrothal of his infant daughter to the dauphin. Maximilian, however, found that for a time he must leave Flanders to put down the rising of the Hook faction in Holland, who, led by Frans van Brederode, and in alliance with the anti-Burgundian party in Utrecht, had made themselves masters of Leyden. Beaten in a bloody fight by the regent, Brederode nevertheless managed to seize Sluis and Rotterdam; and from these ports he and his daring companionin-arms, Jan van Naaldwijk, carried on a guerrilla warfare for some years. Brederode was killed in a fight at Brouwershaven (1490), but Sluis still held out and was not taken till two years later.

Meanwhile Maximilian had to undertake a campaign against the Flemings, who were again in arms at the instigation of the turbulent burghers of Ghent and Bruges. Entering the province at the head of a large force he compelled the rebel towns to submit and obtained possession of the person of his son Philip (July, 1485). Elected in the following year King of the Romans, Maximilian left the Netherlands to be crowned at Aachen (April, 1486). A war with France called him back, in the course of which he suffered a severe defeat at Bethune. At the beginning of 1488 Ghent and Bruges once more rebelled; and the Roman king, enticed to enter Bruges, was there seized and compelled to see his friends executed in the market-place beneath his prison window. For seven months he was held a prisoner; nor was he released until he had sworn to surrender his powers, as regent, to a council of Flemings and to withdraw all his foreign troops from the Netherlands. He was forced to give hostages as a pledge of his good faith, among them his general, Philip of Cleef, who presently joined his captors.

Maximilian, on arriving at the camp of the Emperor Frederick III, who had gathered together an army to release his imprisoned son, was persuaded to break an oath given under duress. He advanced therefore at the head of his German mercenaries into Flanders, but was able to achieve little success against the Flemings, who found in Philip of Cleef an able commander. Despairing of success, he now determined to retire into Germany, leaving Duke Albert of Saxe-Meissen, a capable and tried soldier of fortune, as general-in-chief of his forces and Stadholder of the Netherlands. With the coming of Duke Albert order was at length to be restored, though not without a severe struggle.

Slowly but surely Duke Albert took town after town and reduced province after province into submission. The Hook party in Holland and Zeeland, and their anti-Burgundian allies in Utrecht, and Robert de la Marck in Liège, in turn felt the force of his arm. An insurrection of the peasants in West Friesland and Kennemerland—the "Bread and Cheese Folk," as they were called—was easily put down. Philip of Cleef with his Flemings was unable to make head against him; and, with the fall of Ghent and Sluis in the summer of 1492, the duke was able to announce to Maximilian that the Netherlands, except Gelderland, were pacified. The treaty of Senlis in 1493 ended the war with France. In the following year, after his accession to the imperial throne, Maximilian retired to his ancestral dominions in Germany, and his son, Philip the Fair, took in his hands the reins of government. The young sovereign, who was a Netherlander by birth and had spent all his life in the country, was more popular than his father; and his succession to the larger part of the Burgundian inheritance was not disputed. He received the homage of Zeeland at Roemerswaal, of Holland at Geertruidenburg, and seized the occasion to announce the abrogation of the Great Privilege, and at the same time restored the Grand Council at Mechlin.

In Utrecht the authority of Bishop David of Burgundy was now firmly re-established; and on his death, Philip of Baden, an obsequious adherent of the house of Austria, was elected. These results of the pacification carried out so successfully by Duke Albert had, however, left Maximilian and Philip deeply in debt to the Saxon; and there was no money wherewith to meet the claim, which amounted to 300,000 guilders. After many negotiations extending over several years, compensation was found for Albert in Friesland. That unhappy province and the adjoining territory of Groningen had for a long time been torn by internal dissensions between the two parties, the *Schieringers* and the *Vetkoopers*, who were the counterparts of the Hooks and Cods of Holland. The Schieringers called in the aid of the Saxon duke, who brought the land into subjection. Maximilian now recognised Albert as hereditary Podesta or governor of Friesland on condition that the House of Austria reserved the right of redeeming the territory for 100,000 guilders; and Philip acquiesced in the bargain by which Frisian freedom was sold in exchange for the cancelling of a debt. The struggle with Charles of Egmont in Gelderland was not so easily terminated. Not till 1505 was Philip able to overcome this crafty and skilful adversary. Charles was compelled to do homage and to accompany Philip to Brussels (October, 1505). It was, however, but a brief submission. Charles made his escape once more into Gelderland and renewed the war of independence.

Before these events had taken place, the marriage of Philip with Juana, the daughter of Ferdinand of Aragon and Isabel of Castile, had brought about a complete change in his fortunes. Maximilian, always full of ambitious projects for the aggrandisement of his House, had planned with Ferdinand of Aragon a double marriage between their families, prompted by a common hatred and fear of the growing power of France. The Archduke Philip was to wed the Infanta Juana, the second daughter of Ferdinand and Isabel; the Infante Juan, the heir to the thrones of Aragon and Castile, Philip's sister, Margaret. Margaret had in 1483, aged then three years, been betrothed to the Dauphin Charles, aged twelve, and she was brought up at the French Court, and after the death of Louis XI (August 30, 1483) had borne the title of Queen and had lived at Amboise with other children of the French royal house, under the care of the Regent, Anne de Beaujeu. The marriage, however, of Charles VIII and Margaret was never to be consummated. In August, 1488, the male line of the Dukes of Brittany became extinct; and the hand of the heiress, Anne of Brittany, a girl of twelve, attracted many suitors. It was clearly a matter of supreme importance to the King of France that this important territory should not pass by marriage into the hands of an enemy. The Bretons, on the other hand, clung to their independence and dreaded absorption in the unifying French state. After many intrigues her council advised the young duchess to accept Maximilian as her husband, and she was married to him by proxy in March, 1490. Charles VIII immediately entered Brittany at the head of a strong force and, despite a fierce and prolonged resistance, conquered the country, and gained possession of Anne's person (August, 1491). The temptation was too strong to be resisted. Margaret, after residing in France as his affianced wife for eight years, was repudiated and finally, two years later, sent back to the Netherlands, while Anne was compelled to break off her marriage with Margaret's father, and became Charles' queen. This double slight was never forgiven either by Maximilian or by Margaret, and was the direct cause of the negotiations for the double Spanish marriage, which, though delayed by the suspicious caution of the two chief negotiators, Ferdinand and Maximilian, was at length arranged. In August, 1496, an imposing fleet conveyed the Infanta Juana to Antwerp and she was married to Philip at Lille. In the following April Margaret and Don Juan were wedded in the cathedral of Burgos. The union was followed by a series of catastrophes in the Spanish royal family. While on his way with his wife to attend the marriage of his older sister Isabel with the King of Portugal, Juan caught a malignant fever and expired at Salamanca in October, 1497.

The newly-married Queen of Portugal now became the heiress to the crowns of Aragon and Castile, but she died a year later and shortly afterwards her infant son. The succession therefore passed to the younger sister, Juana; and Philip the Fair, the heir of the House of Austria and already through his mother the ruler of the rich Burgundian domain, became through his wife the prospective sovereign of the Spanish kingdoms of Ferdinand and Isabel. Fortune seemed to have reserved all her smiles for the young prince, when on February 24, 1500, a son was born to him at Ghent, who received the name Charles. But dark days were soon to follow. Philip was pleasure-loving and dissolute, and he showed little affection for his wife, who had already begun to exhibit symptoms of that weakness of mind which was before long to develop into insanity. However in 1501, they journeyed together to Spain, in order to secure Juana's rights to the Castilian succession and also to that of Aragon should King Ferdinand die without an heir-male.

In November, 1504, Isabel the Catholic had died; and Philip and his consort at once assumed the titles of King and Queen of Castile, in spite of the opposition of Ferdinand, who claimed the right of regency during his life-time. Both parties were anxious to obtain the support of Henry VII. Already since the accession of Philip the commercial relations between England and the Netherlands had been placed on what proved to be a permanently friendly basis by the treaty known as the *Magnus Intercursus* of 1496. Flanders and Brabant were dependent upon the supply of English wool for their staple industries, Holland and Zeeland for that freedom of fishery on which a large part of their population was employed and subsisted. In reprisals for the support formerly given by the Burgundian government to the house of York, Henry had forbidden the exportation of wool and of cloth to the Netherlands, had removed the staple from Bruges to Calais, and had withdrawn the fishing rights enjoyed by the Hollanders since the reign of Edward I. But this state of commercial war was ruinous to both countries; and, on condition that Philip henceforth undertook not to allow any enemies of the English government to reside in his dominions, a good understanding was reached, and the *Magnus*

*Intercursus*, which re-established something like freedom of trade between the countries, was duly signed in February, 1496. The treaty was solemnly renewed in 1501, but shortly afterwards fresh difficulties arose concerning Yorkist refugees, and a stoppage of trade was once more threatened. At this juncture a storm drove Philip and Juana, who had set sail in January, 1506, for Spain, to take refuge in an English harbour. For three months they were hospitably entertained by Henry, but he did not fail to take advantage of the situation to negotiate three treaties with his unwilling guest: (1) a treaty of alliance, (2) a treaty of marriage with Philip's sister, the Archduchess Margaret, already at the age of 25 a widow for the second time, (3) a revision of the treaty of commerce of 1496, named from its unfavourable conditions, *Malus Intercursus*. The marriage treaty came to nothing through the absolute refusal of Margaret to accept the hand of the English king.

Philip and Juana left England for Spain, April 23, to assume the government of the three kingdoms, Castile, Leon and Granada, which Juana had inherited from her mother. Owing to his wife's mental incapacity Philip in her name exercised all the powers of sovereignty, but his reign was very short, for he was suddenly taken ill and died at Burgos, September 25, 1506. His hapless wife, after the birth of a posthumous child, sank into a state of hopeless insanity and passed the rest of her long life in confinement. Charles, the heir to so vast an inheritance, was but six years old. The representatives of the provinces, assembled at Mechlin (October 18), offered the regency of the Burgundian dominions to the Emperor Maximilian; he in his turn nominated his daughter, Margaret, to be regent in his place and guardian of his grandson during Charles' minority, and she with the assent of the States-General took the oath on her installation as *Mambour* or Governor-General of the Netherlands, March, 1507. Margaret was but 27 years of age, and for twenty-four years she continued to administer the affairs of the Netherlands with singular discretion, firmness and Statesmanlike ability. The superintendence and training of the young archduke could have been placed in no better hands. Charles, who with his three sisters lived with his aunt at Mechlin, was thus both by birth and education a Netherlander.

One of the first acts of Margaret was a refusal to ratify the *Malus Intercursus* and the revival of the *Magnus Intercursus* of 1496.

This important commercial treaty from that time forward continued in force for more than a century. The great difficulty that Margaret encountered in her government was the lack of adequate financial resources. The extensive privileges accorded to the various provinces and their mutual jealousies and diverse interests made the task of levying taxes arduous and often fruitless. Margaret found that the granting of supplies, even for so necessary a purpose as the raising of troops to resist the raids of Charles of Gelderland, aided by the French king, into Utrecht and Holland, was refused. She fortunately possessed in a high degree those qualities of persuasive address and sound judgment, which gave to her a foremost place among the diplomatists and rulers of her time. Such was the confidence that her brilliant abilities inspired that she was deputed both by the Emperor Maximilian and by Ferdinand of Aragon to be their plenipotentiary at the Peace Congress that assembled at Cambray in November, 1508. Chiefly through her exertions the negotiations had a speedy and successful issue, and the famous treaty known as the League of Cambray was signed on December 10. By this treaty many of the disputes concerning the rights and prerogatives of the French crown in the Burgundian Netherlands were amicably settled; and it was arranged that Charles of Egmont should be provisionally recognised as Duke of Gelderland on condition that he should give up the towns in Holland that he had captured and withdraw his troops within his own borders.

The extant correspondence between Maximilian and Margaret, which is of the most confidential character, on matters of high policy, is a proof of the high opinion the emperor entertained of his daughter's intelligence and capacity. In nothing was his confidence more justified than in the assiduous care and interest that the regent took in the education of the Archduke Charles and his three sisters, who had been placed in her charge. In 1515 Charles, on entering his sixteenth year, was declared by Maximilian to be of age; Margaret accordingly handed over to him the reins of government and withdrew for the time into private life. Her retirement was not, however, to be of long continuance. On January 23, 1516, King Ferdinand of Aragon died, and Charles, who now became King of Castile and of Aragon, was obliged to leave the Netherlands to take possession of his Spanish dominions. Before sailing he reinstated his aunt as governess, and appointed a council to assist her. This post she continued to hold till the day of her death, for Charles was never again able to take up his permanent residence in the Netherlands. During the first years after his accession to the thrones of Ferdinand and Isabel he was much occupied with Spanish affairs; and the death of Maximilian, January 12, 1519, opened out to him a still wider field of ambition and activity. On June 28 Charles was elected emperor, a result which he owed in no small degree to the diplomatic skill and activity of Margaret. Just a year later the emperor visited the Netherlands, where Charles of Gelderland was again giving trouble, and his presence was required both for the purpose of dealing with the affairs of the provinces and also for securing a grant of supply, for he was sorely in need of funds. Margaret had at his request summoned the States-General to meet at Brussels, where Charles personally addressed them, and explained at some length the reasons which led him to ask his loyal and devoted Netherland subjects for their aid on his election to the imperial dignity. The States-General on this, as on other occasions, showed no niggardliness in responding to the request of a sovereign who, though almost always absent, appealed to their patriotism as a born Netherlander, who had been brought up in their midst and spoke their tongue. Charles was crowned at Aachen, October 23, 1520, and some three months later presided at the famous diet of Worms, where he met Martin Luther face to face. Before starting on his momentous journey he again appointed Margaret regent, and gave to her Council, which he nominated, large powers; the Council of Mechlin, the Court of Holland and other provincial tribunals being subjected to its superior authority and jurisdiction. By this action the privileges of the provinces were infringed, but Charles was resolute in carrying out the centralising policy of his ancestors, the Dukes of Burgundy, and he had the power to enforce his will in spite of the protests that were raised. And so under the wise and conciliatory but firm administration of Margaret during a decade of almost continuous religious and international strife—a decade marked by such great events as the rapid growth of the Reformation in Germany, the defeat and capture of Francis I at Pavia, the sack of Rome by the troops of Bourbon and the victorious advance of the Turks in Hungary and along the eastern frontier of the empire— the Netherland provinces remained at peace, save for the restless intrigues of Charles of Egmont in Gelderland, and prospered.

Their wealth furnished indeed no small portion of the funds which enabled Charles to face successfully so many adversaries and to humble the power of France. The last important act of Margaret, like her first, was connected with the town of Cambray. In this town, as the representative and plenipotentiary of her nephew the emperor, she met, July, 1529, Louise of Savoy, who had been granted similar powers by her son Francis I, to negotiate a treaty of peace. The two princesses proved worthy of the trust that had been placed in them, and a general treaty of peace, often spoken of as "the Ladies' Peace," was speedily drawn up and ratified. The conditions were highly advantageous to the interests of Spain and the Netherlands. On November 30 of the following year Margaret died, as the result of a slight accident to her foot which the medical science of the day did not know how to treat properly, in the 50th year of her age and the 24th of her regency.

Charles, who had a few months previously reached the zenith of his power by being crowned with the iron crown of Lombardy and with the imperial crown at the hands of Pope Clement VII at Bologna (February 22 and 24, 1530), appointed as governess in Margaret's place his sister Mary, the widowed queen of Louis, King of Hungary, who had been slain by the Turks at the battle of Mohacs, August 29, 1526.

Mary, who had passed her early life in the Netherlands under the care of her aunt Margaret, proved herself in every way her worthy successor. She possessed, like Margaret, a strong character, statesmanlike qualities and singular capacity in the administration of affairs. She filled the difficult post of regent for the whole period of twenty-four years between the death of Margaret and the abdication of Charles V in 1555. It was fortunate indeed for that great sovereign that these two eminent women of his house should, each in turn for one half of his long reign, have so admirably conducted the government of this important portion of his dominions, as to leave him free for the carrying out of his far-reaching political projects and constant military campaigns in other lands. Two years after Mary entered upon her regency Charles appointed three advisory and administrative bodies—the Council of State, the Council of Finance and the Privy Council—to assist her in the government. The Council of State dealt with questions of external and internal policy and with the appointment of officials; the Council of Finance with the care of the revenue and private domains of the sovereign; to the Privy Council were entrusted the publication of edicts and "placards," and the care of justice and police.

When Charles succeeded Philip the Fair only a portion of the Netherlands was subject to his sway. With steady persistence he set himself to the task of bringing all the seventeen provinces under one sovereign. In 1515 George of Saxe-Meissen sold to him his rights over Friesland. Henry of Bavaria, who in opposition to his wishes had been elected Bishop of Utrecht, was compelled (1528) to cede to him the temporalities of the see, retaining the spiritual office only. Charles thus added the Upper and Lower *Sticht*—Utrecht and Overyssel—to his dominions. He made himself (1536) master of Groningen and Drente after a long and obstinate struggle with Charles of Gelderland, and seven years later he forced Charles' successor, William of Jülich and Cleves, to renounce in his favour his claims to Gelderland and Zutphen. During the reign of Charles V the States-General were summoned many times, chiefly for the purpose of voting subsidies, but it was only on special and solemn occasions, that the representatives of all the seventeen provinces were present, as for instance when Philip received their homage in 1549 and when Charles V announced his abdication in 1555. The names of the seventeen provinces summoned on these occasions were Brabant, Limburg, Luxemburg, Gelderland, Flanders, Holland, Zeeland, Artois, Hainault, Namur, Lille with Douay and Orchies, Tournay and district, Mechlin, Friesland, Utrecht, Overyssel with Drente and Groningen. The bishopric of Liège, though nominally independent, was under the strict control of the government at Brussels. The relations of Charles' Burgundian domains to the empire were a matter of no small moment, and he was able to regulate them in a manner satisfactory to himself. Several times during his reign tentative attempts were made to define those relations, which were of a very loose kind. The fact that the head of the house of Habsburg was himself emperor had not made him any less determined than the Burgundian sovereigns, his ancestors, to assert for his Netherland territories a virtual independence of imperial control or obligation. The various states of which the Netherlands were composed were as much opposed as the central government at Brussels to any recognition of the claims of the empire; and both Margaret of Austria and Mary of Hungary ventured to refuse to send representatives to the imperial diets, even when requested to do so by the emperor. At last in 1548, when all the Netherland provinces had been brought under the direct dominion or control of one sovereign prince, a convention was drawn up at the diet of Augsburg, chiefly by the exertions of the Regent Mary and her tried councillors Viglius and Granvelle, by which the unity of the Netherland territories was recognised and they were freed from imperial jurisdiction. Nominally, they formed a circle of the empire,—the Burgundian circle—and representatives of the circle were supposed to appear at the diets and to bear a certain share of imperial taxation in return for the right to the protection of the empire against attacks by France. As a matter of fact, no representatives were ever sent and no subsidy was paid, nor was the protection of the empire ever sought or given.

This convention, which in reality severed the shadowy links which had hitherto bound the Netherlands to the empire, received the sanction of the States-General in October, 1548; and it was followed by the issuing, with the consent of the Estates of the various provinces, of a "Pragmatic Sanction" by which the inherited right of succession to the sovereignty in each and every province was settled upon the male and female line of Charles' descendants, notwithstanding the existence of ancient provincial privileges to the contrary. In 1549 the emperor's only son Philip was acknowledged by all the Estates as their future sovereign, and made a journey through the land to receive homage.

The doctrines of the Reformation had early obtained a footing in various parts of the Netherlands. At first it was the teaching of Luther and of Zwingli which gained adherents. Somewhat later the Anabaptist movement made great headway in Holland and Friesland, especially in Amsterdam. The chief leaders of the Anabaptists were natives of Holland, including the famous or infamous John of Leyden, who with some thousands of these fanatical sectaries perished at Münster in 1535. Between 1537 and 1543 a more moderate form of Anabaptist teaching made rapid progress through the preaching of a certain Menno Simonszoon. The followers of this man were called Mennonites. Meanwhile Lutheranism and Zwinglianism were in many parts of the country being supplanted by the sterner doctrines of Calvin. All these movements were viewed by the emperor with growing anxiety and detestation. Whatever compromises with the Reformation he might be compelled to make in Germany, he was determined to extirpate heresy from his hereditary dominions. He issued a strong placard soon after the diet of Worms in 1521 condemning Luther and his opinions and forbidding the printing or sale of any of the reformer's writings; and between that date and 1555 a dozen other edicts and placards were issued of increasing stringency. The most severe was the so-called "blood-placard" of 1550. This enacted the sentence of death against all convicted of heresy—the men to be executed with the sword and the women buried alive; in cases of obstinacy both men and women were to be burnt. Terribly harsh as were these edicts, it is doubtful whether the number of those who Suffered the extreme penalty has not been greatly exaggerated by partisan writers. Of the thousands who perished, by far the greater part were Anabaptists; and these met their fate rather as enemies of the state and of society, than as heretics. They were political as well as religious anarchists.

In the time of Charles the trade and industries of the Netherlands were in a highly prosperous state. The Burgundian provinces under the wise administrations of Margaret and Mary, and protected by the strong arm of the emperor from foreign attack, were at this period by far the richest state in Europe and the financial mainstay of the Habsburg power. Bruges, however, had now ceased to be the central market and exchange of Europe, owing to the silting up of the river Zwijn. It was no longer a port, and its place had been taken by Antwerp. At the close of the reign of Charles, Antwerp, with its magnificent harbour on the Scheldt, had become the "counting-house" of the nations, the greatest port and the wealthiest and most luxurious city in the world. Agents of the principal bankers and merchants of every country had their offices within its walls. It has been estimated that, inclusive of the many foreigners who made the town their temporary abode, the population of Antwerp in 1560 was about 150,000. Five hundred vessels sailed in and out of her harbour daily, and five times that number were to be seen thronging her wharves at the same time.

To the north of the Scheldt the condition of things was not less satisfactory than in the south, particularly in Holland. The commercial prosperity of Holland was in most respects different in kind from that of Flanders and Brabant, and during the period with which we are dealing had been making rapid advances, but on independent lines. A manufactory of the coarser kinds of cloth, established at Leyden, had indeed for a time met with a considerable measure of success, but had fallen into decline in the time of Mary of Hungary. The nature of his country led the Hollander to be either a sailor or a dairy-farmer, not an artisan or operative. Akin though he was in race to the Fleming and the Brabanter, his instincts led him by the force of circumstances to turn his energies in other directions. Subsequent history has but emphasised the fact—which from the fourteenth century onwards is clearly evident—that the people who inhabited the low-lying sea-girt lands of dyke, canal and polder in Holland and Zeeland were distinct in character and temper from the citizens of Bruges, Ghent, Ypres, Brussels or Mechlin, who were essentially landsmen and artisans. Ever since the discovery of the art of curing herrings (ascribed to William Beukelsz), the herring fishery had acquired a great importance to the Hollanders and Zeelanders, and formed the chief livelihood of a large part of the entire population of those provinces; and many thousands, who did not themselves sail in the fishing fleets, found employment in the ship and boat-building wharves and in the making of sails, cordage, nets and other tackle. It was in this hazardous occupation that the hardy race of skilled and seasoned seamen, who were destined to play so decisive a part in the coming wars of independence, had their early training. The herring harvest, through the careful and scientific methods that were employed in curing the fish and packing them in barrels, became a durable and much sought for article of commerce. A small portion of the catch served as a supply of food for home consumption, the great bulk in its thousands of barrels was a marketable commodity, and the distribution of the cured herring to distant ports became a lucrative business. It had two important consequences, the formation of a Dutch Mercantile Marine, and the growth of Amsterdam, which from small beginnings had in the middle of the sixteenth century become a town with 40,000 inhabitants and a port second only in importance in the Netherlands to Antwerp. From its harbour at the confluence of the estuary of the Y with the Zuyder Zee ships owned and manned by Hollanders sailed along the coasts of France and Spain to bring home the salt for curing purposes and with it wines and other southern products, while year by year a still larger and increasing number entered the Baltic. In those eastern waters they competed with the German Hanseatic cities, with whom they had many acrimonious disputes, and with such success that the Hollanders gradually monopolised the traffic in grain, hemp and other "Eastland" commodities and became practically the freight-carriers of the Baltic. And be it remembered that they were able to achieve this because many of the North-Netherland towns were themselves members of the Hanse League, and possessed therefore the same rights and privileges commercially as their rivals, Hamburg, Lübeck or Danzig. The great industrial cities of Flanders and Brabant, on the other hand, not being members of the League nor having any mercantile marine of their own, were content to transact business with the foreign agents of the Hanse towns, who had their counting-houses at Antwerp. It will thus be seen that in the middle of the sixteenth century the trade of the northern provinces, though as yet not to be compared in volume to that of the Flemings and Walloons, had before it an opening field for enterprise and energy rich in possibilities and promise for the future.

Such was the state of affairs political, religious and economical when in the year 1555 the Emperor Charles V, prematurely aged by the heavy burden of forty years of world-wide sovereignty, worn out by constant campaigns and weary of the cares of state, announced his intention of abdicating and retiring into a monastery. On October 25, 1555, the act of abdication was solemnly and with impressive ceremonial carried out in the presence of the representatives of the seventeen provinces of the Netherlands specially summoned to meet their sovereign for the last time in the Great Hall of the Palace at Brussels. Charles took an affecting farewell of his Netherland subjects and concluded by asking them to exhibit the same regard and loyalty to his son Philip as they had always displayed to himself. Much feeling was shown, for Charles, despite the many and varied calls and duties which had prevented him from residing for any length of time in the Netherlands, had always been at pains to manifest a special interest in the country of his birth. The Netherlands were to him throughout life his homeland and its people looked upon him as a fellow-countryman, and not even the constant demands that Charles had made for financial aid nor the stern edicts against heresy had estranged them from him. The abdication was the more regretted because at the same time Mary of Hungary laid down her office as regent, the arduous duties of which she had so long and so ably discharged. On the following day, October 26, the Knights of the Golden Fleece, the members of the Councils and the deputies of the provinces took the oath of allegiance to Philip, the emperor's only son and heir; and Philip on his side solemnly undertook to maintain unimpaired the ancient rights and privileges of the several provinces.

# CHAPTER III

# THE PRELUDE TO THE REVOLT

Philip at the time of his accession to the sovereignty of the Netherlands was already King of Naples and Sicily, and Duke of Milan, and, by his marriage in 1554 to Mary Tudor, King-consort of England, in which country he was residing when summoned by his father to assist at the abdication ceremony at Brussels. A few months later (January 16, 1556) by a further act of abdication on the part of Charles V he became King of Castile and Aragon. It was a tremendous inheritance, and there is no reason to doubt that Philip entered upon his task with a deep sense that he had a mission to fulfil and with a self-sacrificing determination to spare himself no personal labour in the discharge of his duties. But though he bore to his father a certain physical likeness, Philip in character and disposition was almost his antithesis. Silent, reserved, inaccessible, Philip had none of the restless energy or the geniality of Charles, and was as slow and undecided in action as he was bigoted in his opinions and unscrupulous in his determination to compass his ends. He found himself on his accession to power faced with many difficulties, for the treasury was not merely empty, it was burdened with debt. Through lack of means he was compelled to patch up a temporary peace (February 5, 1556) with the French king at Vaucelles, and to take steps to reorganise his finances.

One of Philip's first acts was the appointment of Emmanuel Philibert, Duke of Savoy, to the post vacated by his aunt Mary; but it was a position, as long as the king remained in the Netherlands, of small responsibility. Early in 1556 he summoned the States-General to Brussels and asked for a grant of 1,300,000 florins. The taxes proposed were disapproved by the principal provinces and eventually refused. Philip was very much annoyed, but was compelled to modify his proposals and accept what was offered by the delegates. There was indeed from the very outset no love lost between the new ruler and his Netherland subjects. Philip had spent nearly all his life in Spain, where he had received his education and early training, and he had grown up to manhood, in the narrowest sense of the word, a Spaniard. He was as unfamiliar with the laws, customs and privileges of the several provinces of his Netherland dominions as he was with the language of their peoples. He spoke and wrote only Castilian correctly, and during his four years' residence at Brussels he remained coldly and haughtily aloof, a foreigner and alien in a land where he never felt at home. Philip at the beginning of his reign honestly endeavoured to follow in his father's steps and to carry out his policy; but acts, which the great emperor with his conciliatory address and Flemish sympathies could venture upon with impunity, became suspect and questionable when attempted by the son. Philip made the great mistake of taking into his private confidence only foreign advisers, chief among whom was Anthony Perrenot de Granvelle, Bishop of Arras, a Burgundian by birth, the son of Nicholas Perrenot, who for thirty years had been the trusted counsellor of Charles V.

The opening of Philip's reign was marked by signal military successes. War broke out afresh with France, after a brief truce, in 1557. The French arms however sustained two crushing reverses at St Quentin, August 129, 1557, and at Gravelines, July 13, 1558. Lamoral, Count of Egmont, who commanded the cavalry, was the chief agent in winning these victories. By the treaty of Cateau-Cambresis peace was concluded, in which the French made many concessions, but were allowed to retain, at the cost of Philip's ally, the town of Calais which had been captured from the English by a surprise attack in 1558. By the death of Queen Mary, which was said to have been hastened by the news of the loss of Calais, Philip's relations with England were entirely changed, and one of the reasons for a continuance of his residence in the Netherlands was removed. Peace with France therefore was no sooner assured than Philip determined to return to Spain, where his presence was required. He chose his half-sister Margaret, Duchess of Parma, to be regent in place of the Duke of Savoy. In July he summoned the Chapter of the Order of the Golden Fleece—destined to be the last that was ever held—to Ghent in order to announce his intended departure. A little later the States-General were called together, also at Ghent, for a solemn leave-taking. On August 26, Philip embarked at Flushing, and quitted the Netherlands, never again to return.

Philip's choice of Margaret as governess-general was a happy one. She was a natural daughter of Charles V. Her mother was a Fleming, and she had been brought up under the care of her aunts, Margaret of Austria and Mary of Hungary. She resembled those able rulers in being a woman of strong character and statesmanlike qualities, and no doubt she would have been as successful in her administration had she had the same opportunities and the same freedom of action as her predecessors. Philip, however, though henceforth he passed the whole of his life in Spain, had no intention of loosening in any way his grasp of the reins of power or of delegating any share of his sovereign authority. On his return to Madrid he showed plainly that he meant to treat the Netherland provinces as if they were dependencies of the Spanish crown, and he required from Margaret and her advisers that all the details of policy, legislation and administration should be submitted to him for supervision and sanction. This necessitated the writing of voluminous despatches and entailed with a man of his habits of indecision interminable delays. Margaret moreover was instructed that in all matters she must be guided by the advice of her three councils. By far the most important of the three was the Council Of State, which at this time consisted of five members—Anthony Granvelle, Bishop of Arras; Baron de Barlaymont; Viglius van Zwychem van Aytta; Lamoral, Count of Egmont; and William, Prince of Orange. Barlaymont was likewise president of the Council of Finance and Viglius president of the Privy Council. By far the most important member of the Council of State, as he was much the ablest, was the Bishop of Arras; and he, with Barlaymont and Viglius, formed an inner confidential council from whom alone the regent asked advice. The members of this inner council, nicknamed the *Consulta*, were all devoted to the interests of Philip. Egmont and Orange, because of their great influence and popularity with the people, were allowed to be nominally Councillors of State, but they were rarely consulted and were practically shut out from confidential access to the regent. It is no wonder that both were discontented with their position and soon showed openly their dissatisfaction.

Egmont, a man of showy rather than of solid qualities, held in 1559 the important posts of Stadholder of Flanders and Artois. The Prince of Orange was the eldest of the five sons of William, Count of Nassau-Dillenburg, head of the younger or German branch of the famous house of Nassau. Members of the elder or Netherland branch had for several generations rendered distinguished services to their Burgundian and Habsburg sovereigns. This elder branch became extinct in the person of Réné, the son of Henry of Nassau, one of Charles V's most trusted friends and advisers, by Claude, sister of Philibert, Prince of Orange-Châlons. Philibert being childless bequeathed his small principality to Réné; and Réné in his turn, being killed at the siege of St Dizier in 1544, left by will all his possessions to his cousin William, who thus became Prince of Orange. His parents were Lutherans, but Charles insisted that William, at that time eleven years of age, should be brought up as a Catholic at the Court of Mary of Hungary. Here he became a great favourite of the emperor, who in 1550 conferred on him the hand of a great heiress, Anne of Egmont, only child of the Count of Buren. Anne died in 1558, leaving two children, a son, Philip William, and a daughter. At the ceremony of the abdication in 1555, Charles entered the hall leaning on the shoulder of William, on whom, despite his youth, he had already bestowed an important command. Philip likewise specially recognised William's ability and gave evidence of his confidence in him by appointing him one of the plenipotentiaries to conclude with France the treaty of Cateau-Cambresis in 1559. He had also made him a Knight of the Golden Fleece, a Councillor of State and Stadholder of Holland, Zeeland, Utrecht and Burgundy (Franche-Comté). Nevertheless there arose between Philip and Orange a growing feeling of distrust and dislike, with the result that William speedily found himself at the head of a patriotic opposition to any attempts of the Spanish king to govern the Netherlands by Spanish methods. The presence of a large body of Spanish troops in the country aroused the suspicion that Philip intended to use them, if necessary, to support him in overriding by force the liberties and privileges of the provinces. It was largely owing to the influence of Orange that the States-General in 1559 refused to vote the grant of supplies for which

Philip had asked, unless he promised that all foreign troops should be withdrawn from the Netherlands. The king was much incensed at such a humiliating rebuff and is reported, when on the point of embarking at Flushing, to have charged William with being the man who had instigated the States thus to thwart him.

Thus, when Margaret of Parma entered upon her duties as regent, she found that there was a feeling of deep dissatisfaction and general irritation in the provinces; and this was accentuated as soon as it was found that, though Philip had departed, his policy remained. The spirit of the absent king from his distant cabinet in Madrid brooded, as it were, over the land. It was soon seen that Margaret, whatever her statesmanlike qualities or natural inclination might be, had no real authority, nor was she permitted to take any steps or to initiate any policy without the advice and approval of the three confidential councillors placed at her side by Philip—Granvelle, Viglius and Barlaymont. Of these Granvelle, both by reason of his conspicuous abilities and of his being admitted more freely than anyone else into the inner counsels of a sovereign, as secretive in his methods as he was suspicious and distrustful of his agents, held the foremost position and drew upon himself the odium of a policy with which, though it was dictated from Spain, his name was identified.

Orange and Egmont, with whom were joined a number of other leading nobles (among these Philip de Montmorency, Count of Hoorn, his brother the lord of Montigny, the Counts of Meghem and Hoogstraeten and the Marquis of Berghen), little by little adopted an attitude of increasing hostility to this policy, which they regarded as anti-national and tending to the establishment of a foreign despotism in the Netherlands.

The continued presence of the Spanish troops, the severe measures that were being taken for the suppression of heresy, and a proposal for the erection of a number of new bishoprics, aroused popular discontent and suspicion. Orange and Egmont, finding that they were never consulted except on matters of routine, wrote to Philip (July, 1561) stating that they found that their attendance at the meetings of the Council of State was useless and asked to be allowed to resign their posts. Meanwhile, feeling that the presence of the Spanish troops was a source of weakness rather than of strength, Margaret and Granvelle were urging upon the king the necessity of their withdrawal. Neither the nobles nor the regent succeeded in obtaining any satisfactory response. Orange and Egmont accordingly absented themselves from the Council, and Margaret ventured on her own authority to send away the Spanish regiments.

The question of the bishoprics was more serious. It was not a new question. The episcopal organisation in the Netherlands was admittedly inadequate. It had long been the intention of Charles V to create a number of new sees, but in his crowded life he had never found the opportunity of carrying out the proposed scheme, and it was one of the legacies that at his abdication he handed on to his son. One of the first steps taken by Philip was to obtain a Bull from Pope Paul IV for the creation of the new bishoprics, and this Bull was renewed and confirmed by Pius IV, January, 1560. Up to this time the entire area of the seventeen provinces had been divided into three unwieldy dioceses—Utrecht, Arras and Tournay. The See of Utrecht comprised nearly the whole of the modern kingdom of the Netherlands. Nor was there any archiepiscopal see. The metropolitical jurisdiction was exercised by the three foreign Archbishops of Cologne, Rheims and Treves. Philip now divided the land into fourteen dioceses (Charles had proposed six) with three Metropolitans at Mechlin, Utrecht and 'sHertogenbosch[3]. Granvelle, who had obtained the Cardinal's hat, February, 1561, was appointed Archbishop of Mechlin, and by virtue of this office Primate of the Netherlands, December, 1561. This new organisation was not carried out without arousing widespread opposition.

The existing bishops resented the diminution of their jurisdiction and dignity, and still louder were the protests of the abbots, whose endowments were appropriated to furnish the incomes of the new sees. Still more formidable was the hostility of the people generally, a hostility founded on fear, for the introduction of so many new bishops nominated by the king was looked upon as being the first step to prepare the way for the bringing in of the dreaded Spanish Inquisition. Already the edicts against heretics, which Charles V had enacted and severely enforced, were being carried out throughout the length and breadth of the land with increasing and merciless barbarity. Both papal and episcopal inquisitors were active in the work of persecution, and so many were the sentences that in many places the civil authorities, and even some of the stadholders, declined to carry out the executions. Public opinion looked upon Granvelle as the author of the new bishoprics scheme and the instigator of the increased activity of the persecutors. He was accused of being eager to take any measures to repress the ancient liberties of the Netherland provinces and to establish a centralised system of absolute rule, in order to ingratiate himself with the king and so to secure his own advancement. That the cardinal was ambitious of power there can be no question. But to men of Granvelle's great abilities, as administrator and statesman, ambition is not necessarily a fault; and access to the secret records and correspondence of the time has revealed that the part played by him was far from being so sinister as was believed. The Bishop of Arras was not consulted about the bishoprics proposal until after the Papal Bull had been secured, and at first he was unfavourable to it and was not anxious to become archbishop and primate. It was his advice which led Margaret to send away the hated Spanish regiments from Netherland soil; and, far from being naturally a relentless persecutor, there is proof that neither he nor the president of the Privy Council, the jurist Viglius, believed in the policy of harsh and brutal methods for stamping out heretical opinions. They had in this as in other matters to obey their master, and allow the odium to fall upon themselves.

To Orange and Egmont, the two leaders of the opposition to Granvelle, a third name, that of Philip de Montmorency, Count of Hoorn and Admiral of Flanders, has now to be added. These three worked together for the overthrow of the Cardinal, but their opposition at this time was based rather on political than on religious grounds. They all professed the Catholic faith, but the marriage of Orange in August, 1561, with a Lutheran, Anne daughter of Maurice of Saxony and granddaughter of Philip of Hesse, was ominous of coming change in William's religious opinions. In 1562 the discontent of the nobles led to the formation of a league against the cardinal, of which, in addition to the three leaders, the Counts of Brederode, Mansfeld and Hoogstraeten were the principal members. This league, of which Orange was the brain and moving spirit, had as its chief aim the removal of Granvelle from office, and then redress of grievances. It found widespread support. The cardinal was assailed by a torrent of lampoons and pasquinades of the bitterest description. But, though Margaret began to see that the unpopularity of the minister was undermining her position, and was rendering for her the task of government more and more difficult, Philip was obdurate and closed his ears. The long distance between Madrid and Brussels and the procrastinating habits of the Spanish king added immensely to the regent's perplexities. She could not act on her own initiative, and her appeals to Philip were either disregarded or after long delay met by evasive replies.

The discontented nobles in vain tried to obtain redress for their grievances. In the autumn of 1562 Montigny was sent on a special mission to Madrid, but returned without effecting anything. Orange, Egmont and Hoorn thereupon drew up a joint letter containing a bold demand for the dismissal of Granvelle, as the chief cause of all the troubles in the land. The king replied by asking that one of them should go in person to Spain to discuss the grievances with him, and suggesting that Egmont should be sent. Egmont however was averse to the proposal, and another and stronger letter signed by the three leaders was despatched to Madrid. Finding that both Margaret and Granvelle himself were in agreement with Orange, Egmont and Hoorn in their view of the situation, Margaret advising, with the cardinal's acquiescence, the necessity of the minister's removal from his post, Philip determined at last that Granvelle should leave the Netherlands. But in accordance with the counsel of Alva, who was opposed on principle to any concession, he characteristically employed circuitous and clandestine means to conceal from the world any appearance of yielding to the request of his subjects. In January, 1564 he sent a letter to the Duchess of Parma expressing his displeasure at the lords' letter, and saying that they must substantiate their complaints. The same messenger (Armenteros, the duchess' secretary) carried another letter for Granvelle headed "secret," in which the cardinal was told that "owing to the strong feeling that had been aroused against him, he was to ask permission from the regent to go away for a short time to visit his mother." About a week after these letters had reached their destination another courier brought a reply to the three nobles, which, though written on the same day as the others, bore a date three weeks later, in which they were bidden to take their places again in the Council of State, and a promise was given that the charges against Granvelle after substantiation should be maturely considered. This letter was delivered on March

1, after Granvelle had already, in obedience to the king's orders, asked for leave of absence to visit his mother in Franche-Comté. The cardinal actually left Brussels on March 13, to the great joy of every class of the people, never to return.

With the departure of Granvelle, the nobles once more took their seats on the Council of State. The *Consulta* disappeared, and the regent herself appeared to be relieved and to welcome the disappearance of the man whose authority had overshadowed her own. But the change, though it placed large powers of administration and of patronage in the hands of Netherlanders instead of foreigners, did not by any means introduce purer methods of government. Many of the nobles were heavily in debt; most of them were self-seeking; offices and emoluments were eagerly sought for, and were even put up for sale. Armenteros, Margaret's private secretary (to whom the nickname of *Argenteros* was given), was the leading spirit in this disgraceful traffic, and enriched himself by the acceptance of bribes for the nomination to preferments. It was an unedifying state of things; and public opinion was not long in expressing its discontent with such an exhibition of widespread venality and greed. All this was duly reported to Philip by Granvelle, who continued, in his retirement, to keep himself well informed of all that was going on.

Meanwhile by the efforts of Orange, Egmont and Hoorn, chiefly of the former, proposals of reform were being urged for the strengthening of the powers of the Council of State, for the reorganisation of finance, and for the more moderate execution of the placards against heresy. While discussion concerning these matters was in progress, came an order from Philip (August, 1564) for the enforcing of the decrees of the recently concluded Council of Trent. This at once aroused protest and opposition. It was denounced as an infringement of the fundamental privileges of the provinces. Philip's instructions however were peremptory. In these circumstances it was resolved by the Council of State to despatch Egmont on a special mission to Madrid to explain to the king in person the condition of affairs in the Netherlands. Egmont having expressed his willingness to go, instructions were drawn up for him by Viglius. When these were read at a meeting of the council convened for the purpose, Orange in a long and eloquent speech boldly expressed his dissent from much that Viglius had written, and wished that Philip should be plainly told that it was impossible to enforce the decrees and that the severity of religious persecution must be moderated. The council determined to revise the instructions on the lines suggested by Orange, whose words had such an effect upon the aged Viglius, that he had that very night a stroke of apoplexy, which proved fatal.

Egmont set out for Spain, January 15, 1565, and on his arrival was received by Philip with extreme courtesy and graciousness. He was entertained splendidly; presents were made to him, which, being considerably in debt, he gladly accepted; but as regards his mission he was put off with evasions and blandishments, and he returned home with a reply from the king containing some vague promises of reform in financial and other matters, but an absolute refusal to modify the decrees against heresy. Rather would he sacrifice a hundred thousand lives, if he had them, than concede liberty of worship in any form. For some months however no attempt was made to carry out active persecutions; and the regent meanwhile did her utmost to place before the king urgent reasons for the modification of his policy, owing to the angry spirit of unrest and suspicion which was arising in the provinces. She begged Philip to visit the Netherlands and acquaint himself personally with the difficulties of a situation which, unless her advice were taken, would rapidly grow worse and pass beyond her control. Philip however was deaf alike to remonstrance or entreaty. On November 5, 1565, a royal despatch reached Brussels in which the strictest orders were renewed for the promulgation throughout the provinces of the decrees of the Council of Trent and for the execution of the placards against heretics, while the proposals that had been made for an extension of the powers of the Council of State and for the summoning of the States-General were refused. As soon as these fateful decisions were known, and the Inquisition began to set about its fell work in real earnest, the popular indignation knew no bounds. A large number of the magistrates refused to take any part in the cruel persecution that arose, following the example of Orange, Egmont, Berghen and others of the stadholders and leading nobles. A strong spirit of opposition to arbitrary and foreign rule arose and found expression in the action taken by a large number of the members of the so-called "lesser nobility." Many of these had come to Brussels, and at a meeting at the house of the Count of Culemburg the formation of a league to resist arbitrary rule was proposed. The leaders were Lewis of Nassau, brother of the Prince of Orange, Nicolas de Harnes, Philip de Marnix, lord of Sainte Aldegonde, and Henry, Viscount of Brederode. Other meetings were held, and a document embodying the principles and demands of the Confederates was drawn up, known as *the Compromise*, which was widely distributed among the nobles and quickly obtained large and constantly increasing support. The signatories of the Compromise, while professing themselves to be faithful and loyal subjects of the king, denounced the Inquisition in its every form "as being unjust and contrary to all laws human and divine"; and they pledged themselves to stand by one another in resisting its introduction into the Netherlands and in preventing the carrying-out of the placards against heresy, while at the same time undertaking to maintain the royal authority and public peace in the land.

At first the great nobles stood aloof, doubtful what course to pursue. At the instigation of Orange conferences were held, at which, by his advice, a petition or *Request*, setting forth the grievances and asking for redress, should be made in writing for presentation to the regent. The original draft of this document was the work of Lewis of Nassau. These conferences, however, revealed that there was a considerable divergence of views among the leading nobles. Egmont and Meghem were indeed so alarmed at the character of the movement, which seemed to them to savour of treason, that they separated themselves henceforth from Orange and Hoorn and openly took the side of the government. The duchess after some demur agreed to receive the petition. A body of confederates under the leadership of Brederode and Lewis of Nassau marched to the palace, where they were received by Margaret in person. The petitioners asked the regent to send an envoy to Madrid to lay before the king the state of feeling among his loyal subjects in the Netherlands, praying him to withdraw the Inquisition and moderate the placards against heresy, and meanwhile by her own authority to suspend them until the king's answer had been received. The regent replied that she had no power to suspend the Inquisition or the placards, but would undertake, while awaiting the royal reply, to mitigate their operation.

On the last day of their stay at Brussels, April 8, the confederates under the presidency of Brederode, to the number of about three hundred, dined together at the Hotel Culemburg. In the course of the meal Brederode drew the attention of the company now somewhat excited with wine to a contemptuous phrase attributed by common report to Barlaymont. Margaret was somewhat perturbed at the formidable numbers of the deputation, as it entered the palace court, and it was said that Barlaymont remarked that "these beggars" (*ces gueux*) need cause her no fear. Brederode declared that he had no objection to the name and was quite willing to be "a beggar" in the cause of his country and his king. It was destined to be a name famous in history. Immediately loud cries arose from the assembled guests, until the great hall echoed with the shouts of *Vivent les Gueux*. From this date onwards the confederates were known as "les gueux," and they adopted a coarse grey dress with the symbols of beggarhood—the wallet and the bowl—worn as the *insignia* of their league. It was the beginning of a popular movement, which made rapid headway among all classes. A medal was likewise struck, which bore on one side the head of the king, on the other two clasped hands with the inscription—*Fidèles au roy jusques à la besace.*

Thus was the opposition to the tyrannical measures of the government organising itself in the spring of 1566. It is a great mistake to suppose that the majority of those who signed "the Compromise" or presented "the Request" were disloyal to their sovereign or converts to the reformed faith. Among those who denounced the methods of the Inquisition and of the Blood Placards were a large number, who without ceasing to be Catholics, had been disillusioned by the abuses which had crept into the Roman Church, desired their removal only to a less degree than the Protestants themselves, and had no sympathy with the terrible and remorseless persecution on Spanish lines, which sought to crush out all liberty of thought and all efforts of religious reform by the stake and the sword of the executioner. Nevertheless this league of the nobles gave encouragement to the sectaries and was the signal for a great increase in the number and activity of the Calvinist and Zwinglian preachers, who flocked into the land from the neighbouring countries. Such was the boldness of these preachers that, instead of being contented with secret meetings, they began to hold their conventicles in the fields or in the outskirts of the towns. Crowds of people thronged to hear them, and the authority of the magistrates was defied and flouted. The regent was in despair. Shortly after the presentation of the Request it was determined by the advice of the council to send special envoys to lay before the king once more the serious state of things. The Marquis of Berghen and Baron Montigny consented with some demur to undertake the mission, but for various reasons they did not reach Madrid till some two months later. They were received with apparent courtesy, and after several conferences the king, on July 31, despatched a letter to Margaret in which he undertook to do away with the Papal Inquisition and offered to allow such moderation of the Placards as did not imply any recognition of heretical opinions or any injury to the Catholic faith. He refused to consent to the meeting of the States, but he sent letters couched in most friendly terms to Orange and Egmont appealing to their loyalty and asking them to support the regent by their advice and influence. These demonstrations of a conciliatory temper were however mere temporising. He was playing false. A document is in existence, dated August 9, in which Philip states that these concessions had been extorted from him against his will and that he did not regard himself as bound by them, and he informed the Pope that the abolition of the Papal Inquisition was a mere form of words.

Meanwhile events were moving fast in the Netherlands. The open-air preachings were attended by thousands; and at Antwerp, which was one of the chief centres of Calvinism, disorders broke out, and armed conflicts were feared. Orange himself, as burgrave of Antwerp, at the request of the duchess visited the town and with the aid of Brederode and Meghem succeeded in effecting a compromise between the Catholic and Protestant parties. The latter were allowed to hold their preachings undisturbed, so long as they met outside and not within the city walls. The regent in her alarm was even driven to make overtures to the confederates to assist her in the maintenance of order. There was much parleying, in which Orange and Egmont took part; and in July an assembly of the signatories of the Compromise was called together at St Trond in the district of Liège. Some two thousand were present, presided over by Lewis of Nassau. It was resolved to send twelve delegates to Margaret to lay before her the necessity of finding a remedy for the evils which were afflicting and disturbing the land. They offered to consult with Orange and Egmont as to the best means by which they could work together for the country's good, but hinting that, if no redress was given, they might be forced to look for foreign aid. Indeed this was no empty threat, for Lewis had already been in communication with the Protestant leaders both in France and in the Rhinelands, as to the terms on which they would furnish armed assistance; and Orange was probably not altogether in ignorance of the fact. The regent was angry at the tone of the delegates, whom she received on July 26, but in her present impotence thought it best to dissemble. She promised to give consideration to the petition, and summoned a meeting of the Knights of the Golden Fleece to meet at Brussels on August 18, when she would decide upon her answer. But, when that date arrived, other and more pressing reasons than the advice of counsellors compelled her to yield to the confederates a large part of their demands. On August 23 she agreed, in return for help in the restoration of order, to concede liberty of preaching, so long as those who assembled did not bear arms and did not interfere with the Catholic places of worship and religious services. Further an indemnity was promised to all who had signed the Compromise.

The reasons which influenced her were, first the receipt, on August 12, of the conciliatory letter from the king, to which reference has already been made, in which he consented to a certain measure of toleration; and secondly a sudden outburst of iconoclastic fury on the part of the Calvinistic sectaries, which had spread with great rapidity through many parts of the land. On August 14, at St Omer, Ypres, Courtray, Valenciennes and Tournay, fanatical mobs entered the churches destroying and wrecking, desecrating the altars, images, vestments and works of art, and carrying away the sacred vessels and all that was valuable. On August 16 and 17 the cathedral of Antwerp was entered by infuriated and sacrilegious bands armed with axes and hammers, who made havoc and ruin of the interior of the beautiful church. In Holland and Zeeland similar excesses were committed. Such conduct aroused a feeling of the deepest indignation and reprobation in the minds of all right-thinking men, and alienated utterly those more moderate Catholics who up till now had been in favour of moderation. Of the great nobles, who had hitherto upheld the cause of the national liberties and privileges against the encroachments of a foreign despotism, many now fell away. Among these were Aremberg, Meghem and Mansfeld. Egmont hesitated. As might have been expected, the news of the outrages, when it reached Philip's ears, filled him with rage and grief; and he is reported to have exclaimed, "It shall cost them dear. I swear it by the soul of my father." From this time forward he was determined to visit with exemplary punishment not only the rioters and the Protestant sectaries, but more especially the great nobles on whose shoulders he laid the whole blame for the troubles that had arisen.

He was in no hurry to act, and announced that it was his intention to go to the Netherlands in person and enquire into the alleged grievances. So he told his councillors and wrote to Margaret. No one seems to have suspected his deep-laid scheme for allaying the suspicions of his intended victims until the right moment came for laying his hands upon them and crushing all opposition by overwhelming force. Orange alone, who had his paid spies at Madrid, had a presage of what was coming and took measures of precaution betimes. An intercepted letter from the Spanish ambassador at Paris to the Regent Margaret, specifically mentioned Orange, Egmont and Hoorn as deserving of exemplary punishment; and on October 3 the prince arranged a meeting at Dendermonde to consider what should be their course of action. In addition to Egmont and Hoorn, Hoogstraeten and Lewis of Nassau were present. William and Lewis urged that steps should be taken for preparing armed resistance should the necessity arise. But neither Egmont nor Hoorn would consent; they would not be guilty of any act of disloyalty to their sovereign. The result of the meeting was a great disappointment to Orange, and this date marked a turning-point in his life. In concert with his brothers, John and Lewis, he began to enter into negotiations with several of the German Protestant princes for the formation of a league for the protection of the adherents of the reformed faith in the Netherlands. Now for the first time he severed his nominal allegiance to the Roman Church, and in a letter to Philip of Hesse avowed himself a Lutheran.

During these same autumn months Philip furnished his sister with considerable sums of money for the levying of a strong mercenary force, German and Walloon. Possessed now of a body of troops that she could trust, Margaret in the spring of 1567 took energetic steps to suppress all insurrectionary movements and disorders, and did not scruple to disregard the concessions which had been wrung from her on August 23. The confederate nobles, satisfied with her promises, had somewhat prematurely dissolved their league; but one of the most fiery and zealous among them, John de Marnix, lord of Thoulouse, collected at Antwerp a body of some 2000 Calvinists and attempted to make himself master of that city. At Austruweel he was encountered (March 13) by a Walloon force despatched by Margaret with orders to "exterminate the heretics." Thoulouse and almost the whole of his following perished in the fight. In the south at the same time the conventicles were mercilessly suppressed and the preachers driven into exile.

Margaret now felt herself strong enough to demand that the stadholders and leading nobles should, on pain of dismissal from their posts, take an oath "to serve the king and to act for and against whomsoever His Majesty might order." Egmont took the oath; Hoorn, Hoogstraeten and Brederode declined to do so and resigned their offices. Orange offered his resignation, but Margaret was unwilling to accept it and urged him to discuss the matter first with Egmont and Meghem. The three nobles met accordingly at Willebroek, April 2. William used his utmost powers of persuasion in an attempt to convince Egmont that he was courting destruction. But in vain. He himself was not to be moved from his decision, and the two friends, who had worked together so long in the patriot cause, parted, never to meet again. Orange saw that he was no longer safe in the Netherlands and, on April 22, he set out from Breda for the residence of his brother John at Dillenburg. Here in exile he could watch in security the progress of events, and be near at hand should circumstances again require his intervention in the affairs of the Netherlands.

Orange did not take this extreme step without adequate cause. At the very time that he left the Netherlands Philip was taking leave of the Duke of Alva, whom he was despatching at the head of a veteran force to carry out without pity or remorse the stern duty of expelling heresy from the provinces and punishing all those, and especially the leaders, who had ventured to oppose the arbitrary exercise of the royal authority. He had for some time been preparing this expedition. He still kept up the pretence that he was coming in person to enquire into the alleged grievances, but he never had the slightest intention of quitting Madrid. Alva sailed from Cartagena (April 27) for Genoa, and proceeded at once to draw together from the various Spanish garrisons in Italy a picked body of some 12,000 men. With these he set out in June for his long march across the Alps and through Burgundy, Lorraine and Luxemburg. His progress, jealously watched by the French and Swiss, met with no opposition save for the difficulties of the route. He entered the Netherlands on August 8, with his army intact. A number of notables, amongst whom was Egmont, came to meet him on his way to Brussels. He received them, more particularly Egmont, with every appearance of graciousness. Alva as yet bore only the title of Captain-General, but the king had bestowed on him full powers civil and military; and the Duchess of Parma, though still nominally regent, found herself reduced to a nonentity. Alva's first step was to place strong Spanish garrisons in the principal cities, his next to get the leaders who had been marked for destruction into his power. To effect this he succeeded by fair and flattering words in securing the presence of both Egmont and Hoorn at Brussels. Under the pretence of taking part in a consultation they were (September 9) invited to the duke's residence and on their arrival suddenly found themselves arrested. At the same time their secretaries and papers were seized, and Antony van Stralen, the burgomaster of Antwerp, was placed under arrest. These high-handed actions were the prelude to a reign of terror; and Margaret, already humiliated by finding herself superseded, requested her brother to accept her resignation. On October 6 the office of Governor-General was conferred upon Alva; and shortly afterwards the duchess left the Netherlands and returned to Parma.

Alva had now the reins of power in his hand, and with a relentless zeal and cold-blooded ferocity, which have made his name a by-word, he set about the accomplishment of the fell task with which his master had entrusted him. He had to enforce with drastic rigour all the penalties decreed by the placards against heretics and preachers, and to deal summarily with all who had taken any part in opposition to the government. But to attempt to do this by means of the ordinary courts and magistrates would consume time and lead to many acquittals. Alva therefore had no sooner thrown off the mask by the sudden and skilfully planned arrest of Egmont and Hoorn, than he proceeded to erect an extraordinary tribunal, which had no legal standing except such as the arbitrary will of the duke conferred upon it. This so-called Council of Troubles, which speedily acquired in popular usage the name of the Council of Blood, virtually consisted of Alva himself, who was president and to whose final decision all cases were referred, and two Spanish lawyers, his chosen tools and agents, Juan de Vargas and Louis del Rio. The two royalist nobles, Noircarmes and Barlaymont, and five Netherland jurists also had seats; but, as only the Spaniards voted, the others before long ceased to attend the meetings. The proceedings indeed were, from the legal point of view, a mere travesty of justice. A whole army of commissioners was let loose upon the land, and informers were encouraged and rewarded. Multitudes of accused were hauled before the tribunal and were condemned by batches almost without the form of a trial. For long hours day by day Vargas and del Rio revelled in their work of butchery; and in all parts of the Netherlands the executioners were busy. It was of no use for the accused to appeal to the charters and privileges of their provinces. All alike were summoned to Brussels; *non curamus privilegios vestros* declared Vargas in his ungrammatical Latin. Hand in hand with the wholesale sentences of death went the confiscation of property. Vast sums went into the treasury. The whole land for awhile was terror-stricken. All organised opposition was crushed, and no one dared to raise his voice in protest.

The Prince of Orange was summoned to appear in person before the council within six weeks, under pain of perpetual banishment and confiscation of his estates. He refused to come, and energetically denied that the council had any jurisdiction over him. The same sentence was passed upon all the other leaders who had placed themselves out of reach of Alva's arm—Sainte Aldegonde, Hoogstraeten, Culemburg, Montigny, Lewis of Nassau and others. Unable to lay hands upon the prince himself, the governor-general took dastardly advantage of William's indiscretion in leaving his eldest son at Louvain to pursue his studies at the university. At the beginning of 1568 Philip William, Count of Buren in right of his mother, was seized and sent to Madrid to be brought up at the court of Philip to hate the cause to which his father henceforth devoted his life. Already indeed, before the abduction of his son, Orange from his safe retreat at Dillenburg had been exerting himself to raise troops for the invasion of the Netherlands. He still professed loyalty to the king and declared that in the king's name he wished to restore to the provinces those liberties and privileges which Philip himself had sworn that he would maintain. The difficulty was to find the large sum of money required for such an enterprise, and it was only by extraordinary efforts that a sufficient amount was obtained. Part of the money was collected in Antwerp and various towns of Holland and Zeeland, the rest subscribed by individuals. John of Nassau pledged his estates, Orange sold his plate and jewels, and finally a war-chest of 200,000 florins was gathered together. It was proposed to attack the Netherlands from three directions. From the north Lewis of Nassau was to lead an army from the Ems into Friesland; Hoogstraeten on the east to effect an entrance by way of Maestricht; while another force of Huguenots and refugees in the south was to march into Artois. It was an almost desperate scheme in the face of veteran troops in a central position under such a tried commander as Alva. The last-named French force and that under Hoogstraeten were easily defeated and scattered by Spanish detachments sent to meet them. Lewis of Nassau was at first more successful. Entering Groningen at the head of eight or nine thousand undisciplined troops he was attacked, May 23, in a strong position behind a morass by a Spanish force under the Count of Aremberg, Stadholder of Friesland, at Heiligerlee. He gained a complete victory. Aremberg himself was slain, as was also the younger brother of Lewis, Adolphus of Nassau. The triumph of the invaders was of short duration. Alva himself took in hand the task of dealing with the rebels. At the head of 15,000 troops he drove before him the levies of Nassau to Jemmingen on the estuary of the Ems, and here with the loss of only seven men he completely annihilated them. Lewis himself and a few others alone escaped by throwing themselves into the water and swimming for their lives.

The action at Heiligerlee, by compelling the governor-general to take the field, had hastened the fate of Egmont and Hoorn. After their arrest the two noblemen were kept in solitary confinement in the citadel of Ghent for several months, while the long list of charges against them was being examined by the Council of Troubles—in other words by Vargas and del Rio. These charges they angrily denied; and great efforts were made on their behalf by the wife of Egmont and the dowager Countess of Hoorn. Appeals were made to the governor-general and to Philip himself, either for pardon on the ground of services rendered to the State, or at least for a trial, as Knights of the Golden Fleece, before the Court of the Order. The Emperor Maximilian himself pleaded with Philip for clemency, but without avail. Their doom had been settled in advance, and the king was inflexible. Alva accordingly determined that they should be executed before he left Brussels for his campaign in the north. On June 2, the council, after refusing to hear any further evidence in the prisoners' favour, pronounced them guilty of high treason; and Alva at once signed the sentences of death. Egmont and Hoorn the next day were brought by a strong detachment of troops from Ghent to Brussels and were confined in a building opposite the town hall, known as the Broodhuis. On June 5, their heads were struck off upon a scaffold erected in the great square before their place of confinement. Both of them met their death with the utmost calmness and courage. The effect of this momentous stroke of vengeance upon these two patriot leaders, both of them good Catholics, who had always professed loyalty to their sovereign, and one of whom, Egmont, had performed distinguished services for his country and king, was profound. A wave of mingled rage and sorrow swept over the land. It was not only an act of cruel injustice, but even as an act of policy a blunder of the first magnitude, which was sure to bring, as it did bring, retribution in its train.

# CHAPTER IV

# THE REVOLT OF THE NETHERLANDS

The complete failure of the expeditions of Hoogstraeten and of Lewis of Nassau was a great discouragement to the Prince of Orange. Nevertheless after receiving the news of Jemmingen he wrote to his brother, "With God's help I am determined to go on." By great exertions he succeeded in gathering together a heterogeneous force of German and Walloon mercenaries numbering about 18,000 men, and with these in the beginning of October he crossed the frontier. But to maintain such a force in the field required far larger financial resources than William had at his disposal. Alva was aware of this, and, as the prince made his way into Brabant, he followed his steps with a small body of veteran troops, cutting off supplies and stragglers, but declining battle. The mercenaries, debarred from plunder and in arrears of pay, could not be kept together more than a few weeks. In November Orange withdrew into France and disbanded the remnants of his army. In disguise he managed to escape with some difficulty through France to Dillenburg. His brothers, Lewis and Henry, joined the Huguenot army under Coligny and took part in the battles of Moncontour and Jarnac.

Alva was now apparently supreme in the Netherlands; and crowds of refugees fled the country to escape the wholesale persecutions of the Council of Blood. Alva however, like his predecessor and indeed like all Spanish governors engaged in carrying out the policy of Philip II, was always hampered by lack of funds. The Spanish treasury was empty. The governor-general's troops no less than those of Orange clamoured for their regular pay, and it was necessary to find means to satisfy them.

The taxes voted for nine years in 1559 had come to an end. New taxes could only be imposed with the assent of the States-General. Alva, however, after his victory at Jemmingen and the dispersion of the army of Orange, felt himself strong enough to summon the States-General and demand their assent to the scheme of taxation which he proposed. The governor-general asked for (1) a tax of five per cent., the "twentieth penny," on all transfers of real estate, (2) a tax of ten per cent., the "tenth penny," on all sales of commodities. These taxes, which were an attempt to introduce into the Netherlands the system known in Castile as *alcabala*, were to be granted in perpetuity, thus, as the duke hoped, obviating the necessity of having again to summon the States-General. In addition to these annual taxes he proposed a payment once for all of one per cent., "the hundredth penny," on all property, real or personal. Such a demand was contrary to all precedent in the Netherlands and an infringement of time-honoured charters and privileges; and even the terror, which Alva's iron-handed tyranny had inspired, did not prevent his meeting with strong opposition. The proposals had to be referred to the provincial estates, and everywhere difficulties were raised. All classes were united in resistance. Petitions came pouring in protesting against impositions which threatened to ruin the trade and industries of the country. Alva found it impossible to proceed.

The "hundredth penny" was voted, but instead of the other taxes, which were to provide a steady annual income, he had to content himself with a fixed payment of 2,000,000 guilders for two years only. The imposition of these taxes on the model of the *alcabala* had been part of a scheme for sweeping away all the provincial jurisdictions and rights and forming the whole of the Netherlands into a unified state, as subservient to despotic rule as was Castile itself. A greater centralisation of government had been the constant policy of the Burgundian and Habsburg rulers since the time of Philip the Good, a policy to be commended if carried out in a statesmanlike and moderate spirit without any sudden or violent infringement of traditional liberties. The aim of Philip of Spain as it was interpreted by his chosen instrument, the Duke of Alva, was far more drastic. With Alva and his master all restrictions upon the absolute authority of the sovereign were obstacles to be swept remorselessly out of the way; civil and religious liberty in their eyes deserved no better fate than to be suppressed by force. Alva's experience was that of many would-be tyrants before and since his day, that the successful application of force is limited by the power of the purse. His exchequer was empty. Philip was himself in financial difficulties and could spare him no money from Spain. The refusal of the provincial estates of the Netherlands to sanction his scheme of taxation deprived him of the means for imposing his will upon them. His reign of terror had produced throughout the land a superficial appearance of peace. There were at the beginning of 1570 no open disturbances or insurrectionary movements to be crushed, but the people were seething with discontent, and the feeling of hatred aroused by the presence of the Spanish Inquisition and the foreign soldiery and by the proceedings of the Council of Blood was, day by day, becoming deeper and more embittered.

This condition of affairs was duly reported to the king at Madrid; and there was no lack of councillors at his side who were unfriendly to Alva and eager to make the most of the complaints against him. Among these enemies was Ruy Gomez, the king's private secretary, who recommended a policy of leniency, as did Granvelle, who was now at Naples. Philip never had any scruples about throwing over his agents, and he announced his intention of proclaiming an amnesty on the occasion when Anne of Austria, his intended bride and fourth wife, set sail from Antwerp for Spain. The proclamation was actually made at Antwerp by the governor-general in person, July 16, 1570. It was a limited declaration of clemency, for six classes of offenders were excepted, and it only extended to those who within two months made their peace with the Catholic Church and abjured the Reformed doctrines.

During the years 1570-71 there were however few outward signs of the gradual undermining of Alva's authority. There was sullen resentment and discontent throughout the land, but no attempt at overt resistance. The iron hand of the governor-general did not relax its firm grasp of the reins of power, and the fear of his implacable vengeance filled men's hearts. He ruled by force, not by love; and those who refused to submit had either to fly the country or to perish by the hands of the executioner. Nevertheless during these sad years the Prince of Orange and Lewis of Nassau, in spite of the apparent hopelessness of the situation, were unremitting in their efforts to raise fresh forces. William at Dillenburg exerted himself to the uttermost to obtain assistance from the Protestant princes of the Rhineland. With the Calvinists he was, however, as yet strongly suspect. He himself was held to be a lukewarm convert from Catholicism to the doctrines of Augsburg; and his wife was the daughter and heiress of Maurice of Saxony, the champion of Lutheranism. William's repudiation of Anne of Saxony for her repeated infidelities (March, 1571) severed this Lutheran alliance. The unfortunate Anne, after six years' imprisonment, died insane in 1577. At the same time the closest relations of confidence and friendship sprang up between Orange and the well-known Calvinist writer and leader, Philip de Marnix, lord of Sainte Aldegonde. This connection with Sainte Aldegonde ensured for William the support of the Calvinists; and secret agents of the prince were soon busily at work in the different parts of the provinces promising armed assistance and collecting levies for the raising of an invading force. Foremost among these active helpers were Jacob van Wesenbeke, Diedrich Sonoy and Paul Buys; and the chief scene of their operations were the provinces of Holland and Zeeland, already distinguished for their zeal in the cause of freedom. The amount of cash that was raised was, however, for some time very small. There was goodwill in plenty, but the utter failure of the prince's earlier efforts had made people despair.

These earlier efforts had indeed, on land, been disastrous, but they had not been confined entirely to land operations. Orange, in his capacity as a sovereign prince, had given *letters of marque* to a number of vessels under the command of the lord of Dolhain. These vessels were simply corsairs and they were manned by fierce fanatical sectaries, desperadoes inflamed at once by bitter hatred of the papists and by the hope of plunder. These "Beggars of the Sea" (*Gueux de mer*), as they were called, rapidly increased in number and soon made themselves a terror in the narrow seas by their deeds of reckless daring and cruelty. William tried in vain to restrain excesses which brought him little profit and no small discredit. It was to no purpose that he associated the lord of Lumbres in the chief command with Dolhain. Their subordinates, William de Blois, lord of Treslong, and William de la Marck, lord of Lumey, were bold, unscrupulous adventurers who found it to their interest to allow their unruly crews to burn and pillage, as they lusted, not only their enemies' ships in the open sea, but churches and monasteries along the coast and up the estuaries that they infested. The difficulty was to find harbours in which they could take refuge and dispose of their booty. For some time they were permitted to use the English ports freely, and the Huguenot stronghold at La Rochelle was also open to them as a market. Queen Elizabeth, as was her wont, had no scruple in conniving at acts of piracy to the injury of the Spaniard; but at last, at the beginning of 1572, in consequence of strong representations from Madrid, she judged it politic to issue an order forbidding the Sea-Beggars to enter any English harbours. The pirates, thus deprived of the shelter which had made their depredations possible, would have been speedily in very bad case, but for an unexpected and surprising stroke of good fortune. It chanced that a large number of vessels under Lumbres and Treslong were driven by stress of weather into the estuary of the Maas; and finding that the Spanish garrison of Brill had left the town upon a punitive expedition, the rovers landed and effected an entry by burning one of the gates. The place was seized and pillaged, and the marauders were on the point of returning with their spoil to their ships, when at the suggestion of Treslong it was determined to place a garrison in the town and hold it as a harbour of refuge in the name of the Prince of Orange, as Stadholder of Holland. On April 1, 1572, the prince's flag was hoisted over Brill, and the foundation stone was laid of the future Dutch republic.

William himself at first did not realise the importance of this capture, and did not take any steps to express his active approval; but it was otherwise with his brother Lewis, who was at the time using his utmost endeavours to secure if not the actual help, at least the connivance, of Charles IX to his conducting an expedition from France into the Netherlands. Lewis saw at once the great advantage to the cause of the possession of a port like Brill, and he urged the Beggars to try and gain possession of Flushing also, before Alva's orders for the strengthening of the garrison and the defences had been carried out. Flushing by its position commanded the approach by water to Antwerp. When the ships of Lumbres and Treslong appeared before the town, the inhabitants rose in revolt, overpowered the garrison, and opened the gates. This striking success, following upon the taking of Brill, aroused great enthusiasm. The rebels had now a firm foothold both in Holland and Zeeland, and their numbers grew rapidly from day to day. Soon the whole of the island of Walcheren, on which Flushing stands, was in their hands with the exception of the capital Middelburg; and in Holland several important towns hoisted the flag of revolt and acknowledged the Prince of Orange as their lawful Stadholder. From Holland the rebellion spread into Friesland. Finally on June 19 an assembly of the Estates of Holland was, at the instance of Dordrecht, convened to meet in that town. There was but one representative of the nobility present at this meeting, whose legality was more than doubtful, but it included deputies of no less than twelve out of the fourteen towns which were members of the Estates. The prince sent Ste Aldegonde as his plenipotentiary. The step taken was practically an act of insurrection against the king. William had resigned his stadholdership in 1568 and had afterwards been declared an outlaw. Bossu had been by royal authority appointed to the vacant office. The Estates now formally recognised the prince as Stadholder of the king in Holland, Zeeland, West Friesland and Utrecht; and he was further invested with the supreme command of the forces both by land and sea and was charged with the duty of protecting the country against foreign oppression or invasion by foreign troops. Ste Aldegonde in the name of the prince announced his acceptance of the posts that had been conferred on him and declared that he desired, as a condition of such acceptance, that the principle of religious freedom and liberty of worship should be conceded to Catholics and Protestants alike. To this the Estates assented. Orange took an oath to maintain the towns in the rights and privileges of which they had been deprived by Alva and not to enter into any negotiations or conclude any treaty with Spain without their consent. The Court of Holland for the administration of justice was reconstituted and a Chamber of Finance erected. The question of finance was indeed crucial, for the new stadholder asked for a subsidy of 100,000 crowns a month for the support of the army he had raised for the invasion of Brabant; and the Estates agreed to take measures for appropriating certain taxes for the purpose, an undertaking which had, however, in this time of present distress small likelihood of effectual result.

The course of events indeed in the months which followed this historic gathering at Dordrecht was not encouraging to those who had thus dared somewhat prematurely to brave the wrath of Philip and the vengeance of Alva. Lewis of Nassau had for some time been engaged in raising a Huguenot force for the invasion of the southern Netherlands. The news of the capture of Brill and Flushing stirred him to sudden action. He had collected only a small body of men, but, with characteristic impetuosity he now led these across the frontier, and, before Alva was aware of his presence in Hainault, had captured by surprise Valenciennes and Mons (May 24). It was a rash move, for no sooner did the news reach the governor-general than he sent his son, Don Frederick of Toledo, at the head of a powerful force to expel the invader. Don Frederick quickly made himself master of Valenciennes and then proceeded (June 3) to lay siege to Mons, where Lewis, in hopes that relief would reach him, prepared for an obstinate defence. These hopes were not without foundation, for he knew that, beyond the Rhine, Orange with a considerable army was on the point of entering the Netherlands from the east, and that the Huguenot leader, Genlis, was leading another force from France to his succour. William at the head of 20,000 German and 3000 Walloon mercenaries actually entered Gelderland (July 7), captured Roeremonde and then marched into Brabant. Here (July 19) the news reached him of the complete defeat and annihilation of the raw levies of Genlis by Toledo's veteran troops. Hampered by lack of funds William now, as throughout his life, showed himself to be lacking in the higher qualities of military leadership. With an ill-paid mercenary force time was a factor of primary importance, nevertheless the prince made no effort to move from his encampment near Roeremonde for some five weeks. Meanwhile his troops got out of hand and committed many excesses, and when, on August 27, he set out once more to march westwards, he found to his disappointment that there was no popular rising in his favour. Louvain and Brussels shut their gates, and though Mechlin, Termonde and a few other places surrendered, the prince saw only too plainly that his advance into Flanders would not bring about the relief of Mons. All his plans had gone awry. Alva could not be induced to withdraw any portion of the army that was closely blockading Mons, but contented himself in following Orange with a force under his own command while avoiding a general action. And then like a thunderclap, September 5, the news of the massacre of St Bartholomew was brought to the prince, and he knew that the promise of Coligny to conduct 12,000 arquebusiers to the succour of Lewis could not be redeemed. In this emergency William saw that he must himself endeavour to raise the siege. He accordingly marched from Flanders and, September 11, encamped at the village of Harmignies, a short distance from Mons. In the night six hundred Spaniards, each of whom to prevent mistakes wore a white shirt over his armour, surprised the camp. The prince himself was awakened by a little dog that slept in his tent and only narrowly escaped with his life, several hundred of his troops being slain by the *Camisaders*. He was now thoroughly discouraged and on the following day retreated first to Mechlin, then to Roeremonde, where on September 30 the ill-fated expedition was disbanded. The retirement from Harmignies decided the fate of Mons. Favourable conditions were granted and Lewis of Nassau, who was ill with fever, met with chivalrous treatment and was allowed to return to Dillenburg.

William now found himself faced with something like financial ruin. Mercenary armies are very costly, and by bitter experience he had learnt the futility of opposing a half-hearted and badly disciplined force to the veteran troops of Alva. He resolved therefore to go in person to Holland to organise and direct the strong movement of revolt, which had found expression in the meeting of the Estates at Dordrecht. His agents had long been busy going about from town to town collecting funds in the name of the prince and encouraging the people in their resistance to the Inquisition and to foreign tyranny. William's declaration that henceforth he intended to live and die in their midst and to devote himself with all his powers to the defence of the rights and liberties of the land met with willing and vigorous support throughout the greater part of Holland, West Friesland and Zeeland; and contributions for the supply of the necessary ways and means began to flow in. It was, however, a desperate struggle to which he had pledged himself, and to which he was to consecrate without flinching the rest of his life. If, however, the prince's resolve was firm, no less so was that of Alva.

Alva had his enemies at the Spanish court, always ready to excite distrust against the duke in the mind of the suspicious king. In July, 1572, the Duke of Medina-Coeli had been sent from Spain to enquire into the state of affairs in the Netherlands; probably it was intended that he should take over the administration and supersede the governor-general. On his arrival, however, Medina-Coeli quickly saw that the difficulties of the situation required a stronger hand than his, and he did not attempt to interfere with Alva's continued exercise of supreme authority. The governor-general, on his side, knew well what was the meaning of this mission of Medina-Coeli, and no sooner was the army of Orange dispersed than he determined, while the reins of power were still in his hands, to visit the rebellious towns of the north with condign vengeance.

At the head of a powerful force, Frederick of Toledo marched northwards. Mechlin, which had received Orange, was given over for three days to pillage and outrage. Then Zutphen was taken and sacked. Naarden, which had, though without regular defences, dared to resist the Spaniards, was utterly destroyed and the entire population massacred. Amsterdam, one of the few towns of Holland which had remained loyal to the king, served as a basis for further operations. Although it was already December and the season was unfavourable, Toledo now determined to lay siege to the important town of Haarlem. Haarlem was difficult of approach. It was protected on two sides by broad sheets of shallow water, the Haarlem lake and the estuary of the Y, divided from one another by a narrow neck of land. On another side was a thick wood. It was garrisoned by 4000 men, stern Calvinists, under the resolute leadership of Ripperda and Lancelot Brederode. An attempt to storm the place (December 21) was beaten off with heavy loss to the assailants; so Toledo, despite the inclemency of the weather, had to invest the city. Another desperate assault, January 31, disastrously failed, and the siege was turned into a blockade. The position, however, of the besiegers was in some respects worse than that of the besieged; and Toledo would have abandoned his task in despair had not his father ordered him at all costs to proceed. William meanwhile made several efforts to relieve the town. Bodies of skaters in the winter, and when the ice disappeared, numbers of boats crossed over the Haarlem lake from Leyden and managed to carry supplies of food into the town, and resistance might have been indefinitely prolonged had not Bossu put a stop to all intercourse between Haarlem and the outside world by convoying a flotilla of armed vessels from the Y into the lake. Surrender was now only a question of time. On July 11, 1573, after a relieving force of 4000 men, sent by Orange, had been utterly defeated, and the inhabitants were perishing by famine, Toledo gained possession of Haarlem. The survivors of the heroic garrison were all butchered, and Ripperda and Brederode, their gallant leaders, executed. A number of the leading citizens were likewise put to death, but the town was spared from pillage on condition of paying a heavy fine. The siege had lasted seven months, and the army of Toledo, which had suffered terribly during the winter, is said to have lost twelve thousand men.

Alva in his letters to the king laid great stress on the clemency with which he had treated Haarlem. It had been spared the wholesale destruction of Zutphen and Naarden, and the duke hoped that by this exhibition of comparative leniency he might induce the other rebel towns to open their gates without opposition. He was deceived. On July 18 Alkmaar was summoned to surrender, but refused. Alva's indignation knew no bounds, and he vowed that every man, woman and child in the contumacious town should be put to the sword. The threat, however, could not at once be executed. Toledo's army, debarred from the sack of Haarlem, became mutinous through lack of pay. Until they received the arrears due to them, they refused to stir. Not till August 21 was Don Frederick able to invest Alkmaar with a force of 16,000 men. The garrison consisted of some 1300 burghers with 800 troops thrown into the town by Sonoy, Orange's lieutenant in North Holland. Two desperate assaults were repulsed with heavy loss, and then the Spaniards proceeded to blockade the town. Sonoy now, by the orders of the prince, gained the consent of the cultivators of the surrounding district to the cutting of the dykes. The camps and trenches of the besiegers were flooded out; and (October 8) the siege was raised and the army of Don Frederick retired, leaving Alkmaar untaken. Within a week another disaster befell the Spanish arms. Between Hoorn and Enkhuizen the fleet of Bossu on the Zuyder Zee was attacked by the Sea-Beggars and was completely defeated. Bossu himself was taken prisoner and was held as a hostage for the safety of Ste Aldegonde, who fell into the hands of the Spaniards about month later.

This naval victory, following upon the retreat from Alkmaar, strengthened greatly the efforts of Orange and gave fresh life to the patriot cause. It likewise marked the end of the six years of Alva's blood-stained rule in the Netherlands. Weary and disappointed, always hampered by lack of funds, angry at the loss of the king's confidence and chafing at the evidence of it in the presence of Medina-Coeli at his side, the governor-general begged that he might be relieved of his functions. His request was granted, October 29. The chosen successor was the Grand Commander, Don Luis de Requesens, governor of Milan. It was only with much reluctance that Requesens, finding the king's command insistent and peremptory, accepted the charge.

The Grand Commander was indeed far from being a suitable man for dealing with the difficult situation in the Netherlands, for he was a Spanish grandee pure and simple and did not even speak French. Even the loyalists received him coolly. He knew nothing of the country, and whatever his ability or disposition it was felt that he would not be allowed a free hand in his policy or adequate means for carrying it out. That his temper was conciliatory was quickly shown. An amnesty was proclaimed for political offenders except three hundred persons (among these Orange and his principal adherents), and pardon to all heretics who abjured their errors. He went even further than this by entering into a secret exchange of views with William himself through Ste Aldegonde as an intermediary, in the hope of finding some common meeting-ground for an understanding. But the prince was immovable. Unless freedom of worship, the upholding of all ancient charters and liberties and the removal of Spaniards and all foreigners from any share in the government or administration of the land were granted, resistance would be continued to the last. These were conditions Requesens had no power even to consider.

Orange during this time was on his side using all his diplomatic ability to gain help for the oppressed Netherlanders from France and England. But Charles IX had his own difficulties and was in too feeble health (he died May, 1574) to take any decided step, and Queen Elizabeth, though she connived at assistance being given to the rebel cause on strictly commercial terms, was not willing either to show open hostility to Philip or to support subjects in revolt against their sovereign. William's position appeared well-nigh desperate, for at the opening of the year 1574 his authority was only recognised in a few of the towns of Holland and in some of the Zeeland islands, and the Spaniards had sent a large force to invest Leyden. He had, however, made up his mind to cast in his lot with the brave Hollanders and Zeelanders in their gallant struggle against overwhelming odds. To identify himself more completely with his followers, the prince, October, 1573, openly announced his adhesion to Calvinism. There are no grounds for doubting his sincerity in taking this step; it was not an act of pure opportunism. His early Catholicism had probably been little more than an outward profession, and as soon as he began to think seriously about religious questions, his natural bent had led him first to the Lutheran faith of his family, and then to the sterner doctrines, which had gained so firm a foothold in the towns of Holland and Zeeland. Nevertheless William, though henceforth a consistent Calvinist, was remarkable among his contemporaries for the principles of religious toleration he both inculcated and practised. He was constitutionally averse to religious persecution in any form, and by the zealots of his party he was denounced as lukewarm; but throughout his life he upheld the right of the individual, who was peaceful and law-abiding, to liberty of opinion and freedom of worship.

The year 1574 opened favourably. By a remarkable feat of arms the veteran Spanish commander Mondragon had, October, 1572, reconquered several of the Zeeland islands. His men on one occasion at ebb-tide marched across the channel which lies between South Beveland and the mainland, the water reaching up to their necks. The patriot forces had since then recovered much of the lost ground, but Middelburg was strongly held, and so long as the Spaniards had command of the sea, was the key to the possession of Zeeland. On January 29, 1574, the Sea-Beggars under Boisot attacked the Spanish fleet near Roemerswaal and after a bloody encounter gained a complete victory. The siege of Middelburg was now pressed and Mondragon surrendered, February 18. The prince at once set to work to create a patriot government in the province. Four towns had representatives, Middelburg, Zierikzee, Veere and Flushing. William himself acquired by purchase the marquisate of Flushing and thus was able to exercise a preponderating influence in the Provincial Estates, all of whose members were required to be Calvinists and supporters of the rebel cause.

The investment of Leyden by the Spaniards threatened however, now that Haarlem had fallen, to isolate South Holland and Zeeland; and William did not feel himself strong enough to make any serious attempt to raise the siege. Lewis of Nassau therefore, with the help of French money, set himself to work with his usual enthusiastic energy to collect a force in the Rhineland with which to invade the Netherlands from the east and effect a diversion. At the head of 7000 foot and 3000 horse—half-disciplined troops, partly Huguenot volunteers, partly German mercenaries—he tried to cross the Meuse above Maestricht with the intention of effecting a junction with the Prince of Orange. He was accompanied by John and Henry of Nassau, his brothers, and Christopher, son of the Elector Palatine. He found his course blocked by a Spanish force under the command of Sancho d'Avila and Mondragon. The encounter took place on the heath of Mook (April 14) and ended in the crushing defeat of the invaders. Lewis and his young brother, Henry, and Duke Christopher perished, and their army was completely scattered. The death of his brothers was a great grief to William. Lewis had for years been his chief support, and the loss of this dauntless champion was indeed a heavy blow to the cause for which he had sacrificed his life. He was only thirty-six years of age, while Henry, the youngest of the Nassaus, to whom the Prince was deeply attached, was but a youth of twenty-four.

The invasion of Lewis had nevertheless the result of raising the siege of Leyden; but only for a time. After the victory at Mook the Spanish troops were free to continue the task of reconquering rebel Holland for the king. On May 26 a strong force under Valdez advanced to Leyden and completely isolated the town by surrounding it with a girdle of forts. The attack came suddenly, and unfortunately the place had not been adequately provisioned. So strong was the position of the Spaniards that the stadholder did not feel that any relieving force that he could send would have any chance of breaking through the investing lines and revictualling the garrison. In these circumstances he summoned, June 1, a meeting of the Estates of Holland at Rotterdam and proposed, as a desperate resource, that the dykes should be cut and the land submerged, and that the light vessels of the Sea-Beggars under Boisot should sail over the waters, attack the Spanish forts and force an entrance into the town. After considerable opposition the proposal was agreed to and the waters were allowed to flow out upon the low-lying fields, villages and farms, which lie between the sea, the Rhine, the Waal and the Maas. Unfortunately the season was not favourable, and though the water reached nearly to the higher land round Leyden on which the Spanish redoubts were erected, and by alarming Valdez caused him to press the blockade more closely, it was not deep enough even for the light-draught vessels, which Boisot had gathered together, to make their way to the town. So the month of August passed and September began. Meanwhile the prince, who was the soul of the enterprise, was confined to his sickbed by a violent attack of fever, and the pangs of famine began to be cruelly felt within the beleaguered town. A portion of the citizens were half-hearted in the struggle, and began to agitate for surrender and even sent out emissaries to try to make terms with the Spanish commander. But there were within Leyden leaders of iron resolution, the heroic Burgomaster Pieter Adriaanzoon van der Werf; the commandant of the garrison, Jan van der Does; Dirk van Bronkhorst, Jan van Hout and many others who remained staunch and true in face of the appalling agony of a starving population; men who knew the fate in store for them if they fell into the enemy's hands and were determined to resist as long as they had strength to fight. At last in mid-September faint hopes began to dawn. William recovered, and a fierce equinoctial gale driving the flood-tide up the rivers gradually deepened the waters up to the very dyke on which the entrenchments of the besiegers stood. Urged on by Orange, Boisot now made a great effort. Anxiously from the towers was the approach of the relieving fleet watched. The town was at the very last extremity. The people were dying of hunger on every side. Some fierce combats took place as soon as the Sea-Beggars, experts at this amphibious warfare, arrived at the outlying Spanish forts, but not for long. Alarmed at the rising of the waters and fearing that the fleet of Boisot might cut off their escape, the Spaniards retreated in the night; and on the morning of October 3 the vessels of the relieving force, laden with provisions, entered the town. The long-drawn-out agony was over and Leyden saved from the fate of Haarlem, just at the moment when further resistance had become impossible. Had Leyden fallen the probability is that the whole of South Holland would have been conquered, and the revolt might have collapsed. In such a narrow escape well might the people of the town see an intervention of Providence on their behalf. The prince himself hastened to Leyden on the following day, reorganised the government of the town and in commemoration of this great deliverance founded the University, which was to become in the 17th century one of the most famous seats of learning in Europe.

The successful relief of Leyden was followed by a mutiny of the army of Valdez. They were owed long arrears of pay, had endured great hardships, and now that they saw themselves deprived of the hope of the pillage of the town, they put their commander and his officers under arrest and marched under a leader elected by themselves into Utrecht. Other mutinies occurred in various parts of the southern provinces, for Requesens had no funds, and it was useless to appeal to Philip, for the Spanish treasury was empty. This state of things led to a practical cessation of active hostilities for many months; and Requesens seized the opportunity to open negotiations with Orange. These were, however, doomed to be fruitless, for the king would not hear of any real concessions being made to the Protestants. The position of William was equally beset with difficulties, politically and financially. In the month following the relief of Leyden he even threatened to withdraw from the country unless his authority were more fully recognised and adequate supplies were furnished for the conduct of the war. The Estates accordingly, November 12, asked him to assume the title of Regent or Governor, with "absolute might, authority and sovereign control" of the affairs of the country. They also voted him an allowance of 49,000 guilders a month; but, while thus conferring on the man who still claimed to be the "Stadholder of the king" practically supreme power, the burgher-corporations of the towns were very jealous of surrendering in the smallest degree that control over taxation which was one of their most valued rights. The exercise of authority, however, by the prince from this time forward was very great, for he had complete control in military and naval matters, and in the general conduct of affairs he held all the administrative threads in his own hands. He had become indispensable, and in everything but name a sovereign in Holland and Zeeland.

The first part of 1575 was marked by a lull in warlike operations, and conferences were held at Breda between envoys of Orange and Requesens, only to find that there was no common ground of agreement. The marriage of the prince (June 24) with Charlotte de Bourbon, daughter of the Duke of Montpensier, was a daring step which aroused much prejudice against him. The bride, who was of the blood-royal of France, had been Abbess of Jouarre, but had abjured her vows, run away and become a Calvinist. This was bad enough, but the legality of the union was rendered the more questionable by the fact that Anne of Saxony was still alive. On all sides came protests—from Charlotte's father, from John of Nassau, and from Anne's relations in Saxony and Hesse. But William's character was such that opposition only made him more determined to carry out his purpose. The wedding was celebrated at Brill with Calvinist rites. The union, whether legitimate or not, was undoubtedly one of great happiness.

Meanwhile the governor-general, unable to obtain any financial help from Spain, had managed to persuade the provinces, always in dread of the excesses of the mutinous soldiery, to raise a loan of 1,200,000 guilders to meet their demands for arrears of pay. Requesens was thus enabled to put in the late summer a considerable army into the field and among other successes to gain possession of the Zeeland islands, Duiveland and Schouwen. On September 27 a force under the command of the veteran Mondragon waded across the shallow channels dividing the islands, which fell into their hands. Zierikzee, the chief town of Schouwen, made a stout resistance, but had at length to surrender (July, 1576). This conquest separated South Holland from the rest of Zeeland; and, as Haarlem and Amsterdam were in the hands of the Spaniards, the only territory over which the authority of Orange extended was the low-lying corner of land between the Rhine and the Maas, of which Delft was the centre.

The situation again appeared well-nigh desperate, and the stadholder began to look anxiously round in the hope of obtaining foreign assistance. It was to the interest of both France and England to assist a movement which distracted the attention and weakened the power of Spain. But Henry III of France was too much occupied with civil and religious disturbances in his own country, and Elizabeth of England, while receiving with courtesy the envoys both of Orange and Requesens, gave evasive replies to both. She was jealous of France, and pleased to see the growing embarrassment of her enemy Philip, but the Tudor queen had no love either for rebels or for Calvinists. While refusing therefore openly to take the side of the Hollanders and Zeelanders, she agreed to give them secret help; and no obstacle was placed in the way of the English volunteers, who had already since 1572 been enlisting in the Dutch service. It was at this time that those English and Scottish Brigades were first formed which remained for nearly two centuries in that service, and were always to be found in the very forefront of the fighting throughout the great war of Liberation.

On March 4, 1576, Requesens died; and in the considerable interval that elapsed before the arrival of his successor, the outlook for the patriot cause became distinctly brighter. The Estates of Holland and Zeeland met at Delft (April 25, 1576); and the assembly was noteworthy for the passing of an Act of Federation. This Act, which was the work of Orange, bound the two provinces together for common action in defence of their rights and liberties and was the first step towards that larger union, which three years later laid the foundations of the Dutch Republic. By this Act sovereign powers were conferred upon William; he was in the name of the king to exercise all the prerogatives of a ruler. It required all his influence to secure the insertion of articles (1) extending a certain measure of toleration to all forms of religious worship that were not contrary to the Gospel, (2) giving authority to the prince in case of need to offer the Protectorate of the federated provinces to a foreign prince. Orange knew only too well that Holland and Zeeland were not strong enough alone to resist the power of Spain. His hopes of securing the support of the other provinces, in which Catholics were in the majority, depended, he clearly saw, on the numerous adherents to the ancient faith in Holland and Zeeland being protected against the persecuting zeal of the dominant Calvinism of those provinces. In any case—and this continued to be his settled conviction to the end of his life—the actual independence of the whole or any portion of the Netherlands did not seem to him to lie within the bounds of practical politics. The object for which he strove was the obtaining of substantial guarantees for the maintenance of the ancient charters, which exempted the provinces from the presence of foreign officials, foreign tribunals, foreign soldiery and arbitrary methods of taxation. As Philip had deliberately infringed all those privileges which he had sworn to maintain, it was the duty of all patriotic Netherlanders to resist his authority, and, if resistance failed to bring redress, to offer the sovereignty with the necessary restrictions to some other prince willing to accept it on those conditions and powerful enough to protect the provinces from Spanish attack. In order to grasp the principles which guided William's policy during the next few years it is essential to bear in mind (1) that he sought to bring about a union of all the Netherland provinces on a basis of toleration, (2) that he did not aim at the erection of the Netherlands into an independent State.

On the death of Requesens the Council of State had assumed temporary charge of the administration. There had for some time been growing dissatisfaction even amongst the loyalist Catholics of the southern provinces at the presence and over-bearing attitude of so many Spanish officials and Spanish troops in the land and at the severity of the religious persecution. Representations were made to the king by the Council of State of the general discontent throughout the country, of the deplorable results of the policy of force and repression, and urging the withdrawal of the troops, the mitigation of the edicts, and the appointment of a member of the royal house to the governorship. To these representations and requests no answer was sent for months in accordance with Philip's habitual dilatoriness in dealing with difficult affairs of State. He did, however, actually nominate in April his bastard brother, Don John of Austria, the famous victor of Lepanto, as Requesens' successor. But Don John, who was then in Italy, had other ambitions, and looked with suspicion upon Philip's motives in assigning him the thankless task of dealing with the troubles in the Low Countries. Instead of hurrying northwards, he first betook himself to Madrid where he met with a cold reception. Delay, however, so far from troubling Philip, was thoroughly in accordance with the whole bent of his character and policy. For six months Don John remained in Spain, and it was a half-year during which the situation in the Netherlands had been to a very large extent transformed.

The position of Orange and his followers in Holland and Zeeland in the spring of 1576 had again darkened. In June the surrender of Zierikzee to Mondragon was a heavy blow to the patriot cause, for it gave the Spaniards a firm footing in the very heart of the Zeeland archipelago and drove a wedge between South Holland and the island of Walcheren. This conquest was, however, destined to have important results of a very different character from what might have been expected. The town had surrendered on favourable terms and pillage was forbidden. Baulked of their expected booty, the Spanish troops, to whom large arrears of pay were due, mutinied. Under their own "eletto" they marched to Aalst, where they were joined by other mutineers, and soon a large force was collected together, who lived by plunder and were a terror to the country. The Council declared them to be outlaws, but the revolted soldiery defied its authority and scoffed at its threats. This was a moment which, as Orange was quick to perceive, was extremely favourable for a vigorous renewal of his efforts to draw together all the provinces to take common action in their resistance to Spanish tyranny. His agents and envoys in all parts of the Netherlands, but especially in Flanders and Brabant, urged his views upon the more influential members of the provincial estates and upon leading noblemen, like the Duke of Aerschot and other hitherto loyal supporters of the government, who were now suspected of wavering. His efforts met with a success which a few months earlier would have been deemed impossible. The conduct of the Spanish troops, and the lack of any central authority to protect the inhabitants against their insolence and depredations, had effected a great change in public opinion. In Brussels Baron de Héze (a god-child of the prince) had been appointed to the command of the troops in the pay of the Estates of Brabant. De Héze exerted himself to arouse popular opinion in the capital in favour of Orange and against the Spaniards. To such an extent was he successful that he ventured, Sept. 21, to arrest the whole of the Council of State with the exception of the Spanish member Roda, who fled to Antwerp. William now entered into direct negotiations with Aerschot and other prominent nobles of Flanders and Brabant. He took a further step by sending, at the request of the citizens of Ghent, a strong armed force to protect the town against the Spanish garrison in the citadel. In the absence of any lawful government, the States-General were summoned to meet at Brussels on September 22. Deputies from Brabant, Flanders and Hainault alone attended, but in the name of the States-General they nominated Aerschot, Viglius and Sasbout as Councillors of State, and appointed Aerschot to the command of the forces, with the Count of Lalaing as his lieutenant. They then, Sept. 27, approached the prince with proposals for forming a union of all the provinces. As a preliminary it was agreed that the conditions, which had been put forward by William as indispensable—namely, exclusion of all foreigners from administrative posts, dismissal of foreign troops, and religious toleration—should be accepted. The proposals were gladly received by William, and Ghent was chosen as the place where nine delegates from Holland and Zeeland should confer with nine delegates nominated by the States-General as representing the other provinces. They met on October 19. Difficulties arose on two points—the recognition to be accorded to Don John of Austria, and the principle of non-interference with religious beliefs. Orange himself had always been an advocate of toleration, but the representatives of Holland and Zeeland showed an obstinate disinclination to allow liberty of Catholic worship within their borders; and this attitude of theirs might, in spite of the prince's efforts, have led to a breaking-off of the negotiations, had not an event occurred which speedily led to a sinking of differences on the only possible basis, that of mutual concession and compromise.

The citadel of Antwerp was, during this month of October, garrisoned by a body of mutinous Spanish troops under the command of Sancho d'Avila, the victor of Mook. Champagney, the governor, had with him a body of German mercenaries under a certain Count Oberstein; and at his request, such was the threatening attitude of the Spaniards, the States-General sent Havré with a reinforcement of Walloon troops. On Sunday, November 4, the garrison, which had been joined by other bands of mutineers, turned the guns of the citadel upon the town and sallying forth attacked the forces of Champagney. The Germans offered but a feeble resistance. Oberstein perished; Champagney and Havré took refuge on vessels in the river; and the Spaniards were masters of Antwerp. The scene of massacre, lust and wholesale pillage, which followed, left a memory behind it unique in its horror even among the excesses of this blood-stained time. The "Spanish Fury," as it was called, spelt the ruin of what, but a short time before, had been the wealthiest and most flourishing commercial city in the world.

The news of this disaster reached the States-General, as they were in the act of considering the draft proposals which had been submitted to them by the Ghent conference. At the same time tidings came that Don John, who had travelled through France in disguise, had arrived at Luxemburg. They quickly therefore came to a decision to ratify the pact, known as the *Pacification of Ghent,* and on November 8 it was signed. The *Pacification* was really a treaty between the Prince of Orange and the Estates of Holland and Zeeland on the one hand, and the States-General representing the other provinces. It was agreed that the Spanish troops should be compelled to leave the Netherlands and that the States-General of the whole seventeen provinces, as they were convened at the abdication of Charles V, should be called together to decide upon the question of religious toleration and other matters of national importance. Meanwhile the placards against heresy were suspended, and all the illegal measures and sentences of Alva declared null and void. His confiscated property was restored to Orange, and his position, as stadholder in Holland and Zeeland, acknowledged. Don John was informed that he would not be recognised as governor-general unless he would consent to dismiss the Spanish troops, accept the Pacification of Ghent, and swear to maintain the rights and privileges of the Provinces. Negotiations ensued, but for a long time to little purpose; and Don John, who was rather an impetuous knight-errant than a statesman and diplomatist, remained during the winter months at Namur, angry at his reception and chafing at the conditions imposed upon him, which he dared not accept without permission from the king. In December the States-General containing deputies from all the provinces met at Brussels, and in January the Pacification of Ghent was confirmed, and a new compact, to which the name of the Union of Brussels was given, was drawn up by a number of influential Catholics. This document, to which signatures were invited, was intended to give to the Pacification of Ghent the sanction of popular support and to be at the same time a guarantee for the maintenance of the royal authority and the Catholic religion. The Union of Brussels was generally approved throughout the southern provinces, and the signatories from every class were numbered by thousands. Don John, who was at Huy, saw that it was necessary to temporise. He was willing, he declared, to dismiss the foreign troops and send them out of the country and to maintain the ancient charters and liberties of the provinces, provided that nothing was done to subvert the king's authority or the Catholic faith. Finally, on February 12, a treaty called "The Perpetual Edict," a most inappropriate name, was signed, and the States-General acknowledged Don John as governor-general. The agreement was principally the work of Aerschot and the loyalist Catholic party, who followed his leadership, and was far from being entirely acceptable to Orange. He had no trust in the good faith of either Philip or his representative, and, though he recommended Holland and Zeeland to acquiesce in the treaty and acknowledge Don John as governor-general, it was with the secret resolve to keep a close watch upon his every action, and not to brook any attempt to interfere with religious liberty in the two provinces, in which he exercised almost sovereign power and with whose struggles for freedom he had identified himself.

The undertaking of Don John with regard to the Spanish troops was punctually kept. Before the end of April they had all left the country; and on May 1 the new governor-general made his state entry into Brussels. It was to outward appearances very brilliant. But the hero of Lepanto found himself at once distrusted by the Catholic nobles and checkmated by the influence and diplomacy of the ever watchful William of Orange. Chafing at his impotence, and ill-supported by the king, who sent no reply to his appeals for financial help, Don John suddenly left the capital and, placing himself at the head of a body of Walloon troops, seized Namur. Feeling himself in this stronghold more secure, he tried to bring pressure on the States-General to place in his hands wider powers and to stand by him in his efforts to force Orange to submit to the authority of the king. His efforts were in vain. William had warned the States-General and the nobles of the anti-Spanish party in Brabant and Flanders that Don John was not to be trusted, and he now pointed to the present attitude of the governor-general, as a proof that his suspicions were well-founded. Indeed the eyes of all true patriots began to turn to the prince, who had been quietly strengthening his position, not only in Holland and Zeeland, where he was supreme, but also in Utrecht and Gelderland; and popular movements in Brussels and elsewhere took place in his favour. So strongly marked was the Orange feeling in the capital that the States-General acceded to the general wish that the prince should be invited to come in person to Brussels. Confidence was expressed by Catholics no less than by Protestants that only under his leadership could the country be delivered from Spanish tyranny. A deputation was sent, bearing the invitation; but for a while William hesitated in giving an affirmative reply.

On September 23, however, he made his entry into Brussels amidst general demonstrations of joy and was welcomed as "the Restorer and Defender of the Father-land's liberty." Thus, ten years after he had been declared an outlaw and banished, did the Prince of Orange return in triumph to the town which had witnessed the execution of Egmont and Hoorn. It was the proudest day of his life and the supreme point of his career.

## CHAPTER V

## WILLIAM THE SILENT

The position of William at Brussels after his triumphant entry, September 23, 1577, was by no means an easy one. His main support was derived from a self-elected Council of Eighteen, containing representatives of the gilds and of the citizens. This Council controlled an armed municipal force and was really master in the city. In these circumstances the States-General did not venture upon any opposition to the popular wishes, in other words to William, whose influence with the masses was unbounded. The States-General, therefore, under pressure from the Eighteen, informed Don John, October 8, that they no longer recognised him as governor-general; and the Estates of Brabant appointed the prince to the office of *Ruward* or governor of the province. Meanwhile a fresh factor of disturbance had been introduced into the troubled scene. Certain of the Catholic nobles opposed to Spanish rule, but suspicious of Orange, had invited the twenty year old Archduke Matthias, brother of the emperor, to accept the sovereignty of the Netherlands. Matthias, who was of an adventurous spirit, after some parleying agreed. He accordingly left Vienna secretly, and at the end of October arrived in the Netherlands. Not content with this counter-stroke, Aerschot went to Ghent to stir up opposition to the appointment of William as Ruward of Brabant. The populace however in Ghent was Orangist, and, rising in revolt, seized Aerschot and a number of other Catholic leaders and threw them into prison. They were speedily released, but the breach between the Catholic nobles and the Calvinist stadholder of Holland was widened. William himself saw in the coming of Matthias a favourable opportunity for securing the erection of the

Netherlands into a constitutional State under the nominal rule of a Habsburg prince. By his influence, therefore, the States-General entered into negotiations with the Archduke; and Matthias finally was recognised (December 8) as governor on condition that he accepted the Union of Brussels, He was also induced to place the real power in the hands of Orange with the title of Lieutenant-General. Matthias made his state entry into Brussels, January 18, 1578. His position appeared to be strengthened by a treaty concluded with the English queen (January 7) by which Elizabeth promised to send over a body of troops and to grant a subsidy to the States, for the repayment of which the towns of Middelburg, Bruges and Gravelines were to be pledges.

The news however of the step taken by Matthias had had more effect upon Philip II than the despairing appeals of his half-brother. A powerful army of tried Spanish and Italian troops under the command of Alexander Farnese, Prince of Parma, son of the former regent Margaret, was sent to Flanders. Farnese was Don John's nephew, and they had been brought up together at Madrid, being almost of the same age. Already Philip had determined to replace Don John, whose brilliance as a leader in the field did not compensate for his lack of statesmanlike qualities. In Farnese, whether by good fortune or deliberate choice, he had at length found a consummate general who was to prove himself a match even for William the Silent in all the arts of political combination and intrigue. At Gembloux, January 31, Don John and Parma fell upon the levies of the States and gained a complete and almost bloodless victory. Had Philip supplied his governor-general with the money he asked for, Don John might now have conquered the whole of the southern Netherlands, but without funds he could achieve little.

Meanwhile all was confusion. The States-General withdrew from Brussels to Antwerp; and William, finding that Matthias was useless, began negotiations with France, England and Germany in the hope of finding in this emergency some other foreign prince ready to brave the wrath of Philip by accepting the suzerainty of the Netherlands. The Duke of Anjou, brother of the French king, was the favoured candidate of the Catholic party; and William, whose one aim was to secure the aid of a powerful protector in the struggle against Spain, was ready to accept him. Anjou at the head of an army of 15,000 men crossed the frontier at Mons, July 12; and, on the following August 13, a treaty was agreed upon between him and the States-General, by which the French duke, with the title of *Defender of the Liberties of the Netherlands*, undertook to help the States to expel the Spaniards from the Low Countries. But, to add to the complications of the situation, a German force under the command of John Casimir, brother of the Elector Palatine, and in the pay of Queen Elizabeth, invaded the hapless provinces from the east. The advent of John Casimir was greeted with enthusiasm by the Calvinist party; and it required all the skill and sagacity of the Prince of Orange to keep the peace and prevent the rival interests from breaking out into open strife in the face of the common enemy. But Don John was helpless, his repeated appeals for financial help remained unanswered, and, sick at heart and weary of life, he contracted a fever and died in his camp at Namur, October 1, 1578. His successor in the governor-generalship was Alexander of Parma, who had now before him a splendid field for the exercise of his great abilities.

The remainder of the year 1578 saw a violent recrudescence of religious bitterness. In vain did Orange, who throughout his later life was a genuine and earnest advocate of religious toleration, strive to the utmost of his powers and with untiring patience to allay the suspicions and fears of the zealots. John Casimir at Ghent, in the fervour of his fanatical Calvinism, committed acts of violence and oppression, which had the very worst effect in the Walloon provinces. In this part of the Netherlands Catholicism was dominant; and there had always been in the provinces of Hainault, Artois, and in the southern districts generally, a feeling of distrust towards Orange. The upholding of the principle of religious toleration by a man who had twice changed his faith was itself suspect; and Farnese left no means untried for increasing this growing anti-Orange feeling among the Catholic nobles. A party was formed, which bore the name of "The Malcontents," whose leaders were Montigny, Lalaing and La Motte. With these the governor-general entered into negotiations, with the result that an alliance was made between Hainault, Artois, Lille, Douay and Orchies (January 6, 1579), called the Union of Arras, for the maintenance of the Catholic faith, by which these Walloon provinces and towns expressed their readiness to submit to the king on condition that he were willing to agree to uphold their rights and privileges in accordance with the provisions of the Pacification of Ghent. The Union of Arras did not as yet mean a complete reconciliation with the Spanish sovereign, but it did mean the beginning of a breach between the Calvinist north and the Catholic south, which the statecraft of Parma gradually widened into an impossible chasm. Before this took place, Anjou, Matthias and John Casimir had alike withdrawn from the scene of anarchic confusion, in which for a brief time each had been trying to compass his own ambitious ends in selfish indifference to the welfare of the people they were proposing to deliver from the Spanish yoke. The opening of the year 1579 saw Orange and Parma face to face preparing to measure their strength in a grim struggle for the mastery.

In the very same month as witnessed the signing of the Union of Arras, a rival union had been formed in the northern Netherlands, which was destined to be much more permanent. The real author however of the Union of Utrecht was not Orange, but his brother, John of Nassau. In March, 1578, John had been elected Stadholder of Gelderland. He, like William, had devoted himself heart and soul to the cause of Netherland freedom, but his Calvinism was far more pronounced than his brother's. From the moment of his acceptance of the stadholdership he set to work to effect a close union between Holland, Zeeland and Utrecht with Gelderland and the adjoining districts which lay around the Zuyder Zee. It was a difficult task, since the eastern provinces were afraid (and not unjustly) that its much greater wealth would give Holland predominance in the proposed confederation. Nevertheless it was accomplished, and an Act of Union was drawn up and signed at Utrecht, January 29, 1579, by the representatives of Holland, Zeeland, the town and district (*sticht*) of Utrecht, Gelderland and Zutphen, by which they agreed to defend their rights and liberties and to resist all foreign intervention in their affairs by common action as if they were one province, and to establish and maintain freedom of conscience and of worship within their boundaries. William does not seem at first to have been altogether pleased with his brother's handiwork. He still hoped that a confederation on a much wider scale might have been formed, comprising the greater part of those who had appended their signatures to the Pacification of Ghent. It was not until some months had passed and he saw that his dreams of a larger union were not to be realised, that he signed, on May 3, the Act of Union drawn up at Utrecht. By this time he was well aware that Parma had succeeded in winning over the malcontent nobles to accept his terms. On May 19 the Walloon provinces, whose representatives had signed the Union of Arras, agreed to acknowledge, with certain nominal reservations, the sovereignty of Philip and to allow only Catholic worship. In fact the reconciliation was complete.

Thus, despite the efforts of Orange, the idea of the federation of all the seventeen provinces on national lines became a thing of the past, henceforth unattainable. The Netherlands were divided into two camps. Gradually in the course of 1580 Overyssel, Drente and the greater part of Friesland gave in their adherence to the Union of Utrecht, and Groningen and the Ommelanden allied themselves with their neighbours. In the rest of the Low Countries all fell away and submitted themselves to the king's authority, except Antwerp and Breda in Brabant, and Ghent, Bruges and Ypres in Flanders. William felt that Parma was constantly gaining ground. Defection after defection took place, the most serious being that of George Lalaing, Count of Renneberg, the Stadholder of Groningen. Negotiations were indeed secretly opened with William himself, and the most advantageous and flattering terms offered to him, if he would desert the patriot cause. But with him opposition to Spain and to Spanish methods of government was a matter of principle and strong conviction. He was proof alike against bribery and cajolery, even when he perceived, as the year 1580 succeeded 1579, that he had no staunch friends on whom he could absolutely rely, save in the devoted provinces of Holland and Zeeland.

For things had been going from bad to worse. The excesses and cruelties committed by the Calvinists, wherever they found themselves in a position to persecute a Catholic minority, and especially the outrages perpetrated at Ghent under the leadership of two Calvinist fanatics, De Ryhove and De Hembyze, although they were done in direct opposition to the wishes and efforts of Orange, always and at all times the champion of toleration, did much to discredit him in Flanders and Brabant and to excite bitter indignation among the Catholics, who still formed the great majority of the population of the Netherlands. William felt himself to be month by month losing power. The action he was at last compelled to take, in rescuing Ghent from the hands of the ultra-democratic Calvinist party and in expelling De Ryhove and De Hembyze, caused him to be denounced as "a papist at heart." Indeed the bigots of both creeds in that age of intolerance and persecution were utterly unable to understand his attitude, and could only attribute it to a lack of any sincere religious belief at all. Farnese, meanwhile, whose genius for Machiavellian statesmanship was as remarkable as those gifts for leadership in war which entitled him to rank as the first general of his time, was a man who never failed to take full advantage of the mistakes and weaknesses of his opponents. At the head of a veteran force he laid siege in the spring of 1579 to the important frontier town of Maestricht. He encountered a desperate resistance, worthy of the defence of Haarlem or of Leyden, and for four months the garrison held out grimly in the hope of relief. But, despite all the efforts of Orange to despatch an adequate force to raise the siege, at last (June 29) the town was carried by assault and delivered up for three days to the fury of a savage soldiery. By the possession of this key to the Meuse, Parma was now able to cut off communications between Brabant and Protestant Germany. Had he indeed been adequately supported by Philip it is probable that at this time all the provinces up to the borders of Holland might have been brought into subjection by the Spanish forces.

The position of William was beset with perils on every side. One by one his adherents were deserting him; even in the provinces of Holland and Zeeland he was losing ground. He saw clearly that without foreign help the national cause for which he had sacrificed everything was doomed. In this emergency he reopened negotiations with Anjou, not because he had any trust in the French prince's capacity or sincerity, but for the simple reason that there was no one else to whom he could turn. As heir to the throne of France and at this time the favoured suitor of Queen Elizabeth, his acceptance of the sovereignty of the Netherlands would secure, so Orange calculated, the support both of France and England. It was his hope also that the limiting conditions attached to the offer of sovereignty would enable him to exercise a strong personal control over a man of weak character like Anjou. The Duke's vanity and ambition were flattered by the proposal; and on September 19, 1580, a provisional treaty was signed at Plessis-les-Tours by which Anjou accepted the offer that was made to him, and showed himself quite ready to agree to any limitations imposed upon his authority, since he had not any intention, when once he held the reins of power, of observing them.

The first effect of William's negotiations with Anjou was to alienate the Calvinists without gaining over the Catholics. Anjou was suspect to both. The action of the Spanish government, however, at this critical juncture did much to restore the credit of the prince with all to whom the Spanish tyranny and the memory of Alva were abhorrent. Cardinal Granvelle, after fifteen years of semi-exile in Italy, had lately been summoned to Madrid to become chief adviser to the king. Granvelle spared no pains to impress upon Philip the necessity of getting rid of Orange as the chief obstacle to the pacification of the Netherlands, and advised that a price should be placed upon his life. "The very fear of it will paralyse or kill him" was the opinion of the cardinal, who ought to have had a better understanding of the temper and character of his old adversary. Accordingly at Maestricht, March 15, 1581, "a ban and edict in form of proscription" was published against the prince, who was denounced as "a traitor and miscreant, an enemy of ourselves and of our country"; and all and everywhere empowered "to seize the person and goods of this William of Nassau, as enemy of the human race." A solemn promise was also made "to anyone who has the heart to free us of this pest, and who will deliver him dead or alive, or take his life, the sum of 25,000 crowns in gold or in estates for himself and his heirs; and we will pardon him any crimes of which he has been guilty, and give him a patent of nobility, if he be not noble." It is a document which, however abhorrent or loathsome it may appear to us, was characteristic of the age in which it was promulgated and in accordance with the ideas of that cruel time. The ban was a declaration of war to the knife, and as such it was received and answered.

In reply to the ban the prince at the close of the year (December 13) published a very lengthy defence of his life and actions, the famous *Apology*. To William himself is undoubtedly due the material which the document embodies and the argument it contains, but it was almost certainly not written by him, but by his chaplain, Pierre L'Oyseleur, Seigneur de Villiers, to whom it owes its rather ponderous prolixity and redundant verbiage. Historically it is of very considerable value, though the facts are not always to be relied upon as strictly accurate. The *Apology* was translated into several languages and distributed to the leading personages in every neighbouring country, and made a deep impression on men's minds.

The combined effect of the *Ban* and *the Apology* was to strengthen William's position in all the provinces where the patriot party still held the upper hand; and he was not slow to take advantage of the strong anti-Spanish feeling which was aroused. Its intensity was shown by the solemn Act of Abjuration, July 26, 1581, by which the provinces of Brabant, Flanders, Holland, Zeeland, Utrecht and Gelderland renounced their allegiance to Philip II on the ground of his tyranny and misrule. But after signing this Act it never seems to have occurred to the prince or to the representatives of the provinces, that these now derelict territories could remain without a personal sovereign. Orange used all his influence and persuasiveness to induce them to accept Anjou. Anjou, as we have seen, had already agreed to the conditions under which he should, when invited, become "prince and lord" of the Netherlands. In the autumn of 1581 the position was an ambiguous one. The States-General claimed that, after the abjuration of Philip, the sovereignty of the provinces had reverted to them, as the common representative of a group of provinces that were now sovereign in their own right, and that the conferring of that sovereignty on another overlord was their prerogative. The position of Orange was peculiar, for *de facto* under one title or another he exercised the chief authority in each one of the rebel provinces, but in the name of the States-General, instead of the king. His influence indeed was so great as to over-shadow that of the States-General, but great as it was, it had to be exerted to the utmost before that body could be induced to accept a man of Anjou's despicable and untrustworthy character as their new ruler. William however had committed himself to the candidature of the duke, through lack of any fitter choice; and at last both the States-General and the several provincial Estates (Holland and Zeeland excepted) agreed to confer the sovereignty upon the French prince subject to the conditions of the treaty of Plessis-les-Tours.

William himself exercised the powers with which Holland and Zeeland had invested him in the name of the king, whose stadholder he was, even when waging war against him. After the Abjuration this pretence could no longer be maintained. The Estates of Holland and Zeeland had indeed petitioned Orange to become their count, but he refused the title, fearing to give umbrage to Anjou. Finding, however, the two provinces resolute in their opposition to the Valois prince, he consented, July 24, 1581, to exercise provisionally, as if he were count, the powers of "high supremacy," which had already been conferred upon him. Meanwhile Anjou was dallying in England, but on receiving through Ste Aldegonde an intimation that the States could brook no further delay, he set sail and landed at Flushing. Lord Leicester and a brilliant English escort accompanied him; and Elizabeth asked the States to receive her suitor as "her own self." At Antwerp, where he took up his residence, Anjou was (February 19) solemnly invested with the duchy of Brabant, and received the homage of his new subjects. He was far from popular, and William remained at his side to give him support and counsel. On March 18 (Anjou's birthday) an untoward event occurred, which threatened to have most disastrous consequences. As Orange was leaving the dinner-table, a young Biscayan, Juan Jaureguy by name, attempted his assassination, by firing a pistol at him. The ball entered the head by the right ear and passed through the palate. Jaureguy was instantly killed and it was afterwards found that he had, for the sake of the reward, been instigated to the deed by his master, a merchant named Caspar Anastro. Anjou, who was at first suspected of being accessory to the crime, was thus exculpated. It was a terrible wound and William's life was for some time in great danger; but by the assiduous care of his physicians and nurses he very slowly recovered, and was strong enough, on May 2, to attend a solemn service of thanksgiving. The shock of the event and the long weeks of anxiety were however too heavy a strain upon his wife, Charlotte de Bourbon, who had recently given birth to their sixth daughter. Her death, on May 5, was deeply grieved by the prince, for Charlotte had been a most devoted helpmeet and adviser to him throughout the anxious years of their married life. During the whole of the summer and autumn William remained at Antwerp, patiently trying to smooth away the difficulties caused by the dislike and suspicion felt by the Netherlanders for the man whom they were asked to recognise as their sovereign. It was an arduous task, but William, at the cost of his own popularity, succeeded in getting the duke acknowledged in July as Lord of Friesland and Duke of

Gelderland, and in August Anjou was solemnly installed at Bruges, as Count of Flanders. Meanwhile he was planning, with the help of the large French force which Anjou had undertaken to bring into the Netherlands, to take the offensive against Parma. The truth is that he and Anjou were really playing at cross-purposes. Orange wished Anjou to be the *roi-fainéant* of a United Netherland state of which he himself should be the real ruler, but Anjou had no intention of being treated as a second Matthias. He secretly determined to make himself master of Antwerp by a sudden attack and, this achieved, to proceed to seize by force of arms some of the other principal cities and to make himself sovereign in reality as well as in name. He resented his dependence upon Orange and was resolved to rid himself of it. With shameless treachery in the early morning of January 17, 1583, he paid a visit to the prince in Antwerp, and, with the object of gaining possession of his person, tried to persuade him to attend a review of the French regiments who were encamped outside the town. The suspicions of William had however been aroused, and he pleaded some excuse for declining the invitation. At midday some thousands of Anjou's troops rushed into the city at the dinner-hour with loud cries of "Ville gagnée! Tue! Tue!" But the citizens flew to arms; barricades were erected; and finally the French were driven out with heavy loss, leaving some 1500 prisoners in the hands of the town-guard. Many French nobles perished, and the "French Fury," as it was called, was an ignominious and ghastly failure. Indignation was wide and deep throughout the provinces; and William's efforts to calm the excitement and patch up some fresh agreement with the false Valois, though for the moment partially successful, only added to his own growing unpopularity.

The prince in fact was so wedded to the idea that the only hope for the provinces lay in securing French aid that he seemed unable to convince himself that Anjou after this act of base treachery was impossible. His continued support of the duke only served to alienate the people of Brabant and Flanders. The Protestants hated the thought of having as their sovereign a prince who was a Catholic and whose mother and brothers were looked upon by them as the authors of the massacre of St Bartholomew. The Catholics, cajoled by Parma's fair words, and alarmed by the steady progress of his arms, were already inclining to return to their old allegiance.

The marriage of Orange, April 7, 1583, to Louise, daughter of the famous Huguenot leader Admiral Coligny, and widow of the Sieur de Téligny, added to the feelings of distrust and hostility he had already aroused, for the bride was a Frenchwoman and both her father and husband had perished on the fatal St Bartholomew's day.

Finding himself exposed to insult, and his life ever in danger, William, at the end of July, left Antwerp and took up his residence again at Delft in the midst of his faithful Hollanders. They, too, disliked his French proclivities, but his alliance with Louise de Téligny seemed to be an additional pledge to these strong Calvinists of his religious sincerity.

Meanwhile Anjou had already returned to France; and Parma had now a freer field for his advance northwards and, though sorely hampered by lack of funds, was rapidly taking town after town. In the spring of 1584 he took Ypres and Bruges, and a strong party in Ghent was in traitorous correspondence with him. Many nobles had fallen away from the patriot cause, among them William's brother-in-law, Count van den Berg, who had succeeded John of Nassau as Stadholder of Gelderland. The hold of Orange upon Brabant and the Scheldt was, however, still ensured by the possession of Antwerp, of which strongly fortified town the trusty Ste Aldegonde was governor.

Meanwhile the prince, who was still striving hard to persuade the provinces that were hostile to Spanish rule that their only hope lay in obtaining aid from France through Anjou, was living at the old convent of St Agatha, afterwards known as the Prinsenhof at Delft. His manner of life was of the most modest and homely kind, just like that of an ordinary Dutch burgher. He was in fact deeply in debt, terribly worried with the outward aspect of things, and his position became one of growing difficulty, for on June 10, 1584, the miserable Anjou died, and the policy on which he had for so long expended his best efforts was wrecked. Even his own recognition as Count of Holland and Zeeland had led to endless negotiations between the Estates and the various town councils which claimed to have a voice in the matter; and in July, 1584, he had, though provisionally exercising sovereign authority, not yet received formal homage. And all this time, in addition to the other cares that weighed heavily upon him, there was the continual dread of assassination. Ever since the failure of the attempt of Jaureguy, there had been a constant succession of plots against the life of the rebel leader and heretic at the instigation of the Spanish government, and with the knowledge of Parma. Religious fanaticism, loyalty to the legitimate sovereign, together with the more sordid motive of pecuniary reward, made many eager to undertake the murderous commission. It was made the easier from the fact that the prince always refused to surround himself with guards or to take any special precautions, and was always easy of access. Many schemes and proposed attempts came to nothing either through the vigilance of William's spies or through the lack of courage of the would-be assassins. A youth named Balthazar Gérard had however become obsessed with the conviction that he had a special mission to accomplish the deed in which Jaureguy had failed, and he devoted himself to the task of ridding the world of one whom he looked upon as the arch-enemy of God and the king. Under the false name of Francis Guyon he made his way to Delft, pretended to be a zealous Calvinist flying from persecution, and went about begging for alms. The prince, even in his poverty always charitable, hearing of his needy condition sent to the man a present of twelve crowns. With this gift Gérard bought a pair of pistols and on July 10, 1584, having managed on some pretext to gain admittance to the Prinsenhof, he concealed himself in a dark corner by the stairs just opposite the door of the room where William and his family were dining. As the prince, accompanied by his wife, three of his daughters and one of his sisters, came out and was approaching the staircase, the assassin darted forward and fired two bullets into his breast. The wound was mortal; William fell to the ground and speedily expired. Tradition says that, as he fell, he exclaimed in French: "My God, have pity on my soul! My God, have pity on this poor people!" But an examination of contemporary records of the murder throws considerable doubt on the statement that such words were uttered. The nature of the wound was such that the probability is that intelligible speech was impossible.

Balthazar Gérard gloried in his deed, and bore the excruciating tortures which were inflicted upon him with almost superhuman patience and courage. He looked upon himself as a martyr in a holy cause, and as such he was regarded by Catholic public opinion. His deed was praised both by Granvelle and Parma, and Philip bestowed a patent of nobility on his family, and exempted them from taxation.

In Holland there was deep and general grief at the tragic ending of the great leader, who had for so many years been the fearless and indefatigable champion of their resistance to civil and religious tyranny. He was accorded a public funeral and buried with great pomp in the Nieuwe Kerk at Delft, where a stately memorial, recording his many high qualities and services, was erected to his memory.

William of Orange was but fifty-one years of age when his life was thus prematurely ended, and though he had been much aged by the cares and anxieties of a crushing responsibility, his physicians declared that at the time of his death he was perfectly healthy and that he might have been spared to carry on his work for many years, had he escaped the bullets of the assassin. But it was not to be. It is possible that he should be reckoned in the number of those whose manner of death sets the seal to a life-work of continuous self-sacrifice. The title of "Father of his Country," which was affectionately given to him by Hollanders of every class, was never more deservedly bestowed, for it was in the Holland that his exertions had freed and that he had made the impregnable fortress of the resistance to Spain that he ever felt more at home than anywhere else. It was in the midst of his own people that he laid down the life that had been consecrated to their cause. As a general he had never been successful. As a statesman he had failed to accomplish that union of the Netherlands, north and south, which at one triumphant moment had seemed to be well-nigh realised by the Pacification of Ghent. But he had by the spirit that he had aroused in Holland and its sister province of Zeeland created a barrier against Spanish domination in the northern Netherlands which was not to be broken down.

## CHAPTER VI

## THE BEGINNINGS OF THE DUTCH REPUBLIC

At the moment of the assassination of William the Silent it might well have seemed to an impartial observer that the restoration of the authority of the Spanish king over the whole of the Netherlands was only a question of time. The military skill and the statecraft of Alexander Farnese were making slow but sure progress in the reconquest of Flanders and Brabant. Despite the miserable inadequacy of the financial support he received from Spain, the governor-general, at the head of a numerically small but thoroughly efficient and well-disciplined army, was capturing town after town. In 1583 Dunkirk, Nieuport, Lindhoven, Steenbergen, Zutphen and Sas-van-Gent fell; in the spring of 1584 Ypres and Bruges were already in Spanish hands, and on the very day of William's death the fort of Liefkenshoek on the Scheldt, one of the outlying defences of Antwerp, was taken by assault. In August Dendermonde, in September Ghent, surrendered. All West Flanders, except the sea-ports of Ostend and Sluis, had in the early autumn of 1584 been reduced to the obedience of the king. The campaign of the following year was to be even more successful. Brussels, the seat of government, was compelled by starvation to capitulate, March 10; Mechlin was taken, July 19; and finally Antwerp, after a memorable siege, in which Parma displayed masterly skill and resource, passed once more into the possession of the Spaniards. The fall of this great town was a very heavy blow to the patriot cause, and it was likewise the ruin of Antwerp itself. A very large part of its most enterprising inhabitants left their homes rather than abjure their religious faith and took refuge in Holland

and Zeeland, or fled across the Rhine into Germany. Access to the sea down the Scheldt was closed by the fleets of the Sea Beggars, and the commerce and industry of the first commercial port of western Europe passed to Amsterdam and Middelburg. Meanwhile there had been no signs of weakness or of yielding on the part of the sturdy burghers of Holland and Zeeland. On the fatal July 10, 1584, the Estates of Holland were in session at Delft. They at once took energetic action under the able leadership of Paul Buys, Advocate of Holland, and John van Oldenbarneveldt, Pensionary of Rotterdam. They passed a resolution "to uphold the good cause with God's help without sparing gold or blood." Despatches were at once sent to the Estates of the other provinces, to the town councils and to the military and naval commanders, affirming their own determined attitude and exhorting all those who had accepted the leadership of the murdered Prince of Orange "to bear themselves manfully and piously without abatement of zeal on account of the aforesaid misfortune." Their calm courage at such a moment of crisis reassured men's minds. There was no panic. Steps were at once taken for carrying on the government in Holland, Zeeland and Utrecht. Stimulated by the example of Holland, the States-General likewise took prompt action. On August 18 a Council of State was appointed to exercise provisionally the executive powers of sovereignty, consisting of eighteen members, four from Holland, three each from Zeeland and Friesland, two from Utrecht and six from Brabant and Flanders. Of this body Maurice of Nassau, William's seventeen year-old son, was nominated first Councillor, and a pension of 30,000 guilders per annum was granted him. At the same time Louise de Coligny was invited to take up her residence in Holland and suitable provision was made for her. William Lewis, son of Count John of Nassau, was elected Stadholder of Friesland. Count Nieuwenaar was Stadholder of Gelderland and shortly afterwards also of Utrecht and Overyssel. Owing to the youth of Maurice the question as to whether he should become Count of Holland and Zeeland or be elected Stadholder was left in abeyance until it should be settled to which of two foreign rulers the sovereignty of the provinces, now that Anjou was dead, should be offered.

In the revolted provinces the responsible leaders were at this time practically unanimous in their opinion that any attempt on their part to carry on the struggle against the power of Spain without foreign assistance was hopeless; and it was held that such assistance could only be obtained by following in the footsteps of William and offering to confer the overlordship of the provinces on another sovereign in the place of Philip II. There were but two possible candidates, Henry III of France and Elizabeth of England.

There were objections to both, but the rapid successes of Parma made it necessary to take action. The partisans of a French alliance were in the majority, despite the efforts of a strong opposition headed by Paul Buys; and an embassy (January, 1585) was despatched to Paris to offer conditionally to the French king the Protectorship of Holland and Zeeland and sovereignty over the other provinces. The negotiations went on for a couple of months, but Henry III finally declined the offer. Another embassy was sent, July, 1585, to England, but Elizabeth refused absolutely to accept the sovereignty. She however was not averse to the proposal that she should despatch a body of troops to the armed assistance of the provinces, provided that adequate guarantees were given for the outlay. She was afraid of Philip II and, though she had no love for men who were rebels to their lawful sovereign, was quite willing to use them for her own ends. Her motives therefore were mixed and purely self-interested; nevertheless it is doubtful if the negotiations would have led to any definite result, had not the news of the fall of Antwerp made both parties feel that this was no time for haggling or procrastination. Elizabeth therefore promised to send at once 6000 troops under the command of a "gentleman of quality," who should bear the title of governor-general. He was to co-operate with the Council of State (on which two Englishmen were to sit) in restoring order and in maintaining and defending the ancient rights and privileges of the provinces. The governor-general and all other officials were to take an oath of fealty both to the States-General and to the queen. The towns of Flushing and Brill with the fort of Rammekens were to be handed over in pledge to Elizabeth for the repayment of expenses and received English garrisons. They were known as "the cautionary towns."

At the end of October the States were informed that the choice of the queen had fallen upon her favourite, Robert Dudley, Earl of Leicester, and that he would shortly set out for the Netherlands.

Holland and Zeeland, ever jealous of foreign interference with their rights and privileges, resolved now to forestall the arrival of the English governor-general by appointing Maurice of Nassau, with the title of "Excellency," to the offices of Stadholder and Admiral and Captain-General of both provinces; and the Count of Hohenlo was nominated (Maurice being still little more than a boy) to the actual command of the State's forces. Leicester set sail from Harwich accompanied by a fleet of fifty vessels and landed at Flushing on December 19. He met everywhere with an enthusiastic reception. The States-General were eager to confer large powers upon him. Practically he was invested with the same authority as the former regent, Mary of Hungary, with the reservation that the States-General and the Provincial Estates should meet at their own instance, that the present stadholders should continue in office, and that appointments to vacant offices should be made from two or three persons nominated by the Provincial Estates. A new Council of State was created which, as previously agreed, included two Englishmen. On February 4, 1586, Leicester's government was solemnly inaugurated in the presence of Maurice of Nassau and the States-General, and he accepted the title of "Excellency." Elizabeth on hearing this was very angry and even threatened to recall Leicester, and she sent Lord Heneage to express both to the States-General and the governor-general her grave displeasure at what had taken place. She bade Leicester restrict himself to the functions that she had assigned to him, and it was not until July that she was sufficiently appeased to allow him to be addressed as "Excellency."

All this was galling to Leicester's pride and ambition, and did not tend to improve his relations with the States. An English governor would in any case have had a difficult task, and Leicester had neither tact nor capacity as a statesman, and no pretensions as a military leader. He possessed no knowledge of the institutions of the country or the character of the people, and was ignorant of the Dutch language. The measures he took and the arbitrary way in which he tried to enforce them, soon brought him face to face with the stubborn resistance of the Estates of Holland under the leadership of Oldenbarneveldt. In April, 1586, he issued a very stringent placard forbidding all traffic with the enemy's lands and more especially the supplying of the enemy with grain. He meant it well, for he had been informed that the cutting-off of this commerce, which he regarded as illicit, would deprive the Spaniards of the necessaries of life, and Parma's position would become desperate. This carrying trade had, however, for long been a source of much profit to the merchants and shipowners of Holland and Zeeland; indeed it supplied no small part of the resources by which those two provinces had equipped the fleets and troops by which they had defended themselves against the efforts of the Spanish king. Two years before this the States-General had tried to place an embargo on the traffic in grain, but the powerful town-council of Amsterdam had refused obedience and the Estates of Holland supported them in their action. The deputies of the inland provinces, which had suffered most from the Spanish armies, were jealous of the prosperity of the maritime States, and regarded this trade with the Spaniard as being carried on to their injury. But Holland and Zeeland supplied the funds without which resistance would long since have been impossible, and they claimed moreover, as sovereign provinces, the right to regulate their trade affairs. The edict remained a dead-letter, for there was no power to enforce it.

The governor made a still greater mistake when, in his annoyance at the opposition of the Hollanders, he courted the democratic anti-Holland party in Utrecht, which had as its leader the ultra-Calvinist stadholder, Nieuwenaar, and caused one of his confidants, a Brabanter, Gerard Prounick, surnamed Deventer, to be elected burgomaster of Utrecht, although as a foreigner he was disqualified from holding that office. An even more arbitrary act was his creation of a Chamber of Finance armed with inquisitorial powers, thus invading the rights of the Provincial Estates and depriving the Council of State of one of its most important functions. To make matters worse, he appointed Nieuwenaar to preside over the new Chamber, with a Brabanter, Jacques Reingoud, as treasurer-general, and a Fleming, Daniel de Burchgrave, as auditor. The Estates of Holland, under the guidance of Oldenbarneveldt, prepared themselves to resist stubbornly this attempt to thrust upon them a new tyranny.

As a military leader Leicester was quite unfitted to oppose successfully such a general as Parma. Both commanders were in truth much hampered by the preparations that were being made by Philip for the invasion of England. The king could spare Parma but little money for the pay of his troops, and his orders were that the Spanish forces in the Netherlands should be held in reserve and readiness for embarkation, as soon as the Great Armada should hold command of the Channel. England was the first objective. When its conquest was accomplished that of the rebel provinces would speedily follow. On the other hand Elizabeth, always niggardly, was little disposed in face of the threatened danger to dissipate her resources by any needless expenditure. Leicester therefore found himself at the head of far too small a force to deal any effective blows at the enemy. He succeeded in capturing Doesburg, but failed to take Zutphen. It was in a gallant effort to prevent a Spanish convoy from entering that town that Sir Philip Sidney met his death at the combat of Warnsfeld (Sept. 22, 1586). An important fort facing Zutphen was however stormed, and here Leicester left Sir Robert Yorke with a strong garrison, and at the same time sent Sir William Stanley with 1200 men to be governor of Deventer. These appointments gave rise to much criticism that proved later to be fully justified, for both these officers were Catholics and had formerly been in the Spanish service. Leicester had also taken other steps that were ill-judged. West Friesland had for many years been united to Holland and was known as the North-Quarter. The governor-general, however, appointed Sonoy Stadholder of West Friesland, and was thus infringing the rights and jurisdiction of Maurice of Nassau. Maurice also held the post of Admiral-General of Holland and Zeeland, but Leicester took it upon himself to create three distinct Admiralty Colleges, those of Holland, Zeeland, and the North-Quarter, thus further dividing authority in a land where greater unity was the chief thing to be aimed at. Leicester was equally unwise in the part he took in regard to religious matters. Oldenbarneveldt, Paul Buys and the great majority of burgher-regents in Holland belonged to the moderate or, as it was called, the "libertine" party, to which William the Silent had adhered and whose principles of toleration he had strongly upheld. Leicester, largely influenced by spite against Oldenbarneveldt and the Hollanders for their opposition to his edict about trade with the enemy and to his appointment of Sonoy, threw himself into the arms of the extreme Calvinists, who were at heart as fanatical persecutors as the Spanish inquisitors themselves. These "precisian" zealots held, by the governor-general's permission and under his protection, a synod at Dort, June, 1586, and endeavoured to organise the Reformed Church in accordance with their strict principles of exclusiveness.

By this series of maladroit acts Leicester had made himself so unpopular and distrusted in Holland that the Estates of that predominant province lost no opportunity of inflicting rebuffs upon him. Stung by the opposition he met and weary of a thankless task, the governor determined at the end of November to pay a visit to England. The Council of State was left in charge of the administration during his absence.

His departure had the very important effect of bringing the question of State-rights acutely to the front. The dislike and distrust felt by the Hollanders towards the English governor-general was greatly increased by the treachery of Yorke and Stanley, who delivered the fort at Zutphen and the town of Deventer, with the defence of which they had been charged, into the hands of the Spaniards. The town of Gelder and the fort at Wouw were likewise betrayed, and there can be small doubt that, had Parma at this time been able to take advantage of the dissensions in the ranks of his adversaries, he would have met with little effectual resistance to his arms. His whole attention was, however, centred in preparations for the proposed invasion of England. Leicester had no sooner left the country than the Estates of Holland, under the strong leadership of Oldenbarneveldt, took measures to assert their right to regulate their own affairs, independently of the Council of State. A levy of troops was made (in the pay of the province of Holland), who were required to take an oath to the Provincial Estates and the stadholder. To Maurice the title of "Prince" was given; and Sonoy in the North-Quarter and all the commanders of fortified places were compelled to place themselves under his orders. The States-General, in which the influence of Holland and its chief representative, Oldenbarneveldt, was overpoweringly great, upheld the Provincial Estates in the measures they were taking. As a result of their action the trade restrictions were practically repealed, the Council of State was reconstituted, and a strong indictment of Leicester's conduct and administration was drawn up in the name of the States-General and forwarded to the absent governor in England.

Elizabeth was indignant at the language of this document, but at this particular time the dangers which were threatening her throne and people were too serious for her to take any steps to alienate the States. It was her obvious policy to support them in their resistance, and to keep, if possible, Parma's forces occupied in the Netherlands. Accordingly Leicester returned to his post, July 1587, but in an altogether wrong spirit. He knew that he had a strong body of partisans in Utrecht, Friesland and elsewhere, for he had posed as the friend of the people's rights against the nobles and those burgher-aristocracies in the cities in whose hands all real power rested, and by his attitude in religious matters he had won for himself the support of the Calvinist preachers. His agents, Deventer in Utrecht, Aysma in Friesland and Sonoy in the North-Quarter, were able men, who could count on the help of the democracy, whom they flattered. So Leicester came back with the determination to override the opposition of the Estates of Holland and compel their submission to his will. But he found that he only succeeded in making that opposition more resolute. His attempts to overthrow the supremacy of the "regents" in Amsterdam, Leyden, Enkhuizen and other towns were complete failures. Oldenbarneveldt and Maurice were supreme in Holland and Zeeland; and the power of the purse gave to Holland a controlling voice in the States-General. The position of Leicester was shaken also by his inability to relieve Sluis, which important seaport fell after a long siege into Parma's hands, August 5. Its capture was attributed by rumour, which in this case had no foundation, to the treachery of the English governor and garrison. Moreover it was discovered that for some months secret peace negotiations had been passing between the English government and Parma; and this aroused violent suspicions that the Netherlands were merely being used as pawns in English policy, and alienated from the governor-general the sympathy of the preachers, who had been his strongest supporters. Humiliated and broken in spirit, Leicester, after many bickerings and recriminations, finally left the Netherlands (December 10), though his formal resignation of his post did not reach the States-General until the following April. Lord Willoughby was placed in command of the English troops.

The year 1588 was the beginning of a decade full of fate for the Dutch Republic. The departure of Leicester left the seven provinces of the Union of Utrecht weak, divided, torn by factions, without allies, the country to the east of the Yssel and to the south of the Scheldt and the Waal already in the hands of the enemy. Moreover the armed forces of that enemy were far stronger than their own and under the command of a consummate general. But this was the year of the Spanish Armada, and Parma's offensive operations were, by the strictest orders from Madrid, otherwise directed. And Elizabeth on her side, though highly offended at the treatment which her favourite, Leicester, had received from the Hollanders, was too astute to quarrel at such a moment with a people whose ships kept a strict blockade in the Scheldt and before the Flemish harbours. Thus a respite was obtained for the States at this critical time, which was turned to good account and was of vital import for their constitutional development. The Leicestrian period, despite its record of incompetence and failure, had however the distinction of being the period which for good or for evil gave birth to the republic of the United Netherlands, as we know it in history. The curious, amorphous, hydra-headed system of government, which was to subsist for some two centuries, was in its origin the direct result of the confused welter of conflicting forces, which was the legacy of Leicester's rule. As a preliminary to a right understanding of the political system, which was now, more by accidental force of circumstances than by design, developing into a permanent constitution, it will be necessary to trace the events of the years which immediately followed the departure of Leicester, and which under the influence and by the co-operation of three striking personalities were to mould the future of the Dutch republic.

Those three personalities were John van Oldenbarneveldt, Maurice of Nassau and his cousin William Lewis of Nassau, the Stadholder of Friesland. Born in 1547, Oldenbarneveldt, after studying Jurisprudence at Louvain, Bourges and Heidelberg, became a devoted adherent of William the Silent and took part in the defence of Haarlem and of Leyden. His abilities, however, fitted him to take a prominent part as a politician and administrator rather than as a soldier; and his career may be said to have begun by his appointment to the post of Pensionary of Rotterdam in 1576. In this capacity his industry and his talent speedily won for him a commanding position in the Estates of Holland, and he became one of the Prince of Orange's confidential friends and advisers. In 1586 he was appointed Advocate of Holland in succession to Paul

Buys. This office included the duties of legal adviser, secretary and likewise in a sense that of "Speaker" to the Provincial Estates. In addition to all this he was the mouthpiece in the States-General of the deputation representing the Provincial Estates, and exercised in that assembly all the authority attaching to the man who spoke in the name of Holland. At this time of transition, by his predominance alike in his own province of Holland and in the States-General, he was able to secure for the general policy of the Union, especially in the conduct of foreign affairs, a continuity of aim and purpose that enabled the loosely-cemented and mutually jealous confederacy of petty sovereign states to tide-over successfully the critical years which followed the departure of Leicester, and to acquire a sense of national unity.

The brain and the diplomatic skill of the great statesman would, however, have been of little avail without the aid of the military abilities of Maurice of Nassau. Maurice was twenty years of age when Leicester left Holland. He was a man very different from his father in opinions and in the character of his talents. Maurice had nothing of his father's tolerance in religious matters or his subtle skill in diplomacy. He was a born soldier, but no politician, and had no wish to interfere in affairs of State. He had the highest respect for Oldenbarneveldt and complete confidence in his capacity as a statesman, and he was at all times ready to use the executive powers, which he exercised by virtue of the numerous posts he was speedily called upon to fill, for the carrying out of Oldenbarneveldt's policy; while the Advocate on his side found in the strong arm of the successful general the instrument that he needed for the maintenance of his supremacy in the conduct of the civil government. Already in 1587 Maurice was Stadholder of Holland and Zeeland. In 1588 he became Captain-General and Admiral-General of the Union with the control and supervision of all the armed forces of the Provinces by sea and by land. The death of Nieuwenaar in the following year created a vacancy in the stadholderates of Utrecht, Gelderland and Overyssel. Maurice was in each province elected as Nieuwenaar's successor. The Advocate therefore and the Prince, through the close accord which was for many years to subsist between them, gathered thus into their hands (except in Friesland) practically the entire administrative, executive and military powers of the United Provinces and by their harmonious co-operation with William Lewis, the wise and capable Stadholder of Friesland, were able to give something of real unity to a group of states, each claiming to be a sovereign entity, and to give them the outward semblance of a federal republic. There was no "eminent head," but the sovereignty in reality, if not in name, was vested during the period with which we have now to deal in this triumvirate.

Circumstances provided a favourable field for the display of the youthful Maurice's military abilities. In 1589 the assassination of Henry III placed Henry of Navarre on the throne of France. The accession of the brilliant Huguenot leader led to civil war; and the Catholic opposition was encouraged and supported by Philip II, who regarded Henry IV as a menace and danger to the Spanish power. Parma, therefore, whose active prosecution of the war against the rebel provinces had been so long hindered by having to hold his army in readiness for the projected invasion of England, found himself, after the failure and destruction of the Armada, in no better position for a campaign in the northern Netherlands. Disappointment and false charges against him brought on a serious illness, and on his recovery he received orders to conduct an expedition into France. William Lewis of Nassau had for sometime been urging upon the States-General that the time for remaining upon the strict defensive was past, and that, when the enemy's efforts were weakened and distracted, the best defence was a vigorous offensive. At first he spoke to deaf ears, but he found now a powerful supporter in Maurice, and the two stadholders prevailed. They had now by careful and assiduous training created a strong and well-disciplined army for the service of the States. This army was made up by contingents of various nationalities, English, Scottish, French and German as well as Netherlanders. But the material was on the whole excellent, and the entire force was welded together by confidence in their leaders.

In 1590 the capture of Breda by a ruse (seventy men hidden beneath a covering of peat making their entrance into the town and opening the gates to their comrades outside) was a good omen for the campaign that was planned for 1591. For the first time Maurice had an opportunity for showing his genius for war and especially for siege warfare. By rapid movements he took first Zutphen, then Deventer and Delfzijl, and relieved the fort of Knodsenburg (near

Nijmwegen). Thus successful on the eastern frontier, the stadholder hurried to Zeeland and captured Hulst, the key to the land of Waas. He then turned his steps again to the east and appearing suddenly before Nijmwegen made himself master of this important city. Such a succession of brilliant triumphs established Maurice's fame, and to a lesser degree that of William Lewis, whose co-operation and advice were of the greatest service to the younger man. This was markedly the case in the following year (1592) when the two stadholders set to work to expel the Spaniards from the two strongly fortified towns of Steenwijk and Coevorden, whose possession enabled a strong force under the veteran Verdugo to retain their hold upon Friesland. The States army was not at its full strength, for the English contingent under Sir Francis Vere had been sent to France; and Verdugo was confident that any attempt to capture these well-garrisoned fortresses was doomed to failure. He had to learn how great was the scientific skill and resource of Maurice in the art of beleaguering. Steenwijk after an obstinate defence capitulated on June 5. Coevorden was then invested and in its turn had to surrender, on September 12. During this time Parma had been campaigning with no great success in northern France. In the autumn he returned to the Netherlands suffering from the effects of a wound and broken in spirit. Never did any man fill a difficult and trying post with more success and zeal than Alexander Farnese during the sixteen years of his governor-generalship. Nevertheless Philip was afraid of his nephew's talents and ambition, and he despatched the Count of Fuentes with a letter of recall. It was never delivered. Parma set out to meet him, but fell ill and died at Spa, December 2, 1592. He appointed the Count of Mansfeld to take his place, until the Archduke Ernest of Austria, who had been appointed to succeed him, arrived in the Netherlands.

The campaign of 1593 was marked by the taking of Geertruidenberg, a fortress which barred the free access of the Hollanders and Zeelanders to the inland waters. The science which Maurice displayed in the siege of this town greatly increased his renown. In the following year the stadholders turned their attention to the north-east corner of the land, which was still in the possession of the Spaniards. After a siege of two months Groningen surrendered; and the city with the surrounding district was by the terms of the capitulation—known as "The Treaty of

Reduction"—admitted as a province into the Union under the name of *Stad en Landen*. William Lewis was appointed stadholder, and Drente was placed under his jurisdiction. The northern Netherlands were now cleared of the enemy, and Maurice at the conclusion of the campaign made a triumphal entry into the Hague amidst general rejoicing. William Lewis lost no time in taking steps to establish Calvinism as the only recognised form of faith in his new government. His strong principles did not allow him to be tolerant, and to Catholicism he was a convinced foe. Everywhere throughout the United Provinces the reformed religion was now dominant, and its adherents alone could legally take part in public worship.

In January, 1595, Henry IV declared war against Spain and was anxious for an alliance with the States against the common enemy. The Archduke Ernest, on whose coming into the Netherlands great hopes had been placed, found himself now in a difficult position with hostile armies threatening from both sides and no hope of efficient financial or other support from Spain. He was instructed therefore to enter into negotiations at the Hague with a view to the conclusion of a peace, based upon the terms of the Pacification of Ghent. But there was never any prospect of an agreement being reached; and the sudden death of the archduke (February 20, 1595) brought the negotiations to an end. Archduke Ernest was succeeded by the Count of Fuentes as governor *ad interim*. Fuentes proved himself to be a strong and capable commander; and the summer was marked by a series of successes against the hostile forces both of the French and the Netherlanders. There was no decisive encounter, but the Spanish forces foiled the efforts of their adversaries to effect an invasion or capture any towns.

The Cardinal Archduke Albert arrived at Brussels to replace Fuentes in January, 1596. Albert was the favourite nephew of King Philip, and had been brought up at Madrid. Although an ecclesiastic, he proved himself to be a statesman and soldier of more than ordinary capacity. It was intended that he should, as soon as the Pope's consent could be obtained, divest himself of his orders and marry his cousin the Infanta Isabel. The bankrupt condition of Spain prevented Philip from furnishing the archduke with adequate financial help on entering upon his governorship, but Albert was provided with some money, and he found in the Netherlands the well-disciplined and war-tried force of which Fuentes had made such good use in the previous campaign. He was anxious to emulate that general's success, and as the veteran leaders, Mondragon and Verdugo, had both died, he gave the command to the Seigneur de Rosne, a French refugee. This man was a commander of skill and enterprise, and special circumstances enabled him by two brilliant offensive strokes to capture first Calais and afterwards Hulst. Hulst was only taken after a severe struggle, in which De Rosne himself fell.

The special circumstances which favoured these operations were brought about by the conclusion of a treaty of alliance between France, England and the States. This treaty was the result of prolonged negotiations; it was of short duration and its conditions were far from favourable to the United Provinces, but it was of great importance from the fact that for the first time the new-fledged republic was recognised by the neighbouring sovereigns of France and England as an independent state and was admitted into alliance on terms of equality. It was, however, only with difficulty and through the insistence of Henry IV that Elizabeth was induced to acknowledge the independent status of the rebel provinces. In return the republic was required to keep up a force of 8000 men for service in the Netherlands, and to despatch 4000 men to act with the French army in northern France—this auxiliary force to include the five English regiments in the States' service. Thus Maurice was deprived of a considerable part of his army and obliged to act on the defensive. Elizabeth also insisted upon the carrying out of Leicester's placard forbidding trade with the enemy. This clause of the treaty was very unpalatable to Amsterdam and the Hollanders generally, and only a sullen acquiescence was given to it. From the first it was systematically evaded. The English government on their part undertook to support the French king with a force equal in strength to that furnished by the Provinces, *i.e.* 4000 men, but at the same time a secret treaty was drawn up by which Henry agreed to a reduction of the English troops by one-half. This piece of underhand work was in due time discovered by the States, who saw that their allies were not to be trusted and that they must be on the watch lest their interests should be sacrificed to the selfish policy of France. The issue showed that Henry IV was in fact ready to make terms with Spain, as soon as it was to his advantage to do so. Meanwhile in 1597 the French king, by advancing in force into Picardy, drew upon this frontier the chief attention of the Spaniards; and Maurice seized the opportunity that was offered to him to conduct an offensive campaign with signal success.

He began the year brilliantly by surprising in January, while still in its winter quarters, a Spanish force of 4500 near Turnhout. More than half the force was destroyed. On the side of the Netherlands eight men only fell. With the spring began a series of sieges; and, one after the other, Rheinberg, Meurs, Groenloo, Breedevoort, Enschede, Ootmarsum, Oldenzaal and Lingen were captured. Gelderland, Overyssel and Drente were entirely freed from the presence of the enemy. With the opening of 1598 Henry IV and Philip II entered upon negotiations for a peace. The French king felt the necessity of a respite from war in order to reorganise the resources of his country, exhausted by a long continuance of civil strife; and Philip was ill and already feeling his end approaching. The States strove hard to prevent what they regarded as desertion, and two embassies were despatched to France and to England to urge the maintenance of the alliance. Oldenbarneveldt himself headed the French mission, but he failed to turn Henry from his purpose. A treaty of peace between France and Spain was signed at Vervins, May 2, 1598. Oldenbarneveldt went from Paris to England and was more successful. Elizabeth bargained however for the repayment of her loan by annual installments, and for armed assistance both by land and sea should an attack be made by the Spaniards on England. The queen, however, made two concessions. Henceforth only one English representative was to have a seat in the Council of State; and all the English troops in the Netherlands, including the garrisons of the cautionary towns, were to take an oath of allegiance to the States.

This year saw the accomplishment of a project on which the Spanish king had for some time set his heart—the marriage of the Cardinal Archduke Albert to his cousin the Infanta Isabel Clara Eugenia, and the erection of the Netherlands into an independent sovereignty under their joint rule. Philip hoped in this way to provide suitably for a well-beloved daughter and at the same time, by the grant of apparent independence to the Netherland provinces, to secure their allegiance to the new sovereigns. The use of the word "apparent" is justified, for provision was made in the deed of cession that the Netherlands should revert to the Spanish crown in case the union should prove childless; and there was a secret agreement that the chief fortresses should still be garrisoned by Spanish troops and that the archdukes, as they were officially styled, should recognise the suzerainty of the King of Spain.

Philip did not actually live to carry his plan into execution. His

death took place on September 13, 1598. But all the necessary arrangements for the marriage and the transfer of sovereignty had already been made. Albert, having first divested himself of his ecclesiastical dignities, was married by proxy to Isabel at Ferrara in November. It was not until the end of the following year that the new rulers made their *joyeuse entrée* into Brussels, but their marriage marks the beginning of a fresh stage in the history of the Netherlands. Albert and Isabel were wise and capable, and they succeeded in gaining the affection and willing allegiance of the southern provinces. The States-General of the revolted provinces of the north had, however, already enjoyed for some years a real independence won by suffering and struggle and they showed no disposition to meet the overtures of the archdukes. They were resolved to have no further connection with Spain or with Spanish rulers, and from this time forward the cleavage in character, sentiment, and above all in religion, between north and south was to become, as time went on, more and more accentuated. The Dutch republic and the Spanish Netherlands were henceforth destined to pursue their separate course along widely divergent paths.

The ten years which had elapsed between the departure of Leicester and the advent of Albert and Isabel had witnessed a truly marvellous transformation in the condition of the rebel provinces, and especially of Holland and Zeeland. Gradually they had been freed from the presence of the Spaniard, while at the same time the Spanish yoke had been firmly riveted upon Flanders and Brabant. These provinces were now devastated and ruined. The quays of Antwerp were deserted, the industries of Ghent and Bruges destroyed. The most enterprising and skilful of their merchants and artisans had fled over the frontier into Holland or across the sea into England. Holland and Zeeland were thronged with refugees, Flemings and Brabanters, French Huguenots and numerous Spanish and Portuguese Jews, driven out by the pitiless persecution of Philip II. The Hollanders and Zeelanders had long been a seafaring people, who had derived the chief part of their wealth from their fisheries and their carrying trade; and this influx of new and vigorous blood, merchants, traders, and textile workers, bringing with them their knowledge, skill and energy, aroused such a phenomenal outburst of maritime and commercial activity and adventure as the world had never seen before. The fleets of the Hollanders and Zeelanders had during the whole of the war of independence been the main defence of those provinces against Spanish invasion; but, great as had been the services they had rendered, it was the carrying-trade which had furnished the rebel states with the sinews of war, and of this a large part had been derived from that very trading with the enemy which Leicester had striven in vain to prevent. The Spaniards and Portuguese were dependent upon the Dutch traders for the supply of many necessaries of life; and thus Spanish gold was made to pay for the support of the war which was waged against the Spanish king. The dues in connection with this trade, known as licences and convoys, alone furnished large sums to replenish the war-chest; and it is said that from 25,000 to 30,000 seamen found employment by it.

Amsterdam during this decade had been rapidly growing in importance and it was soon to be the first seaport in the world. It had become the *emporium* of the Baltic trade. In 1601 it is stated that between 800 and 900 ships left its quays in three days, carrying commodities to the Baltic ports. They came back laden with corn and other "east-sea" goods, which they then distributed in French, Portuguese and Spanish havens, and even as far as Italy and the Levant. Ship-building went on apace at Enkhuizen, Hoorn and other towns on the Zuyder Zee; and Zaandam was soon to become a centre of the timber trade. In Zeeland, Middelburg, through the enterprise of an Antwerp refugee of French extraction, by name Balthazar de Moucheron, was second only to Amsterdam as a sea-port, while Dordrecht and Rotterdam were also busy with shipping.

The energies of the Dutch at this springtide of their national life were far from being confined to European, waters. Dutch sailors already knew the way to the East-Indies round the Cape of Good Hope through employment on Portuguese vessels; and the trade-routes by which the Spaniards brought the treasures of the New World across the Atlantic were likewise familiar to them and for a similar reason. The East-Indies had for the merchants of Holland and Zeeland, ever keenly on the look-out for fresh markets, a peculiar attraction. At first the Cape route was thought to be too dangerous, and several attempts were made to discover a northwest passage along the coast of Siberia. Balthazar de Moucheron was the pioneer in these northern latitudes. He established a regular traffic with the Russians by way of the White Sea, and had a factory (built in 1584) at Archangel. Through his instances, aided by those of the famous geographer Petrus Plancius (likewise a refugee from Antwerp), an expedition was fitted out and despatched in 1594 to try to sail round northern Asia, but it was driven back after passing through the Waigat by ice and storms. A like fate befell a second expedition in the following year. Discouraged, but still not despairing, a third fleet set out in 1596 under the command of Jacob van Heemskerk with William Barendtsz as pilot. Forced to winter in Spitsbergen, after terrible sufferings, Heemskerk returned home in the autumn of 1597 with the remnant of his crews. Barendtsz was one of those who perished. This was the last effort in this direction, for already a body of Amsterdam merchants had formed a company for trafficking to India by the Cape; and four ships had sailed, April 2, 1596, under the command of Cornelis Houtman, a native of Gouda. A certain Jan Huyghen van Linschoten, who had been in the Portuguese service, had published in 1595 a book containing a description from personal knowledge of the route to the East and the character of the Portuguese commerce. It was the information contained in this work that led the Amsterdam merchants to venture their money upon Houtman's expedition, which Linschoten himself accompanied as guide. They reached Madagascar, Java and the Moluccas, and, after much suffering and many losses by sickness, what was left of the little fleet reached home in July, 1597. The rich cargo they brought back, though not enough to defray expenses, proved an incentive to further efforts. Three companies were formed at Amsterdam, two at Rotterdam, one at Delft and two in Zeeland, for trading in the East-Indies, all vying with one another in their eagerness to make large profits from these regions of fabled wealth, hitherto monopolised by the Portuguese. One expedition sent out by two Amsterdam companies under the command of Jacob van Neck and Wybrand van Waerwyck was very successful and came back in fifteen months richly laden with East-Indian products. The year 1598 was one of great commercial activity. Two-and-twenty large vessels voyaged to the East-Indies; others made their way to the coasts of Guinea, Guiana and Brazil; and one daring captain, Olivier van Noort, sailing through the Straits of Magellan, crossed the Pacific. It was in this year that Philip II prohibited by decree all trading in Spain with the Dutch, and all the Dutch ships in the harbours of the Peninsula were confiscated. But the Spanish trade was no longer of consequence to the Hollanders and Zeelanders. They had sought and found compensation elsewhere.

The small companies formed to carry out these ventures in the far-Eastern seas continued to grow in number, and by the very keenness of their competition threatened each other's enterprises with ruin. In these circumstances the States-General and the Estates of Holland determined, under the leadership of Oldenbarneveldt, to take a step which was to be fraught with very important consequences. The rival companies were urged to form themselves into a single corporation to which exclusive rights would be given for trading in the East-Indies. Such a proposal was in direct contradiction to that principle of free trade which had hitherto been dear to the Netherlanders, and there was much opposition, and many obstacles had to be overcome owing to the jealousies of the various provinces, towns and bodies of merchants who were interested. But at length the patience and statesmanship of Oldenbarneveldt overcame all difficulties, and on March 20, 1601, a charter was issued creating the United East-India Company and giving it a monopoly of the East-India trade (for 21 years) with all lands east of the Cape of Good Hope and west of the Straits of Magellan. The executive control was vested in a College known as the Seventeen. Extensive sovereign privileges were conferred upon the company and exercised by the Seventeen in the name of the States-General. They might make treaties with native rulers and potentates, erect forts for the protection of their factories, appoint governors and officials with administrative and judicial functions, and enlist troops, but these officials and troops were required to take an oath of allegiance to the States-General. The States-General themselves became "participants" by investing the 25,000 pounds, which the company had paid them for the grant of the charter.

The capital speedily reached the amount of six and a half million guilders.

The warlike operations of the year 1599 were uneventful and in the main defensive, except on the eastern frontier where the Spanish forces under the command of the Admiral of Aragon, Mendoza, captured Wesel and Rheinberg. The new rulers of the Netherlands, Albert and Isabel, did not make their entry into Brussels until the end of 1599; and almost before they had had time to organise the new government and gain firm possession of the reins of power in the Belgic provinces, they found themselves confronted with a serious danger. The seaport of Dunkirk had for many years been a nest of pirates, who preyed upon Dutch commerce in the narrow seas. The States-General, urged on by Oldenbarneveldt, resolved in the spring of 1606 to despatch an expedition to besiege and capture Dunkirk. Both Maurice and William Lewis were opposed to the project, which they regarded as rash and risky. The States-General, however, hearing reports of the archduke's soldiery being mutinous for lack of pay, persisted in their purpose, and Maurice, against his better judgment, acquiesced. A body of picked troops, 12,000 foot and 3000 horse, was assembled on the island of Walcheren. A succession of contrary winds delaying the sailing of the force, it was determined to march straight through West Flanders to Nieuport and then along the shore to Dunkirk. A deputation of the States-General, of which Oldenbarneveldt was the leading member, went to Ostend to supervise, much to Maurice's annoyance, the military operations. The stadholder, however, reached Nieuport without serious opposition and proceeded to invest it. Meanwhile the Archduke Albert had been acting with great energy. By persuasive words and large promises he succeeded in winning back the mutineers, and at the head of a veteran force of 10,000 infantry and 1500 cavalry he followed Maurice and, advancing along the dunes, came on July 1 upon a body of 2000 men under the command of Ernest Casimir of Nassau, sent by the stadholder to defend the bridge of Leffingen. At the sight of the redoubtable Spanish infantry a panic seized these troops and they were routed with heavy loss. The fight, however, gave Maurice time to unite his forces and draw them up in battle order in front of Nieuport. Battle was joined the following afternoon, and slowly, foot by foot, after a desperate conflict the archduke's Spanish and Italian veterans drove back along the dunes the troops of the States. Every hillock and sandy hollow was fiercely contested, the brunt of the conflict falling on the English and Frisians under the command of Sir Francis Vere. Vere himself was severely wounded, and the battle appeared to be lost. At this critical moment the Spaniards began to show signs of exhaustion through their tremendous exertions in two successive fights under a hot sun in the yielding sand-hills; and the prince, at the critical moment, throwing himself into the midst of his retreating troops, succeeded in rallying them. At the same time he ordered some squadrons of cavalry which he had kept in reserve to charge on the flank of the advancing foe. The effect was instantaneous. The Spaniards were thrown into confusion, broke and fled. The victory was complete. The archduke only just escaped capture, and of his army 5000 perished and a large number were taken prisoners, among these the Admiral of Aragon. Almost by a miracle was the States' army thus rescued from a desperate position. Maurice's hard-won triumph greatly enhanced his fame, for the battle of Nieuport destroyed the legend of the invincibility of the Spanish infantry in the open field. The victorious general, however, was not disposed to run any further risks. He accordingly retreated to Ostend and there embarked his troops for the ports from which they had started. The expedition had been very costly and had been practically fruitless. Oldenbarneveldt and those who had acted with him were deeply disappointed at the failure of their plans for the capture of Dunkirk and were far from satisfied with Maurice's obstinate refusal to carry out any further offensive operations. From this time there arose a feeling of soreness between the advocate and the stadholder, which further differences of opinion were to accentuate in the coming years.

The vigour and powers of leadership displayed by their new sovereigns in meeting the invasion of Flanders by the States' army, though a defeat in the field had been suffered at Nieuport, had inspired their subjects in the southern Netherlands with confidence and loyalty. Albert had proved himself a brave commander, and his efforts had at least been successful in compelling the enemy to withdraw within his own borders.

Ostend had long been a thorn in the side of the government at Brussels and energetic steps were soon taken to besiege it. But the possession of Ostend was important also to Elizabeth, and she promised active assistance. The larger part of the garrison was, indeed, formed of English troops, and Sir Francis Vere was governor of the town. The siege which ensued was one of the memorable sieges of history, it lasted for more than three years (July 15,1601, to September 20,1604) and was productive of great feats of valour, skill and endurance on the part alike of besiegers and besieged. The States' army under Maurice, though it did not march to the relief of Ostend, endeavoured to divert the attention of Albert from his objective by attacks directed elsewhere. In 1601 the fortresses of Rheinberg and Meurs on the Rhine were captured, and an attack made upon Hertogenbosch. In 1602 the important town of Grave on the Meuse was taken and a raid made into Brabant and Luxemburg.

Meanwhile the defenders of Ostend had been making a desperate resistance, and little progress was made by the besiegers, with the result that a great drain was made upon the finances of the archdukes and there were threatenings of mutiny among the troops. But the situation was saved by the intervention of a wealthy Genoese banker, Ambrosio de Spinola, who offered his services and his money to the archdukes and promised that if he, though inexperienced in warfare, were given the command, he would take Ostend. He fulfilled his promise. Without regard to loss of life he pressed on the siege, and though as fast as one line of defences was taken another arose behind it to bar his progress, little by little he advanced and bit by bit the area held by the garrison grew less. At last in the spring of 1604, under the pressure of the States-General, Maurice led an army of 11,000 men into Flanders in April, 1604, and laid siege to Sluis on May 19. Both Maurice and William Lewis were still unwilling to run the risk of an attack on Spinola's army in its lines, and so the two sieges went on side by side, as it were independently. Sluis fell at the end of August, and Ostend was then at its last gasp. Urged now by the deputies of the States to make a direct effort to relieve the heroic garrison, Maurice and his cousin, after wasting some precious time in protesting against the step, began to march southward. It was too late. What was left of Ostend surrendered on September 20, and Spinola became the master of a heap of ruins. It is said that this three years' siege cost the Spaniards 80,000 lives, to say nothing of the outlay of vast expenditure. Whether Maurice and William

Lewis were right or wrong in their reluctance to assail Spinola's entrenched camp, it is certain that they were better judges of the military situation than the civilian deputies of the States. In any case the capture of Sluis was an offset to the loss of Ostend; and its importance was marked by the appointment of Frederick Henry, the young brother of the stadholder, as governor of the seaport and the surrounding district, which received the name of States-Flanders. The tremendous exertions put forward for the defence of Ostend had been a very serious drain upon the resources of the United Provinces, especially upon those of Holland. Taxation was already so high that Oldenbarneveldt and many other leading members of the States-General and Provincial Estates began to feel despondent and to doubt whether it were possible to continue the war. No longer could the States rely upon the assistance of England. James I had concluded peace with Spain; and, though he made professions of friendship and goodwill to the Dutch, wary statesmen, like the Advocate, did not trust him, and were afraid lest he should be tempted to deliver up the cautionary towns into the hands of the enemy. Reverting to the policy of William the Silent, Oldenbarneveldt even went so far as to make tentative approaches to Henry IV of France touching the conditions on which he would accept the sovereignty of the Provinces. Indeed it is said that such was the despair felt by this great statesman, who knew better than any man the economic difficulties of the situation, that he even contemplated the possibility of submission to the archdukes. Had he suggested submission, there would have been no question, however, that he could not have retained office, for Maurice, William Lewis and the military leaders on the one hand, and on the other the merchants and the adventurous seamen, whom they employed in the profitable Indian traffic, would not have listened for a moment to any thought of giving up a struggle which had been so resolutely and successfully maintained for so many years. For financially the archdukes were in even worse plight than the Netherlanders, even though for a short time, with the help of Spinola, appearances seemed to favour the Belgic attacks on the Dutch frontier districts. In 1605 the Genoese general, at the head of a mixed but well-disciplined force in his own pay, made a rapid advance towards Friesland, and, after capturing Oldenzaal and Lingen and ravaging the eastern provinces, concluded the campaign with a brilliant success against a body of the States cavalry commanded by Frederick Henry, who nearly lost his life. Maurice with inferior forces kept strictly on the defensive, skilfully covering the heart of the land from attack, but steadily refusing a pitched battle. In the following year Spinola with two armies attempted to force the lines of the Waal and the Yssel, but, though thwarted in this aim by the wariness of the stadholder and by a very wet season, he succeeded in taking the important fortresses of Groll and Rheinberg. Maurice made no serious effort to relieve them, and his inactivity caused much discontent and adverse comment. His military reputation suffered, while that of his opponent was enhanced. But subsequent events showed that Maurice, though perhaps erring on the side of caution, had acted rightly. The armies which had threatened the safety of the Provinces had been raised at the charges of a private individual, but the financial resources, even of a Spinola, were not capable of a prolonged effort; there was no money in the State treasury; and the soldiery, as soon as their pay was in arrears, began once more to be mutinous. The bolt had been shot without effect, and the year 1607 found both sides, through sheer lack of funds, unable to enter upon a fresh campaign on land with any hope of definite success. But though the military campaigns had been so inconclusive, it had been far different with the fortunes of maritime warfare in these opening years of the seventeenth century. The sea-power of the Dutch republic was already a formidable factor which had to be reckoned with and which was destined to be decisive.

The East-India Company was no sooner founded than active steps were taken to make full use of the privileges granted by the Charter. A fleet of 17 vessels was despatched in 1602 under Wybrand van Waerwyck. Waerwyck visited Ceylon and most of the islands of the Malay Archipelago, established a factory at Bantam with a staff of officials for developing trade relations with the natives, and even made his way to Siam and China. He sent back from time to time some of his vessels richly laden, and finally returned himself with the residue of his fleet after an absence of five years in June, 1607. Another expedition of thirteen ships sailed in 1604 under Steven van der Hagen, whose operations were as widespread and as successful as those of Waerwyck. Van der Hagen took possession of Molucca and built factories at Amboina, Tidor and other places in the spice-bearing islands. On his way back in 1606 with his cargo of cloves, spices and other products of the far Orient, he encountered at Mauritius another westward-bound fleet of eleven ships under Cornelis Matelief. Matelief's first objective was the town of Malacca, held by the Portuguese and commanding the straits to which it gave its name. Alphonso de Castro, the Viceroy of India, hastened however with a naval force far more powerful than the Dutch squadron to the relief of this important fortress; and after a hardly-fought but indecisive action Matelief raised the siege on August 17. Returning, however, about a month later, the Dutch admiral found that De Castro had sailed away, leaving only a detachment of ten vessels before Malacca. Matelief at once attacked this force, whose strength was about equal to his own, and with such success that he sank or burnt every single ship of the enemy with scarcely any loss, September 21, 1606.

These successful incursions into a region that the Spaniards and Portuguese had jealously regarded as peculiarly their own aroused both anger and alarm. All available forces in the East (the Portuguese from the Mozambique and Goa, the Spaniards from the Philippines) were equipped and sent to sea with the object of expelling the hated and despised Netherlanders from East-Indian waters. Paulus van Caerden, Matelief's successor in command, was defeated and himself taken prisoner. Nor were the Spaniards content with attacking the Dutch fleets in the far East. As the weather-worn and heavily-laden Company's vessels returned along the west coast of Africa, they had to pass within striking distance of the Spanish and Portuguese harbours and were in constant danger of being suddenly assailed by a superior force and captured. In 1607 rumours reached Holland of the gathering of a large Spanish fleet at Gibraltar, whose destination was the East-Indies. The directors of the Company were much alarmed, an alarm which was shared by the States-General, many of whose deputies were cargo-shareholders. Accordingly, in April, 1607, a fleet of twenty-six vessels set sail for the purpose of seeking out and attacking the Spaniards whether in harbour or on the open sea. The command was given to one of the most daring and experienced of Dutch seamen, Jacob van Heemskerk. He found twenty-one ships still at anchor in Gibraltar Bay, ten of them large galleons, far superior in size and armament to his own largest vessels. Heemskerk at once cleared for action. Both Heemskerk and the Spanish commander, d'Avila, were killed early in the fight, the result of which however was not long doubtful. The Spanish fleet was practically destroyed. On the Dutch side no vessel was lost and the casualties were small. Such a disaster was most humiliating to Castilian pride, and its effect in hastening forward the peace negotiations, which were already in progress, was considerable.

The initial steps had been taken by the archdukes. Through the secret agency of Albert's Franciscan Confessor, Father John Neyen, both Oldenbarneveldt and Maurice were approached in May, 1606, but without any result. Early in 1607 however the efforts were renewed, and negotiations were actively set on foot for the purpose of concluding a peace or a truce for a term of twelve, fifteen or twenty years. There were, however, almost insuperable difficulties in the way. In the first place the stadholders, the military and naval leaders, the Calvinist clergy, and the great majority of the traders honestly believed that a peace would be detrimental to all the best interests of the States, and were thoroughly distrustful of the motives which had prompted the archdukes and the Spanish government to make these advances. Oldenbarneveldt on the other hand thought that peace was necessary for the land to recuperate after the exhausting struggle, which had already lasted for forty years; and he found strong support among the burgher-regents and that large part of the people who were over-burdened and impoverished by the weight of taxation, and sick and weary of perpetual warfare. There were, however, certain preliminary conditions, which all were agreed must be assented to, and without which it would be useless to continue the negotiations. The independence of the United Provinces must be recognised, freedom of trade in the Indies conceded, and the public exercise of Catholic worship prohibited. After some parleying the archdukes agreed to treat with the United Provinces "in the quality and as considering them free provinces and states," and an armistice was concluded in April, 1607, for eight months, in order that the matters in dispute might be referred to the King of Spain and his views upon them ascertained. Not till October did the king's reply arrive at Brussels. He consented to negotiate with the States "as free and independent" parties, but he required that liberty of Catholic worship should be permitted during the truce, and no mention was made of the Indian trade. This was by no means satisfactory; nevertheless the influence of Oldenbarneveldt prevailed and the negotiations were not broken off. On February 1, 1608, the archdukes' envoys, the two leading members being Ambrosio de Spinola and the president of the Privy Council, Ricardot, arrived in Holland. They were met at Ryswyck by Maurice and William Lewis in person, and with much ceremony and splendour a solemn entry was made into the Hague, the procession with the brilliant retinues forming a memorable spectacle, as it made its way through the crowds which lined the roads. The negotiations were conducted in the Binnenhof. The Special Commissioners to represent the States-General were William Lewis of Nassau, Walraven, lord of Brederode, and a deputy from each of the provinces under the leadership of Oldenbarneveldt. Envoys from France, England, Denmark, the Palatinate and Brandenburg were present, took part in the discussions, and acted as friendly mediators.

The question of treating the United Provinces "as free States" was soon settled. The archdukes, who were aiming at the conclusion of a truce in which to recuperate and not of a definitive peace, showed an unexpected complaisance in granting a concession which they regarded as only temporary. Then came the really serious questions as to freedom of trade in the Indies and the liberty of Catholic worship. Of these the first was of most immediate interest, and showed irreconcilable differences between the two parties. The Spaniards would never consent to any trespassing in the closed area, which they regarded as their own peculiar preserve. The Dutch traders and sailors were fired with the spirit of adventure and of profit, and their successful expeditions had aroused an enthusiasm for further effort in the distant seas, which had hardened into a fixed resolve not to agree to any peace or truce shutting them out from the Indian trade. For months the subject was discussed and re-discussed without result. Some of the foreign delegates left. The armistice was prolonged, in order that Father Neyen might go to Madrid for further instructions. It was found, however, that the King of Spain would yield nothing. The negotiations came to a standstill, and both sides began to make preparations for a renewal of the war. President Jeannin on behalf of the French king, by his skilful mediation, in which he was supported by his English colleague, saved the situation. He proposed as a compromise a twelve years' truce, pointing out that whatever terms were arranged would only be binding for that short period. He managed to bring about a personal interview between Oldenbarneveldt and Maurice, who had respectively headed the peace and war parties in the provinces; and henceforth both consented to work together for this proposal of a limited truce, during which the trade to the Indies should be open and the religious question be untouched. The assent of the States-General and of the several Provincial Estates was obtained. The two most interested, Holland and Zeeland, were won over, Holland by the arguments and persuasions of the Advocate, Zeeland, which was the last to agree, by the influence of Maurice. Jeannin was aware that the finances of Spain were at their last gasp, and that both the archdukes and Philip III were most anxious for a respite from the ever-consuming expense of the war. At last the long and wearisome negotiations came to an end, and the treaty concluding a truce for twelve years was signed at the Hague on April 9,1609. The territorial *status quo* was recognised. The United Provinces were treated "as free States over which the archdukes made no pretensions." Nothing was said about the religious difficulty nor about trade in the Indies, but in a secret treaty the King of Spain undertook not to interfere with Dutch trade, wherever carried on. Thus access to the Indies was conceded, though to save appearances the word was not mentioned. This result was due solely to the diplomatic tact and resource of Jeannin, who was able to announce to Henry IV that he had accomplished his task "to the satisfaction of everyone, and even of Prince Maurice."

# CHAPTER VII

# THE SYSTEM OF GOVERNMENT

One of the reasons which influenced the archdukes and the King of Spain to make large concessions in order to secure the assent of the States-General to the conclusion of a twelve years' truce was their firm belief that the unstable political condition of the United Provinces must lead to civil discord, as soon as the relaxing of the pressure of war loosened the bonds which had, since Leicester's departure, held together a number of separate authorities and discordant interests. They were right in their supposition. In order, therefore, to understand the course of events in the republic, which had been correctly recognised by the treaty not as a single state, but as a group of "free and independent States," it is necessary to give a brief account of one of the most strangely complicated systems of government that the world has ever seen—especially strange because no one could ever say positively where or with whom the sovereignty really resided.

Let us take into separate consideration the powers and functions of (1) the Council of State, (2) the States-General, (3) the Provincial Estates, (4) the Stadholders, (5) the Advocate (later the *Raad-Pensionarius* or Council-Pensionary) of Holland, (6) the Admiralty Colleges.

The Council of State was not a legislative, but an executive, body. In the time of Leicester the Council was the executive arm of the governor-general and had large powers. After his departure the presence of the English ambassador, who by treaty had a seat in the Council, caused the States-General gradually to absorb its powers, and to make its functions subordinate to their own, until at last its authority was confined to the administration of the affairs of war and of finance. The right of the English representative to sit in the Council and take an active part in its deliberations continued till 1626. The Stadholders were also *ex officio* members. The Provinces, since 1588, were represented by twelve councillors. Holland had three; Gelderland, Zeeland and Friesland two each; Utrecht, Overyssel and Groningen (*Stad en Landen*) one each. The treasurer-general and the clerk (*Griffier*) of the States-General took part in the deliberations and had great influence. The chief duty of the Council, during the period with which we are dealing, was the raising of the "quotas" from the various provinces for the military defence of the State. The General Petition or War Budget was prepared by the Council and presented to the States-General at the end of each year, providing for the military expenses in the following twelve months. The "quotas" due towards these expenses from the several provinces were set forth in smaller petitions sent to the Provincial Estates, whose consent was necessary. The so-called *repartitie* fixing the amount of these quotas was likewise drawn up by the Council of State, and was the subject at times of considerable haggling and discontent. In 1612 it was settled that the proportions to be borne by the provinces should be Holland 57.1 per cent.; Friesland 11.4; Zeeland 11 (afterwards reduced to 9); Utrecht and Groningen 5.5; Overyssel 3.5. It will thus be seen that the quota of Holland was considerably more than half of the whole; and, as the naval expenditure was to an even larger extent borne by Holland, the preponderating influence of this province in the Union can be easily understood. The forces of the republic that were distributed in the several provinces received their pay from the provinces, but those maintained by the Council, as troops of the State, were paid by monies received from the Generality lands, *i.e.* lands such as the conquered portions of Brabant and Flanders, governed by the States-General, but without representation in that body. The Council of State, though its political powers were curtailed and absorbed by the States-General, continued to exercise, as a court of justice, appellate jurisdiction in military and financial questions.

The States-General consisted of representatives of the Estates of the seven sovereign provinces of Gelderland, Holland, Zeeland, Utrecht, Friesland, Overyssel, and Groningen (*Stad en Landen*) in the order of precedence given above. Gelderland, having been a duchy, ranked before those that had formerly been counties or lordships. The provinces sent deputations varying in number; Holland and Gelderland generally six, the others less. Each province had but a single vote. The president changed week by week, being chosen in turn from each province according to their order of precedence. Holland had nominally no more weight than the others; its practical influence, however, was great in proportion to the burden of taxation that it bore and was increased by the fact that the sessions, which after 1593 were permanent, were held at the Hague in the same building with the Estates of Holland, and that the Council-Pensionary of Holland was the spokesman of the province in the States-General. The States-General had control of the foreign affairs of the Union. To them belonged the supreme control of military and naval matters. The Captain-General and Admiral-General of the Union were appointed by them; and a deputation of the States-General accompanied the army into the field and the commanders were bound to consult it. They exercised a strong supervision of finance, and sovereign authority over the entire administration of the "Generality" lands. Ambassadors were appointed by them, also the Treasurer-General of the Union, and numerous other important officials. Yet with all these attributes and powers the States-General possessed only a derived, not an inherent, authority. To foreigners the sovereignty of the republic of the United Netherlands appeared to be vested in their "High-Mightinesses." In reality the States-General was, as already stated, a gathering of deputations from the seven sovereign provinces. Each deputation voted as a unit; and in all important affairs of peace and war, treaties and finance, there must be no dissentient. A single province, however small, could, by obstinate opposition, block the way to the acceptance of any given proposal. Moreover the members, despite their lofty designation as High-Mightinesses, did not vote according to their convictions or persuasions, but according to the charge they had received from their principals. The deputation of a province had no right to sanction any disputable measure or proposal without referring it back to the Estates of that province for approval or disapproval. Hence arose endless opportunities and occasions for friction and dissension and manifold delays in the transaction of the business of the republic, oftentimes in a manner inimical to its vital interests.

The Provincial Estates in their turn were by no means homogeneous or truly representative bodies. In Holland the nobles had one vote; and eighteen towns, Dordrecht, Haarlem, Delft, Leyden, Amsterdam, Gouda, Rotterdam, Gorkum, Schiedam, Schoonhoven, Brill, Alkmaar, Hoorn, Enkhuizen, Edam, Monnikendam, Medemblik and Purmerend, had one each. The nobles, though they had only one vote, were influential, as they represented the rural districts and the small towns which had no franchise, and they voted first. Here again, as in the States-General, though each of the privileged towns counted equal in the voting, as a matter of fact their weight and influence was very different. The opposition of wealthy and populous Amsterdam was again and again sufficient to override the decision of the majority, for there was no power to enforce its submission, except the employment of armed force. For at this point it may be as well to explain that each one of these municipalities (*vroedschappen*) claimed to be a sovereign entity, and yet, far from being bodies representing the citizens as a whole, they were close corporations of the narrowest description. The ordinary inhabitants of these towns had no voice whatever in the management of their own affairs. The governing body or *vroedschap* consisted of a limited number of persons, sometimes not more than forty, belonging to certain families, which filled up vacancies by co-option and chose the burgomasters and sheriffs (*schepenen*). Thus it will be seen that popular representation had no place in Holland. The regent-burghers were a small patrician oligarchy, in whose hands the entire government and administration of the towns rested, and from their number were chosen the deputies, who represented the eighteen privileged cities in the Provincial Estates.

The other provinces do not need such detailed notice. In Zeeland the Estates consisted of seven members, the "first noble" (who presided) and six towns. There was but one noble, the Marquis of Flushing and Veere. William the Silent in 1581 obtained this marquisate by purchase; and his heirs, through its possession, continued to exercise great influence in the Provincial Estates. As Philip William, Prince of Orange, was in Madrid, Maurice sat in the assembly as "first noble" in his place. In Utrecht the three Estates were represented, *i.e.* the nobles, the towns (four in number) and the clergy. The representatives of the clergy were, however, chosen no longer from the Chapter but from the possessors of what had been Church lands and property. They were elected by the knights and the small towns out of a list drawn up by the corporation of Utrecht. They necessarily belonged to the Reformed (Calvinist) faith. Gelderland was divided into three (so-called) quarters, Nijmwegen, Zutphen and Arnhem. Each of these quarters had its separate assembly; and there was also a general diet. The nobles, who were numerous and had large estates, were here very influential. Friesland was divided into four quarters, three of which (Oostergoo, Westergoo and Zevenwolden) were country districts, the fourth a gathering of the deputies of eleven towns. The Diet of Friesland was not formed of Estates, the nobles and the town representatives sitting together in the same assembly, which was elected by a popular vote, all who had a small property-qualification possessing the franchise, Roman Catholics excepted. The system of administration and divided authority was in Friesland a very complicated one, inherited from mediaeval times, but here again the nobles, being large land-owners, had much influence. The stadholder presided at the diet and had a casting vote. The Estates of Groningen were divided into two parts—town and districts—each with one vote. The districts were those of Hunsingoo, Fivelingoo and the West-Quarter. Here also the stadholder had a casting vote. In Overyssel the Estates, like those of Groningen, consisted of two members, the nobles from the three quarters, Sallant, Twente and Vollenhove, and the deputies of the three towns, Deventer, Kampen and Zwolle.

The ordinary executive and administrative work of Provincial government was carried out in Holland by a body known as the Commissioned-Councillors—*Gecommitteerde-Raden;* in the other provinces by Deputed-Estates—*Gedeputeerde-Staten.* The Commissioned-Councillors were to the Estates of Holland what the Council of State was to the States-General. They enjoyed considerable independence, for they were not appointed by the Estates but directly by the nobles and cities according to a fixed system of rotation, and they sat continuously, whereas the Estates only met for short sessions. Their duty was to see that all provincial edicts and ordinances decreed by the Estates were published and enforced, to control the finances and to undertake the provision and oversight of all military requirements; and to them it belonged to summon the meetings of the Estates. The Deputed-Estates in the other provinces had similar but generally less extensive and authoritative functions.

Such a medley of diverse and often conflicting authorities within a state of so small an area has no counterpart in history. It seemed impossible that government could be carried on, or that there could be any concerted action or national policy in a republic which was rather a many-headed confederation than a federal state. That the United Netherlands, in spite of all these disadvantages, rapidly rose in the 17th century to be a maritime and commercial power of the first rank was largely due to the fact that the foreign policy of the republic and the general control of its administration was directed by a succession of very able men, the stadholders of the house of Orange-Nassau and the council-pensionaries of Holland. For a right understanding of the period of Dutch history with which we are about to deal, it is necessary to define clearly what was the position of the stadholder and of the council-pensionary in this cumbrous and creaking machinery of government that has just been described, and the character of those offices, which conferred upon their holders such wide-reaching influence and authority.

The Stadholder or governor was really, both in title and office, an anomaly in a republic. Under the Burgundian and Habsburg rulers the Stadholder exercised the local authority in civil and also in military matters as representing the sovereign duke, count or lord in the province to which he was appointed, and was by that fact clothed with certain sovereign attributes during his tenure of office. William the Silent was Stadholder of Holland and Zeeland at the outbreak of the revolt, and, though deprived of his offices, he continued until the time of the Union of Utrecht to exercise authority in those and other provinces professedly in the name of the king. After his death one would have expected that the office would have fallen into abeyance, but the coming of Leicester into the Netherlands led to a revival of the stadholderate. Holland and Zeeland, in their desire to exercise a check upon the governor-general's arbitrary exercise of his powers, appointed Maurice of Nassau to take his father's place; and at the same time William Lewis of Nassau became Stadholder of Friesland, and stadholders were also appointed in Utrecht, Gelderland and Overyssel. In 1609 Maurice was Stadholder in the five provinces of Holland,

Zeeland, Gelderland, Utrecht and Overyssel; his cousin William Lewis in Friesland and Groningen with Drente. The powers of the stadholder were not the same in the different provinces, but generally speaking he was the executive officer of the Estates; and in Holland, where his authority was the greatest, he had the supervision of the administration of justice, the appointment of a large number of municipal magistrates, and the prerogative of pardon, and he was charged with the military and naval defence of the province. The stadholder received his commission both from the Provincial Estates and from the States-General and took an oath of allegiance to the latter. In so far, then, as he exercised quasi-sovereign functions, he did it in the name of the States, whose servant he nominally was. But when the stadholder, as was the case with Maurice and the other Princes of Orange, was himself a sovereign-prince and the heir of a great name, he was able to exercise an authority far exceeding those of a mere official. The descendants of William the Silent—Maurice, Frederick Henry, William II and William III—were, moreover, all of them men of exceptional ability; and the stadholderate became in their hands a position of almost semi-monarchical dignity and influence, the stadholder being regarded both by foreign potentates and by the people of the Netherlands generally as "the eminent head of the State." Maurice, as stated above, was stadholder in five provinces; Frederick Henry, William II and William III in six; the seventh province, Friesland, remaining loyal, right through the 17th century, to their cousins of the house of Nassau-Siegen, the ancestors of the present Dutch royal family. That the authority of the States-General and States-Provincial should from time to time come into conflict with that of the stadholder was to be expected, for the relations between them were anomalous in the extreme. The Stadholder of Holland for instance appointed, directly or indirectly, the larger part of the municipal magistrates; they in their turn the representatives who formed the Estates of the Province. But, as the stadholder was the servant of the Estates, he, in a sense, may be said to have had the power of appointing his own masters. The stadholders of the house of Orange had also, in addition to the prestige attaching to their name, the possession of large property and considerable wealth, which with the emoluments they received from the States-General, as Captain-General and Admiral-General of the Union, and from the various provinces, where they held the post of stadholder, enabled them in the days of Frederick Henry and his successors to maintain the state and dignity of a court.

The office of Land's Advocate or Council-Pensionary was different altogether in character from the stadholderate, but at times scarcely less influential, when filled by a man of commanding talents. The Advocate in the time of Oldenbarneveldt combined the duties of being legal adviser to the Estates of Holland, and of presiding over and conducting the business of the Estates at their meetings, and also those of the Commissioned-Councillors. He was the leader and spokesman of the Holland deputies in the States-General. He kept the minutes, introduced the business and counted the votes at the provincial assemblies. It was his duty to draw up and register the resolutions. What was perhaps equally important, he carried on the correspondence with the ambassadors of the republic at foreign courts, and received their despatches, and conducted negotiations with the foreign ambassadors at the Hague. It is easy to see how a man like Oldenbarneveldt, of great industry and capacity for affairs, although nominally the paid servant of the Estates, gradually acquired an almost complete control over every department of administration and became, as it were, a Minister of State of all affairs. In Oldenbarneveldt's time the post was held for life; and, as Maurice did not for many years trouble himself about matters of internal government and foreign diplomacy, the Advocate by the length of his tenure of office had at the opening of the 17th century become the virtual director and arbiter of the policy of the State. After his death the title of advocate and the life-tenure ceased. His successors were known as Council-Pensionaries, and they held office for five years only, but with the possibility of re-election. The career of John de Witt showed, however, that in the case of a supremely able man these restrictions did not prevent a *Raad-Pensionarius*[4] from exercising for eighteen years an authority and influence greater even than that of Oldenbarneveldt.

An account of the multiplied subdivision of administrative control in the United Provinces would not be complete without some mention of the Admiralty Colleges in Holland. Holland with Zeeland furnished the fleets on which the existence and well-being of the republic depended. Both William the Silent and his son Maurice were, as stadholders, admirals of Holland and of Zeeland,

and both likewise were by the States-General appointed Admirals-General of the Union. They thus wielded a double authority over maritime affairs in the two provinces. In 1574 William had at his side a Council of Admiralty erected by the Provincial Estates, but Leicester in 1585 was annoyed by the immediate control of naval matters being withdrawn from the governor-general and the Council of State. He succeeded therefore in obtaining a division of the Council of Admiralty into three Chambers, shortly afterwards increased to five—Rotterdam, Hoorn with Enkhuizen, Veere, Amsterdam and Harlingen with Dokkum. In 1597 it was determined that each Admiralty should consist of seven members nominated by the States-General. The Admiral-General presided over each College and over joint meetings of the five Colleges. The Admiralties nominated the lieutenants of the ships and proposed a list of captains to be finally chosen by the States-General. The Lieutenant-Admiral and Vice-Admirals of Holland and the Vice-Admiral of Zeeland were chosen by the Provincial Estates. The States-General appointed the Commander-in-Chief. Such a system seemed to be devised to prevent any prompt action or swift decision being taken at times of emergency or sudden danger.

# CHAPTER VIII

# THE TWELVE YEARS' TRUCE

The first years of the truce were for the United Provinces, now recognised as "free and independent States," a period of remarkable energy and enterprise. The young republic started on its new career with the buoyant hopefulness that comes from the proud consciousness of suffering and dangers bravely met and overcome, and, under the wise and experienced guidance of Oldenbarneveldt, acquired speedily a position and a weight in the Councils of Europe out of all proportion to its geographical area or the numbers of its population. The far-seeing statecraft and practised diplomatic skill of the Advocate never rendered greater services to his country than during these last years of his long tenure of power. A difficult question as to the succession to the Jülich-Cleves duchies arose at the very time of the signing of the truce, which called for delicate and wary treatment.

In March, 1609, the Duke of Jülich and Cleves died without leaving a male heir, and the succession to these important border territories on the Lower Rhine became speedily a burning question. The two principal claimants through the female line were the Elector of Brandenburg and William, Count-Palatine of Neuburg. The Emperor Rudolph II, however, under the pretext of appointing imperial commissioners to adjudicate upon the rival claims, aroused the suspicions of Brandenburg and Neuburg; and these two came to an agreement to enter into joint possession of the duchies, and were styled "the possessors." The Protestant Union at Heidelberg recognised "the possessors," for it was all-important for the balance of power in Germany that these lands should not pass into the hands of a Catholic ruler of the House of Austria. For the same reason

Brandenburg and Neuburg were recognised by the States-General, who did not wish to see a partisan of Spain established on their borders. The emperor on his part not only refused to acknowledge "the possessors," but he also sent his cousin Archduke Leopold, Bishop of Passau, to intervene by armed force. Leopold seized the fortress of Jülich and proceeded to establish himself.

It was an awkward situation, for neither the United Provinces nor the archdukes nor the King of Spain had the smallest desire to make the Jülich succession the cause of a renewal of hostilities, immediately after the conclusion of the truce. The eagerness of the French king to precipitate hostilities with the Habsburg powers however forced their hands. Henry IV had for some time been making preparations for war, and he was at the moment irritated by the protection given by the archdukes to the runaway Princess of Condé, who had fled to Brussels. He had succeeded in persuading the States to send an auxiliary force into Germany to assist the French army of invasion in the spring of 1610, when just as the king was on the point of leaving Paris to go to the front he was assassinated on May 14. This event put an end to the expedition, for the regent, Marie de' Medici, was friendly to Austria. The States nevertheless did not feel disposed to leave Leopold in possession of Jülich. Maurice led an army into the duchy and laid siege to the town. It capitulated on September 1. As might have been anticipated, however, the joint rule of the "possessors" did not turn out a success. They quarrelled, and Neuburg asked for Catholic help. Maurice and Spinola in 1614 found themselves again face to face at the head of rival forces, but actual hostilities were avoided; and by the treaty of Nanten (November 12, 1614) it was arranged that the disputed territory should be divided, Brandenburg ruling at Cleves, Neuburg at Jülich. Thus, in the settlement of this thorny question, the influence of Oldenbarneveldt worked for a temporary solution satisfactory to the interests of the United Provinces; nor was his successful intervention in the Jülich-Cleves affair an isolated instance of his diplomatic activity. On the contrary it was almost ubiquitous.

The growth of the Dutch trade in the Baltic had for some years been advancing by leaps and bounds, and now far exceeded that of their old rivals, the Hanseatic league. Christian IV, the ambitious and warlike King of Denmark, had been seriously interfering with this trade by imposing such heavy dues for the passage of the Sound as on the one hand to furnish him with a large revenue, and on the other hand to support his claim to sovereign rights over all traffic with the inland sea. The Hanse towns protested strongly and sought the support of the States-General in actively opposing the Danish king. It was granted. A force of 7000 men under Frederick Henry was sent into Germany to the relief of Brunswick, which was besieged by Christian IV. The siege was raised; and an alliance was concluded between the republic and the Hanse towns for common action in the protection of their commercial interests. Nor was this all. Oldenbarneveldt entered into diplomatic relations with Charles IX of Sweden and with Russia. Cornelis Haga was sent to Stockholm; and from this time forward a close intimacy was established between Sweden and the States. The seaport of Gotheborg, just outside the entrance to the Sound, was founded by a body of Dutch colonists under a certain Abraham Cabelliau, an Amsterdam merchant, and continued to be for years practically a Dutch town.

Scarcely less important was the enterprise shown in the establishment of friendly relations with distant Russia. Balthazar de Moucheron established a Dutch factory at Archangel so early as 1584; and a growing trade sprang up with Russia by way of the White Sea, at first in rivalry with the English Muscovy Company. But a Dutch merchant, by name Isaac Massa, having succeeded in gaining the ear and confidence of the Tsar, Russian commerce gradually became a Dutch monopoly. In 1614 a Muscovite embassy conducted by Massa came to the Hague, and access to the interior of Russia was opened to the traders of Holland and to them only.

In the Mediterranean no less foresight and dexterity was shown in forwarding the interests of the States. The Advocate's son-in-law, Van der Myle, went in 1609 as ambassador to Venice; and the following year the first Venetian envoy, Tommaso Contarini, arrived in Holland. In 1612 Cornelis Haga, who had been in Sweden, was sent to Constantinople to treat with the Turks about commercial privileges in the Levant and for the suppression of piracy, and he remained in the East in charge of the republic's interests for many years.

More difficult was the maintenance of friendly relations with England. In 1604 James I had made peace with Spain; and the growing rivalry upon the seas between the Dutch and English tended to alienate his sympathies from the rising maritime power of the republic. He outwardly maintained friendly relations; his ambassador had a seat on the Council of State; he retained his garrisons in the cautionary towns; and after the signing of the truce he bestowed the Garter upon Prince Maurice. But at this very time, May, 1609, James took a step which was most hurtful to that industry which had laid the foundation of the commercial prosperity of Holland—this was the issuing of an edict imposing a tax on all foreigners fishing in English waters. Though general in its form, this edict was really directed against the right heretofore enjoyed by the Netherlanders to fish on the English coast, a right conferred by a series of treaties and never challenged since its confirmation by the *Magnus Intercursus* of 1496. Dutch public opinion was strongly aroused and a special embassy was sent to London, April, 1610, to protest against the edict and endeavour to procure its withdrawal or its modification. This was by no means an easy matter. The fisheries, on which a large part of the population of Holland and Zeeland depended for their livelihood, were of vital importance to the States. On the other hand their virtual monopoly by the Dutch caused keen resentment in England. In the latter part of the reign of Elizabeth that adventurous sea-faring spirit, which was destined eventually to plant the flag of England on the shores of every ocean, had come to the birth, and everywhere it found, during this early part of the 17th century, Dutch rivals already in possession and Dutch ships on every trading route. The Dutch mercantile marine in fact far exceeded the English in numbers and efficiency. The publication of Hugo Grotius' famous pamphlet, *Mare Liberum*, in March, 1609, was probably the final cause which decided James to issue his Fisheries' proclamation. The purpose of Grotius was to claim for every nation, as against the Portuguese, freedom of trade in the Indian Ocean, but the arguments he used appeared to King James and his advisers to challenge the *dominium maris*, which English kings had always claimed in the "narrow seas." The embassy of 1610, therefore, had to deal not merely with the fisheries, but with the whole subject of the maritime relations of the two countries; and a crowd of published pamphlets proves the intense interest that was aroused. But the emergence of the dispute as to the Jülich-Cleves succession, and the change in the policy of the French government owing to the assassination of Henry IV, led both sides to desire an accommodation; and James consented, not indeed to withdraw the edict, but to postpone its execution for two years. It remained a dead letter until 1616, although all the time the wranglings over the legal aspects of the questions in dispute continued. The Republic, however, as an independent State, was very much hampered by the awkward fact of the cautionary towns remaining in English hands. The occupation of Flushing and Brill, commanding the entrances to important waterways, seemed to imply that the Dutch republic was to a certain extent a vassal state under the protection of England. Oldenbarneveldt resolved therefore to take advantage of King James' notorious financial embarrassments by offering to redeem the towns by a ready-money payment. The nominal indebtedness of the United Provinces for loans advanced by Elizabeth was £600,000; the Advocate offered in settlement £100,000 in cash and £150,000 more in half-yearly payments. James accepted the offer, and the towns were handed over, the garrisons being allowed to pass into the Dutch service, June 1616. Sir Dudley Carleton, however, who about this time succeeded Sir Ralph Winwood as English envoy at the Hague, continued to have a seat in the Council of State.

Oldenbarneveldt thus, at a time when his dominant position in the State was already being undermined and his career drawing to an end, performed a great service to his country, the more so as King James, in his eagerness to negotiate a marriage between the Prince of Wales and a Spanish infanta, was beginning to allow his policy to be more and more controlled by the Count of Gondomar, the Spanish ambassador at Whitehall. James' leaning towards Spain naturally led him to regard with stronger disfavour the increasing predominance of the Dutch flag upon the seas, and it was not long before he was sorry that he had surrendered the cautionary towns. For the fishery rights and the principle of the *dominium maris* in the narrow seas were no longer the only questions in dispute between England and the States. English seamen and traders had other grievances to allege against the Hollanders in other parts of the world. The exclusive right to fish for whales in the waters of Spitsbergen and Greenland was claimed by the English on the ground of Hugh Willoughby's alleged discovery of Spitsbergen in 1553. The Dutch would not admit any such claim, and asserted that

Heemskerk was the first to visit the archipelago, and that he planted in 1596 the Dutch flag on the shores of the island, to which he gave the name of Spitsbergen. In 1613 James conferred the monopoly upon the English Muscovy Company, who sent out a fishing fleet with orders to drive off any interlopers; and certain Dutch vessels were attacked and plundered. The reply of the States-General was the granting of a charter, January 27, 1614, to a company, known as the Northern or Greenland Company, with the monopoly of fishing between Davis' Straits and Nova Zembla; and a fishing fleet was sent out accompanied by warships. The result was a temporary agreement between the English and Dutch companies for using separate parts of Spitsbergen as their bases, all others being excluded. Meanwhile the dispute was kept open; and despite conferences and negotiations neither side showed any disposition to yield. Matters reached an acute stage in 1618. English and Dutch fishing fleets of exceptional strength sailed into the northern waters in the early summer of that year, and a fierce fight took place, which, as two Dutch war vessels were present, resulted in the scattering of the English vessels and considerable loss of life and property.

The rivalry and opposition between the Dutch and English traders in the East-Indies was on a larger scale, but here there was no question of the Dutch superiority in force, and it was used remorselessly. The Dutch East India Company had thriven apace. In 1606 a dividend of 50 per cent, had been paid; in 1609 one of 325 per cent. The chief factory was at Bantam, but there were many others on the mainland of India, and at Amboina, Banda, Ternate and Matsjan in the Moluccas; and from these centres trade was carried on with Ceylon, with Borneo and even with distant China and Japan. But the position of the company was precarious, until the secret article of the treaty of 1609 conceded liberty of trade during the truce. The chief need was to create a centre of administration, from which a general control could be exercised over all the officials at the various trading factories throughout the East-Indian archipelago. It was resolved, therefore, by the Council of Seventeen to appoint a director-general, who should reside at Bantam, armed with powers which made him, far removed as he was from interference by the home authorities, almost a sovereign in the extensive region which he administered. Jan Pieterszoon Koen, appointed in 1614, was the first of a series of capable men by whose vigorous and sometimes unscrupulous action the Dutch company became rapidly the dominant power in the eastern seas, where their trade and influence overshadowed those of their European competitors. The most enterprising of those competitors were the English. Disputes quickly arose between the rival companies as to trading rights in the Moluccas, the Banda group and Amboina; and some islands, where the English had made treaties with the natives, were occupied by the Dutch, and the English expelled.

Another grievance was the refusal of the States-General in 1616 to admit English dyed cloths into the United Provinces. This had caused especial irritation to King James. The manufacture of woollen cloth and the exportation of wool had for long been the chief of English industries; and the monopoly of the trade was, when James ascended the throne, in the hands of the oldest of English chartered companies, the Fellowship of Merchant Adventurers. The Adventurers held since 1598 their Court and Staple at Middelburg in Zeeland. The English had not learnt the art of finishing and dyeing the cloth that they wove; it was imported in its unfinished state, and was then dyed and prepared for commerce by the Dutch. Some thousands of skilled hands found employment in Holland in this work. James, always impecunious, determined in 1608, on the proposal of a certain Alderman Cockayne, to grant Cockayne a patent for the creation of a home-dyeing industry, reserving to the crown a monopoly for the sale of the goods. The Adventurers complained of this as a breach of their charter; and, after much bickering, the king in 1615 settled the dispute by withdrawing the charter. Cockayne now hoped that the company he had formed would be a profitable concern, but he and the king were doomed to disappointment. The Estates of Holland refused to admit the English dyed cloths, and their example was followed by the other provinces and by the States-General. Cockayne became bankrupt, and in 1617 the king had to renew the charter of the Adventurers. James was naturally very sore at this rebuff, and he resolved upon reprisals by enforcing the proclamation of 1609 and exacting a toll from all foreign vessels fishing in British waters. Great was the indignation in Holland, and the fishing fleet in 1617 set sail with an armed convoy. A Scottish official named Browne, who came to collect the toll, was seized and carried as a prisoner to Holland. James at once laid hands on two Dutch skippers in the Thames, as hostages, and demanded satisfaction for the outrage upon his officer. Neither side would at first give way, and it was not until after some months that an accommodation was patched up. The general question of the fishery privileges remained however just as far from settlement as ever, for the States stood firm upon their treaty rights. At length it was resolved by the States to send a special mission to England to discuss with the king the four burning questions embittering the relations between the two countries. The envoys arrived in London, December, 1618. For seven months the parleyings went on without any definite result being reached, and in August, 1619, the embassy returned. Very important events had meanwhile been occurring both in the United Provinces and in Germany, which made it necessary to both parties that the decision on these trade questions, important as they were, should be postponed for awhile, as they were overshadowed by the serious political crises in Holland and in Bohemia, which were then occupying all men's attention.

# CHAPTER IX

# MAURICE AND OLDENBARNEVELDT

The conclusion of the truce did not bring, with material progress and trade expansion, internal peace to the United Provinces. The relations between the Prince-stadholder and the all-powerful Advocate had long been strained. In the long-drawn-out negotiations Maurice had never disguised his dislike to the project of a truce, and, though he finally acquiesced, it was a sullen acquiescence. At first there was no overt breach between the two men, but Maurice, though he did not refuse to meet Oldenbarneveldt, was cold and unfriendly. He did not attempt to interfere with the old statesman's control of the machinery of administration or with his diplomatic activities, for he was naturally indolent and took little interest in politics. Had he been ambitious, he might many years before have obtained by general consent sovereign power, but he did not seek it. His passion was the study of military science. From his early youth he had spent his life in camps, and now he found himself without occupation. The enemies of Oldenbarneveldt seized the opportunity to arouse Maurice's suspicions of the Advocate's motives in bringing about the truce, and even to hint that he had been bribed with Spanish gold. Chief among these enemies was Francis van Aerssens, for a number of years ambassador of the States at Paris. Aerssens owed much to the Advocate, but he attributed his removal from his post at the French court to the decision of Oldenbarneveldt to replace him by his son-in-law, Van der Myle. He never forgave his recall, and alike by subtle insinuation and unscrupulous accusation, strove to blacken the character and reputation of his former benefactor.

By a curious fatality it was the outbreak of fierce sectarian strife and dissension between the extreme and the moderate Calvinists which was eventually to change the latent hostility of Maurice to Oldenbarneveldt into open antagonism. Neither of the two men had strong religious convictions, but circumstances brought it about that they were to range themselves irrevocably on opposite sides in a quarrel between fanatical theologians on the subject of predestination and grace.

From early times Calvinism in the northern Netherlands had been divided into two schools. The strict Calvinists or "Reformed," known by their opponents as "Precisians," and the liberal Calvinists, "the Evangelicals," otherwise "the Libertines." To this Libertine party belonged William the Silent, Oldenbarneveldt and the majority of the burgher-regents of Holland. These men regarded the religious question from the statesman's point of view. Having risen in rebellion against the tyranny of the Spanish Inquisition, they were anxious to preserve their countrymen (only a minority of whom were Protestants) from being placed under the heel of a religious intolerance as narrow and bigoted as that from which they had escaped. The "Reformed" congregations on the other hand, led by the preachers, were anxious to summon a National Synod for the purpose of creating a State Church to whose tenets, rigidly defined by the Heidelberg catechism and the Netherland confession, all would be required to conform on pain of being deprived of their rights as citizens. The Libertines were opposed to such a scheme, as an interference with the rights of each province to regulate its own religious affairs, and as an attempt to assert the supremacy of Church over State.

The struggle between the two parties, which had continued intermittently for a number of years, suddenly became acute through the appointment by Maurice of Jacob Harmensz, better known as Arminius, to the Chair of Theology at Leyden, vacated by the death of Junius in 1602. The leader of the strict Calvinist school, the learned Franciscus Gomarus, had at the time of the appointment of Arminius already been a professor at Leyden for eight years. Each teacher gathered round him a following of devoted disciples, and a violent collision was inevitable. Prolonged and heated controversy on the high doctrines of Predestination and Freewill led to many appeals being made to the States-General and to the Estates of

Holland to convene a Synod to settle the disputed questions, but neither of these bodies in the midst of the negotiations for the truce was willing to complicate matters by taking a step that could not fail to accentuate existing discords. Six months after the truce was signed Arminius died. The quarrel, however, was only to grow more embittered. Johannes Uyttenbogaert took the leadership of the Arminians, and finally, after consultation with Oldenbarneveldt, he called together a convention of Arminian preachers and laymen at Gouda (June, 1610). They drew up for presentation to the Estates a petition, known as the *Remonstratie,* consisting of five articles, in which they defined the points wherein they differed from the orthodox Calvinist doctrines on the subjects of predestination, election and grace. The Gomarists on their part drew up a *Contra-Remonstratie* containing seven articles, and they declined to submit to any decision on matters of doctrine, save from a purely Church Synod. These two weighty declarations gained for the two parties henceforth the names of Remonstrants and Contra-Remonstrants. For the next three years a fierce controversy raged in every province, pulpit replying to pulpit, and pamphlet to pamphlet. The Contra-Remonstrants roundly accused their adversaries of holding Pelagian and Socinian opinions and of being Papists in disguise. This last accusation drew to their side the great majority of the Protestant population, but the Remonstrants had many adherents among the burgher-regents, and they could count upon a majority in the Estates of Holland, Utrecht and Overyssel, and they had the powerful support of Oldenbarneveldt.

The Advocate was no theologian, and on the doctrinal points in dispute he probably held no very clear views. He inclined, however, to the Arminians because of their greater tolerance, and above all for their readiness to acknowledge the authority of the State as supreme, in religious as well as in civil matters. He was anxious to bring about an accommodation which should give satisfaction to both parties, but he was dealing with fanatics, and the fires of religious bigotry when once kindled are difficult to quench. And now was seen a curious object lesson in the many-headed character of the government of the United Netherlands. A majority of the provinces in the States-General favoured the Contra-Remonstrants. The Estates of Holland, however, under the influence of Oldenbarneveldt by a small majority refused the

Contra-Remonstrant demand and resolved to take drastic action against the Gomarists. But a number of the representative towns in Holland, and among them Amsterdam, declined to enforce the resolution. At Rotterdam, on the other hand, and in the other town-councils, where the Arminians had the majority, the Gomarist preachers were expelled from their pulpits; and the Advocate was determined by coercion, if necessary, to enforce the authority of the Estates throughout the province. But coercion without the use of the military force was impossible in face of the growing uprising of popular passion; and the military forces could not be employed without the consent of the stadholder. Thus in 1617, with the question of civil war in Holland trembling in the balance, the ultimate decision lay with the stadholder; and Maurice after long hesitation determined to throw the sword of the soldier into the scale against the influence of the statesman.

Maurice had not as yet openly broken with his father's old friend, whose immense services to the republic during the greater part of four decades he fully recognised. As to the questions now in dispute the stadholder was to an even less degree than the Advocate a zealous theologian. It is reported that he declared that he did not know whether predestination was blue or green. His court-chaplain, Uyttenbogaert, was a leading Arminian; and both his step-mother, Louise (see p. 78), to whose opinions he attached much weight, and his younger brother, Frederick Henry, were by inclination "libertines." On the other hand William Lewis, the Frisian Stadholder, was a zealous Calvinist, and he used all his influence with his cousin to urge him to make a firm stand against Oldenbarneveldt, and those who were trying to overthrow the Reformed faith. Sir Dudley Carleton, the new English ambassador, ranged himself also as a strong opponent of the Advocate. While Maurice, however, was hesitating as to the action he should take, Oldenbarneveldt determined upon a step which amounted to a declaration of war. In December, 1616, he carried in the Estates of Holland a proposal that they should, in the exercise of their sovereign rights, enlist a provincial force of 4000 militia (*waardgelders*) in their pay. Thus Holland, though a strong minority in the Estates was in opposition, declared its intention of upholding the principle of provincial sovereignty against the authority of the States-General. The States-General at the instance of the two stadholders, May,

1617, declared for the summoning of a National Synod by a vote of four provinces against three. The Estates of Holland, again with a sharp division of opinion but by a majority, declined to obey the summons. An impasse was thus reached and Maurice at last openly declared for the Contra-Remonstrant side.

On July 23 the Prince, accompanied by his suite, ostentatiously attended divine service at the Cloister Church at the Hague, where the Contra-Remonstrants had a fortnight before, in face of the prohibition of the Estates, established themselves. This step was countered by decisive action on the part of Oldenbarneveldt. A proposal was made in the Estates of Holland, August 4, known as the "Sharp Resolution"—and it well merited its name, for it was of the most drastic character. It was a most unqualified declaration of provincial sovereignty, and yet it was only passed in the teeth of a strong minority by the exertion of the Advocate's personal influence. By this resolution Holland declined to assent to the summoning of any Synod, National or Provincial, and asserted the supremacy of the Estates in matters of religion. The municipal authorities were ordered to raise levies of *Waardgelders* to keep the peace; and all officials, civil or military, were required to take an oath of obedience to the Estates on pain of dismissal. A strong protest was made by the representatives of the dissenting cities headed by Reinier Pauw, burgomaster of Amsterdam.

On the plea of ill-health Oldenbarneveldt now left the Hague, and took up his residence at Utrecht. His object was to keep this province firm in its alliance with Holland. He did not return till November 6, but all the time he was in active correspondence with his party in Holland, at whose head were the three pensionaries of Rotterdam, Leyden and Haarlem—De Groot, Hoogerbeets and De Haan. Under their leadership levies of *Waardgelders* were made in a number of towns; but other towns, including Amsterdam, refused, and the total levy did not amount to more than 1800 men. Meanwhile the majority of the States-General, urged on by Maurice and William Lewis, were determined, despite the resistance of Holland and Utrecht, to carry through the proposal for the summoning of a National Synod. Overyssel had been overawed and persuaded to assent, so that there were five votes against two in its favour. All through the winter the wrangling went on, and estrangement between the contending parties grew more bitter and acute. A perfect flood of pamphlets, broadsheets and pasquinades issued from the press; and in particular the most violent and envenomed attacks were made upon the character and administration of the Advocate, in which he was accused of having received bribes both from Spanish and French sources and to have betrayed the interests of his country. The chief instigator of these attacks was Oldenbarneveldt's personal enemy, Francis van Aerssens, whose pen was never idle. The defenders of the Remonstrant cause and of the principles of provincial sovereignty were not lacking in the vigour and virulence of their replies; and the Advocate himself felt that the accusations which were made against him demanded a formal and serious rejoinder. He accordingly prepared a long and careful defence of his whole career, in which he proved conclusively that the charges made against him had no foundation. This *Remonstratie* he addressed to the Estates of Holland, and he also sent a copy to the Prince. If this document did not at the time avail to silence the voices of prejudiced adversaries whose minds were made up, it has at least had the effect of convincing posterity that, however unwise may have been the course now deliberately pursued by the Advocate, he never for the sake of personal gain betrayed the interests of his country. Had he now seen that the attempt of a majority in the Estates of Holland to resist the will of the majority in the States-General could only lead to civil war, and had he resigned his post, advising the Estates to disband the *Waardgelders* and yield to superior force, a catastrophe might have been averted. There is no reason to believe that in such circumstances Maurice would have countenanced any extreme harshness in dealing with the Advocate. But Oldenbarneveldt, long accustomed to the exercise of power, was determined not to yield one jot of the claim of the sovereign province of Holland to supremacy within its own borders in matters of religion. The die was cast and the issue had to be decided by force of arms.

On June 28, 1618, a solemn protest was made by the Advocate in the States-General against the summoning of a National Synod in opposition to the expressed opinion of the Estates of Holland; and a threat was made that Holland might withhold her contribution to the general fund. The majority of the States-General (July 9) declared the raising of local levies illegal, and (July 23) it was resolved that a commission be sent to Utrecht with Maurice at its head to demand the disbanding of the *Waardgelders* in that town.

The Estates of Holland[5] impelled by Oldenbarneveldt now took a very strong step, a step which could not be retrieved. They resolved also to despatch commissioners to Utrecht to urge the town-council to stand firm. De Groot, Hoogerbeets and two others were nominated, and they at once set out for Utrecht. Maurice, with the deputation from the States-General and a large suite, left the Hague only a little later than De Groot and his companions, and reached Utrecht on the evening of the 25th. This strange situation lasted for several days, and much parleying and several angry discussions took place. Matters were further complicated by the news that the dissentient towns of Holland were also sending a deputation. This news had a considerable effect upon Colonel Ogle, the commander of the *Waardgelders* in Utrecht, and his officers. They were already wavering; they now saw that resistance to the orders of the States-General would be useless. The Prince, who had been collecting a body of troops, now determined on action. His force entered the city on the evening of the 31st, and on the following morning he commanded the local levies to lay down their arms. They at once obeyed, and Maurice took possession of the city. The Holland commissioners and the members of the town-council fled. Maurice appointed a new town-council entirely Contra-Remonstrant; and changes were made in both branches of the Estates, so as to secure a Contra-Remonstrant majority and with it the vote of the province in the States-General for the National Synod. Holland now stood alone, and its opposition had to be dealt with in a fashion even sterner than that of Utrecht.

The Remonstrant cities of Holland were still for resistance, and attempts were made to influence the stadholder not to resort to extreme measures. Maurice had, however, made up his mind. On August 18 the States-General passed a resolution demanding the dismissal of the *Waardgelders* in Holland within twenty-four hours. The placard was published on the 20th and was immediately obeyed. The Estates of Holland had been summoned to meet on the 21st, and were at once called upon to deal with the question of the National Synod. A few days later (August 28) a secret resolution was adopted by the majority in the States-General, without the knowledge of the Holland deputies, to arrest Oldenbarneveldt, De

Groot, Hoogerbeets and Ledenburg, the secretary of the Estates of Utrecht, on the ground that their action in the troubles at Utrecht had been dangerous to the State. On the following day the Advocate, on his way to attend the meeting of the Estates, was arrested and placed in confinement. De Groot, Hoogerbeets and Ledenburg met with similar treatment. After protesting the Estates adjourned on the 30th until September 12, the deputies alleging that it was necessary to consult their principals in this emergency, but in reality because the suddenness of the blow had stricken them with terror. It was a prudent step, for Maurice was resolved to purge the Estates and the town-councils of Holland, as he had already purged those of Utrecht. Attended by a strong body-guard he went from town to town, changing the magistracies, so as to place everywhere the Contra-Remonstrants in power. As a consequence of this action the deputies sent by the towns were likewise changed; and, when the Estates next met, the supporters of Oldenbarneveldt and his policy had disappeared. A peaceful revolution had been accomplished. All opposition to the summoning of the Synod was crushed; and (November 9) the Estates passed a vote of thanks to the stadholder for "the care and fidelity" with which he had discharged a difficult and necessary duty.

Meanwhile Oldenbarneveldt and the other prisoners had been confined in separate rooms in the Binnenhof and were treated with excessive harshness and severity. They were permitted to have no communication with the outside world, no books, paper or writing materials; and the conditions of their imprisonment were such as to be injurious to health. A commission was appointed by the States-General to examine the accused, and it began its labours in November. The method of procedure was unjust and unfair in the extreme, even had it been a case of dealing with vile criminals. The treatment of Oldenbarneveldt in particular was almost indecently harsh. The aged statesman had to appear sixty times before the commission and was examined and cross-examined on every incident of the forty years of his administration and on every detail of his private life. He was allowed not only to have no legal adviser, but also was forbidden access to any books of reference or to any papers or to make any notes. It was thus hoped that, having to trust entirely to his memory, the old man might be led into self-contradictions or to making damaging admissions against himself.

De Groot and Hoogerbeets had to undergo a similar, though less protracted, inquisition. Such was its effect upon Ledenburg that he committed suicide.

It was not until February 20, 1619, that the States-General appointed an extraordinary court for the trial of the accused. It consisted of twenty-four members, of whom twelve were Hollanders.

It is needless to say that such a court had no legal status; and the fact that nearly all its members were the Advocate's personal or political enemies is a proof that the proceedings were judicial only in name. It was appointed not to try, but to condemn the prisoners. Oldenbarneveldt protested in the strongest terms against the court's competence. He had been the servant of the Estates of the sovereign province of Holland, and to them alone was he responsible. He denied to the States-General any sovereign rights; they were simply an assembly representing a number of sovereign allies. These were bold statements, and they were accompanied by an absolute denial of the charges brought against him. It was quite useless. All the prisoners were condemned, first De Groot, then Hoogerbeets, then Oldenbarneveldt. The trials were concluded on May 1, but it was resolved to defer the sentences until after the close of the National Synod, which had been meeting at Dordrecht. This took place on May 9.

Meanwhile strong and influential efforts were made for leniency. The French ambassador, Aubrey du Maurier, during the trial did his utmost to secure fair treatment for the Advocate; and a special envoy, Châtillon, was sent from Paris to express the French king's firm belief in the aged statesman's integrity and patriotism based on an intimate knowledge of all the diplomatic proceedings during and after the negotiations for the Truce. But these representations had no effect and were indeed resented. Equally unfruitful were the efforts made by Louise de Coligny to soften the severity of her step-son's attitude. Even William Lewis wrote to Maurice not to proceed too harshly in the matter. All was in vain. The Prince's heart was steeled. He kept asking whether the Advocate or his family had sued for pardon. But Oldenbarneveldt was far too proud to take any step which implied an admission of guilt; and all the members of his family were as firmly resolved as he was not to supplicate for grace. Few, however, believed that capital punishment would be carried out. On Sunday, May 12, however, sentence of death was solemnly pronounced; and on the following morning the head of the great statesman and patriot was stricken off on a scaffold erected in the Binnenhof immediately in front of the windows of Maurice's residence. The Advocate's last words were a protestation of his absolute innocence of the charge of being a traitor to his country; and posterity has endorsed the declaration.

That Oldenbarneveldt had in the last two years of his life acted indiscreetly and arrogantly there can be no question. His long tenure of power had made him impatient of contradiction; and, having once committed himself to a certain course of action, he determined to carry it through in the teeth of opposition, regardless of consequences and with a narrow obstinacy of temper that aroused bitter resentment. His whole correspondence and private papers were however seized and carefully scrutinised by his personal enemies; and, had they found any evidence to substantiate the charges brought against him, it would have been published to the world. It is clear that not a shred of such evidence was discovered, and that the Advocate was perfectly innocent of the treasonable conduct for which a packed court condemned him to suffer death. Such was the reward that Oldenbarneveldt received for life-long services of priceless value to his country. He more than any other man was the real founder of the Dutch Republic; and it will remain an ineffaceable stain on Maurice's memory that he was consenting unto this cruel and unjust sentence.

Sentences of imprisonment for life were passed upon De Groot and Hoogerbeets. They were confined in the castle of Loevestein. The conditions of captivity were so far relaxed that the famous jurist was allowed to receive books for the continuance of his studies. Through the ingenuity and daring of his wife De Groot contrived to escape in 1621 by concealing himself in a trunk supposed to be filled with heavy tomes. The trunk was conveyed by water to Rotterdam, from whence the prisoner managed to make his way safely to France.

Concurrently with the political trials the National Synod had been pursuing its labours at Dordrecht. On November 13 rather more than one hundred delegates assembled under the presidency of Johannes Bogerman of Leeuwarden. Fifty-eight of the delegates were preachers, professors and elders elected by the provincial synods, fifteen were commissioners appointed by the States-General, twenty-eight were members of foreign Reformed churches. English and Scottish representatives took an active part in the proceedings. The Synod decided to summon the Remonstrants to send a deputation to make their defence. On December 6 accordingly, a body of twelve leading Remonstrants with Simon Episcopius at their head took their seats at a table facing the assembly. Episcopius made a long harangue in Latin occupying nine sessions. His eloquence was, however, wasted on a court that had already prejudged the cause for which he pleaded. After much wrangling and many recriminations Bogerman ordered the Remonstrants to withdraw. They did so only to meet in an "anti-synod" at Rotterdam at which the authority of the Dordrecht assembly to pronounce decisions on matters of faith was denied. Meanwhile the Contra-Remonstrant divines at Dordrecht during many weary sessions proceeded to draw up a series of canons defining the true Reformed doctrine and condemning utterly, as false and heretical, the five points set forth in the Remonstrance. On May 1 the Netherland confession and the Heidelberg catechism were unanimously adopted, as being in conformity with Holy Scripture, and as fixing the standard of orthodox teaching. The Synod was dissolved eight days later. The final session was the 154th; and this great assembly of delegates from many lands, the nearest approach to a general council of the Protestant churches that has ever been held, came to a close amidst much festivity and no small congratulation. No time was lost in taking action by the dominant party against their opponents. Two hundred Remonstrant preachers were driven into exile; and the congregations were treated with the same spirit of intolerance as had hitherto been the lot of the Catholics, and were forbidden the exercise of public worship.

After the Advocate's death, except for the persecution directed against the Remonstrant party, the course of public affairs went on smoothly. Maurice, who by the death of his brother, Philip William, had in February, 1618, become Prince of Orange, was virtually sovereign in the United Provinces. His name appeared in treaties with eastern potentates and in diplomatic despatches, just as if he were a reigning monarch; and the people of the Netherlands were even at times spoken of as his subjects. But Maurice never cared to trouble himself about the details of politics, and he now left the management of affairs in the hands of a few men that he could trust, notably in those of Francis van Aerssens (henceforth generally known as lord of Sommelsdijk) and Reinier Pauw, the influential burgomaster of Amsterdam. Aerssens had shown himself spiteful and vindictive in his conduct towards his earlier patron, Oldenbarneveldt, but being a clever diplomatist and gifted with considerable powers of statesmanship, he became henceforth for many years the trusted adviser and confidant not only of Maurice, but of his successor Frederick Henry.

The year 1620 was marked by the sudden death in June of William Lewis, the Stadholder of Friesland. His loss was much deplored by Maurice, who had for years been accustomed to rely upon the tried experience and sound judgment of his cousin both in peace and war. A few months earlier (March) Louise de Coligny had died at Fontainebleau. She too had been from his youth the wise adviser of her step-son, but she was deeply grieved at the fate of Oldenbarneveldt, and after his execution left the Netherlands to take up her residence in her native country. By the death of William Lewis the two stadholderates of Groningen with Drente and of Friesland became vacant. Maurice succeeded to that of Groningen, but the Frieslanders remained faithful to the house of Nassau-Siegen and elected Ernest Casimir, the younger brother of William Lewis, as their stadholder.

## CHAPTER X

## FROM THE END OF THE TWELVE YEARS' TRUCE TO THE PEACE OF MUENSTER (1621-48). THE STADHOLDERATE OF FREDERICK HENRY OF ORANGE

Civil disturbances and religious persecutions were not the only causes of anxiety to the political leaders in the United Provinces during the crisis of 1618-19; foreign affairs were also assuming a menacing aspect. The year 1618 saw the opening in Germany of the Thirty Years' War. The acceptance of the Crown of Bohemia by Frederick, Elector Palatine, meant that the long-delayed struggle for supremacy between Catholics and Protestants was to be fought out; and it was a struggle which neither Spain nor the Netherlands could watch with indifference. Maurice was fully alive to the necessity of strengthening the defences of the eastern frontier; and subsidies were granted by the States-General to Frederick and also to some of the smaller German princes. This support would have been larger, but the unexpected refusal of James I to give aid to his son-in-law made the Dutch doubtful in their attitude. The States, though friendly, were unwilling to commit themselves. In the spring of 1620, however, by James' permission, the English regiments in the Dutch service under the command of Sir Horace Vere were sent to oppose Spinola's invasion of the Rhineland. Accompanied by a Dutch force under Frederick Henry, they reached the Palatinate, but it was too late. The fate of the King of Bohemia was soon to be decided elsewhere than in his hereditary dominions. Completely defeated at the battle of Prague, Frederick with his wife and family fled to Holland to seek the protection of their cousin, the Prince of

Orange. They met with the most generous treatment at his hands, and they were for many years to make the Hague the home of their exile.

As the date at which the Twelve Years' Truce came to an end drew near, some efforts were made to avert war. There were advocates of peace in the United Provinces, especially in Gelderland and Overyssel, the two provinces most exposed to invasion.

The archdukes had no desire to re-open hostilities; and Pecquinius, the Chancellor of Brabant, was sent to the Hague to confer with Maurice, and was authorised to name certain conditions for the conclusion of a peace. These conditions proved, however, to be wholly unacceptable, and the early summer of 1621 saw Maurice and Spinola once more in the field at the head of rival armies. The operations were, however, dilatory and inconclusive. The stadholder now, and throughout his last campaigns, was no longer physically the same man as in the days when his skilful generalship had saved the Dutch republic from overthrow; he had lost the brilliant energy of youth. The deaths in the course of this same year, 1621, of both the Archduke Albert and Philip III of Spain, were also hindrances to the vigorous prosecution of the war. In 1622 there was much marching and counter-marching, and Maurice was successful in compelling Spinola to raise the siege of Bergen-op-Zoom, the last success he was destined to achieve. In the course of this year the prince's life was in serious danger. A plot was laid to assassinate him on his way to Ryswyck, the leading conspirator being William van Stoutenberg, the younger son of Oldenbarneveldt. Stoutenberg had, in 1619, been deprived of his posts and his property confiscated, and he wished to avenge his father's death and his own injuries. The plot was discovered, but Stoutenberg managed to escape and took service under the Archduchess Isabel. Unfortunately he had implicated his elder brother, Regnier, lord of Groeneveldt, in the scheme. Groeneveldt was seized and brought to the scaffold.

From this time nothing but misfortune dogged the steps of Maurice, whose health began to give way under the fatigues of campaigning. In 1623 a carefully planned expedition against Antwerp, which he confidently expected to succeed, was frustrated by a long continuance of stormy weather. Spinola in the following year laid siege to Breda. This strongly fortified town, an ancestral domain of the Princes of Orange, had a garrison of 7000 men.

The Spanish commander rapidly advancing completely invested it. Maurice, who had been conducting operations on the eastern frontier, now hastened to Breda, and did his utmost by cutting off Spinola's own supplies to compel him to raise the blockade. All his efforts however failed, and after holding out for many months Breda surrendered. In the spring of 1625 the prince became so seriously ill that he asked the States-General to appoint his brother commander-in-chief in his stead. Feeling his end drawing near, Maurice's chief wish was to see Frederick Henry married before his death. Frederick Henry, like Maurice himself, had never shown any inclination for wedlock and there was no heir to the family. He had, however, been attracted by the Countess Amalia von Solms, a lady of the suite of Elizabeth of Bohemia. Under pressure from the dying man the preliminaries were speedily arranged, and the wedding was quietly celebrated on April 4. Though thus hastily concluded, the marriage proved to be in every way a thoroughly happy one. Amalia was throughout his life to be the wise adviser of her husband and to exercise no small influence in the conduct of public affairs. Maurice died on April 23, in the fifty-eighth year of his age. His forty years of continuous and strenuous service to the State had made him prematurely old; and there can be but little doubt that the terrible anxieties of the crisis of 1618-19 told upon him. Above all a feeling of remorse for his share in the tragedy of Oldenbarneveldt's death preyed upon his mind.

The new Prince of Orange succeeded to a difficult position, but he was endowed with all the qualities of a real leader of men. Forty-one years old and brought up from boyhood in camps under the eye of his brother, Frederick Henry was now to show that he was one of the most accomplished masters of the military art, and especially siege-craft, in an age of famous generals, for Bernard of Saxe-Weimar, Torstenson, Turenne, Charles Gustavus and the Great Elector were all trained in his school. He was, however, much more than an experienced and resourceful commander in the field. He inherited much of his father's wary and tactful statesmanship and skill in diplomacy. He was, moreover, deservedly popular. He was a Hollander born and bred, and his handsome face, chivalrous bearing, and conciliatory genial temper, won for him an influence, which for some years was to give him almost undisputed predominance in the State. To quote the words of a contemporary,

Van der Capellen, "the prince in truth disposed of everything as he liked; everything gave way to his word."

The offices and dignities held by Maurice were at once conferred on Frederick Henry. He was elected Stadholder of Holland, Zeeland, Utrecht, Gelderland and Overyssel, and was appointed Captain-General and Admiral-General of the Union and head of the Council of State. During practically the whole of his life the prince spent a considerable part of the year in camp, but he was able all the time to keep in touch with home affairs, and to exercise a constant supervision and control of the foreign policy of the State by the help of his wife, and through the services of Francis van Aerssens. The Court of the Princess of Orange, graced as it was by the presence of the exiled King and Queen of Bohemia, was brilliant and sumptuous, and gave to the reality of power possessed by the stadholder more than a semblance of sovereign pomp. During her husband's absence she spared no pains to keep him well-acquainted with all the currents and undercurrents of action and opinion at the Hague, and was not only able to give sound advice, but was quite ready, when necessity called, to meet intrigue with intrigue and render abortive any movements or schemes adverse to the prince's policy or authority. The obligations of Frederick Henry to Aerssens were even greater. The stadholder was at first suspicious of the man, whom he disliked for the leading part he had taken against Oldenbarneveldt. But he did not allow personal prejudice to prevent him from employing a diplomatist of Aerssens' experience and capacity, and, with acquaintance, he learned to regard him, not merely as a clever and wise councillor, but as a confidential friend.

The right conduct of foreign affairs was of peculiar importance at the moment, when Frederick Henry became stadholder, for a change of *régime* took place almost simultaneously both in France and England. In Paris Cardinal Richelieu had just laid firm hands upon the reins of power, and the timorous and feeble James I died in the autumn of 1625. Richelieu and Charles I were both hostile to Spain, and the republic had reason to hope for something more than friendly neutrality in the coming years of struggle with the united forces of the two Habsburg monarchies.

One of the chief difficulties which confronted the new stadholder was the religious question. The prince himself, as was well known, was inclined to Remonstrant opinions. He was, however, anxious not to stir up the smouldering embers of sectarian strife, and he made no effort to withdraw the placards against the Remonstrants, but confined himself to moderate in practice their severity. He recalled from exile Van der Myle, Oldenbarneveldt's son-in-law; made Nicholas van Reigersberg, De Groot's brother-in-law, a member of the council; and released Hoogerbeets from his captivity at Loevestein. When, however, De Groot himself, presuming on the stadholder's goodwill, ventured to return to Holland without permission, the prince refused to receive him and he was ordered to leave the country once more.

The year 1626 was marked by no events of military importance; both sides were in lack of funds and no offensive operations were undertaken. Much rejoicing, however, attended the birth of a son and heir to the Prince of Orange, May 27. The child received the name of William. Early in the following year Sir Dudley Carleton, as envoy-extraordinary of King Charles I, invested Frederick Henry at the Hague with the Order of the Garter. This high distinction was not, however, a mark of really friendlier relations between the two countries. The long-standing disputes as to fishing rights in the narrow seas and at Spitsbergen, and as to trading spheres in the East Indian Archipelago, remained unsettled; and in the unfortunate and ill-considered war, which broke out at this time between England and France, the sympathies of the States were with the latter. Already those close relations between the French and the Dutch, which for the next decade were to be one of the dominating factors in determining the final issue of the Thirty Years' War, were by the diplomatic efforts of Richelieu and of Aerssens being firmly established. France advanced to the States a large subsidy by the aid of which the stadholder was enabled to take the field at the head of a really fine army and to give to the world a brilliant display of his military abilities. Throughout his stadholderate the persistent aim which Frederick Henry held before himself was never aggression with a view to conquest, but the creation of a scientific frontier, covered by strong fortresses, within which the flat lands behind the defensive lines of the great rivers could feel reasonably secure against sudden attack. It was with this object that in 1629 he determined to lay siege to the town of Hertogenbosch. A force of 24,000 infantry and 4000 cavalry were gathered together for the enterprise. It was composed of many nationalities, like all the armies commanded by Maurice and Frederick Henry, but was admirably disciplined and devoted to its commander. Four English, three Scottish and four French regiments, all choice troops, raised by permission of their sovereigns for the service of the States, formed the backbone of the force. On April 30 the town was invested.

Hertogenbosch, or Bois-le-duc, was strongly fortified, and so surrounded by marshy ground, intersected by a number of small streams, that the only way of approach for a besieging force was a single causeway defended by the forts of St Isabella and St Anthony. The garrison consisted of 8000 men, and the governor, Grobendonc, was an experienced and resolute soldier.

The stadholder began by surrounding the town with a double line of circumvallation. The marshes were crossed by dykes, and two streams were dammed so as to fill a broad deep moat round the lines and flood the country outside. Other lines, three miles long, connected the investing lines with the village of Crèveceeur on the Meuse, Frederick Henry's base of supplies, which were brought by water from Holland. These works completed, approaches were at once opened against the forts of St Anthony and St Isabella, the task being entrusted to the English and French troops. The court of Brussels now began to take serious measures for relieving the town. At first regarding *Bolduc la pucelle* as impregnable, they had been pleased to hear that the prince had committed himself to an enterprise certain to be a dismal failure. Then came the news of the circumvallation, and with it alarm. The Count de Berg was therefore ordered (June 17) at the head of an army of 30,000 foot and 7000 horse to advance into North Brabant and raise the siege. But the stadholder was prepared and ceaselessly on his guard; and the Spanish general, after several vain attempts, found the Dutch lines unassailable. With the view of compelling Frederick Henry to follow him, Berg now marched into the heart of the United Provinces, devastating as he went with fire and sword, took Amersfoort and threatened Amsterdam. But the prince confined himself to despatching a small detached force of observation; and meanwhile a happy stroke, by which a certain Colonel Dieden surprised and captured the important frontier fortress of Wesel, forced the Spaniards to retreat, for Wesel was Berg's depot of supplies and munitions.

While all this was going on the Prince of Orange had been pushing forward the siege operations. On July 17 the forts of St Isabella and St Anthony were stormed. The attack against the main defences, in which the English regiments specially distinguished themselves, was now pressed with redoubled vigour. The resistance at every step was desperate, but at last the moat was crossed and a lodgment effected within the walls. On September 14 Hertogenbosch surrendered; and the virgin fortress henceforth became the bulwark of the United Provinces against Spanish attack on this side. The consummate engineering skill, with which the investment had been carried out, attracted the attention of all Europe to this famous siege. It was a signal triumph and added greatly to the stadholder's popularity and influence in the republic.

It was needed. The Estates of Holland were at this time once more refractory. The interests of this great commercial and maritime province differed from those of the other provinces of the Union; and it bore a financial burden greater than that of all the others put together. The Estates, then under the leadership of Adrian Pauw, the influential pensionary of Amsterdam, declined to raise the quota of taxation assigned to the province for military needs and proceeded to disband a number of troops that were in their pay. Inconsistently with this action they declined to consider certain proposals for peace put forward by the Infanta Isabel, for they would yield nothing on the questions of liberty of worship or of freedom to trade in the Indies. Their neglect to furnish the requisite supplies for the war, however, prevented the prince from undertaking any serious military operations in 1630. Fortunately the other side were in no better case financially, while the death of Spinola and the withdrawal of the Count de Berg from the Spanish service deprived them of their only two competent generals. This attitude of Holland, though it thwarted the stadholder's plans and was maintained in opposition to his wishes, by no means however implied any distrust of him or lack of confidence in his leadership. This was conclusively proved by the passing, at the instigation of Holland, of the *Acte de Survivance* (April 19, 1631). This Act declared all the various offices held by the prince hereditary in the person of his five-year-old son. He thus became, in all but name, a constitutional sovereign.

An expedition planned for the capture of Dunkirk at this time, spring 1631, proved too hazardous and was abandoned, but later in the year the Dutch sailors gave a signal proof of their superiority at sea. Encouraged by the failure of the attempted attack on Dunkirk the government at Brussels determined on a counter-stroke. A flotilla of 35 frigates, accompanied by a large number of smaller vessels to carry supplies and munitions and having on board a body of 6000 soldiers, set sail from Antwerp under the command of Count John of Nassau (a cousin of the stadholder) and in the presence of Isabel herself to effect the conquest of some of the Zeeland islands. As soon as the news reached Frederick Henry, detachments of troops were at once despatched to various points; and about a dozen vessels were rapidly equipped and ordered to follow the enemy and if possible bring him to action. A landing at Terscholen was foiled by Colonel Morgan, who, at the head of 2000 English troops, waded across a shallow estuary in time to prevent a descent. At last (September 12) the Dutch ships managed to come up with their adversaries in the Slaak near the island of Tholen. They at once attacked and though so inferior in numbers gained a complete victory. Count John of Nassau just contrived to escape, but his fleet was destroyed and 5000 prisoners were taken.

The year 1632 witnessed a renewal of military activity and was memorable for the famous siege and capture of Maestricht. This fortress held the same commanding position on the eastern frontier as Hertogenbosch on the southern; and, though its natural position was not so strong as the capital of North Brabant, Maestricht, lying as it did on both sides of the broad Meuse, and being strongly fortified and garrisoned, was very difficult to invest. The stadholder, at the head of a force of 17,000 infantry and 4000 horse, first made himself master of Venloo and Roeremonde and then advanced upon Maestricht. Unfortunately before Roeremonde, Ernest Casimir, the brave stadholder of Friesland and Groningen, was killed. He was succeeded in his offices by his son, Henry Casimir. Arriving (June 10) before Maestricht, Frederick Henry proceeded to erect strongly entrenched lines of circumvallation round the town connecting them above and below the town by bridges. Supplies reached him plentifully by the river. To the English and French regiments were once more assigned the place of honour in the attack. All went well until July 2, when Don Gonzales de Cordova led a superior Spanish force from Germany, consisting of 18,000 foot and 6000 horse, to raise the siege, and encamped close to the Dutch lines on the south side of the river. Finding however no vulnerable spot, he awaited the arrival at the beginning of August of an Imperialist army of 12,000 foot and 4000 horse, under the renowned Pappenheim. This impetuous leader determined upon an assault, and the Dutch entrenchments were attacked suddenly with great vigour at a moment when the prince was laid up with the gout. He rose, however, from his bed, personally visited all the points of danger, and after desperate fighting the assailants were at last driven off with heavy loss. The Spaniards and Imperialists, finding that the stadholder's lines could not be forced, instituted a blockade, so that the besiegers were themselves besieged. But Frederick Henry had laid up such ample stores of munitions and provisions that he paid no heed to the cutting of his communications, and pushed on his approaches with the utmost rapidity. All difficulties were overcome by the engineering skill of the scientific commander; and finally two tunnels sixty feet deep were driven under the broad dry moat before the town walls. The English regiments during these operations bore the brunt of the fighting and lost heavily, Colonels Harwood and the Earl of Oxford being killed and Colonel Morgan dangerously wounded. After exploding a mine, a forlorn hope of fifty English troops rushed out from one of the tunnels and made good their footing upon the ramparts. Others followed, and the garrison, fearing that further resistance might entail the sacking of the town, surrendered (August 23) with honours of war.

One result of the fall of Maestricht was a renewal on the part of the Archduchess Isabel of negotiations for peace or a long truce. On the authority of Frederick Henry's memoirs the terms first offered to him in camp were favourable and might have been accepted. When, however, the discussion was shifted to the Hague, the attitude of the Belgic representatives had stiffened. The cause was not far to seek, for on November 6, 1632 the ever-victorious Gustavus Adolphus had fallen in the hour of triumph in the fatal battle of Lützen. The death of the Swedish hero was a great blow to the Protestant cause and gave fresh heart to the despondent Catholic alliance. The negotiations dragged however their slow length along, the chief point of controversy being the old dispute about freedom to trade in the Indies. On this point agreement was impossible. Spain would yield nothing of her pretensions; and the Hollanders would hear of no concessions that threatened the prosperity of the East and West India Companies in which so many merchants and investors were deeply interested. Any admission of a Spanish monopoly or right of exclusion would have spelt ruin to thousands. The diplomatic discussions, however, went on for many months in a desultory and somewhat futile manner; and meanwhile though hostilities did not actually cease, the campaign of 1633 was conducted in a half-hearted fashion. The death of Isabel on November 29, 1633, shattered finally any hopes that the peace party in the Provinces (for there was a strong peace party) might have had of arriving at any satisfactory agreement. By the decease of the arch-duchess, who had been a wise and beneficent ruler and had commanded the respect and regard not only of her own subjects but of many northerners also, the Belgic provinces reverted to the crown of Spain and passed under the direct rule of Philip IV. The Cardinal Infante Ferdinand, fresh from his crushing victory over the Swedes at Nördlingen, came as governor to Brussels in 1634, at the head of considerable Spanish forces, and an active renewal of the war in 1635 was clearly imminent.

In these circumstances Frederick Henry determined to enter into negotiations with France for the conclusion of an offensive and defensive alliance against Spain, the common enemy. He had many difficulties to encounter. The Estates of Holland, though opposed to the terms actually offered by the Brussels government, were also averse to taking any step which shut the door upon hopes of peace. Richelieu on his side, though ready, as before, to grant subsidies and to permit the enrolment of French regiments for the Dutch service, shrank from committing France to an open espousal of the Protestant side against the Catholic powers. The stadholder, however, was not deterred by the obstacles in his way; and the diplomatic skill and adroitness of Aerssens, aided by his own tact and firmness of will, overcame the scruples of Richelieu. The opposition of the Estates of Holland, without whose consent no treaty could be ratified, was likewise surmounted. Adrian Pauw, their leader, was despatched on a special embassy to Paris, and in his absence his influence was undermined, and Jacob Cats was appointed Council-Pensionary in his stead. In the spring of 1635 a firm alliance was concluded between France and the United

Provinces, by which it was agreed that neither power should make peace without the consent of the other, each meanwhile maintaining a field force of 25,000 foot and 5000 horse and dividing conquests in the Southern Netherlands between them. This treaty was made with the concurrence and strong approval of the Swedish Chancellor, Oxenstierna, and was probably decisive in its effect upon the final issue of the Thirty Years' War.

In the early spring of 1635, therefore, a French force entered the Netherlands and, after defeating Prince Thomas of Savoy at Namur, joined the Dutch army at Maestricht. Louis XIII had given instructions to the French commanders, Châtillon and de Brézé, to place themselves under the orders of the Prince of Orange; and Frederick Henry at the head of 32,000 foot and 9000 horse now entered the enemy's territory and advanced to the neighbourhood of Louvain. Here however, owing to the outbreak of disease among his troops, to lack of supplies and to differences of opinion with his French colleagues, the prince determined to retreat. His action was attended by serious results. His adversary, the Cardinal Infante Ferdinand, was a wary and skilful general. He now seized his opportunity, rapidly made himself master of Diest, Gennep, Goch and Limburg, and took by surprise the important fort of Schenck at the junction of the Waal and the Rhine. Vexed at the loss of a stronghold which guarded two of the main waterways of the land, the stadholder at once laid siege to Schenck. But the Spanish garrison held out obstinately all through the winter and did not surrender until April 26,1636. The Dutch army had suffered much from exposure and sickness during this long investment and was compelled to abstain for some months from active operations. Ferdinand thereupon, as soon as he saw that there was no immediate danger of an attack from the north, resolved to avenge himself upon the French for the part they had taken in the preceding year's campaign. Reinforced by a body of Imperialist troops under Piccolomini he entered France and laid the country waste almost to the gates of Paris. This bold stroke completely frustrated any plans that the allies may have formed for combined action in the late summer.

The following year the States determined, somewhat against the wishes of Frederick Henry, to send an expedition into Flanders for the capture of Dunkirk. This was done at the instance of the French ambassador, Charnacé, acting on the instructions of Richelieu, who promised the assistance of 5000 French troops and undertook, should the town be taken, to leave it in the possession of the Dutch. The stadholder accordingly assembled (May 7) an army of 14,000 foot and a considerable body of horse at Rammekens, where a fleet lay ready for their transport to Flanders. Contrary winds, however, continued steadily to blow for many weeks without affording any opportunity for putting to sea. At last, wearied out with the long inaction and its attendant sickness the prince (July 20) suddenly broke up his camp and marched upon Breda. Spinola, after capturing Breda in 1625, had greatly strengthened its defences; and now, with a garrison of 4000 men under a resolute commander, it was held to be secure against any attack. The siege was a repetition of those of Hertogenbosch and Maestricht. In vain did the Cardinal Infante with a powerful force try to break through the lines of circumvallation, which the prince had constructed with his usual skill. Called away by a French invasion on the south, he had to leave Breda to its fate. The town surrendered on October 10.

During the years 1637 and 1638 the ever-recurring dissensions between the province of Holland and the Generality became acute once more. The Provincial Estates insisted on their sovereign rights and refused to acknowledge the authority of the States-General to impose taxes upon them. This opposition of Holland was a great hindrance to the prince in the conduct of the war, and caused him constant anxiety and worry. It was impossible to plan or to carry out a campaign without adequate provision being made for the payment and maintenance of the military and naval forces, and this depended upon Holland's contribution. Amsterdam was the chief offender. On one occasion a deputation sent to Amsterdam from the States-General was simply flouted. The burgomaster refused to summon the council together, and the members of the deputation had to return without an audience. All the prince's efforts to induce the contumacious city to consider his proposals in a reasonable and patriotic spirit were of no avail; they were rejected insultingly. In his indignation Frederick Henry is reported to have exclaimed, "I have no greater enemy, but if only I could take Antwerp, it would bring them to their senses."

The immense and growing prosperity of Amsterdam at this time was indeed mainly due to the fall of Antwerp from its high estate. To reconquer Antwerp had indeed long been a favourite project of Frederick Henry. In 1638 he made careful and ample preparations for its realisation. But it was not to be. Misfortune this year was to dog his steps. The advance was made in two bodies. The larger under the prince was to march straight to Antwerp. The second, of 6000 men, commanded by Count William of Nassau, was instructed to seize some outlying defences on the Scheldt before joining the main force before the town. Count William began well, but, hearing a false rumour that a fleet was sailing up the Scheldt to intercept his communications, he hastily retreated. While his ranks were in disorder he was surprised by a Spanish attack, and practically his entire force was cut to pieces. On hearing of this disaster the stadholder had no alternative but to abandon the siege.

Constant campaigning and exposure to the hardships of camp life year after year began at this time seriously to affect the health of the stadholder. He was much troubled by attacks of gout, which frequently prevented him from taking his place in the field. In 1639 there were no military events of importance; nevertheless this year was a memorable one in the annals of the Dutch republic.

It was the year of the battle of the Downs. A great effort was made by Spain to re-establish her naval supremacy in the narrow seas, and the finest fleet that had left the harbours of the peninsula since 1588 arrived in the Channel in September, 1639. It consisted of seventy-seven vessels carrying 24,000 men, sailors and soldiers, and was under the command of an experienced and capable seaman, Admiral Oquendo. His orders were to drive the Dutch fleet from the Channel and to land 10,000 men at Dunkirk as a reinforcement for the Cardinal Infante. Admiral Tromp had been cruising up and down the Channel for some weeks on the look-out for the Spaniards, and on September 16 he sighted the armada. He had only thirteen vessels with him, the larger part of his fleet having been detached to keep watch and ward over Dunkirk. With a boldness, however, that might have been accounted temerity, Tromp at once attacked the enemy and with such fury that the Spanish fleet sought refuge under the lee of the Downs and anchored at the side of an English squadron under Vice-Admiral Pennington. Rejoined by seventeen ships from before Dunkirk, the Dutch admiral now contented himself with a vigilant blockade, until further reinforcements could reach him. Such was the respect with which he had inspired the Spaniards, that no attempt was made to break the blockade; and in the meantime Tromp had sent urgent messages to Holland asking the Prince of Orange and the admiralties to strain every nerve to give him as many additional ships as possible. The request met with a ready and enthusiastic response. In all the dockyards work went on with relays of men night and day. In less than a month Tromp found himself at the head of 105 sail with twelve fire-ships. They were smaller ships than those of his adversary, but they were more than enough to ensure victory. On October 21, after detaching Vice-Admiral Witte de with 30 ships to watch Pennington's squadron, Tromp bore down straight upon the Spanish fleet though they were lying in English waters. Rarely has there been a naval triumph more complete. Under cover of a fog Oquendo himself with seven vessels escaped to Dunkirk; all the rest were sunk, burnt, or captured. It is said that 15,000 Spaniards perished. On the side of the Dutch only 100 men were killed and wounded. The Spanish power at sea had suffered a blow from which it never recovered.

Charles I was very angry on learning that English ships had been obliged to watch the fleet of a friendly power destroyed in English waters before their eyes. The king had inherited from his father a long series of grievances against the Dutch; and, had he not been involved in serious domestic difficulties, there would probably have been a declaration of war. But Charles' finances did not permit him to take a bold course, and he was also secretly irritated with the Spaniards for having sought the hospitality of English waters (as written evidence shows) without his knowledge and permission. Aerssens was sent to London to smooth over the matter. He had no easy task, but by skill and patience he contrived, in spite of many adverse influences at the court, so to allay the bitter feelings that had been aroused by "the scandal of the Downs" that Charles and his queen were willing, in the early months of 1640, to discuss seriously the project of a marriage between the stadholder's only son and one of the English princesses. In January a special envoy, Jan van der Kerkoven, lord of Heenvlict, joined Aerssens with a formal proposal for the hand of the princess royal; and after somewhat difficult negotiations the marriage was at length satisfactorily arranged. The ceremony took place in London, May

12, 1641. As William was but fifteen years of age and Mary, the princess royal, only nine, the bridegroom returned to Holland alone, leaving the child-bride for a time at Whitehall with her parents. The wedding took place at an ominous time. Ten days after it was celebrated Strafford was executed; and the dark shadow of the Great Rebellion was already hanging over the ill-fated Charles. In the tragic story of the House of Stewart that fills the next two decades there is perhaps no more pathetic figure than that of Mary, the mother of William III. At the time this alliance gave added lustre to the position of the Prince of Orange, both at home and abroad, by uniting his family in close bonds of relationship with the royal houses both of England and France.

In 1640, as the Spaniards remained on the defensive, the stadholder entered Flanders and by a forced march attempted to seize Bruges. His effort, however, was foiled, as was a later attempt to capture Hulst, when Frederick Henry and the States sustained a great loss in the death of the gallant Henry Casimir of Nassau, who was killed in a chance skirmish at the age of 29 years. This regrettable event caused a vacancy in the stadholderates of Friesland and Groningen with Drente. A number of zealous adherents of the House of Orange were now anxious that Frederick Henry should fill the vacant posts to the exclusion of his cousin, William Frederick, younger brother of Henry Casimir. They urged upon the prince, who was himself unwilling to supplant his relative, that it was for the good of the State that there should be a unification of authority in his person; and at last he expressed himself ready to accept the offices, if elected. The result of the somewhat mean intrigues that followed, in which Frederick Henry himself took no part, gave a curious illustration of the extreme jealousy of the provinces towards anything that they regarded as outside intrusion into their affairs. The States-General ventured to recommend the Estates of Friesland to appoint the Prince of Orange; the recommendation was resented, and William Frederick became stadholder. The Frieslanders on their part sent a deputation to Groningen in favour of William Frederick, and Groningen-Drente elected the Prince of Orange. This dispute caused an estrangement for a time between the two branches of the House of Nassau, which was afterwards healed by the marriage of the Friesland stadholder with Albertine

Agnes, a daughter of Frederick Henry. From this union the present royal family of Holland trace their descent.

The military operations of the years 1641, 1642 and 1643 were dilatory and featureless. Both sides were sick of the war and were content to remain on the defensive. This was no doubt largely due to the fact that in rapid succession death removed from the stage many of those who had long played leading parts in the political history of the times. Aerssens died shortly after his return from his successful mission to England in the autumn of 1641; and almost at the same time the Cardinal Infante Ferdinand, who during his tenure of the governor-generalship had shown great capacity and prudence both as a statesman and as a commander, expired. In 1642, after eighteen years of almost autocratic rule, Richelieu passed away, his death (December 4, 1642) coming almost half-way between those of his enemy, the intriguing Marie de' Medici (July 3, 1642), and that of her son, Louis XIII (May 18, 1643). Anne of Austria, the sister of the King of Spain, became regent in France; but this did not imply any change of policy with regard to the United Provinces, for Cardinal Mazarin, who, through his influence over the regent succeeded to the power of Richelieu, was a pupil in the school of that great statesman and followed in his steps. Moreover, during this same period the outbreak of civil war in England had for the time being caused that country to be wholly absorbed in its own domestic concerns, and it ceased to have any weight in the councils of western Europe. Thus it came to pass that there was a kind of lull in the external affairs of the United Provinces; and her statesmen were compelled to take fresh stock of their position in the changed situation that had been created.

Not that this meant that these years were a time of less pressure and anxiety to the Prince of Orange. His new relations with the English royal family were a source of difficulty to him. Henrietta Maria (March, 1642) came to Holland, bringing with her the princess royal, and for a whole year took up her residence at the Hague. She was received with kindliness and courtesy not only by the stadholder and his family, but by the people of Holland generally. Her presence, together with that of the Queen of Bohemia, at the Princess of Orange's court gave to it quite a regal dignity and splendour, which was particularly gratifying to Amalia von Solms. But the English queen had other objects in view than those of courtesy. She hoped not merely to enlist the sympathies of Frederick Henry for the royal cause in the English civil war, but to obtain through his help supplies of arms and munitions from Holland for King Charles. But in this she did not succeed. The Parliament had sent an envoy, William Strickland, to counteract the influence of Henrietta Maria, and to represent to the States-General that it was fighting in defence of the same principles which had led to the revolt against Spain. The prince was far too prudent to allow his personal inclinations to override his political judgment as a practical statesman. He knew that public opinion in the United

Provinces would never sanction in any form active support of King Charles against his parliament, and he did not attempt it. Intervention was confined to the despatch of an embassy to England with instructions to mediate between the two parties. When the unfortunate queen found that all her efforts on behalf of King Charles were in vain, she determined to leave the safe refuge where she had been so hospitably entertained and to return to her husband's side. She sailed from Scheveningen on March 9, 1643, and reached the royal camp at York in safety.

In the autumn of this year, 1643, two special envoys were sent by Cardinal Mazarin to the Hague; and one of the results of their visit was a renewal of the treaty of 1635 by which France and the United Provinces had entered upon an offensive and defensive alliance and had agreed to conclude no peace but by mutual consent. Nevertheless Frederick Henry, whom long experience had made wary and far-sighted, had been growing for some little time suspicious of the advantage to the republic of furthering French aggrandisement in the southern Netherlands. He saw that France was a waxing, Spain a waning power, and he had no desire to see France in possession of territory bordering on the United Provinces. This feeling on his part was possibly the cause of the somewhat dilatory character of his military operations in 1641 and 1642. The revolt of Portugal from Spain in December, 1640, had at first been welcomed by the Dutch, but not for long. The great and successful operations of the East and West India Companies had been chiefly carried on at the expense of the Portuguese, not of the Spaniards. The great obstacle to peace with Spain had been the concession of the right to trade in the Indies. It was Portugal, rather than Spain, which now stood in the way of the Dutch merchants obtaining that right, for the Spanish government, in its eagerness to stamp out a rebellion which had spread from the Peninsula to all the Portuguese colonies, was quite ready to sacrifice these to secure Dutch neutrality in Europe. The dazzling victory of the French under the young Duke of Enghien over a veteran Spanish army at Rocroi (May, 1643) also had its effect upon the mind of the prince. With prophetic foresight, he rightly dreaded a France too decisively victorious. In the negotiations for a general peace between all the contending powers in the Thirty Years' War, which dragged on their slow length from 1643 to 1648, the stadholder became more and more convinced that it was in the interest of the Dutch to maintain Spain as a counterpoise to the growing power of France, and to secure the favourable terms, which, in her extremity, Spain would be ready to offer.

At first, however, there was no breach in the close relations with France; and Frederick Henry, though hampered by ill-health, showed in his last campaigns all his old skill in siege-craft. By the successive captures of Hertogenbosch, Maestricht and Breda he had secured the frontiers of the republic in the south and south-east. He now turned to the north-west corner of Flanders. In 1644 he took the strongly fortified post of Sas-van-Gent, situated on the Ley, the canalised river connecting Ghent with the Scheldt. In 1645 he laid siege to and captured the town of Hulst, and thus gained complete possession of the strip of territory south of the Scheldt, known as the Land of Waes, which had been protected by these two strongholds, and which has since been called Dutch Flanders.

Very shortly after the capitulation of Hulst, the ambassadors plenipotentiary of the United Provinces set out (November, 1645) to take their places at the Congress of Münster on equal terms with the representatives of the Emperor and of the Kings of France and Spain. The position acquired by the Dutch republic among the powers of Europe was thus officially recognised *de facto* even before its independence had been *de jure* ratified by treaty. The parleyings at Münster made slow headway, as so many thorny questions had to be settled. Meanwhile, with the full approval of the prince, negotiations were being secretly carried on between Madrid and the Hague with the view of arriving at a separate understanding, in spite of the explicit terms of the treaty of 1635. As soon as the French became aware of what was going on, they naturally protested and did their utmost to raise every difficulty to prevent a treaty being concluded behind their backs. The old questions which had proved such serious obstacles in the negotiations of 1607-9 were still sufficiently formidable. But the situation was very different in 1646-7. The Spanish monarchy was actually *in extremis*. Portugal and Catalonia were in revolt; a French army had crossed the Pyrenees; the treasury was exhausted. Peace with the Dutch Republic was a necessity; and, as has been already said, the vexed question about the Indies had resolved itself rather into a Portuguese than a Spanish question. By a recognition of the Dutch conquests in Brazil and in the Indian Ocean they were acquiring an ally without losing anything that they had not lost already by the Portuguese declaration of independence. But, as the basis of an agreement was on the point of being reached, an event happened which caused a delay in the proceedings.

The Prince of Orange, who had been long a martyr to the gout, became in the autumn of 1646 hopelessly ill. He lingered on in continual suffering for some months and died on March 14, 1647. Shortly before his death he had the satisfaction of witnessing the marriage of his daughter Louise Henrietta to Frederick William of Brandenburg, afterwards known as the Great Elector. He was not, however, destined to see peace actually concluded, though he ardently desired to do so. Frederick Henry could, however, at any rate feel that his life-work had been thoroughly and successfully accomplished. The services he rendered to his country during his stadholderate of twenty-two years can scarcely be over-estimated. It is a period of extraordinary prosperity and distinction, which well deserves the title given to it by Dutch historians—"the golden age of Frederick Henry." The body of the stadholder was laid, amidst universal lamentation and with almost regal pomp, besides those of his father and brother in the Nieuwe Kerk at Delft.

The removal of a personality of such authority and influence at this critical time was a dire misfortune, for there were many cross-currents of policy in the different provinces and of divergence of interests between the seafaring and merchant classes and other sections of the population. Finally the skill and perseverance of the two leading Dutch plenipotentiaries, Pauw and Van Knuyt, and of the Spanish envoys, Peñaranda and Brun, brought the negotiations to a successful issue. The assent of all the provinces was necessary, and for a time Utrecht and Zeeland were obstinately refractory, but at length their opposition was overcome; and on January 30, 1648, the treaty of Münster was duly signed. Great rejoicings throughout the land celebrated the end of the War of Independence, which had lasted for eighty years. Thus, in spite of the solemn engagement made with France, a separate peace was concluded with Spain and in the interests of the United Provinces. Their course of action was beyond doubt politically wise and defensible, but, as might be expected, it left behind it a feeling of soreness, for the French naturally regarded it as a breach of faith. The treaty of Münster consisted of 79 articles, the most important of which were: the King of Spain recognised the United Provinces as free and independent lands; the States-General kept all their conquests in Brabant, Limburg and Flanders, the so-called Generality lands; also their conquests in Brazil and the East Indies made at the expense of Portugal; freedom of trading both in the East and West Indies was conceded; the Scheldt was declared closed, thus shutting out Antwerp from access to the sea; to the House of Orange all its confiscated property was restored; and lastly a treaty of trade and navigation with Spain was negotiated. On all points the Dutch obtained all and more than all they could have hoped for.

# CHAPTER XI

# THE EAST AND WEST INDIA COMPANIES. COMMERCIAL AND ECONOMIC EXPANSION

An account of the foundation, constitution and early efforts of the Dutch East India Company has been already given. The date of its charter (March 20, 1602) was later than that of its English rival (Dec. 31, 1600), but in reality the Dutch were the first in the field, as there were several small companies in existence and competing with one another in the decade previous to the granting of the charter, which without extinguishing these companies incorporated them by the name of chambers under a common management, the Council of Seventeen. The four chambers however—Amsterdam, Zeeland, the Maas (Rotterdam and Delft) and the North Quarter (Enkhuizen and Hoorn)—though separately administered and with different spheres, became gradually more and more unified by the growing power of control exercised by the Seventeen. This was partly due to the dominating position of the single Chamber of Amsterdam, which held half the shares and appointed eight members of the council. The erection of such a company, with its monopoly of trade and its great privileges including the right of maintaining fleets and armed forces, of concluding treaties and of erecting forts, was nothing less than the creation of an *imperium in imperio*; and it may be said to have furnished the model on which all the great chartered companies of later times have been formed. The English East India Company was, by the side of its Dutch contemporary, almost insignificant; with its invested capital of £30,000 it was in no position to struggle successfully against a competitor which started with subscribed funds amounting to £540,000.

The conquest of Portugal by Spain had spelt ruin to that unhappy country and to its widespread colonial empire and extensive commerce. Before 1581 Lisbon had been a great centre of the Dutch carrying-trade; and many Netherlanders had taken service in Portuguese vessels and were familiar with the routes both to the East Indies and to Brazil. It was the closing of the port of Lisbon to Dutch vessels that led the enterprising merchants of Amsterdam and Middelburg to look further afield. In the early years of the seventeenth century a large number of expeditions left the Dutch harbours for the Indian Ocean and made great profits; and very large dividends were paid to the shareholders of the company. How far these represented the actual gain it is difficult to discover, for the accounts were kept in different sets of ledgers; and it is strongly suspected that the size of the dividends may, at times when enhanced credit was necessary for the raising of loans, have been to some extent fictitious. For the enterprise, which began as a trading concern, speedily developed into the creation of an empire overseas, and this meant an immense expenditure.

The Malay Archipelago was the chief scene of early activity, and more especially the Moluccas. Treaties were made with the native chiefs; and factories defended by forts were established at Tidor, Ternate, Amboina, Banda and other places. The victories of Cornelis Matelief established that supremacy of the Dutch arms in these eastern waters which they were to maintain for many years. With the conclusion of the truce the necessity of placing the general control of so many scattered forts and trading posts in the hands of one supreme official led, in 1609, to the appointment of a governor-general by the Seventeen with the assent of the States-General. The governor-general held office for five years, and he was assisted by a council, the first member of which, under the title of director-general, was in reality minister of commerce. Under him were at first seven (afterwards eight) local governors. These functionaries, though exercising considerable powers in their respective districts, were in all matters of high policy entirely subordinate to the governor-general. The first holders of the office were all men who had risen to that position by proving themselves to possess energy and enterprise, and being compelled by the distance from home to act promptly on their own initiative, were practically endowed with autocratic authority. In consequence of this the Dutch empire in the East became in their hands rapidly extended and consolidated, to the exclusion of all competitors. This meant not only that the Portuguese and Spaniards were ousted from their formerly dominant position in the Orient, but that a collision with the English was inevitable.

The first governor-general, Pieter Both, had made Java the centre of administration and had established factories and posts at Bantam, Jacatra and Djapara, not without arousing considerable hostility among the local rulers, jealous of the presence of the intruders. This hostility was fostered and encouraged by the English, whose vessels had also visited Java and had erected a trading-post close to that of the Dutch at Jacatra. Already the spice islands had been the scene of hostile encounters between the representatives of the two nations, and had led to many altercations. This was the state of things when Jan Pieterzoon Koen became governor-general in 1615. This determined man, whose experience in the East Indies was of long date, and who had already served as director-general, came into his new office with an intense prejudice against the English, and with a firm resolve to put an end to what he described as their treachery and intrigues. "Were they masters," he wrote home, "the Dutch would quickly be out of the Indies, but praise be to the Lord, who has provided otherwise. They are an unendurable nation." With this object he strongly fortified the factory near Jacatra, thereby arousing the hostility of the *Pangeran*, as the native ruler was styled. The English in their neighbouring post also began to erect defences and to encourage the *Pangeran* in his hostile attitude. Koen thereupon fell upon the English and destroyed and burnt their factory, and finding that there was a strong English fleet under Sir Thomas Dale in the neighbourhood, he sailed to the Moluccas in search of reinforcements, leaving Pieter van der Broeck in command at the factory. The *Pangeran* now feigned friendship, and having enticed Broeck to a conference, made him prisoner and attacked the Dutch stronghold. The garrison however held out until the governor-general returned with a strong force. With this he stormed and destroyed the town of Jacatra and on its site erected a new town, as the seat of the company's government, to which the name Batavia was given. From this time the Dutch had no rivalry to fear in Java. The conquest of the whole island was only a question of time, and the "pearl of the Malay Archipelago" has from 1620 to the present been the richest and most valuable of all the Dutch colonial possessions. Koen was planning to follow up his success by driving the English likewise from the Moluccas, when he heard that the home government had concluded a treaty which tied his hands.

The position in the Moluccas had for some years been one of continual bickering and strife; the chief scene being in the little group known as the Banda islands. The lucrative spice-trade tempted both companies to establish themselves by building forts; and the names of Amboina and Pulo Rum were for many years to embitter the relations of the two peoples. Meanwhile the whole subject of those relations had been in 1619 discussed at London by a special embassy sent nominally to thank King James for the part he had taken in bringing the Synod of Dort to a successful termination of its labours, but in reality to settle several threatening trade disputes. Almost the only result of the prolonged conferences was an agreement (June 2, 1619) by which the East India Companies were for twenty years to be virtually amalgamated. The English were to have half the pepper crop in Java and one-third of the spices in the Moluccas, Amboina and the Banda islands. Forts and posts were to remain in their present hands, but there was to be a joint council for defence, four members from each company, the president to be appointed alternately month by month. Such a scheme was a paper scheme, devised by those who had no personal acquaintance with the actual situation. There was no similarity between a great military and naval organisation like the Dutch Company and a body of traders like the English, whose capital was small, and who were entirely dependent on the political vagaries of an impecunious sovereign, whose dearest wish at the time was to cultivate close relations with the very power in defiance of whose prohibition the East India Company's trade was carried on. The agreement received indeed a fresh sanction at another conference held in London (1622-23), but it never was a working arrangement. The bitter ill-feeling that had arisen between the Dutch and English traders was not to be allayed by the diplomatic subterfuge of crying peace when there was no peace. Events were speedily to prove that this was so.

The trade in spices had proved the most lucrative of all, and measures had been taken to prevent any undue lowering of the price by a glut in the market. The quantity of spices grown was carefully regulated, suitable spots being selected, and the trees elsewhere destroyed. Thus cloves were specially cultivated at Amboina; nutmegs in the Banda islands. Into this strictly guarded monopoly, from which the English had been expelled by the energy of Koen, they were now by the new treaty to be admitted to a share.

It was only with difficulty that the Dutch were induced to acquiesce sullenly in the presence of the intruders. A fatal collision took place almost immediately after the convention between the Companies, about the trade in the spice islands, had been renewed in London, 1622-3.

In 1623 Koen was succeeded, as governor-general, by Pieter Carpentier, whose name is still perpetuated by the Gulf of Carpentaria on the north of Australia. At this time of transition the Governor of Amboina, Van Speult, professed to have discovered a conspiracy of the English settlers, headed by Gabriel Towerson, to make themselves masters of the Dutch fort. Eighteen Englishmen were seized, and though there was no evidence against them, except what was extorted by torture and afterwards solemnly denied, twelve, including Towerson, were executed. Carpentier admitted that the proceedings were irregular, and they were in any case unnecessary, for a despatch recalling Towerson was on its way to Amboina. It was a barbarous and cruel act; and when the news of the "massacre of Amboina," as it was called, reached England, there was loud indignation and demands for redress. But the quarrel with Spain over the marriage of the Prince of Wales had driven James I at the very end of his life, and Charles I on his accession, to seek the support of the United Provinces. By the treaty of Southampton, September 17, 1625, an offensive and defensive alliance was concluded with the States-General; and Charles contented himself with a demand that the States should within eighteen months bring to justice those who were responsible "for the bloody butchery on our subjects." However, Carleton again pressed for the punishment of the perpetrators of "the foule and bloody act" of Amboina. The Dutch replied with evasive promises, which they never attempted to carry out; and Charles' disastrous war with France and his breach with his parliament effectually prevented him from taking steps to exact reparation. But Amboina was not forgotten; the sore rankled and was one of the causes that moved Cromwell to war in 1654.

The activity of the Dutch in eastern waters was, however, by no means confined to Java, their seat of government, or to the Moluccas and Banda islands with their precious spices. Many trading posts were erected on the large islands of Sumatra and Borneo. Trading relations were opened with Siam from 1613 onwards. In 1623 a force under Willem Bontekoe was sent by Koen to Formosa. The island was conquered and a governor appointed with his residence at Fort Zelandia. Already under the first governor-general, Pieter Both, permission was obtained from the Shogun for the Dutch, under close restrictions, to trade with Japan, a permission which was still continued, after the expulsion of the Portuguese and the bloody persecution of the Christian converts (1637-42), though under somewhat humiliating conditions. But, with the Dutch, trade was trade, and under the able conduct of Francis Caron it became of thriving proportions. During the next century no other Europeans had any access to the Japanese market except the agents of the Dutch East India Company.

Among the governors-general of this early period the name of Antony van Diemen (1636-45) deserves special recognition. If Koen laid the firm foundations of Dutch rule in the East, Van Diemen built wisely and ably on the work of Koen. Carpentier's rule had been noteworthy for several voyages of discovery along the coasts of New Guinea and of the adjoining shore of Australia, but the spirit of exploration reached its height in the days of Van Diemen. The north and north-west of Australia being to some extent already known, Abel Tasman was despatched by Van Diemen to find out, if possible, how far southward the land extended. Sailing in October, 1642, from Mauritius, he skirted portions of the coast of what is now Victoria and New South Wales and discovered the island which he named after his patron Van Diemen's land, but which is now very appropriately known as Tasmania. Pressing on he reached New Zealand, which still bears the name that he gave to it, and sailed through the strait between the northern and southern islands, now Cook's strait. In the course of this great voyage he next discovered the Friendly or Tonga islands and the Fiji archipelago. He reached Batavia in June, 1643, and in the following year he visited again the north of Australia and voyaged right round the

Gulf of Carpentaria. Even in a modern map of Australia Dutch names will be found scattered round certain portions of the coast of the island-continent, recording still, historically, the names of the early Dutch explorers, their patrons, ships and homes. Along the shores of the Gulf of Carpentaria may be seen Van Diemen river, gulf and cape; Abel Tasman, Van Alphen, Nassau and Staten rivers; capes Arnhem, Caron and Maria (after Francis Caron and Maria van Diemen) and Groote Eylandt. In Tasmania, with many other names, may be found Frederick Henry bay and cape, Tasman's peninsula and Tasman's head and Maria island; while the wife of the governor-general is again commemorated, the northernmost point of New Zealand bearing the name of Maria van Diemen cape.

To Van Diemen belongs the credit of giving to the Dutch their first footing (1638) in the rich island of Ceylon, by concluding a treaty with the native prince of Kandy. The Portuguese still possessed forts at Colombo, Galle, Negumbo and other places, but Galle and Negumbo were now taken by the Dutch, and gradually the whole island passed into their hands and became for a century and a half their richest possession in the East, next to Java. On the Coromandel coast posts were also early established, and trade relations opened up with the Persians and Arabs. At the time when the Treaty of Münster gave to the United Provinces the legal title to that independence for which they had so long fought, and conceded to them the freedom to trade in the Indies, that trade was already theirs, safe-guarded by the fleets, the forts and the armed forces of the chartered company. The governor-general at Batavia had become a powerful potentate in the Eastern seas; and a succession of bold and able men, by a policy at once prudent and aggressive, had in the course of a few decades organised a colonial empire. It was a remarkable achievement for so small a country as the United Provinces, and it was destined to have a prolonged life. The voyage round by the cape was long and hazardous, so Van Diemen in 1638 caused the island of Mauritius to be occupied as a refitting station; and in 1652 one of his successors (Reinierz) sent a body of colonists under Jan van Riebeck to form a settlement, which should be a harbour of refuge beneath the Table mountain at the Cape itself. This was the beginning of the Cape colony.

Quite as interesting, and even more exciting, was the history of Dutch enterprise in other seas during this eventful period. The granting of the East India Company's charter led a certain Willem Usselincx to come forward as an earnest and persistent advocate for the formation of a West India Company on the same lines. But Oldenbarneveldt, anxious to negotiate a peace or truce with Spain and to maintain good relations with that power, refused to lend any countenance to his proposals, either before or after the truce was concluded. He could not, however, restrain the spirit of enterprise that with increasing prosperity was abroad in Holland. The formation of the Northern or Greenland Company in 1613, specially created in order to contest the claims of the English Muscovy Company to exclusive rights in the whale fishery off Spitsbergen, led to those violent disputes between the fishermen of the two countries, of which an account has been given. The granting of a charter to the Company of New Netherland (1614) was a fresh departure. The voyage of Henry Hudson in the Dutch service when, in 1610, he explored the coast of North America and sailed up the river called by his name, led certain Amsterdam and Hoorn merchants to plan a settlement near this river; and they secured a charter giving them exclusive rights from Chesapeake bay to Newfoundland. The result was the founding of the colony of New Netherland, with New Amsterdam on Manhattan island as its capital. This settlement was at first small and insignificant, but, being placed midway between the English colonies on that same coast, it added one more to the many questions of dispute between the two sea-powers.

Willem Usselincx had all this time continued his agitation for the erection of a West India Company; and at last, with the renewal of the war with Spain in 1621, his efforts were rewarded. The charter granted by the States-General (June 3, 1621) gave to the company for twenty-four years the monopoly of navigation and trade to the coast-lands of America and the West Indies from the south-end of Newfoundland to the Straits of Magellan and to the coasts and lands of Africa from the tropic of Cancer to the Cape of Good Hope. The governing body consisted of nineteen representatives, the Nineteen. The States-General contributed to the capital 1,000,000 fl., on half of which only they were to receive dividends. They also undertook in time of war to furnish sixteen ships and four yachts, the company being bound to supply a like number. The West India Company from the first was intended to be an instrument of war. Its aims were buccaneering rather than commerce. There was no secret about its object; it was openly proclaimed. Its historian De Laet (himself a director) wrote, "There is no surer means of bringing our Enemy at last to reason, than to infest him with attacks everywhere in America and to stop the fountain-head of his best finances." After some tentative efforts, it was resolved to send out an expedition in great force; but the question arose, where best to strike? By the advice of Usselincx and others acquainted with the condition of the defences of the towns upon the American coast, Bahia, the capital of the Portuguese colony of Brazil, was selected, as specially vulnerable. Thus in the West, as in the East, Portugal was to suffer for her unwilling subjection to the crown of Castile.

The consent of the States-General and of the stadholder being obtained, some months were spent in making preparations on an adequate scale. The fleet, which consisted of twenty-three ships of war with four yachts, armed with 500 pieces of ordnance, and carrying in addition to the crews a force of 1700 troops, sailed in two contingents, December, 1623, and January, 1624. Jacob Willekens was the admiral-in-chief, with Piet Hein as his vice-admiral. Colonel Jan van Dorth, lord of Horst, was to conduct the land operations and to be the governor of the town, when its conquest was achieved. On May 9 the fleet sailed into the Bay of All Saints (*Bahia de todos os Santos*) and proceeded to disembark the troops on a sandy beach a little to the east of the city of San Salvador, commonly known as Bahia. It was strongly situated on heights rising sheer from the water; and, as news of the Dutch preparations had reached Lisbon and Madrid, its fortifications had been repaired and its garrison strengthened. In front of the lower town below the cliffs was a rocky island, and on this and on the shore were forts well provided with batteries, and under their lee were fifteen ships of war. On May 10 Piet Hein was sent with five vessels to contain the enemy's fleet and cover the landing of the military forces. But Hein, far from being content with a passive role, attacked the Portuguese, burnt or captured all their ships and then, embarking his men in launches, stormed the defences of the island and spiked the guns. Meanwhile the troops had, without opposition, occupied a Benedictine convent on the heights opposite the town. But the daring of Piet Hein had caused a panic to seize the garrison.

Despite the efforts of the governor, Diogo de Mendoça Furdado, there was a general exodus in the night, both of the soldiery and the inhabitants. When morning came the Dutch marched into the undefended town, the governor and his son, who had refused to desert their posts, being taken prisoners. They, with much booty, were at once sent to Holland as a proof of the completeness of the victory. Events, however, were to prove that it is easier for an expeditionary force to capture a town at such a distance from the home-base of supplies, than to retain it.

Governor Van Dorth had scarcely entered upon his duties when he fell into an ambush of native levies near San Salvador and was killed. His successor, Willem Schouten, was incompetent and dissolute; and, when the fleet set sail on its homeward voyage at the end of July, the garrison soon found itself practically besieged by bodies of Portuguese troops with Indian auxiliaries, who occupied the neighbouring woods and stopped supplies. Meanwhile the news of the capture of San Salvador reached Madrid and Lisbon; and Spaniards and Portuguese vied with one another in their eagerness to equip a great expedition to expel the invaders. It was truly a mighty armada which set sail, under the supreme command of Don Fadrique de Toledo, from the Iberian ports at the beginning of 1625, for it consisted of fifty ships with five caravels and four pinnaces, carrying 12,566 men and 1185 guns. On Easter Eve (March 29) the fleet entered All Saints' Bay in the form of a vast crescent measuring six leagues from tip to tip. The Dutch garrison of 2300 men, being strongly fortified, resisted for a month but, shut in by sea and by land and badly led, they capitulated on April 28, on condition that they were sent back to Holland.

That the brilliant success of 1624 was thus so soon turned into disaster was in no way due to the supineness of the home authorities. The Nineteen were in no way surprised to hear of great preparations being made by the King of Spain to retake the town, and they on their part were determined to maintain their conquest by meeting force with force. Straining all their resources, three squadrons were equipped; the first two, numbering thirty-two ships and nine yachts, were destined for Brazil; the third, a small flying squadron of seven vessels, was despatched early to watch the Spanish ports. The general-in-chief of the Brazilian expedition was Boudewyn Hendrikszoon. Driven back by a succession of storms, it was not until April 17, 1625, that the fleet was able to leave the Channel and put out to sea. The voyage was a rapid one and on May 23, Hendrikszoon sailed into the bay in battle order, only to see the Spanish flag waving over San Salvador and the mighty fleet of Admiral Toledo drawn up under the protection of its batteries. Hendrikszoon sailed slowly past the Spaniards, who did not stir, and perceiving that it would be madness to attack a superior force in such a position he reluctantly gave orders to withdraw. On the homeward journey by the West Indies a number of rich prizes were made, but sickness made great ravages among the crews, and counted Hendrikszoon himself among its victims.

The events of the following year seem to show that with audacity he might have at least inflicted heavy losses on the enemy. For in 1626 the directors, ignorant of his failure, sent out a reinforcement of nine ships and five yachts under the command of the redoubtable Piet Hein. Hein sailed on May 21 for the West Indies, where he learnt that Hendrikszoon was dead and that the remnant of his expedition had returned after a fruitless voyage of misadventure. Hein however was not the man to turn back. He determined to try what he could effect at Bahia by a surprise attack. He reached the entrance to the bay on March 1, 1627, but was unluckily becalmed; and the Portuguese were warned of his presence. On arriving before San Salvador he found thirty ships drawn up close to the land; sixteen of these were large and armed, and four were galleons with a considerable number of troops on board. The Dutch admiral with great daring determined to attack them by sailing between them and the shore, making it difficult for the guns on shore to fire on him without injury to their own ships. It was a hazardous stroke, for the passage was narrow, but entirely successful. One of the four galleons, carrying the admiral's flag, was sunk, the other three struck. Taking to their launches, the Dutchmen now fiercely assailed the other vessels, and in a very short time were masters of twenty-two prizes. It was a difficult task to carry them off at the ebb-tide, and it was not achieved without loss. Hein's own ship, the *Amsterdam,* grounded and had to be burnt, and another ship by some mischance blew up. The total loss, except through the explosion, was exceedingly small. The captured vessels contained 2700 chests of sugar, besides a quantity of cotton, hides and tobacco. The booty was stored in the four largest ships and sent to Holland; the rest were burnt.

Hein now made a raid down the coast as far as Rio de Janeiro and then returned. The "Sea Terror of Delft" for some weeks after this remained in unchallenged mastery of the bay, picking up prizes when the opportunity offered. Then he sailed by the West Indies homewards and reached Dutch waters on October 31, 1627, having during this expedition captured no less than fifty-five enemy vessels. The value of the booty was sufficient to repay the company for their great outlay, and it was wisely used in the equipment of fresh fleets for the following year.

This next year, 1628, was indeed an *annus mirabilis* in the records of the Dutch West India Company. On January 24 two fleets put to sea, one under Dirk Simonsz Uitgeest for the coast of Brazil; another under Pieter Adriansz Ita for the West Indies. Both were successful and came back laden with spoil. It was reserved, however, for the expedition under Piet Hein to make all other successes seem small. This fleet, consisting of thirty-one ships of war, left Holland at the end of May for the West Indies with instructions to lie in wait for the Spanish Treasure Fleet. Many attempts had been made in previous years to intercept the galleons, which year by year carried the riches of Mexico and Peru to Spain, but they had always failed. After some weeks of weary cruising, Piet Hein, when off the coast of Cuba, was rewarded (September 8) by the sight of the Spanish fleet approaching, and at once bore down upon them. After a sharp conflict, the Spaniards took refuge in the bay of Matanzas and, running the galleons into shoal-water, tried to convey the rich cargoes on shore. It was in vain. The Dutch sailors, taking to their boats, boarded the galleons and compelled them to surrender. The spoil was of enormous value, comprising 177,537 lbs. of silver, 135 lbs. of gold, 37,375 hides, 2270 chests of indigo, besides cochineal, logwood, sugar, spices and precious stones. It brought 11,509,524 fl. into the coffers of the company, and a dividend of 50 per cent, was paid to the shareholders. It was a wrong policy thus to deal with the results of a stroke of good fortune not likely to be repeated. This year was, however, to be a lucky year unto the end. A fourth expedition under Adrian Jansz Pater which left on August 15 for the Caribbean sea, sailed up the Orinoco and destroyed the town of San Thomé de Guiana, the chief Spanish settlement in those parts. All this, it may be said, partook of the character of buccaneering, nevertheless these were shrewd blows struck at the very source from whence the Spanish power obtained means for carrying on the war. The West India Company was fulfilling triumphantly one of the chief purposes for which it was created, and was threatening Philip IV with financial ruin.

The successes of 1628 had the effect of encouraging the directors to try to retrieve the failure at Bahia by conquest elsewhere.

Olinda, on the coast of Pernambuco, was selected as the new objective. An expeditionary force of exceptional strength was got ready; and, as Piet Hein, at the very height of his fame, unfortunately lost his life in the spring of 1629 in an encounter with the Dunkirk pirates, Hendrik Cornelisz Lonck, who had served as vice-admiral under Hein at Matanzas bay, was made admiral-in-chief, with Jonckheer Diederik van Waerdenburgh in command of the military forces. A considerable delay was caused by the critical position of the United Provinces when invaded by the Spanish-Imperialist armies at the time of the siege of Hertogenbosch, but the capture of that fortress enabled the last contingents to sail towards the end of the year; and Lonck was able to collect his whole force at St Vincent, one of the Canary islands, on Christmas Day to start on their voyage across the Atlantic. That force consisted of fifty-two ships and yachts and thirteen sloops, carrying 3780 sailors and 3500 soldiers, and mounting 1170 guns. Adverse weather prevented the arrival of the fleet in the offing of Olinda until February 13. Along the coast of Pernambuco runs a continuous reef of rock with narrow openings at irregular intervals, forming a barrier against attack from the sea. Olinda, the capital of the provinces, was built on a hill a short distance inland, having as its port a village known as Povo or the Reciff, lying on a spit of sand between the mouths of the rivers Biberibi and Capibaribi. There was a passage through the rocky reef northwards about two leagues above Olinda and three others southwards (only one of which, the *Barra*, was navigable for large ships) giving access to a sheet of water of some 18 ft. in depth between the reef and the spit of sand, and forming a commodious harbour, the Pozo.

The problem before the Dutch commander was a difficult one, for news of the expedition had reached Madrid; and Matthias de Albuquerque, brother of "the proprietor" of Pernambuco, Duarte de Albuquerque, a man of great energy and powers of leadership, had arrived in October to put Olinda and the Reciff into a state of defence. Two forts strongly garrisoned and armed, San Francisco and San Jorge, defended the entrances through the reef and the neck of the spit of sand; sixteen ships chained together and filled with combustibles barred access to the harbour; and the village of the Reciff was surrounded by entrenchments. Within the fortifications of Olinda, Albuquerque held himself in readiness to oppose any body of the enemy that should effect a landing above the town. Lonck, after consultation with Waerdenburgh, determined to make with the main body of the fleet under his own command an attempt to force the entrances to the Pozo, while Waerdenburgh, with the bulk of the military contingent on sixteen ships, sailed northwards to find some spot suitable for disembarkation.

The naval attack was made on February 15, but was unavailing. All the efforts of the Dutch to make their way through any of the entrances to the Pozo, though renewed again and again with the utmost bravery, were beaten off. In the evening Lonck withdrew his ships. He had learnt by an experience, to which history scarcely offers an exception, that a naval attack unsupported by military co-operation against land defences cannot succeed. But Waerdenburgh had used the opportunity, while the enemy's attention was directed to the repelling of the assault on the Reciff, to land his army without opposition. At dawn the Dutch general advanced and, after forcing the crossing of the river Doce in the teeth of the resistance of a body of irregular troops led by Albuquerque in person, marched straight on Olinda. There was no serious resistance. The fortifications were carried by storm and the town fell into the hands of Waerdenburgh. The garrison and almost all the inhabitants fled into the neighbouring forest.

Aware of the fact that the occupation of Olinda was useless without a harbour as a base of supplies, it was resolved at once with the aid of the fleet to lay siege to the forts of San Francisco and San Jorge. Despite obstinate resistance, first San Jorge, then San Francisco surrendered; and on March 3 the fleet sailed through the Barra, and the Reciff with the island of Antonio Vaz behind it was occupied by the Dutch. No sooner was the conquest made than steps were taken for its administration. A welcome reinforcement arrived from Holland on March 11, having on board three representatives sent by the Nineteen, who were to form with Waerdenburgh, appointed governor, an administrative council, or Court of Policy. The Reciff, rather than Olinda, was selected as the seat of government, and forts were erected for its defence. The position, however, was perilous in the extreme. Albuquerque, who was well acquainted with the country and skilled in guerrilla warfare, formed an entrenched camp to which he gave the name of the *Arreyal de Bom Jesus*, a position defended by marshes and thick woods. From this centre, by the aid of large numbers of friendly Indians, he was able to cut off all supplies of fresh water, meat or vegetables from reaching the Dutch garrison. They had to depend for the necessaries of life upon stores sent to them in relief fleets from Holland. It was a strange and grim struggle of endurance, in which both Dutch and Portuguese suffered terribly, the one on the barren sea-shore, the other in the pathless woods under the glare of a tropical sun, both alike looking eagerly for succour from the Motherland. The Dutch succours were the first to arrive. The first detachment under Marten Thijssen reached the Reciff on December 18, 1630; the main fleet under Adrian Jansz Pater on April 14, 1631. The whole fleet consisted of sixteen ships and yachts manned by 1270 sailors and 860 soldiers. Their arrival was the signal for offensive operations. An expedition under Thijssen's command sailed on April 22 for the large island of Itamaraca about fifteen miles to the north of the Reciff. It was successful. Itamaraca was occupied and garrisoned, and thus a second and advantageous post established on the Brazilian coast.

Meanwhile the Spanish government had not been idle. After many delays a powerful fleet set sail from Lisbon on May 5 for Pernambuco, consisting of fifteen Spanish and five Portuguese ships and carrying a large military force, partly destined for Bahia, but principally as a reinforcement for Matthias de Albuquerque. The expedition was commanded by Admiral Antonio de Oquendo, and was accompanied by Duarte de Albuquerque, the proprietor of Pernambuco. After landing troops and munitions at Bahia, the Spaniards wasted several weeks before starting again to accomplish the main object of blockading the Dutch in the Reciff and compelling their surrender by famine. But Pater had learnt by his scouts of the presence of Oquendo at Bahia, and though his force was far inferior he determined to meet the hostile armada at sea. The Spanish fleet was sighted at early dawn on September 12, and Pater at once gave orders to attack. His fleet consisted of sixteen ships and yachts, that of the enemy of twenty galleons and sixteen caravels. The Dutch admiral had formed his fleet in two lines, himself in the *Prins Willem* and Vice-Admiral Thijssen in the *Vereenigte Provintien* being the leaders. On this occasion the sight of the great numbers and size of the Spanish galleons caused a great part of the Dutch captains to lose heart and hang back. Pater and Thijssen, followed by only two ships, bore down however on the Spaniards. *The Prins Willem* with the *Walcheren* in attendance laid herself alongside the *St Jago*, flying the flag of Admiral Oquendo; the *Vereenigte Provintien* with the *Provintie van Utrecht* in its wake drew up to the *St Antonio de Padua*, the ship of Vice-Admiral Francisco de Vallecilla. For six hours the duel between the *Prins Willem* and the *St Jago* went on with fierce desperation, the captain of the *Walcheren* gallantly holding at bay the galleons who attempted to come to the rescue of Oquendo. At 4 p. m. the *St Jago* was a floating wreck with only a remnant of her crew surviving, when suddenly a fire broke out in the *Prins Willem*, which nothing could check. With difficulty the *St Jago* drew off and, finding that his vessel was lost, Pater, refusing to surrender, wrapped the flag round his body and threw himself into the sea. Meanwhile success had attended Thijssen. The lagging Dutch ships coming up gradually threatened the convoy of Spanish transports and drew off many of the galleons for their protection. The *Provintie van Utrecht* indeed, like the *Prins Willem*, caught fire and was burnt to the water's edge; but the vice-admiral himself sank the *St Antonio de Padua* and another galleon that came to Vallecilla's help, and captured a third. It was a bloody and apparently indecisive fight, but the Dutch enjoyed the fruits of victory. Oquendo made no attempt to capture the Reciff and Olinda, but, after landing the troops he convoyed at a favourable spot, sailed northwards, followed by Thijssen.

But though relieved the position was still very serious. Albuquerque, now considerably reinforced from his impregnable post at the *Arreyal de Bom Jesus*, cut off all intercourse inland. The Dutch even abandoned Olinda and concentrated themselves at the

Reciff, where they remained as a besieged force entirely dependent upon supplies sent from Holland. Several expeditions were despatched with the hope of seizing other positions on the coast, but all of them proved failures; and, when Waerdenburgh returned home in 1633, having reached the end of his three years' service as governor, all that could be said was that the Dutch had retained their foothold on the coast of Pernambuco, but at vast cost to the company in men, vessels and treasure, and without any apparent prospect for the future. But pertinacity was to be rewarded. For the period of success that followed special histories must be consulted. In the year following the return of Waerdenburgh the efforts of the Dutch authorities to extend their possessions along the coast at the various river mouths were steadily successful; and with the advent of Joan Maurice of Nassau to the governorship, in 1637, the dream of a Dutch empire in Brazil seemed to be on the point of realisation. This cousin of the Prince of Orange was endowed with brilliant qualities, and during the seven years of his governorship he extended the Dutch dominion from the Rio Grande in the south to the island of Maranhão on the north and to a considerable distance inland, indeed over the larger part of seven out of the fourteen captaincies into which Portuguese Brazil was divided. On his arrival, by a wise policy of statesmanlike conciliation, he contrived to secure the goodwill of the Portuguese planters, who, though not loving the Dutch heretics, hated them less than their Spanish oppressors, and also of the Jews, who were numerous in the conquered territory. Under his rule the Reciff as the seat of the Dutch government was beautified and enlarged; many fine buildings and gardens adorned it, and the harbour made commodious for commerce with rows of warehouses and ample docks. To the new capital he gave the name of Mauritsstad.

During the earlier part of his governor-generalship Joan Maurice was called upon to face a really great danger. The year 1639 was to witness what was to be the last great effort (before the Portuguese revolt) of the still undivided Spanish monarchy for supremacy at sea. Already it has been told how a great fleet sent under Antonio de Oquendo to drive the Dutch from the narrow seas was crushed by Admiral Tromp at the battle of the Downs. In the same year the most formidable armada ever sent from the Peninsula across the ocean set sail for Brazil. It consisted of no less than eighty-six vessels manned by 12,000 sailors and soldiers under the command of the Count de Torre. Unpropitious weather conditions, as so often in the case of Spanish naval undertakings, ruined the enterprise. Making for Bahia they were detained for two months in the Bay of All Saints by strong northerly winds. Meanwhile Joan Maurice, whose naval force at first was deplorably weak, had managed by energetic efforts to gather together a respectable fleet of forty vessels under Admiral Loos, which resembled the English fleet of 1588 under Effingham and Drake, in that it made up for lack of numbers and of size by superior seamanship and skill in manoeuvring. At length, the wind having shifted, the Count de Torre put to sea; and on January 12, 1640, the Dutch squadrons sighted the Spaniards, who were being driven along by a southerly gale which had sprung up. Clinging to their rear and keeping the weather-gauge, the Dutch kept up a running fight, inflicting continual losses on their enemies, and, giving them no opportunity to make for land and seek the shelter of a port, drove them northwards in disorder never to return. By this signal deliverance the hold of the Netherlanders upon their Brazilian conquests appeared to be assured; and, as has been already stated, Joan Maurice took full advantage of the opportunity that was offered to him to consolidate and extend them. A sudden change of political circumstances was, however, to bring to a rapid downfall a dominion which had never rested on a sound basis.

The revolt of Portugal in 1641 was at first hailed in the United Provinces as the entry of a new ally into the field against their ancient enemy the Spaniard. But it was soon perceived that there could be no friendship with independent Portugal, unless both the East and West India Companies withdrew from the territories they had occupied overseas entirely at the expense of the Portuguese. King João IV and his advisers at Lisbon, face to face as they were with the menacing Spanish power, showed willingness to make great concessions, but they could not control the spirit which animated the settlers in the colonies themselves. Everywhere the Spanish yoke was repudiated, and the Dutch garrisons in Brazil suddenly found themselves confronted in 1645 with a loyalist rising, with which they were not in a position to deal successfully. The West India Company had not proved a commercial success. The fitting out of great fleets and the maintenance of numerous garrisons of mercenaries at an immense distance from the home country had exhausted their resources and involved the company in debt. The building of Mauritsstad and the carrying out of Joan Maurice's ambitious schemes for the administration and organisation of a great Brazilian dominion were grandiose, but very costly. The governor, moreover, who could brook neither incompetence nor interference on the part of his subordinates, had aroused the enmity of some of them, notably of a certain Colonel Architofsky, who through spite plotted and intrigued against him with the authorities at home. The result was that, the directors having declined to sanction certain proposals made to them by Joan Maurice, he sent in his resignation, which was accepted (1644). It must be remembered that their position was a difficult one. The charter of the company had been granted for a term of twenty-four years, and it was doubtful whether the States-General, already beginning to discuss secretly the question of a separate peace with Spain, would consent to renew it. The relations with Portugal were very delicate; and a formidable rebellion of the entire body of Portuguese settlers, aided by the natives, was on the point of breaking out. Indeed the successors of Joan Maurice, deprived of any adequate succour from home, were unable to maintain themselves against the skill and courage of the insurgent Portuguese leaders. The Dutch were defeated in the field, and one by one their fortresses were taken. The Reciff itself held out for some time, but it was surrendered at last in 1654; and with its fall the Dutch were finally expelled from the territory for the acquisition of which they had sacrificed so much blood and treasure.

The West India Company at the peace of Münster possessed, besides the remnant of its Brazilian dominion, the colony of New Netherland in North America, and two struggling settlements on the rivers Essequibo and Berbice in Guiana. New Netherland comprised the country between the English colonies of New England and Virginia; and the Dutch settlers had at this time established farms near the coast and friendly relations with the natives of the interior, with whom they trafficked for furs. The appointment of Peter Stuyvesant as governor, in 1646, was a time of real development in New Netherland. This colony was an appanage of the Chamber of Amsterdam, after which New Amsterdam, the seat of government on the island of Manhattan, was named. The official trading posts on the Essequibo and the Berbice, though never abandoned, had for some years a mere lingering existence, but are deserving of mention in that they were destined to survive the vicissitudes of fortune and to become in the 18th century a valuable possession. Their importance also is to be measured not by the meagre official reports and profit and loss accounts that have survived in the West India Company's records, but by the much fuller information to be derived from Spanish and Portuguese sources, as to the remarkable daring and energy of Dutch trading agents in all that portion of the South American continent lying between the rivers Amazon and Orinoco. Expelled from the Amazon itself in 1627 by the Portuguese from Para, the Dutch traders established themselves at different times at the mouths of almost all the rivers along what was known as the Wild Coast of Guiana, and penetrating inland through a good understanding with the natives, especially with the ubiquitous Carib tribes, carried on a barter traffic beyond the mountains into the northern watershed of the Amazon, even as far as the Rio Negro itself. This trade with the interior finds no place in the company's official minutes, for it was strictly speaking an infringement of the charter, and therefore illegitimate. But it was characteristically Dutch, and it was winked at, for the chief offenders were themselves among the principal shareholders of the company.

No account of Dutch commerce during the period of Frederick Henry would be complete, however, which did not refer to the relations between Holland and Sweden, and the part played by an Amsterdam merchant in enabling the Swedish armies to secure the ultimate triumph of the Protestant cause in the Thirty Years' War. Louis de Geer sprang from an ancient noble family of Liège. His father fled to Dordrecht in 1595 to escape from the Inquisition and became prosperous in business. Liège was then, as now, a great centre of the iron industry; and after his father's death Louis de Geer in 1615 removed to Amsterdam, where he became a merchant in all kinds of iron and copper goods, more especially of ordnance and fire-arms. In close alliance with him, though not in partnership, was his brother-in-law, Elias Trip, the head of a firm reputed to have the most extensive business in iron-ware and weapons in the Netherlands. The commanding abilities of de Geer soon gave to the two firms, which continued to work harmoniously together as a family concern, a complete supremacy in the class of wares in which they dealt. At this time the chief supply of iron and copper ore came from Sweden; and in 1616 de Geer was sent on a mission by the States-General to that country to negotiate for a supply of these raw materials for the forging of ordnance. This mission had important results, for it was the first step towards bringing about those close relations between Sweden and the United Provinces which were to subsist throughout the whole of the Thirty Years' War. In the following year, 1617, Gustavus Adolphus, then about to conduct an expedition into Livonia, sent an envoy to Holland for the purpose of securing the good offices of the States-General for the raising of a loan upon the security of the Swedish copper mines. The principal contributor was Louis de Geer. He had, during his visit to Sweden, learnt how great was the wealth of that country in iron ore, and at the same time that the mines were lying idle and undeveloped through lack of capital and skilled workmen. He used his opportunity therefore to obtain from Gustavus the lease of the rich mining domain of Finspong. The lease was signed on October 12, 1619, and de Geer at once began operations on the largest scale. He introduced from Liège a body of expert Walloon iron-workers, built forges and factories, and was in a few years able to supply the Swedish government with all the ordnance and munitions of war that they required, and to export through the port of Norrköping large supplies of goods to his warehouses at Amsterdam. His relations with Gustavus Adolphus soon became intimate. The king relied upon de Geer for the supply of all the necessaries for his armies in the field, and even commissioned him to raise troops for the Swedish service. In 1626 the Dutch merchant was appointed by the king acting-manager of the copper mines, which were royal property; and, in order to regularise his position and give him greater facilities for the conduct of his enterprises, the rights of Swedish citizenship were conferred by royal patent upon him. It was a curious position, for though de Geer paid many visits to Sweden, once for three consecutive years, 1626-29, he continued to make Amsterdam his home and principal residence. He thus had a dual nationality. Year after year saw an increasing number of mines and properties passing into the great financier's hands, and in return for these concessions he made large advances to the king for his triumphant expedition into

Germany; advancing him in 1628 50,000 rixdalers, and somewhat later a further sum of 32,000 rixdalers. So confidential were the relations between them that Gustavus sent for de Geer to his camp at Kitzingen for a personal consultation on business matters in the spring of 1632. It was their last interview, for before that year closed the Swedish hero was to perish at Lützen.

The death of Gustavus made no difference to the position of Louis de Geer in Sweden, for he found Axel Oxenstierna a warm friend and powerful supporter. Among other fresh enterprises was the formation of a Swedo-Dutch Company for trading on the West Coast of Africa. In this company Oxenstierna himself invested money. In reward for his many services the Swedish Council of Regency conferred upon de Geer and his heirs a patent of nobility (August 4, 1641); and as part repayment of the large loans advanced by him to the Swedish treasury he obtained as his own the districts containing his mines and factories in different parts of Sweden, making him one of the largest landed proprietors in the country. He on his part in return for this was able to show in a remarkable way that he was not ungrateful for the favours that he had received.

With Christian IV of Denmark for many years the Swedes and the Dutch had had constant disputes and much friction. This able and ambitious king, throughout a long and vigorous reign, which began in 1593, had watched with ever-increasing jealousy the passing of the Baltic trade into Dutch hands, and with something more than jealousy the rapid advance to power of the sister Scandinavian kingdom under Gustavus Adolphus. Of the 1074 merchant ships that passed through the Sound between June 19 and November 16, 1645, all but 49 came from Dutch ports, by far the largest number from Amsterdam; and from these Christian IV drew a large revenue by the exaction of harsh and arbitrary toll-dues. Again and again the States-General had complained and protested; and diplomatic pressure had been brought to bear upon the high-handed king, but without avail. Between Sweden and Denmark there had been, since Gustavus Adolphus came to the throne in 1613, no overt act of hostility; but smouldering beneath the surface of an armed truce were embers of latent rivalries and ambitions ready at any moment to burst into flame. Christian IV was a Protestant, but his jealousy of Sweden led him in 1639 openly to take sides with the Catholic powers, Austria and Spain. Fearing that he might attempt to close the passage of the Sound, the States-General and the Swedish Regency in 1640 concluded a treaty "for securing the freedom and protection of shipping and commerce in the Baltic and North Seas"; and one of the secret articles gave permission to Sweden to buy or hire ships in the Netherlands and in case of necessity to enlist crews for the same. Outward peace was precariously maintained between the Scandinavian powers, when the seizure of a number of Swedish ships in the Sound in 1643 made Oxenstierna resolve upon a bold stroke. Without any declaration of war the Swedish general, Torstensson, was ordered to lead his victorious army from North Germany into Denmark and to force King Christian to cease intriguing with the enemy. Holstein, Schleswig and Jutland were speedily in Torstensson's hands, but the Danish fleet was superior to the Swedish, and he could make no further progress. Both sides turned to the United Provinces. Christian promised that the grievances in regard to the Sound dues should be removed if the States-General would remain neutral. Oxenstierna addressed himself to Louis de Geer. The merchant on behalf of the Swedish government was instructed to approach the stadholder and the States-General, and to seek for naval assistance under the terms of the treaty of 1640; and, if he failed in obtaining their assent, then he—de Geer—should himself (in conformance with the secret article of that treaty) raise on his own account and equip a fleet of thirty ships for the Swedish service.

De Geer soon discovered that Frederick Henry, being intent on peace negotiations, was averse to the proposal. The stadholder, and the States-General acting under his influence, did not wish to create fresh entanglements by embroiling the United Provinces in a war with Denmark. De Geer therefore at once began on his own responsibility to equip ships in the various seaports of Holland and Zeeland which had been the chief sufferers by the vexatious Sound dues, and he succeeded in enlisting the connivance of the Estates of Holland to his undertaking. Before the end of April, 1644, a fleet of thirty-two vessels was collected under the command of Marten Thijssen. Its first efforts were unsuccessful. The Danish fleet effectually prevented the junction of Thijssen with the Swedes, and for a time he found himself blockaded in a narrow passage called the Listerdiep. Taking advantage of a storm which dispersed the Danes, the Dutch admiral at last was able to put to sea again, and early in July somewhat ignominiously returned to Amsterdam to refit. For the moment King Christian was everywhere triumphant. On July 11 he gained a signal victory over the Swedish fleet at Colberg Heath, and he had the satisfaction of seeing Torstensson compelled by the Imperialists to retreat from Jutland. But the energy and pertinacity of the Amsterdam merchant saved the situation. Though the retreat of Thijssen meant for him a heavy financial loss, de Geer never for a moment faltered in his purpose. Within three weeks Thijssen again put to sea with twenty-two ships, and by skilful manoeuvring he succeeded in making his way through the Skagerak and the Sound, and finally brought his fleet to anchor in the Swedish harbour of Calmar. From this harbour the united Swedo-Dutch squadrons sailed out and on October 23, between Femern and Laaland, met the Danish fleet, and after a desperate conflict completely defeated and destroyed it. Thus were the wealth and resources of a private citizen of Amsterdam able to intervene decisively at a critical moment in the struggle for supremacy in the Baltic between the two Scandinavian powers. But it is not in the victory won by Marten Thijssen that de Geer rendered his greatest service to Sweden. As the Swedish historian Fryxell truly says, "all that was won by the statesmanship of Oxenstierna, by the sword of Baner, Torstensson and Wrangel, in a desolated Germany streaming with blood, has been already lost again; but the benefits which Louis de Geer brought to Sweden, by the path of peaceful industry and virtue, these still exist, and bear wholesome fruit to a late posterity."

This expedition under Marten Thijssen, who after his victory was created a Swedish noble and definitely entered the Swedish naval service, though connived at by Frederick Henry and the States-General, did not express any desire on their part to aggrandise Sweden unduly at the expense of Denmark. If some great merchants such as Louis de Geer and Elias Trip were exploiting the resources of Sweden, others, notably a certain Gabriel Marcelis, had invested their capital in developing the Danish grazing lands; and politically and commercially the question of the Sound dues, pre-eminently a Danish question, overshadowed all others in importance. The Dutch had no desire to give Sweden a share in the control of the Sound; they preferred in the interests of their vast Baltic trade to have to deal with Christian IV alone.

The Swedish threat was useful in bringing diplomatic pressure to bear on the Danish king, but ultimately they felt confident that, if he refused to make concessions in the matter of the dues, they could compel him to do so. As one of their diplomatists proudly declared, "the wooden keys of the Sound were not in the hands of King Christian, but in the wharves of Amsterdam." In June, 1645, his words were put to a practical test. Admiral Witte de With at the head of a fleet of fifty war-ships was ordered to convoy 300 merchantmen through the Sound, peacefully if possible, if not, by force. Quietly the entire fleet of 350 vessels sailed through the narrow waters. The Danish fleet and Danish forts made no attempt at resistance. All the summer De With cruised to and fro and the Dutch traders suffered no molestation. Christian's obstinacy at last gave way before this display of superior might, and on August 23, by the treaty of Christianopel he agreed to lower the tolls for forty years and to make many other concessions that were required from him. At the same time by Dutch mediation peace was concluded between Denmark and Sweden, distinctly to the advantage of the former, by the treaty of Brömsebro.

To pass to other regions. In the Levant, during the long residence of Cornelis Haga at Constantinople, trade had been greatly extended. Considerable privileges were conceded to the Dutch by the so-called "capitulation" concluded by his agency with the Porte in 1612; and Dutch consuls were placed in the chief ports of Turkey, Asia Minor, Syria, Egypt, Tunis, Greece and Italy. The trading however with the Mediterranean and the Levant was left to private enterprise, the States-General which had given charters to the different Companies—East India, West India and Northern—not being willing to create any further monopolies.

The lack of coal and of metals has always seriously hindered industrial development in the United Provinces. Nevertheless the advent into Holland of so many refugees who were skilled artisans, from the southern Netherlands, led to the establishment of various textile industries at Leyden, Haarlem and other towns. One of the chief of these was the dressing and dyeing of English cloth for exportation.

Amsterdam, it should be mentioned, had already at this time become the home of the diamond industry. The art of cutting and polishing diamonds was a secret process brought to the city on the Y by Portuguese Jews, who were expelled by Philip II; and in Amsterdam their descendants still retain a peculiar skill and craftmanship that is unrivalled. Jewish settlers were indeed to be found in many of the Dutch towns; and it was through them that Holland became famous in 17th century Europe for the perfection of her goldsmiths' and silversmiths' art and for jewelry of every kind. Another industry, which had its centre at Delft, was that of the celebrated pottery and tiles known as "delfware." It will be evident from what has been said above that vast wealth flowed into Holland at this period of her history, but, as so often happens, this sudden growth of riches had a tendency to accumulate in the hands of a minority of the people, with the inevitable consequence, on the one hand, of the widening of the gulf which divided poverty from opulence; on the other, with the creation among rich and poor alike of a consuming eagerness and passion for gain, if not by legitimate means, then by wild speculation or corrupt venality. Bubble companies came into existence, only to bring disaster on those who rashly invested their money in them. The fever of speculation rose to its height in the mania for the growing of bulbs and more especially of tulips, which more and more absorbed the attention of the public in Holland in the years 1633-6. Perfectly inordinate sums were offered in advance for growing crops or for particular bulbs; most of the transactions being purely paper speculations, a gambling in futures. Millions of guilders were risked, and hundreds of thousands lost or won. In 1637 the crash came, and many thousands of people, in Amsterdam, Haarlem, Leyden, Alkmaar and other towns in Holland, were brought to ruin. The Estates of Holland and the various municipal corporations, numbers of whose members were among the sufferers, were compelled to take official action to extend the time for the liquidation of debts, and thus to some extent limit the number of bankruptcies. The tulip mania reduced, however, so many to beggary that it came as a stern warning. It was unfortunately only too typical of the spirit of the time.

Even worse in some ways was the venality and corruption which began to pervade the public life of the country. The getting of wealth, no matter how, was an epidemic, which infected not merely the business community, but the official classes of the republic. There was malversation in the admiralties and in the military administration. The government was in the hands of narrow oligarchies, who took good care to oppose jealously any extension of the privileges which placed so much valuable patronage at their disposal. Even envoys to foreign courts were reputed not to be inaccessible to the receipt of presents, which were in reality bribes; and in the law-courts the wealthy suitor or offender could generally count on a charitable construction being placed upon all points in his favour. The severe placards, for instance, against the public celebration of any form of worship but that of the Reformed religion, according to the decrees of the Synod of Dort, were notoriously not enforced. Those who were able and willing to pay for a dispensation found a ready and judicious toleration.

This toleration was not entirely due to the venality of the officials, but rather to the spirit of materialistic indifference that was abroad among the orthodox Calvinists, who were alone eligible for public office. Large numbers of those who professed the established faith were in reality either nominal conformists too much immersed in affairs to trouble about religious questions, or actually free-thinkers in disguise. It must never be forgotten that in the United Provinces taken as a whole, the Calvinists, whether orthodox or arminian, formed a minority of the population. Even in Holland itself more than half the inhabitants were Catholics, including many of the old families and almost all the peasantry. Likewise in Utrecht, Gelderland and Overyssel the Catholics were in the majority. The Generality lands, North Brabant and Dutch Flanders, were entirely of the Roman faith. In Holland, Zeeland and especially in Friesland and Groningen the Mennonite Baptists and other sects had numerous adherents. Liberty of thought and to a large extent of worship was in fact at this time the characteristic of the Netherlands, and existed in spite of the unrepealed placards which enforced under pain of heavy penalties a strict adherence to the principles of Dort.

# CHAPTER XII

# LETTERS, SCIENCE AND ART

The epithet "glorious"—*roemrijke*—has been frequently applied by Dutch historians to the period of Frederick Henry—and deservedly. The preceding chapter has told that it was a time of wonderful maritime and colonial expansion, of commercial supremacy and material prosperity. But the spirit of the Holland, which reached its culminating point of national greatness in the middle of the 17th century, was far from being wholly occupied with voyages of adventure and conquest on far distant seas, or engrossed in sordid commercialism at home. The rapid acquisition of wealth by successful trade is dangerous to the moral health and stability alike of individuals and of societies; and the vices which follow in its train had, as we have already pointed out, infected to a certain extent the official and commercial classes in the Dutch republic at this epoch. There is, however, another side of the picture. The people of the United Provinces in their long struggle for existence, as a free and independent state, had had all the dormant energies and qualities of which their race was capable called into intense and many-sided activity, with the result that the quickening impulse, which had been sent thrilling through the veins, and which had made the pulses to throb with the stress of effort and the eagerness of hope, penetrated into every department of thought and life. When the treaty of Münster was signed, Holland had taken her place in the very front rank in the civilised world, as the home of letters, science and art, and was undoubtedly the most learned state in Europe.

In an age when Latin was the universal language of learning, it was this last fact which loomed largest in the eyes of contemporaries. The wars and persecutions which followed the Reformation made Holland the place of refuge of many of the most adventurous spirits, the choicest intellects and the most independent thinkers of the time. Flemings and Walloons, who fled from Alva and the Inquisition, Spanish and Portuguese Jews driven out by the fanaticism of Philip II, French Huguenots and German Calvinists, found within the borders of the United Provinces a country of adoption, where freedom of the press and freedom of opinion existed to a degree unknown elsewhere until quite modern times. The social condition of the country, the disappearance of a feudal nobility, and the growth of a large and well-to-do burgher aristocracy in whose hands the government of the republic really lay, had led to a widespread diffusion of education and culture. All travellers in 17th century Holland were struck by the evidences which met their eyes, in all places that they visited, of a general prosperity combined with great simplicity of life and quiet domesticity. Homely comfort was to be seen everywhere, but not even in the mansions of the merchant princes of Amsterdam was there any ostentatious display of wealth and luxury. Probably of no other people could it have been said that "amongst the Dutch it was unfashionable not to be a man of business[6]." And yet, in spite of this, there was none of that narrowness of outlook, which is generally associated with burgher-society immersed in trade. These men, be it remembered, were necessarily acquainted with many languages, for they had commercial relations with all parts of the world. The number too of those who had actually voyaged and travelled in far distant oceans, in every variety of climate, amidst every diversity of race, was very large; and their presence in their home circles and in social gatherings and all they had to tell of their experiences opened men's minds, stirred their imaginations, and aroused an interest and a curiosity, which made even the stay-at-home Hollanders alert, receptive and eager for knowledge.

The act of William the Silent in founding the University of Leyden, as a memorial of the great deliverance of 1574, was prophetic of the future that was about to dawn upon the land, which, at the moment of its lowest fortunes, the successful defence of Leyden had done so much to save from utter disaster. For the reasons which have been already stated, scholars of renown driven by intolerance from their own countries found in the newly-founded Academy in Holland a home where they could pursue their literary work undisturbed, and gave to it a fame and celebrity which speedily attracted thousands of students not only from the Netherlands, but also from foreign lands. This was especially the case during the terrible time when Germany was devastated by the Thirty Years' War. Among the scholars and philologists, who held chairs at Leyden during the first century of its existence, are included a long list of names of European renown. Justus Lipsius and Josephus Justus Scaliger may be justly reckoned among the founders of the science of critical scholarship. These were of foreign extraction, as was Salmasius, one of their successors, famous for his controversy with John Milton. But only less illustrious in the domain of philology and classical learning were the Netherlanders Gerardus Johannes Vossius (1577-1649) and his five sons, one of whom Isaac (1618-89) may be even said to have surpassed his father; Daniel Heinsius (1580-1665) and his son Nicolas (1620-1681), men of immense erudition and critical insight; and the brilliant Latinist Caspar Barlaeus (1584-1648). Of theologians and their bitter disputes posterity retains a less grateful remembrance. Gomarus and Arminius by their controversies were the authors of party strife and civil dissensions which led to the death of Oldenbarneveldt on the scaffold; and with them may be mentioned Episcopius, Voetius, Coecaeus, Bogerman and Uyttenbogaert. Not all these men had a direct connection with Leyden, for the success which attended the creation of the academy in that town quickly led to the erection of similar institutions elsewhere. Universities were founded at Franeker, 1584; Groningen, 1614; Amsterdam, 1632; Utrecht, 1636; and Harderwijk, 1646. These had not the same attraction as Leyden for foreigners, but they quickly became, one and all, centres for the diffusion of that high level of general culture which was the distinguishing mark of the 17th century Netherlands.

All the writers, whose names have just been mentioned, used Latin almost exclusively as their instrument of expression. But one name, the most renowned of them all, has been omitted, because through political circumstances he was compelled to spend the greater part of his life in banishment from his native land. Hugo Grotius (Huig van Groot), after his escape from the castle of Loevestein in 1621, though he remained through life a true patriot, never could be induced to accept a pardon, which implied an admission of guilt in himself or in Oldenbarneveldt. So the man, who was known to have been the actual writer of the Advocate's *Justification*, continued to live in straitened circumstances at Paris, until Oxenstierna appointed him Swedish ambassador at the French court. This post he held for eleven years. Of his extraordinary ability, and of the variety and range of his knowledge, it is not possible to speak without seeming exaggeration. Grotius was in his own time styled "the wonder of the world"; he certainly stands intellectually as one of the very foremost men the Dutch race has produced. Scholar, jurist, theologian, philosopher, historian, poet, diplomatist, letter-writer, he excelled in almost every branch of knowledge and made himself a master of whatever subject he took in hand. For the student of International Law the treatise of Grotius, *De Jure belli et pacis*, still remains the text-book on which the later superstructure has been reared. His *Mare liberum*, written expressly to controvert the Portuguese claim of an exclusive right to trade and navigate in the Indian Ocean, excited much attention in Europe, and was taken by James I to be an attack on the oft-asserted *dominium maris* of the English crown in the narrow seas. It led the king to issue a proclamation forbidding foreigners to fish in British waters (May, 1609). Selden's *Mare clausum* was a reply, written by the king's command, to the *Mare liberum*. Of his strictly historical works the *Annales et Historiae de Rebus Belgicis*, for its impartiality and general accuracy no less than for its finished and lucid style, stands out as the best of all contemporary accounts from the Dutch side of the Revolt of the Netherlands. As a theologian Grotius occupied a high rank. His *De Veritate Religionis Christianae* and his *Annotationes in Vetus et in Novum Testamentum* are now out of date; but the *De Veritate* was in its day a most valuable piece of Christian apologetic and was quickly translated into many languages. The *Annotationes* have, ever since they were penned, been helpful to commentators on the Scriptures for their brilliancy and suggestiveness on many points of criticism and interpretation. His voluminous correspondence, diplomatic, literary, confidential, is rich in information bearing on the history and the life of his time. Several thousands of these letters have been collected and published.

But if the smouldering embers of bitter sectarian and party strife compelled the most brilliant of Holland's own sons to spend the last twenty-three years of his life in a foreign capital and to enter the service of a foreign state, Holland was at the same time, as we have seen, gaining distinction by the presence within her hospitable boundaries of men of foreign extraction famous for their learning.

It was thus that both the Cartesian and Spinozan systems of philosophy had their birth-place on Dutch soil. René Descartes sought refuge from France at Amsterdam in 1629, and he resided at different places in the United Provinces, among them at the university towns of Utrecht, Franeker and Leyden, for twenty years. During this time he published most of his best known works, including the famous *Discours de la méthode*. His influence was great. He made many disciples, who openly or secretly became "Cartesians." Among his pupils was Baruch Spinoza (1632-1677) the apostle of pantheism. A Portuguese Jew by descent, Spinoza was born in Amsterdam and was a resident in his native city throughout life.

The fame of Holland in 17th century Europe as the chosen home of learning had thus been established by scholars and thinkers whose literary language was ordinarily Latin. It is now time to speak of the brilliant band of poets, dramatists and stylists, who cultivated the resources of their native tongue with such success as to make this great era truly the Golden Age of Dutch Literature properly so-called. The growth of a genuine national literature in the Netherlands, which had produced during the latter part of the 13th century a Maerlandt and a Melis Stoke, was for some considerable time checked and retarded by the influence of the Burgundian *régime*, where French, as the court language, was generally adopted by the upper classes. The Netherland or Low-German tongue thus became gradually debased and corrupted by the introduction of bastard words and foreign modes of expression. Nevertheless this period of linguistic degradation witnessed the uprise of a most remarkable institution for popularising "the Art of Poesy." I refer to the literary gilds, bearing the name of "Chambers of Rhetoric," which, though of French origin, became rapidly acclimatised in the Netherlands. In well-nigh every town one or more of these "gilds" were established, delighting the people with their quaint pageantry and elaborate ritual, and forming centres of light and culture throughout the land. Rhyming, versifying, acting, became through their means the recreation of many thousands of shop-keepers, artisans and even peasants. And with all their faults of style and taste, their endless effusion of bad poetry, their feeble plays and rude farces, the mummery and buffoonery which were mingled even with their gravest efforts, the "Rhetoricians" effectually achieved the great and important work of attracting an entire people in an age of ignorance and of darkness towards a love of letters, and thereby broke the ground for the great revival of the 17th century. Amsterdam at one time possessed several of these Chambers of Rhetoric, but towards the end of the 16th century they had all disappeared, with one brilliant exception, that of the "Blossoming Eglantine," otherwise known as the "Old Chamber." Founded in 1518 under the special patronage of Charles V, the "Eglantine" weathered safely the perils and troubles of the Revolt, and passed in 1581 under the joint direction of a certain notable triumvirate, Coornheert, Spiegel and Visscher. These men banded themselves together "to raise, restore and enrich" their mother-tongue. But they were not merely literary purists and reformers; the "Eglantine" became in their hands and through their efforts the focus of new literary life and energy, and Amsterdam replaced fallen Antwerp as the home of Netherland culture.

The senior member of the triumvirate, Dirk Volkertz Coornheert, led a stormy and adventurous life. He was a devoted adherent of William the Silent and for a series of years, through good and ill-fortune, devoted himself with pen and person to the cause of his patron. As a poet he did not attain any very high flight, but he was a great pamphleteer, and, taking an active part in religious controversy, by his publications he drew upon himself a storm of opposition and in the end of persecution. He was, like his patron, a man of moderate and tolerant views, which in an age of religious bigotry brought upon him the hatred of all parties and the accusation of being a free-thinker. His stormy life ended in 1590. Hendrik Laurensz Spiegel (1549-1612) was a member of an old Amsterdam family. In every way a contrast to Coornheert, Spiegel was a Catholic. A prosperous citizen, simple, unostentatious and charitable, he spent the whole of his life in his native town, and being disqualified by his religion from holding public office he gave all his leisure to the cultivation of his mind and to literary pursuits. The work on which his fame chiefly rests was a didactic poem entitled the *Hert-Spiegel*. In his pleasant country house upon the banks of the Amstel, beneath a wide and spreading tree, which he was wont to call the "Temple of the Muses" he loved to gather a circle of literary friends, irrespective of differences of opinion or of faith, and with them to spend the afternoon in bright congenial converse on books and men and things. Roemer Visscher, the youngest member of the triumvirate, was like Spiegel an Amsterdammer, a Catholic and a well-to-do merchant. His poetical efforts did not attain a high standard, though his epigrams, which were both witty and quaint, won for him from his contemporaries the name of the "Second Martial." Roemer Visscher's fame does not, however, rest chiefly upon his writings. A man of great affability, learned, shrewd and humorous, he was exceedingly hospitable, and he was fortunate in having a wife of like tastes and daughters more gifted than himself. During the twenty years which preceded his death in 1620 his home was the chosen rendezvous of the best intelligence of the day. To the young he was ever ready to give encouragement and help; and struggling talent always found in him a kindly critic and a sympathising friend. He lived to see and to make the acquaintance of Brederôo, Vondel, Cats and Huyghens, the men whose names were to make the period of Frederick Henry the most illustrious in the annals of Dutch literature.

Gerbrand Adriansz Brederôo, strictly speaking, did not belong to that period. He died prematurely in 1618, a victim while still young to a wayward life of dissipation and disappointment. His comedies, written in the rude dialect of the fish-market and the street, are full of native humour and originality and give genuine glimpses of low life in old Amsterdam. His songs show that Brederôo had a real poetic gift. They reveal, beneath the rough and at times coarse and licentious exterior, a nature of fine susceptibilities and almost womanly tenderness. Joost van den Vondel was born in the same year as Brederôo, 1587, but his career was very different. Vondel survived till 1679, and during the whole of his long life his pen was never idle. His dramas and poems (in the edition of Van Lennep) fill twelve volumes. Such a vast production, as is inevitable, contains material of very unequal merit; but it is not too much to say that the highest flights of Vondel's lyric poetry, alike in power of expression and imagery, in the variety of metre and the harmonious cadence of the verse, deserve a far wider appreciation than they have ever received, through the misfortune of having been written in a language little known and read. Vondel was the son of an Antwerp citizen compelled as a Protestant to fly from his native town after its capture by Parma. He took refuge at Cologne, where the poet was born, and afterwards settled at Amsterdam. In that town Vondel spent all his life, first as a shopkeeper, then as a clerk in the City Savings' Bank. He was always a poor man; he never sought for the patronage of the great, but rather repelled it. His scathing attacks on those who had compassed the death of Oldenbarneveldt, and his adhesion to the Remonstrant cause brought him in early life into disfavour with the party in power, while later his conversion to Catholicism—in 1641—and his eager and zealous advocacy of its doctrines, were a perpetual bar to that public recognition of his talents which was his due. Vondel never at any time sacrificed his convictions to his interest, and he wrote poetry not from the desire of wealth or fame, but because he was a born poet and his mind found in verse the natural expression of its thought and emotions.

But, though Vondel was a poor man, he was not unlearned. On the contrary he was a diligent student of Greek and Latin literature, and translated many of the poetical masterpieces in those languages into Dutch verse. Indeed so close was his study that it marred much of his own work. Vondel wrote a great number of dramas, but his close imitation of the Greek model with its chorus, and his strict adherence to the unities, render them artificial in form and lacking in movement and life. This is emphasised by the fact that many of them are based on Scriptural themes, and by the monotony of the Alexandrine metre in which all the dialogues are written. It is in the choruses that the poetical genius of Vondel is specially displayed. Lyrical gems in every variety of metre are to be found in the Vondelian dramas, alike in his youthful efforts and in those of extreme old age. Of the dramas, the finest and the most famous is the *Lucifer*, 1654, which treats of the expulsion of Lucifer and his rebel host of angels from Heaven. We are here in the presence of a magnificent effort to deal grandiosely with a stupendous theme. The conception of the personality of Lucifer is of heroic proportions; and a comparison of dates renders it at least probable that this Dutch drama passed into John Milton's hands, and that distinct traces of the impression it made upon him are to be found in certain passages of the *Paradise Lost*. Vondel also produced hundreds of occasional pieces, besides several lengthy religious and didactic poems. He even essayed an epic poem on Constantine the Great, but it was never completed. Of the occasional poems the finest are perhaps the triumph songs over the victories of Frederick Henry, and of the great admirals Tromp and De Ruyter.

Jacob Cats (1577-1660) lived, like Vondel, to a great age, but in very different circumstances. He was a native of Dordrecht and became pensionary of that town, and, though not distinguished as a statesman or politician, he was so much respected for his prudence and moderation that for twenty-two years he filled the important office of Council-Pensionary of Holland and was twice sent as an Envoy Extraordinary to England. He was a prolific writer and was undoubtedly the most popular and widely-read of the poets of his time. His works were to be found in every Dutch homestead, and he was familiarly known as "Father Cats." His gifts were, however, of a very different order from those of Vondel. His long poems dealt chiefly with the events of domestic, every-day existence; and the language, simple, unpretentious and at times commonplace, was nevertheless not devoid of a certain restful charm. There are no high flights of imagination or of passion, but there are many passages as rich in quaint fancy as in wise maxims. With Constantine Huyghens (1596-1687) the writing of verse was but one of the many ways in which one of the most cultured, versatile, and busy men of his time found pleasant recreation in his leisure hours. The trusted secretary, friend and counsellor of three successive Princes of Orange, Huyghens in these capacities was enabled for many years to render great service to Frederick Henry, William II and William III, more especially perhaps to the last-named during the difficult and troubled period of his minority. Nevertheless all these cares and labours of the diplomatist, administrator, courtier and man of the world did not prevent him from following his natural bent for intellectual pursuits. He was a man of brilliant parts and of refined and artistic tastes. Acquainted with many languages and literatures, an accomplished musician and musical composer, a generous patron of letters and of art, his poetical efforts are eminently characteristic of the personality of the man. His volumes of short poems—*Hofwijck, Cluijswerck, Voorhout* and *Zeestraet*—contain exquisite and witty pictures of life at the Hague—"the village of villages"—and are at once fastidious in form and pithy in expression.

It remains to speak of the man who may truly be described as the central figure among his literary contemporaries. Pieter Cornelisz Hooft (1583-1647) was indisputably the first man of letters of his time. He sprang from one of the first families of the burgher-aristocracy of Amsterdam, in which city his father, Cornelis Pietersz Hooft, filled the office of burgomaster no less than thirteen times. He began even as a boy to write poetry, and his strong bent to literature was deepened by a prolonged tour of more than three years in France, Germany and Italy, almost two years of which were spent at Florence and Venice. After his return he studied jurisprudence at Leyden, but when he was only twenty-six years old he received an appointment which was to mould and fix the whole of his future career. In 1609 Prince Maurice, in recognition of his father's great services, nominated Hooft to the coveted post of Drost, or Governor, of Muiden and bailiff of Gooiland. This post involved magisterial and administrative duties of a by-no-means onerous kind; and the official residence of the Drost, the "High House of Muiden," an embattled feudal castle with pleasant gardens, lying at the point where at no great distance from Amsterdam the river Vecht sleepily empties itself into the Zuyder Zee, became henceforth for thirty years a veritable home of letters.

Hooft's literary life may be divided into two portions. In the decade after his settlement at Muiden, he was known as a dramatist and a writer of pretty love songs. His dramas—*Geerard van Velzen, Warenar* and *Baeto*—caught the popular taste and were frequently acted, but are not of high merit. His songs and sonnets are distinguished for their musical rhythm and airy lightness of touch, but they were mostly penned, as he himself tells us, for his own pleasure and that of his friends, not for general publication. There are, nevertheless, charming pieces in the collected edition of Hooft's poems, and he was certainly an adept in the technicalities of metrical craft. But Hooft himself was ambitious of being remembered by posterity as a national historian. He aimed at giving such a narrative of the struggle against Spain as would entitle him to the name of "the Tacitus of the Netherlands." He wished to produce no mere chronicle like those of Bor or Van Meteren, but a literary history in the Dutch tongue, whose style should be modelled on that of the great Roman writer, whose works Hooft is said to have read through fifty-two times. He first, to try his hand, wrote a life of Henry IV of France, which attained great success. Louis XIII was so pleased with it that he sent the author a gold chain and made him a Knight of St Michael. Thus encouraged, on August 19, 1628, Hooft began his *Netherland Histories*, and from this date until his death in 1647 he worked ceaselessly at the *magnum opus*, which, beginning with the abdication of Charles V, he intended to carry on until the conclusion of the Twelve Years' Truce. He did not live to bring the narrative further than the end of the Leicester régime. In a small tower in the orchard at Muiden he kept his papers; and here, undisturbed, he spent all his leisure hours for nineteen years engaged on the great task, on which he concentrated all his energies. He himself tells us of the enormous pains that he took to get full and accurate information, collecting records, consulting archives and submitting every portion as it was written to the criticism of living authorities, more especially to Constantine Huyghens and through him to the Prince of Orange himself. Above all Hooft strove, to use his own words, "never to conceal the truth, even were it to the injury of the fatherland"; and the carrying-out of this principle has given to the great prose-epic that he wrote a permanent value apart altogether from its merits as a remarkable literary achievement. And yet perhaps the most valuable legacy that Hooft has left to posterity is his collection of letters. Of these a recent writer[7] has declared "that, though it could not be asserted that they [Hooft's letters] threw into the shade the whole of the rest of Netherland literature, still the assertion would not be far beyond the mark." They deal with every variety of subject, grave and gay; and they give us an insight into the literary, social and domestic life of the Holland of his time, which is of more value than any history.

In these letters we find life-like portraits of the scholars, poets, dramatists, musicians, singers, courtiers and travellers, who formed that brilliant society which received from their contemporaries the name of the "Muiden Circle"—*Muidener Kring*. The genial and hospitable Drost loved to see around him those "five or six couple of friends," whom he delighted to invite to Muiden. Hooft was twice married; and both his wives, Christina van Erp and Heleonore

Hellemans, were charming and accomplished women, endowed with those social qualities which gave an added attractiveness to the Muiden gatherings. Brandt, Hooft's biographer, describes Christina as "of surpassing capacity and intelligence, as beautiful, pleasing, affable, discreet, gentle and gracious, as such a man could desire to have"; while, of Heleonore, Hooft himself writes: "Within this house one ever finds sunshine, even when it rains without."

This reference to the two hostesses of Muiden calls attention to one of the noteworthy features of social life in the Holland of this period—namely, the high level of education among women belonging to the upper burgher-class. Anna and Maria Tesselschade Visscher, and Anna Maria Schuurman may be taken as examples. Anna, the elder of the two daughters of Roemer Visscher (1584-1651), was brought up amidst cultured surroundings. For some years after her mother's death she took her place as mistress of the house which until 1620 had been the hospitable rendezvous of the literary society of Amsterdam. She was herself a woman of wide erudition, and her fame as a poet was such as to win for her, according to the fashion of the day, the title of "the Dutch Sappho." Tesselschade, ten years younger than her sister and educated under her fostering care, was however destined to eclipse her, alike by her personal charms and her varied accomplishments. If one could believe all that is said in her praise by Hooft, Huyghens, Barlaeus, Brederôo, Vondel and Cats, she must indeed have been a very marvel of perfect womanhood. As a singer she was regarded as being without a rival; and her skill in painting, carving, etching on glass and tapestry work was much praised by her numerous admirers. Her poetical works, including her translation into Dutch verse of Tasso's *Gerusalemme Liberata*, have almost all unfortunately perished, but a single ode that survives—"the Ode to a Nightingale"—is an effort not unworthy of Shelley and shows her possession of a true lyrical gift. At Muiden the presence of the "beautiful" Tesselschade was almost indispensable. "What feast would be complete," wrote Hooft to her, "at which you were not present? Favour us then with your company if it be possible"; and again: "that you will come is my most earnest desire. If you will but be our guest, then, I hope, you will cure all our ills." He speaks of her to Barlaeus as "the priestess"; and it is clear that at her shrine all the frequenters of Muiden were ready to burn the incense of adulation. Both Anna and Tesselschade, like their father, were devout Catholics.

Anna Maria van Schuurman (1607-84) was a woman of a different type. She does not seem to have loved or to have shone in society, but she was a very phenomenon of learning. She is credited with proficiency in painting, carving and other arts; but it is not on these, so to speak, accessory accomplishments that her fame rests, but on the extraordinary range and variety of her solid erudition. She was at once linguist, scholar, theologian, philosopher, scientist and astronomer. She was a remarkable linguist and had a thorough literary and scholarly knowledge of French, English, German, Italian, Latin, Greek, Hebrew, Syriac, Chaldee, Arabic and Ethiopic. Her reputation became widespread; and, in the latter part of her long life, many strangers went to Utrecht, where she resided, to try to get a glimpse of so great a celebrity, which was not easy owing to her aversion to such visits.

Turning to the domain of mathematical and physical science and of scientific research and discovery, we find that here also the 17th century Netherlanders attained the highest distinction. As mathematicians Simon Stevin, the friend and instructor of Maurice of Orange, and Francis van Schooten, the Leyden Professor, who numbered among his pupils Christian Huyghens and John de Witt, did much excellent work in the earlier years of the century. The published writings of De Witt on "the properties of curves" and on "the theory of probabilities" show that the greatest of Dutch statesmen might have become famous as a mathematician had the cares of administration permitted him to pursue the abstract studies that he loved. Of the scientific achievements of Christian Huyghens (1629-95), the brilliant son of a brilliant father, it is difficult to speak in adequate terms. There is scarcely any name in the annals of science that stands higher than his. His abilities, as a pure mathematician, place him in the front rank among mathematicians of all time; and yet the services that he rendered to mathematical science were surpassed by his extraordinary capacity for the combination of theory with practice. His powers of invention, of broad generalisation, of originality of thought were almost unbounded. Among the mathematical problems with which he dealt successfully were the theory of numbers, the squaring of the circle and the calculation of chances. To him we owe the conception of the law of the conservation of energy, of the motion of the centre of gravity, and of the undulatory theory of light. He expounded the laws of the motion of the pendulum, increased the power of the telescope, invented the micrometer, discovered the rings and satellites of Saturn, constructed the first pendulum clock, and a machine, called the gunpowder machine, in principle the precursor of the steam engine. For sheer brain power and inventive genius Christian Huyghens was a giant. He spent the later years of his life in Paris, where he was one of the founders and original members of the *Académie des Sciences*. Two other names of scientists, who gained a European reputation for original research and permanent additions to knowledge, must be mentioned; those of Antoni van Leeuwenhoek (1632-1723), and of Jan Swammerdam (1637-80). Leeuwenhoek was a life-long observer of minute life. The microscope (the invention of which was due to a Dutchman, Cornelius Drebbel) was the favourite instrument of his patient investigations, and he was able greatly to improve its mechanism and powers. Among the results of his labours was the discovery of the infusoria, and the collection of a valuable mass of information concerning the circulation of the blood and the structure of the eye and brain. Swammerdam was a naturalist who devoted himself to the study of the habits and the metamorphoses of insects, and he may be regarded as the founder of this most important branch of scientific enquiry. His work forms the basis on which all subsequent knowledge on this subject has been built up.

To say that the school of Dutch painting attained its zenith in the period of Frederick Henry and the decades which preceded and followed it, is scarcely necessary. It was the age of Rembrandt. The works of that great master and of his contemporaries, most of whom were influenced and many dominated by his genius, are well known to every lover of art, and are to be seen in every collection of pictures in Europe. One has, however, to visit the Rijks Museum at Amsterdam and the Mauritshuis at the Hague to appreciate what an extraordinary outburst of artistic skill and talent had at this time its birth within the narrow limits of the northern Netherlands. To the student of Dutch history these two galleries are a revelation, for there we see 17th century Holland portrayed before us in every phase of its busy and prosperous public, social and domestic life. Particularly is this the case with the portraits of individuals and of civic and gild groups by Rembrandt, Frans Hals, Van der Helst and their followers, which form an inimitable series that has rarely been equalled. To realise to what an extent in the midst of war the fine arts flourished in Holland, a mere list of the best-known painters of the period will suffice, it tells its own tale. They are given in the order of their dates: Frans Hals (1584-1666), Gerard Honthorst (1592-1662), Jan van Goyen (1596-1656), Jan Wyvants (1600–87), Albert Cuyp (1606-72), Jan Lievens (1607-63), Rembrandt van Rhyn (1608-69), Gerard Terburg (1608-81), Adrian Brouwer (1608-41), Ferdinand Bol (1609-81), Salomon Koning (1609-74), Andreas Both (1609-60), Jan Both (1610-62), Adrian van Ostade (1610-85), Bartolomaus van der Helst (1613-70), Gerard Douw (1613-80), Gabriel Metzu (1615-58), Govaert Flinck (1615-60), Isaac van Ostade (1617-71), Aart van der Neer (1619-83), Pieter de Koningh (1619-89), Philip Wouvermans (1620-68), Pieter van der Hoogh (?), Nicolas Berchem (1624-83), Paul Potter (1625-54), Jacob Ruysdael (1625-81), Meindert Hobbema (?), Jan Steen (1626-79), Samuel van Hoogstraeten (1627-78), Ludolf Backhuizen (1631-1709), Jan van der Meer of Delft (1632-?), Nicholas Maes (1632-93), William van der Velde (1633-1707), Frans van Mieris (1635-81), Caspar Netscher (1639-84), Adrian van der Velde (1639-72).

It is strange that little is known of the lives of the great majority of these men; they are scarcely more than names, but their memory survives in their works. No better proof could be brought of the general abundance of money and at the same time of the widespread culture of the land than the fact that art found among all classes so many patrons. The aristocratic burgher-magistrates and the rich merchants loved to adorn their houses with portraits and a choice selection of pictures; it was a favourite investment of capital, and there was a certain amount of rivalry among the principal families in a town like Amsterdam in being possessed of a fine collection. The "Six" collection still remains as an example upon the walls of the 17th century house of Burgomaster Six, where it was originally placed. The governing bodies of gilds and boards, members of corporations, the officers of the town *schutterij* or of archer companies delighted to have their portraits hung around their council chambers or halls of assembly. In the well-to-do farmer-homesteads and even in the dwellings of the poorer classes pictures were to be found, as one may see in a large number of the "interiors" which were the favourite subject of the *genre* painters of the day. But with all this demand the artists themselves do not seem to have in any case been highly paid. The prices were low. Even Rembrandt himself, whose gains were probably much larger than those of any of his contemporaries, and whose first wife, Saskia Uilenburg, was a woman of means, became bankrupt in 1656, and this at a time when he was still in his prime, and his powers at their height. Some of his most famous pictures were produced at a later date.

During the Thirty Years' War Holland became the centre of the publishing and book-selling trade; and Leyden and Amsterdam were famed as the foremost seats of printing in Europe. The devastation of Germany and the freedom of the press in the United Provinces combined to bring about this result. The books produced by the Elseviers at Leyden and by Van Waesberg and Cloppenburch at Amsterdam are justly regarded as fine specimens of the printer's art, while the maps of Willem Jansz Blaeu and his Dutch contemporaries were quite unrivalled, and marked a great step forward in cartography.

This chapter must not conclude without a reference to the part taken by the Netherlanders in the development of modern music and the modern stage. The love of music was widespread; and the musicians of the Netherlands were famed alike as composers and executants. It was from its earlier home in the Low Countries that the art of modern music spread into Italy and Germany and indeed into all Europe. Similarly in the late Middle Ages the people of the Netherlands were noted for their delight in scenic representations and for the picturesque splendour with which they were carried out. The literary gilds, named Chambers of Rhetoric, never took such deep root elsewhere; and in the performance of Mystery Plays and Moralities and of lighter comic pieces (*chuttementen* and *cluyten*) many thousands of tradespeople and artisans took part. In the 17th century all the Chambers of Rhetoric had disappeared with the single exception of the famous "Old Chamber" at Amsterdam, known as *The Blossoming Eglantine*, to which the leading spirits of the Golden Age of Dutch Literature belonged and which presided over the birth of the Dutch Stage. From the first the stage was popular and well-supported; and the new theatre of Amsterdam, the Schouburg (completed in 1637), became speedily renowned for the completeness of its arrangements and the ability of its actors. Such indeed was their reputation that travelling companies of Dutch players visited the chief cities of Germany, Austria and Denmark, finding everywhere a ready welcome and reaping a rich reward, whilst at Stockholm for a time a permanent Dutch theatre was established.

# CHAPTER XIII

# THE STADHOLDERATE OF WILLIAM II.

# THE GREAT ASSEMBLY

Upon the death of Frederick Henry of Orange (March, 1647), his only son succeeded to his titles and estates and also by virtue of the Act of Survivance to the offices of Stadholder in six provinces and to the Captain-Generalship and Admiral-Generalship of the Union. William was but twenty-one years of age and, having been excluded during Frederick Henry's lifetime from taking any active part in affairs of state, he had turned his energies into the pursuit of pleasure, and had been leading a gay and dissolute life. His accession to power was, however, speedily to prove that he was possessed of great abilities, a masterful will and a keen and eager ambition. He had strongly disapproved of the trend of the peace negotiations at Münster, and would have preferred with the help of the French to have attempted to drive the Spaniards out of the southern Netherlands. The preliminaries were, however, already settled in the spring of 1647; and the determination of the province of Holland and especially of the town of Amsterdam to conclude an advantageous peace with Spain and to throw over France rendered the opposition of the young Stadholder unavailing. But William, though he had perforce to acquiesce in the treaty of Münster, was nevertheless resolved at the earliest opportunity to undo it. Thus from the outset he found himself in a pronounced antagonism with the province of Holland, which could only issue in a struggle for supremacy similar to that with which his uncle

Maurice was confronted in the years that followed the truce of 1609, and, to a less degree, his father after 1640.

Commerce was the predominant interest of the burgher-aristocracies who held undisputed sway in the towns of Holland; and they, under the powerful leadership of Amsterdam, were anxious that the peace they had secured should not be disturbed. They looked forward to lightening considerably the heavy load of taxation which burdened them, by reducing the number of troops and of ships of war maintained by the States. To this policy the young prince was resolutely opposed, and he had on his side the prestige of his name and a vast body of popular support even in Holland itself, among that great majority of the inhabitants, both of town and country, who were excluded from all share in government and administration and were generally Orangist in sympathy. He had also with him the officers of the army and navy and the preachers. His chief advisers were his cousin William Frederick, Stadholder of Friesland, and Cornelis van Aerssens (son of Francis) lord of Sommelsdijk. By the agency of Sommelsdijk he put himself in secret communication with Count d'Estrades, formerly French ambassador at the Hague, now Governor of Dunkirk, and through him with Mazarin, with the view of concluding an alliance with France for the conquest of the Spanish Netherlands, and for sending a joint expedition to England to overthrow the Parliamentary forces and establish the Stewarts on the throne. Mazarin was at this time, however, far too much occupied by his struggle with the Fronde to listen to the overtures of a young man who had as yet given no proof of being in a position to give effect to his ambitious proposals. Nevertheless the prince was in stern earnest. In April, 1648, his brother-in-law, James, Duke of York, had taken refuge at the Hague, and was followed in July by the Prince of Wales. William received them with open arms and, urged on by his wife, the Princess Royal, and by her aunt the exiled Queen of Bohemia, who with her family was still residing at the Hague, he became even more eager to assist in effecting a Stewart restoration than in renewing the war with Spain. The difficulties in his way were great. In 1648 public opinion in the States on the whole favoured the Parliamentary cause. But, when the Parliament sent over Dr Doreslaer and Walter Strickland as envoys to complain of royal ships being allowed to use Dutch harbours, the States-General, through the influence of the prince, refused them an audience. The Estates of Holland on this gave a signal mark of their independence and antagonism by receiving Doreslaer and forbidding the royal squadron to remain in any of the waters of the Province.

The news of the trial of King Charles for high-treason brought about a complete revulsion of feeling. The Prince of Wales himself in person begged the States-General to intervene on his father's behalf; and the proposal met with universal approval. It was at once agreed that Adrian Pauw, the now aged leader of the anti-Orange party in Holland, should go to London to intercede for the king's life. He was courteously received on January 26 o.s., and was granted an audience by the House of Commons, but the decision had already been taken and his efforts were unavailing. The execution of the king caused a wave of horror to sweep over the Netherlands, and an address of condolence was offered by the States-General to the Prince of Wales; but, to meet the wishes of the delegates of Holland, he was addressed not as King of Great Britain, but simply as King Charles II, and it was agreed that Joachimi, the resident ambassador in London, should not be recalled at present. The new English Government on their part sent over once more Dr Doreslaer with friendly proposals for drawing the two republics into closer union. Doreslaer, who had taken part in the trial of Charles I, was specially obnoxious to the royalist exiles, who had sought refuge in Holland. He landed on May 9. Three days later he was assassinated as he was dining at his hotel. The murderers, five or six in number, managed to make their escape and were never apprehended.

Although highly incensed by this outrage, the English Government did not feel itself strong enough to take decided action. The Estates of Holland expressed through Joachimi their abhorrence at what had occurred; and the Parliament instructed Strickland to approach the States-General again with friendly advances. The States-General refused to grant him an audience, while receiving the envoy despatched by Charles II from Scotland to announce his accession. The English Council of State had no alternative but to regard this as a deliberate insult. Strickland was recalled and left Holland, July 22. On September 26 Joachimi was ordered to leave London. The breach between the two countries seemed to be complete, but the Estates of Holland, who for the sake of their commerce dreaded the thought of a naval war, did all in their power to work for an accommodation. They received Strickland in a public audience before his departure, and they ventured to send a special envoy to Whitehall, Gerard Schaep, January 22, to treat with the Parliament. By this action the Provincial Estates flouted the authority of the States-General and entered into negotiations on their own account, as if they were an independent State. The Hollanders were anxious to avoid war almost at any price, but circumstances proved too strong for them.

In order to carry out this pacifist policy the Estates of Holland now resolved to effect a large reduction of expenditure by disbanding a portion of the troops and ships. When the peace of Münster was signed the States possessed an army of 60,000 men, and all parties were agreed that this large force might safely be reduced. In July 1648, a drastic reduction was carried out, twenty-five thousand men being disbanded. The Estates of Holland, however, demanded a further retrenchment of military charges, but met with the strong opposition of the Prince and his cousin William Frederick, who declared that an army of at least 30,000 was absolutely necessary for garrisoning the frontier fortresses and safeguarding the country against hostile attack. Their views had the support of all the other provinces, but Holland was obdurate. In Holland commerce reigned supreme; and the burgher-regents and merchants were suspicious of the prince's warlike designs and were determined to thwart them. Finding that the States-General refused to disband at their dictation some fifty-five companies of the excellent foreign troops who formed the kernel of the States' army, the Provincial Estates proceeded to take matters into their own hands, and discharged a body of 600 foreign troops which were paid by the Province. In doing this they were acting illegally. The old question of the sovereign rights of the Provinces, which had been settled in 1619 by the sword of Maurice, was once more raised. The States-General claimed to exercise the sole authority in military matters. There were not seven armies in the Union, but one army under the supreme command of the captain-general appointed by the States-General. The captain-general was now but a young and inexperienced man, but he had none of the hesitation and indecision shown by his uncle Maurice in the troubles of 1618-

19, and did not shrink from the conflict with the dominant province to which he was challenged.

For some time, indeed, wrangling went on. There was a strong minority in the Estates of Holland opposed to extreme measures; and the council-pensionary, Jacob Cats, was a moderate man friendly to the House of Orange. An accommodation was reached on the subject of the disbanding of the 600 foreign troops, but the conflict was renewed, and in the middle of 1650 it assumed grave proportions. The heart and soul of the opposition to the prince was Amsterdam. William had for some time been urged by his Friesland cousin to take action, since the attitude of Amsterdam threatened the dissolution of the Union. The prince was at this time engaged in negotiating with France, but nothing had as yet been settled, and his projects were not ripe for execution. Nevertheless it was absolutely necessary for their realisation that the military forces should not be excessively reduced. Under his influence the States-General decided that, though the number of troops in the several regiments should be decreased, the *cadres* of all regiments with their full quota of officers should be retained. To this the Estates of Holland dissented, and finding that they could not prevail, they determined on a daring step. Orders were sent (June 1, 1650) to the colonels of the regiments on the Provincial war-sheet to disband their regiments on pain of stoppage of pay. The colonels refused to take any orders save from the Council of State and the captain-general. The prince accordingly, with William Frederick and the Council of State, appeared in the States-General and appealed to them to uphold the colonels in their refusal. There could be no question that the Estates of Holland were hopelessly in the wrong, for their representatives in the States-General had in 1623, 1626, 1630 and 1642 voted for the enforcement on recalcitrant provinces of the full quota at which they were assessed for the payment of the army of the Union. The States-General, June 5, therefore determined to send a "notable deputation" to the towns of Holland. The prince was asked to head the deputation, the members of which were to be chosen by him; and he was invested with practically dictatorial powers to take measures for the keeping of the peace and the maintenance of the Union. In doing this the Generality were themselves acting *ultra vires*. The States-General was an assembly consisting of the representatives of the Provincial

Estates. It could deal or treat therefore only with the Estates of the several provinces, not with the individual towns within a province. In resisting the interference of the Estates of Holland with matters that concerned the Union as a whole, they were themselves infringing, by the commission given to the "notable deputation," the jurisdiction of the Provincial Estates over their own members.

The prince set out on June 8, and visited all the "privileged" towns. The result was more than disappointing. The Council of the premier municipality, Dordrecht, set the example by declaring that they were answerable only to the Estates of the Province. Schiedam, Alkmaar, Edam and Monnikendam gave the same reply. Delft and Haarlem were willing to receive the prince as stadholder, but not the deputation. Amsterdam, under the influence of the brothers Andries and Cornelis Bicker, went even further and after some parleying declined to admit either the deputation or the prince. On June 25 William returned to the Hague bitterly chagrined by his reception and determined to crush resistance by force.

The stroke he planned was to seize the representatives of six towns which had been specially obstinate in their opposition, and at the same time to occupy Amsterdam with an armed force. His preparations were quickly made. On July 30 an invitation was sent to Jacob de Witt, ex-burgomaster of Dordrecht, and five other prominent members of the Estates of Holland, to visit the prince. On their arrival they were arrested by the stadholder's guard, and carried off as prisoners to the Castle of Loevestein. William had meanwhile left the execution of the *coup-de-main* against Amsterdam to his cousin William Frederick. The arrangements for gathering together secretly a large force from various garrisons were skilfully made, and it was intended at early dawn to seize unexpectedly one of the gates, and then to march in and get possession of the town without opposition. The plan, however, accidentally miscarried. Some of the troops in the night having lost their way, attracted the notice of a postal messenger on his way to Amsterdam, who reported their presence to the burgomaster, Cornelis Bicker. Bicker at once took action. The gates were closed, the council summoned, and vigorous measures of defence taken. William Frederick therefore contented himself with surrounding the city, so as to prevent ingress or egress from the gates. On the next morning, July 31, William, having learnt that the surprise attack had failed, set out for Amsterdam, determined to compel its surrender. The council, fearing the serious injury a siege would cause to its commerce, opened negotiations (August 1). The prince, however, insisting on unconditional submission, no other course was open. Amsterdam undertook to offer no further opposition to the proposals of the States-General, and was compelled to agree to the humiliating demand of the stadholder that the brothers Bicker should not only resign their posts in the municipal government, but should be declared ineligible for any official position in the future.

The Prince of Orange had now secured the object at which he had aimed. His authority henceforth rested on a firm basis. His opponents had been overthrown and humiliated. The Estates of six provinces thanked him for the success of his efforts, and he on his part met the general wish for economy by agreeing to a reduction of the foreign troops in the pay of the States on the distinct understanding that only the States-General had the right to disband any portion of the forces, not the provincial paymasters. In the flush of triumph William at the end of August left the Hague for his country seat at Dieren, nominally for hunting and for rest, in reality to carry on secret negotiations with France for the furtherance of his warlike designs. The complete defeat of Charles II at the battle of Worcester, September 3, must have been a severe blow to his hopes for the restoration of the Stuarts, but it did not deter him from pursuing his end. With d'Estrades, now Governor of Dunkirk, the prince secretly corresponded, and through him matters were fully discussed with the French Government. In a letter written from the Hague on October 2, William expressed a strong wish that d'Estrades should come in person to visit him; and it was the intention of d'Estrades to accept this invitation as soon as he had received from Paris the copy of a draft-treaty, which was being prepared. This draft-treaty, which was probably drawn up by Mazarin, reached d'Estrades in the course of October, but circumstantial evidence proves that it was never seen by William. Its provisions were as follows. Both Powers were to declare war on Spain and attack Flanders and Antwerp. The Dutch were to besiege Antwerp, which city, if taken, was to become the personal appanage of the Prince, of Orange. When the Spanish power in the southern Netherlands had been overthrown, then France and the United Provinces were to send a joint expedition to England to place Charles II on the throne. Whether the prince would have approved these proposals we know not; in all probability he would have declined to commit himself to a plan of such a far-reaching and daring character, for he was aware of the limitations of his power, and knew that even his great influence would have been insufficient to obtain the consent of the States-General to an immediate renewal of war. Speculation however is useless, for an inexorable fate raised other issues.

On October 8 the stadholder returned to Dieren, on the 27th he fell ill with an attack of small-pox. He was at once taken back to the Hague and for some days he progressed favourably, but the illness suddenly took a turn for the worse and he expired on November 6. The news of the prince's death fell like a shock upon the country. Men could scarcely believe their ears. William was only 24 years old; and, though his wife gave birth to a son a week later, he left no heir capable of succeeding to the high offices that he had held. The event was the more tragic, following, as it did, so swiftly upon the *coup d'état* of the previous summer, and because of the youth and high promise of the deceased prince. William II was undoubtedly endowed with high and brilliant qualities of leadership, and he had proved his capacity for action with unusual decision and energy. Had his life not been cut short, the course of European politics might have been profoundly changed.

As was to be expected, the burgher-regents of Holland, when once the first shock was over, lost no time in taking advantage of the disappearance of the man who had so recently shown that he possessed the power of the sword and meant to be their master. The States-General at once met and requested the Provincial Estates to take steps to deal with the situation. The Estates of Holland proposed that an extraordinary assembly should be summoned. This was agreed to by the States-General; and "the Great Assembly" met on January 11, 1651. In the meantime the Holland regents had been acting. The Estates of that province were resolved to abolish the stadholderates and to press the States-General to suspend the offices of Captain-and Admiral-General of the Union. Utrecht, Gelderland, Overyssel and Zeeland were induced to follow their example. Groningen, however, elected William Frederick of Friesland to be stadholder in the place of his cousin.

The "States party" in Holland had for their leaders the aged Adrian Pauw, who had for so many years been the moving spirit of the opposition in powerful Amsterdam to Frederick Henry's authority, and Jacob de Witt, the imprisoned ex-burgomaster of Dordrecht. The "Orange party" was for the moment practically impotent. Stunned by the death of their youthful chief, they were hopelessly weakened and disorganised by the dissensions and rivalries which surrounded the cradle of the infant Prince of Orange. The princess royal quarrelled with her mother-in-law, Amalia von Solms, over the guardianship of the child. Mary asserted her right to be sole guardian; the dowager-princess wished to have her son-in-law, the Elector of Brandenburg, associated with her as co-guardian. After much bickering the question was at last referred to the Council of State, who appointed the princess royal, the dowager-princess and the elector jointly to the office. This decision however was far from effecting a reconciliation between the mother and the grandmother. Mary did not spare the Princess Amalia the humiliation of knowing that she regarded her as inferior in rank and social standing to the eldest daughter of a King of England. There was rivalry also between the male relatives William Frederick, Stadholder of Friesland, and Joan Maurice, the "Brazilian," both of them being ambitious of filling the post of captain-general, either in succession to the dead prince, or as lieutenant in the name of his son. In these circumstances a large number of the more moderate Orangists were ready to assist the "States party" in preventing any breach of the peace and securing that the government of the republic should be carried on, if not in the manner they would have wished, at least on stable and sound lines, so far as possible in accordance with precedent.

The Great Assembly met on January 11,1651, in the Count's Hall in the Binnenhof at the Hague. The sittings lasted until September, for there were many important matters to be settled on which the representatives of the seven provinces were far from being in entire agreement. The chief controversies centred around the interpretation of the Utrecht Act of Union, the Dordrecht principles, and military affairs. The last-named proved the most thorny. The general result was decentralisation, and the strengthening of the Provincial Estates at the expense of the States-General. It was agreed that the established religion should be that formulated at Dordrecht, that the sects should be kept in order, and the placards against Roman Catholicism enforced. In accordance with the proposal of Holland there was to be no captain- or admiral-general. Brederode, with the rank of field-marshal, was placed at the head of the army. The Provincial Estates were entrusted with considerable powers over the troops in their pay. The effect of this, and of the decision of five provinces to dispense with a stadholder and to transfer his power and prerogatives to the Estates, was virtually the establishment in permanent authority of a number of close municipal corporations. It meant the supersession alike of monarchy and popular government, both of which were to a certain extent represented by the authority vested in, and the influence exerted by, the stadholder princes of Orange, in favour of a narrow oligarchic rule. Moreover, in this confederation of seven semi-sovereign provinces, Holland, which contributed to the strength, the finances and the commerce of the Union more than all the other provinces added together, obtained now, in the absence of an "eminent head," that position of predominance, during the stadholderless period which now follows, for which its statesmen had so long striven. When the amiable Jacob Cats, the Council-Pensionary of Holland, closed the Great Assembly in a flowery speech describing the great work that it had accomplished, a new chapter in the history of the republic may be said to have begun.

# CHAPTER XIV

# THE RISE OF JOHN DE WITT.

# THE FIRST ENGLISH WAR

Before the sittings of the Great Assembly had come to an end, a young statesman, destined to play the leading part in the government of the Dutch republic during two decades, had already made his mark. After the death of William II Jacob de Witt was not only reinstated in his former position at Dordrecht but on December 21, 1650, John, his younger son, at the age of 25 years was appointed pensionary of that town. In this capacity he was *ex officio* spokesman of the deputation sent to represent Dordrecht in the Great Assembly. His knowledge, his readiness and persuasiveness of speech, his industry and his gifts at once of swift insight and orderly thoroughness, quickly secured for him a foremost place both in the deliberations of the Assembly and in the conduct of the negotiations with the English Parliament, which at this time required very delicate handling.

The many disputes, which had arisen between England and the United Provinces during the period between the accession of James I and the battle of the Downs in 1639, had never been settled. The minds of Englishmen were occupied with other and more pressing matters while the Civil War lasted. But the old sores remained open. Moreover the refusal of the States-General to receive the Parliamentary envoys, the murder of Doreslaer, and the protection afforded to royalist refugees, had been additional causes of resentment; but the English Council had not felt strong enough to take action. The death of the Prince of Orange, following so quickly upon the complete overthrow of Charles II at Worcester, appeared at first to open out a prospect of friendlier relations between the two neighbouring republics. In January, 1651, the Great Assembly formally recognised the Commonwealth and determined to send back to his old post in London the veteran ambassador, Joachimi, who had been recalled. The English government on their part anticipated his return by despatching, in March, Oliver St John and Walter Strickland on a special embassy to the Hague. They reached that city on March 27, 1651, and presented their credentials to the Great Assembly two days later. Their reception in the streets was anything but favourable. The feeling among the populace was predominantly Orangist and Stewart; and St John and Strickland, greeted with loud cries of "regicides" and many abusive epithets, remembering the fate of Doreslaer, were in fear of their lives.

On April 4 a conference was opened between the envoys and six commissioners appointed by the States to consider the proposals of the English Government for "a more strict and intimate alliance and union" between the two states. The Dutch quickly perceived that what the English really wanted was nothing less than such a binding alliance or rather coalition as would practically merge the lesser state in the greater. But the very idea of such a loss of the independence that they had only just won was to the Netherlanders unthinkable. The negotiations came to a deadlock. Meanwhile St John and Strickland continued to have insults hurled at them by Orangists and royalist refugees, foremost amongst them Prince Edward, son of the Queen of Bohemia. The Parliament threatened to recall the envoys, but consented that they should remain, on the undertaking of the Estates of Holland to protect them from further attacks, and to punish the offenders. New proposals were accordingly made for an offensive and defensive alliance (without any suggestion of a union), coupled with the condition that both States should bind themselves not to allow the presence within their boundaries of avowed enemies of the other—in other words the expulsion of the members and adherents of the house of Stewart, including the princess royal and the Queen of Bohemia with their children. In the face of the strong popular affection for the infant Prince of Orange and his mother, even the Estates of Holland dared not consider such terms, and the States-General would have angrily rejected them. After some further parleying therefore about fisheries and trade restrictions, it was felt that no agreement could be reached; and St John and Strickland returned to England on July 31, 1651.

Their failure created a very bad impression upon the Parliament. All the old complaints against the Dutch were revived; and, as they had refused the offer of friendship that had been made to them, it was resolved that strong measures should be taken to obtain redress for past grievances and for the protection of English trade interests.

At the instance of St John, the famous Navigation Act was passed by the Parliament, October 9, 1651. This Act struck a mortal blow at the Dutch carrying trade by forbidding the importation of foreign goods into English ports except in English bottoms, or in those of the countries which had produced the goods. Scarcely less injurious was the prohibition to aliens to fish in British waters, and the withdrawal of the rights based on the *Magnus Intercursus*, for the maintenance of which Dutch statesmen had so long and strenuously fought. There was consternation in Holland, and the States-General determined to send a special embassy to London. At the same time the Estates of Holland replaced Jacob Cats by appointing the aged Adrian Pauw, a man in whose ripe judgment they had confidence, to the office of council-pensionary. The chosen envoys were Jacob Cats and Gerard Schaep from Holland, Paulus van der Perre from Zeeland, all three representative of the two maritime and trading provinces. They arrived in England on December 27, 1651. Their instructions were to secure the withdrawal of the Navigation Act and to try to negotiate a new treaty of commerce on the basis of the *Magnus Intercursus*. They were also to protest strongly against the action of English privateers, who, having been given letters of marque to prey upon French commerce, had been stopping and searching Dutch merchantmen on the ground that they might be carrying French goods. The English government, however, met the Dutch complaints by raking up the long list of grievances that had stirred up a bitter feeling of popular hatred against the United Provinces in England, and by demanding reparation. They further demanded that Dutch commanders should acknowledge England's sovereignty by striking flag and sail and by firing a salute, whenever any of their squadrons met English ships "in the narrow seas."

It was these last two questions, the right of search and the striking of the flag, that were to be the real causes of the outbreak of a war that was desired by neither of the two governments. But popular feeling and the course of events was too strong for them. The news of the seizure of their vessels, not merely by privateers, but by an English squadron under Ayscue in the West Indies, had caused intense indignation and alarm in Holland, and especially in Amsterdam. Pressure was brought to bear on the States-General and the Admiralties, who in pursuance of economy had reduced the fleet to seventy-five ships. It was resolved therefore, on February 22, to fit out an additional 150 vessels. The Council of State, on hearing of this, began also to make ready for eventualities. Negotiations were still proceeding between the two countries, when Martin Tromp, the victor of the battle of the Downs, now lieutenant-admiral of Holland, was sent to sea with fifty ships and instructions to protect Dutch merchantmen from interference, and to see that the States suffered no affront. Nothing was actually said about the striking of the flag.

The situation was such that an armed collision was almost certain to happen with such an admiral as Tromp in command. It came suddenly through a misunderstanding. The Dutch admiral while cruising past Dover met, on May 29, fifteen English ships under Blake. The latter fired a warning shot across the bows of Tromp's ship to signify that the flag should be struck. Tromp declared that he had given orders to strike the flag, but that Blake again fired before there was time to carry them out. Be this as it may, the two fleets were soon engaged in a regular fight, and, the English being reinforced, Tromp withdrew at nightfall to the French coast, having lost two ships. Great was the anger aroused in England, where the Dutch were universally regarded as the aggressors. In the Netherlands, where the peace party was strong, many were disposed to blame Tromp despite his protests. Adrian Pauw himself left hastily for London, John de Witt being appointed to act as his deputy during his absence. Pauw's strenuous efforts however to maintain peace were all in vain, despite the strong leanings of Cromwell towards a peaceful solution. But popular feeling on both sides was now aroused. The States-General, fearing that the Orangists would stir up a revolt, if humiliating terms were submitted to, stiffened their attitude. The result was that the envoys left London on June 30, 1652; and war was declared.

The Dutch statesmen who sought to avoid hostilities were right. All the advantages were on the side of their enemies. The Dutch merchant-fleets covered the seas, and the welfare of the land depended on commerce. The English had little to lose commercially. Their war-fleet too, though inferior in the number of ships, was superior in almost all other respects. The Stuarts had devoted great attention to the fleet and would have done more but for lack of means. Charles' much abused ship-money was employed by him for the creation of the first English professional navy. It had been largely increased by the Parliament after 1648; and its "generals," Blake, Penn and Ayscue, had already acquired much valuable experience in their encounters with the royalist squadron under Prince Rupert, and in long cruises to the West Indies for the purpose of forcing the English colonies to acknowledge parliamentary rule. The crews therefore were well trained, and the ships were larger, stronger and better armed than those of the Dutch. The position of England, lying as it did athwart the routes by which the Dutch merchant-fleets must sail, was a great advantage. Even more important was the advantage of having a central control, whereas in the Netherlands there were five distinct Boards of Admiralty, to some extent jealous of each other, and now lacking the supreme direction of an admiral-general.

The war began by a series of English successes and of Dutch misfortunes. Early in July, 1652, Blake at the head of sixty ships set sail for the north to intercept the Dutch Baltic commerce, and to destroy their fishing fleet off the north of Scotland. He left Ayscue with a small squadron to guard the mouth of the Thames. Tromp meanwhile had put to sea at the head of nearly a hundred ships. Ayscue succeeded in intercepting a fleet of Dutch merchantmen near Calais, all of them being captured or burnt, while Blake with the main force off the north coast of Scotland destroyed the Dutch fishing fleet and their convoy. After these first blows against the enemy's commerce good fortune continued to attend the English. Tromp was prevented from following Blake by strong northerly winds. He then turned upon Ayscue, whose small force he must have overwhelmed, but for a sudden change to a southerly gale. The Dutch admiral now sailed northwards and (July 25) found the

English fleet off the Shetlands. A violent storm arose, from the force of which Blake was protected, while the Dutch vessels were scattered far and wide. On the following day, out of ninety-nine ships Tromp could only collect thirty-five, and had no alternative but to return home to refit.

Before Tromp's return another Dutch fleet under Michael de Ruyter had put to sea to escort a number of outward-bound merchantmen through the Channel, and to meet and convoy back the home-coming ships. He had twenty-three warships and three fireships under his command. Ayscue had previously sailed up Channel with forty men-of-war and five fireships for a similar purpose. The two fleets met on August 16, and despite his inferiority of force De Ruyter forced Ayscue to withdraw into Plymouth, and was able to bring his convoy home to safety.

The ill-success of Tromp, though he was in no way to blame for it, caused considerable alarm and discontent in Holland. His enemies of the States party in that province took advantage of it to suspend the gallant old seaman from his command. He was an Orangist; and, as the Orange partisans were everywhere clamorously active, the admiral was suspect. In his place Cornelisz Witte de With was appointed, a capable sailor, but disliked in the fleet as much as Tromp was beloved. De With effected a junction with De Ruyter and with joint forces they attacked Blake on October 8, near the shoal known as the Kentish Knock. The English fleet was considerably more powerful than the Dutch, and the desertion of De With by some twenty ships decided the issue. The Dutch had to return home with some loss. The English were elated with their victory and thought that they would be safe from further attack until the spring. Blake accordingly was ordered to send a squadron of twenty sail to the Mediterranean, where the Dutch admiral Jan van Galen held the command of the sea. But they were deceived in thinking that the struggle in the Channel was over for the winter. The deserters at the Kentish Knock were punished, but the unpopularity of De With left the authorities with no alternative but to offer the command-in-chief once more to Martin Tromp. Full of resentment though he was at the bad treatment he had received, Tromp was too good a patriot to refuse. At the end of November the old admiral at the head of 100 warships put to sea for the purpose of convoying some 450 merchantmen through the

Straits. Stormy weather compelled him to send the convoy with an escort into shelter, but he himself with sixty ships set out to seek the English fleet, which lay in the Downs. After some manoeuvring the two fleets met on December 10, off Dungeness. A stubborn fight took place, but this time it was some of the English ships that were defaulters. The result was the complete victory of the Dutch; and Blake's fleet, severely damaged, retreated under cover of the night into Dover roads. Tromp was now for a time master of the Channel and commerce to and from the ports of Holland and Zeeland went on unimpeded, while many English prizes were captured.

This state of things was however not to last long. Towards the end of February, 1653, Blake put to sea with nearly eighty ships, and on the 25th off Portland met Tromp at the head of a force nearly equal to his own in number. But the Dutch admiral was convoying more than 150 merchantmen and he had moreover been at sea without replenishment of stores ever since the fight at Dungeness, while the English had come straight from port. The fight, which on the part of the Dutch consisted of strong rear-guard actions, had lasted for two whole days, when Tromp found that his powder had run out and that on the third day more than half his fleet were unable to continue the struggle. But, inspiring his subordinates De Ruyter, Evertsen and Floriszoon with his own indomitable courage, Tromp succeeded by expert seamanship in holding off the enemy and conducting his convoy with small loss into safety. Four Dutch men-of-war were taken and five sunk; the English only lost two ships.

Meanwhile both nations had been getting sick of the war. The Dutch were suffering terribly from the serious interference with their commerce and carrying trade and from the destruction of the important fisheries industry, while the English on their side were shut out from the Baltic, where the King of Denmark, as the ally of the United Provinces, had closed the Sound, and from the Mediterranean, where Admiral van Galen, who lost his life in the fight, destroyed a British squadron off Leghorn (March 23). In both countries there was a peace party. Cromwell had always wished for a closer union with the United Provinces and was averse to war. In the Dutch republic the States party, especially in Holland the chief sufferer by the war, was anxious for a cessation of hostilities; and it found its leader in the youthful John de Witt, who on the death of Adrian Pauw on February 21, 1653, had been appointed council-pensionary. Cromwell took pains to let the Estates of Holland know his favourable feelings towards them by sending over, in February, a private emissary, Colonel Dolman, a soldier who had served in the Netherland wars. On his part John de Witt succeeded in persuading the Estates of Holland to send secretly, without the knowledge of the States-General, letters to the English Council of State and the Parliament expressing their desire to open negotiations. Thus early did the new council-pensionary initiate a form of diplomacy in which he was to prove himself an adept. This first effort was not a success. The Parliament published the letter with the title "Humble Supplication of the States of Holland." The indignation of the Orange partisans was great, and they threatened internal disturbances throughout the country. Such however was the skill of De Witt that, on Parliament showing a willingness to resume the negotiations that had been broken off in the previous summer, he induced the States-General by a bare majority (four provinces to three) to send a conciliatory letter, the date of which (April 30, 1653) coincided with Cromwell's forcible dissolution of the Rump Parliament and the assumption by him, with the support of the army, of dictatorial powers. The English Council of State, however, was well informed of the serious economical pressure of the war upon Holland; and their insistence now on the full satisfaction of all the English demands made a continuation of hostilities inevitable.

Tromp, after successfully bringing in two large convoys of merchantmen, encountered (June 12), near the Gabbard, the English fleet under Monk and Deane. Each fleet numbered about 100 sail, but the Dutch ships were inferior in size, solidity and weight of metal. For two days the fight was obstinately and fiercely contested, but on Blake coming up with a reinforcement of thirteen fresh ships, Tromp was obliged to retreat, having lost twenty ships. He complained bitterly, as did his vice-admirals De Ruyter and De With, to the Board of Admiralty of the inferiority of the vessels of his fleet, as compared with those of the adversary.

The English now instituted a blockade of the Dutch coast, which had the effect of reducing to desperate straits a land whose welfare and prosperity depended wholly on commerce. Amsterdam was ruined. In these circumstances direct negotiation was perforce attempted. Four envoys were sent representing the three maritime provinces. At first it seemed impossible that any common ground of agreement could be found. Cromwell was obsessed with the idea of a politico-religious union between the two republics, which would have meant the extinction of Dutch independence. The Council of State met the Dutch envoys with the proposal *una gens, una respublica,* which nothing but sheer conquest and dire necessity would ever induce the Dutch people to accept. Accordingly the war went on, though the envoys did not leave London, hoping still that some better terms might be offered. But in order to gain breathing space for the efforts of the negotiators, one thing was essential— the breaking of the blockade. The Admiralties made a supreme effort to refit and reinforce their fleet, but it lay in two portions; eighty-five sail under Tromp in the Maas, thirty-one under De With in the Texel. Monk with about 100 ships lay between them to prevent their junction. On August 4 Tromp sailed out and, after a rearguard action off Katwijk, out-manoeuvred the English commander and joined De With. He now turned and with superior numbers attacked Monk off Scheveningen. The old hero fell mortally wounded at the very beginning of what proved to be an unequal fight. After a desperate struggle the Dutch retired with very heavy loss. Monk's fleet also was so crippled that he returned home to refit. The action in which Tromp fell thus achieved the main object for which it was fought, for it freed the Dutch coast from blockade. It was, moreover, the last important battle in the war. The States, though much perplexed to find a successor to Martin Tromp, were so far from being discouraged that great energy was shown in reorganising the fleet. Jacob van Wassenaer, lord of Obdam, was appointed lieutenant-admiral of Holland, with De Ruyter and Evertsen under him as vice-admirals. De With retained his old command of a detached squadron, with which he safely convoyed a large fleet of East Indiamen round the north of Scotland into harbour. After this there were only desultory operations on both sides and no naval engagement.

    Meanwhile negotiations had been slowly dragging on. The accession of Cromwell to supreme power in December, 1653, with the title of Lord Protector seemed to make the prospects of the negotiations brighter, for the new ruler of England had always professed himself an opponent of the war, which had shattered his fantastic dream of a union between the two republics. Many conferences took place, but the Protector's attitude and intentions were ambiguous and difficult to divine. The fear of an Orange restoration appears to have had a strange hold on his imagination and to have warped at this time the broad outlook of the statesman. At last Cromwell formulated his proposals in twenty-seven articles. The demands were those of the victor, and were severe. All the old disputes were to be settled in favour of England. An annual sum was to be paid for the right of fishing; compensation to be made for "the massacre of Amboina" and the officials responsible for it punished; the number of warships in English waters was to be limited; the flag had to be struck when English ships were met and the right of search to be permitted. These demands, unpalatable as they were, might at least have furnished a basis of settlement, but there was one demand besides these which was impossible. Article 12 stipulated that the Prince of Orange should not at any time hold any of the offices or dignities which had been held by his ancestors, or be appointed to any military command. De Witt, in whose hands were all the threads of the negotiations, was perfectly aware that it would be useless to present such proposals to the States-General. Not only would they indignantly reject them, but he had not the slightest hope of getting any single province, even Holland, to allow a foreign power to interfere with their internal affairs and to bid them to treat with harsh ingratitude the infant-heir of a family to which the Dutch people owed so deep a debt. There was nothing for it but to prepare for a vigorous resumption of the war. Strong efforts were therefore made at De Witt's instigation to increase the fleet and secure the active co-operation of Denmark and France, both friendly to the States. But Cromwell really wanted peace and showed himself ready to yield on certain minor points, but he continued to insist on the exclusion of the Prince of Orange. Not till the Dutch envoys had demanded their passports did the Protector give way so far as to say he would be content to have the exclusion guaranteed by a secret article.

What followed forms one of the strangest chapters in the history of diplomacy. De Witt had all this time been keeping up, in complete secrecy, a private correspondence with the leading envoy, his confidant Van Beverningh. Through Van Beverningh he was able to reach the private ear of Cromwell, and to enter into clandestine negotiations with him. The council-pensionary knew well the hopelessness of any attempt to get the assent of the States-General to the proposed exclusion, even in a secret article. Van Beverningh was instructed to inform Cromwell of the state of public feeling on this point, with the result that the Protector gave the envoy to understand that he would be satisfied if the Estates of Holland alone would affirm a declaration that the Prince should never be appointed stadholder or captain-general. Whether this concession was offered by Cromwell *proprio motu* or whether it was in the first instance suggested to him by De Witt through Van Beverningh is unknown. In any case the council-pensionary, being convinced of the necessity of peace, resolved to secure it by playing a very deep and dangerous game. Not only must the whole affair be kept absolutely from the cognisance of the States-General, but also De Witt was fully aware that the assent of the Estates of Holland to the proposed exclusion article could only be obtained with the greatest difficulty. He was to prove himself a very past master in the art of diplomatic chicanery and intrigue.

The council-pensionary first set to work to have the treaty, from which the exclusion article had been cut out, ratified rapidly by the States-General, before bringing the secret article to the knowledge of the Estates of Holland. The Estates adjourned for a recess on April 21, 1654. On the following day he presented the treaty to the States-General, and such was his persuasive skill that he accomplished the unprecedented feat of getting this dilatory body to accept the conditions of peace almost without discussion. On April 23 the treaty ratified and signed was sent back to London. Only one article aroused opposition (Art. 32), the so-called "temperament clause"; but Cromwell had insisted upon it. By this article the States-General and the Provincial Estates separately undertook that every stadholder, captain-general or commander of military or naval forces should be required to take an oath to observe the treaty. Meanwhile De Witt had received a letter from Van Beverningh and his colleague Nieuwpoort addressed to the

Estates of Holland (not at the moment in session) stating that Cromwell refused on his part to ratify the treaty until he received the Act of Exclusion[8] from the Estates, who were until now wholly ignorant that any such proposal would be made to them.

The cleverness and skill now shown by the council-pensionary were truly extraordinary. A summons was sent out to the Estates to meet on April 28 without any reason being assigned. The members on assembly were sworn to secrecy, and then the official letter from London was read to them. The news that Cromwell refused to sign the treaty until he received the assent of the Province of Holland to the Act of Exclusion came upon the Estates like a thunder-bolt. The sudden demand caused something like consternation, and the members asked to be allowed to consider the matter with their principals before taking so momentous a decision. Three days were granted but, as it was essential to prevent publicity, it was settled that only the burgomasters should be consulted, again under oath of secrecy. At the meeting on May 1 another despatch from Van Beverningh was read in which the envoy stated that the demand of Cromwell—that the Act should be placed in his hands within two days after the ratification of the treaty—was peremptory and threatening. Unless he received the Act he would consider the treaty as not binding upon him. Using all his powers of advocacy, De Witt succeeded after an angry debate in securing a majority for the Act. Five towns however obstinately refused their assent, and claimed that it could not be passed without it. But De Witt had made up his mind to risk illegality, and overruled their protest. The Act was declared to have been passed and was on May 5 sent to Van Beverningh and Nieuwpoort with instructions not to deliver it until circumstances compelled them to do so. The proclamation of peace followed amidst general rejoicing both in England and the Netherlands; but for some five weeks the existence of the Act was unknown to the States-General, and during that period, as a fact, it remained in Van Beverningh's possession still undelivered.

Early in June a bribe induced one of De Witt's clerks to betray the secret to Count William Frederick. The news soon spread, and loud was the outcry of the Orange partisans and of the two princesses, who at once addressed a remonstrance to the States-General. All the other provinces strongly protested against the action of the Estates of Holland and of the council-pensionary. De Witt attempted to defend himself and the Estates, by vague statements, avoiding the main issue, but insisting that nothing illegal had been done. His efforts were in vain. On June 6 the States-General passed a resolution that the envoys in England should be ordered to send back at once all the secret instructions they had received from Holland, and the Act of Exclusion. Meanwhile the Estates of Holland themselves, frightened at the clamour which had been aroused, began to show signs of defection. They went so far as to pass a vote of thanks to the envoys for not having delivered the Act to Cromwell. De Witt's position appeared hopeless. He extricated himself and outwitted his opponents by the sheer audacity and cleverness of the steps that he took. His efforts to prevent the resolution of the States-General from taking immediate effect proving unavailing, he put forward the suggestion that on account of its importance the despatch should be sent to the envoys in cipher. This was agreed to, and on June 7 the document was duly forwarded to London by the council-pensionary; but he enclosed a letter from himself to Van Beverningh and Nieuwpoort informing them that the Estates of Holland assented to the request made by the States-General, and that they were to send back the secret correspondence and also the Act, *if it were still undelivered*. The result answered to his expectations. While the clerk was laboriously deciphering the despatch, the envoys read between the lines of De Witt's letter, and without a moment's delay went to Whitehall and placed the Act in Cromwell's hands. The States-General had thus no alternative between acceptance of the *fait accompli* and the risk of a renewal of the war. No further action was taken, and the Protector professed himself satisfied with a guarantee of such doubtful validity.

It is impossible to withhold admiration from De Witt's marvellous diplomatic dexterity, and from the skill and courage with which he achieved his end in the face of obstacles and difficulties that seemed insurmountable; but for the course of double-dealing and chicanery by which he triumphed, the only defence that can be offered is that the council-pensionary really believed that peace was an absolute necessity for his country, and that peace could only be maintained at the cost of the Act of Exclusion. Whether or no Cromwell would have renewed the war, had the Act been withdrawn, it is impossible to say. There is, however, every reason to believe that De Witt was prompted to take the risks he did by purely patriotic motives, and not through spite against the house of Orange. Be this as it may, the part that he now played was bitterly resented, not merely by the Orange partisans, but by popular opinion generally in the United Provinces, and it was never forgiven.

# CHAPTER XV

## THE ADMINISTRATION OF JOHN DE WITT 1654-1665

## FROM THE PEACE OF WESTMINSTER TO THE OUT-BREAK OF THE SECOND ENGLISH WAR

The position of John de Witt in July, 1654, was a difficult one. The conduct of the council-pensionary in the matter of the Act of Exclusion was openly attacked in the States-General. Had the leaders of the Orange party been united, the attack might have had serious consequences; but notoriously the princess royal, the princess dowager and William Frederick were on bad terms, and De Witt, with his usual adroitness, knew well how to play off one against another. To meet the accusations of his assailants in the States-General he drew up however an elaborate defence of the action taken by the Estates of Holland and by himself. The document bore the title "Deduction of the Estates of Holland." It was laborious rather than convincing, and it did not convince opponents. Nevertheless, though resentment continued to smoulder, the fact that peace had been assured soon reconciled the majority to allow the doubtful means by which it had been obtained to be overlooked. The tact, the persuasiveness, the great administrative powers of the council-pensionary effected the rest; and his influence from this time forward continued to grow, until he attained to such a control over every department of government, as not even Oldenbarneveldt had possessed in the height of his power.

John de Witt was possibly not the equal of the famous Advocate in sheer capacity for great affairs, but he had practical abilities of the highest order as a financier and organiser, and he combined with these more solid qualifications a swiftness of courageous decision in moments of emergency which his almost infinite resourcefulness in extricating himself from difficult and perilous situations, enabled him to carry to a successful issue. His marriage in February, 1655, to Wendela Bicker, who belonged to one of the most important among the ruling burgher-families of Amsterdam, brought to him enduring domestic happiness. It was likewise of no slight political value. Andries and Cornelis Bicker, who had headed the opposition to William II and had been declared by him in 1650 incapable of holding henceforth any municipal office, were her uncles; while her maternal uncle, Cornelis de Graeff, was a man of weight and influence both in his native town and in the Provincial Estates. By this close relationship with such leading members of the regent-aristocracy of Amsterdam the council-pensionary became almost as secure of the support of the commercial capital in the north of Holland, as he was already of Dordrecht in the south. Two of his cousins, Slingelandt and Vivien, were in turn his successors, as pensionaries of Dordrecht, while for his predecessor in that post, Nicolas Ruysch, he obtained the extremely influential office of *griffier* or secretary to the States-General. Nor did he scruple to exercise his powers of patronage for other members of his family. His father, Jacob de Witt, was made a member of the Chamber of Finance; his elder brother, Cornelis, Ruwaard of Putten. By these and other appointments of men who were his friends and supporters, to important positions diplomatic, military and naval, De Witt contrived to strengthen more and more his personal authority and influence. And yet in thus favouring his relatives and friends, let us not accuse De Witt of base motives or of venality. He firmly believed in his own ability to serve the State, and, without doubt, he was convinced that it was for the best interest of his country for him to create for himself, as far as was possible amidst the restrictions by which he was hemmed in on every side, a free field of diplomatic and administrative action. No one, not even his bitterest enemies, ever charged John de Witt with personal corruption. Throughout his whole career he lived quietly and unostentatiously, as a simple citizen, on a very moderate income, and he died a poor man.

One of the first cares of the council-pensionary after the peace with England was to deal with the internal troubles which were disturbing certain parts of the land, notably Groningen, Zeeland and Overyssel. In the last-named province a serious party struggle arose out of the appointment of a strong Orangist, named Haersolte, to the post of Drost or governor of Twente. The Estates were split up, the Orange partisans meeting at Zwolle, the anti-Orange at Deventer. Both enlisted troops, but those of Zwolle were the stronger and laid siege to Deventer. The victorious Orangists then nominated William III as stadholder with William Frederick as his lieutenant. At last, after three years' strife, the parties called in De Witt and William Frederick as mediators. But De Witt was far too clever for the Friesland stadholder. It happened that the post of field-marshal had just fallen vacant by the death of Brederode. Both William Frederick and his cousin Joan Maurice aspired to the office. The council-pensionary induced his co-mediator, with the hope of becoming Brederode's successor, to yield on all points. Haersolte was deprived of office; the prince's appointment as stadholder was suspended until his majority; and therefore William Frederick could not act as his lieutenant. Thus peace was restored to Overyssel, but William Frederick was not appointed field-marshal. In the other provinces the tact and skill of De Witt were equally successful in allaying discord. He would not have been so successful had the Orange party not been hopelessly divided and had it possessed capable leaders.

As an administrator and organiser the council-pensionary at once applied himself to two most important tasks, financial reform and naval reconstruction. The burden of debt upon the province of Holland, which had borne so large a part of the charges of the war, was crushing. The rate of interest had been reduced in 1640 from 6 J to 5 per cent. But the cost of the English war, which was wholly a naval war, had caused the debt of Holland to mount to 153,000,000 guilders, the interest on which was 7,000,000 guilders per annum. De Witt first took in hand a thorough overhauling of the public accounts, by means of which he was enabled to check unnecessary outlay and to effect a number of economies. Finding however that, despite his efforts to reduce expenditure, he could not avoid an annual deficit, the council-pensionary took the bold step of proposing a further reduction of interest from 5 to 4 per cent. He had some difficulty in persuading the investors in government funds to consent, but he overcame opposition by undertaking to form a sinking fund by which the entire debt should be paid off in 41 years. Having thus placed the finances of the province on a sound basis, De Witt next brought a similar proposal before the States-General with the result that the interest on the Generality debt was likewise reduced to 4 per cent.

The English war had conclusively proved to the Dutch their inferiority in the size and armament of their war-vessels, and of the need of a complete reorganisation of the fleet. De Witt lost no time in taking the necessary steps. The custom which had hitherto prevailed of converting merchantmen into ships of war at the outbreak of hostilities was abandoned. Steps were taken to build steadily year by year a number of large, strongly-constructed, powerfully armed men-of-war, mounting 60,70 and 80 guns. These vessels were specially adapted for passing in and out of the shallow waters and were built for strength rather than for speed. Again, the part taken in the war by the light, swift-sailing English frigates led to a large flotilla of these vessels being built, so useful for scouting purposes and for preying upon the enemy's commerce. The supply and training of seamen was also dealt with, and the whole system of pay and of prize-money revised and reorganised. It was a great and vitally necessary task, and subsequent events were to show how admirably it had been carried out.

No one knew better than John de Witt that peace was the chief interest of the United Provinces, but his lot was cast in troubled times, and he was one of those prescient statesmen who perceive that meekness in diplomacy and willingness to submit to injury do not promote the cause of peace or further the true interests of any country.

The conquests of France in the southern Netherlands caused great anxiety to the Dutch; and the high-handed action of French pirates in searching and seizing Dutch merchantmen in the Mediterranean aroused much indignation. The States, acting on De Witt's advice, replied by sending a squadron under De Ruyter to put a stop to these proceedings. The Dutch admiral took vigorous action and captured some French freebooters. The French government thereupon forbade Dutch vessels to enter French harbours. The Dutch replied by a similar embargo and threatened to blockade the French coast. This threat had the desired effect, and an accommodation was reached. The peace of the Pyrenees in 1659, by which the French retained a large part of their conquests in Flanders, Hainault and Namur, while the English acquired possession of Dunkirk, was disquieting. For the relations with England, despite the goodwill of the Protector, were far from satisfactory. The trade interests of the two republics clashed at so many points that a resumption of hostilities was with difficulty prevented. More especially was this the case after the outbreak of war with Portugal in November, 1657.

The Dutch accused the Portuguese government of active connivance with the successful revolt of the Brazilian colonists against Dutch rule. What was once Dutch Brazil was now claimed by the Lisbon government as a Portuguese possession, and De Witt demanded an indemnity. As this was not conceded, a squadron under Obdam, November, 1657, blockaded the Portuguese coast, while another under De Ruyter made many seizures of merchant vessels. Cromwell was disposed to intervene, but his death on September 3, 1658, removed any fears of English action. Meanwhile the Dutch captured Ceylon and Macassar and practically cut off Portuguese intercourse with the East Indies. At last in August, 1661, a treaty was signed by which the Dutch abandoned all territorial claims in Brazil, but were granted freedom of trade and an indemnity of 8,000,000 fl. to be paid in sixteen years, and, what was more valuable, they retained possession of their conquests in the East.

The protracted dispute with Portugal was however of quite subordinate importance to the interest of the Dutch in the complications of the so-called Northern War. On the abdication of Christina in 1654, Charles X Gustavus had succeeded to the Swedish throne. The new king was fired with the ambition of following in the footsteps of Gustavus Adolphus, and of rendering Sweden supreme in the Baltic by the subjection of Poland and Denmark. Charles was a man of great force of character and warlike energy, and he lost no time in attempting to put his schemes of conquest into execution. Having secured the alliance of the Great Elector, anxious also to aggrandise himself in Polish Prussia, the Swedish king declared war against Poland, and in the early summer of 1656 laid siege to Danzig. But the importance of the Baltic trade to Holland was very great and Danzig was the corn emporium of the Baltic. Under pressure therefore of the Amsterdam merchants the States-General despatched (July) a fleet of forty-two ships under Obdam van Wassenaer through the Sound, which raised the siege of Danzig and with Polish consent left a garrison in the town. Thus checked, the Swedish king at Elbing (September, 1656) renewed amicable relations with the republic, and Danzig was declared a neutral port. At the same time a defensive alliance was concluded between the States and Denmark. It was obvious from, this that the Dutch were hostile to Swedish pretensions and determined to resist them. De Witt was anxious to preserve peace, but he had against him all the influence of Amsterdam, and that of the able diplomatist, Van Beuningen, who after being special envoy of the States at Stockholm had now been sent to Copenhagen. Van Beuningen held that, whatever the risks of intervention on the part of the States, the control of the Sound must not fall into the hands of Sweden. The emergency came sooner than was expected.

Brandenburg having changed sides, the Swedes were expelled from Poland; and Frederick III of Denmark, despite the advice of De Witt, seized the opportunity to declare war on Sweden. Although it was the depth of winter Charles Gustavus lost no time in attacking Denmark. He quickly drove the Danes from Schonen and Funen and invaded Seeland. Frederick was compelled at Roeskilde (February, 1658) to accept the terms of the conqueror. Denmark became virtually a Swedish dependency, and undertook to close the Sound to all foreign ships. Involved as the republic was in disputes at this time with both France and England, and engaged in war with Portugal, De Witt would have been content to maintain a watchful attitude in regard to Scandinavian matters and to strive by diplomacy to secure from Sweden a recognition of Dutch rights. But his hand was forced by Van Beuningen, who went so far as to urge the Danish king to rely on his defensive alliance with the republic and to break the treaty of Roeskilde. Charles Gustavus promptly invaded Denmark, drove the Danish fleet from the sea, placed strong garrisons at Elsinore and Kronborg, and laid siege to Copenhagen. Van Beuningen had proudly asserted that "the oaken keys of the Sound lay in the docks of Amsterdam," and his boast was no empty one. At the beginning of October a force of thirty-five vessels under Obdam carrying 4000 troops sailed for the Sound with orders to destroy the Swedish fleet, and to raise the siege of Copenhagen. On November 8 Obdam encountered the Swedes in the entrance to the Baltic. The Swedish admiral Wrangel had forty-five ships under his command, and the battle was obstinate and bloody. Obdam carried out his instructions. Only a remnant of the Swedish fleet found refuge in the harbour of Landskrona, but the Dutch also suffered severely. The two vice-admirals, Witte de With and Floriszoon, were killed, and Obdam himself narrowly escaped capture, but Copenhagen was freed from naval blockade.

Charles Gustavus however held military possession of a large part of Denmark, and in the spring began to press the attack on the capital from the land side. As both England and France showed a disposition to interfere in the conflict, the States-General now acted with unexpected vigour, recognising that this question to them was vital. An imposing force of seventy-five warships, carrying 12,000 troops and mounting 3000 guns, was despatched in May, 1659, under De Ruyter to the Baltic. Negotiations for peace between the Scandinavian powers under the mediation of France, England and the United Provinces, were now set on foot and dragged on through the summer. But neither Charles Gustavus nor Frederick could be brought to agree to the terms proposed, and the former in the autumn again threatened Copenhagen. In these circumstances De Ruyter was ordered to expel the Swedes from Funen. On November 24 the town of Nyborg was taken by storm and the whole Swedish force compelled to surrender. De Ruyter was now supreme in the Baltic and closely blockaded the Swedish ports. The spirit of Charles Gustavus was broken by these disasters; he died on February 20, 1660. Peace was now concluded at Oliva on conditions favourable to Sweden, but securing for the Dutch the free passage of the Sound. The policy of De Witt was at once firm and conciliatory. Without arousing the active opposition of England and France, he by strong-handed action at the decisive moment succeeded in maintaining that balance of power in the Baltic which was essential in the interest of Dutch trade. The republic under his skilful leadership undoubtedly gained during the northern wars fresh weight and consideration in the Councils of Europe.

The peace of the Pyrenees, followed by the peace of Oliva and the settlement with Portugal, seemed to open out to the United Provinces a period of rest and recuperation, but probably no one knew better than the council-pensionary that outward appearances were deceptive. In the spring of 1660 a bloodless revolution had been accomplished in England, and Charles II was restored to the throne. The hostility of De Witt and of the States party to the house of Stuart had been marked. It happened that Charles was at Breda when he received the invitation recalling him to England. The position was a difficult one, but the council-pensionary at once saw, with his usual perspicacity, that there was but one course to pursue. Acting under his advice, every possible step was taken by the States-General and the Estates of Holland to propitiate the prince, who from being a forlorn exile had suddenly become a powerful king. Immense sums were spent upon giving him a magnificent reception at the Hague; and, when he set sail from Scheveningen, deputations from the States-General and the Estates of Holland attended in state his embarkation and lavish promises of friendship were exchanged. It was significant, however, that Charles handed to the council-pensionary a declaration commending to the care of their High Mightinesses "the Princess my sister and the Prince of Orange my nephew, persons who are extremely dear to me." He had previously expressed the same wish to De Witt privately; and compliance with it, *i.e.* the annulling of the Act of Exclusion, was inevitable. But all the actors in this comedy were playing a part. Charles was not deceived by all this subservience, and, continuing to entertain a bitter grudge against De Witt and his party, only waited his time to repay their enmity in kind. De Witt on his side, though in his anxiety to conciliate the new royalist government he consented to deliver up three regicides who were refugees in Holland (an act justly blamed), refused to restore the Prince of Orange to any of the ancient dignities and offices of his forefathers. Acting however on his advice, the Estates of Holland passed a unanimous resolution declaring William a ward of the Estates and voting a sum of money for his maintenance and education.

Very shortly after this momentous change in the government of England, Cardinal Mazarin died (March, 1661); and the youthful Louis XIV took the reins of power into his own hands. Outwardly all seemed well in the relations between France and the republic, and in point of fact an offensive and defensive alliance for twenty-five years was concluded between them on April 27, 1662. Later in the same year Count D'Estrades, formerly ambassador in the time of Frederick Henry, resumed his old post. The relations between him and De Witt were personally of the friendliest character, but the conciliatory attitude of D'Estrades did not deceive the far-sighted council-pensionary, who was seriously disquieted as to the political aims of France in the southern Netherlands.

By the treaty of the Pyrenees, 1659, the French had already acquired a large slice of territory in Flanders and Artois. They had since obtained Dunkirk by purchase from Charles II. Moreover Louis XIV had married the eldest daughter of Philip IV, whose only son was a weakly boy. It is true that Maria Theresa, on her marriage, had renounced all claims to the Spanish succession. But a large dowry had been settled upon her, and by the treaty the renunciation was contingent upon its payment. The dowry had not been paid nor was there any prospect of the Spanish treasury being able to find the money. Besides it was no secret that Louis claimed the succession to Brabant for his wife and certain other portions of the Netherlands under what was called the Law of Devolution. By this law the female child of a first wife was the heir in preference to the male child of a later marriage. The Dutch dreaded the approach of the French military power to their frontiers, and yet the decrepitude of Spain seemed to render it inevitable. There appeared to De Witt to be only two solutions of the difficulty. Either what was styled "the cantonment" of the southern Netherlands, *i.e.* their being formed into a self-governing republic under Dutch protection guaranteed by a French alliance, or the division of the Belgic provinces between the two powers. The latter proposal, however, had two great disadvantages: in the first place it gave to France and the Republic the undesirable common frontier; in the second place Amsterdam was resolved that Antwerp should not be erected into a dangerous rival. The last objection proved insuperable; and, although De Witt had many confidential discussions with D'Estrades, in which the French envoy was careful not to commit himself to any disclosure of the real intentions of his government, no settlement of any kind had been arrived at, when the threatening state of relations with England threw all other questions into the background.

The accession of Charles II placed upon the throne of England a man who had no goodwill to Holland and still less to the council-pensionary, and who, like all the Stewart kings, had a keen interest in naval and maritime matters. The Navigation Act, far from being repealed, was vigorously enforced, as were the English claims to the sovereignty of the narrow seas. The grievances of the English East India Company against its Dutch rival with regard to the seizure of certain ships and especially as to the possession of a small island named Poeloe-Rum in the Moluccas led to a growing feeling of bitterness and hostility. A special embassy, headed by De Witt's cousin, Beverweert, was sent to London in the autumn of 1660 to try to bring about a friendly understanding, but was fruitless. At the same time George Downing, a skilful intriguer and adventurer, who after serving Cromwell had succeeded in gaining the confidence of the royal government, had been sent as ambassador to the Hague, where he worked underhand to exacerbate the disputes and to prevent a settlement of the differences between the two peoples. The position and treatment of the Prince of Orange had likewise been a source of difficulty and even of danger to the supremacy of the States party. There arose a general movement among the provinces, headed by Gelderland and Zeeland, to nominate William captain-and admiral-general of the Union and stadholder. The lack of leadership in the Orangist party, and the hostility between the two princesses, rendered, however, any concentrated action impossible. De Witt, with his usual adroitness, gained the ear of the princess royal, who accepted the proposal that the Estates of Holland should undertake the education of the prince, and even consented that De Witt himself and his wife's uncle, De Graef, should superintend the prince's studies. This arranged, Mary, for the first time since her marriage, paid a visit to her native land, being desirous to consult her brother on various subjects. Unfortunately she died of small-pox in January, 1661, having nominated Charles as her son's guardian. This nomination did not tend to smooth matters between the two countries.

There was a powerful war party in England, supported by the Duke of York. It was at his instigation that a strong-handed act took place which aroused intense indignation in Holland. A company called "The Royal African Company" had been formed in which the duke had a large interest. A fleet fitted out by this company under the command of Admiral Holmes seized, in February, 1664, a portion of the coast of Guinea on which the Dutch had settlements. Strong protests meeting with nothing but evasive replies, in all secrecy a squadron was got ready to sail under De Ruyter, nominally to the Mediterranean. Dilatory negotiations were in the meantime being conducted by Beverweert in London, and by Downing at the Hague in regard to this and other grievances, but without any approach to a settlement. Downing in fact was surreptitiously doing his best not to reconcile, but to aggravate differences. Matters were brought to a head by the news that an English fleet had crossed the Atlantic and had taken possession of the Dutch colony of New Netherland (September), and that Holmes had made himself master of Cabo Corso on the West African coast, and was threatening further conquests. This was too much. De Ruyter received orders to proceed to Guinea, where he speedily drove out the English intruders and reoccupied the lost settlements. During the winter both powers prepared for a struggle for maritime supremacy which had become inevitable; and at last war was declared by England (March 4, 1665).

# CHAPTER XVI

# THE LAST YEARS OF DE WITT'S ADMINISTRATION, 1665-1672. THE SECOND ENGLISH WAR. THE TRIPLE ALLIANCE. THE FRENCH INVASION

THE declaration of war in March, 1665, found the Dutch navy, thanks to the prescience and personal care of the council-pensionary, far better prepared for a struggle with the superior resources of its English rival than was the case in 1654. John de Witt, aided by his brother Cornelis, had supplied the lack of an admiral-general by urging the various Admiralty Boards to push on the building of vessels in size, construction and armaments able to contend on equal terms with the English men-of-war. He had, moreover, with his usual industry taken great pains to study the details of admiralty-administration and naval science; and now, in company with the Commissioners of the States-General, he visited all the ports and dockyards and saw that every available ship was got ready for immediate service, provided with seasoned crews, and with ample stores and equipment. The English on their side were equally ready for the encounter. After the death of Cromwell the fleet had been neglected, but during the five years that had passed since the Restoration steps had been taken to bring it to an even greater strength and efficiency than before. Whatever may have been the faults of the Stewart kings, neglect of the navy could not be laid to their charge. One of the first steps of Charles II was to appoint his brother James, Duke of York, to the post of Lord-High-Admiral; and James was unremitting in his attention to his duties, and a most capable naval administrator and leader, while Charles himself never ceased during his reign to take a keen interest in naval matters. In his case, as previously in the case of his father, it was lack of the necessary financial means that alone prevented him from creating an English fleet that would be capable of asserting that "sovereignty in the narrow seas," which was the traditional claim of the English monarchy.

The English were ready before the Dutch, who were hampered in their preparations by having five distinct Boards of Admiralty. The Duke of York put to sea with a fleet of 100 ships at the end of April and, cruising off the coast of Holland, cut off the main Dutch fleet in the Texel from the Zeeland contingent. It was unfortunate for Holland that Michael Adriansz de Ruyter, one of the greatest of seamen, was at this time still in the Mediterranean Obdam, to whom the chief command was given, waited until a storm drove the enemy to their harbours. He then united all the Dutch squadrons and crossing to Southwold Bay found the English fleet ready for battle. After some manoeuvring the action was joined on June 13, and after a bloody fight ended most disastrously for the Dutch. The flag-ships in the course of the struggle became closely engaged, with the result that Obdam's vessel suddenly blew up, while that of the English admiral was seriously damaged and he himself wounded. The Dutch line had already been broken, and the fate of their commander decided the issue. The Dutch in great confusion sought the shelter of their shoals, but their habit of firing at the masts and rigging had so crippled their opponents that a vigorous pursuit was impossible. Nevertheless the English had gained at the first encounter a decided victory. Sixteen Dutch ships were sunk or destroyed, nine captured, and at least 2000 men were killed, including three admirals, and as many more taken prisoners. The English had but one vessel sunk, and their casualties did not amount to more than a third of the Dutch losses. The consternation and anger in Holland was great. Jan Evertsen, the second-in-command, and a number of the captains were tried by court-martial; and the reorganisation of the fleet was entrusted to Cornells Tromp, who, encouraged and aided by the council-pensionary, set himself with great energy to the task.

The English meanwhile were masters of the sea, though administrative shortcomings, defects of victualling and shortage of men prevented them from taking full advantage of their success.

Early in August, however, a fleet under the Earl of Sandwich attempted to capture a number of Dutch East Indiamen, who had sailed round the north of Scotland. The East Indiamen took refuge in the neutral port of Bergen. Here Sandwich ventured to attack them but was driven off by the forts. While he was thus engaged in the north the Channel was left free; and De Ruyter with his squadron seized the opportunity to return to home-waters without opposition. His arrival was of the greatest value to the Dutch, and he was with universal approval appointed to succeed Obdam as lieutenant-admiral of Holland, and was given the supreme command on the sea. Tromp, angry at being superseded, was with difficulty induced to serve under the new chief, but he had to yield to the force of public opinion. De Ruyter at once gave proof of his skill by bringing back safely the East Indiamen from Bergen, though a severe storm caused some losses, both to the fleet and the convoy. The damage was however by the energy of De Witt and the admiral quickly repaired; and De Ruyter again sailed out at the beginning of October to seek the English fleet. He cruised in the Channel and off the mouth of the Thames, but no enemy vessels were to be seen; and at the end of the month fresh storms brought the naval campaign of 1665 to a close, on the whole to the advantage of the English.

Nor were the misfortunes of the Dutch confined to maritime warfare. Between England and Holland indeed the war was entirely a sea affair, neither of them possessing an army strong enough to land on the enemy's coast with any hope of success; but the United Provinces were particularly vulnerable on their eastern frontier, and Charles II concluded an alliance with the Bishop of Münster, who had a grievance against the States on account of a disputed border-territory, the lordship of Borkelo. Subsidised by England, the bishop accordingly at the head of 18,000 men (September, 1665) overran a considerable part of Drente and Overyssel and laid it waste. There was at first no organised force to oppose him. It had been the policy of Holland to cut down the army, and the other provinces were not unwilling to follow her example. No field-marshal had been appointed to succeed Brederode; there was no army of the Union under a captain-general, but seven small provincial armies without a military head. Some thousands of fresh troops were now raised and munitions of war collected, but to whom should the chief command be given? William Frederick was dead (October 31, 1664) and had been succeeded by his youthful son, Henry Casimir, in the Stadholderate of Friesland. Joan Maurice of Nassau had withdrawn from the Netherlands and was Governor of Cleves in the service of Brandenburg. He was however persuaded to place himself at the head of the army, though complaining bitterly of the inadequacy of the forces placed at his disposal. De Witt, however, had not been idle. He secured the assistance of Brunswick-Lüneburg, and an army of 12,000 Brunswickers under the command of George Frederick von Waldeck attacked Münster; while a force of 6000 French likewise, under the terms of the treaty of 1662, advanced to the help of the Dutch. Threatened also by Brandenburg, the bishop was compelled to withdraw his troops for home defence and in April, 1666, was glad to conclude peace with the States.

French naval co-operation against England was also promised; and war was actually declared by Louis XIV in the early spring of 1666. The real cause of this strong action was due to other motives than enmity to England. The death of Philip IV of Spain in September, 1665, had brought nearer the prospect of there being no heir-male to the vast Spanish monarchy. The French Queen, Maria Theresa, was the eldest child of Philip; and, though on her marriage she had renounced her claim to the Spanish throne, it was well known that Louis intended to insist upon her rights, particularly in regard to the Spanish Netherlands. He was afraid that the States, always suspicious of his ambitious projects, might be tempted to come to terms with England on the basis of a defensive alliance against French aggression in Flanders and Brabant, for both powers were averse to seeing Antwerp in French hands. To avert this danger Louis determined to take part in the war on the side of the Dutch. The move however was diplomatic rather than serious, for the French admiral, de Beaufort, never sailed into the North Sea or effected a junction with the Dutch fleet. Nevertheless, as will be seen, his presence in the Atlantic exercised an important effect upon the naval campaign of 1666.

The English fleet was not ready until the beginning of June. The ravages of the plague and financial difficulties had caused delay; and the fleet only numbered about eighty sail, including a squadron which had been recalled from the Mediterranean. The "Generals-at-Sea," as they were called, were Monk and Rupert.

They began by committing the great blunder of dividing their force. Rupert was detached with twenty ships to keep watch over de Beaufort, a diversion which had serious consequences for the English. The Dutch fleet, consisting of seventy-two men-of-war with twelve frigates, was the most powerful that the Admiralties had ever sent to sea, not in numbers but in the quality of the ships. De Witt himself had supervised the preparations and had seen that the equipment was complete in every respect. De Ruyter was in supreme command and led the van, Cornelis Evertsen the centre, Cornelis Tromp the rear. On June 11 the English fleet under Monk was sighted between the North Foreland and Dunkirk, and the famous Four Days' Battle was begun. The English had only fifty-four ships, but having the weather gauge Monk attacked Tromp's squadron with his whole force; nor was it till later in the day that De Ruyter and Evertsen were able to come to the relief of their colleague. Night put an end to an indecisive contest, in which both sides lost heavily. The next day Monk renewed the attack, at first with some success; but, De Ruyter having received a reinforcement of sixteen ships, the weight of numbers told and Monk was forced to retreat. On the third morning De Ruyter pursued his advantage, but the English admiral conducted his retirement in a most masterly manner, his rear squadron covering the main body and fighting stubbornly. Several ships, however, including the flagship of Vice-Admiral Ayscue, had to be abandoned and were either destroyed or captured by the Dutch. At the end of the day Monk had only twenty-eight ships left fit for service. Very opportunely he was now rejoined by Rupert's squadron and other reinforcements; and on the fourth morning the two fleets confronted one another in almost equal numbers, each having some sixty vessels. Once more therefore the desperate struggle was resumed and with initial advantage to the English. Rupert forced his way through the Dutch fleet, which was for awhile divided. But the English habit of firing at the hulls, though it did most damage, was not so effective as the Dutch system of aiming at the masts and rigging in crippling the freedom of tacking and manoeuvring; and Monk and Rupert were unable to prevent De Ruyter from re-uniting his whole force, and bearing down with it upon the enemy. The English were forced to retreat again, leaving several of their "lamed" vessels behind. They lost in all ten ships besides fireships, something like 3000 killed and wounded and 2500 prisoners. Vice-Admiral Berkeley was killed, Vice-Admiral Ayscue taken prisoner. Nor were the Dutch much better off. Four or five of their ships were sunk, a number severely damaged, and their casualty list was probably as large as that of their foes. Nevertheless the victory was undoubtedly theirs; and the fleet on its return was greeted with public rejoicings in Holland and Zeeland. The triumph was of short duration.

By vigorous efforts on both sides the damaged fleets were rapidly repaired. De Ruyter was the first to put to sea (July 9) with some ninety ships; three weeks later Monk and Rupert left the Thames with an equal force. The encounter took place on August 4. It ended in a decisive English victory after some fierce and obstinate fighting. The Dutch van, after losing its two admirals, Evertsen and De Vries, gave way. Monk and Rupert then attacked with a superior force the centre under De Ruyter himself, who to save his fleet from destruction was compelled to take refuge behind the Dutch shoals. Meanwhile the squadron under Tromp, driving before it the rear squadron of the English, had become separated and unable to come to De Ruyter's assistance. For this abandonment he was bitterly reproached by De Ruyter and accused of desertion. The quarrel necessitated Tromp's being deprived of his command, as the States-General could not afford to lose the services of the admiral-in-chief.

For a time the English were now masters of the narrow seas, and, cruising along the Dutch coast, destroyed a great number of Dutch merchantmen, made some rich prizes and even landed on the island of Terschelling, which was pillaged. Lack of supplies at length compelled them to withdraw for the purpose of revictualling. On this De Ruyter, accompanied by Cornelis de Witt as special commissioner, sailed out in the hopes of effecting a junction with De Beaufort. Rupert also put to sea again, but storms prevented a meeting between the fleets and sickness also seriously interfered with their efficiency. De Ruyter himself fell ill; and, though John de Witt was himself with the fleet, no further operations were attempted. Both sides had become weary and exhausted and anxious for peace.

To De Witt the war had been from the outset distasteful; and he had been much disturbed by the constant intrigues of the Orangist party to undermine his position. He was aware that in this hour of the country's need the eyes of a considerable part of the people, even in Holland, were more and more directed to the young prince. There was a magic in his name, which invested the untried boy with the reflected glory of his ancestor's great deeds. The council-pensionary, a past-master in the arts of expediency, was driven to avert the danger which threatened the supremacy of the States party, by proposing to the Princess Amalia that the province of Holland should not only charge themselves with William's education, but should adopt him as "a Child of State." It was a short-sighted device for, as the princess shrewdly saw, this exceptional position assigned to her grandson must ensure, when he grew to man's estate, the reversion of his ancestral dignities. She willingly assented; and in April, 1666, the Estates of Holland appointed a Commission, of which John de Witt was himself the head, which was entrusted with the religious and political instruction of the prince. A few months later De Witt was to discover that Orangist intrigues were being still clandestinely carried on. An officer of French extraction, the lord of Buat, though an Orange partisan, had been employed by the pensionary to make tentative proposals of peace to the English court through Lord Arlington. In August a packet of intercepted letters showed that Buat had played him false and was seeking to compass his overthrow. Buat was brought to trial, condemned to death, and executed on October 11.

This strong action by the council-pensionary did not prevent, however, the preliminaries of a peaceful settlement being discussed both at the Hague and in London during the winter months, with the result that a conference of delegates representing Great Britain, the United Provinces and France, met at Breda in May, 1667, to discuss the terms of peace. But the negotiations did not progress. The English envoys raised afresh all the old questions, while the Dutch were not ready to concede anything unless the Navigation Act was largely modified. In these circumstances De Witt determined by bold action to try to expedite the negotiations in a sense favourable to Holland. He knew that the English were unprepared. Charles II, in opposition to the advice of Rupert, Monk and the Duke of York, had refused to spend money in preparation for a campaign at sea, which he felt confident would never take place. The ravages of the plague and of the Great Fire of London had made the year 1666 one of the darkest in English history and had caused the heavy financial drain and losses of the war to be more severely felt. There was widespread discontent in the country; and the king in sore financial distress was immovable in his resolve that no steps should be taken for refitting the fleet. The ships remained laid up in port, although the Dutch despatched in April a squadron to the Firth of Forth and dominated the Channel.

In deep secrecy De Witt now made preparations for the despatch of a great fleet with orders to sail up the estuary of the Thames and attack the English ships in harbour. De Ruyter, accompanied by Cornelis de Witt, left the Texel on June 14, at the head of a fleet numbering more than eighty vessels. A squadron under Admiral Van Ghent sailed up the Thames on June 19, followed by the main body. Sheerness was captured, and on the 22nd De Ruyter determined to force his way up the Medway. The river had been blocked by drawing up a line of ships behind a heavy chain. The Dutch fire-ships broke through the chain and burnt the vessels, and then proceeding upwards burnt, scuttled or captured some sixteen vessels, among the latter the flag-ship, *Royal Charles*. The sound of the Dutch guns was heard in London and for a time panic reigned. But the narrowness of the river and the prompt measures that were taken to call out the militia and man the forts prevented any further success. The Dutch fleet withdrew to the Nore and, beyond blocking the mouth of the river, were able to effect no further damage. The blow to English prestige was however irreparable, and the people felt deeply humiliated that short-sightedness and lack of preparation on the part of the government should have exposed them to an insult galling to the national pride. One of its consequences, as had been anticipated by De Witt, was a more conciliatory attitude on the part of the English envoys at Breda. Peace was concluded on July 26, on terms more favourable than the Dutch could have expected. The Navigation Act was modified, various commercial advantages were conceded and Poeloe-Rum was retained. On the other hand, the custom of the striking of the flag remained unchanged. It was agreed that the English colony of Surinam, which had been captured in March, 1667, by a Zeeland squadron should be kept in exchange for New York, an exchange advantageous to both parties.

By the treaty of Breda the Dutch republic attained the summit of its greatness, and the supremacy of De Witt appeared to be not only secure but unassailable. Yet events were preparing which were destined to undermine the prosperity of Holland and the position of the statesman to whom in so large a measure that prosperity was due. France under the absolute rule of Louis XIV had become by far the most powerful State in Europe, and the king was bent upon ambitious and aggressive projects. It has already been explained that after the death of Philip IV of Spain he claimed for his queen, Maria Theresa, the succession, by the so-called "law of devolution," to a large part of the southern Netherlands. He now determined that the hour had come for enforcing his claim. In May, 1667, before the treaty of Breda had been signed, a French army of 50,000 men crossed the Belgic frontier. Castel-Rodrigo, the Spanish governor, had no force at his disposal for resisting so formidable an invasion; fortress after fortress fell into French hands; and Flanders, Brabant and Hainault were speedily overrun. This rapid advance towards their borders caused no small consternation in Holland, and De Witt's efforts to reach an understanding with King Louis proved unavailing. The States were not in a position to attempt an armed intervention, and the once formidable Spanish power was now feeble and decrepit. The only hope lay in the formation of a coalition. De Witt therefore turned to England and Sweden for help.

The anti-French party in Sweden was then predominant; and Dohna, the Swedish ambassador at the Hague, was ordered to go to London, there to further the efforts of the newly appointed Dutch envoy, John Meerman, for the formation of a coalition to check French aggrandisement. They had difficulties to overcome. The English were sore at the results of the peace of Breda. Charles disliked the Dutch and was personally indebted to Louis XIV for many favours. But the feeling in England was strongly averse to French aggression towards Antwerp. The fall of Clarendon from power at this time and the accession of Arlington, who was son-in-law to Beverweert, turned the scale in favour of the proposals of De Witt; and Charles found himself obliged to yield. Sir William Temple, whose residence as English minister at Brussels had convinced him of the gravity of the French menace, was ordered to go to the Hague to confer personally with the council-pensionary and then to proceed to London. His mission was most promptly and skilfully carried out. His persuasiveness overcame all obstacles.

After a brief stay in London he returned to the Hague, January 17, 1668. Even the proverbial slowness of the complicated machinery of the Dutch government did not hinder him from carrying out his mission with almost miraculous rapidity. Having first secured the full support of De Witt to his proposals, he next, with the aid of the council-pensionary, pressed the urgency of the case upon the States-General with such convincing arguments that the treaty between England and the United Provinces was signed on January 23. Three days afterwards Dohna was able to announce the adhesion of the Swedish government; and on January 26, the Triple Alliance was an accomplished fact. It was essentially a defensive alliance, and its main object was to offer mediation between France and Spain in order to moderate the French claims and to back up their mediation, if necessity should arise, by joint action. As a preliminary precaution, a strong force was promptly placed under the command of Joan Maurice of Nassau, and a fleet of forty-eight ships was fitted out.

These steps had their effect. Louis, suddenly confronted by this formidable coalition, preferred to accept mediation, though it involved his waiving a portion of his pretensions. Knowing well that the alliance was a very unstable one, for the consent of Charles was given under duress and the aims of Sweden were mercenary, he foresaw that by biding his time, he could have ample revenge later upon the republic of traders who had ventured to thwart him. At a meeting at St Germain-en-Laye between the French Foreign Minister, Lionne, and the Dutch and English ambassadors, Van Beuningen and Trevor, preliminaries were settled on April 15. These were confirmed by a conference of representatives of all the interested States at Aix-la-Chapelle (May 2), in which Temple took an active part. Louis gave up Franche-Comté, which he had conquered, but retained Mons, Courtrai, Tournai, Lille, Charleroi and other frontier towns. This treaty, following on that of Breda, was the crowning triumph of De Witt's administration, for it had given to the Dutch Republic a decisive voice in the Councils of the Great Powers of Europe.

But, though he had proved himself so successful in the fields of diplomacy and statesmanship, the position of the council-pensionary had, during the course of the English war, become distinctly weaker. De Witt's authoritative ways, his practical monopoly of power, and his bestowal of so many posts upon his relatives and friends, aroused considerable jealousy and irritation. Cabals began to be formed against him and old supporters to fall away. He lost the help of Van Beverningh, who resigned the office of Treasurer-General, and he managed to estrange Van Beuningen, who had much influence in Amsterdam. The Bickers and De Graeffs were no longer supreme in that city, where a new party under the leadership of Gillis Valckenier had acceded to power. This party, with which Van Beuningen now associated himself, was at present rather anti-De Witt than pro-Orange. Valckenier and Beuningen became in succession burgomasters; and De Witt's friend, Pieter de Groot, had to resign the office of pensionary. In the Estates of Holland, therefore, De Witt had to face opposition, one of the leaders being the able Pensionary of Haarlem, Caspar Fagel. And all this time he had ever before his eyes the fact that the Prince of Orange could not much longer remain "the Child of State"; and that, when he passed out of the tutelage of the Estates of Holland, his future position would have to be settled. De Witt had himself devoted much personal care to William's instruction; and the prince had submitted patiently and apparently with contentment to the restrictions with which he was surrounded. Physically weakly, his health was at all times delicate, but his intelligence was remarkable and his will-power extraordinary. Cold and impenetrable in manner and expression, unbending in his haughty aloofness, he knew how with perfect courtesy to keep his own counsel and to refrain from giving utterance to an unguarded word. But behind this chilling and sphinx-like exterior was a mind of singular precocity, already filled with deep-laid schemes and plans for the future, confident that his opportunity would come, and preparing when the hour struck to seize it. One can well imagine how anxiously in their many personal interviews the council-pensionary must have tried to read what was passing in his pupil's inmost thoughts, only to be baffled.

So early as August, 1667, steps had been taken by the Estates of Holland to forestall the danger that threatened. On the proposal of Van Beuningen and Valckenier, who had not yet detached themselves from the States party, an edict was passed to which, somewhat infelicitously, the name of the "Eternal Edict" was given. It abolished in Holland the office of stadholder for ever and affirmed the right of the town-corporations (*vroedschappen*) to elect their own magistrates. It was further resolved to invite the other provinces to declare that no stadholder could hold either the captain-or admiral-generalship of the Union. This resolution was styled the "Concept of Harmony." Deputations were sent to urge the acceptation of the Concept; and De Witt himself used his utmost power of persuasion to bring about a general agreement. He was successful in Utrecht, Gelderland and Overyssel. But Zeeland, Friesland and Groningen, where the Orangists were strong, refused to give their assent; and the approval of the States-General was only carried by a bare majority. De Witt himself doubtless knew that the erection of this paper barrier against the inherited influence of one bearing the honoured title of Prince of Orange was of little real value. It is reported that Vivien, the Pensionary of Dordrecht, De Witt's cousin, stuck his pen-knife into a copy of the Eternal Edict as it lay on the table before him, and in reply to a remonstrance said: "I was only trying what steel can do against parchment."

The second period of five years during which De Witt had held the post of council-pensionary was now drawing to an end. For a decade he had wielded a power which had given to him almost supreme authority in the republic, especially in the control of foreign affairs. But all the time he had lived the life of a simple burgher, plainly dressed, occupying the same modest dwelling-house, keeping only a single manservant. He was devotedly attached to his wife and children, and loved to spend the hours he could spare from public affairs in the domestic circle. The death of Wendela on July 1, 1668, was a great blow to him and damped the satisfaction which must have filled him at the manner in which he was reelected at the end of that month to enter upon his third period of office. In recognition of his great services his salary of 6000 guilders was doubled, and a gratuity of 45,000 guilders was voted to him, to which the nobles added a further sum of 15,000 guilders. De Witt again obtained an Act of Indemnity from the Estates of Holland and likewise the promise of a judicial post on his retirement.

The Prince of Orange had received the announcement of the passing of the Eternal Edict without showing the slightest emotion, or making any protest. He now, two months after the re-election of the council-pensionary, took the first step towards self-assertion. Under cover of a visit to his ancestral town of Breda,

William made his way to Middelburg, where the Estates of Zeeland were assembled. Being now eighteen years of age he claimed his inherited right to take his seat as "first noble," and after being duly installed he appointed his relative, Seigneur van Odijk, to act as his deputy. This done, he quietly returned to the Hague, having given a clear indication of the course he meant to pursue.

The peace of Aix-la-Chapelle had left a deep feeling of humiliation and rancour in the heart of Louis XIV; and he was resolved to leave no stone unturned to wreak his vengeance on Holland and its council-pensionary. The Triple Alliance was plainly an ill-assorted combination. Charles II cared nothing about the fate of the Spanish Netherlands, and there was a strong party in England which hated the Dutch and wished to wipe out the memory of Chatham and to upset the treaty of Breda. Grievances about the settlement of questions concerning the East Indies and Surinam were raked up. Both Van Beuningen in London and Pieter de Groot in Paris sent warnings that the States should be prepared for war and at an early date, but the council-pensionary pinned his faith on Temple and the Alliance, and kept his eyes shut to the imminent danger. Meanwhile Louis had been bribing freely both in England and Sweden, and he had no difficulty in detaching the latter power from the Alliance. To England he sent over the beautiful Henrietta, Duchess of Orleans, Charles' favourite sister, on a secret mission to the king, and she was speedily successful. The offer of an annual payment of 3,000,000 francs and the possession of Walcheren, which commanded the entrance to the Scheldt, effected their purpose. A secret treaty was signed at Dover on December 31, 1670, between Louis and Charles, by which the latter agreed, on being called upon to do so, to declare war upon Holland in conjunction with the French.

Meanwhile De Witt was so absorbed in domestic politics and in the maintenance of the burgher-aristocratic party in power, that he seemed to have lost his usual statesmanlike acumen. He never ceased to work for the general acceptance of the Concept of Harmony. At last the three recalcitrant provinces (Friesland, Groningen and Zeeland), when William had reached his twenty-first year, agreed to accept it on condition that the prince were at once admitted to the Council of State. Even now De Witt tried to prevent the prince from having more than an advisory vote, but he was overruled through the opposition of Amsterdam to his views. All this time Louis was preparing his great plan for the crushing of the republic. He succeeded in gaining the promised assistance of England, Münster and Cologne, and in detaching from the Dutch the Emperor and the Swedes. The finances under Colbert were in a flourishing state, and a splendid army had been equipped by the great war minister, Louvois. It was in vain that Pieter de Groot sent warnings of coming peril. The council-pensionary was deaf, and the States-General still deafer. Temple had left (August, 1670) for a visit to London, and he never returned. For some months there was no resident English ambassador at the Hague. Finally, at the end of the year, Downing arrived, the very man who had done his utmost to bring about the war of 1665. De Witt still placed his hopes in the anti-French views of the English Parliament; but in August, 1671, it was dissolved by the king and was not summoned to meet again for a year and a half. Charles had therefore a free-hand, and the secret treaty of Dover was the result. The reports of De Groot became more and more alarming; and De Witt found it necessary to urge the States to make preparations both by sea and land to resist attack. But he met with a luke-warm response. The fleet indeed was considerably strengthened, but the army was in a miserable state. At no time during the English wars had a powerful army been required, and the lesson taught by the invasion of the Bishop of Münster had had little effect. The heavy charges of the naval war compelled the States and especially Holland, on whom the chief burden fell, to economise by cutting down the military expenses. Politically also the ruling burgher-regents in Holland had from past experience a wholesome fear lest the power of the sword wielded by another Maurice or William II should again overthrow the civil power. The consequence was that when Charles II declared war on March 28, 1672, and Louis on the following April 6, and a great French army of 120,000 men under Condé, Turenne and Luxemburg marched through Liège to invade the States, while another army of 30,000 men from Münster and Cologne attacked farther north, all was confusion and panic, for it was felt that there was no possibility of effective resistance. The Bishop of Münster was eager to take vengeance for his defeat in 1666, and the Elector-Archbishop of Cologne was a Bavarian prince friendly to France. His help was the more valuable, as he was likewise Bishop of Liège, and thus able to offer to the French armies a free passage through his territory.

Not until the storm was actually bursting on them by sea and land at once were the various authorities in the threatened land induced to move in earnest. Confronted by the sudden crisis, De Witt however made the most strenuous efforts to meet it. A fleet of 150 ships was got ready and an army of some 50,000 men, mercenaries of many nationalities, hastily gathered together. It was a force without cohesion, discipline or competent officers. In the peril of the country all eyes were turned towards the Prince of Orange. William was now twenty-one years of age, but by the provisions of the Concept of Harmony his name was not to be proposed as captain-general until he had reached the age of twenty-two. But in the wave of feeling which swept over the country the paper barrier was dashed aside. In the Estates of Holland, which De Witt had so long controlled, and despite his strong opposition, the proposal to confer the post on William for one year was carried. All that the council-pensionary could effect was to surround the exercise of the office with so many restrictions as to deprive the prince of any real authority. These restrictions did not, however, meet the approval of the other provinces, and William himself refused to accept them. De Witt had to give way. William was appointed captain-general for one year (February 25, 1672). It appeared to be an absolutely hopeless task that this utterly inexperienced young man had to face. But the mere fact that once more a Prince of Orange was in command gave new hope. It was a name to conjure with; and the holder of it, young as he was and with no previous military training, faced his task with the calm confidence which comes from conscious power and an inherited aptitude for the leadership of men.

## CHAPTER XVII

## WAR WITH FRANCE AND ENGLAND. WILLIAM III, STADHOLDER. MURDER OF THE BROTHERS DE WITT, 1672

The advance of the French armies and those of Münster and Cologne to attack the eastern frontier of the United Provinces met with little serious resistance. Fortress after fortress fell; the line of the Yssel was abandoned. Soon the whole of Gelderland, Overyssel, Drente and Utrecht were in the possession of the enemy. Even the castle of Muiden, but ten miles from Amsterdam, was only saved from capture at the last moment by Joan Maurice throwing himself with a small force within the walls. The Prince of Orange had no alternative but to fall back behind the famous waterline of Holland. He had at his disposal, after leaving garrisons in the fortresses, barely 4000 men as a field-force. With some difficulty the people were persuaded to allow the dykes to be cut, as in the height of the struggle against Spain, and the country to be submerged. Once more behind this expanse of flood, stretching like a gigantic moat from Muiden on the Zuyder Zee to Gorkum on the Maas, Holland alone remained as the last refuge of national resistance to an overwhelming foe. True the islands of Zeeland and Friesland were yet untouched by invasion, but had Holland succumbed to the French armies their resistance would have availed little. At the end of June the aspect of affairs looked very black, and despite the courageous attitude of the young captain-general, and the ceaseless energy with which the council-pensionary worked for the equipment of an adequate fleet, and the provision of ways and means and stores, there seemed to be no ray of hope. Men's hearts failed them for fear, and a panic of despair filled the land.

Had the combined fleets of England and France been able at this moment to obtain a victory at sea and to land an army on the coast, it is indeed difficult to see how utter and complete disaster could have been avoided. Fortunately, however, this was averted. It had been De Witt's hope that De Ruyter might have been able to have struck a blow at the English ships in the Thames and the Medway before they had time to put to sea and effect a junction with the French. But the Zeeland contingent was late and it was the middle of May before the famous admiral, accompanied as in 1667 by Cornelis de Witt as the representative of the States-General, sailed at the head of seventy-five ships in search of the Anglo-French fleet. After delays through contrary winds the encounter took place in Southwold Bay on June 7. The Duke of York was the English admiral-in-chief, D'Estrées the French commander, and they had a united force of ninety ships. The Dutch, who had the wind-gauge, found the hostile squadrons separated from one another. De Ruyter at once took advantage of this. He ordered Vice-Admiral Banckers with the Zeeland squadron to contain the French, while he himself with the rest of his force bore down upon the Duke of York. The battle was contested with the utmost courage and obstinacy on both sides and the losses were heavy. The advantage, however, remained with the Dutch. The English flag-ship, the *Royal James*, was burnt; and the duke was afterwards three times compelled to shift his flag. Both fleets returned to the home ports to refit; and during the rest of the summer and early autumn no further attack was made on De Ruyter, who with some sixty vessels kept watch and ward along the coasts of Holland and Zeeland. The Dutch admiral had gained his object and no landing was ever attempted.

But the battle of Southwold Bay, though it relieved the immediate naval danger, could do nothing to stay the advancing tide of invasion on land. The situation appeared absolutely desperate; trade was at a standstill; and the rapid fall in the State securities and in the East India Company's stock gave alarming evidence of the state of public opinion. In these circumstances De Witt persuaded the States-General and the Estates of Holland to consent to the sending of two special embassies to Louis, who was now at

Doesburg, and to London, to sue for peace. They left the Hague on June 13, only to meet with a humiliating rebuff. Charles II refused to discuss the question apart from France. Pieter de Groot and his colleagues were received at Doesburg with scant courtesy and sent back to the Hague to seek for fuller powers. When they arrived they found the council-pensionary lying on a sick-bed. The country's disasters had been attributed to the De Witts, and the strong feeling against them led to a double attempt at assassination. John de Witt, while walking home at the close of a busy day's work was (June 21) attacked by four assailants and badly wounded. The leader, Jacob van der Graeff, was seized and executed; the others were allowed to escape, it was said by the prince's connivance. A few days later an attack upon Cornells de Witt at Dordrecht likewise failed to attain its object. That such dastardly acts could happen without an outburst of public indignation was ominous of worse things to come. It was a sign that the whole country had turned its back upon the States party and the whole system of government of which for nineteen years John de Witt had been the directing spirit, and had become Orangist. Revolutionary events followed one another with almost bewildering rapidity. On July 2 the Estates of Zeeland appointed William to the office of Stadholder. The Estates of Holland repealed the Eternal Edict on July 3; and on the next day it was resolved on the proposal of Amsterdam to revive the stadholdership with all its former powers and prerogatives in favour of the Prince of Orange. The other provinces followed the lead of Holland and Zeeland; and on July 8 the States-General appointed the young stadholder captain-and admiral-general of the Union. William thus found himself invested with all the offices and even more than the authority that had been possessed by his ancestors. Young and inexperienced as he was, he commanded unbounded confidence, and it was not misplaced.

Meanwhile, despite the strong opposition of Amsterdam and some other towns, the fuller powers asked for by De Groot were granted, and he returned to the camp of Louis to endeavour to obtain more favourable terms of peace. He was unsuccessful. The demands of the French king included concessions of territory to Cologne, to Münster and to England, and for himself the greater part of the Generality-lands with the great fortresses of Hertogenbosch and Maestricht, a war indemnity of 16,000,000 francs, and complete freedom for Catholic worship. On July 1 De Groot returned to the Hague to make his report. The humiliating terms were rejected unanimously, but it was still hoped that now that the Prince of Orange was at the head of affairs negotiations might be resumed through the mediation of England. William even went so far as to send a special envoy to Charles II, offering large concessions to England, if the king would withdraw from the French alliance. But it was in vain. On the contrary at this very time (July 16) the treaty between Louis and Charles was renewed; and the demands made on behalf of England were scarcely less exorbitant than those put forward by Louis himself—the cession of Sluis, Walcheren, Cadsand, Voorne and Goerce, an indemnity of 25,000,000 francs, the payment of an annual subsidy for the herring fishery, and the striking of the flag. If all the conditions made by the two kings were agreed to, the sovereignty of the remnants of the once powerful United Provinces, impoverished and despoiled, was offered to the prince. He rejected it with scorn. When the Estates of Holland on the return of De Groot asked his advice about the French terms, the stadholder replied, "all that stands in the proposal is unacceptable; rather let us be hacked in pieces, than accept such conditions"; and when an English envoy, after expressing King Charles' personal goodwill to his nephew, tried to persuade him to accept the inevitable, he met with an indignant refusal. "But don't you see that the Republic is lost," he is reported to have pleaded. "I know of one sure means of not seeing her downfall," was William's proud reply, "to die in defence of the last ditch."

The firm attitude of the prince gave courage to all; and, whatever might be the case with the more exposed provinces on the eastern and south-eastern frontiers, the Hollanders and Zeelanders were resolved to sacrifice everything rather than yield without a desperate struggle. But the fact that they were reduced to these dire straits roused the popular resentment against the De Witts and the system of government which had for more than two decades been in possession of power. Their wrath was especially directed against the council-pensionary. Pamphlets were distributed broadcast in which he was charged amongst other misdoings with appropriating public funds for his private use. While yet suffering from the effects of his wounds De Witt appeared (July 23) before the Estates and vigorously defended himself. A unanimous vote declared him free from blame.

Cornelis de Witt was, no less than his brother, an object of popular hatred. In the town of Dordrecht where the De Witt influence had been so long supreme his portrait in the Town-hall was torn to pieces by the mob and the head hung on a gallows. On July 24 he was arrested and imprisoned at the Hague on the charge brought against him by a barber named Tichelaer, of being implicated in a plot to assassinate the prince. Tichelaer was well known to be a bad and untrustworthy character. On the unsupported testimony of this man, the Ruwaard, though indignantly denying the accusation, was incarcerated in the Gevangenpoort, to be tried by a commission appointed by the Estates. Great efforts were made by his friends and by his brother to obtain his release; but, as the prince would not interfere, the proceedings had to take their course. John de Witt meanwhile, wishing to forestall a dismissal which he felt to be inevitable, appeared before the Estates on August 4, and in an impressive speech voluntarily tendered his resignation of the post of council-pensionary, asking only for the redemption of the promise made to him that at the close of his tenure of office he should receive a judicial appointment. The resignation was accepted, the request granted, but owing to opposition no vote of thanks was given. Caspar Fagel was appointed council-pensionary in his place.

The enemies of John de Witt were not content with his fall from power. A committee of six judges were empanelled to try his brother Cornelis for his alleged crime. On August 17, to their eternal disgrace, they by a majority vote ordered the prisoner, who was suffering from gout, to be put to the torture. The illustrious victim of their malice endured the rack without flinching, insisting on his absolute innocence of any plot against the prince's life. Nevertheless, early on August 19, sentence was pronounced upon him of banishment and loss of all his offices. Later on the same day Cornelis sent a message to his brother that he should like to see him. John, in spite of strong warnings, came to the Gevangenpoort and was admitted to the room where the Ruwaard, as a result of the cruel treatment he had received, was lying in bed; and the two brothers had a long conversation. Meanwhile a great crowd had gathered round the prison clamouring for vengeance upon the De Witts. Three companies of soldiers were however drawn up under the command of Count Tilly with orders from the Commissioned-Councillors to maintain order. At the same time the *schutterij*—the civic guard—was called out. These latter, however, were not to be trusted and were rather inclined to fraternise with the mob. So long as Tilly's troops were at hand, the rioters were held in restraint and no acts of violence were attempted. It was at this critical moment that verbal orders came to Tilly to march his troops to the gates to disperse some bands of marauding peasants who were said to be approaching. Tilly refused to move without a written order. It came, signed by Van Asperen, the president of the Commissioned-Councillors, a strong Orange partisan. On receiving it Tilly is said to have exclaimed, "I will obey, but the De Witts are dead men." The soldiers were no sooner gone than the crowd, under the leadership of Verhoef, a goldsmith, and Van Bankhem, a banker, forced the door of the prison (the *schutterij* either standing aloof, or actually assisting in the attack), and rushing upstairs found John de Witt sitting calmly at the foot of his brother's bed reading aloud to him a passage of Scripture. Hands were laid upon both with brutal violence; they were dragged into the street; and there with blows of clubs and repeated stabs done to death. It was 4 p.m. when Tilly departed, at 4.30 all was over, but the infuriated rabble were not content with mere murder. The bodies were shamefully mis-handled and were finally hung up by the feet to a lamppost, round which to a late hour in the evening a crowd shouted, sang and danced. It is impossible to conceive a fate more horrible or less deserved. The poor dishonoured remains were taken down when night fell by faithful hands and were at dawn in the presence of a few relatives and friends interred in the Nieuwe Kerk.

That William III had any complicity in this *execrable faict*, as it was well styled by the new council-pensionary Fagel, there is not the slightest evidence. He was absent from the Hague at the time and wholly preoccupied with the sore necessities of the military position; and it is said that he was much affected at hearing the dreadful news. But his naturally cold and self-contained nature had been hardened in the school of adversity during the long years of humiliation which had been imposed upon him by John de Witt and his party. He had endured in proud patience awaiting the hour when he could throw off the yoke, and now that it had come he could not forgive. Under the plea that the number of those implicated in the deed was so large that it was impossible to punish them and thus stir up party passions at a time when the whole energies of the nation were needed for the war, he took no steps to bring the offenders to justice. Unfortunately for his reputation he was not content with a neutral attitude, but openly protected and rewarded the three chief offenders Tichelaer, Verhoef and Van Bankhem, all of them men of disreputable character.

Thus two of the greatest statesmen and patriots that Holland has produced, John van Oldenbarneveldt and John de Witt, both perished miserably, victims of the basest national ingratitude; and it will ever remain a stain upon the national annals and upon the memory of two illustrious Princes of Orange, Maurice and William III, that these tragedies were not averted.

# CHAPTER XVIII

# THE STADHOLDERATE OF WILLIAM III, 1672-1688

In the early summer of 1672, when William resolved to concentrate all his available forces for the defence of Holland covered by its water-line, the military situation was apparently hopeless. Had Turenne and Luxemburg made a united effort to force this line at the opening of the campaign the probability is that they would have succeeded. Instead of doing so they expended their energies in the capture of a number of fortified places in Gelderland, Overyssel and North Brabant; and in the meantime the stadholder was week by week strengthening the weak points in his defences, encouraging his men, personally supervising every detail and setting an example of unshaken courage and of ceaseless industry. He had at his side, as his field-marshal, George Frederick, Count of Waldeck, an officer of experience and skill who had entered the Republic's service, and Van Beverningh as Commissioner of the States-General. With their help and counsel he had before autumn an efficient army of 57,000 men on guard behind entrenchments at all assailable points, while armed vessels patrolled the waterways. Outside the line Nijmwegen, Grave, Coevorden, Steenwijk and other smaller places had fallen; but the Münster-Cologne forces, after a siege lasting from July 9 to August 28, had to retire from Groningen. The French armies were all this time being constantly weakened by having to place garrisons in the conquered provinces; and neither Turenne nor Luxemburg felt strong enough to attack the strongly-protected Dutch frontiers behind the water-line.

The prince, however, was not content with inaction. Assuming the offensive, he ventured on a series of attacks on Naarden and on Woerden, raised the siege of Maestricht, and finally made an attempt to cut the French communications by a march upon Charleroi. All these raids were more or less failures, since in each case William had to retreat without effecting anything of importance. Nevertheless the enterprise shown by the young general had the double effect of heartening his own troops and of undermining the overweening confidence of the enemy. A hard frost in December enabled Luxemburg to penetrate into Holland, but a rapid thaw compelled a hasty withdrawal. The only road open to him was blocked by a fortified post at Nieuwerbrug, but Colonel Vin et Pain, who was in command of the Dutch force, retired to Gouda and left the French a free passage, to the stadholder's great indignation. The colonel was tried on the charge of deserting his post, and shot.

The year 1673 was marked by a decisive change for the better in the position of the States. Alarm at the rapid growth of the French power brought at last both Spanish and Austrian assistance to the hard-pressed Netherlands; and the courage and skill of De Ruyter held successfully at bay the united fleets of England and France, and effectually prevented the landing of an army on the Dutch coast. Never did De Ruyter exhibit higher qualities of leadership than in the naval campaign of 1673. His fleet was greatly inferior in numbers to the combined Anglo-French fleet under Prince Rupert and D'Estrées. A stubborn action took place near the mouth of the Scheldt on June 7, in which the English had little assistance from the French squadron and finally retired to the estuary of the Thames. Another fierce fight at Kijkduin on August 21 was still more to the advantage of the Dutch. Meanwhile on land the French had scored a real success by the capture of the great fortress of Maestricht with its garrison of 6000 men, after a siege which lasted from June 6 to July 1. All attempts, however, to pass the water-line and enter Holland met with failure; and, as the summer drew to its close, the advance of Imperial and Spanish forces began to render the position of the French precarious. William seized his opportunity in September to capture Naarden before Luxemburg could advance to its relief. He then took a bolder step. In October, at the head of an army of 25,000 men, of whom 15,000 were Spanish, he marched to Cologne and, after effecting a junction with the Imperial army, laid siege to Bonn, which surrendered on November 15. This brilliant stroke had great results. The French, fearing that their communications might be cut, withdrew from the Dutch frontier; and at the same time the Münster-Cologne forces hastily evacuated the eastern provinces. The stadholder before the end of the year entirely freed the country from its invaders. Once more a Prince of Orange had saved the Dutch Republic in its extremity.

The effect of this was to place almost supreme power in his hands. Had the prince at this moment set his heart upon obtaining the title of sovereign, he would have had but little difficulty in gratifying his ambition. Leading statesmen like the Council-Pensionary Fagel, the experienced Van Beverningh, and Valckenier, the most influential man in Amsterdam, would have supported him. But William was thoroughly practical. The freeing of the Provinces from the presence of the enemy was but the beginning of the task which he had already set before himself as his life-work, *i.e.* the overthrow of the menacing predominance of the French power under Louis XIV. His first care was the restoration of the well-nigh ruined land. The country outside the water-line had been cruelly devastated by the invaders, and then impoverished by having for a year and a half to maintain the armies of occupation. Large tracts on the borders of Holland, Utrecht and Friesland, submerged by the sea-waters through the cutting of the dams, had been rendered valueless for some years to come, while those parts of Holland and Zeeland on which the enemy had not set foot had been crushed beneath heavy taxes and the loss of commerce.

The position of the three provinces, Utrecht, Gelderland and Overyssel, which had been overrun by the French at the opening of hostilities and held by them ever since, had to be re-settled. They had, during this period, paid no taxes, and had no representation in the States-General. Holland was in favour of reducing them to the status of Generality-lands until they had paid their arrears. The prince was opposed to any harshness of treatment, and his will prevailed. The three provinces were re-admitted into the Union, but with shorn privileges; and William was elected stadholder by each of them with largely increased powers. The nomination, or the choice out of a certain number of nominees, of the members of the Town-Corporations, of the Courts of Justice and of the delegates to the States-General, was granted to him. The Dutch Republic was full of anomalies. In Utrecht, Gelderland and Overyssel we have the curious spectacle in the days of William III of the stadholder, who was nominally a servant of the Sovereign Estates, himself appointing his masters. As a matter of fact, the voice of these provinces was his voice; and, as he likewise controlled the Estates in Zeeland, he could always count upon a majority vote in the States-General in support of his foreign policy. Nor was this all.

Holland itself, in gratitude for its deliverance, had become enthusiastically Orangist. It declared the stadholdership hereditary in the male-line, and its example was followed by Zeeland, Utrecht, Gelderland and Overyssel, while the States-General in their turn made the captain-and admiral-generalship of the Union hereditary offices. Nor was gratitude confined to the conferring of powers and dignities which gave the prince in all but name monarchical authority. At the proposal of Amsterdam, the city which so often had been and was yet to be the stubborn opponent of the Princes of Orange, William II's debt of 2,000,000 fl. was taken over by the province of Holland; Zeeland presented him with 30,000 fl.; and the East India Company with a grant of 1/33 of its dividends.

From the very first William had kept steadily in view a scheme of forming a great coalition to curb the ambitious designs of Louis XIV; and for effecting this object an alliance between England and the United Provinces was essential. The first step was to conclude peace. This was not a difficult task. The English Parliament, and still more the English people, had throughout been averse from fighting on the side of the French against the Dutch. Charles II, with the help of French money, had been carrying on the war in opposition to the wishes of his subjects, who saw their fleets but feebly supported by their French allies, their trade seriously injured, and but little chance of gaining any advantageous return for the heavy cost. Charles himself had a strong affection for his nephew, and began to turn a favourable ear to his proposals for negotiations, more especially as his heroic efforts to stem the tide of French invasion had met with so much success. In these circumstances everything was favourable to an understanding; and peace was concluded at Westminster on February 19,1674. The terms differed little from those of Breda, except that the Republic undertook to pay a war indemnity of 2,000,000 fl. within three years. The striking of the flag was conceded. Surinam remained in

Dutch hands. New York, which had been retaken by a squadron under Cornelis Evertsen, August, 1673, was given back to the English crown. Negotiations were likewise opened with Münster and Cologne; and peace was concluded with Münster (April 22) and with Cologne (May 11) on the basis of the evacuation of all conquered territory. France was isolated and opposed now by a strong coalition, the Republic having secured the help of Austria, Spain, Brandenburg and Denmark. The campaign of the summer of 1674 thus opened under favouring circumstances, but nothing of importance occurred until August 11, when William at the head of an allied force of some 70,000 men encountered Condé at Seneff in Hainault. The battle was fought out with great obstinacy and there were heavy losses on both sides. The French, however, though inferior in numbers had the advantage in being a more compact force than that of the allies; and William, poorly supported by the Imperialist contingents, had to retire from the field. He was never a great strategist, but he now conducted a retreat which extracted admiration from his opponents. His talents for command always showed themselves most conspicuously in adverse circumstances. His coolness and courage in moments of peril and difficulty never deserted him, and, though a strict disciplinarian, he always retained the confidence and affection of his soldiers. On October 27 Grave was captured, leaving only one of the Dutch fortresses, Maestricht, in the hands of the French.

The war on land dragged on without any decisive results during 1675. The stadholder was badly supported by his allies and reduced to the defensive; but, though tentative efforts were made by the English government to set on foot negotiations for peace, and a growing party in Holland were beginning to clamour for the cessation of a war which was crippling their trade and draining the resources of the country, the prince was resolutely opposed to the English offer of mediation, which he regarded as insincere and premature. He was well aware that there was in England a very strong and widespread opposition to the succession of James Duke of York, who made no secret of his devoted attachment to the Roman Catholic faith. So strong was the feeling that he had been compelled to resign his post of Lord-High-Admiral. The dislike and distrust he aroused had been accentuated by his second marriage to Mary of Modena, a zealous Catholic. William was the son of the eldest daughter of Charles I, and to him the eyes of a large party in England were turning. The prince was keenly alive to the political advantages of his position. He kept himself well informed of the intrigues of the court and of the state of public opinion by secret agents, and entered into clandestine correspondence with prominent statesmen. Charles II himself, though he had not the smallest sympathy with his nephew's political views, was as kindly disposed to him as his selfish and unprincipled nature would allow, and he even went so far as to encourage in 1674 an alliance between him and his cousin Mary, the elder daughter of the Duke of York. But William had at that time no inclination for marriage. He was preoccupied with other things, and the age of Mary—she was only twelve—rendered it easy for him to postpone his final decision.

Events were to force his hand. In 1676 the French king, fearing the power of the coalition that was growing in strength, endeavoured to detach the republic by offering to make a separate peace on generous terms. Despite the opposition of the stadholder, Dutch and French representatives met at Nijmwegen; but William by his obdurate attitude rendered any settlement of the points in dispute impossible. In 1677, however, the capture of Valenciennes by the French and their decisive defeat of the allied army under William's command at Mont-Cassel (April 11) made it more difficult for him to resist the growing impatience of the burgher-class in Holland and especially of the merchants of Amsterdam at his opposition to peace. He was accused of wishing to continue the war from motives of personal ambition and the desire of military glory. In February of this year, however, Charles II after a period of personal rule was through lack of resources compelled to summon parliament. It no sooner met than it showed its strong sympathy with the Netherlands; and the king speedily saw that he could no longer pursue a policy opposed to the wishes of his people. When, therefore, William sent over his most trusted friend and counsellor, Bentinck, to London on a secret mission in the summer, he met with a most favourable reception; and the prince himself received an invitation to visit his uncle with the special object of renewing the proposal for his marriage with the Princess Mary. William accordingly arrived in London on October 19; and, the assent of the king and the Duke of York being obtained, the wedding was celebrated with almost indecent haste. It was a purely political union;

and when, early in December, the Prince and Princess of Orange set sail for Holland, the young girl wept bitterly at having to leave her home for a strange land at the side of a cold, unsympathetic husband. The weeks he spent in England had been utilised by the prince to good purpose. He persuaded Charles to promise his support by land and sea to the Netherlands in case the terms of peace offered by the allies were rejected by the French. A treaty between the States and Great Britain giving effect to this promise was actually signed on January 29, 1678. The results, however, did not answer William's expectations. The English Parliament and the States alike had no trust in King Charles, nor was the English match at first popular in Holland. A strong opposition arose against the prince's war policy. The commercial classes had been hard hit by the French invasion, and they were now suffering heavy losses at sea through the Dunkirk privateers led by the daring Jean Bart. The peace party included such tried and trusted statesmen as Van Beverningh, Van Beuningen and the Council-Pensionary Fagel, all of them loyal counsellors of the stadholder. So resolute was the attitude of Amsterdam that the leaders of both municipal parties, Valckenier and Hooft, were agreed in demanding that the French offers of a separate peace should be accepted. On the same side was found Henry Casimir, Stadholder of Friesland, who was jealous of his cousin's autocratic exercise of authority.

The *pourparlers* at Nijmwegen were still going on, but made no progress in face of William's refusal to treat except in concert with his allies. Louis XIV, however, fully informed of the state of public opinion and of the internal dissensions both in the United Provinces and in England, was not slow to take advantage of the situation. A powerful French army invaded Flanders and made themselves masters of Ypres and Ghent and proceeded to besiege Mons. William, despite the arrival of an English auxiliary force under Monmouth, could do little to check the enemy's superior forces. Meanwhile French diplomacy was busy at Amsterdam and elsewhere in the States, working against the war parties; and by the offer of favourable terms the States-General were induced to ask for a truce of six weeks. It was granted, and the Dutch and Spanish representatives at Nijmwegen (those of the emperor, of Brandenburg and of Denmark refusing to accede) speedily agreed to conclude peace on the following terms: the French to restore

Maestricht and to evacuate all occupied Dutch territory, and to make a commercial treaty. Spain to surrender an important slice of southern Flanders, but to be left in possession of a belt of fortresses to cover their Netherland possessions against further French attack. But, though these conditions were accepted, the French raised various pretexts to delay the signature of the treaty, hoping that meanwhile Mons, which was closely beleaguered by Luxemburg, might fall into their hands, and thus become an asset which they could exchange for some other possession. The States and the Spanish Government were both anxious to avoid this; and the Prince of Orange, who steadily opposed the treaty, returned towards the end of July to his camp to watch the siege of Mons and prevent its falling into the hands of the enemy. At the same time (July 26) King Charles, who had been working through Sir William Temple for the conclusion of peace, now declared that, unless the treaty was signed before August 11, he would assist the allies to enforce it. The French diplomatists at Nijmwegen had hitherto declared that their troops would not evacuate Maestricht and the other places which they had agreed to restore to the States, until Brandenburg and Denmark had evacuated the territory they had conquered from Sweden. On August 10, just before time for resuming hostilities had been reached, they tactfully conceded this point and promised immediate evacuation, if the treaty were at once concluded. Van Beverningh and his colleagues accordingly, acting on their instructions, affixed their signatures just before midnight.

They fell into the trap laid for them, for the treaty between France and Spain was not yet signed, and it was the intention of the French to make further pretexts for delay in the hope that Mons meanwhile would fall. The report of the conclusion of peace reached the stadholder in his camp on August 13, but unofficially. On the morning of August 14 D'Estrades came personally to bring the news to Luxemburg; and the French marshal was on the point of forwarding the message to the Dutch camp, when he heard that Orange was advancing with his army to attack him, and he felt that honour compelled him to accept the challenge. A sanguinary fight took place at St Denis, a short distance from Mons. William exposed his life freely, and though the result was nominally a drawn battle, he achieved his purpose. Luxemburg raised the siege of Mons, and the negotiations with Spain were pressed forward. The treaty was signed on September 17, 1678. The peace of Nijmwegen thus brought hostilities to an end, leaving the United Provinces in possession of all their territory. It lasted ten years, but it was only an armed truce. Louis XIV desired a breathing space in which to prepare for fresh aggressions; and his tireless opponent, the Prince of Orange, henceforth made it the one object of his life to form a Grand Alliance to curb French ambition and uphold in Europe what was henceforth known as "the Balance of Power."

In setting about this task William was confronted with almost insuperable difficulties. The Dutch people generally had suffered terribly in the late invasions and were heartily sick of war. The interest of the Hollanders and especially of the Amsterdammers was absorbed in the peaceful pursuits of commerce. The far-reaching plans and international combinations, upon which William concentrated his whole mind and energies, had no attraction for them, even had they understood their purpose and motive. The consequence was that the prince encountered strong opposition, and this not merely in Holland and Amsterdam, but from his cousin Henry Casimir and the two provinces of which he was stadholder. In Amsterdam the old "States" party revived under the leadership of Valckenier and Hooft; and in his latter days Van Beuningen was ready to resist to the utmost any considerable outlay on the army or navy or any entangling alliances. They held that it was the business of the Republic to attend to its own affairs and to leave Louis to pursue his aggressive policy at the expense of other countries, so long as he left them alone. The ideal which William III had set before him was the exact reverse of this; and, unfortunately for his own country, throughout his life he often subordinated its particular interests to the wider European interests which occupied his attention.

The work of building up afresh a coalition to withstand the ever-growing menace of the formidable French power could scarcely have been more unpromising than it now appeared. Spain was utterly exhausted and feeble. Brandenburg and Denmark had been alienated by the States concluding a separate peace at Nijmwegen and leaving them in the lurch. The attention of the emperor was fully occupied in defending Hungary and Vienna itself against the Turks. England under Charles II was untrustworthy and vacillating, almost a negligible quantity. A visit made by William to London convinced him that nothing was at present to be hoped for from that quarter. At the same time the very able French ambassador at the Hague, D'Avaux, did his utmost to foment the divisions and factions in the Provinces. He always insisted that he was accredited to the States-General and not to the Prince of Orange, and carried on correspondence and intrigues with the party in Amsterdam opposed to the stadholder's anti-French policy. The cumbrous and complicated system of government enabled him thus to do much to thwart the prince and to throw obstacles in his way. The curious thing is, that William was so intent on his larger projects that he was content to use the powers he had without making any serious attempt, as he might have done, to make the machine of government more workable by reforms in the direction of centralisation. Immersed in foreign affairs, he left the internal administration in the hands of subordinates chosen rather for their subservience than for their ability and probity; and against several of them, notably against his relative Odijk, serious charges were made. Odijk, representing the prince as first noble in Zeeland, had a large patronage; and he shamelessly enriched himself by his venal traffic in the disposal of offices without a word of rebuke from William, in whose name he acted. On the contrary, he continued to enjoy his favour. Corruption was scarcely less rife in Holland, though no one practised it quite on the same scale as Odijk in Zeeland. William indeed cared little about the domestic politics of the Republic, except in so far as they affected his diplomatic activities; and in this domain he knew how to employ able and devoted men. He had Waldeck at his side not merely as a military adviser, but as a skilful diplomatist well versed in the intricate politics of the smaller German states; Everhard van Weede, lord of Dijkveld, and Godard van Rheede, lord of Amerongen, proved worthy successors of Van Beverningh and Van Beuningen. Through the Council-Pensionary Fagel he was able to retain the support of the majority in the Estates of Holland, despite the strong opposition he encountered at Amsterdam and some other towns, where the interests of commerce reigned supreme. The death of Gillis Valckenier, the ablest of the leaders of the opposition in Amsterdam, in 1680 left the control of affairs in that city in the hands of Nicolaes Witsen and Johan Hudde, but these were men of less vigour and determination than Valckenier.

Louis XIV meanwhile had been actively pushing forward his schemes of aggrandisement. Strasburg was seized in August, 1681; Luxemburg was occupied; claims were made under the treaty of Nijmwegen to certain portions of Flanders and Brabant, and troops were despatched to take possession of them. There was general alarm; and, with the help of Waldeck, William was able to secure the support of a number of the small German states in the Rhenish circle, most of them always ready to hire out their armed forces for a subsidy. Sweden also offered assistance. But both England and Brandenburg were in secret collusion with France, and the emperor would not move owing to the Turkish menace.

In these circumstances Spain was compelled (1684) by the entry of the armies of Louis into the southern Netherlands to declare war upon France, and called upon the States for their military aid of 8000 men in accordance with the terms of the treaty of Nijmwegen. Orange at once referred the matter to the Council of State, and himself proposed that 16,000 should be sent. As this, however, could only mean a renewal of the war with France, the proposal met with strong opposition in many quarters, and especially in Amsterdam. Prosperity was just beginning to revive, and a remembrance of past experiences filled the hearts of many with dread at the thought of the French armies once more invading their land. The Amsterdam regents even went so far as to enter into secret negotiations with D'Avaux; and they were supported by Henry Casimir, who was always ready to thwart his cousin's policy. William was checkmated and at first, in his anger, inclined to follow his father's example and crush the opposition of Amsterdam by force. He possessed however, which William II had not, the support of a majority in the Estates of Holland. He used this with effect. The raising of the troops was sanctioned by the Estates (January 31, 1684), an intercepted cipher-letter from D'Avaux being skilfully used to discredit the Amsterdam leaders, who were accused of traitorous correspondence with a foreign power. Nevertheless the prince, although he was able to override any active opposition at home, did not venture, so long as England and Brandenburg were on friendly relations with France, to put pressure upon the States-General. The French troops, to the prince's chagrin, overran Flanders; and he had no alternative but to concur in the truce for twenty years concluded at Ratisbon, August 15, 1684, which left the French king in possession of all his conquests.

No more conclusive proof of the inflexible resolve of William III can be found than the patience he now exhibited. His faith in himself was never shaken, and his patience in awaiting the favourable moment was inexhaustible. To him far more appropriately than to his great-grandfather might the name of William the Silent have been given. He had no confidants, except Waldeck and William Bentinck; and few could even guess at the hidden workings of that scheming mind or at the burning fires of energy and will-power beneath the proud and frigid reserve of a man so frail in body and always ailing. Very rarely could a born leader of men have been more unamiable or less anxious to win popular applause, but his whole demeanour inspired confidence and, ignoring the many difficulties and oppositions which thwarted him, he steadfastly bided his time and opportunity. It now came quickly, for the year 1685 was marked by two events—the accession of James II to the throne of England, and the Revocation of the Edict of Nantes—which were to have far-reaching consequences.

The new King of England was not merely a strong but a bigoted Roman Catholic. Had he been a wise and patriotic prince, he would have tried by a studiously moderate policy to win the loyal allegiance of his subjects, but he was stubborn, wrong-headed and fanatical, and from the first he aimed at the impossible. His attempts to establish absolute rule, to bring back the English nation to the fold of the Catholic Church and, as a means to that end, to make himself independent of Parliament by accepting subsidies from the French king, were bound to end in catastrophe. This was more especially the case as Louis XIV had, at the very time of King James' accession, after having for a number of years persecuted the Huguenots in defiance of the Edict of Nantes, taken the step of revoking that great instrument of religious toleration on November 17, 1685. The exile of numerous families, who had already been driven out by the *dragonnades*, was now followed by the expulsion of the entire Huguenot body, of all at least who refused to conform to the Catholic faith. How many hundreds of thousands left their homes to find refuge in foreign lands it is impossible to say, but amongst them were great numbers of industrious and skilled artisans and handicraftsmen, who sought asylum in the Dutch Republic and there found a ready and sympathetic welcome. The arrival of these unhappy immigrants had the effect of arousing a strong feeling of indignation in Holland, and indeed throughout the provinces, against the government of Louis XIV. They began to see that the policy of the French king was not merely one of territorial aggression, but was a crusade against Protestantism. The governing classes in Holland, Zeeland, Friesland and Groningen were stirred up by the preachers to enforce more strictly the laws against the Catholics in those provinces, for genuine alarm was felt at the French menace to the religion for which their fathers had fought and suffered. The cause of Protestantism was one with which the Princes of Orange had identified themselves; but none of his ancestors was so keen an upholder of that cause as was William III. The presence in their midst of the Huguenot refugees had the effect of influencing public opinion powerfully in the States in favour of their stadholder's warlike policy. Nor was the Dutch Republic the only State which was deeply moved by the ruthless treatment of his Protestant subjects by the French king. The Elector of Brandenburg, as head of the principal Protestant State in Germany, had also offered an asylum to the French exiles and now reverted once more to his natural alliance with the United Provinces. He sent his trusted councillor, Paul Fuchs, in May, 1685, to offer to his nephew, the Prince of Orange, his friendly co-operation in the formation of a powerful coalition against France. Fuchs was a skilled diplomatist, and by his mediation an understanding was arrived at between the stadholder and his opponents in Amsterdam. At the same time strong family influence was brought to bear upon Henry Casimir of Friesland, and a reconciliation between the two stadholders was effected. William thus found himself, before the year 1685 came to an end, able to pursue his policy without serious let or hindrance. He was quite ready to seize his opportunity, and by tactful diplomacy he succeeded by August, 1686, in forming an alliance between the United Provinces, Brandenburg, Sweden, Austria, Spain and a number of the smaller Rhenish states, to uphold the treaties of Westphalia and Nijmwegen against the encroachments of French military aggression. But the design of William was still incomplete. The naval power and financial resources of England were needed to enable the coalition to grapple successfully with the mighty centralised power of Louis XIV.

In England the attempt of James II to bring about a Catholic reaction by the arbitrary use of the royal prerogative was rapidly alienating the loyalty of all classes, including many men of high position, and even some of his own ministers. William watched keenly all that was going on and kept himself in close correspondence with several of the principal malcontents. He was well aware that all eyes were turning to him (and he accepted the position) as the natural defender, should the need arise, of England's civil and religious liberties. The need arose and the call came in the summer of 1688, and it found William prepared. The climax of the conflict between King James and his people was reached with the acquittal of the Seven Bishops in May, 1688, amidst public rejoicings, speedily followed on June 10 by the birth of a Prince of Wales. The report was spread that the child was supposititious and it was accepted as true by large numbers of persons, including the Princess Anne, and also, on the strength of her testimony, by the Prince and Princess of Orange.

The secret relations of William with the leaders of opposition had for some time been carried on through his trusted confidants, Dijkveld, the State's envoy at the English Court, and William of Nassau, lord of Zuilestein. A bold step was now taken. Several Englishmen of note signed an invitation to the prince to land in England with an armed force in defence of the religion and liberties of the country; and it was brought to him by Admiral Russell, one of the signatories. After some hesitation William, with the consent and approval of the princess, decided to accept it. No man ever had a more loyal and devoted wife than William III of Orange, and he did not deserve it. For some years after his marriage he treated Mary with coldness and neglect. He confessed on one occasion to Bishop Burnet that his churlishness was partly due to jealousy; he could not bear the thought that Mary might succeed to the English throne and he would in that country be inferior in rank to his wife. The bishop informed the princess, who at once warmly declared that she would never accept the crown unless her husband received not merely the title of king, but the prerogatives of a reigning sovereign. From that time forward a complete reconciliation took place between them, and the affection and respect of William for this loyal, warm-hearted and self-sacrificing woman deepened as the years went on. Mary's character, as it is revealed in her private diaries, which have been preserved, deserves those epithets. Profoundly religious and a convinced Protestant, Mary with prayers for guidance and not without many tears felt that the resolve of her husband to hazard all on armed intervention in England was fully justified; and at this critical juncture she had no hesitation in allowing her sense of duty to her husband and her country to override that of a daughter to her father. Already in July vigorous preparations in all secrecy began to be made for the expedition. The naval yards were working at full pressure with the ostensible object of sending out a fleet to suppress piracy in the Mediterranean. The stadholder felt that he was able to rely upon the willing co-operation of the States in his project. His difficulty now, as always, was to secure the assent of Amsterdam. But the opposition of that city proved less formidable than was anticipated. The peril to Protestantism should England under James II be leagued with France, was evident, and scarcely less the security of the commerce on which Amsterdam depended for its prosperity. The support of Amsterdam secured that of the Estates of Holland; and finally, after thus surmounting successfully the elements of opposition in the town and the province, where the anti-Orange party was most strongly represented, the prince had little difficulty in obtaining, on October 8, the unanimous approval of the States-General, assembled in secret session, to the proposed expedition. By that time an army of 14,000 men had been gathered together and was encamped at Mook. Of these the six English and Scottish regiments, who now, as throughout the War of Independence, were maintained in the Dutch service, formed the nucleus. The force also comprised the prince's Dutch guards and other picked Dutch troops, and also some German levies. Marshal Schomberg was in command. The pretext assigned was the necessity of protecting the eastern frontier of the Republic against an attack from Cologne, where Cardinal Fürstenberg, the nominee and ally of Louis XIV, had been elected to the archiepiscopal throne.

Meanwhile diplomacy was active. D'Avaux was far too clear-sighted not to have discerned the real object of the naval and military preparations, and he warned both Louis XIV and James II. James, however, was obdurate and took no heed, while Louis played his enemy's game by declaring war on the Emperor and the Pope, and by invading the Palatinate instead of the Republic.

For William had been doing his utmost to win over to his side, by the agency of Waldeck and Bentinck, the Protestant Princes of Germany, with the result that Brandenburg, Hanover, Saxony, Brunswick and Hesse had undertaken to give him active support against a French attack; while the constant threat against her possessions in the Belgic Netherlands compelled Spain to join the anti-French league which the stadholder had so long been striving to bring into existence. To these were now added the Emperor and the Pope, who, being actually at war with France, were ready to look favourably upon an expedition which would weaken the common enemy. The Grand Alliance of William's dreams had thus (should his expedition to England prove successful) come within the range of practical politics; and with his base secured Orange now determined to delay no longer, but to stake everything upon the issue of the English venture.

The prince bade farewell to the States-General on October 26, and four days later he set sail from Helvoetsluis, but was driven back by a heavy storm, which severely damaged the fleet. A fresh start was made on November 11. Admiral Herbert was in command of the naval force, which convoyed safely through the Channel without opposition the long lines of transports. Over the prince's vessel floated his flag with the words *Pro Religione et Libertate* inscribed above the motto of the House of Orange, *Je maintiendray*. Without mishap a landing was effected at Torbay, November 14 (5 o.s.), which was William's birthday, and a rapid march was made to Exeter. He met with no armed resistance. James' troops, his courtiers, his younger daughter the Princess Anne, all deserted him; and finally, after sending away his wife and infant son to France, the king himself left his palace at Whitehall by night and fled down the river to Sheerness. Here he was recognised and brought back to London. It was thought, however, best to connive at his escape, and he landed on the coast of France at Christmas. The expedition had achieved its object and William, greeted as a deliverer, entered the capital at the head of his army.

On February 13, 1689, a convention, specially summoned for the purpose, declared that James by his flight had vacated the throne; and the crown was offered to William and Mary jointly, the executive power being placed in the hands of the prince.

# CHAPTER XIX

# THE KING-STADHOLDER, 1688-1702

The accession of William III to the throne of England was an event fraught with important consequences to European politics and to the United Provinces. The king was enabled at last to realise the formation of that Grand Alliance for which he had so long been working. The treaty of Vienna, signed on May 12, 1689, encircled France with a ring of enemies, and saw the Emperor and Spain united with the Protestant powers, England, the States and many of the German princes in a bond of alliance for the maintenance of the treaties of Westphalia and the Pyrenees. It was not without some difficulty that William succeeded in inducing the States to enter into an offensive and defensive alliance with England. A special embassy consisting of Witsen, Odijk, Dijkveld and others was sent to London early in 1689 to endeavour to bring about some mutually advantageous arrangement of the various conflicting maritime and commercial interests of the two countries. But they could effect nothing. The English government refused either to repeal or modify the Navigation Act or to reduce the toll for fishing privileges; and it required all the personal influence of William to secure the signing of a treaty (September 3), which many leading Hollanders considered to be a subordinating of Dutch to English interests. And they were right; from this time began that decline of Dutch commercial supremacy which was to become more and more marked as the 18th century progressed. The policy of William III, as Frederick the Great remarked most justly, placed Holland in the position of a sloop towed behind the English ship-of-the-line.

The carrying trade of the world was still, however, in the reign of William III practically in the hands of the Dutch, despite the losses that had been sustained during the English wars and the French invasion. The only competitor was England under the shelter of the Navigation Act. The English had, under favourable conditions, their staple at Dordrecht, the Scots their staple at Veere; and the volume of trade under the new conditions of close alliance was very considerable. But the imports largely exceeded the exports; and both exports and imports had to be carried in English bottoms. The Baltic (or Eastern) trade remained a Dutch monopoly, as did the trade with Russia through Archangel. Almost all the ships that passed through the Sound were Dutch; and they frequented all the Baltic ports, whether Russian, Scandinavian or German, bringing the commodities of the South and returning laden with hemp, tallow, wood, copper, iron, corn, wax, hides and other raw products for distribution in other lands. The English had a small number of vessels in the Mediterranean and the Levant, and frequented the Spanish and Portuguese harbours, but as yet they hardly interfered with the Dutch carrying-trade in those waters. The whole trade of Spain with her vast American dominions was by law restricted to the one port of Cadiz; but no sooner did the galleons bringing the rich products of Mexico and Peru reach Cadiz than the bulk of their merchandise was quickly transhipped into Dutch vessels, which here, as elsewhere, were the medium through which the exchange of commodities between one country and another was effected. It was a profitable business, and the merchants of Amsterdam and of the other Dutch commercial centres grew rich and prospered.

The position of the Dutch in the East Indies at the close of the 17th century is one of the marvels of history. The East India Company, with its flourishing capital at Batavia, outdistanced all competitors. It was supreme in the Indian archipelago and along all the shores washed by the Indian Ocean. The governor-general was invested with great powers and, owing to his distance from the home authority, was able to make unfettered use of them during his term of office. He made treaties and conducted wars and was looked upon by the princes and petty rulers of the Orient as a mighty potentate. The conquest of Macassar in 1669, the occupation of Japara and Cheribon in 1680, of Bantam in 1682, of Pondicherry in 1693, together with the possession of Malacca and of the entire coast of Ceylon, of the Moluccas, and of the Cape of Good Hope, gave to the Dutch the control of all the chief avenues of trade throughout those regions. By treaties of alliance and commerce with the Great Mogul and other smaller sovereigns and chieftains factories were established at Hooghly on the Ganges, at Coelim, Surat, Bender Abbas, Palembang and many other places. In the Moluccas they had the entire spice trade in their hands. Thus a very large part of the products of the Orient found its way to Europe by way of Amsterdam, which had become increasingly the commercial emporium and centre of exchange for the world.

The West India Company, on the other hand, had been ruined by the loss of its Brazilian dominion followed by the English wars. Its charter came to an end in 1674, but it was replaced by a new Company on a more moderate scale. Its colonies on the Guiana coast, Surinam, Berbice and Essequibo were at the end of the 17th century in an impoverished condition, but already beginning to develop the sugar plantations which were shortly to become a lucrative industry; and the island of Curaçoa had the unenviable distinction of being for some years one of the chief centres of the negro slave trade.

In the United Provinces themselves one of the features of this period was the growth of many new industries and manufactures, largely due to the influx of Huguenot refugees, many of whom were skilled artisans. Not only did the manufacturers of cloth and silk employ a large number of hands, but also those of hats, gloves, ribbons, trimmings, laces, clocks and other articles, which had hitherto been chiefly produced in France. One of the consequences of the rapid increase of wealth was a change in the simple habits, manners and dress, which hitherto travellers had noted as one of the most remarkable characteristics of the Hollanders. Greater luxury began to be displayed, French fashions and ways of life to be imitated, and the French language to be used as the medium of intercourse among the well-to-do classes. Another sign of the times was the spread of the spirit of speculation and of gambling in stocks and shares, showing that men were no longer content to amass wealth by the slow process of ordinary trade and commerce. This state of prosperity, which was largely due to the security which the close alliance with England brought to the Republic, explains in no small measure the acquiescence of the Dutch in a state of things which made the smaller country almost a dependency of the larger. They were proud that their stadholder should reign as king in Britain; and his prolonged absences did not diminish their strong attachment to him or lessen his authority among them. So much greater indeed was the power exercised by William in the Republic than that which, as a strictly constitutional sovereign, he possessed in the kingdom, that it was wittily said that the Prince of Orange was stadholder in England and king in Holland.

It must not be supposed, however, that William in his capacity as stadholder was free from worries and trials. He had many; and, as usual, Amsterdam was the chief centre of unrest. After the expedition set sail for Torbay, William was continuously absent for no less than two and a half years. It is no wonder therefore that during so long a period, when the attention of the king was absorbed by other pressing matters, difficulties should have arisen in his administration of the affairs of the Republic. It was very unfortunate that his most able and trusted friend and adviser, the Council-Pensionary Fagel, should have died, in December, 1688, just when William's enterprise in England had reached its most critical stage. Fagel was succeeded, after a brief interval, in his most important and influential office by Antony Heinsius. Heinsius, who had been for some years Pensionary of Delft, was a modest, quiet man, already forty-five years of age, capable, experienced and business-like. His tact and statesmanlike qualities were of the greatest service to William and scarcely less to his country, at a time when urgent duties in England made it so difficult for the stadholder to give personal attention to the internal affairs of the Republic. No other Prince of Orange had ever so favourable an opportunity as William III for effecting such changes in the system of government and administration in the Dutch Republic as would simplify and co-ordinate its many rival and conflicting authorities, and weld its seven sovereign provinces into a coherent State with himself (under whatever title) as its "eminent head." At the height of his power his will could have over-ridden local or partisan opposition, for he had behind him the prestige of his name and deeds and the overwhelming support of popular opinion. But William had little or no interest in these constitutional questions. Being childless, he had no dynastic ambitions. The nearest male representative of his house was Henry Casimir, the stadholder of Friesland, with whom his relations had been far from friendly. In his mind, everything else was subordinate to the one and overruling purpose of his life, the overthrow of the power of Louis XIV and of French ascendancy in Europe.

The great coalition which had been formed in 1689 by the treaty of Vienna was, in the first years of the war which then broke out, attended with but mediocre success. The French armies laid waste the Palatinate with great barbarity, and then turned their attentions to the southern Netherlands. The attempted invasion was, however, checked by an allied force (August 25) in a sharp encounter near Charleroi. The next year, 1690, was particularly unfortunate for the allies. William was still absent, having been obliged to conduct an expedition to Ireland. He had placed the aged Marshal Waldeck in command of the Coalition forces. Waldeck had the redoubtable Luxemburg opposed to him and on July 1 the two armies met at Fleurus, when, after a hard-fought contest, the allies suffered a bloody defeat. An even greater set-back was the victory gained by Admiral Tourville over the combined Anglo-Dutch fleet off Beachy Head (July 10). The Dutch squadron under Cornelis Evertsen bore the brunt of the fight and suffered heavily. They received little help from the English contingent; and the English Admiral Torrington was accused of having wilfully sacrificed his allies. The effect was serious, for the French enjoyed for a while the rare satisfaction of holding the command of the Channel. The complete triumph of King William at the battle of the Boyne (July 12) relieved somewhat the consternation felt at this naval disaster, and set him free to devote his whole attention to the Continental war. His return to the Hague early in 1691 caused general rejoicing, and he was there able to concert with his allies the placing of a large force in the field for the ensuing campaign. The operations were, however, barren of any satisfactory results. Luxemburg advanced before the allies were ready, and burnt and plundered a large tract of country. William, acting on the defensive, contented himself with covering the capital and the rest of Flanders and Brabant from attack; and no pitched battle took place.

Great preparations were made by Louis XIV in the spring of 1692 for the invasion of England. Troops were collected on the coast, and the squadron under D'Estrées at Toulon was ordered to join the main fleet of Tourville at Brest. Contrary winds delayed the junction; and Tourville rashly sailed out and engaged off La Hogue a greatly superior allied fleet on May 29. The conflict this time chiefly fell upon the English, and after a fierce fight the French were defeated and fled for refuge into the shoal waters. Here they were followed by the lighter vessels and fire-ships of the allies; and the greater part of the French fleet was either burnt or driven upon the rocks (June 1). The maritime power of France was for the time being destroyed, and all fears of invasion dissipated. On land ill-success continued to dog the footsteps of the allies. The strong fortress of Namur was taken by the French; and, after a hotly contested battle at Steinkirk, William was compelled by his old adversary Luxemburg to retreat. William, though he was rarely victorious on the field of battle, had great qualities as a leader. His courage and coolness won the confidence of his troops, and he was never greater than in the conduct of a retreat. This was shown conspicuously in the following year (1693), when, after a disastrous defeat at Neerwinden (July 29), again at the hands of Luxemburg, he succeeded at imminent personal risk in withdrawing his army in good order in face of the superior forces of the victorious enemy.

In 1694 the allies confined themselves to defensive operations. Both sides were growing weary of war; and there were strong parties in favour of negotiating for peace both in the Netherlands and in England. Some of the burgher-regents of Amsterdam, Dordrecht and other towns even went so far as to make secret overtures to the French government, and they had the support of the Frisian Stadholder; but William was resolutely opposed to accepting such conditions as France was willing to offer, and his strong will prevailed.

The position of the king in England was made more difficult by the lamented death of Queen Mary on January 2,1695. William had become deeply attached to his wife during these last years, and for a time he was prostrated by grief. But a strong sense of public duty roused him from his depression; and the campaign of 1695 was signalised by the most brilliant military exploit of his life, the recapture of Namur. That town, strong by its natural position, had been fortified by Vauban with all the resources of engineering skill, and was defended by a powerful garrison commanded by Marshal Boufflers. But William had with him the famous Coehoorn, in scientific siege-warfare the equal of Vauban himself. At the end of a month the town of Namur was taken, but Boufflers withdrew to the citadel. Villeroy, at the head of an army of 90,000 men, did his utmost to compel the king to raise the siege by threatening Brussels; but a strong allied force watched his movements and successfully barred his approach to Namur. At last, on September 5, Boufflers capitulated after a gallant defence on the condition that he and his troops should march out with all the honours of war.

The campaign of 1696 was marked by no event of importance; indeed both sides were thoroughly tired out by the protracted and inconclusive contest. Moreover the failing health of Charles II of Spain threatened to open out at any moment the vital question of the succession to the Spanish throne. Louis XIV, William III and the emperor were all keenly alive to the importance of the issue, and wished to have their hands free in order to prepare for a settlement, either by diplomatic means or by a fresh appeal to arms. But peace was the immediate need, and overtures were privately made by the French king to each of the allied powers in 1696. At last it was agreed that plenipotentiaries from all the belligerents should meet in congress at Ryswyck near the Hague with the Swedish Count Lilienrot as mediator. The congress was opened on May 9, 1697, but many weeks elapsed before the representatives of the various powers settled down to business. Heinsius and Dijkveld were the two chief Dutch negotiators. The emperor, when the other powers had come to terms, refused to accede; and finally England, Spain and the United Provinces determined to conclude a separate peace. It was signed on September 20 and was based upon the treaties of Nijmwegen and Münster. France, having ulterior motives, had been conciliatory. Strasburg was retained, but most of the French conquests were given up. William was recognised as King of England, and the Principality of Orange was restored to him. With the Dutch a commercial treaty was concluded for twenty-five years on favourable terms.

It was well understood, however, by all the parties that the peace of Ryswyck was a truce during which the struggle concerning the Spanish Succession would be transferred from the field of battle to the field of diplomacy, in the hope that some solution might be found. The question was clearly of supreme importance to the States, for it involved the destiny of the Spanish Netherlands. England, too, had great interests at stake, and was determined to prevent the annexation of the Belgic provinces by France. With Charles II the male line of the Spanish Habsburgs became extinct;

and there were three principal claimants in the female line of succession. The claim of the Dauphin was much the strongest, for he was the grandson of Anne of Austria, Philip III's eldest daughter, and the son of Maria Theresa of Austria, Charles II's eldest sister. But both these queens of France had on their marriage solemnly renounced their rights of succession. Louis XIV, however, asserted that his wife's renunciation was invalid, since the dowry, the payment of which was guaranteed by the marriage contract, had never been received. The younger sister of Maria Theresa had been married to the emperor; and two sons and a daughter had been the fruit of the union. This daughter in her turn had wedded the Elector of Bavaria, and had issue one boy of ten years. The Elector himself, Maximilian Emmanuel, had been for five years Governor of the Spanish Netherlands, where his rule had been exceedingly popular. William knew that one of the chief objects of the French king in concluding peace was to break up the Grand Alliance and so prepare the way for a masterful assertion of his rights as soon as the Spanish throne was vacant; and with patient diplomatic skill he set to work at once to arrange for such a partition of the Spanish monarchy among the claimants as should prevent the Belgic provinces from falling into the hands of a first-class power and preserve Spain itself with its overseas possessions from the rule of a Bourbon prince. He had no difficulty in persuading the States to increase their fleet and army in case diplomacy should fail, for the Dutch were only too well aware of the seriousness of the French menace to their independence. In England, where jealousy of a standing army had always been strong, he was less successful, and Parliament insisted on the disbanding of many thousands of seasoned troops. The object at which William aimed was a partition treaty; and a partition was actually arranged (October 11, 1698). This arrangement, according to the ideas of the time, paid no respect whatever to the wishes of the peoples, who were treated as mere pawns by these unscrupulous diplomatists. The Spanish people, as might be expected, were vehemently opposed to any partition of the empire of Charles V and Philip II; and, in consequence of the influences that were brought to bear upon him, Charles II left by will the young electoral prince, Joseph Ferdinand, heir to his whole inheritance. By the secret terms of the partition treaty the crown of Spain together with the Netherlands and the

American colonies had been assigned to the Bavarian claimant, but the Spanish dominions in Italy were divided between the two other claimants, the second son of the Dauphin, Philip, Duke of Anjou, receiving Naples and Sicily; the second son of the emperor, the Archduke Charles, the Milanese. Unfortunately, Joseph Ferdinand fell sick of the small-pox and died (March, 1699). With William and Heinsius the main point now was to prevent the French prince from occupying the Spanish throne; and in all secrecy negotiations were again opened at the Hague for a second partition treaty. They found Louis XIV still willing to conclude a bargain. To the Duke of Anjou was now assigned, in addition to Naples and Sicily, the duchy of Lorraine (whose duke was to receive the Milanese in exchange); the rest of the Spanish possessions were to fall to the Archduke Charles (March, 1700). The terms of this arrangement between the French king and the maritime powers did not long remain a secret; and when they were known they displeased the emperor, who did not wish to see French influence predominant in Italy and his own excluded, and still more the Spanish people, who objected to any partition and to the Austrian ruler. The palace of Charles II became a very hot-bed of intrigues, and finally the dying king was persuaded to make a fresh will and nominate Anjou as his universal heir. Accordingly on Charles' death (November 1, 1700) Philip V was proclaimed king.

For a brief time Louis was doubtful as to what course of action would be most advantageous to French interests, but not for long. On November 11 he publicly announced to his court at Versailles that his grandson had accepted the Spanish crown. This step was followed by the placing of French garrisons in some of the frontier fortresses of the Belgic Netherlands by consent of the governor, the Elector of Bavaria. The following months were spent in the vain efforts of diplomacy to obtain such guarantees from the French king as would give security to the States and satisfaction to England and the emperor, and so avoid the outbreak of war. In the States Heinsius, who was working heart and soul with the stadholder in this crisis, had no difficulty in obtaining the full support of all parties, even in Holland, to the necessity of making every effort to be ready for hostilities. William had a more difficult task in England, but he had the support of the Whig majority in Parliament and of the commercial classes; and he laboured hard, despite constant and increasing ill-health, to bring once more into existence the Grand Alliance of 1689. In July negotiations were opened between the maritime powers and the emperor at the Hague, which after lengthy discussions were brought to a conclusion in September, in no small degree through the tact and persuasiveness of Lord Marlborough, the English envoy, who had now begun that career which was shortly to make his name so famous. The chief provisions of the treaty of alliance, signed on September 7, 1701, were that Austria was to have the Italian possessions of Spain; the Belgic provinces were to remain as a barrier and protection for Holland against French aggression; and England and the States were to retain any conquests they might make in the Spanish West Indies. Nothing was said about the crown of Spain, a silence which implied a kind of recognition of Philip V. To this league were joined Prussia, Hanover, Lüneburg, Hesse-Cassel, while France, to whom Spain was now allied, could count upon the help of Bavaria. War was not yet declared, but at this very moment Louis XIV took a step which was wantonly provocative. James II died at St Germain on September 6; and his son was at once acknowledged by Louis as King of England, by the title of James III. This action aroused a storm of indignation among the English people, and William found himself supported by public opinion in raising troops and obtaining supplies for war. The preparations were on a vast scale. The emperor undertook to place 90,000 men in the field; England, 40,000; the German states, 54,000; and the Republic no less than 100,000. William had succeeded at last in the object of his life; a mighty confederation had been called into being to maintain the balance of power in Europe, and overthrow the threatened French domination. This confederation in arms, of which he was the soul and the acknowledged head, was destined to accomplish the object for which it was formed, but not under his leadership. The king had spent the autumn in Holland in close consultation with Heinsius, visiting the camps, the arsenals and the dockyards, and giving instructions to the admirals and generals to have everything in readiness for the campaign of the following spring. Then in November he went to England to hurry on the preparations, which were in a more backward condition than in the States. But he had overtaxed his strength. Always frail and ailing, William had for years by sheer force of will-power conquered his bodily weakness and endured the fatigue of campaigns in which he was content to share all hardships with his soldiers. In his double capacity, too, of king and stadholder, the cares of government and the conduct of foreign affairs had left him no rest. Especially had this been the case in England during the years which had followed Queen Mary's death, when he found himself opposed and thwarted and humiliated by party intrigues and cabals, to such an extent that he more than once thought of abdicating. He was feeling very ill and tired when he returned, and he grew weaker, for the winter in England always tried him. His medical advisers warned him that his case was one for which medicine was of no avail, and that he was not fit to bear the strain of the work he was doing. But the indomitable spirit of the man would not give way, and he still hoped with the spring to be able to put himself at the head of his army. It was not to be; an accident was the immediate cause by which the end came quickly. He was riding in Bushey Park when his horse stumbled over a mole-hill and the king was thrown, breaking his collar-bone (March 14, 1702). The shock proved fatal in his enfeebled state; and, after lingering for four days, during which, in full possession of his mental faculties, he continued to discuss affairs of state, he calmly took leave of his special friends, Bentinck, Earl of Portland and Keppel, Earl of Albemarle, and of the English statesmen who stood round his death-bed, and, after thanking them for their services, passed away. For four generations the House of Orange had produced great leaders of men, but it may be said without disparagement to his famous predecessors that the last heir-male of that House was the greatest of them all. He saved the Dutch Republic from destruction; and during the thirty years of what has well been called his reign he gave to it a weighty place in the Councils of Europe and raised it to a height of great material prosperity. But even such services as these were dwarfed by the part that he played in laying the foundation of constitutional monarchy in England, and of the balance of power in Europe. It is difficult to say whether Holland, England or Europe owed the deepest debt to the life-work of William III.

# CHAPTER XX

# THE WAR OF THE SPANISH SUCCESSION AND THE TREATIES OF UTRECHT, 1702-1715

William III left no successor to take his place. The younger branch of the Nassau family, who had been, from the time of John of Nassau, stadholders of Friesland and, except for one short interval, of Groningen, and who by the marriage of William Frederick with Albertina Agnes, younger daughter of Frederick Henry, could claim descent in the female line from William the Silent, had rendered for several generations distinguished services to the Republic, but in 1702 had as its only representative a boy of 14 years of age, by name John William Friso. As already narrated, the relations between his father, Henry Casimir, and William III had for a time been far from friendly; but a reconciliation took place before Henry Casimir's untimely death, and the king became god-father to John William Friso, and by his will left him his heir. The boy had succeeded by hereditary right to the posts of stadholder and captain-general of Friesland and Groningen under the guardianship of his mother, but such claims as he had to succeed William III as stadholder in the other provinces were, on account of his youth, completely ignored. As in 1650, Holland, Zeeland, Utrecht, Gelderland and Overyssel reverted once more to a stadholderless form of government.

Fortunately this implied no change of external policy. The men who had for years been fellow-workers with King William and were in complete sympathy with his aims continued to hold the most important posts in the government of the Republic, and to control its policy. That policy consisted in the maintenance of a close alliance with England for the purpose of curbing the ambitious designs of Louis XIV. Foremost among these statesmen were Antony Heinsius, the council-pensionary of Holland, Simon van Slingelandt, secretary of the Council of State since 1690, and Jan Hop, the treasurer-general of the Union. In England the recognition by Louis of the Prince of Wales as King James III had thoroughly aroused the popular feeling against France; and Anne the new queen determined to carry out her predecessor's plans. The two maritime powers, closely bound together by common interests, and the ties which had arisen between them during the thirteen years of the reign of the king-stadholder, were to form the nucleus of a coalition with Austria and a number of the German states, including Prussia and Hanover (to which Savoy somewhat later adhered), pledged to support the claims of the Archduke Charles to the Spanish throne. For the Dutch it was an all-important question, for with Philip V reigning at Madrid the hegemony of France in Europe seemed to be assured. Already French troops were in possession of the chief fortresses of the so-called Spanish Netherlands. Face to face with such a menace it was not difficult for Heinsius to obtain not only the assent of the States-General, but of the Estates of Holland, practically without a dissenting voice, to declare war upon France and Spain (May 8, 1702); and this was quickly followed by similar declarations by England and Austria.

The Grand Alliance had an outward appearance of great strength, but in reality it had all the weaknesses of a coalition, its armies being composed of contingents from a number of countries, whose governments had divergent aims and strategic objects, and it was opposed by a power under absolute rule with numerous and veteran armies inspired by a long tradition of victory under brilliant leaders. In 1702, however, the successors of Turenne and Luxemburg were by no means of the same calibre as those great generals. On the other hand, the allies were doubly fortunate in being led by a man of exceptional gifts. John Churchill, Earl (and shortly afterwards Duke) of Marlborough, was placed in supreme command of the Anglo-Dutch armies. Through the influence of his wife with the weak Queen Anne, the Whig party, of which Marlborough and his' friend Godolphin the lord-treasurer were the heads, was maintained in secure possession of power; and Marlborough thus entered upon his command in the full confidence of having the unwavering support of the home government behind him. Still this would have availed little but for the consummate abilities of this extraordinary man. As a general he displayed a military genius, both as a strategist and a tactician, which has been rarely surpassed. For ten years he pursued a career of victory not marred by a single defeat, and this in spite of the fact that his army was always composed of heterogeneous elements, that his subordinates of different nationalities were jealous of his authority and of one another, and above all, as will be seen, that his bold and well-laid plans were again and again hindered and thwarted by the timidity and obstinacy of the civilian deputies who were placed by the States-General at his side. Had Marlborough been unhampered, the war would probably have ended some years before it did; as it was, the wonderful successes of the general were made possible by his skill and tact as a diplomatist. He had, moreover, the good fortune to have at his side in the Imperialist general, Prince Eugene of Savoy, a commander second only to himself in brilliance and leadership. In almost all wars the Austrian alliance has proved a weak support on which to trust; but now, thanks to the outstanding capacity of Eugene, the armies of Austria were able to achieve many triumphs. The vigorous participation of the emperor in this war, in support of the claims of his second son, was only made possible by the victories of the Italian general over the Turks, who had overrun Hungary and threatened Vienna. And now, in the still more important sphere of operations in the West in which for a series of years he had to co-operate with Marlborough, it is to the infinite credit of both these great men that they worked harmoniously and smoothly together, so that at no time was there even a hint of any jealousy between them. In any estimate of the great achievements of Marlborough it must never be forgotten that he not only had Eugene at his right hand in the field, but Heinsius in the council chamber. Heinsius had always worked loyally and sympathetically with William III; and it was in the same spirit that he worked with the English duke, who brought William's life-task to its triumphant accomplishment. Between Marlborough and Heinsius, as between Marlborough and Eugene, there was no friction—surely a convincing tribute to the adroit and tactful persuasiveness of a commanding personality.

In July, 1702, Marlborough at the head of 65,000 men faced Marshal Boufflers with a French army almost as strong numerically, the one in front of Nijmwegen, the other in the neighbourhood of Liège. Leaving a force of 25,000 Dutch and Brandenburgers to besiege Kaiserswerth, Marlborough by skilful manoeuvring prevented Boufflers from attempting a relief, and would on two occasions have been able to inflict a severe defeat upon him had he not been each time thwarted by the cautious timidity of the Dutch deputies. Kaiserswerth, however, fell, and in turn Rheinberg, Venloo, Roeremonde and Liège; and the campaign ended successfully, leaving the allies in command of the lower Rhine and lower Meuse.

That of 1703 was marred even more effectually than that of the previous year by the interference of the deputies, and the ill-concealed opposition to Marlborough of certain Dutch generals, notably of Slangenburg. The duke was very angry, and bitter recriminations ensued. In the end Slangenburg was removed from his command; and the appointment of Ouwerkerk, as field-marshal of the Dutch forces, relieved the tension, though the deputies were still present at headquarters, much to Marlborough's annoyance. The campaign resulted in the capture of Bonn, Huy and Limburg, but there was no general action.

The year 1704 saw the genius of Marlborough at length assert itself. The French had placed great armies in the field, Villeroy in the Netherlands, Tallard in Bavaria, where in conjunction with the Bavarian forces he threatened to descend the Danube into the heart of Austria. Vienna itself was in the greatest danger. The troops under Lewis of Baden and under Eugene were, even when united, far weaker than their adversaries. In these circumstances Marlborough determined by a bold strategical stroke to execute a flank march from the Netherlands right across the front of the Franco-Bavarian army and effect a junction with the Imperialists. He had to deceive the timid Dutch deputies by feigning to descend the Meuse with the intention of working round Villeroy's flank; then, leaving Ouwerkerk to contain that marshal, he set out on his daring adventure early in May and carried it out with complete success. His departure had actually relieved the Netherlands, for Villeroy had felt it necessary with a large part of his forces to follow Marlborough and reinforce the Franco-Bavarians under Marshal Tallard and the

Elector. The two armies met at Blenheim (Hochstädt) on August 13. The battle resulted in the crushing victory of the allies under Marlborough and Eugene. Eleven thousand prisoners were taken, among them Tallard himself. The remnant of the French army retired across the Rhine. Vienna was saved, and all Bavaria was overrun by the Imperialists.

Meanwhile at sea the Anglo-Dutch fleet was incontestably superior to the enemy; and the operations were confined to the immediate neighbourhood of the Peninsula. William III had before his death been preparing an expedition for the capture of Cadiz. His plan was actually carried out in 1702, when a powerful fleet under the supreme command of Admiral Sir George Rooke sailed for Cadiz; but the attack failed owing to the incompetence of the Duke of Ormonde, who commanded the military forces. In this expedition a strong Dutch squadron under Philip van Almonde participated. Almonde was a capable seaman trained in the school of Tromp and De Ruyter; and he took a most creditable part in the action off Vigo, October 23, in which a large portion of the silver fleet was captured, and the Franco-Spanish fleet, which formed its escort, destroyed. The maritime operations of 1703 were uneventful, the French fleet being successfully blockaded in Toulon harbour.

The accession of Portugal in the course of this year to the Grand Alliance was important in that it opened the estuary of the Tagus as a naval base, and enabled the Archduke Charles to land with a body of troops escorted by an Anglo-Dutch fleet under Rooke and Callenberg. This fleet later in the year (August 4) was fortunate in capturing Gibraltar without much loss, the defences having been neglected and inadequately garrisoned. In this feat of arms, which gave to the English the possession of the rock fortress that commands the entrance into the Mediterranean, the Dutch under Callenberg had a worthy share, as also in the great sea-fight off Malaga on August 24, against the French fleet under the Count of Toulouse. The French had slightly superior numbers, and the allies, who had not replenished their stores after the siege of Gibraltar, were short of ammunition. Though a drawn battle, so far as actual losses were concerned, it was decisive in its results. The French fleet withdrew to the shelter of Toulon harbour; and the allies' supremacy in the midland sea was never again throughout the war seriously challenged. The Dutch ships at the battle of Malaga were twelve in number and fought gallantly, but it was the last action of any importance in which the navy of Holland took part. There had been dissensions between the English and Dutch commanders, and from this time forward the admiralties made no effort to maintain their fleet in the state of efficiency in which it had been left by William III. The cost of the army fell heavily upon Holland, and money was grudged for the maintenance of the navy, whose services, owing to the weakness of the enemy, were not required.

The military campaign of 1705 produced small results, the plans of Marlborough for an active offensive being thwarted by the Dutch deputies. The duke's complaints only resulted in one set of deputies being replaced by another set of civilians equally impracticable. There was also another reason for a slackening of vigour. The Emperor Leopold I died on May 5. His successor Joseph I had no children, so that the Archduke Charles became the heir-apparent to all the possessions of the Austrian Habsburgs. Louis XIV therefore seized the opportunity to make secret overtures of peace to some of the more influential Dutch statesmen through the Marquis D'Allègne, at that time a prisoner in the hands of the Dutch. The French were willing to make many concessions in return for the recognition of Philip V as King of Spain. In the autumn conversations took place between Heinsius, Buys the pensionary of Amsterdam, and others, with D'Allègne and Rouillé, an accredited agent of the French government. Matters went so far that Buys went to London on a secret mission to discuss the matter with the English minister. The English cabinet, however, refused to recognise Philip V; and, as the Dutch demand for a strong barrier of fortresses along the southern frontier of the Netherlands was deemed inadmissible at Versailles, the negotiations came to an end.

In 1706 Marlborough's bold proposal to join Eugene in Italy, and with their united forces to drive the French out of that country and to march upon Toulon, failed to gain the assent of the Dutch deputies. The duke, after much controversy and consequent delay, had to content himself with a campaign in Belgium. It was brilliantly carried out. On Whit Sunday, May 23, at Ramillies the allies encountered the enemy under the command of Marshal Villeroi and the Elector of Bavaria. The French were utterly defeated with very heavy loss; and such was the vigour of the pursuit that the shattered army was obliged to retire to Courtrai, leaving Brabant and Flanders undefended. In rapid succession Louvain, Antwerp, Ghent, Bruges and other towns surrendered to Marlborough, and a little later Ostend, Dendermonde, Menin and Ath; and the Archduke Charles was acknowledged as sovereign by the greater part of the southern Netherlands. In Italy and Spain also things had gone well with the allies. This series of successes led Louis XIV to make fresh overtures of peace to the States-General, whom the French king hoped to seduce from the Grand Alliance by the bait of commercial advantages both with Spain and France and a good "barrier." He was even ready to yield the crown of Spain to the Archduke Charles on condition that Philip of Anjou were acknowledged as sovereign of the Spanish possessions in Italy. Heinsius however was loyal to the English alliance; and, in face of the determination of the English government not to consent to any division of the Spanish inheritance, the negotiations again came to nothing.

The year 1707 saw a change of fortune. Austria was threatened by the victorious advance of Charles XII of Sweden through Poland into Saxony. A French army under Villars crossed the Rhine (May 27) and advanced far into south-eastern Germany. The defence of their own territories caused several of the German princes to retain their troops at home instead of sending them as mercenaries to serve in the Netherlands under Marlborough. The duke therefore found himself unable to attack the superior French army under Vendôme, and acted steadfastly on the defensive. An attempt by Eugene, supported by the English fleet, to capture Toulon ended in dismal failure and the retreat of the Imperialists with heavy loss into Italy. In Spain the victory of Berwick at Almanza (April 27) made Philip V the master of all Spain, except a part of Catalonia.

But, though Marlborough had been reduced to immobility in 1707, the following campaign was to witness another of his wonderful victories. At the head of a mixed force of 80,000 men he was awaiting the arrival of Eugene with an Imperialist army of 35,000, when Vendôme unexpectedly took the offensive while he still had superiority in numbers over his English opponent. Rapidly overrunning western Flanders he made himself master of Bruges and Ghent and laid siege to Oudenarde. By a series of brilliant movements Marlborough out-marched and out-manoeuvred his adversary and, interposing his army between him and the French frontier, compelled him to risk a general engagement. It took place on July 11, 1708, and ended in the complete defeat of the French, who were only saved by the darkness from utter destruction. Had the bold project of Marlborough to march into France forthwith been carried out, a deadly blow would have been delivered against the very vitals of the enemy's power and Louis XIV probably compelled to sue for peace on the allies' terms. But this time not only the Dutch deputies, but also Eugene, were opposed to the daring venture, and it was decided that Eugene should besiege Lille, while Marlborough with the field army covered the operations. Lille was strongly fortified, and Marshal Boufflers made a gallant defence. The siege began in mid-August; the town surrendered on October 22, but the citadel did not fall until December 9. Vendôme did his best to cut off Eugene's supplies of munitions and stores, and at one time the besiegers were reduced to straits. The French marshal did not, however, venture to force an engagement with Marlborough's covering army, a portion of which under General Webb, after gaining a striking victory over a French force at Wynendael, (September 30), conducted at a critical moment a large train of supplies from Ostend into Eugene's camp. As a consequence of the capture of Lille, the French withdrew from Flanders into their own territory, Ghent and Bruges being re-occupied by the allies with a mere show of resistance.

The reverses of 1708 induced the French king to be ready to yield much for the sake of peace. He offered the Dutch a strong barrier, a favourable treaty of commerce and the demolition of the defences of Dunkirk; and there were many in Holland who would have accepted his terms. But their English and Austrian allies insisted on the restoration of Louis' German conquests, and that the king should, by force if necessary, compel his grandson to leave Spain. Such was the exhaustion of France that Louis would have consented to almost any terms however harsh, but he refused absolutely to use coercion against Philip V. The negotiations went on through the spring nor did they break down until June, 1709, when the exorbitant demands of the allies made further progress impossible. Louis issued a manifesto calling upon his subjects to support him in resisting terms which were dishonouring to France.

He met with a splendid response from all classes, and a fine army of 90,000 men was equipped and placed in the field under the command of Marshal Villars. The long delay over the negotiations prevented Marlborough and Eugene from taking the field until June. They found Villars had meanwhile entrenched himself in Artois in a very strong position. Marlborough's proposal to advance by the sea-coast and outflank the enemy being opposed both by Eugene and the Dutch deputies as too daring, siege was laid to Tournay. Campaigns in those days were dilatory affairs. Tournay was not captured until September 3; and the allies, having overcome this obstacle without any active interference, moved forward to besiege Mons. They found Villars posted at Malplaquet on a narrow front, skilfully fortified and protected on both flanks by woods. A terrible struggle ensued (September 11, 1709), the bloodiest in the war. The Dutch troops gallantly led by the Prince of Orange attacked the French right, but were repulsed with very heavy losses. For some time the fight on the left and centre of the French line was undecided, the attacking columns being driven back many times, but at length the allies succeeded in turning the extreme left and also after fearful slaughter in piercing the centre; and the French were compelled to retreat. They had lost 12,000 men, but 23,000 of the allies had fallen; the Dutch divisions had suffered the most severely, losing almost half their strength. The immediate result of this hard-won victory was the taking of Mons, October 9. The lateness of the season prevented any further operations. Nothing decisive had been achieved, for on all the other fields of action, on the Rhine, on the Piedmont frontier and in Spain, the advantage had on the whole been with the French and Spaniards. Negotiations proceeded during the winter (1709-10), Dutch and French representatives meeting both at the Hague and at Geertruidenberg. The States were anxious for peace and Louis was willing to make the concessions required of him, but Philip V refused to relinquish a crown which he held by the practically unanimous approval of the Spanish people. The emperor on the other hand was obstinate in claiming the undivided Spanish inheritance for the Archduke Charles. The maritime powers, however, would not support him in this claim; and the maritime powers meant England, for Holland followed her lead, being perfectly satisfied with the conditions of the First Barrier Treaty, which had been drawn up and agreed upon between the States-General and the English government on October 29, 1709. By this secret treaty the Dutch obtained the right to hold and to garrison a number of towns along the French frontier, the possession of which would render them the real masters of Belgium. Indeed it was manifest that, although the Dutch did not dispute the sovereign rights of the Archduke Charles, they intended to make the southern Netherlands an economic dependency of the Republic, which provided for its defence.

The negotiations at Geertruidenberg dragged on until July, 1710, and were finally broken off owing to the insistence of the Dutch envoys, Buys and Van Dussen, upon conditions which, even in her exhausted state, France was too proud to concede. Meanwhile Marlborough and Eugene, unable to tempt Villars to risk a battle, contented themselves with a succession of sieges. Douay, Béthune, St Venant and Aine fell, one after the other, the French army keeping watch behind its strongly fortified lines. This was a very meagre result, but Marlborough now felt his position to be so insecure that he dared not take any risks. His wife, so long omnipotent at court, had been supplanted in the queen's favour; Godolphin and the Whig party had been swept from power; and a Tory ministry bent upon peace had taken their place. Marlborough knew that his period of dictatorship was at an end, and he would have resigned his command but for the pressing instances of Eugene, Heinsius and other leaders of the allies.

The desire of the Tory ministry to bring the long drawn-out hostilities to an end was accentuated by the death, on April 17, 1711, of the Emperor Joseph, an event which left his brother Charles heir to all the possessions of the Austrian Habsburgs. The Grand Alliance had been formed and the war waged to maintain the balance of power in Europe. But such a result would not be achieved by a revival of the empire of Charles V in the person of the man who had now become the head of the House of Austria. Even had the Whigs remained in office, they could hardly have continued to give active support to the cause of the Habsburg claimant in Spain.

One of the consequences of the death of Joseph I, then, was to render the Tory minister, Henry St John, more anxious to enter

313

into negotiations for peace; another was the paralysing of active operations in the field. Eugene had been summoned to Germany to watch over the meeting of the Imperial Diet at Frankfort, and Marlborough was left with an army considerably inferior in numbers to that of his opponent Villars. Thus the only fruit of the campaign was the capture of Bouchain. Meanwhile the French minister Torcy entered into secret communications with St John, intimating that France was ready to negotiate directly with England, but at first without the cognisance of the States. The English ministry on their part, under the influence of St John, showed themselves to be ready to throw over their allies, to abandon the Habsburg cause in Spain, and to come to an agreement with France on terms advantageous to England. For French diplomacy, always alert and skilful, these proceedings were quite legitimate; but it was scarcely honourable for the English government, while the Grand Alliance was still in existence, to carry on these negotiations in profound secrecy.

In August matters had so far advanced that Mesnager was sent over from Paris to London entrusted with definite proposals. In October the preliminaries of peace were virtually settled between the two powers. Meanwhile the Dutch had been informed through Lord Strafford, the English envoy at the Hague, of what was going on; and the news aroused no small indignation and alarm. But great pressure was brought to bear upon them; and, knowing that without England they could not continue the war, the States-General at last, in fear for their barrier, consented, on November 21, to send envoys to a peace congress to be held at Utrecht on the basis of the Anglo-French preliminaries. It was in vain that the Emperor Charles VI protested both at London and the Hague, or that Eugene was despatched on a special mission to England in January, 1712. The English ministry had made up their minds to conclude peace with or without the emperor's assent; and the congress opened at the beginning of the year 1712 without the presence of any Austrian plenipotentiaries, though they appeared later. The Dutch provinces sent two envoys each. The conferences at Utrecht were, however, little more than futile debates; and the congress was held there rather as a concession to save the *amour propre* of the States than to settle the terms of peace. The real negotiations were carried on secretly between England and France; and after a visit by St John, now Viscount Bolingbroke, in person to Paris in August, all points of difference between the two governments were amicably arranged. Spain followed the lead of France; and the States, knowing that they could not go on with the war without England, were reluctantly obliged to accept the Anglo-French proposals. Their concurrence might not have been so easily obtained, but for the unfortunate course of the campaign of 1712. Marlborough had now been replaced in the chief command by the Duke of Ormonde. Eugene, counting upon English support, had taken Quesnoy on July 4, and was about to invest Landrecies, when Ormonde informed him that an armistice had been concluded between the French and English governments. On July 16 the English contingent withdrew to Dunkirk, which had been surrendered by the French as a pledge of good faith. Villars seized the opportunity to make a surprise attack on the isolated Dutch at the bridge of Denain (July 24) and, a panic taking place, completely annihilated their whole force of 12,000 men with slight loss to himself. Eugene had to retreat, abandoning his magazines; and Douay, Quesnoy and Bouchain fell into the hands of the French marshal.

These disasters convinced the Dutch of their helplessness when deprived of English help; and instructions were given to their envoys at Utrecht, on December 29, to give their assent to the terms agreed upon and indeed dictated by the governments of England and France. Making the best of the situation, the Dutch statesmen, confronted with the growing self-assertion of the French plenipotentiaries, concluded, on January 30, 1713, a new offensive and defensive alliance with England. This treaty of alliance is commonly called the Second Barrier Treaty, because it abrogated the Barrier Treaty of 1709, and was much more favourable to France. It was not until all these more or less secret negotiations were over that the Congress, after being suspended for some months, resumed its sittings at Utrecht. The Peace of Utrecht which ensued is really a misnomer. No general treaty was agreed upon and signed, but a series of separate treaties between the belligerent powers. This was what France had been wishing for some time and, by the connivance of England, she achieved it. The treaty between these two countries was signed on April 11, 1713; and such was the dominant position of England that her allies, with the single exception of the emperor, had to follow her lead.

Treaties with the States-General, with Savoy, Brandenburg and Portugal, were all signed on this same day.

Louis XIV had good right to congratulate himself upon obtaining far more favourable terms than he could have dared to hope in 1710 or 1711. Philip V was recognised as King of Spain and the Indies, but had solemnly to renounce his right of succession to the French throne and his claim to the Spanish possessions in the Netherlands and in Italy. The treaty between England and Spain was signed on July 13, 1713; that between the States-General and Spain was delayed until June 26, 1714, owing to the difficulties raised by the emperor, who, though deserted by his allies, continued the war single-handed, but with signal lack of success. He was forced to yield and make peace at Rastatt in a treaty, which was confirmed by the Imperial Diet at Baden in Switzerland on September 7, 1714. By this treaty the French king retained practically all his conquests, while Charles VI, though he did not recognise the title of Philip V, contented himself with the acquisition of the "Spanish" Netherlands, and of the Milanese and Naples. Into the details of these several treaties it is unnecessary here to enter, except in so far as they affected the United Provinces. The power that benefited more than any other was Great Britain, for the Peace of Utrecht laid the foundation of her colonial empire and left her, from this time forward, the first naval and maritime power in the world. Holland, though her commerce was still great and her colonial possessions both rich and extensive, had henceforth to see herself more and more overshadowed and dominated by her former rival. Nevertheless the treaties concluded by the States-General at this time were decidedly advantageous to the Republic.

That with France, signed on April 11, 1713, placed the Spanish Netherlands in the possession of the States-General, to be held by them in trust for Charles VI until such time as the emperor came to an agreement with them about a "Barrier." France in this matter acted in the name of Spain, and was the intermediary through whose good offices Spanish or Upper Gelderland was surrendered to Prussia. Most important of all to the Dutch was the treaty with the emperor concluded at Antwerp, November 15, 1715. This is generally styled the Third Barrier Treaty, the First being that of 1709, the Second that of 1713 at Utrecht. The States-General finally obtained what was for their interest a thoroughly satisfactory settlement. They obtained the right to place garrisons amounting in all to 35,000 men in Furnes, Warneton, Ypres, Knocke, Tournay, Menin and Namur; and three-fifths of the cost were to be borne by the Austrian government, who pledged certain revenues of their newly-acquired Belgic provinces to the Dutch for the purpose. The strong position in which such a treaty placed the Republic against aggression, either from the side of France or Austria, was made stronger by being guaranteed by the British government.

# CHAPTER XXI

# THE STADHOLDERLESS REPUBLIC, 1715-1740

The thirty-four years which followed the Peace of Utrecht are a period of decadence and decay; a depressing period exhibiting the spectacle of a State, which had played a heroic part in history, sinking, through its lack of inspiring leadership and the crying defects inherent in its system of government, to the position of a third-rate power. The commanding abilities of the great stadholders of the house of Orange-Nassau, and during the stadholderless period which followed the untimely death of William II, those of the Council-Pensionary, John de Witt, had given an appearance of solidarity to what was really a loose confederation of sovereign provinces. Throughout the 17th century maritime enterprise, naval prowess and world-wide trade had, by the help of skilled diplomacy and wise statesmanship, combined to give to the Dutch Republic a weight in the council of nations altogether disproportionate to its size and the number of its population. In the memorable period of Frederick Henry the foundations were laid of an empire overseas; Dutch seamen and traders had penetrated into every ocean and had almost monopolised the carrying-trade of Europe; and at the same time Holland had become the chosen home of scholarship, science, literature and art. In the great days of John de Witt she contended on equal terms with England for the dominion of the seas; and Amsterdam was the financial clearing-house of the world. To William III the Republic owed its escape from destruction in the critical times of overwhelming French invasion in 1672, when by resolute and heroic leadership he not only rescued the United Provinces from French domination, but before his death had raised them to the rank of a great power. Never did the prestige of the States stand higher in Europe than at the opening of the 18th century. But, as has already been pointed out, the elevation of the great stadholder to the throne of England had been far from an unmixed blessing to his native land. It brought the two maritime and commercial rivals into a close alliance, which placed the smaller and less favoured country at a disadvantage, and ended in the weaker member of the alliance becoming more and more the dependent of the stronger. What would have been the trend of events had William survived for another ten or fifteen years or had he left an heir to succeed him in his high dignities, one can only surmise. It may at least be safely said, that the treaty which ended the war of the Spanish succession would not have been the treaty of Utrecht.

William III by his will made his cousin, John William Friso of Nassau-Siegen, his heir. Friso (despite the opposition of the Prussian king, who was the son of Frederick Henry's eldest daughter) assumed the title of Prince of Orange; and, as he was a real Netherlander, his branch of the house of Nassau having been continuously stadholders of Friesland since the first days of the existence of the Republic, he soon attracted to himself the affection of the Orangist party. But at the time of William III's death Friso was but fourteen years of age; and the old "States" or "Republican" party, which had for so many years been afraid to attempt any serious opposition to the imperious will of King William, now saw their opportunity for a return once more to the state of things established by the Great Assembly in 1651. Under the leadership of Holland five provinces now declared for a stadholderless government. The appointment of town-councillors passed into the hands of the corporations or of the Provincial Estates, not, however, without serious disturbances in Gelderland, Utrecht, Overyssel and also in Zeeland, stirred up partly by the old regent-families, who had been excluded from office under William, partly by the gilds and working folk, who vainly hoped that they would be able to exercise a larger share in the government. In many places faction-fights ensued. In Amersfoort two burghers were tried and beheaded; in Nijmwegen the burgomaster, Ronkens, met the same fate. But after a short while the aristocratic States party everywhere gained control in the town-corporations and through them in the Provincial Estates. In Zeeland the dignity of "first noble" was abolished.

The effect of all this was that decentralisation reached its extreme point. Not only were there seven republics, but each town asserted sovereign rights, defying at times the authority of the majority in the Provincial Estates. This was especially seen in the predominant province of Holland, where the city of Amsterdam by its wealth and importance was able to dictate its will to the Estates, and through the Estates to the States-General. Money-making and trade profits were the matters which engrossed everybody's interest. War interfered with trade; it was costly, and was to be avoided at any price. During this time the policy of the Republic was neutrality; and the States-General, with their army and navy reduced more and more in numbers and efficiency, scarcely counted in the calculations of the cabinets of Europe.

But this very time that was marked by the decline and fall of the Republic from the high position which it occupied during the greater part of the 17th century, was the golden age of the burgher-oligarchies. A haughty "patrician" class, consisting in each place of a very limited number of families, closely inter-related, had little by little possessed themselves, as a matter of hereditary right, of all the offices and dignities in the town, in the province and in the state. Within their own town they reigned supreme, filling up vacancies in the *vroedschap* by co-option, exercising all authority, occupying or distributing among their relatives all posts of profit, and acquiring great wealth. Their fellow-citizens were excluded from all share in affairs, and were looked down upon as belonging to an inferior caste. The old simple habits of their forefathers were abandoned. French fashions and manners were the vogue amongst them, and English clothes, furniture and food. In the country—*platteland*—people had no voice whatever in public affairs; they were not even represented, as the ordinary townspeople were by their regents. Thus the United Netherlands had not only ceased to be a unified state in any real sense of the word, but had ceased likewise to be a free state. It consisted of a large number of semi-independent oligarchies of the narrowest description; and the great mass of its population was deprived of every vestige of civic rights.

That such a State should have survived at all is to be explained by the fact that the real control over the foreign policy of the Republic and over its general government continued to be exercised by the band of experienced statesmen who had served under William III and inherited his traditions. Heinsius, the wise and prudent council-pensionary, continued in office until his death cm August 3, 1720, when he was succeeded by Isaac van Hoornbeck, pensionary of Rotterdam. Hoornbeck was not a man of great parts, but he was sound and safe and he had at his side Simon van Slingelandt, secretary of the Council of State since 1690, and others whose experience in public office dated from the preceding century. In their hands the external policy of the Republic, conducted with no lack of skill, was of necessity non-interventionist. In internal matters they could effect little. The finances after the war were in an almost hopeless condition, and again and again the State was threatened with bankruptcy. To make things worse an epidemic of wild speculation spread far and wide during the period 1716-1720 in the bubble companies, the Mississippi Company and the South Sea Company, associated with the name of Edward Law, which proved so ruinous to many in England and France, as well as in Holland. In 1716 such was the miserable condition of the country that the Estates of Overyssel, under the leadership of Count van Rechteren, proposed the summoning of a Great Assembly on the model of that of 1651 to consider the whole question of government and finance. The proposal was ultimately accepted, and the Assembly met at the Hague on November 28. After nine months of ineffectual debate and wrangling it finally came to an end on September 14, 1717, without effecting anything, leaving all who had the best interests of the State at heart in despair.

In the years immediately succeeding the Peace of Utrecht difficulties arose with Charles XII of Sweden; whose privateers had been seizing Dutch and English merchantmen in the Baltic. Under De Witt or William III the fleet of the Republic would speedily have brought the Swedish king to reason. But now other counsels prevailed. Dutch squadrons sailed into the Baltic with instructions to convoy the merchant vessels, but to avoid hostilities. With some difficulty this purpose was achieved; and the death of Charles at the siege of Frederikshald brought all danger of war to an end. And yet in the very interests of trade it would have been good policy for the States to act strongly in this matter of Swedish piracy in the Baltic. Russia was the rising power in those regions. The Dutch had really nothing to fear from Sweden, whose great days came to an end with the crushing defeat of Charles XII at Pultova in 1709. Trade relations had been opened between Holland and Muscovy so early as the end of the 16th century; and, despite English rivalry, the opening out of Russia and of Russian trade had been almost entirely in Dutch hands during the 17th century. The relations between the two countries became much closer and more important after the accession of the enterprising and reforming Tsar, Peter the Great. It is well known how Peter in 1696 visited Holland to learn the art of ship-building and himself toiled as a workman at Zaandam. As a result of this visit he carried back with him to Russia an admiration for all things Dutch. He not only favoured Dutch commerce, but he employed numbers of Hollanders in the building and training of his fleet and in the construction of waterways and roads. In 1716-17 Peter again spent a considerable time in Holland. Nevertheless Dutch policy was again timid and cautious; and no actual alliance was made with Russia, from dread of entanglements, although the opportunity seemed so favourable.

It was the same when in this year 1717 Cardinal Alberoni, at the instigation of Elizabeth of Parma the ambitious second wife of Philip V, attempted to regain Spain's lost possessions in Italy by an aggressive policy which threatened to involve Europe in war. Elizabeth's object was to obtain an independent sovereignty for her sons in her native country. Austria, France and England united to resist this attempt to reverse the settlement of Utrecht, and the States were induced to join with them in a quadruple alliance. It was not, however, their intention to take any active part in the hostilities which speedily brought Spain to reason, and led to the fall of Alberoni. But the Spanish queen had not given up her designs, and she found another instrument for carrying them out in Ripperda, a Groningen nobleman, who had originally gone to Spain as ambassador of the States. This able and scheming statesman persuaded Elizabeth that she might best attain her ends by an alliance with Austria, which was actually concluded at Vienna on April 1, 1725. This alliance alarmed France, England and Prussia, but was especially obnoxious to the Republic, for the emperor had in 1722 erected an East India Company at Ostend in spite of the prohibition placed by Holland and Spain in the treaties of 1714-15 upon Belgian overseas commerce. By the Treaty of Alliance in

1725 the Spanish crown recognised the Ostend Company and thus gave it a legal sanction. The States therefore, after some hesitation, became parties to a defensive alliance against Austria and Spain that had been signed by France, England and Prussia at Hanover in September, 1728. These groupings of the powers were of no long duration. The emperor, fearing an invasion of the Belgian provinces, first agreed to suspend the Ostend Company for seven years, and then, in order to secure the assent of the maritime powers to the Pragmatic Sanction, which guaranteed to his daughter, Maria Theresa, the succession to the Austrian hereditary domains, he broke with Spain and consented to suppress the Ostend Company altogether. The negotiations which took place at this time are very involved and complicated, but they ended in a revival of the old alliance between Austria and the maritime powers against the two Bourbon monarchies of France and Spain. This return to the old policy of William III was largely the work of Slingelandt, who had become council-pensionary on July 27, 1727.

Simon van Slingelandt, with the able assistance of his brother-in-law Francis Fagel, clerk of the States-General, was during the nine years in which he directed the foreign policy of the Republic regarded as one of the wisest and most trustworthy, as he was the most experienced statesman of his time. His aim was, in co-operation with England, to maintain by conciliatory and peaceful methods the balance of power. Lord Chesterfield, at that time the British envoy at the Hague, had the highest opinion of Slingelandt's powers; and the council-pensionary's writings, more especially his *Pensées impartiales*, published in 1729, show what a thorough grasp he had of the political situation. Fortunately the most influential ministers in England and France, Robert Walpole and Cardinal Fleury, were like-minded with him in being sincere seekers after peace. The Treaty of Vienna (March 18, 1731), which secured the recognition by the powers of the Pragmatic Sanction, was largely his work; and he was also successful in preventing the question of the Polish succession, after the death of Augustus of Saxony in 1733, being the cause of the outbreak of a European war. In domestic policy Slingelandt, though profoundly dissatisfied with the condition of the Republic, took no steps to interfere with the form of government. He saw the defects of the stadholderless system plainly enough, but he had not, like Fagel, strong Orangist sympathies; and on his appointment as council-pensionary he pledged himself to support during his tenure of office the existing state of things. This undertaking he loyally kept, and his strong personality during his life-time alone saved Holland, and through Holland the entire Republic, from falling into utter ruin and disaster. At his death Antony van der Heim became council-pensionary under the same conditions as his predecessor. But Van der Heim, though a capable and hard-working official, was not of the same calibre as Slingelandt. The narrow and grasping burgher-regents had got a firm grip of power, and they used it to suppress the rights of their fellow-citizens and to keep in their own hands the control of municipal and provincial affairs. Corruption reigned everywhere; and the patrician oligarchy, by keeping for themselves and their relations all offices of profit, grew rich at the same time that the finances of the State fell into greater confusion. It was not a condition of things that could endure, should any serious crisis arise.

John William Friso, on whom great hopes had been fixed, met with an untimely death in 1711, leaving a posthumous child who became William IV, Prince of Orange. Faithful Friesland immediately elected William stadholder under the regency of his mother, Maria Louisa of Hesse-Cassel. By her fostering care the boy received an education to fit him for service to the State. Though of weakly bodily frame and slightly deformed, William had marked intelligence, and a very gentle and kindly disposition. Though brave like all his family, he had little inclination for military things. The Republican party had little to fear from a man of such character and disposition. The burgher-regents, secure in the possession of power, knew that the Frisian stadholder was not likely to resort either to violence or intrigue to force on a revolution. Nevertheless the prestige of the name in the prevailing discontent counted for much. William was elected stadholder of Groningen in 1718, of Drente and of Gelderland in 1722, though in each case with certain restrictions. But the other provinces remained obstinate in their refusal to admit him to any place in their councils or to any military post. The Estates of Zeeland went so far as to abolish the marquisate of Flushing and Veere, which carried with it the dignity of first noble and presidency in the meetings of the Estates, and offered to pay 100,000 fl. in compensation to the heir of the Nassaus. William refused to receive it, saying that either the marquisate did not belong to him, in which case he could not accept money for it, or it did belong to him and was not for sale. William's position was advanced by his marriage in 1734 to Anne, eldest daughter of George II. Thus for the third time a Princess Royal of England became Princess of Orange. The reception of the newly married pair at Amsterdam and the Hague was, however, cool though polite; and despite the representatives of Gelderland, who urged that the falling credit and bad state of the Republic required the appointment of an "eminent head," Holland, Utrecht, Zeeland and Overyssel remained obdurate in their refusal to change the form of government. William had to content himself with the measure of power he had obtained and to await events. He showed much patience, for he had many slights and rebuffs to put up with. His partisans would have urged him to more vigorous action, but this he steadily refused to take.

The Republic kept drifting meanwhile on the downward path. Its foreign policy was in nerveless hands; jobbery was rampant; trade and industry declined; the dividends of the East India Company fell year by year through the incompetence and greed of officials appointed by family influence; the West India Company was practically bankrupt. Such was the state of the country in 1740, when the outbreak of the Austrian Succession War found the Republic without leadership, hopelessly undecided what course of action it should take, and only seeking to evade its responsibilities.

# CHAPTER XXII

# THE AUSTRIAN SUCCESSION WAR. WILLIAM IV, 1740-1751

The death of the Emperor Charles VI in October, 1740, was the signal for the outbreak of another European war. All Charles' efforts on behalf of the Pragmatic Sanction proved to have been labour spent in vain. Great Britain, the United Provinces, Spain, Saxony, Poland, Russia, Sardinia, Prussia, most of the smaller German States, and finally France, had agreed to support (1738) the Pragmatic Sanction. The assent of Spain had been bought by the cession of the two Sicilies; of France by that of Lorraine, whose Duke Francis Stephen had married Maria Theresa and was compensated by the Grand Duchy of Tuscany for the loss of his ancestral domain. The only important dissentient was Charles Albert, Elector of Bavaria, who had married the younger daughter of Joseph I and who claimed the succession not only through his wife, but as the nearest male descendant of Ferdinand I. On the death of Charles VI, then, it might have been supposed that Maria Theresa would have succeeded to her inheritance without opposition. This was far from being the case. The Elector of Bavaria put forward his claims and he found unexpected support in Frederick II of Prussia. Frederick had just succeeded his father Frederick William I, and being at once ambitious and without scruples he determined to seize the opportunity for the purpose of territorial aggression. While lulling the suspicions of Vienna by friendly professions, he suddenly, in December, 1740, invaded Silesia. Maria Theresa appealed to the guarantors of the Pragmatic Sanction. She met no active response, but on the part of Spain, Sardinia and France veiled hostility. Great Britain, at war with Spain since 1739, and fearing the intervention of France, confined her efforts to diplomacy; and the only anxiety of the United Provinces was to avoid being drawn into war. An addition was made to the army of 11,000 men and afterwards in 1741, through dread of an attack on the Austrian Netherlands, a further increase of 20,000 was voted. The garrisons and fortifications of the barrier towns were strengthened and some addition was made to the navy. But the policy of the States continued to be vacillating and pusillanimous. The Republican party, who held the reins of power, desiring peace at any price, were above all anxious to be on good terms with France. The Orangist opposition were in favour of joining with England in support of Maria Theresa; but the prince would not take any steps to assert himself, and his partisans, deprived of leadership, could exert little influence. Nor did they obtain much encouragement from England, where Walpole was still intent upon a pacific policy.

The events of 1741, however, were such as to compel a change of attitude. The Prussians were in possession of Silesia; and spoliation, having begun so successfully, became infectious. The aged Fleury was no longer able to restrain the war party in France. In May at Nymphenburg a league was formed by France, Spain, Sardinia, Saxony and Poland, in conjunction with Prussia and Bavaria, to effect the overthrow of Maria Theresa and share her inheritance between them. Resistance seemed hopeless. A Franco-Bavarian army penetrated within a few miles of Vienna, and then overran Bohemia. Charles Albert was crowned King of Bohemia at Prague and then (January, 1742) was elected Emperor under the title of Charles VII.

Before this election took place, however, English mediation had succeeded by the convention of Klein-Schnellendorf in securing a suspension of hostilities (October 9) between Austria and Prussia. This left Frederick in possession of Silesia, but enabled the Queen of Hungary, supported by English and Dutch subsidies, not only to clear Bohemia from its invaders, but to conquer Bavaria. At the very time when Charles Albert was elected Emperor, his own capital was occupied by his enemies. In February, 1742, the long ministry of Walpole came to an end; and the party in favour of a more active participation in the war succeeded to office. George II was now thoroughly alarmed for the safety of his

Hanoverian dominions; and Lord Stair was sent to the Hague on a special mission to urge the States to range themselves definitely on the side of Maria Theresa. But fears of a French onslaught on the southern Netherlands still caused timorous counsels to prevail. The French ambassador, De Fénélon, on his part was lavish in vague promises not unmingled with veiled threats, so that the feeble directors of Dutch policy, torn between their duty to treaty obligations urged upon them by England, and their dread of the military power of France, helplessly resolved to cling to neutrality as long as possible. But events proved too strong for them. Without asking their permission, an English force of 16,000 men landed at Ostend and was sent to strengthen the garrison of the barrier fortresses (May, 1742). The warlike operations of this year were on the whole favourable to Maria Theresa, who through English mediation, much against her will, secured peace with Prussia by the cession of Silesia. The treaty between the two powers was signed at Berlin on July 28. Hostilities with France continued; but, though both the Maritime Powers helped Austria with subsidies, neither Great Britain nor the States were at the close of the year officially at war with the French king.

Such a state of precarious make-believe could not last much longer. The Austrians were anxious that the English force in the Netherlands, which had been reinforced and was known as the *Pragmatic Army*, should advance into Bavaria to co-operate with the Imperial forces. Accordingly the army, commanded by George II in person, advanced across the Main to Dettingen. Here the king, shut in by French forces and cut off from his supplies, was rescued from a very difficult position by the valour of his troops, who on June 27, 1743 attacked and completely routed their opponents. The States-General had already, on June 22, recognised their responsibilities; and by a majority vote it was determined that a force of 20,000 men under the command of Count Maurice of Nassau-Ouwerkerk should join the *Pragmatic Army*.

The fiction that the Maritime Powers were not at war with France was kept up until the spring of 1744, when the French king in alliance with Spain declared war on England. One of the projects of the war party at Versailles was the despatch of a powerful expedition to invade England and restore the Stewarts. As soon as news of the preparations reached England, a demand was at once made, in accordance with treaty, for naval aid from the States. Twenty ships were asked for, but only eight were in a condition to sail; and the admiral in command, Grave, was 73 years of age and had been for fifteen years in retirement. What an object lesson of the utter decay of the Dutch naval power! Fortunately a storm dispersed the French fleet, and the services of the auxiliary squadron were not required.

The news that Marshal Maurice de Saxe was about to invade the Austrian Netherlands with a French army of 80,000 men came like a shock upon the peace party in the States. The memory of 1672 filled them with terror. The pretence of neutrality could no longer be maintained. The choice lay between peace at any price or war with all its risks; and it was doubtful which of the two alternatives was the worse. Was there indeed any choice? It did not seem so, when De Fénélon, who had represented France at the Hague for nineteen years, came to take leave of the States-General on his appointment to a command in the invading army (April 26). But a last effort was made. An envoy-extraordinary, the Count of Wassenaer-Twickel, was sent to Paris, but found that the king was already with his army encamped between Lille and Tournay. Wassenaer was amused with negotiations for awhile, but there was no pause in the rapid advance of Marshal Saxe. The barrier fortresses, whose defences had been neglected, fell rapidly one after another. All west Flanders was overrun. The allied forces, gathered at Oudenarde, were at first too weak to offer resistance, and were divided in counsels. Gradually reinforcements came in, but still the Pragmatic army remained inactive and was only saved from inevitable defeat by the invasion of Alsace by the Imperialists. Marshal Saxe was compelled to despatch a considerable part of the invading army to meet this attack on the eastern frontier, and to act on the defensive in Flanders. Menin, Courtrai, Ypres, Knocke and other places remained, however, in French hands.

All this time the Dutch had maintained the fiction that the States were not at war with France; but in January, 1745, the pressure of circumstances was too strong even for the weak-kneed Van der Heim and his fellow-statesmen, and a quadruple alliance was formed between England, Austria, Saxony and the United Provinces to maintain the Pragmatic Sanction. This was followed in March by the declaration of war between France and the States.

Meanwhile the position of Austria had improved. The Emperor Charles VII died on January 20; and his youthful successor Maximilian Joseph, in return for the restoration of his electorate, made peace with Maria Theresa and withdrew all Bavarian claims to the Austrian succession. Affairs in Flanders however did not prosper. The command-in-chief of the allied army had been given to the Duke of Cumberland, who was no match for such an opponent as Maurice de Saxe. The Prince of Waldeck was in command of the Dutch contingent.

The provinces of Friesland, Groningen, Overyssel and Gelderland had repeatedly urged that this post should be bestowed upon the Prince of Orange; and the States-General had in 1742 offered to give William the rank of lieutenant-general in the army, but Holland and Zeeland steadily refused. The campaign of 1745 was disastrous. The battle of Fontenoy (May 11) resulted in a victory for Marshal Saxe over the allied forces, a victory snatched out of the fire through the pusillanimous withdrawal from the fight of the Dutch troops on the left wing. The British infantry with magnificent valour on the right centre had pierced through the French lines, only to find themselves deserted and overwhelmed by superior forces. This victory was vigorously followed up. The Jacobite rising under Charles Edward, the young Pretender, had necessitated the recalling not only of the greater part of the English expeditionary force, but also, under the terms of the treaties between Great Britain and the United Provinces, of a body of 6000 Dutch. Before the year 1745 had ended, Tournay, Ghent, Bruges, Oudenarde, Dendermonde, Ostend, Nieuport, Ath fell in succession into the hands of Marshal Saxe, and after a brave defence Brussels itself was forced to capitulate on February 19, 1746.

Van der Heim and the Republican conclave in whose hands was the direction of foreign affairs, dreading the approach of the French armies to the Dutch frontier, sent the Count de Larrey on a private mission to Paris in November, 1745, to endeavour to negotiate terms of peace. He was unsuccessful; and in February, 1746 another fruitless effort was made, Wassenaer and Jacob Gilles being the envoys. The French minister, D'Argenson, was not unwilling to discuss matters with them; and negotiations went on for some time in a more or less desultory way, but without in any way checking the alarming progress of hostilities. An army 120,000 strong under Marshal Saxe found for some months no force strong enough to resist it. Antwerp, Louvain, Mechlin, Mons, Charleroi, Huy and finally Namur (September 21) surrendered to the French. At last (October 11) a powerful allied army under the command of Charles of Lorraine made a stand at Roucoux. A hardly-fought battle, in which both sides lost heavily, ended in the victory of the French. Liège was taken, and the French were now masters of Belgium.

These successes made the Dutch statesmen at the Hague the more anxious to conclude peace. D'Argenson had always been averse to an actual invasion of Dutch territory; and it was arranged between him and the Dutch envoys, Wassenaer and Gilles, at Paris, and between the council-pensionary Van der Heim and the Abbé de la Ville at the Hague, that a congress should meet at Breda in August, in which England consented to take part. Before it met, however, Van der Heim had died (August 15). He was succeeded by Jacob Gilles. The congress was destined to make little progress, for several of the provinces resented the way in which a small handful of men had secretly been committing the Republic to the acceptance of disadvantageous and humiliating terms of peace, without obtaining the consent of the States-General to their proposals. The congress did not actually assemble till October, and never got further than the discussion of preliminaries, for the war party won possession of power at Paris, and Louis XV dismissed D'Argenson. Moderate counsels were thrown to the winds; and it was determined in the coming campaign to carry the war into Dutch territory.

Alarm at the threatening attitude of the French roused the allies to collect an army of 90,000 men, of whom more than half were Austrian; but, instead of Charles of Lorraine, the Duke of Cumberland was placed in command. Marshal Saxe, at the head of the main French force, held Cumberland in check, while he despatched Count Löwenthal with 20,000 to enter Dutch Flanders. His advance was a triumphal progress. Sluis, Cadsand and Axel surrendered almost without opposition. Only the timely arrival of an English squadron in the Scheldt saved Zeeland from invasion.

The news of these events caused an immense sensation. For some time popular resentment against the feebleness and jobbery of the stadholderless government had been deep and strong.

Indignation knew no bounds; and the revolutionary movement to which it gave rise was as sudden and complete in 1747 as in 1672. All eyes were speedily turned to the Prince of Orange as the saviour of the country. The movement began on April 25 at Veere and Middelburg in the island of Walcheren. Three days later the Estates of the Province proclaimed the prince stadholder and captain- and admiral-general of Zeeland. The province of Holland, where the stadholderless form of government was so deeply rooted and had its most stubborn and determined supporters, followed the example of Zeeland on May 3, Utrecht on May 5, and Overyssel on May 10. The States-General appointed him captain-and admiral-general of the Union. Thus without bloodshed or disturbance of any kind or any personal effort on the part of the prince, he found himself by general consent invested with all the posts of dignity and authority which had been held by Frederick Henry and William III. It was amidst scenes of general popular rejoicing that William visited Amsterdam, the Hague and Middelburg, and prepared to set about the difficult task to which he had been called.

One of the first results of the change of government was the closing of the Congress of Breda. There was no improvement, however, in the military position. The allied army advancing under Cumberland and Waldeck, to prevent Marshal Saxe from laying siege to Maestricht, was attacked by him at Lauffeldt on July 2. The fight was desperately contested, and the issue was on the whole in favour of the allies, when at a critical moment the Dutch gave way; and the French were able to claim, though at very heavy cost, a doubtful victory. It enabled Saxe nevertheless to despatch a force under Löwenthal to besiege the important fortress of Bergen-op-Zoom. It was carried by assault on September 16, and with it the whole of Dutch Brabant fell into the enemy's hands.

Indignation against the rule of the burgher-regents, which had been instrumental in bringing so many disasters upon the Republic, was very general; and there was a loudly expressed desire that the prince should be invested with greater powers, as the "eminent head" of the State. With this object in view, on the proposal of the nobles of Holland, the Estates of that province made the dignity of stadholder and of captain-and admiral-general hereditary in both the male and female lines. All the other provinces passed resolutions to the same effect; and the States-General made the offices of captain-and admiral-general of the Union also hereditary. In the case of a minority, the Princess-Mother was to be regent; in that of a female succession the heiress could only marry with the consent of the States, it being provided that the husband must be of the Reformed religion, and not a king or an elector.

Strong measures were taken to prevent the selling of offices and to do away with the system of farming out the taxes. The post-masterships in Holland, which produced a large revenue, were offered to the prince; but, while undertaking the charge, he desired that the profits should be applied to the use of the State. Indeed they were sorely needed, for though William would not hear of peace and sent Count Bentinck to England to urge a vigorous prosecution of the war in conjunction with Austria and Russia in 1748, promising a States contingent of 70,000 men, it was found that, when the time for translating promises into action came, funds were wanting. Holland was burdened with a heavy debt; and the contributions of most of the provinces to the Generality were hopelessly in arrears. In Holland a "voluntary loan" was raised, which afterwards extended to the other provinces and also to the Indies, at the rate of 1 per cent. on properties between 1000 fl. and 2000 fl.; of 2 per cent. on those above 2000 fl. The loan (*mildegift*) produced a considerable sum, about 50,000,000 fl.; but this was not enough, and the prince had the humiliation of writing and placing before the English government the hopeless financial state of the Republic, and their need of a very large loan, if they were to take any further part in the war. This pitiful revelation of the condition of their ally decided Great Britain to respond to the overtures for peace on the part of France. The representatives of the powers met at Aix-la-Chapelle; and, as the English and French were both thoroughly tired of the war, they soon came to terms. The preliminaries of peace between them were signed on April 30, 1748, on the principle of a restoration of conquests. In this treaty of Aix-la-Chapelle the United Provinces were included, but no better proof could be afforded of the low estate to which the Dutch Republic had now fallen than the fact that its representatives at Aix-la-Chapelle, Bentinck and Van Haren, were scarcely consulted and exercised practically no influence upon the decisions. The French evacuated the southern Netherlands in return for the restoration to them of the colony of Cape Breton, which had fallen into the hands of the English; and the barrier towns were again allowed to receive Dutch garrisons. It was a useless concession, for their fortifications had been destroyed, and the States could no longer spare the money to make them capable of serious defence.

The position of William IV all this time was exceptionally responsible, and therefore the more trying. Never before had any Prince of Orange been invested with so much power. The glamour attaching to the name of Orange was perhaps the chief asset of the new stadholder in facing the serious difficulties into which years of misgovernment had plunged the country. He had undoubtedly the people at his back, but unfortunately they expected an almost magical change would take place in the situation with his elevation to the stadholderate. Naturally they were disappointed. The revolution of 1747 was not carried out in the spirit of "thorough," which marked those of 1618, 1650 and 1672. William IV was cast in a mould different from that of Maurice or William II, still more from that of his immediate predecessor William III. He was a man of wide knowledge, kindly, conciliatory, and deeply religious, but only a mediocre statesman. He was too undecided in his opinions, too irresolute in action, to be a real leader in a crisis.

The first business was to bring back peace to the country; and this was achieved, not by any influence that the Netherlands government was able to exercise upon the course of the negotiations at Aix-la-Chapelle, but simply as a part of the understanding arrived at by Great Britain and France. It was for the sake of their own security that the English plenipotentiaries were willing to give up their conquests in North America as compensation for the evacuation of those portions of Belgium and of the Republic that the French forces occupied, and the restoration of the barrier fortresses.

After peace was concluded, not only the Orange partisans but the great mass of the people, who had so long been excluded from all share of political power, desired a drastic reform of the government. They had conferred sovereign authority upon William, and would have willingly increased it, in the hope that he would in his person be a centre of unity to the State, and would use his power for the sweeping away of abuses. It was a vain hope. He never attempted to do away, root and branch, with the corrupt municipal oligarchies, but only to make them more tolerable by the infusion of a certain amount of new blood.

The birth of an heir on March 8, 1748, caused great rejoicings, for it promised permanence to the new order of things. Whatever the prince had firmly taken in hand would have met with popular approval, but William had little power of initiative or firmness of principle. He allowed his course of action to be swayed now by one set of advisers, now by their opponents. Even in the matter of the farmers of the revenue, the best-hated men throughout the Republic and especially in Holland, it required popular tumults and riots at Haarlem, Leyden, the Hague and Amsterdam, in which the houses of the obnoxious officials were attacked and sacked, to secure the abolition of a system by which the proceeds of taxation were diverted from the service of the State to fill the pockets of venal and corrupt officials. In Amsterdam the spirit of revolt against the domination of the Town Council by a few patrician families led to serious disorders and armed conflicts in which blood was shed; and in September, 1748, the prince, at the request of the Estates, visited the turbulent city. As the Town Council proved obstinate in refusing to make concessions, the stadholder was compelled to take strong action. The Council was dismissed from office, but here, as elsewhere, the prince was averse from making a drastic purge; out of the thirty-six members, more than half, nineteen, were restored. The new men, who thus took their seats in the Town Council, obtained the *sobriquet* of "Forty-Eighters."

The state of both the army and navy was deplorable at the end of the war in which the States had played so inglorious a part. William had neither the training nor the knowledge to undertake their reorganisation. He therefore sought the help of Lewis Ernest, Duke of Brunswick-Wolfenbüttel (1718-86), who, as an Austrian field-marshal, had distinguished himself in the war. Brunswick was with difficulty persuaded, in October, 1749, to accept the post of Dutch field-marshal, a salary of 60,000 fl. being guaranteed to him, the governorship of Hertogenbosch, and the right to retain his rank in the Austrian army. The duke did not actually arrive in Holland and take up his duties until December, 1750.

The prince's efforts to bring about a reform of the Admiralties, to make the Dutch navy an efficient force and to restore the commerce and industries of the country were well meant, but were marred by the feebleness of his health. All through the year 1750 he had recurring attacks of illness and grew weaker. On October 22, 1751, he died. It is unfair to condemn William IV because he did not rise to the height of his opportunities. When in 1747 power was thrust upon him so suddenly, no man could have been more earnest in his wish to serve his country. But he was not gifted with the great abilities and high resolve of William III; and there can be no doubt that the difficulties with which he had to contend were manifold, complex and deep-rooted. A valetudinarian like William IV was not fitted to be the physician of a body-politic suffering from so many diseases as that of the United Provinces in 1747.

# CHAPTER XXIII

# THE REGENCY OF ANNE AND OF BRUNSWICK. 1751-1766

On the death of William IV, his widow, Anne of England, was at once recognised as regent and guardian of her son William V. Bentinck and other leaders of the Orangist party took prompt measures to secure that the hereditary rights of the young prince did not suffer by his father's early death. During the minority Brunswick was deputed to perform the duties of captain-general. The new regent was a woman of by no means ordinary parts. In her domestic life she possessed all the virtues of her mother, Queen Caroline; and in public affairs she had been of much help to her husband and was deeply interested in them. She was therefore in many ways well-fitted to undertake the serious responsibilities that devolved upon her, but her good qualities were marred by a self-willed and autocratic temperament, which made her resent any interference with her authority. William Bentinck, who was wont to be insistent with his advice, presuming on the many services he had rendered, the Duke of Brunswick, and the council-pensionary Steyn were all alike distrusted and disliked by her. Her professed policy was not to lean on any party, but to try and hold the balance between them. Unfortunately William IV, after the revolution of 1747, had allowed his old Frisian counsellors (with Otto Zwier van Haren at their head) to have his ear and to exercise an undue influence upon his decisions. This Frisian court-cabal continued to exercise the same influence with Princess Anne; and the Hollanders not unnaturally resented it. For Holland, as usual, in the late war had borne the brunt of the cost and had a debt of 70,000,000 fl. and an annual deficit of 28,000,000 fl. The council-pensionary Steyn was a most competent financier, and he with Jan Hop, the treasurer-general of the Union, and with William Bentinck, head and spokesman of the nobles in the Estates of Holland, were urgent in impressing upon the Regent the crying need of retrenchment. Anne accepted their advice as to the means by which economies might be effected and a reduction of expenses be brought about. Among these was the disbanding of some of the military forces, including a part of the body-guard. To this the regent consented, though characteristically without consulting Brunswick. The captain-general felt aggrieved, but allowed the reduction to be made without any formal opposition. No measure, however, of a bold and comprehensive financial reform, like that of John de Witt a century earlier, was attempted.

The navy had at the peace of Aix-la-Chapelle been in an even worse condition than the army; and the stadholder, as admiral-general, had been urging the Admiralties to bestir themselves and to make the fleet more worthy of a maritime power. But William's premature death brought progress to a standstill; and it is noteworthy that such was the supineness of the States-General in 1752 that, while Brunswick was given the powers of captain-general, no admiral-general was appointed. The losses sustained by the merchants and ship-owners through the audacity of the Algerian pirates roused public opinion, however; and in successive years squadrons were despatched to the Mediterranean to bring the sea-robbers to reason. Admiral Boudaen in 1755 contented himself with the protection of the merchantmen, but Wassenaer in 1756 and 1757 was more aggressive and compelled the Dey of Algiers to make terms.

Meanwhile the rivalry between France and England on the one hand, and between Austria and Prussia on the other, led to the formation of new alliances, and placed the Dutch Republic in a difficult position. The peace of Aix-la-Chapelle was but an armed truce. The French lost no time in pushing forward ambitious schemes of colonial enterprise in North America and in India. Their progress was watched with jealous eyes by the English; and in 1755 war broke out between the two powers. The Republic was bound to Great Britain by ancient treaties; but the activities of the French ambassador, D'Affry, had been successful in winning over a number of influential Hollanders and also the court-cabal to be inclined to France and to favour strict neutrality. The situation was immensely complicated by the alliance concluded between Austria and France on May 1, 1756.

This complete reversal of the policy, which from the early years of William III had grouped England, Austria and the States in alliance against French aggression, caused immense perturbation amongst the Dutch statesmen. By a stroke of the pen the Barrier Treaty had ceased to exist, for the barrier fortresses were henceforth useless. The English ambassador, Yorke, urged upon the Dutch government the treaty right of Great Britain to claim the assistance of 6000 men and twenty ships; Austria had the able advocacy of D'Affry in seeking to induce the States to become parties to the Franco-Austrian alliance. The regent, though an English princess, was scarcely less zealous than were the council-pensionary Steyn, Brunswick and most of the leading burgher-regents in desiring to preserve strict neutrality. To England the answer was made that naval and military help were not due except in case of invasion. The French had meanwhile been offering the Dutch considerable commercial privileges in exchange for their neutrality, with the result that Dutch merchantmen were seized by the English cruisers and carried into English ports to be searched for contraband.

The princess had a very difficult part to play. Delegations of merchants waited upon her urging her to exert her influence with the English government not to use their naval supremacy for the injury of Dutch trade. Anne did her best, but without avail. England was determined to stop all commercial intercourse between France and the West Indies. Dutch merchantmen who attempted to supply the French with goods did so at their own risk. Four deputations from Amsterdam and the maritime towns waited upon the princess, urging an increase of the fleet as a protection against England. Other deputations came from the inland provinces, asking for an increase of the army against the danger of a French invasion. The French were already in occupation of Ostend and Nieuport, and had threatening masses of troops on the Belgian frontier. The regent, knowing on which side the peril to the security of the country was greatest, absolutely refused her consent to an increase of the fleet without an increase of the army. The Estates of Holland refused to vote money for the army; and, having the power of the purse, matters were at a deadlock. The Republic lay helpless and without defence should its enemies determine to attack it. In the midst of all these difficulties and anxieties, surrounded by intrigues and counter-intrigues, sincerely patriotic and desirous to do her utmost for the country, but thwarted and distrusted on every side, the health of the regent, which had never been strong, gradually gave way. On December 11, 1758, she went in person to the States-General, "with tottering steps and death in her face," to endeavour to secure unity of action in the presence of the national danger, but without achieving her object. The maritime provinces were obdurate. Seeing death approaching, with the opening of the new year she made arrangements for the marriage of her daughter Caroline with Charles Christian, Prince of Nassau-Weilburg, and after committing her two children to the care of the Duke of Brunswick (with whom she had effected a reconciliation) and making him guardian of the young Prince of Orange, Anne expired on January 12, 1759, at the early age of forty-nine.

The task Brunswick had to fulfil was an anxious one, but by the exercise of great tact, during the seven years of William's minority, he managed to gather into his hands a great deal of the powers of a stadholder, and at the same time to ingratiate himself with the anti-Orange States party, whose power especially in Holland had been growing in strength and was in fact predominant. By politic concessions to the regents, and by the interest he displayed in the commercial and financial prosperity of the city of Amsterdam, that chief centre of opposition gave its support to his authority; and he was able to do this while keeping at the same time on good terms with Bentinck, Steyn, Fagel and the Orange party.

The political position of the United Provinces during the early part of the Brunswick guardianship was impotent and ignominious in the extreme. Despite continued protests and complaints, Dutch merchantmen were constantly being searched for contraband and brought as prizes into English ports; and the lucrative trade that had been carried on between the West Indies and France in Dutch bottoms was completely stopped. Even the fitting out of twenty-one ships of the line, as a convoy, effected nothing, for such a force could not face the enormous superiority of the English fleet, which at that time swept the seas. The French ambassador, D'Affry, made most skilful use of his opportunities to create a pro-French party in Holland and especially in Amsterdam, and he was not unsuccessful in his intrigues. But the Dutch resolve to remain neutral at any cost remained as strong as ever, for, whatever might be the case with maritime Holland, the inland provinces shrank from running any risks of foreign invasion. When at last the Peace of Paris came in 1763, the representatives of the United Provinces, though they essayed to play the part of mediators between the warring powers, no longer occupied a position of any weight in the councils of the European nations. The proud Republic, which had treated on equal terms with France and with Great Britain in the days of John de Witt and of William III, had become in the eyes of the statesmen of 1763 a negligible quantity.

One of the effects of the falling-off in the overseas trade of Amsterdam was to transform this great commercial city into the central exchange of Europe. The insecurity of sea-borne trade caused many of the younger merchants to deal in money securities and bills of exchange rather than in goods. Banking houses sprang up apace, and large fortunes were made by speculative investments in stocks and shares; and loans for foreign governments, large and small, were readily negotiated. This state of things reached its height during the Seven Years' War, but with the settlement which followed the peace of 1763 disaster came. On July 25 the chief financial house in Amsterdam, that of De Neufville, failed to meet its liabilities and brought down in its crash a very large number of other firms, not merely in Holland, but also in Hamburg and other places; for a veritable panic was caused, and it was some time before stability could be restored.

The remaining three years of the Brunswick *régime* were uneventful in the home country. Differences with the English East India Company however led to the expulsion of the Dutch from their trading settlements on the Hooghley and Coromandel; and in Berbice there was a serious revolt of the negro slaves, which, after hard fighting in the bush, was put down with much cruelty. The young Prince of Orange on the attainment of his eighteenth year, March 8, 1766, succeeded to his hereditary rights. His grandmother, Maria Louisa, to whose care he had owed much, had died on April 9, in the previous year. During the interval the Princess Caroline had taken her place as regent in Friesland.

## CHAPTER XXIV

## WILLIAM V. FIRST PERIOD, 1766-1780

Of all the stadholders of his line William V was the least distinguished. Neither in appearance, character nor manner was he fitted for the position which he had to fill. He had been most carefully educated, and was not wanting in ability, but he lacked energy and thoroughness, and was vacillating and undecided at moments when resolute action was called for. Like his contemporary Louis XVI, had he been born in a private station, he would have adorned it, but like that unhappy monarch he had none of the qualities of a leader of men in critical and difficult times. It was characteristic of him that he asked for confirmation from the Provincial Estates of the dignities and offices which were his by hereditary right. In every thing he relied upon the advice of the Duke of Brunswick, whose methods of government he implicitly followed. To such an extent was this the case that, soon after his accession to power, a secret Act was drawn up (May 3, 1766), known as the Act of Consultation, by which the duke bound himself to remain at the side of the stadholder and to assist him by word and deed in all affairs of State. During the earlier years therefore of William V's stadholderate he consulted Brunswick in every matter, and was thus encouraged to distrust his own judgment and to be fitful and desultory in his attention to affairs of State.

One of the first of Brunswick's cares was to provide for the prince a suitable wife. William II, William III and William IV had all married English princesses, but the feeling of hostility to England was strong in Holland, and it was not thought advisable for the young stadholder to seek for a wife in his mother's family. The choice of the duke was the Prussian Princess Wilhelmina. The new

Princess of Orange was niece on the paternal side of Frederick the Great and on the maternal side of the Duke of Brunswick himself. The marriage took place at Berlin on October, 4 1767. The bride was but sixteen years of age, but her attractive manners and vivacious cleverness caused her to win the popular favour on her first entry into her adopted country.

The first eight years of William's stadholdership passed by quietly. There is little to record. Commerce prospered, but the Hollanders were no longer content with commerce and aimed rather at the rapid accumulation of wealth by successful financial transactions. Stock-dealing had become a national pursuit. Foreign powers came to Amsterdam for loans; and vast amounts of Dutch capital were invested in British and French funds and in the various German states. And yet all the time this rich and prosperous country was surrounded by powerful military and naval powers, and, having no strong natural frontiers, lay exposed defenceless to aggressive attack whether by sea or land. It was in vain that the stadholder, year by year, sent pressing memorials to the States-General urging them to strengthen the navy and the army and to put them on a war footing. The maritime provinces were eager for an increase of the navy, but the inland provinces refused to contribute their quota of the charges. Utrecht, Gelderland, Overyssel and Groningen on the other hand, liable as they were to suffer from military invasion, were ready to sanction a considerable addition to the land forces, but were thwarted by the opposition of Holland, Zeeland and Friesland. So nothing was done, and the Republic, torn by divided interests and with its ruling classes lapped in self-contented comfort and luxury, was a helpless prey that seemed to invite spoliation.

This was the state of things when the British North American colonies rose in revolt against the mother-country. The sympathies of France were from the first with the colonials; and a body of volunteers raised by Lafayette with the connivance of the French overnment crossed the Atlantic to give armed assistance to the rebels. Scarcely less warm was the feeling in the Netherlands. The motives which prompted it were partly sentimental, partly practical. There was a certain similarity between the struggle for independence on the part of the American colonists against a mighty state like Great Britain, and their own struggle with the world-power of Spain. There was also the hope that the rebellion would have the practical result of opening out to the Dutch merchants a lucrative trade with the Americans, one of whose chief grievances against the mother-country had been the severity of the restrictions forbidding all trading with foreign lands. At the same time the whole air was full of revolutionary ideas, which were unsettling men's minds. This was no less the case in the Netherlands than elsewhere; and the American revolt was regarded as a realisation and vindication in practical politics of the teaching of Montesquieu, Voltaire and Rousseau, whose works were widely read, and of the Englishmen Hume, Priestley and Richard Price. Foremost among the propagandists of these ideas were Jan Dirk van der Capellen tot de Pol, a nobleman of Overyssel, and the three burgomasters of Amsterdam, Van Berckel, De Vrij Temminck and Hooft, all anti-Orange partisans and pro-French in sentiment. Amidst all these contending factions and opinions, the State remained virtually without a head, William V drifting along incapable of forming an independent decision, or of making a firm and resolute use of the great powers with which he was entrusted.

Torn by internal dissensions, the maintenance of neutrality by the Republic became even more difficult than in the Seven Years' War. The old questions of illicit trade with the enemy and the carrying of contraband arose. The Dutch islands of St Eustatius and Curaçoa became centres of smuggling enterprise; and Dutch merchant vessels were constantly being searched by the British cruisers and often carried off as prizes into English ports. Strong protests were made and great irritation aroused. Amsterdam was the chief sufferer. Naturally in this hot-bed of Republican opinion and French sympathies, the prince was blamed and was accused of preferring English interests to those of his own country. The arrival of the Duke de la Vauguyon, as French ambassador, did much to fan the flame. Vauguyon entered into close relations with the Amsterdam regents and did all in his power to exacerbate the growing feeling of hostility to England, and to persuade the Republic to abandon the ancient alliance with that country in favour of one with France.

The British ambassador, Yorke, lacked his ingratiating manners; and his language now became imperative and menacing in face of the flourishing contraband trade that was carried on at St Eustatius. In consequence of his strong protest the governor of the island,

Van Heyliger, was replaced by De Graeff, but it was soon discovered that the new governor was no improvement upon his predecessor. He caused additional offence to the British government by saluting the American flag on November 16, 1776. The threats of Yorke grew stronger, but with small result. The Americans continued to draw supplies from the Dutch islands. The entry of France into the war on February 6, 1778, followed by that of Spain, complicated matters. England was now fighting with her back to the wall; and her sea-power had to be exerted to its utmost to make head against so many foes. She waged relentless war on merchant ships carrying contraband or suspected contraband, whether enemy or neutral. At last money was voted under pressure from Amsterdam, supported by the prince, for the building of a fleet for protection against privateers and for purposes of convoy. But a fleet cannot be built in a day; and, when Admiral van Bylandt was sent out in 1777, his squadron consisted of five ships only. Meanwhile negotiations with England were proceeding and resulted in certain concessions, consent being given to allow what was called "limited convoy." The States-General, despite the opposition of Amsterdam, accepted on November 13, 1778, the proffered compromise. But the French ambassador Vauguyon supported the protest of Amsterdam by threatening, unless the States-General insisted upon complete freedom of trade, to withdraw the commercial privileges granted to the Republic by France. Finding that the States-General upheld their resolution of November 13, he carried his threat into execution. This action brought the majority of the Estates of Holland to side with Amsterdam and to call for a repeal of the "limited convoy" resolution. The English on their part, well aware of all this, continued to do their utmost to stop all supplies reaching their enemies in Dutch bottoms, convoy or no convoy. The British government, though confronted by so many foes, now took strong measures. Admiral van Bylandt, convoying a fleet of merchantmen through the Channel, was compelled by a British squadron to strike his flag; and all the Dutch vessels were taken into Portsmouth. This was followed by a demand under the treaty of 1678 for Dutch aid in ships and men, or the abrogation of the treaty of alliance and of the commercial privileges it carried with it. Yorke gave the States-General three weeks for their decision; and on April 17, 1779, the long-standing alliance, which William III had made the keystone of his policy, ceased to exist. War was not declared, but the States-General voted for "unlimited convoy" on April 24; and every effort was made by the Admiralties to build and equip a considerable fleet. The reception given to the American privateer, Paul Jones, who, despite English protests, was not only allowed to remain in Holland for three months, but was feted as a hero (October-December, 1779), accentuated the increasing alienation of the two countries.

At this critical stage the difficult position of England was increased by the formation under the leadership of Russia of a League of Armed Neutrality. Its object was to maintain the principle of the freedom of the seas for the vessels of neutral countries, unless they were carrying contraband of war, *i.e.*military or naval munitions. Further a blockade would not be recognised if not effective. Sweden and Denmark joined the league; and the Empress Catherine invited the United Provinces and several other neutral powers to do likewise. Her object was to put a curb upon what was described by Britain's enemies as the tyranny of the Mistress of the Seas. The Republic for some time hesitated. Conscious of their weakness at sea, the majority in the States-General were unwilling to take any overt steps to provoke hostilities, when an event occurred which forced their hands.

In 1778 certain secret negotiations had taken place between the Amsterdam regents and the American representatives at Paris, Franklin and Lee. It chanced that Henry Lawrence, a former President of the Congress, was on his way from New York to Amsterdam in September, 1780, for the purpose of raising a loan. Pursued by an English frigate, the ship on which he was sailing was captured off Newfoundland; and among his papers were found copies of the negotiations of 1778 and of the correspondence which then took place. Great was the indignation of the British government, and it was increased when the Estates of Holland, under the influence of Amsterdam, succeeded in bringing the States-General (by a majority of four provinces to three) to join the League of Armed Neutrality. Better open war than a sham peace. Instructions were therefore sent to the ambassador Yorke to demand the punishment of the Amsterdam regents for their clandestine transactions with the enemies of England. The reply was that the matter should be brought before the Court of Holland; and Van Welderen, the Dutch ambassador in London, in vain endeavoured to give assurances that the States were anxious to maintain a strict neutrality. Yorke demanded immediate satisfaction and once more called upon the Republic to furnish the aid in men and ships in accordance with the treaty. Further instructions were therefore sent to Van Welderen, but they were delayed by tempestuous weather. In any case they would have been of no avail. The British government was in no mood for temporising. On December 20, 1780 war was declared against the United Provinces; and three days later Yorke left the Hague.

# CHAPTER XXV

# STADHOLDERATE OF WILLIAM V, *CONTINUED*, 1780-1788

The outbreak of war meant the final ruin of the Dutch Republic. Its internal condition at the close of 1780 made it hopelessly unfitted to enter upon a struggle with the overwhelming sea-power of England. Even had William V possessed the qualities of leadership, he would have had to contend against the bitter opposition and enmity of the anti-Orange party among the burgher-regents, of which Van der Capellen was one of the most moving spirits, and which had its chief centre in Amsterdam. But the prince, weak and incompetent, was apparently intent only on evading his responsibilities, and so laid himself open to the charges of neglect and mal-administration that were brought against him by his enemies.

Against an English fleet of more than 300 vessels manned by a force of something like 100,000 seamen, the Dutch had but twenty ships of the line, most of them old and of little value. Large sums of money were now voted for the equipment of a fleet; and the Admiralties were urged to press forward the work with all possible vigour. But progress was necessarily slow. Everything was lacking—material, munitions, equipment, skilled labour—and these could not be supplied in time to prevent Dutch commerce being swept from the seas and the Dutch colonies captured. The Republicans, or Patriots, as they began to name themselves, were at first delighted that the Orange stadholder and his party had been compelled to break with England and to seek the alliance of France; but their joy was but short-lived. Bad tidings followed rapidly one upon another. In the first month of the war 200 merchantmen were captured, of the value of 15,000,000 florins. The fishing fleets dared not put out to sea. In 1780 more than 2000 vessels passed through the Sound, in 1781 only eleven. On February 3 St Eustatius surrendered to Admiral Rodney, when one hundred and thirty merchantmen together with immense stores fell into the hands of the captors. Surinam and Curaçoa received warning and were able to put themselves into a state of defence, but the colonies of Demerara, Berbice and Essequibo were taken, also St Martin, Saba and the Dutch establishments on the coast of Guinea. In the East Indies Negapatam and the factories in Bengal passed into English possession; and the Cape, Java and Ceylon would have shared the same fate, but for the timely protection of a French squadron under the command of Suffren, one of the ablest and bravest of French seamen.

The losses were enormous, and loud was the outcry raised in Amsterdam and elsewhere against the prince of being the cause of his country's misfortunes. "Orange," so his enemies said, "is to blame for everything. He possessed the power to do whatsoever he would, and he neglected to use it in providing for the navy and the land's defences." This was to a considerable extent unjust, for William from 1767 onwards had repeatedly urged an increase of the sea and land forces, but his proposals had been thwarted by bitter opposition, especially in Amsterdam itself. The accusations were to this extent correct that he was undoubtedly invested with large executive power which he had not the strength of will to use. It was at this period that Van der Capellen and others started a most violent press campaign not only against the stadholder, but against the hereditary stadholdership and all that the house of Orange-Nassau stood for in the history of the Dutch Republic. Brunswick was attacked with especial virulence. The "Act of Consultation" had become known; and, had the prince been willing to throw responsibility upon the duke for bad advice he might have gained some fleeting popularity by separating himself from the hated "foreigner." But William, weak though he was, would not abandon the man who in his youth had been to him and to his house a wise and staunch protector and friend; and he knew, moreover, that the accusations against Brunswick were really aimed at himself. The duke, however, after appealing to the States-General, and being by them declared free from blame, found the spirit of hostility so strong at Amsterdam and in several of the Provincial Estates that he withdrew first (1782) to Hertogenbosch, of which place he was governor, and finally left the country in 1784.

The war meanwhile, which had been the cause, or rather the pretext, for this outburst of popular feeling against Brunswick, was pursuing its course. In the summer of 1781 Rear-Admiral Zoutman, at the head of a squadron of fifteen war-ships, was ordered to convoy seventy-two merchantmen into the Baltic. He met an English force of twelve vessels, which were larger and better armed than the Dutch, under Vice-Admiral Hyde Parker. A fierce encounter took place at the Doggerbank on August 5, which lasted all day without either side being able to claim the victory. Parker was the first to retreat, but Zoutman had likewise to return to the Texel to repair his disabled ships, and his convoy never reached the Baltic. The Dutch however were greatly elated at the result of the fight, and Zoutman and his captains were feted as heroes.

Doggerbank battle was but, at the most, an indecisive engagement on a very small scale, and it brought no relaxation in the English blockade. No Dutch admiral throughout all the rest of the war ventured to face the English squadrons in the North Sea and in the Channel; and the Dutch mercantile marine disappeared from the ocean. England was strong enough to defy the Armed Neutrality, which indeed proved, as its authoress Catherine II is reported to have said, "an armed nullity." There was deep dissatisfaction throughout the country, and mutual recriminations between the various responsible authorities, but there was some justice in making the stadholder the chief scapegoat, for, whatever may have been the faults of others, a vigorous initiative in the earlier years of his stadholdership might have effected much, and would have certainly gained for him increased influence and respect.

The war lasted for two years, if war that could be called in which there was practically no fighting. There were changes of government in England during that time, and the party of which Fox was the leader had no desire to press hardly upon the Dutch. Several efforts were made to induce them to negotiate in London a separate peace on favourable terms, but the partisans of France in Amsterdam and elsewhere rendered these tentative negotiations fruitless. Being weak, the Republic suffered accordingly by having to accept finally whatever terms its mightier neighbour thought fit to dictate. On November 30, 1782, the preliminary treaty by which Great Britain conceded to the United States of America their independence was concluded. A truce between Great Britain and France followed in January, 1783, in which the United Provinces, as a satellite of France, were included. No further hostilities took place, but the negotiations for a definitive peace dragged on, the protests of the Dutch plenipotentiaries at Paris against the terms arranged between England and France being of no avail. Finally the French government concluded a separate peace on September 3; but it was not till May 20, 1784, that the Dutch could be induced to surrender Negapatam and to grant to the English the right of free entry into the Moluccas. Nor was this the only humiliation the Republic had at this time to suffer, for during the course of the English war serious troubles with the Emperor Joseph II had arisen.

Joseph had in 1780 paid a visit to his Belgian provinces, and he had seen with his own eyes the ruinous condition of the barrier fortresses. On the pretext that the fortresses were now useless, since France and the Republic were allies, Joseph informed the States-General of his intention to dismantle them all with the exception of Antwerp and Luxemburg. This meant of course the withdrawal of the Dutch garrisons. The States-General, being unable to resist, deemed it the wiser course to submit. The troops accordingly left the barrier towns in January, 1782. Such submission, as was to be expected, inevitably led to further demands.

The Treaty of Münster (1648) had left the Dutch in possession of territory on both banks of the Scheldt, and had given them the right to close all access by river to Antwerp, which had for a century and a quarter ceased to be a sea-port. In 1781, during his visit to Belgium, Joseph had received a number of petitions in favour of the liberation of the Scheldt. At the moment he did not see his way to taking action, but in 1783 he took advantage of the embarrassments of the Dutch government to raise the question of a disputed boundary in Dutch Flanders; and in the autumn of that year a body of Imperial troops took forcible possession of some frontier forts near Sluis. Matters were brought to a head in May, 1784, by the emperor sending to the States-General a detailed summary of all his grievances, *Tableau sommaire des prétentions*. In this he claimed, besides cessions of territory at Maestricht and in Dutch

Flanders, the right of free navigation on the Scheldt, the demolition of the Dutch forts closing the river, and freedom of trading from the Belgian ports to the Indies. This document was in fact an ultimatum, the rejection of which meant war. For once all parties in the Republic were united in resistance to the emperor's demands; and when in October, 1784, two ships attempted to navigate the Scheldt, the one starting from Antwerp, the other from Ostend, they were both stopped; the first at Saftingen on the frontier, the second at Flushing. War seemed imminent. An Austrian army corps was sent to the Netherlands; and the Dutch bestirred themselves with a vigour unknown in the States for many years to equip a strong fleet and raise troops to repel invasion. It is, however, almost certain that, had Joseph carried out his threat of sending a force of 80,000 men to avenge the insult offered to his ships, the hastily enlisted Dutch troops would not have been able to offer effectual resistance. But the question the emperor was raising was no mere local question. He was really seeking to violate important clauses of two international treaties, to which all the great powers were parties, the Treaty of Münster and the Treaty of Utrecht. His own possession of the Belgian Netherlands and the independence and sovereign rights of the Dutch Republic rested on the same title. Joseph had counted upon the help or at least the friendly neutrality of his brother-in-law, Louis XVI, but France had just concluded an exhausting war in which the United Provinces had been her allies. The French, moreover, had no desire to see the Republic overpowered by an act of aggression that might give rise to European complications. Louis XVI offered mediation, and it was accepted.

It is doubtful indeed whether the emperor, whose restless brain was always full of new schemes, really meant to carry his threats into execution. In the autumn of 1784 a plan for exchanging the distant Belgian Netherlands for the contiguous Electorate of Bavaria was beginning to exercise his thoughts and diplomacy. He showed himself therefore ready to make concessions; and by the firmness of the attitude of France both the disputants were after lengthy negotiations brought to terms, which were embodied in a treaty signed at Fontainebleau on November 8,1785. The Dutch retained the right to close the Scheldt, but had to dismantle some of the forts; the frontier of Dutch Flanders was to be that of 1664; and Joseph gave up all claim to Maestricht in consideration of a payment of 9,500,000 florins. A few days later an alliance between France and the Republic, known as "the Defensive Confederacy" of Fontainebleau, was concluded, the French government advancing 4,500,000 florins towards the ransom of Maestricht. The return of peace, however, far from allaying the spirit of faction in the Republic, was to lead to civil strife.

The situation with which William V now had to deal was in some ways more difficult and dangerous than in the days of his greater predecessors. It was no longer a mere struggle for supremacy between the Orange-Stadholder party (*prins-gezinderi*) and the patrician-regents of the town corporations (*staats-gezinderi*); a third party had come into existence, the democratic or "patriot" party, which had imbibed the revolutionary ideas of Rousseau and others about the Rights of Man and the Social Contract. These new ideas, spread about with fiery zeal by the two nobles, Van der Capellen tot de Pol and his cousin Van der Capellen van den Marsch, had found a fertile soil in the northern Netherlands, and among all classes, including other nobles and many leading burgomasters. Their aim was to abolish all privileges whether in Church or State, and to establish the principle of the sovereignty of the people. These were the days, be it remembered, which immediately succeeded the American Revolution and preceded the summoning of the States-General in France with its fateful consequences. The atmosphere was full of revolution; and the men of the new ideas had no more sympathy with the pretensions of an aristocratic caste of burgher-regents to exclude their fellow-citizens from a voice in the management of their own affairs, than they had with the quasi-sovereign position of an hereditary stadholder. Among the Orange party were few men of mark. The council-pensionary Bleiswijk was without character, ready to change sides with the shifting wind; and Count Bentinck van Rhoon had little ability. They were, however, to discover in burgomaster Van de Spiegel of Goes a statesman destined soon to play a great part in the history of the country. During this period of acute party strife Patriot and Orangeman were not merely divided from one another on questions of domestic policy. The one party were strong adherents of the French alliance and leant upon its support; the other sought to renew the bonds which had so long united the Republic with England. Indeed the able representatives of France and England at the Hague at this time, the Count de Vérac and Sir James Harris (afterwards Lord Malmesbury), were the real leaders and advisers, behind the scenes, of the opposing factions.

The strength of parties varied in the different provinces. Holland, always more or less anti-stadholder, was the chief centre of the patriots. With Holland were the majority of the Estates of Friesland, Groningen and Overyssel. In Utrecht the nobles and the regents were for the stadholder, but the townsmen were strong patriots. Zeeland supported the prince, who had with him the army, the preachers and the great mass of small *bourgeoisie* and the country folk. Nothing could exceed the violence and unscrupulousness of the attacks that were directed against the stadholder in the press; and no efforts were spared by his opponents to curtail his rights and to insult him personally. Corps of patriot volunteers were enrolled in different places with self-elected officers. The wearing of the Orange colours and the singing of the *Wilhelmus* was forbidden, and punished by fine and imprisonment. In September, 1785, a riot at the Hague led to the Estates of Holland taking from the stadholder the command of the troops in that city. They likewise ordered the foot-guards henceforth to salute the members of the Estates, and removed the arms of the prince from the standards and the facings of the troops. As a further slight, the privilege was given to the deputies, while the Estates were in session, to pass through the gate into the Binnenhof, which had hitherto been reserved for the use of the stadholder alone. Filled with indignation and resentment, William left the Hague with his family and withdrew to his country residence at Het Loo. Such a step only increased the confusion and disorder that was filling every part of the country, for it showed that William had neither the spirit nor the energy to make a firm stand against those who were resolved to overthrow his authority.

In Utrecht the strife between the parties led to scenes of violence. The "patriots" found an eloquent leader in the person of a young student named Ondaatje. The Estates of the province were as conservative as the city of Utrecht itself was ultra-democratic; and a long series of disturbances were caused by the burgher-regents of the Town Council refusing to accede to the popular demand for a drastic change in their constitution. Finally they were besieged in the town hall by a numerous gathering of the "free corps" headed by Ondaatje, and were compelled to accede to the people's demands. A portion of the Estates thereupon assembled at Amersfoort; and at their request a body of 400 troops were sent there from Nijmwegen. Civil war seemed imminent, but it was averted by the timely mediation of the Estates of Holland.

Scarcely less dangerous was the state of affairs in Gelderland. Here the Estates of the Gelderland had an Orange majority, but the patriots had an influential leader in Van der Capellen van den Marsch. Petitions and requests were sent to the Estates demanding popular reforms. The Estates not only refused to receive them but issued a proclamation forbidding the dissemination of revolutionary literature in the province. The small towns of Elburg and Hattem not only refused to obey, but the inhabitants proceeded by force to compel their Councils to yield to their demands. The Estates thereupon called upon the stadholder to send troops to restore order. This was done, and garrisons were placed in Elburg and Hattem. This step caused a very great commotion in Holland and especially at Amsterdam; and the patriot leaders felt that the time had come to take measures by which to unite all their forces in the different parts of the country for common defence and common action. The result of all this was that the movement became more and more revolutionary in its aims. To such an extent was this the case that many of the old aristocratic anti-stadholder regents began to perceive that the carrying out of the patriots' programme of popular reform would mean the overthrow of the system of government which they upheld, at the same time as that of the stadholderate.

The reply of the Estates of Holland to the strong measures taken against Elburg and Hattem was the "provisional" removal of the prince from the post of captain-general, and the recalling, on their own authority, of all troops in the pay of the province serving in the frontier fortresses (August, 1786). As the year went on the agitation grew in volume; increasing numbers were enrolled in the free corps. The complete ascendancy of the ultra-democratic patriots was proved and assured by tumultuous gatherings at Amsterdam (April 21, 1787), and a few days later at Rotterdam, compelling the Town Councils to dismiss at Amsterdam nine regents and at Rotterdam seven, suspected of Orange leanings. Holland was now entirely under patriot control; and the democrats in other districts were eagerly looking to the forces which Holland could bring into the field to protect the patriot cause from tyrannous acts of oppression by the stadholder's troops. In the summer of 1787 the forces on both sides were being mustered on the borders of the province of Utrecht, and frequent collisions had already taken place. Nothing but the prince's indecision had prevented the actual outbreak of a general civil war. At the critical moment of suspense an incident occurred, however, which was to effect a dramatic change in the situation.

William's pusillanimous attitude (he was actually talking of withdrawing from the country to Nassau) was by no means acceptable to his high-spirited wife. The princess was all for vigorous action, and she wrung from William a reluctant consent to her returning from Nijmwegen, where for security she had been residing with her family, to the Hague. In that political centre she would be in close communication with Sir J. Harris and Van de Spiegel, and would be able to organise a powerful opposition in Holland to patriot ascendancy. It was a bold move, the success of which largely depended on the secrecy with which it was carried out. On June 28 Wilhelmina started from Nijmwegen, but the commandant of the free corps at Gouda, hearing that horses were being ordered at Schoonhoven and Haasrecht for a considerable party, immediately sent to headquarters for instructions. He was told not to allow any suspicious body of persons to pass. He accordingly stopped the princess and detained her at a farm until the arrival at Woerden of the members of the Committee of Defence. By these Her Highness was treated (on learning her quality) with all respect, but she was informed that she could not proceed without the permit of the Estates of Holland. The indignant princess did not wait for the permit to arrive, but returned to Nijmwegen.

The British ambassador, Harris, at once brought the action of the Estates of Holland before the States-General and demanded satisfaction; and on July 10 a still more peremptory demand was made by the Prussian ambassador, von Thulemeyer. Frederick William II was incensed at the treatment his sister had received; and, when the Estates of Holland refused to punish the offending officials, on the ground that no insult had been intended, orders were immediately given for an army of 20,000 men under Charles, Duke of Brunswick, to cross the frontier and exact reparation. The Prussians entered in three columns and met with little opposition.

Utrecht, where 7000 "patriot" volunteers were encamped, was evacuated, the whole force taking flight and retreating in disorder to Holland. Gorkum, Dordrecht, Kampen and other towns surrendered without a blow; and on September 17 Brunswick's troops entered the Hague amidst general rejoicings. The populace wore Orange favours, and the streets rang with the cry of *Oranje boven*. Amsterdam still held out and prepared for defence, hoping for French succour; and thither the leaders of the patriot party had fled, together with the representatives of six cities. The nobility, the representatives of eight cities, and the council-pensionary remained at the Hague, met as the Estates of Holland, repealed all the anti-Orange edicts, and invited the prince to return. Amidst scenes of great enthusiasm the stadholder made his entry into the Binnenhof on September 20. The hopes held by the patriot refugees at Amsterdam of French aid were vain, for the French government was in no position to help anyone. As soon as the Prussian army appeared before the gates, the Town Council, as in 1650, was unwilling to jeopardise the welfare of the city by armed resistance, and negotiations were opened with Brunswick. On October 3 Amsterdam capitulated, and the campaign was over.

The princess was now in a position to demand reparation for the insult she had received; and, though her terms were severe, the Estates of Holland obsequiously agreed to carry them out (October 6). She demanded the punishment of all who had taken part in her arrest, the disbanding of the free corps, and the purging of the various Town Councils of obnoxious persons. All this was done. In the middle of November the main body of the Prussians departed, but a force of 4000 men remained to assist the Dutch troops in keeping order. The English ambassador, Harris, and Van de Spiegel were the chief advisers of the now dominant Orange government; and drastic steps were taken to establish the hereditary stadholderate henceforth on a firm basis. All persons filling any office were required to swear to maintain the settlement of 1766, and to declare that "the high and hereditary dignities" conferred upon the Princes of Orange were "an essential part not only of the constitution of each province but of the whole State." An amnesty was proclaimed by the prince on November 21, but it contained so many exceptions that it led to a large number of the patriots seeking a place of refuge in foreign countries, as indeed many of the leaders had already done, chiefly in France and the Belgian Netherlands. It has been said that the exiles numbered as many as 40,000, but this is possibly an exaggeration. The victory of the Orange party was complete; but a triumph achieved by the aid of a foreign invader was dearly purchased. The Prussian troops, as they retired laden with booty after committing many excesses, left behind them a legacy of hatred.

# CHAPTER XXVI

# THE ORANGE RESTORATION. DOWNFALL OF THE REPUBLIC, 1788-1795

One of the first steps taken, after the restoration of the stadholder's power had been firmly established, was the appointment of Laurens Pieter van de Spiegel to the post of council-pensionary of Holland in place of the trimmer Bleiswijk. It was quite contrary to usage that a Zeelander should hold this the most important post in the Estates of Holland, but the influence of the princess and of Harris secured his unanimous election on December 3, 1787. Van de Spiegel proved himself to be a statesman of high capacity, sound judgment and great moderation, not unworthy to be ranked among the more illustrious occupants of his great office. He saw plainly the hopeless deadlock and confusion of the machinery of government and its need of root-and-branch revision, but he was no more able to achieve it than his predecessors. The feebleness of the stadholder, the high-handedness of the princess, and the selfish clinging of the patrician-regents to their privileged monopoly of civic power were insuperable hindrances to any attempts to interfere with the existing state of things. Such was the inherent weakness of the Republic that it was an independent State in little more than name; its form of government was guaranteed by foreign powers on whom it had to rely for its defence against external foes.

Prussia by armed force, England by diplomatic support, had succeeded in restoring the hereditary stadholderate to a predominant position in the State. It was the first care of the triumvirate, Harris, Van de Spiegel and the princess, to secure what had been achieved by bringing about a defensive alliance between the Republic, Great Britain and Prussia. After what had taken place this was not a difficult task; and two separate treaties were signed between the States-General and the two protecting powers on the same day, April 15, 1788, each of the three states undertaking to furnish a definite quota of troops, ships or money, if called upon to do so. Both Prussia and England gave a strong guarantee for the upholding of the hereditary stadholderate. This was followed by the conclusion of an Anglo-Prussian alliance directed against France and Austria (August 13). The marriage of the hereditary prince with Frederika Louise Wilhelmina of Prussia added yet another to the many royal alliances of the House of Orange; but, though it raised the prestige of the stadholder's position, it only served to make that position more dependent on the support of the foreigner.

The council-pensionary, Van de Spiegel, did all that statesman could do in these difficult times to effect reforms and bring order out of chaos. It was fortunate for the Republic that the stadholder should have discerned the merits of this eminent servant of the state and entrusted to him so largely the direction of affairs. Internally the spirit of faction had, superficially at least, been crushed by Prussian military intervention, but externally there was serious cause for alarm. Van de Spiegel watched with growing disquietude the threatening aspect of things in France, preluding the great Revolution; and still more serious was the insurrection, which the reforming zeal of Joseph II had caused to break out in the Austrian Netherlands. Joseph's personal visit to his Belgian dominions had filled him with a burning desire to sweep away the various provincial privileges and customs and to replace them by administrative uniformity. Not less was his eagerness to free education from clerical influence. He stirred up thereby the fierce opposition of clericals and democrats alike, ending in armed revolt in Brabant and elsewhere. A desultory struggle went on during the years 1787, '88 and '89, ending in January, 1790, in a meeting of the States-General at Brussels and the formation of a federal republic under the name of "the United States of Belgium." All this was very perturbing to the Dutch government, who were most anxious lest an Austrian attempt at reconquest might lead to a European conflict close to their borders. The death of Joseph on February 24, 1790, caused the danger to disappear. His brother, Leopold II, at once offered to re-establish ancient privileges, and succeeded by tact and moderation in restoring Austrian rule under the old conditions.

That this result was brought about without any intervention of foreign powers was in no small measure due to a conference at the Hague, in which Van de Spiegel conducted negotiations with the representatives of Prussia, England and Austria for a settlement of the Belgian question without disturbance of the peace.

The council-pensionary found the finances of the country in a state of great confusion. One of his first cares was a re-assessment of the provincial quotas, some of which were greatly in arrears and inadequate in amount, thus throwing a disproportionate burden upon Holland. It was a difficult task, but successfully carried out. The affairs of the East and West India Companies next demanded his serious attention. Both of them were practically bankrupt.

The East India Company had, during the 18th century, been gradually on the decline. Its object was to extract wealth from Java and its other eastern possessions; and, by holding the monopoly of trade and compelling the natives to hand over to the Company's officials a proportion of the produce of the land at a price fixed by the Company far below its real value (*contingent-en leverantie-stelsel*), the country was drained of its resources and the inhabitants impoverished simply to increase the shareholder's dividends. This was bad enough, but it was made worse by the type of men whom the directors, all of whom belonged to the patrician regent-families, sent out to fill the posts of governor-general and the subordinate governorships. For many decades these officials had been chosen, not for their proved experience or for their knowledge of the East or of the Indian trade, but because of family connection; and the nominees went forth with the intention of enriching themselves as quickly as possible. This led to all sorts of abuses, and the profits of the Company from all these causes kept diminishing. But, in order to keep up their credit, the Board of XVII continued to pay large dividends out of capital, with the inevitable result that the Company got into debt and had to apply for help to the State. The English war completed its ruin. In June, 1783, the Estates of Holland appointed a Commission to examine into the affairs of the Company. Too many people in Holland had invested their money in it, and the Indian trade was too important, for an actual collapse of the Company to be permitted. Accordingly an advance of 8,000,000 florins was made to the directors, with a guarantee for 38,000,000 of debt. But things went from bad to worse. In 1790 the indebtedness of the Company amounted to 85,000,000 florins. Van de Spiegel and others were convinced that the only satisfactory solution would be for the State to dissolve the Company and take over the Indian possessions in full sovereignty at the cost of liquidating the debt, A commission was appointed in 1791 to proceed to the East and make a report upon the condition of the colonies. Before their mission was accomplished the French armies were overrunning the Republic. It was not till 1798 that the existence of the Company actually came to an end. To the West India Company the effect of the English war was likewise disastrous. The Guiana colonies, whose sugar plantations had been a source of great profit, had been conquered first by the English, then by the French; and, though they were restored after the war, the damage inflicted had brought the Company into heavy difficulties. Its charter expired in 1791, and it was not renewed. The colonies became colonies of the State, the shareholders being compensated by exchanging their depreciated shares for Government bonds.

The Orange restoration, however, and the efforts of Van de Spiegel to strengthen its bases by salutary reforms were doomed to be short-lived. The council-pensionary, in spite of his desire to relinquish office at the end of his quinquennial term, was reelected by the Estates of Holland on December 6, 1792, and yielded to the pressure put upon him to continue his task. A form of government, which had been imposed against their will on the patriot party by the aid of foreign bayonets, was certain to have many enemies; and such prospect of permanence as it had lay in the goodwill and confidence inspired by the statesmanlike and conciliatory policy of Van de Spiegel. But it was soon to be swept away in the cataclysm of the French Revolution now at the height of its devastating course.

In France extreme revolutionary ideas had made rapid headway, ending in the dethronement and imprisonment of the king on August 10, 1792. The invasion of France by the Prussian and Austrian armies only served to inflame the French people, intoxicated by their new-found liberty, to a frenzy of patriotism. Hastily raised armies succeeded in checking the invasion at Valmy on September 20, 1792; and in their turn invading Belgium under the leadership of Dumouriez, they completely defeated the Austrians at Jemappes on November 6. The whole of Belgium was overrun and by a decree of the French Convention was annexed.

The fiery enthusiasts, into whose hands the government of the French Republic had fallen, were eager to carry by force of arms the principles of liberty, fraternity and equality to all Europe, declaring that "all governments are our enemies, all peoples are our friends." The southern Netherlands having been conquered, it was evident that the northern Republic would speedily invite attack. The Dutch government, anxious to avoid giving any cause for hostilities, had carefully abstained from offering any encouragement to the emigrants or support to the enemies of the French Republic. Van de Spiegel had even expressed to De Maulde, the French ambassador, a desire to establish friendly relations with the Republican government. But the Jacobins looked upon the United Provinces as the dependent of their enemies England and Prussia; and, when after the execution of the king the English ambassador was recalled from Paris, the National Convention immediately declared war against England and at the same time against the stadholder of Holland "because of his slavish bondage to the courts of St James and Berlin."

Dumouriez at the head of the French army prepared to enter the United Provinces at two points. The main body under his own command was to cross the Moerdijk to Dordrecht and then advance on Rotterdam, the Hague, Leyden and Haarlem. He was accompanied by the so-called *Batavian legion*, enlisted from the patriot exiles under Colonel Daendels, once the fiery anti-Orange advocate of Hattem. General Miranda, who was besieging Maestricht, was to march by Nijmwegen and Venloo to Utrecht. The two forces would then unite and make themselves masters of Amsterdam. The ambitious scheme miscarried. At first success attended Dumouriez. Breda fell after a feeble resistance, also De Klundert and Geertruidenberg. Meanwhile the advance of an Austrian army under Coburg relieved Maestricht and inflicted a defeat upon the French at Aldenhoven on March 1, 1793. Dumouriez, compelled to retreat, was himself beaten at Neerwinden on March 18, and withdrew to Antwerp. For the moment danger was averted. Revolutionary movements at Amsterdam and elsewhere failed to realise the hopes of the patriots, and the Dutch government was able to breathe again.

It indeed appeared that the French menace need no longer be feared. Dumouriez changed sides and, failing to induce his troops to follow him, took refuge in the enemy's camp. A powerful coalition had now been formed by the energy of Pitt against revolutionary France; and, in April, 1794, a strong English army under the Duke of York had joined Coburg. They were supported by 22,000 Dutch troops commanded by the two sons of the Prince of Orange.

New French armies, however, organised by the genius of Carnot, proved more than a match for the allied forces acting without any unity of place under slow-moving and incompetent leaders. Coburg and the Austrians were heavily defeated at Fleurus by Jourdan on June 26. York and Prince William thereupon retreated across the frontier, followed by the French under Pichegru, while another French general, Moreau, took Sluis and overran Dutch Flanders. This gave fresh encouragement to the patriot party, who in Amsterdam formed a revolutionary committee, of which the leaders were Gogel, Van Dam and Kraijenhoff. Nothing overt was done, but by means of a large number of so-called reading-societies (*leesgezelschappen*) secret preparations were made for a general uprising so soon as circumstances permitted, and communications were meanwhile kept up with the exiled patriots. But Pichegru, though he captured Maestricht and other towns, was very cautious in his movements and distrustful of the promises of the Amsterdam Convention that a general revolt would follow upon his entry into Holland.

In this way the year 1794 drew to its end; and, as no further help from England or Prussia could be obtained, the States-General thought it might be possible to save the Republic from the fate of Belgium by opening negotiations for peace with the enemy. Accordingly two envoys, Brantsen and Repelaer, were sent on December 16 to the French headquarters, whence they proceeded to Paris. Fearing lest their plans for an uprising should be foiled, the Amsterdam committee also despatched two representatives, Blauw and Van Dam, to Paris to counteract the envoys of Van de Spiegel, and to urge upon the French commanders an immediate offensive against Holland. The withdrawal of the remains of the English army under the Duke of York, and the setting in of a strong frost, lent force to their representations. The army of Pichegru, accompanied by Daendels and his Batavian legion, were able to cross the rivers; and Holland lay open before them. It was in vain that the two young Orange princes did their utmost to organise resistance. In

January, 1795 one town after another surrendered; and on the 19th Daendels without opposition entered Amsterdam.

The revolution was completely triumphant, for on this very day the stadholder, despite the protests of his sons and the efforts of the council-pensionary, had left the country. The English government had offered to receive William V and his family; and arrangements had been quietly made for the passage across the North Sea. The princess with her daughter-in-law and grandson were the first to leave; and on January 17, 1795, William himself, on the ground that the French would never negotiate so long as he was in the country, bade farewell to the States-General and the foreign ambassadors. On the following day he embarked with his sons and household on a number of fishing-pinks at Scheveningen and put to sea. With his departure the stadholderate and the Republic of the United Netherlands came to an end.

# CHAPTER XXVII

# THE BATAVIAN REPUBLIC, 1795-1806

On January 19, 1795, Amsterdam fell into the hands of the advancing French troops. Daendels had previously caused a proclamation to be distributed which declared "that the representatives of the French people wished the Dutch nation to make themselves free; that they do not desire to oppress them as conquerors, but to ally themselves with them as with a free people." A complete change of the city government took place without any disturbance or shedding of blood. At the summons of the Revolutionary Committee the members of the Town Council left the Council Hall and were replaced by twenty-one citizens "as provisional representatives of the people of Amsterdam." Of this body Rutger Jan Schimmelpenninck, a former advocate of the Council, was appointed president. The other towns, one after the other, followed in the steps of the capital. The patrician corporations were abolished and replaced by provisional municipal assemblies. Everywhere the downfall of the old *régime* was greeted with tumultuous joy by those large sections of the Dutch population which had imbibed revolutionary principles; and the French troops were welcomed by the "patriots" as brothers and deliverers. "Trees of Liberty," painted in the national colours, were erected in the principal squares; and the citizens, wearing "caps of liberty" danced round them hand in hand with the foreign soldiers. Feast-making, illuminations and passionate orations, telling that a new era of "liberty, fraternity and equality" had dawned for the Batavian people, were the order of the day. The Revolution was not confined to the town-corporations. At the invitation of the Amsterdam Committee and under the protection of the French representatives, deputations from fourteen towns met at the Hague on January 26. Taking possession of the Assembly Hall of the Estates of Holland and choosing as their president Pieter Paulus, a man generally respected, this Provisional Assembly proceeded to issue a series of decrees subverting all the ancient institutions of the land. The representation by Estates and the offices of stadholder and of council-pensionary were abolished. The old colleges such as the Commissioned Councillors, the Admiralties, the Chamber of Accounts, were changed into Committees for General Welfare, for War, for Marine, for Finance, etc. The other provinces in turn followed Holland's example; and the changes in the provincial administrations were then quickly extended to the States-General. These retained their name, but were now to be representative of the citizens of the whole land. The Council of State was transformed into a Committee for General Affairs; and a Colonial Council replaced the East and West India Companies and the Society of Surinam. To the Committee for General Affairs was entrusted the task of drawing up a plan for the summoning of a National Convention on March 4.

So far all had gone smoothly with the course of the revolutionary movement, so much so that its leaders seem almost to have forgotten that the land was in the occupation of a foreign conqueror. The unqualified recognition of Batavian independence, however, in the proclamation by Daendels had caused dissatisfaction in Paris. The Committee of Public Safety had no intention of throwing away the fruits of victory; and two members of the Convention, Cochon and Ramel, were despatched to Holland to report upon the condition of affairs. They arrived at the Hague on February 7. Both reports recommended that a war-indemnity should be levied on the Republic, but counselled moderation, for, though the private wealth of the Dutch was potentially large, the State was practically insolvent. These proposals were too mild to please the Committee of Public Safety. The new States-General had sent (March 3) two envoys, Van Blauw and Meyer, to Paris with instructions to propose a treaty of alliance and of commerce with France, to ask for the withdrawal of the French troops and that the land should not be flooded with *assignats*. The independence of the Batavian Republic was taken for granted. Very different were the conditions laid before them by Merlin de Douat, Rewbell and

Siéyès. A war contribution of 100,000,000 florins was demanded, to be paid in ready money within three months, a loan of like amount at 3 per cent, and the surrender of all territory south of the Waal together with Dutch Flanders, Walcheren and South Beveland. Moreover there was to be no recognition of Batavian independence until a satisfactory treaty on the above lines was drawn up.

These hard conditions were on March 23 rejected by the States-General. Wiser counsels however prevented this point-blank refusal being sent to Paris, and it was hoped that a policy of delay might secure better terms. The negotiations went on slowly through March and April; and, as Blauw and Meyer had no powers as accredited plenipotentiaries, the Committee determined to send Rewbell and Siéyès to the Hague, armed with full authority to push matters through.

The envoys reached the Hague on May 8, and found the States-General in a more yielding mood than might have been expected from their previous attitude. Rewbell and Siéyès knew how to play upon the fears of the Provisional Government by representing to them that, if the terms they offered were rejected, their choice lay between French annexation or an Orange restoration. Four members were appointed by the States-General with full powers to negotiate. The conferences began on May 11; and in five days an agreement was reached. The Batavian Republic, recognised as a free and independent State, entered into an offensive and defensive alliance with the French Republic. But the Dutch had to cede Maestricht, Venloo and Dutch Flanders and to pay an indemnity of 100,000,000 florins. Flushing was to receive a French garrison, and its harbour was to be used in common by the two powers; 25,000 French troops were to be quartered in the Republic and were to be fed, clothed and paid. The Dutch were compelled to permit the free circulation of the worthless *assignats* in their country.

One of the first results of this treaty was a breach with Great Britain. The Dutch coast was blockaded; British fleets stopped all sea-borne commerce; and the Dutch colonies in the East and West Indies were one after the other captured. The action of the Prince of Orange made this an easy task. William placed in the hands of the British commanders letters addressed to the governors of the Dutch colonies ordering them "to admit the troops sent out on behalf of his Britannic Majesty and to offer no resistance to the British warships, but to regard them as vessels of a friendly Power." The Cape of Good Hope surrendered to Admiral Rodney; and in quick succession followed Malacca, Ceylon and the Moluccas. A squadron of nine ships under Rear-Admiral Lucas, sent out to recover the Cape and the other East Indian possessions, was compelled to surrender to the English in Saldanha Bay on August 17, 1796, almost without resistance, owing to the Orange sympathies of the crews. The West Indian Colonies fared no better. Demerara, Essequibo and Berbice capitulated in the spring of 1796; Surinam remained in Dutch hands until 1799; Java until 1801. The occupation by the English of this island, the most important of all the Dutch overseas possessions, made the tale of their colonial losses complete. The offensive and defensive alliance with France had thus brought upon the Republic, as a trading and colonial power, a ruin which the efforts of the provisional government under French pressure to re-organise and strengthen their naval and military forces had been unable to prevent. The erstwhile exiles, Daendels and Dumonceau, who had attained the rank of generals in the French service, were on their return entrusted with the task of raising an army of 36,000 men, disciplined and equipped on the French system. The navy was dealt with by a special Committee, of which Pieter Paulus was the energetic president. Unfortunately for the Committee, a large proportion of the officers and crews were strongly Orangist. Most of the officers resigned, and it was necessary to purge the crews. Their places had to be supplied by less experienced and trustworthy material; but Vice-Admiral Jan de Winter did his utmost to create a fleet in fit condition to join the French and Spanish fleets in convoying an expeditionary force to make a descent upon the coast of Ireland. In July, 1797, eighty ships were concentrated at the Texel with troops on board, ready to join the Franco-Spanish squadrons, which were to sail from Brest. But the junction was never effected. Week after week the Dutch admiral was prevented from leaving the Texel by contrary winds. The idea of an invasion of Ireland was given up, but so great was the disappointment in Holland and such the pressure exerted on De Winter by the Commission of Foreign Affairs, that he was obliged against his will to put to sea on October 7, and attack the English fleet under the command of Admiral Duncan, who was blockading the Dutch coast. The number of vessels on the two sides was not unequal, but neither officers nor crews under De Winter could compare in seamanship and experience with their opponents. The fleets met off Camperdown and the Dutch fought with their traditional bravery, but the defeat was complete. Out of sixteen ships of the line nine were taken, including the flag-ship of De Winter himself.

Meanwhile there had arisen strong differences of opinion in the Republic as to the form of government which was to replace the old confederacy of seven sovereign provinces. No one probably wished to continue a system which had long proved itself obsolete and unworkable. But particularism was still strong, especially in the smaller provinces. The country found itself divided into two sharply opposed parties of Unitarians and federalists. The Unitarians were the most active, and meetings were held all over the country by the local Jacobin clubs. Finally it was determined to hold a central meeting of delegates from all the clubs at the Hague. The meeting took place on Jan. 26, 1796, and resolutions were passed in favour of summoning a National Convention to draw up a new constitution on Unitarian lines. Holland and Utrecht pressed the matter forward in the States-General, and they had the support of Gelderland and Overyssel, but Zeeland, Friesland and Groningen refused their assent. Their action was very largely financial, as provinces whose indebtedness was small dreaded lest unification should increase their burden. But even in the recalcitrant provinces there were a large number of moderate men; and through the intervention of the French ambassador, Nöel, who gave strong support to the Unitarians, the proposal of Holland for a National Assembly to meet on March 1 was carried (February 18) by a unanimous vote. The following Provisional Regulation was then rapidly drawn up by a special committee. The land was divided into districts each containing 15,000 inhabitants; these again into fundamental assemblies (*grondvergaderingen*) of 500 persons; each of these assemblies chose an "elector" (*kiezer*); and then the group of thirty electors chose a deputy to represent the district. The National Assembly was in this way to consist of one hundred and twenty-six members; its deliberations were to be public, the voting individualistic and the majority to prevail. A Commission of twenty-one deputies was to be appointed, who were to frame a draft-Constitution, which after approval by the Assembly was to be submitted to the whole body of the people for acceptance or rejection.

The Assembly, having duly met on March 1, 1796, in the Binnenhof at the Hague, elected Pieter Paulus as their president, but had the misfortune to lose his experienced direction very speedily. He had for some time been in bad health, and on March 17 he died. It fell to his lot to assist at the ceremonial closing of the last meeting of the States-General, which had governed the Republic of the United Netherlands for more than two centuries.

The National Assembly reflected the pronounced differences of opinion in the land. Orangist opinion had no representatives, although possibly more than half the population had Orange sympathies. All the deputies had accepted in principle French revolutionary ideas, but there were three distinct parties, the unitarians, the moderates and the federalists. The moderates, who were in a majority, occupied, as their name implied, an intermediate position between the unitarians or revolutionary party, who wished for a centralised republic after the French model, and the federalists or conservatives, who aimed at retaining so far as possible the rights of the several provinces and towns to manage their own affairs. The leaders of the unitarians were Vreede, Midderigh, Valckenier and Gogel; of the moderates Schimmelpenninck, Hahn and Kantelaur; of the federalists, Vitringa, Van Marle and De Mist. After the death of Pieter Paulus the most influential man in an Assembly composed of politicians mostly without any parliamentary experience was the eloquent and astute Schimmelpenninck, whose opportunist moderation sprang from a natural dislike of extreme courses.

One of the first cares of the Assembly was the appointment of the Commission of twenty-one members to draw up a draft Constitution. The (so-styled) Regulation, representing the views of the moderate majority, was presented to the Assembly on November 10. The Republic was henceforth to be a unified state governed by the Sovereign People; but the old provinces, though now named departments, were to retain large administrative rights and their separate financial quotas. The draft met fierce opposition from the unitarians, but after much discussion and many amendments it was at length accepted by the majority. It had, however, before becoming law, to be submitted to the people; and the network of Jacobin clubs throughout the country, under the leadership of the central club at Amsterdam, carried on a widespread and secret revolutionary propaganda against the Regulation. They tried to enlist the open co-operation of the French ambassador, Noël, but he, acting under the instruction of the cautious Talleyrand, was not disposed to commit himself.

The unitarian campaign was so successful that the Regulation, on being submitted to the Fundamental Assemblies, was rejected by 136,716 votes to 27,955. In these circumstances, as had been previously arranged by the Provisional Government, it was necessary to summon another National Assembly to draw up another draft Constitution. It met on September 1, 1797. The moderates, though they lost some seats, were still in a majority; and the new Commission of Twenty-One had, as before, federalistic leanings. The Unitarians, therefore, without awaiting their proposals, under the leadership of the stalwart revolutionary, Vreede, determined to take strong action. The *coup d'état* they planned was helped forward by two events. The first was the revolution in Paris of September 4, 1797, which led to the replacing of ambassador Noël by the pronounced Jacobin, Charles Delacroix. The other event was the disaster which befell the Dutch fleet at Camperdown, the blame for which was laid upon the Provisional Government.

Vreede and his confederates being assured by Delacroix of the support of the new French Directory, and of the co-operation of the French General Joubert and of Daendels, the commander of the Batavian army, chose for the execution of their plan the week in which Midderigh, one of the confederates, took his turn as president of the Assembly. Midderigh, by virtue of his office, being in command of the Hague civic force, on January 22, 1798, seized and imprisoned the members of the Committee for Foreign Affairs and twenty-two members of the Assembly. The "Rump" then met, protected by a strong body of troops, and declared itself a Constituent Assembly representing the Batavian people. After the French model, an Executive Council was nominated, consisting of five members, Vreede, Fijnje, Fokker, Wildrik and Van Langen, and a new Commission of Seven to frame a Constitution. The "Regulation" was rejected; and the Assembly solemnly proclaimed its "unalterable aversion" to the stadholderate, federalism, aristocracy and governmental decentralisation.

French influence was henceforth paramount; and the draft of the new Constitution, in the framing of which Delacroix took a leading part, was ready on March 6. Eleven days later it was approved by the Assembly. The Fundamental Assemblies in their turn assented to it by 165,520 votes to 11,597, considerable official pressure being exerted to secure this result; and the Constitution came thus into legal existence. Its principal provisions were directed to the complete obliteration of the old provincial particularism. The land was divided into eight departments, whose boundaries in no case coincided with those of the provinces. Holland was split up among five departments; that of the Amstel, with Amsterdam as its capital, being the only one that did not contain portions of two or more provinces. Each department was divided into seven circles; each of these returned one member; and the body of seven formed the departmental government. The circles in their turn were divided into communes, each department containing sixty or seventy. All these local administrations were, however, quite subordinate to the authority exercised by the central Representative Body. For the purpose of electing this body the land was divided into ninety-four districts; each district into forty "Fundamental Assemblies," each of 500 persons. The forty "electors" chosen by these units in their turn elected the deputy for the department. The ninety-four deputies formed the Representative Body, which was divided into two Chambers. The Second Chamber of thirty members was annually chosen by lot from the ninety-four, the other sixty-four forming the First Chamber. The framing and proposing of all laws was the prerogative of the First Chamber. The Second Chamber accepted or rejected these proposed laws, but for a second rejection a two-thirds majority was required. The Executive Power was vested in a Directorate of five persons, one of whom was to retire every year. To supply his place the Second Chamber chose one out of three persons selected by the First Chamber. The Directorate had the assistance of eight agents or ministers: Foreign Affairs, War, Marine, Finance, Justice, Police, Education, and Economy. Finance was nationalised, all charges and debts being borne in common. Church and State were separated, payments to the Reformed ministers from the State ceasing in three years.

Such was the project, but it was not to be carried into effect without another *coup d'état*. It was now the duty of the Constituent

Assembly to proceed to the election of a Representative Body. Instead of this, on May 4, 1798, the Assembly declared itself to be Representative, so that power remained in the hands of the Executive Council, who were afraid of an election returning a majority of "moderates." But this autocratic act aroused considerable discontent amongst all except the extreme Jacobin faction. The opponents of the Executive Council found a leader in Daendels, who, strong "unionist" though he was, was dissatisfied with the arbitrary conduct of this self-constituted government, and more especially in matters connected with the army. Daendels betook himself to Paris, where he was favourably received by the Foreign Secretary, Talleyrand, and with his help was able to persuade the French Directory that it was not in their interest to support the Jacobin Council in their illegal retention of office. Daendels accordingly returned to Holland, where he found the French commander, Joubert, friendly to his project, and three of the "agents," including Pijman, the Minister of War, ready to help him. Placed in command of the troops at the Hague, Daendels (June 12, 1798) arrested the directors and the presidents of the two Chambers. The Constituent Assembly was dissolved and a new Representative Body was (July 31) elected. The moderates, as was expected, were in a considerable majority; and five members of that party, Van Hasselt, Hoeth, Van Haersolte, Van Hoeft and Ermerius were appointed Directors.

The country was now at length in the enjoyment of a settled constitution based upon liberal principles and popular representation. Daendels, though his influence was great, never attempted to play the part of a military dictator; and, though party passions were strong, no political persecutions followed. Nevertheless troubled times awaited the Batavian Republic, and the Constitution of 1798 was not to have a long life.

The Emperor Paul of Russia had taken up arms with Great Britain and Austria against revolutionary France, and the hopes of the Orange party began to rise. The hereditary prince was very active and, though he was unable to move his brother-in-law, the King of Prussia, to take active steps in his favour, he succeeded in securing the intervention of an Anglo-Russian force on his behalf. In August, 1798, a strong English fleet under Admiral Duncan appeared off Texel and in the name of the Prince of Orange demanded the surrender of the Batavian fleet which lay there under Rear-Admiral Story. Story refused. A storm prevented the English from taking immediate action; but on the 26th a landing of troops was effected near Callantroog and the Batavian forces abandoned the Helder. Story had withdrawn his fleet to Vlieter, but Orangist sympathies were strong among his officers and crews, and he was compelled to surrender. The ships, hoisting the Orange flag, became henceforth a squadron attached to the English fleet. Such was the humiliating end of the Batavian navy. The efforts of the hereditary prince to stir up an insurrection in Overyssel and Gelderland failed; and he thereupon joined the Anglo-Russian army, which, about 50,000 strong, was advancing under the command of the Duke of York to invade Holland. But York was an incompetent commander; there was little harmony between the British and Russian contingents; and the French and Batavians under Generals Brune and Daendels inflicted defeats upon them at Bergen (September 19), and at Castricum (October 6). York thereupon entered upon negotiations with Brune and was allowed to re-embark his troops for England, after restoration of the captured guns and prisoners. The expedition was a miserable fiasco.

At the very time when the evacuation of North Holland by invading armies was taking place, the Directory in Paris had been overthrown by Bonaparte (18 Brumaire, or Nov. 20), who now, with the title of First Consul, ruled France with dictatorial powers. The conduct of the Batavian government during these transactions had not been above suspicion; and Bonaparte at once replaced Brune by Augereau, and sent Sémonville as ambassador in place of Deforgues. He was determined to compel the Batavian Republic to comply strictly with the terms imposed by the treaty of 1795, and demanded more troops and more money. In vain the Executive Council, by the mouth of its ambassador, Schimmelpenninck, protested its inability to satisfy those demands. Augereau was inexorable, and there was no alternative but to obey. But the very feebleness of the central government made Bonaparte resolve on a revision of the constitution in an anti-democratic direction. Augereau acted as an intermediary between him and the Executive Council. Three of the directors favoured his views, the other two opposed them. The Representative Body, however, rejected all proposals for a revision. On this the three called in the aid of

Augereau, who suspended the Representative Body and closed the doors of its hall of meeting. The question was now referred to the Fundamental Assemblies. On October 1, 1801, the voting resulted in 52,279 noes against 16,771 yeas. About 350,000 voters abstained, but these were declared to be "yeas"; and the new constitution became on October 16 the law of the land.

The Constitution of 1801 placed the executive power in the hands of a State-Government of twelve persons. The three directors chose seven others, who in their turn chose five more, amongst these the above-named three, to whom they owed their existence. With this State-Government was associated a Legislative Body of 35 members, who met twice in the year and whose only function was to accept without amendment, or to reject, the proposals of the Executive Body. The "agents" were abolished and replaced by small councils, who administered the various departments of State. Considerable administrative powers were given to the local governments, and the boundaries of the eight departments, Holland, Zeeland, Utrecht, Overyssel (in which Drente was included), Gelderland, Groningen, Friesland, and Brabant, were made to coincide largely with those of the old provinces. The aim of the new Constitution was efficiency, the reconciliation of the moderate elements both of the federalist and unitarian parties, and the restraint alike of revolutionary and Orangist intrigues.

It began its course in fortunate circumstances. The long-wished-for peace was concluded at Amiens on March 27, 1802. It was signed by Schimmelpenninck, as the representative of the Batavian Republic, but he had not been allowed to have any influence upon the decisions. Great Britain restored all the captured colonies, except Ceylon; and the house of Orange was indemnified by the grant of the secularised Bishopric of Fulda, the abbeys of Korvey and Weingarten, together with the towns of Dortmund, Isny and Buchhorn. The hereditary prince, as his father refused to reside in this new domain, undertook the duties of government. William V preferred to live on his Nassau Estates. He died at Brunswick in 1806.

The peace was joyfully welcomed in Holland, for it removed the British blockade and gave a promise of the revival of trade. But all the hopes of better times were blighted with the fresh outbreak of war in 1803. All the colonial possessions were again lost; and a new treaty of alliance, which the State-Government was compelled to conclude with France, led to heavy demands. The Republic was required to provide for the quartering and support of 18,000 French troops and 16,000 Batavians under a French general. Further, a fleet of ten ships of war was to be maintained, and 350 flat-bottomed transports built for the conveyance of an invading army to England. These demands were perforce complied with. Nevertheless Napoleon was far from satisfied with the State-Government, which he regarded as inefficient and secretly hostile. In Holland itself it was hated, because of the heavy charges it was obliged to impose. Bonaparte accordingly determined to replace it and to concentrate the executive power in a single person. The Legislative Body was to remain, but the head of the State was to bear the title of council-pensionary, and was to be elected for a period of five years. Schimmelpenninck was designated for this post. Referred to a popular vote, the new Constitution was approved by 14,230 against 136; about 340,000 abstained from voting. On April 29, 1805, Schimmelpenninck entered into office as council-pensionary. He was invested with monarchical authority. The executive power, finance, the army and navy, the naming of ambassadors, the proposing of legislation, were placed in his hands. He was assisted by a Council of State, nominated by himself, of five members, and by six Secretaries of State. The Legislative Body was reduced to nineteen members, appointed by the Departmental Governments. They met twice in the year and could accept or reject the proposals of the council-pensionary, but not amend them.

Schimmelpenninck was honest and able, and during the brief period of his administration did admirable work. With the aid of the accomplished financier Gogel, who had already done much good service to his country in difficult circumstances, he, by spreading the burdens of taxation equally over all parts of the land and by removing restrictive customs and duties, succeeded in reducing largely the deficits in the annual balance-sheet. He also was the first to undertake seriously the improvement of primary education. But it was not Napoleon's intention to allow the council-pensionary to go on with the good work he had begun. The weakening of Schimmelpenninck's eyesight, through cataract, gave the emperor the excuse for putting an end to what he regarded as a provisional system of government, and for converting Holland into a dependent kingdom under the rule of his brother Louis. Admiral Verhuell, sent to Paris at Napoleon's request on a special mission, was bluntly informed that Holland must choose between the acceptance of Louis as their king, or annexation. On Verhuell's return with the report of the emperor's ultimatum, the council-pensionary (April 10, 1806) summoned the Council of State, the Secretaries and the Legislative Body to meet together as an Extraordinary Committee and deliberate on what were best to be done. It was resolved to send a deputation to Paris to try to obtain from Napoleon the relinquishment, or at least a modification, of his demand. Their efforts were in vain; Napoleon's attitude was peremptory. The Hague Committee must within a week petition that Louis Bonaparte might be their king, or he would take the matter into his own hands. The Committee, despite the opposition of Schimmelpenninck, finding resistance hopeless, determined to yield. The deputation at Paris was instructed accordingly to cooperate with the emperor in the framing of a new monarchical constitution. It was drawn up and signed on May 23; and a few days later it was accepted by the Hague Committee. Schimmelpenninck, however, refused to sign it and resigned his office on June 4, explaining in a dignified letter his reasons for doing so. Verhuell, at the head of a deputation (June 5), now went through the farce of begging the emperor in the name of the Dutch people to allow his brother, Louis, to be their king. Louis accepted the proffered sovereignty "since the people desires and Your Majesty commands it." On June 15 the new king left Paris and a week later arrived at the Hague, accompanied by his wife, Hortense de Beauharnais, Napoleon's step-daughter.

# CHAPTER XXVIII

# THE KINGDOM OF HOLLAND AND THE FRENCH ANNEXATION, 1806-1814

Louis Bonaparte was but 28 years old, and of a kindly, gentle character very unlike his self-willed, domineering brother. He was weakly, and his ill-health made him at times restless and moody. He had given great satisfaction by his declaration that "as soon as he set foot on the soil of his kingdom he became a Hollander," and he was well received. The constitution of the new kingdom differed little from that it superseded. The Secretaries of State became Ministers, and the number of members of the Legislative Body was raised to thirty-nine. The king had power to conclude treaties with foreign States without consulting the Legislative Body. The partition of the country was somewhat changed, Holland being divided into two departments, Amstelland and Maasland. Drente became a separate department; and in 1807 East Friesland with Jever was made into an eleventh department, as compensation for Flushing, which was annexed to France.

Louis came to the Hague with the best intentions of doing his utmost to promote the welfare of his kingdom, but from the first he was thwarted by the deplorable condition of the national finances. Out of a total income of fifty million florins the interest on the national debt absorbed thirty-five millions. The balance was not nearly sufficient to defray the costs of administration, much less to meet the heavy demands of Napoleon for contributions to war expenditure. All the efforts of the finance minister Gogel to reduce the charges and increase the income were of small avail. The king was naturally lavish, and he spent considerable sums in the maintenance of a brilliant court, and in adding to the number of royal residences. Dissatisfied with the Hague, he moved first to Utrecht, then to Amsterdam, where the Stadhuis was converted into a palace; and he bought the Pavilion at Haarlem as a summer abode. All this meant great expenditure. 'Louis was vain, and was only prevented from creating marshals of his army and orders of chivalry by Napoleon's stern refusal to permit it. He had to be reminded that by the Bonaparte family-law he was but a vassal king, owning allegiance to the emperor.

Despite these weaknesses Louis did much for the land of his adoption. The old Rhine at Leyden, which lost itself in the dunes, was connected by a canal with Katwijk on the sea, where a harbour was created. The dykes and waterways were repaired and improved, and high-roads constructed from the Hague to Leyden, and from Utrecht to Het Loo. Dutch literature found in Louis a generous patron. He took pains to learn the language from the instruction of Bilderdijk, the foremost writer of his day. The foundation in 1808 of the "Royal Netherland Institute for Science, Letters and the Fine Arts" was a signal mark of his desire to raise the standard of culture in Holland on a national basis. The introduction of the *Code Napoléon,* with some necessary modifications, replaced a confused medley of local laws and customs, varying from province to province, by a general unified legal system. As a statesman and administrator Louis had no marked ability, but the ministers to whom he entrusted the conduct of affairs, Verhuell, minister of marine, Roëll, of foreign affairs, Kragenhoff, of war, Van Maanen, of justice, and more especially the experienced Gogel, in control of the embarrassed finances, were capable men.

The state of the finances indeed was the despair of the Dutch government. The imperious demands of Napoleon for the maintenance of an army of 40,000 men, to be employed by him on foreign campaigns, and also of a considerable navy, made all attempts at economy and re-organisation of the finances almost hopeless. By the war with England the Dutch had lost their colonies and most of their great sea-borne trade; and the situation was rendered more difficult by the Decree of Berlin in 1806 and the establishment of the "Continental System" by the emperor, as a reply to the British blockade. All trade and even correspondence with England were forbidden. He hoped thus to bring England to her knees; but, though the decree did not achieve this object, it did succeed in bringing utter ruin upon the Dutch commercial classes. In vain Louis protested; he was not heard and only met with angry rebukes from his brother for not taking more vigorous steps to stop smuggling, which the character of the Dutch coast rendered a comparatively easy and, at the same time, lucrative pursuit.

The overthrow of Austria and Prussia by Napoleon in 1805 and 1806, followed in 1807 by the Peace of Tilsit with Russia, made the emperor once more turn his attention to the project of an invasion of his hated enemy, England. A great French fleet was to be concentrated on the Scheldt, with Antwerp and Flushing for its bases. For this purpose large sums of money were expended in converting Antwerp into a formidable naval arsenal. But the British government were well aware of "the pistol that was being aimed at England's breast"; and in 1809 a powerful expedition under the command of Lord Chatham was despatched, consisting of more than 100 warships and transports, with the object of destroying these growing dockyards and arsenals, and with them the threat of invasion. The attack was planned at a favourable moment, for the defensive force was very small, the bulk of the Dutch army having been sent to fight in the Austrian and Spanish campaigns, and the French garrisons greatly reduced. Chatham landed on the island of Walcheren, captured Middelburg and Veere and on August 15 compelled Flushing to surrender after such a furious bombardment that scarcely any houses remained standing. The islands of Schouwen, Duiveland and Zuid-Beveland were overrun; and, had the British general pushed on without delay, Antwerp might have fallen. But this he failed to do; and meanwhile Louis had collected, for the defence of the town, a force of 20,000 men, which, to his deep chagrin, Napoleon did not allow him to command. No attack however was made on Antwerp by the British, who had suffered severely from the fevers of Walcheren; and on the news of Wagram and the Treaty of Schönbrunn they slowly evacuated their conquests. Before the end of the year the whole force had returned to England.

This invasion, though successfully repelled, only accentuated the dissensions between the two brothers. French troops remained in occupation of Zeeland; and the French army of the north at Antwerp, now placed under the command of Marshal Oudinot, lay ready to enforce the demands of the emperor should the Dutch government prove recalcitrant. Those demands included the absolute suppression of smuggling, the strictest enforcement of the decrees against trading with England, conscription, and a repudiation of a portion of the State debt. Napoleon overwhelmed his brother with bitter gibes and angry threats, declaring that he wished to make Holland an English colony, and that the whole land, even his own palace, was full of smuggled goods. At last, though unwillingly, Louis consented to go in person to Paris and try to bring about an amicable settlement of the questions at issue. He arrived on December 26, intending to return at the New Year, meanwhile leaving the Council of Ministers in charge of the affairs of the kingdom. He soon found not only that his mission was in vain, but that he was regarded virtually as a prisoner. For three months he remained in Paris under police *surveillance*; and his interviews with his brother were of the most stormy description. The Dutch Council, alarmed by the constant threat of French invasion, at first thought of putting Amsterdam into a state of defence, but finally abandoned the idea as hopeless. The king did his utmost to appease Napoleon by the offer of concessions, but his efforts were scornfully rejected, and at last he was compelled (March 16, 1810) to sign a treaty embodying the terms dictated by the emperor. "I must," he said, "at any price get out of this den of murderers." By this treaty Brabant and Zeeland and the land between the Maas and the Waal, with Nijmwegen, were ceded to France. All commerce with England was forbidden. French custom-house officers were placed at the mouths of the rivers and at every port. Further, the Dutch were required to deliver up fifteen men-of-war and one hundred gunboats.

Louis was compelled to remain at Paris for the marriage of Napoleon with Marie Louise, but was then allowed to depart. Discouraged and humiliated, he found himself, with the title of king, practically reduced to the position of administrative governor of some French departments. Oudinot's troops were in occupation of the Hague, Utrecht and Leyden; and, when the emperor and his bride paid a state visit to Antwerp, Louis had to do him homage. The relations between the two brothers had for some time been strained, Napoleon having taken the part of his step-daughter Hortense, who preferred the gaiety of Paris to the dull court of her husband, reproached the injured man for not treating better the best of wives. Matters were now to reach their climax. The coachman of the French ambassador, Rochefoucault, having met with maltreatment in the streets of Amsterdam, the emperor angrily ordered Rochefoucault to quit the Dutch capital (May 29), leaving only a chargé d'affaires, and at the same time dismissed Verhuell, the Dutch envoy, from Paris. This was practically a declaration of war. The Council of Ministers, on being consulted, determined that it was useless to attempt the defence of Amsterdam; and, when the king learned towards the end of June that Oudinot had orders to occupy the city, he resolved to forestall this final humiliation by abdication. On July 1, 1810, he signed the deed by which he laid down his crown in favour of his elder son, Napoleon Louis, under the guardianship of Queen Hortense. He then left the country, and retired into Bohemia.

To this disposition of the kingdom Napoleon, who had already made up his mind, paid not the slightest heed. On July 9 an Imperial Decree incorporated Holland in the French empire. "Holland," said the emperor, "being formed by the deposits of three French rivers, the Rhine, the Meuse and the Scheldt, was by nature a part of France." Not till January 1, 1811, was the complete incorporation to take place; meanwhile Le Brun, Duke of Piacenza, a man of 72 years of age, was sent to Amsterdam to be governor-general during the period of transition. It was a wise appointment, as Le Brun was a man of kindly disposition, ready to listen to grievances and with an earnest desire to carry out the transformation of the government in a conciliatory spirit. With him was associated, as Intendant of Home Affairs, Baron D'Alphonse, like himself of moderate views, and a Council of Ministers. A deputation of twenty-two persons from the Legislative Assembly was summoned to Paris for consultation with the Imperial Government. To Amsterdam was given the position of the third city in the empire, Paris being the first and Rome the second. The country was divided into nine departments—Bouches de l'Escaut, Bouches de la Meuse, Bouches du Rhin, Zuiderzee, Issel supérieur, Bouches de Issel, Frise, Ems Occidental and Ems Oriental. Over the departments, as in France, were placed *préfets* and under them *sous-préfets* and *maires*. All the *préfets* now appointed were native Dutchmen with the exception of two, De Celles at

Amsterdam and De Standaart at the Hague; both were Belgians and both rendered themselves unpopular by their efforts to gain Napoleon's favour by a stringent enforcement of his orders. The Dutch representation in the Legislative Assembly at Paris was fixed at twenty-five members; in the Senate at six members. When these took their seats, the Council of Affairs at Amsterdam was dissolved and at the same time the *Code Napoléon* unmodified became the law of the land.

Napoleon's demands upon Holland had always been met with the reply that the land's finances were unequal to the strain. The debt amounted to 40,000,000 fl.; and, despite heavy taxation, there was a large annual deficit in the budget. The emperor at once took action to remedy this state of things by a decree reducing the interest on the debt to one-third. This was a heavy blow to those persons whose limited incomes were mainly or entirely derived from investments in the State Funds—including many widows, and also hospitals, orphanages and other charitable institutions. At the same time this step should not be regarded as a mere arbitrary and dishonest repudiation of debt. The State was practically bankrupt. For some years only a portion of the interest or nothing at all had been paid; and the reduction in 1810 was intended to be but a temporary measure. The capital amount was left untouched, and the arrears of 1808 and 1809 were paid up at the new rate. That financial opinion was favourably impressed by this drastic action was shown by a considerable rise in the quotation of the Stock on the Bourse.

A far more unpopular measure was the introduction of military and naval conscription in 1811. There never had been any but voluntary service in Holland. Indeed during the whole period of the Republic, though the fleet was wholly manned by Dutch seamen, the army always included a large proportion of foreign mercenaries. By the law of 1811 all youths of twenty were liable to serve for five years either on land or sea; and the contingent required was filled by the drawing of lots. Deep and strong resentment was felt throughout the country, the more so that the law was made retrospective to all who had reached the age of twenty in the three preceding years. The battalions thus raised were treated as French troops, and were sent to take part in distant campaigns—in Spain and in Russia. Of the 15,000 men who marched with Napoleon into Russia in 1812 only a few hundreds returned.

The strict enforcement of the Continental System entailed great hardships upon the population. To such an extent was the embargo carried that all English manufactured goods found in Holland were condemned to be burnt; and the value of what was actually consumed amounted to millions of florins. A whole army of custom-house officers watched the coast, and every fishing smack that put to sea had one on board. At the same time not till 1812 was the customs barrier with France removed. In consequence of this prices rose enormously, industries were ruined, houses were given up and remained unoccupied, and thousands upon thousands were reduced to abject poverty. Such was the state of the treasury that in 1812 the reformed preachers received no stipends, and officials of all kinds had to be content with reduced salaries.

Nor were these the only causes of discontent. The police regulations and the censorship of the press were of the severest description, and the land swarmed with spies. No newspaper was permitted to publish any article upon matters of State or any political news except such as was sanctioned by the government, and with a French translation of the Dutch original. This applied even to advertisements. All books had to be submitted for the censor's *imprimatur*. Every household was subject to the regular visitation of the police, who made the most minute inquisition into the character, the opinions, the occupations and means of subsistence of every member of the household.

Nevertheless the French domination, however oppressive, had good results in that for the first time in their history the Dutch provinces acquired a real unity. All the old particularism disappeared with the burgher-aristocracies, and the party feuds of Orangists and patriots. A true sense of nationality was developed. All classes of the population enjoyed the same political rights and equality before the law. Napoleon himself was not unpopular. In the autumn of 1811 he, accompanied by Marie Louise, made a state-progress through this latest addition to his empire. Almost every important place was visited, and in all parts of the country he was received with outward demonstrations of enthusiasm and almost servile obsequiency. It is perhaps not surprising, as the great emperor was now at the very topmost height of his dazzling fortunes.

But for Holland Napoleon's triumphs had their dark side, for his chief and most determined enemy, England, was mistress of the seas; and the last and the richest of the Dutch colonies, Java, surrendered to the English almost on the very day that the Imperial progress began. Hearing of the activity of the British squadron in the Eastern seas, King Louis had, shortly after his acceptance of the crown, taken steps for the defence of Java by appointing Daendels, a man of proved vigour and initiative, governor-general. The difficulties of reaching Java in face of British vigilance were however well-nigh insurmountable, and it was not until a year after his nomination to the governorship that Daendels reached Batavia, on January 1, 1808. His measures for the defence of the island, including the construction of important highways, were most energetic, but so oppressive and high-handed as to arouse hostility and alienate the native chiefs. Napoleon, informed of Daendels' harsh rule, sent out Janssens with a body of troops to replace him. The new governor-general landed on April 27, 1811, but he could make no effective resistance to a powerful British expedition under General Auchmuty, which took possession of Batavia on August 4, and after some severe fighting compelled (September 17) the whole of the Dutch forces to capitulate.

The year of Napoleon's invasion of Russia, 1812, was a year of passive endurance. The safety of the remnant of the Grand Army was secured (November 28) by the courage and staunchness of the Dutch pontoon-engineers, who, standing in the ice-cold water of the Beresina, completed the bridge over which, after a desperate battle, the French troops effected their escape. The Moscow catastrophe was followed in 1813 by a general uprising of the oppressed peoples of Europe against the Napoleonic tyranny. In this uprising the Dutch people, although hopes of freedom were beginning to dawn upon them, did not for some time venture to take any part. The Prince of Orange however had been in London since April, trying to secure a promise of assistance from the British government in case of a rising; and he was working in collaboration with a number of patriotic men in Holland, who saw in an Orange restoration the best hopes for their country's independence. The news of Leipzig (October 14-16) roused them to action.

Foremost among these leaders was Gijsbert Karel van Hogendorp. He had been one of the Orangist leaders at the time of the restoration of 1787 and had filled the post of pensionary of Rotterdam. After the French conquest he had withdrawn from public life. With him were associated Count Van Limburg-Stirum and Baron Van der Duyn van Maasdam, like himself residents at the Hague. Van Hogendorp could also count on a number of active helpers outside the Hague, prominent among whom were Falck, Captain of the National Guard at Amsterdam, and Kemper, a professor at Leyden. Plans were made for restoring the independence of the country under the rule of the Prince of Orange; but, in order to escape the vigilance of the French police, great care was taken to maintain secrecy, and nothing was committed to writing. The rapid march of allied troops, Russians and Prussians, towards the Dutch frontiers after Leipzig necessitated rapid action.

Van Hogendorp and his friends wished that Holland should free herself by her own exertions, for they were aware that reconquest by the allied forces might imperil their claims to independence. Their opportunity came when General Melliton, by order of the governor-general Le Brun, withdrew on November 14 from Amsterdam to Utrecht. One of the Orangist confederates, a sea-captain, named Job May, on the following day stirred up a popular rising in the city; and some custom-houses were burnt. Le Brun himself on this retreated to Utrecht and, on the 16th, after transferring the government of the country to Melliton, returned to France. Falck at the head of the National Guard had meanwhile re-established order at Amsterdam, and placed the town in charge of a provisional government. No sooner did this news reach the Hague than Van Hogendorp and Van Limburg-Stirum determined upon instant action (November 17). With a proclamation drawn up by Van Hogendorp, and at the head of a body of the National Guard wearing Orange colours, Van Limburg-Stirum marched through the streets to the Town Hall, where he read the proclamation declaring the Prince of Orange "eminent head of the State." No opposition being offered, after discussion with their chief supporters, the triumvirate, Van Hogendorp, Van Limburg-Stirum and Van der Duyn van Maasdam, took upon themselves provisionally the government of the country, until the arrival of the

Prince. Emissaries were at once sent to Amsterdam to announce what had taken place at the Hague. At first the Amsterdammers showed some hesitation; and it was not until the arrival of a body of Cossacks at their gates (November 24), that the city openly threw in its lot with the Orangist movement, which now rapidly spread throughout the country. Without delay the provisional government despatched two envoys, Fagel and De Perponcher, to London, to inform the Prince of Orange of what had occurred and to invite him to Holland.

William had been in England since April and had met with a favourable reception. In an interview with the British Foreign Secretary, Lord Castlereagh, support had been promised him (April 27, 1813) on the following conditions: (1) the frontiers of Holland should be extended "either by a sort of new Barrier, more effective than the old one, or by the union of some portions of territory adjacent to the ancient Republic; (2) Holland must wait until such time as Great Britain should deem convenient in her own interests for the restoration of the Dutch colonies, which she had conquered during the war; (3) a system of government must be set up which would reconcile the wishes of Holland with those of the Powers called to exercise so powerful an influence upon her future." William had gone to London knowing that he could rely on the active assistance of his brother-in-law, Frederick William of Prussia, and of the Emperor Alexander I, and that the goodwill of England was assured by the projected marriage of his son (now serving under Wellington in Spain) with the Princess Charlotte, heiress-presumptive to the British throne. He now therefore without hesitation accepted the invitation, and landed at Scheveningen, November 30. He was received with unspeakable enthusiasm. At first there was some doubt as to what title William should bear and as to what should be the form of the new government. Van Hogendorp had drawn up a draft of a constitution on the old lines with an hereditary stadholder, a council-pensionary and a privileged aristocracy, but with large and necessary amendments, and the prince was himself inclined to a restoration of the stadholdership with enlarged powers. To the arguments of Kemper is the credit due of having persuaded him that a return to the old system, however amended, had now become impossible. The prince visited Amsterdam, December 2, and was there proclaimed by the title and quality of William I, Sovereign-Prince of the Netherlands. He refused the title of king, but the position he thus accepted with general approval was that of a constitutional monarch, and the promise was given that as soon as possible a Commission should be appointed to draw up a Fundamental Law *(Grondwet)* for the Dutch State.

# CHAPTER XXIX

# THE FORMATION OF THE KINGDOM OF THE NETHERLANDS, 1814-1815

When the Prince of Orange assumed the title of William I, Sovereign-Prince of the Netherlands, at Amsterdam, on December 2, 1813, the principal towns were still occupied by French garrisons; but with the help of the allied forces, Russians and Prussians, these were, in the opening months of 1814, one by one conquered. The Helder garrison, under the command of Admiral Verhuell, did not surrender till May. By the end of that month the whole land was freed.

The first step taken by the Sovereign-Prince (December 21) was to appoint a Commission to draw up a Fundamental Law according to his promise. The Commission consisted of fifteen members, with Van Hogendorp as president. Their labours were concluded early in March. The concept was on March 29 submitted to an Assembly of six hundred notables, summoned for the purpose, the voting to be 'for' or 'against' without discussion. The gathering took place in the Nieuwe Kerk at Amsterdam, Of the 474 who were present, 448 voted in favour of the new Constitution. On the following day the Prince of Orange took the oath in the Nieuwe Kerk and was solemnly inaugurated as Sovereign-Prince of the Netherlands.

The principal provisions of the Fundamental Law of March, 1814, were as follows:

The Sovereign shares the Legislative Power with the States-General, but alone exercises the Executive Power. All the sovereign prerogatives formerly possessed by provinces, districts or towns are now transferred to the Sovereign. He is assisted by a Council of

State of twelve members, appoints and dismisses ministers, declares war and makes peace, has the control of finance and governs the overseas-possessions. The States-General consist of fifty-five members, elected by the nine provinces, Holland, Zeeland, Utrecht, Overyssel, Gelderland, Groningen, Friesland, Brabant and Drente on the basis of population. The members are elected for three years, but one-third vacate their seats every year. They have the right of legislative initiative, and of veto. The finances are divided into ordinary and extraordinary expenditure, over the former the States-General exercise no control, but a general Chamber of Accounts *(Algemeene Rekenkamer)* has the supervision over ways and means. The Sovereign must be a member of the Reformed Church, but equal protection is given by the State to all religious beliefs.

It was essentially an aristocratic constitution. At least one quarter of the States-General must belong to the nobility. The Provincial Estates had the control of local affairs only, but had the privilege of electing the members of the States-General. They were themselves far from being representative. For the country districts the members were chosen from the nobility and the landowners; in the towns by colleges of electors *(kiezers)*, consisting of those who paid the highest contributions in taxes. Except for the strengthening of the central executive power and the abolition of all provincial sovereign rights, the new Constitution differed little from the old in its oligarchic character.

It was, however, to be but a temporary arrangement. It has already been pointed out that, months before his actual return to Holland, the prince had received assurances from the British government that a strong Netherland State should be created, capable of being a barrier to French aggression. The time had now arrived for the practical carrying-out of this assurance. Accordingly Lord Castlereagh in January, 1814, when on his way, as British plenipotentiary, to confer with the Allied Sovereigns at Basel, visited the Sovereign-Prince at the Hague. The conversations issued in a proposal to unite (with the assent of Austria) the Belgic provinces as far as the Meuse to Holland together with the territory between the Meuse and the Rhine as far as the line Maestricht-Düren-Cologne. Castlereagh submitted this project to the allies at Basel; and it was discussed and adopted in principle at the Conference of Châtillon (February 3 to March 15), the Austrian Emperor having renounced all claim to his Belgian dominions in favour of an equivalent in Venetia. This was done without any attempt to ascertain the wishes of the Belgian people on the proposed transference of their allegiance, and a protest was made. An assembly of notables, which had been summoned to Brussels by the military governor, the Duke of Saxe-Weimar, sent a deputation to the allied headquarters at Chaumont to express their continued loyalty to their Habsburg sovereign and to ask that, if the Emperor Francis relinquished his claim, they might be erected into an independent State under the rule of an Austrian archduke. A written reply (March 14) informed them that the question of union with Holland was settled, but assurances were given that in matters of religion, representation, commerce and the public debt their interests would be carefully guarded. Meanwhile General Baron Vincent, a Belgian in the Austrian service, was made governor-general.

The idea, however, of giving to Holland a slice of cis-Rhenan territory had perforce to be abandoned in the face of Prussian objections. The preliminary Treaty of Peace signed at Paris on May 30, 1814, was purposely vague, Art. VI merely declaring that "Holland placed under the sovereignty of the House of Orange shall receive an increase of territory—*un accroissement de territoire*"; but a secret article defined this increase as "the countries comprised between the sea, the frontiers of France, as defined by the present treaty; and the Meuse shall be united in perpetuity to Holland. The frontiers on the right bank of the Meuse shall be regulated in accordance with the military requirements of Holland and her neighbours." In other words the whole of Belgium as far as the Meuse was to be annexed to Holland; beyond the Meuse the military requirements of Prussia were to be consulted.

Previously to this, Castlereagh had written to the British Minister at the Hague, Lord Clancarty, suggesting that the Sovereign-Prince should summon a meeting of an equal number of Dutch and Belgian notables to draw up a project of union to be presented to the Allied Sovereigns at Paris for their approbation. But William had already himself, with the assistance of his minister Van Nagell, drawn up in eight articles the fundamental conditions for the constitution of the new State; and, after revision by Falck and Lord Clancarty, he in person took them to Paris. They were laid by Clancarty before the plenipotentiaries, and were adopted by the Allied Sovereigns assembled in London on June 21, 1814. The principles which animated them were set forth in a protocol which breathes throughout a spirit of fairness and conciliation—but all was marred by the final clause—*Elles mettent ces principes en exécution en vertu de leur droit de conquete de la Belgique.* To unite Belgium to Holland, as a conquered dependency, could not fail to arouse bad feelings; and thus to proclaim it openly was a very grave mistake. It was not thus that that "perfect amalgamation" of the two countries, at which, according to the protocol, the Great Powers aimed, was likely to be effected.

At the same time, as a standing proof of William's own excellent intentions, the text of the Eight Articles is given in full:

(1) *The union shall be intimate and complete, so that the two countries shall form but one State, to be governed by the Fundamental Law already established in Holland, which by mutual consent shall be modified according to the circumstances.*

(2) *There shall be no change in those Articles of the Fundamental Law which secure to all religious cults equal protection and privileges, and guarantee the admissibility of all citizens, whatever be their religious creed, to public offices and dignities.*

(3) *The Belgian provinces shall be in a fitting manner represented in the States-General, whose sittings in time of peace shall be held by turns in a Dutch and a Belgian town.*

(4) *All the inhabitants of the Netherlands thus having equal constitutional rights, they shall have equal claim to all commercial and other rights, of which their circumstances allow, without any hindrance or obstruction being imposed on any to the profit of others.*

(5) *Immediately after the union the provinces and towns of Belgium shall be admitted to the commerce and navigation of the colonies of Holland upon the same footing as the Dutch provinces and towns.*

(6) *The debts contracted on the one side by the Dutch, and on the other side by the Belgian provinces, shall be charged to the public chest of the Netherlands.*

(7) *The expenses required for the building and maintenance of the frontier fortresses of the new State shall be borne by the public chest as serving the security and independence of the whole nation.*

(8) *The cost of the making and upkeep of the dykes shall be at the charge of the districts more directly interested, except in the case of an extraordinary disaster.*

It is not too much to say that, if the provisions of these Articles had been carried out fully and generously, there might have been at the present moment a strong and united Netherland State.

On July 21 the Articles, as approved by the Powers, were returned to the Sovereign-Prince, who officially accepted them, and on August 1 took over at Brussels the government of the Belgic provinces, while awaiting the decisions of the Congress, which was shortly to meet at Vienna, as to the boundaries and political status of the territories over which he ruled. The work of the Congress, however, which met in October, was much delayed by differences between the Powers. Prussia wished to annex the entire kingdom of Saxony; and, when it was found that such a claim, if persisted in, would be opposed by Great Britain, Austria and France, compensation was sought in the Rhenish provinces. Thus the idea of strengthening the new Netherland buffer-state by an addition of territory in the direction of the Rhine had to be abandoned. It must be remembered that the Sovereign-Prince on his part was not likely to raise any objection to having an enlarged and strengthened Prussia as his immediate neighbour on the east. William was both brother-in-law and first cousin of the King of Prussia, and had spent much of his exile at Berlin; and he no doubt regarded the presence of this strong military power on his frontier as the surest guarantee against French aggression. His relations with Prussia were indeed of the friendliest character, as is shown by the fact that secret negotiations were at this very time taking place for the cession to Prussia of his hereditary Nassau principalities of Dillenburg, Siegen, Dietz and Hadamar in exchange for the Duchy of Luxemburg.

The proceedings of the inharmonious Congress of Vienna were, however, rudely interrupted by the sudden return of Napoleon from Elba. Weary of waiting for a formal recognition of his position, William now (March 15, 1815) issued a proclamation in which he assumed the title of King of the Netherlands and Duke of Luxemburg. No protest was made; and the *fait accompli* was duly accepted by the Powers (May 23). The first act of the king was to call upon all his subjects, Dutch and Belgians alike, to unite in opposing the common foe. This call to arms led to a considerable force under the command of the hereditary prince being able to join the small British army, which Wellington had hurriedly collected for the defence of Brussels. The sudden invasion of Belgium by Napoleon (June 14) took his adversaries by surprise, for the Anglo-Netherland forces were distributed in different cantonments and were separated from the Prussian army under Blücher, which had entered Belgium from the east. Napoleon in person attacked and defeated Blücher at Ligny on June 16; and on the same day a French force under Ney was, after a desperate encounter, held in check by the British and Dutch regiments, which had been pushed forward to Quatre Bras. Blücher retreated to Wavre and Wellington to Waterloo on the following day. The issue of the battle of Waterloo, which took place on June 18, is well known. The Belgian contingent did not play a distinguished part at Waterloo, but it would be unfair to place to their discredit any lack of steadiness that was shown. These Belgian troops were all old soldiers of Napoleon, to whom they were attached, and in whose invincibility they believed. The Prince of Orange distinguished himself by great courage both at Quatre Bras and Waterloo.

William, after his assumption of the regal title, at once proceeded to regularise his position by carrying out that necessary modification of the Dutch Fundamental Law to which he was pledged by the Eight Articles. He accordingly summoned a Commission of twenty-four members, half Dutch and half Belgian, Catholics and Protestants being equally represented, which on April 22 met under the presidency of Van Hogendorp. Their activity was sharpened by the threat of French invasion, and in three months (July 18) their difficult task was accomplished. The new Fundamental Law made no change in the autocratic powers conferred on the king. The executive authority remained wholly in his hands. The States-General were now to consist of two Chambers, but the First Chamber was a nominated Chamber. It contained forty to sixty members appointed by the king for life. The Second Chamber of 110 members, equally divided between north and south, *i.e.* fifty-five Dutch and fifty-five Belgian representatives, was elected under a very restricted franchise by the seventeen provinces into which the whole kingdom was divided. The ordinary budget was voted for ten years, and it was only extraordinary expenses which had to be considered annually. The other provisions strictly followed the principles and the liberties guaranteed in advance by the Eight Articles.

The new Fundamental Law was presented to the Dutch States-General on August 8, and was approved by a unanimous vote. Very different was its reception in Belgium. The king had summoned a meeting of 1603 notables to Brussels, of these 1323 were present. The majority were hostile. It had been strongly urged by the Belgian delegates on the Commission that the Belgic provinces, with three and a half millions of inhabitants, ought to return to the Second Chamber of the States-General a number of members proportionately greater than the Dutch provinces, which had barely two millions. The Dutch on their part argued that their country had been an independent State for two centuries and possessed a large colonial empire, while Belgium had always been under foreign rule, and had now been added to Holland "as an increase of territory." It was finally arranged, however, that the representation of the northern and southern portions of the new kingdom should be equal, 55 each. Belgian public opinion loudly protested, especially as the 55 Belgian deputies included four representatives of Luxemburg, which had been created a separate State under the personal rule of King William. Still more bitter and determined was the opposition of the powerful clerical party to the principle of religious equality. About 99 per cent, of the Belgian population was Catholic; and the bishops were very suspicious of what might be the effect of this principle in the hands of an autocratic Calvinist king, supported by the predominant Protestant majority in Holland. A further grievance was that the heavy public debt incurred by Holland should be made a common burden.

Considerable pressure was brought to bear upon the notables, but without avail. The Fundamental Law was rejected by 796 votes to 527. Confronted with this large hostile majority, the king took upon himself to reverse the decision by an arbitrary and dishonest manipulation of the return. He chose to assume that the 280 notables who had not voted were in favour of the Law, and added their votes to the minority. He then declared that 126 votes had been wrongly given in opposition to the principle of religious equality, which, by the Second of the Eight Articles approved by the Powers was binding and fundamental to the Union, and he then not only deducted them from the majority, but added them also to the minority. He then announced that the Fundamental Law had been accepted by a majority of 263 votes. Such an act of chicanery was not calculated to make the relations between north and south work smoothly. Having thus for reasons of state summarily dealt with the decision of the Belgian notables, William (September 26), made his state entry into Brussels and took his oath to the Constitution.

Already the Congress of Vienna had given the official sanction of the Powers to the creation of the kingdom of the Netherlands by a treaty signed at Paris on May 31, 1815. By this treaty the whole of the former Austrian Netherlands (except the province of Luxemburg) together with the territory which before 1795 had been ruled by the prince-bishops of Liège, the Duchy of Bouillon and several small pieces of territory were added to Holland; and the new State thus created was placed under the sovereignty of the head of the House of Orange-Nassau. As stated above, however, it had been necessary in making these arrangements to conciliate Prussian claims for aggrandisement in the cis-Rhenan provinces. This led to a number of complicated transactions. William ceded to Prussia his ancient hereditary Nassau principalities—Dillenburg, Dietz, Siegen and Hadamar. The equivalent which William received was the sovereignty of Luxemburg, which for this purpose was severed from the Belgian Netherlands, of which it had been one of the provinces since the time of the Burgundian dukes, and was erected into a Grand-Duchy. Further than this, the Grand-Duchy was made one of the states of the Germanic Confederation; and the town of Luxemburg was declared to be a federal fortress, the garrison to consist of Prussian and Dutch detachments under a Prussian commandant. There was a double object in this transaction: (1) to preserve to the Grand-Duke his rights and privileges as a German prince, (2) to secure the defence of this important borderland against French attack. Another complication arose from the fact that in the 14th century the House of Nassau had been divided into two branches, Walram and Otto, the younger branch being that of which the Prince of Orange was the head. But by a family-pact[9], agreed upon in 1735 and renewed in 1783, the territorial possessions of either line in default of male-heirs had to pass to the next male-agnate of the other branch. This pact therefore, by virtue of the exchange that had taken place, applied to the new Grand-Duchy. It is necessary here to explain what took place in some detail, for this arbitrary wrenching of Luxemburg from its historical position as an integral part of the Netherlands was to have serious and disconcerting consequences in the near future.

The new kingdom of the Netherlands naturally included Luxemburg, so that William was a loser rather than a gainer by the cession of his Nassau possessions; but his close relation by descent and marriage with the Prussian Royal House made him anxious to meet the wishes of a power on whose friendship he relied. All evidence also points to the conclusion that in accepting the personal sovereignty of the Grand-Duchy he had no intention of treating Luxemburg otherwise than as part of his kingdom. The Fundamental Law was made to apply to Luxemburg, in the same way as to Brabant or Flanders; and of the 55 members allotted to the Belgic provinces, four were representatives of the Grand-Duchy, which was subject to the same legislation and taxes as the kingdom. At first the king had thought of nominating his second son Frederick as his successor in Luxemburg, but he changed his mind and gave him an indemnity elsewhere; and he himself states the reason, "since we have judged it advisable *(convenable)* in the general interest of the kingdom to unite the Grand-Duchy to it and to place it under the same constitutional laws."

The boundaries of the new kingdom and of the Grand-Duchy were fixed by the treaty of May 31, 1815, and confirmed by the General Act of the Congress of Vienna. By this treaty Prussia received a considerable part of the old province of Luxemburg as well as slices of territory taken from the bishopric of Liège. A separate boundary treaty a year later (June 26, 1816) between the Netherlands and Prussia filled in the details of that of 1815; and that Prussia herself acquiesced in the fusion of the kingdom and the Grand-Duchy is shown by the fact that the boundary between Prussia and Luxemburg is three times referred to in the later treaty as the boundary between Prussia and the kingdom of the Netherlands.

# CHAPTER XXX

# THE KINGDOM OF THE NETHERLANDS—UNION OF HOLLAND AND BELGIUM, 1815-1830

The autocratic powers that were conferred upon King William by the Fundamental Law rendered his personality a factor of the utmost importance in the difficult task which lay before him. William's character was strong and self-confident, and he did not shrink from responsibility. His intentions were of the best; he was capable, industrious, a good financier, sparing himself no trouble in mastering the details of State business. But he had the defects of his qualities, being self-opinionated, stubborn and inclined, as in the matter of the vote of the Belgian notables, to override opposition with a high hand. He had at the beginning of his reign the good fortune of being on the best of terms with Castlereagh, the British Foreign Minister. To Castlereagh more than to any other statesman the kingdom of the Netherlands owed its existence. The Peace of Paris saw Great Britain in possession by conquest of all the Dutch colonies. By the Convention of London (August 13, 1814), which was Castlereagh's work, it was arranged that all the captured colonies, including Java, the richest and most valuable of all, should be restored, with the exception of the Cape of Good Hope and the Guiana colonies—Demerara, Berbice and Essequibo. In the latter the plantations had almost all passed into British hands during the eighteen years since their conquest; and Cape Colony was retained as essential for the security of the sea-route to India. But these surrenders were not made without ample compensation. Great Britain contributed £2,000,000 towards erecting fortresses along the French frontier; £1,000,000 to satisfy a claim of Sweden with regard to the island of Guadeloupe; and £3,000,000 or one-half of a debt from Holland to Russia, *i.e.* a sum of £6,000,000 in all.

One of the most urgent problems with which the Sovereign-Prince had to deal on his accession to power was the state of the finances. Napoleon by a stroke of the pen had reduced the public debt to one-third of its amount. William, however, was too honest a man to avail himself of the opportunity for partial repudiation that was offered him. He recalled into existence the two-thirds on which no interest had been paid and called it "deferred debt" (*uitgestelde schuld*); the other third received the name of "working debt" (*werkelijke schuld*). The figures stood at 1200 million florins and 600 million florins respectively. Every year four millions of the "working debt" were to be paid off, and a similar amount from the "deferred" added to it. Other measures taken in 1814 for effecting economies were of little avail, as the campaign of Waterloo in the following year added 40 million florins to the debt. Heavier taxation had to be imposed, but even then the charges for the debt made it almost impossible to avoid an annual deficit in the budget. It was one of the chief grievances of the Belgians that they were called upon to share the burden of a crushing debt which they had not incurred. The voting of ways and means for ten years gave the king the control over all ordinary finance; it was only extraordinary expenditure that had to be submitted annually to the representatives of the people.

The dislike of the Catholic hierarchy in Belgium to Dutch rule had been intensified by the manner in which the king had dealt with the vote of the notables. Their leader was Maurice de Broglie, Bishop of Ghent, a Frenchman by birth. His efforts by speech and by pen to stir up active enmity in Belgium to the union aroused William's anger, and he resolved to prosecute him. It was an act of courage rather than of statesmanship, but the king could not brook opposition. Broglie refused to appear before the court and fled to France. In his absence he was condemned to banishment and the payment of costs. The powerful clerical party regarded him as a martyr and continued to criticise the policy of the Protestant king with watchful and hostile suspicion. Nor were the Belgian liberal party more friendly. They did not indeed support the clerical claim to practical predominance in the State, but they were patriotic Belgians who had no love for Holland and resented the thought that they were being treated as a dependency of their northern neighbours. They were at one with the clericals in claiming that the Belgian representation in the Second Chamber of the States-General should be proportional to their population. But this grievance might have been tolerated had the king shown any inclination to treat his Belgian subjects on a footing of equality with the Dutch. He was, as will be seen, keenly interested in the welfare and progress of the south, but in spirit and in his conduct of affairs he proved himself to be an out-and-out Hollander. The provision of the Fundamental Law that the seat of government and the meetings of the States-General should be alternately from year to year at the Hague and at Brussels was never carried out. All the ministries were permanently located at the Hague; and of the seven ministers who held office in 1816 only one, the Duke d'Ursel, was a Belgian, and he held the post of Minister of Public Works and Waterways. Fourteen years later (at the time of the revolt) six out of seven were still northerners. The military establishments were all in Holland, and nearly all the diplomatic and civil posts were given to Dutchmen. Nor was this merely due to the fact that, when the union took place, Holland already possessed an organised government and a supply of experienced officials, while Belgium lacked both. On the contrary, the policy of the king remained fixed and unwavering. In 1830 out of 39 diplomatists 30 were Dutch. All the chief military posts were filled by Dutchmen. Nor was it different in the civil service. In the home department there were 117 Dutch, 11 Belgians; in the war department 102 Dutch, 3 Belgians; in finance 59 Dutch, 5 Belgians. Such a state of things was bound to cause resentment. Parties in the Belgic provinces were in the early days of the Union divided very much as they have been in recent years. The Catholic or Clerical party had its stronghold in the two Flanders and Antwerp, *i.e.* in the Flemish-speaking districts. In Walloon Belgium the Liberals had a considerable majority. The opposition to the Fundamental Law came overwhelmingly from Flemish Belgium; the support from Liège, Namur, Luxemburg and other Walloon districts. But the sense of injustice brought both parties together, so that in the representative Chamber the Belgian members were soon found voting solidly together, as a permanent opposition, while the Dutch voted *en bloc* for the government. As the representation of north and south was equal, 55 members each, the result would have been a deadlock, but there were always two or three Belgians who held government offices; and these were compelled, on pain of instant dismissal, to vote for a government measure or at least to abstain. Thus the king could always rely on a small but constant majority, and by its aid he did not hesitate to force through financial and legislative proposals in the teeth of Belgian opposition. It is only fair, however, to the arbitrary king to point out how earnestly he endeavoured to promote the material and industrial welfare of the whole land, and to encourage to the best of his power literary, scientific and educational progress. In Holland the carrying-trade, which had so long been the chief source of the country's wealth, had been utterly ruined by Napoleon's Continental System. On the other hand, Belgian industries, which had been flourishing through the strict embargo placed upon the import of British goods, were now threatened with British competition. The steps taken by the energy and initiative of the king were, considering the state of the national finances, remarkable in the variety of their aims and the results that they achieved. The old Amsterdam Bank was transformed into a Bank of the Netherlands. A number of canals were planned and constructed. Chief among these was the North Holland Canal, connecting Amsterdam with the Helder. The approaches to Rotterdam were improved, so that this port became the meeting-point of sea-traffic from England and river-traffic by the Rhine from Germany. But both these ports were quickly overshadowed by the rapid recovery of Antwerp, now that the Scheldt was free and open to commerce. Other important canals, begun and wholly or in part constructed, during this period were the Zuid-Willemsvaart, the Zederik, the Appeldoorn and the Voorne canals. Water communication was not so necessary in the south as in the north, but care was there also bestowed upon the canals, especially upon the canal of Terneuzen connecting Ghent with the western Scheldt, and many highways were constructed. To restore the prosperity of the Dutch carrying-trade, especially that with their East Indies, in 1824 a Company—*de Nederlandsche Handekmaatschappij*—was founded; and at the same time a commercial treaty was concluded with Great Britain, by which both nations were to enjoy free trade with each other's East Indian possessions. The *Handekmaatschappij* had a capital of 37 million florins; to this the king contributed four millions and guaranteed to the shareholders for 20 years a dividend of 4 1/2 per cent. The Company at first worked at a loss, and in 1831 William had to pay four million florins out of his privy purse to meet his guarantee. This was partly due to the set-back of a revolt in Java which lasted some years.

Agriculture received equal attention. Marshy districts were impoldered or turned into pasture-land. More especially did the *Maatschappij van Weldadigheid*, a society founded in 1818 by General van den Bosch with the king's strong support, undertake the task of reclaiming land with the special aim of relieving poverty. No less zealous was the king for the prosperity of Belgian industries; Ghent with its cotton factories and sugar refineries, Tournai with its porcelain industry, and Liège with its hardware, all were the objects of royal interest. The great machine factory at Seraing near Liège under the management of an Englishman, Cockerill, owed its existence to the king. Nor was William's care only directed to the material interests of his people. In 1815 the University at Utrecht was restored; and in Belgium, besides Louvain, two new foundations for higher education were in 1816 created at Ghent and Liège. Royal Academies of the Arts were placed at Amsterdam and Antwerp, which were to bear good fruit. His attention was also given to the much-needed improvement of primary education, which in the south was almost non-existent in large parts of the country. Here the presence of a number of illiterate dialects was a great obstacle and was the cause of the unfortunate effort to make literary Dutch into a national language for his whole realm.

Nevertheless the king's political mistakes (of which the attempted compulsory use of Dutch was one) rendered all his thoughtful watchfulness over his people's welfare unavailing. Great as were the autocratic powers conferred upon the sovereign, he overstepped them. Plans, in which he was interested, he carried out without consulting the States-General. His ministers he regarded as bound to execute his orders. If their views differed from his, they were dismissed. This was the fate even of Van Hogendorp, to whom he owed so much; Roëll and Falck also had to make way for less competent but more obsequious ministers.

The chief difficulty with which the king had to contend throughout this period was the ceaseless and irreconcilable opposition of the Catholic hierarchy and clergy to the principle of absolute religious equality established by the Fundamental Law (Articles CXC-CXCIII). Their leader, Maurice de Broglie, Bishop of Ghent, actually published a *jugement doctrinal* in which he declared that the taking of the oath to the Constitution was an act of treason to the Catholic Church. In this defiance to the government he had the support of the Pope, who only permitted the Count de Méan to take the oath on his appointment to the Archbishopric of Malines on the understanding that he held Articles CXC-CXCIII to refer only to civil matters. From this time to take the oath "dans le sens de M. Méan" became with the ultra-clerical party a common practice.

Other measures of the government aroused Catholic hostility. In this year, 1819, a decree forbade the holding of more than two religious processions in a year. In such a country as Belgium this restriction was strongly resented. But the establishment in 1825 by the king of a *Collegium Philosophicum* at Louvain, at which all candidates for the priesthood were by royal decree required (after 1826) to have a two-years' course before proceeding to an episcopal seminary, met with strenuous resistance. The instruction was in ancient languages, history, ethics and canon-law; and the teachers were nominated by the king. The first effect of this decree was that young men began to seek education in foreign seminaries. Another royal decree at once forbade this, and all youths were ordered to proceed either to the *Collegium* or to one of the High Schools of the land; unless they did so, access to the priesthood or to any public office was barred to them. This was perhaps the most serious of all the king's mistakes. He miscalculated both the strength and the sincerity of the opposition he thus deliberately courted. His decrees were doomed to failure. The bishops on their part refused to admit to their seminaries or to ordination anyone who attended the *Collegium Philosophicum*. The king, in the face of the irrevocable decision of the Belgian hierarchy, found himself in an untenable position. He could not compel the bishops to ordain candidates for Holy Orders, and his decrees were therefore a dead letter; nor on the other hand could he trample upon the convictions of the vast majority of his Belgian subjects by making admission to the priesthood impossible. He had to give way and to send a special envoy—De Celles—to the Pope in 1827 to endeavour to negotiate a Concordat. It was accomplished. By Article III of the Concordat, there were to be eight bishops in the Netherlands instead of five. They were to be chosen by the Pope, but the king was to have the right of objection, and they were required to take the oath of allegiance. The course at the *Collegium Philosophicum* was made optional. William thus yielded on practically all the points at issue, but prided himself on having obtained the right of rejecting a papal nominee. The Pope, however, in an allocution made no mention of this right, and declared that the decree about the *Collegium* was annulled, and that in matters of education the bishops would act in accordance with instructions from Rome. The government immediately issued a confidential notice to the governors of provinces, that the carrying-out of the Concordat was indefinitely postponed. Thus the effort at conciliation ended in the humiliation of the king, and the triumph of the astute diplomacy of the Vatican.

The financial situation, as we have seen, was from the outset full of difficulty. The king was personally parsimonious, but his many projects for the general welfare of the land involved large outlay, and the consequence was an annual average deficit of seven million florins. At first the revenue was raised by the increase of customs and excise, including colonial imports. This caused much dissatisfaction in Holland, especially when duties were placed on coffee and sugar. The complaint was that thus an undue share of taxation fell on the maritime north. In order to lighten these duties on colonial wares, other taxes had to be imposed. In 1821 accordingly it was proposed to meet the deficit by two most unwise and obnoxious taxes, known as *mouture* and *abbatage*. The first was on ground corn, the second on the carcases of beasts, exacted at the mill or the slaughter-house—in other words on bread and on butcher's meat. Both were intensely unpopular, and the *mouture* in particular fell with especial severity on the Belgian working classes and peasantry, who consumed much more bread per head than the Dutch. Nevertheless by ministerial pressure the bill was passed (July 21, 1821) by a narrow majority of four—55 to 51. All the minority were Belgians, only two Belgians voted with the majority. It is inconceivable how the government could have been so impolitic as to impose these taxes in face of such a display of national animosity.

The *mouture* only produced a revenue of 5,500,000 fl.; the *abbatage* 2,500,000 fl.

This amount, though its exaction pressed heavily on the very poor, afforded little relief; and to meet recurring deficits the only resource was borrowing. To extricate the national finances from ever-increasing difficulties the *Amortisatie-Syndikaat* was created in December, 1822. Considerable sources of income from various public domains and from tolls passed into the hands of the seven members of the Syndicate, all of whom were bound to secrecy, both as to its public and private transactions. Its effect was to diminish still further the control of the Representative Chamber over the national finances. The Syndicate did indeed assist the State, for between 1823 and 1829 it advanced no less than 58,885,443 fl. to meet the deficits in the budget, but the means by which it achieved this result were not revealed.

Yet another device to help the government in its undertakings was the *million de l'industrie*, which was voted every year, as an extraordinary charge, but of which no account was ever given. That this sum was beneficially used for the assistance of manufacturing and industrial enterprise, as at Seraing and elsewhere, and that it contributed to the growing prosperity of the southern provinces, is certain. But the needless mystery which surrounded its expenditure led to the suspicion that it was used as a fund for secret service and political jobbery.

The autocratic temper of the king showed itself not merely in keeping the control of finance largely in his own hands, but also in carrying out a series of measures arousing popular discontent by simple *arrêtés* or decrees of the Council of State without consultation with the representative Chamber. Such were the decree of November 6,1814, abolishing trial by jury and making certain other changes in judicial proceedings; that of April 15, 1815, imposing great restrictions on the liberty of the press; that of September 15, 1819, making Dutch the official language of the country; that of June 25,1825, establishing the *Collegium Philosophicum*; and finally that of June 21, 1830, making the Hague the seat of the supreme court of justice. All these produced profound discontent and had a cumulative effect.

The language decree of 1819 was tentative, declaring a knowledge of Dutch obligatory for admission to all public offices, but it was followed by a much more stringent decree in 1822 by which, in the two Flanders, South Brabant and Limburg, Dutch was to be used in the law-courts and in all public acts and notices. Although the operation of this decree was confined to the Flemish-speaking districts, it must be remembered that, from the time of the Burgundian dukes right through the Spanish and Austrian periods, French had always been the official language of the country, the upper classes only spoke French, and with few exceptions the advocates could only plead in that language. This was a great hardship upon the Belgian bar, which would have been greatly increased had the royal decree (June 21, 1830), placing the court of appeal for the whole kingdom at the Hague, been carried into effect.

More serious in its results was the infringement of Art. CCXXVII of the Fundamental Law guaranteeing liberty of the press. The return of Napoleon from Elba, and the imminent danger to which the, as yet, unorganised kingdom of the Netherlands was exposed, led to the issue of an *arrêté* of the severest character. By it all persons publishing news of any kind, or giving information injurious to the State, or writing or distributing political pamphlets, were to be brought before a special tribunal of nine judges holding office at the king's pleasure; and, if condemned, were liable to be sentenced to exposure in the pillory, deprivation of civic rights, branding, imprisonment, and fines varying from 100 to 10,000 francs. This harsh measure was possibly justifiable in an extreme emergency upon the plea that it was necessary for the safety of the State. When the danger was over, and the Fundamental Law was passed, there was no excuse for its further maintenance on the Statute-book. Yet before this court Abbé de Foere was summoned for having defended in the *Spectateur Beige* the *jugement doctrinal* of Bishop de Broglie, and he was sentenced to two years' imprisonment. In the following year, 1818, the government obtained the approval of the States-General (with slight modification) for the continuance of this war-time censorship of the press. The penalties remained, but the court consisted of a judge and four assessors, all government nominees. Under this law a Brussels advocate, Van der Straeten, was fined 3000 fl. for a brochure attacking the ministers; and several other advocates were disbarred for protesting that this sentence was in conflict with the Fundamental Law. Prosecutions henceforth followed prosecutions, and the press was gagged.

As a result of these press persecutions, the two Belgian political parties, the clericals and the liberals, poles apart as they were in their principles, drew closer together. All differences of religious and political creed were fused in a common sense of national grievances under what was regarded as a foreign tyranny. This brought about in 1828 the formation of the *Union*, an association for the co-operation of Belgians of all parties in defence of liberty of worship, liberty of instruction and liberty of the press. The ultra-clericals, who looked to the Vatican for their guidance, and the advanced liberals who professed the principles of the French Revolution were thus by the force of events led on step by step to convert an informal into a formal alliance. The Abbe de Foere in the *Spectateur* and MM. D'Ellougue and Donker in the *Observateur* had been for some years advocating united action; and it was their success in winning over to their side the support and powerful pen of Louis de Potter, a young advocate and journalist of Franco-radical sympathies, that the *Union*, as a party, was actually effected. From this time the onslaughts in the press became more and more violent and embittered, and stirred up a spirit of unrest throughout the country. Petitions began to pour in against the *mouture* and *abbatage* taxes and other unpopular measures, especially from the Walloon provinces. These were followed by a National Petition, signed by representatives of every class of the community asking for redress of grievances, but it met with no response from the unyielding king. He had in the early summer of this year, 1828, made a tour in Belgium and had in several towns, especially in Antwerp and Ghent, met with a warm reception, which led him to underestimate the extent and seriousness of the existing discontent. At Liège, a centre of Walloon liberalism, he was annoyed by a number of petitions being presented to him; and, in a moment of irritation, he described the conduct of those who there protested against "pretended grievances" as infamous, "une conduite in-fâme." The words gave deep offence; and the incident called forth a parody of the League of the Beggars in 1566, an Order of Infamy being started with a medal bearing the motto *fidèles jusqu' à l'infamie*. The movement spread rapidly, but it remains a curious fact that the animosity of the Belgians, as yet, was directed against the Dutch ministers (especially Van Maanen the Minister of Justice) and the Dutch people, whose overbearing attitude was bitterly resented, rather than against the king or the House of Orange. William's good deeds for the benefit of the country were appreciated; his arbitrary measures in contravention to the Fundamental Law were attributed chiefly to his bad advisers.

The month of December, 1829, was however to bring the king and his Belgian subjects into violent collision. A motion was brought forward in the Second Chamber (December 8) by M. Charles de Broukère, an eminent Belgian liberal supported by the Catholics under the leadership of M. de Gerlache, for the abolition of the hated Press Law of 1815. The motion was defeated by the solid Dutch vote, supplemented by the support of seven Belgians. The decennial budget was due, and opposition to it was threatened unless grievances were remedied—the cry was "point de redressements de griefs, point d'argent." On December 11 came a royal message to the States-General which, while promising certain concessions regarding the taxes, the *Collegium Philosophicum* and the language decree, stated in unequivocal terms the principle of royal absolutism. To quote the words of a competent observer of these events:

The message declared in substance that the constitution was an act of condescension on the part of the throne; that the king had restrained rather than carried to excess the rights of his house; that the press had been guilty of sowing discord and confusion throughout the State; and that the opposition was but the fanatic working of a few misguided men, who, forgetting the benefits they enjoyed, had risen up in an alarming and scandalous manner against a paternal government[10].

The Minister of Justice, Van Maanen, on the next day issued a circular calling upon all civil officials to signify their adherence to the principles of the message within 24 hours. Several functionaries, who had taken part in the petition-agitation, were summarily dismissed; and prosecutions against the press were instituted with renewed energy. From this time Van Maanen became the special object of Belgian hatred.

The threat of the Belgian deputies to oppose the decennial budget was now carried out. At the end of December the ministerial proposals were brought before the States-General. The expenditure was sanctioned, the ways and means to meet it were rejected by 55 votes to 52. The Finance Minister in this emergency was obliged to introduce fresh estimates for one year only, from which the *mouture* and *abbatage* taxes were omitted. This was passed without opposition, but in his vexation at this rebuff the king acted unworthily of his position by issuing an *arrêté* (January 8, 1830) depriving six deputies, who had voted in the majority, of their official posts. Meanwhile the virulence of the attacks in the press against the king and his ministers from the pens of a number of able and unscrupulous journalists were too daring and offensive to be overlooked by any government. Foremost in the bitterness of his onslaught was Louis de Potter, whose *Lettre de Démophile au Roi* was throughout a direct challenge to the autocratic claims advanced by the royal message. Nor was De Potter content only with words. An appeal dated December 11, of which he and his friend Tielemans were originators, appeared (January 31,1830) in seventeen news-papers, for raising a national subscription to indemnify the deputies who had been ejected from their posts and salaries for voting against the budget. Proceedings were taken against De Potter and Tielemans, and also against Barthels, editor of the *Catholique*, and the printer, De Nève, and all were sentenced by the court to banishment—De Potter for eight years, Tielemans and Barthels for seven years, DeNève for five years. These men had all committed offences which the government were fully justified in punishing, for their language had passed the limits not only of good order but of decency, and was subversive of all authority. Nevertheless they were regarded by their Belgian compatriots as political martyrs suffering for the cause of their country's liberties. Their condemnation was attributed to Van Maanen, already the object of general detestation.

The ministry had meanwhile taken the wise step of starting an organ, the *National*, at Brussels to take their part in the field of controversy. But in the circumstances it was an act of almost inconceivable folly to select as the editor a certain Libri-Bagnano, a man of Italian extraction, who, as it was soon discovered by his opponents, had twice suffered heavy sentences in France as a forger. He was a brilliant and caustic writer, well able to carry the polemical war into his adversaries' camp. But his antecedents were against him, and he aroused a hatred second only to the aversion felt for Van Maanen.

We have now arrived at the eve of the Belgian Revolt, which had its actual origin in a riot. But the riot was not the cause of the revolt; it was but the spark which brought about an explosion, the materials for which had been for years preparing. The French secret agent, Julian, reports a conversation which took place between the king and Count Bylandt on July 20,1823[11]. The following extract proves that, so early as this date, William had begun to perceive the impossibility of the situation:

> I say it and I repeat it often to Clancarty (the British Minister) that I should love much better to have my Holland quite alone. I should be then a hundred times happier . . . When I am exerting myself to make a whole of this country, a party, which in collusion with the foreigner never ceases to gain ground, is working to disunite it. Besides the allies have not given me this kingdom to submit it to every kind of influence. This situation cannot last.

Another extract from a despatch of the French Minister at the Hague, Lamoussaye, dated December 26, 1828, depicts a state of things in the relations between the two peoples, tending sooner or later to make a political separation of some kind inevitable:

> The Belgian hates the Hollander and he (the Hollander) despises the Belgian, besides which he assumes an infinite *hauteur*, both from his national character, by the creations of his industry and by the memories of his history. Disdained by their neighbour of the North, governed by a prince whose confidence they do not possess, hindered in the exercise of their worship, and, as they say, in the enjoyment of their liberties, overburdened with taxes, having but a share in the National Representation disproportionate to the population of the South, the Belgians ask themselves whether they have a country, and are restless in a painful situation, the outcome of which they seek vainly to discover[12].

From an intercepted letter from Louvain, dated July 30, 1829[12]:

> What does one see? Hesitation uncertainty, embarrassment and fear in the march of the government; organisation, re-organisation and finally disorganisation of all and every administration. Again a rude shock and the machine crumbles.

A true forecast of coming events.

# CHAPTER XXXI

# THE BELGIAN REVOLUTION, 1830-1842

During the last days of July, 1830, came the revolution at Paris that overthrew Charles X and placed the Duke of Orleans at the head of a constitutional monarchy with the title of Louis Philippe, King of the French. The Belgian liberals had always felt drawn towards France rather than Holland, and several of the more influential among them were in Paris during the days of July. Through their close intercourse with their friends in Brussels the news of all that had occurred spread rapidly, and was eagerly discussed. Probably at this time few contemplated the complete separation of Belgium from Holland, but rather looked to the northern and southern provinces becoming administratively autonomous under the same crown. This indeed appeared to be the only practical solution of the *impasse* which had been reached. Even had the king met the complaints of the Belgians by large concessions, had he dismissed Van Maanen, removed Libri-Bagnano from the editorship of the *National*, and created a responsible ministry—which he had no intention of doing—he could not have granted the demand for a representation of the south in the Second Chamber proportionate to the population. For this would have meant that the position of Holland would have henceforth been subordinate to that of Belgium; and to this the Dutch, proud of their history and achievements, would never have submitted. It had been proved that amalgamation was impossible, but the king personally was popular with those large sections of the Belgian mercantile and industrial population whose prosperity was so largely due to the royal care and paternal interest; and, had he consented to the setting-up of a separate administration at Brussels, he might by a conciliatory attitude have retained the loyalty of his Belgian subjects.

He did none of these things; but, when in August, he and his two sons paid a visit to Brussels at a time when the town was celebrating with festivities the holding of an exhibition of national industry, he was well received and was probably quite unaware of the imminence of the storm that was brewing. It had been intended to close the exhibition by a grand display of fireworks on the evening of August 23, and to have a general illumination on the king's birthday (August 24). But the king had hurried back to the Hague to keep his birthday, and during the preceding days there were abundant signs of a spirit of revolutionary ferment. Inscriptions were found on blank walls—*Down with Van Maanen; Death to the Dutch; Down with Libri-Bagnano and the National*; and, more ominous still, leaflets were distributed containing the words *le 23 Août, feu d'artifice; le 24 Août, anniversaire du Roi; le 25 Août, révolution.*

In consequence of these indications of subterranean unrest, which were well known to Baron van der Fosse, the civil governor of Brabant, and to M. Kuyff, the head of the city police, the municipal authorities weakly decided on the ground of unfavourable weather to postpone the fireworks and the illumination. The evening of the 23rd, as it turned out, was exceedingly fine. At the same time the authorities permitted, on the evening of the 25th, the first performance of an opera by Scribe and Auber, entitled *La Muette de Portici*, which had been previously proscribed. The hero, Masaniello, headed a revolt at Naples in 1648 against foreign (Spanish) rule. The piece was full of patriotic, revolutionary songs likely to arouse popular passion.

The evening of the performance arrived, and the theatre was crowded. The excitement of the audience grew as the play proceeded; and the thunders of applause were taken up by the throng which had gathered outside. Finally the spectators rushed out with loud cries of vengeance against Libri-Bagnano and Van Maanen, in which the mob eagerly joined. Brussels was at that time a chosen shelter of political refugees, ready for any excesses; and a terrible riot ensued. The house of Van Maanen and the offices of the *National* were attacked, pillaged and burnt. The city was given over to wild confusion and anarchy; and many of the mob secured arms by the plunder of the gun-smiths' shops. Meanwhile the military authorities delayed action. Several small patrols were surrounded and compelled to surrender, while the main body of troops, instead of attacking and dispersing the rioters, was withdrawn and stationed in front of the royal palace. Thus by the extraordinary passiveness of Lieut.-General Bylandt, the military governor of the province, and of Major-General Wauthier, commandant of the city, who must have been acting under secret orders, the wild outbreak of the night began, as the next day progressed and the troops were still inactive, to assume more of the character of a revolution.

This was checked by the action of the municipal authorities and certain of the principal inhabitants, who called together the civic-guard to protect any further tumultuary attacks by marauders and ne'er-do-wells on private property. The guard were joined by numbers of volunteers of the better classes and, under the command of Baron D'Hoogvoort, were distributed in different quarters of the town, and restored order. The French flags, which at first were in evidence, were replaced at the Town Hall by the Brabant tricolor—red, yellow and black. The royal insignia had in many places been torn down, and the Orange cockades had disappeared; nevertheless there was at this time no symptom of an uprising to overthrow the dynasty, only a national demand for redress of grievances. Meanwhile news arrived that reinforcements from Ghent were marching upon the city. The notables however informed General Bylandt that no troops would be allowed to enter the city without resistance; and he agreed to stop the advance and to keep his own troops in their encampment until he received further orders from the Hague. For this abandonment of any attempt to re-assert the royal authority he has been generally blamed.

There is no lack of evidence to show that the riot of August 25 and its consequences were not the work of the popular leaders. The correspondence of Gendebien with De Potter at this time, and the tone of the Belgian press before and after the outbreak, are proofs of this. The *Catholique* of Ghent (the former organ of Barthels) for instance declared:

> There is no salvation for the throne, but in an ample concession of our rights. The essential points to be accorded are royal inviolability and ministerial responsibility; the dismissal of Van Maanen; liberty of education and the

press; a diminution of taxation... in short, justice and liberty in all and for all, in strict conformity with the fundamental law.

The *Coursier des Pays Bos* (the former organ of De Potter), after demanding the dismissal of Van Maanen as the absolute condition of pacification, adds:

> We repeat that we are neither in a state of insurrection nor revolution; all we want is a mitigation of the grievances we have so long endured, and some guarantees for a better future.

In accordance with such sentiments an infuencial meeting on the on the 28th at the townhall appointed a deputation of five, headed by Alexandre de Gendebien and Felix, count de Mérode, to bear to the king a loyal address setting forth the just grievances which had led to the Brussels disturbances, and asking respectfully for their removal.

The news of the uprising reached the king on the 27th, and he was much affected. At a Council held at the Hague the Prince of Orange earnestly besought his father to accept the proffered resignation of Van Maanen, and to consider in a conciliatory spirit the grievances of the Belgians. But William refused flatly to dismiss the minister or to treat with rebels. He gave the prince, however, permission to visit Brussels, not armed with powers to act, but merely with a mission of enquiry. He also consented to receive the deputation from Brussels, and summoned an extraordinary meeting of the States-General at the Hague for September 13. Troops were at once ordered to move south and to join the camp at Vilvoorde, where the regiments sent to reinforce the Brussels garrison had been halted. The Prince of Orange and his brother Frederick meanwhile had left the Hague and reached Vilvoorde on August 31. Here Frederick assumed command of the troops; and Orange sent his *aide-de-camp* to Baron D'Hoogvoort to invite him to a conference at headquarters. The news of the gathering troops had aroused immense excitement in the capital; and it was resolved that Hoogvoort, at the head of a representative deputation, should go to Vilvoorde to urge the prince to stop any advance of the troops on Brussels, as their entrance into the town would be resisted, unless the citizens were assured that Van Maanen was dismissed, and that the other grievances were removed. They invited Orange to come to Brussels attended only by his personal suite, and offered to be sureties for his safety.

The prince made his entry on September 1, the streets being lined with the civic guard. He was personally popular, but, possessing no powers, he could effect nothing. After three days of parleying he returned to the camp, and his mission was a failure. On the same day when Orange entered Brussels the deputation of five was received by King William at the Hague. His reply to their representations was that by the Fundamental Law he had the right to choose his ministers, that the principle of ministerial responsibility was contrary to the Constitution, and that he would not dismiss Van Maanen or deal with any alleged grievances with a pistol at his head.

William, however, despite his uncompromising words, did actually accept the resignation of Van Maanen (September 3); but when the Prince of Orange, returning from his experiences at Brussels, urged the necessity of an administrative separation of north and south, and offered to return to the Belgian capital if armed with full authority to carry it out, his offer was declined. The king would only consent to bring the matter to the consideration of the States-General, which was to meet on the 13th. Instead of taking any immediate action he issued a proclamation, which in no way faced the exigencies of the situation, and was no sooner posted on the walls at Brussels than it was torn down and trampled underfoot. It is only just to say that the king had behind him the unanimous support of the Dutch people, especially the commercial classes. To them separation was far preferable to admitting the Belgians to that predominant share of the representation which they claimed on the ground of their larger population.

Meanwhile at Brussels, owing to the inaction of the government, matters were moving fast. The spirit of revolt had spread to other towns, principally in the Walloon provinces. Liège and Louvain were the first to move. Charles Rogier, an advocate by profession and a Frenchman by birth, was the leader of the revolt at Liège; and such was his fiery ardour that at the head of some 400 men, whom he had supplied with arms from the armourer's warehouses, he marched to Brussels, and arrived in that disturbed city without encountering any Dutch force. The example of Liège was followed by Jemappes, Wavre, and by the miners of the Borinage; and Brussels was filled with a growing crowd of men filled with a revolutionary spirit. Their aim was to proclaim the independence of Belgium, and set up a provisional government.

For such a step even pronounced liberals like Gendebien, Van de Weyer and Rouppe, the veteran burgomaster of the city, were not yet prepared; and they combined with the moderates, Count Felix de Mérode and Ferdinand Meeus, to form a Committee of Public Safety. They were aided, in the maintenance of order, by the two Barons D'Hoogvoort (Emmanuel and Joseph), the first the commander of the civic guard, and both popular and influential, and by the municipality. While these were still struggling to maintain their authority, the States-General had met at the Hague on September 13. It was opened by a speech from the king which announced his firm determination to maintain law and order in the face of revolutionary violence. He had submitted two questions to the consideration of the States-General: (1) whether experience had shown the necessity for a modification of the Fundamental Law; (2) whether any change should be made in the relations between the two parts of the kingdom. Both questions were, after long debate (September 29) answered in the affirmative; but, before this took place, events at Brussels had already rendered deliberations at the Hague futile and useless.

The contents of the king's speech were no sooner known in Brussels than they were used by the revolutionary leaders to stir up the passions of the mob by inflammatory harangues. Rogier and Ducpétiaux, at the head of the Liègeois and the contingents from the other Walloon towns, with the support of the lowest elements of the Brussels population, demanded the dissolution of the Committee of Public Safety and the establishment of a Provisional Government. The members of the Committee and of the Municipality, sitting in permanence at the Hotel de Ville, did their utmost to maintain order with the strong support of Baron D'Hoogvoort and the Civic Guard. But it was in vain. On the evening of September 20 an immense mob rushed the Hotel de Ville, after disarming the Civic Guard; and Rogier and Ducpétiaux were henceforth masters of the city. The Committee of Public

Safety disappeared and is heard of no more. Hoogvoort resigned his command. On receipt of this news Prince Frederick at Vilvoorde was ordered to advance upon the city and compel submission. But the passions of the crowd had been aroused, and the mere rumour that the Dutch troops were moving caused the most vigorous steps to be taken to resist *à outrance* their penetrating into the town.

The royal forces, on the morning of September 23, entered the city at three gates and advanced as far as the Park. But beyond that point they were unable to proceed, so desperate was the resistance, and such the hail of bullets that met them from barricades and from the windows and roofs of the houses. For three days almost without cessation the fierce contest went on, the troops losing ground rather than gaining it. On the evening of the 26th the prince gave orders to retreat, his troops having suffered severely.

The effect of this withdrawal was to convert a street insurrection into a national revolt. The moderates now united with the liberals, and a Provisional Government was formed, having amongst its members Rogier, Van de Weyer, Gendebien, Emmanuel D'Hoogvoort, Felix de Mérode and Louis de Potter, who a few days later returned triumphantly from banishment. The Provisional Government issued a series of decrees declaring Belgium independent, releasing the Belgian soldiers from their allegiance, and calling upon them to abandon the Dutch standard. They were obeyed. The revolt, which had been confined mainly to the Walloon districts, now spread rapidly over Flanders. Garrison after garrison surrendered; and the remnants of the disorganised Dutch forces retired upon Antwerp (October 2). Two days later the Provisional Government summoned a National Congress to be elected by all Belgian citizens of 25 years of age. The news of these events caused great perturbation at the Hague. The Prince of Orange, who had throughout advocated conciliation, was now permitted by his father to go to Antwerp (October 4) and endeavour to place himself at the head of the Belgian movement on the basis of a grant of administrative separation, but without severance of the dynastic bond with Holland.

King William meanwhile had already (October 2) appealed to the Great Powers, signatories of the Articles of London in 1814, to intervene and to restore order in the Belgic provinces. The difficulties of the prince at Antwerp were very great, for he was hampered throughout by his father's unwillingness to grant him full liberty of action. He issued a proclamation, but it was coldly received; and his attempts to negotiate with the Provisional Government at Brussels met with no success. Things had now gone too far, and any proposal to make Belgium connected with Holland by any ties, dynastic or otherwise, was unacceptable. The well-meaning prince returned disappointed to the Hague on October 24. A most unfortunate occurrence now took place. As General Chassé, the Dutch commander at Antwerp, was withdrawing his troops from the town to the citadel, attacks were made upon them by the mob, and some lives were lost. Chassé in reprisal (October 27) ordered the town to be bombarded from the citadel and the gunboats upon the river. This impolitic act increased throughout Belgium the feeling of hatred against the Dutch, and made the demand for absolute independence deeper and stronger.

The appeal of William to the signatory Powers had immediate effect; and representatives of Austria, Prussia, Russia and Great Britain, to whom a representative of France was now added, met at London on November 4. This course of action was far from what the king expected or wished. Their first step was to impose an armistice; their next to make it clear that their intervention would be confined to negotiating a settlement on the basis of separation. A Whig ministry in England had (November 16) taken the place of that of Wellington; and Lord Palmerston, the new Foreign Secretary, was well-disposed to Belgium and found himself able to work in accord with Talleyrand, the French plenipotentiary. Austria and Russia were too much occupied with their own internal difficulties to think of supporting the Dutch king by force of arms; and Prussia, despite the close family connection, did not venture to oppose the determination of the two western Powers to work for a peaceful settlement. While they were deliberating, the National Congress had met at Brussels, and important decisions had been taken. By overwhelming majorities (November 18) Belgium was declared to be an independent State; and four days later, after vigorous debates, the Congress (by 174 votes to 13) resolved that the new State should be a constitutional monarchy and (by 161 votes to 28) that the house of Orange-Nassau be for ever excluded from the throne. A committee was appointed to draw up a constitution.

William had appealed to the Powers to maintain the Treaties of Paris and Vienna and to support him in what he regarded, on the basis of those treaties, as his undoubted rights; and it was with indignation that he saw the Conference decline to admit his envoy, Falck, except as a witness and on precisely the same terms as the representatives of the Brussels Congress. On December 20 a protocol was issued by the Powers which defined their attitude. They accepted the principle of separation and independence, subject to arrangements being made for assuring European peace. The Conference, however, declared that such arrangements would not affect the rights of King William and of the German Confederation in the Grand Duchy of Luxemburg. This part of the protocol was as objectionable to the Belgians as the former part was to the Dutch king. The London Plenipotentiaries had in fact no choice, for they were bound by the unfortunate clauses of the treaties of 1815, which, to gratify Prussian ambition for cis-Rhenan territory, converted this ancient Belgian province into a German state. This ill-advised step was now to be the chief obstacle to a settlement in 1831. The mere fact that William had throughout the period of union always treated Luxemburg as an integral part of the southern portion of his kingdom made its threatened severance from the Belgic provinces a burning question. For Luxemburgers had taken a considerable part in the revolt, and Luxemburg representatives sat in the National Congress. Of these eleven voted for the perpetual exclusion of the Orange-Nassau dynasty, one only in its favour. It is not surprising, therefore, that a strong protest was made against the decision of the London Conference to treat the status of Luxemburg as outside the subject of their deliberations. The Conference, however, unmoved by this protest, proceeded in a protocol of January 20,1831, to define the conditions of separation. Holland was to retain her old boundaries of the year 1790, and Belgium to have the remainder of the territory assigned to the kingdom of the Netherlands in 1815. Luxemburg was again excluded. The Five Powers, moreover, declared that within these limits the new Belgian State was to be perpetually neutral, its integrity and inviolability being guaranteed by all and each of the Powers. A second protocol (January 27) fixed the proportion of the national debt to be borne by Belgium at sixteen parts out of thirty-one. The sovereign of Belgium was required to give his assent to these protocols, as a condition to being recognised by the Powers. But the Congress of Brussels was in no submissive mood. They had already (January 19) resolved to proceed to the election of a king without consulting anyone. The territorial boundaries assigned to Belgium met with almost unanimous reprobation, a claim being made to the incorporation not merely of Luxemburg, but also of Maestrieht, Limburg and Dutch Flanders, in the new State. Nor were they more contented with the proportion of the debt Belgium was asked to bear. On February 1 the Five Powers had agreed that they would not assent to a member of any of the reigning dynasties being elected to the throne of Belgium. Nevertheless (February 3) the Duc de Nemours, son of Louis Philippe, was elected by 94 votes, as against 67 recorded for the Duke of Leuchtenberg, son of Eugène Beauharnais. The Conference took immediate action by refusing to permit either Nemours or Leuchtenberg to accept the proffered crown.

These acute differences between the Conference and the Belgian Congress were a cause of much satisfaction to the Dutch king, who was closely watching the course of events; and he thought it good policy (February 18) to signify his assent to the conditions set forth in the protocols of January 20 and 27. He had still some hopes of the candidature of the Prince of Orange (who was in London) being supported by the Powers, but for this the time was past.

At this juncture the name of Leopold of Saxe-Coburg, who had resided in England since the death of his wife the Princess Charlotte, was put forward. This candidature was supported by Great Britain; France raised no objection; and in Belgium it met with official support. Early in April a deputation of five commissioners was sent to offer the crown provisionally to the prince, subject to his endeavouring to obtain some modification of the protocols of January 20 and 27. The Five Powers, however, in a protocol, dated April 15, announced to the Belgian Government that the conditions of separation as laid down in the January protocols were final and irrevocable, and, if not accepted, relations would be broken off. Leopold was not discouraged, however; and such was his influence that he did succeed in obtaining from the Conference an undertaking that they would enter into negotiations with King

William in regard both to the territorial and financial disputes with a view to a settlement, *moyennant de justes compensations*.

The Saxe-Coburg prince was elected king by the Congress (June 4); and in redemption of their undertaking the Conference promulgated (June 26) the preliminary treaty, generally known as the Treaty of the XVIII Articles. By this treaty the question of Luxemburg was reserved for a separate negotiation, the *status quo* being meanwhile maintained. Other boundary disputes (Maestricht, Limburg and various *enclaves*) were to be amicably arranged, and the share of Belgium in the public debt was reduced. Leopold had made his acceptance of the crown depend upon the assent of the Congress being given to the Treaty. This assent was given, but in the face of strong opposition (July 9); and the new king made his public entry into Brussels and took the oath to the Constitution twelve days later. On the same day (July 21) the Dutch king refused to accept the XVIII Articles, declaring that he adhered to the protocols of January 20 and 27, which the plenipotentiaries had themselves declared (April 15) to be fundamental and irrevocable. Nor did he confine himself to a refusal. He declared that if any prince should accept the sovereignty of Belgium or take possession of it without having assented to the protocols as the basis of separation he could only regard such prince as his enemy. He followed this up (August 2) by a despatch addressed to the Foreign Ministers of the Five Powers, announcing his intention "to throw his army into the balance with a view to obtaining more equitable terms of separation."

These were no empty words. The facile success of the Belgian revolution had led to the Dutch army being branded as a set of cowards. The king, therefore, despite a solemn warning from the Conference, was determined to show the world that Holland was perfectly able to assert her rights by armed force if she chose to do so. In this course he had the whole-hearted support of his people. It was a bold act politically justified by events. Unexpectedly, on August 2, the Prince of Orange at the head of an army of 30,000 picked men with 72 guns crossed the frontier. The Belgians were quite taken by surprise. Their army, though not perhaps inferior in numbers to the invaders, was badly organised, and was divided into two parts—the army of the Scheldt and the army of the Meuse. The prince knew that he must act with promptness and decision, and he thrust his army by rapid movements between the two Belgian corps. That of the Meuse fell back in great disorder upon Liège; that of the Scheldt was also forced to beat a rapid retreat. Leopold, whose reign was not yet a fortnight old, joined the western corps and did all that man could do to organise and stiffen resistance. At Louvain (August 12) he made a last effort to save the capital and repeatedly exposed his life, but the Belgians were completely routed and Brussels lay at the victor's mercy. It was a terrible humiliation for the new Belgian state. But the prince had accomplished his task and did not advance beyond Louvain. On hearing that a French army, at the invitation of King Leopold, had entered Belgium with the sanction of the Powers, he concluded an armistice, by the mediation of the British Minister, Sir Robert Adair, and undertook to evacuate Belgian territory. His army recrossed the Dutch frontier (August 20), and the French thereupon withdrew.

The Ten Days' Campaign had effected its purpose; and, when the Conference met to consider the new situation, it was felt that the XVIII Articles must be revised. Belgium, saved only from conquest by French intervention, had to pay the penalty of defeat. A new treaty in XXIV Articles was drawn up, and was (October 14) again declared to be final and irrevocable. By this treaty the northwestern (Walloon) portion of Luxemburg was assigned to Belgium, but at the cost of ceding to Holland a considerable piece of Belgian Limburg giving the Dutch the command of both banks of the river Meuse from Maestricht to the Gelderland frontier. The proportion of the debt was likewise altered in favour of Holland. King William was informed that he must obtain the assent of the Germanic Confederation and of the Nassau agnates to the territorial adjustments.

These conditions created profound dissatisfaction both in Belgium and Holland. It was again the unhappy Luxemburg question which caused so much heart-burning. The Conference however felt itself bound by the territorial arrangements of the Congress of Vienna; and Palmerston and Talleyrand, acting in concert throughout, could not on this matter overrule the opposition of Prussia and Austria supported by Russia. All they could do was to secure the compromise by which Walloon Luxemburg was given to Belgium in exchange for territorial compensation in Limburg. Belgian feeling was strong against surrendering any part either of

Luxemburg or Limburg; but King Leopold saw that surrender was inevitable and by a threat of abdication he managed to secure, though against vehement opposition, the acceptance of the Treaty of the XXIV Articles by the Belgian Chambers (November 1). The treaty was signed at London by the plenipotentiaries of the Five Great Powers and by the Belgian envoy, Van de Weyer, on November 15, 1831; and Belgium was solemnly recognised as an independent State, whose perpetual neutrality and inviolability was guaranteed by each of the signatories severally[13].

Once more the obstinacy of King William proved an insuperable obstacle to a settlement. He had expected better results from the Ten Days' Campaign, and he emphatically denied the right of the Conference to interfere with the Grand Duchy of Luxemburg, as this was not a Belgian question, but concerned only the House of Nassau and the Germanic Confederation. He also objected to the proposed regulations regarding the navigation of the river Scheldt, and refused to evacuate Antwerp or other places occupied by Dutch troops. He was aware that Great Britain and France had taken the leading part in drawing up the treaty, but he relied for support upon his close family relations with Prussia and Russia[14], with whom Austria acted. But, although these Powers bore him good will, they had no intention of encouraging his resistance. Their object in delaying their ratification of the treaty was to afford time to bring good advice to bear upon the unbending temper of the Dutch king. The Tsar even sent Count Alexis Orloff on a special mission to the Hague, with instructions to act with the Prussian and Austrian envoys in urging William to take a reasonable course. All their efforts ended in failure.

During the first nine months of the year 1832 a vigorous exchange of notes took place between London and the Hague; and the Conference did its utmost to effect an accommodation. At last patience was exhausted, and the Powers had to threaten coercion. The three eastern Powers declined indeed to take any active share in coercive measures, but were willing that Great Britain and France should be their delegates. Palmerston and Talleyrand, however, were determined that the King of Holland should no longer continue to defy the will of the European Great Powers; and on October 22 the English and French governments concluded a Convention for joint action. Notice was given to King William (November 2) that he must withdraw his troops before November 13 from all places assigned to Belgium by the Treaty of the XXIV Articles. If he refused, the Dutch ports would be blockaded and an embargo placed upon Dutch ships in the allies' harbours. Further, if on November 13 any Dutch garrisons remained on Belgian soil, they would be expelled by armed force. William at once (November 2) replied to the notice by a flat refusal. In so acting he had behind him the practically unanimous support of Dutch public opinion. The allies took prompt measures. An Anglo-French squadron set sail (November 7) to blockade the Dutch ports and the mouth of the Scheldt; and in response to an appeal from the Belgian government (as was required by the terms of the Convention) a French army of 60,000 men under Marshal Gérard crossed the Belgian frontier (November 15) and laid siege to the Antwerp citadel, held by a garrison of 5000 men commanded by General Chassé. The siege began on November 20, and it was not until December 22 that Chassé, after a most gallant defence, was compelled to capitulate. Rear-Admiral Koopman preferred to burn his twelve gunboats rather than surrender them to the enemy. Marshal Gérard offered to release his prisoners if the Dutch would evacuate the forts of Lillo and Liefkenshoeck, lower down the river. His offer was refused; and the French army, having achieved its purpose, withdrew. For some time longer the blockade and embargo continued, to the great injury of Dutch trade. An interchange of notes between the Hague and London led to the drawing up of a convention, known as the Convention of London, on May 21, 1833. By this agreement King William undertook to commit no acts of hostility against Belgium until a definitive treaty of peace was signed, and to open the navigation of the Scheldt and the Meuse for commerce. The Convention was in fact a recognition of the *status quo* and was highly advantageous to Belgium, as both Luxemburg and Limburg were *ad interim* treated as if they were integral parts of the new kingdom.

The cessation of hostilities, however, led to a fresh attempt to reach a settlement. In response to an invitation sent by the western Powers to Austria, Prussia and Russia, the Conference again met in London on July 15. The thread of the negotiations was taken up; but the Belgian government insisted, with the full support of Palmerston, that as a preliminary to any further discussion the King of Holland must obtain the assent of the German Confederation and of the Nassau agnates to the proposed territorial rearrangements. William declined to ask for this assent. The Conference on this was indefinitely suspended. That the king's refusal in August was a part of his fixed policy of waiting upon events was shown by his actually approaching the Confederation and the agnates in the following November (1833). Neither of these would consent to any partition of Luxemburg, unless they received full territorial compensation elsewhere. So matters drifted on through the years 1834-1837. Meanwhile in Holland a change of opinion had been gradually taking place. The heavy taxes consequent upon the maintenance of an army on a war footing pressed more and more upon a country whose income was insufficient to meet its expenses. People grew tired of waiting for a change in the political position that became every year more remote. Luxemburg was of little interest to the Dutch; they only saw that Belgium was prosperous, and that the maintenance of the *status quo* was apparently all to her advantage. The dissatisfaction of the Dutch people, so long patient and loyal, made itself heard with increasing insistence in the States-General; and the king saw that the time had arrived for abandoning his obstinate *non-possumus* attitude. Accordingly, in March, 1838, he suddenly instructed his minister in London (Dedel) to inform Palmerston that he (the king) was ready to sign the treaty of the XXIV Articles, and to agree *pleinement et entièrement* to the conditions it imposed.

The unexpected news of this sudden step came upon the Belgians like a thunderclap. From every part of the kingdom arose a storm of protest against any surrender of territory. The people of Luxemburg and Limburg appealed to their fellow-citizens not to abandon them; and their appeal met with the strongest support from all classes and in both Chambers. They argued that Holland had refused to sign the treaty of 1831, which had been imposed on Belgium in her hour of defeat; and that now, after seven years, the treaty had ceased to be in force and required revision. The Belgians expected to receive support from Great Britain and France, and more especially from Palmerston, their consistent friend. But Palmerston was tired of the endless wrangling; and, acting on his initiative, the Five Powers determined that they would insist on the Treaty of the XXIV Articles being carried out as it stood. The

Conference met again in October, 1838; and all the efforts of the Belgian government, and of King Leopold personally, to obtain more favoured terms proved unavailing. An offer to pay sixty million francs indemnity for Luxemburg and Limburg was rejected both by King William and the Germanic Confederation. Such was the passionate feeling in Belgium that there was actually much talk of resisting in the last resort by force of arms. Volunteers poured in; and in Holland also the government began to make military preparations. But it was an act of sheer madness for isolated Belgium to think of opposing the will of the Great Powers of Europe. The angry interchange of diplomatic notes resulted only in one modification in favour of Belgium. The annual charge of 8,400,000 francs placed upon Belgium on account of her share in the public debt of the Netherlands was reduced to a payment of 5,000,000 francs. The Dutch king signed the treaty on February 1, 1839. Finally the proposal that the treaty should be signed, opposition being useless, met with a sullen assent from the two Belgian Chambers. On April 19, 1839, the Belgian envoy, Van de Weyer, affixed his signature at the Foreign Office in London and so brought to an end the long controversy, which had lasted for nine years. There were still many details to be settled between the two kingdoms, which from this time became two separate and distinct political entities; but these were finally arranged in an amicable spirit, and were embodied in a subsidiary treaty signed November 5, 1842.

# CHAPTER XXXII

# WILLIAM II. REVISION OF THE CONSTITUTION. 1842-1849

The Dutch nation welcomed the final separation from Belgium with profound relief. The national charges had risen from 15 million florins in 1815 to 38 million florins in 1838. Taxation was oppressive, trade stagnant, and the financial position growing more and more intolerable. The long-tried loyalty of the people, who had entrusted their sovereign with such wide and autocratic powers, had cooled. The king's Belgian policy had obviously been a complete failure; and the rotten state of public finance was naturally in large part attributed to the sovereign, who had so long been practically his own finance minister. Loud cries began to be raised for a revision of the constitution on liberal lines. To the old king any such revision was repugnant; but, unable to resist the trend of public opinion, he gave his assent to a measure of constitutional reform in the spring of 1840. Its limited concessions satisfied no one. Its principal modifications of the Fundamental Law were: (1) the division of the province of Holland into two parts; (2) the reduction of the Civil List; (3) the necessary alteration of the number of deputies in the Second Chamber due to the separation from Belgium; (4) abolition of the distinction between the ordinary and the extraordinary budget; (5) a statement of the receipts and expenditure of the colonies to be laid before the States-General. Finally the principle of ministerial responsibility was granted most reluctantly, the king yielding only after the Chambers had declined to consider the estimates without this concession. But William had already made up his mind to abdicate, rather than reign under the new conditions. He knew that he was unpopular and out-of-touch with the times; and his unpopularity had been increased by his announced intention of marrying the Countess Henriette D'Oultremont, a Belgian and a Catholic. On October 7 he issued a proclamation by which he handed over the government to his son William Frederick, Prince of Orange. He then retired quietly to his private estates in Silesia. He died at Berlin in 1843.

William II was forty-eight years of age on his accession to the throne. He was a man of a character very different from that of his father. Amiable, accessible, easily influenced, liberal-handed even to extravagance, he was deservedly popular. He had shown himself in the Peninsula, at Quatre Bras and Waterloo and later in the Ten Days' Campaign, to be a capable and courageous soldier, but he possessed few of the qualities either of a statesman or a financier. He had married in 1816 Anna Paulovna, sister of the Tsar Alexander I, after his proposed marriage with the Princess Charlotte of England had been broken off.

He entered upon his reign in difficult times. There was a loud demand for a further sweeping revision of the constitution. Religious movements, which had been gathering force during the reign of William I, required careful handling. One minister after another had tried to grapple with the financial problem, but in vain. In 1840 the public debt amounted to 2200 million florins; and the burden of taxation, though it had become almost unendurable, failed to provide for the interest on the debt and the necessary expenses of administration. The State was in fact on the verge of bankruptcy. The appointment in 1842 of F.A. van Hall (formerly an Amsterdam advocate, who had held the post of minister of justice) to be finance minister opened out a means of salvation. The arrears to 1840 amounted to 35 million florins; the deficit for 1841-3 had to be covered, and means provided for the expenditure for 1843-4. Van Hall's proposals gave the people the choice between providing the necessary money by an extraordinary tax of one and a half per cent, on property and income, and raising a voluntary loan of 150 million florins at 3 per cent. After long debates the States-General accepted the proposal for the voluntary loan, but the amount was reduced to 126 millions. The success of the loan, though at first doubtful, was by March, 1844, complete. The Amsterdam Bourse gave its utmost support; and the royal family set a good example by a joint subscription of 11 million florins. By this means, and by the capitalisation of the annual Belgian payment of five million francs, Van Hall was able to clear off the four years' arrears and to convert the 5 and 4-1/2 per cent. scrip into 4 per cent. He was helped by the large annual payments, which now began to come in from the Dutch East Indies; and at length an equilibrium was established in the budget between receipts and expenditure.

In the years preceding the French Revolution the Reformed Church in the United Provinces had become honey-combed with rationalism. The official orthodoxy of the Dort synod had become "a fossilised skeleton." By the Constitution of 1798 Church and State were separated, and the property of the Church was taken by the State, which paid however stipends to the ministers. Under King Louis subsidies were paid from the public funds to teachers of every religious persuasion; and this system continued during the union of Holland and Belgium. A movement known as the *Reveil* had meanwhile been stirring the dry-bones of Calvinistic orthodoxy in Holland. Its first leaders were Bilderdijk, De Costa and Capadose. Like most religious revivals, this movement gave rise to extravagancies and dissensions. In 1816 a new sect was founded by a sea-captain, Staffel Mulder, on communistic principles after the example of the first Jerusalem converts, which gathered a number of followers among the peasantry. The "New Lighters"—such was the name they assumed—established in 1823 their headquarters at Zwijndrecht. The first enthusiasm however died down, and the sect gradually disappeared. More serious was the liberal revolt against the cut-and-dried orthodoxy of Dort. Slowly it made headway, and it found leaders in Hofstede de Groot, professor at Groningen, and in two eloquent preachers, De Cocq at Ulrum and Scholte at Deventer. These men, finding that their views met with no sympathy or recognition by the synodal authorities, resolved (October 14, 1834) on the serious step of separating from the Reformed Church and forming themselves and their adherents into a new church body. They were known as "the Separatists" (*de Afgescheidenen*). Though deprived of their pulpits, fined and persecuted, the Separatists grew in number. In 1836 the government refused to recognise them as a Church, but permitted local congregations to hold meetings in houses. In 1838 more favourable conditions were offered, which De Cocq and Scholte finally agreed to accept, but no subsidies were paid to the sect by the State. William II, in 1842, made a further concession by allowing religious teaching to be given daily in the public schools (out of school hours) by the Separatist ministers, as well as by those of other denominations. All this while, however, certain congregations refused to accept the compromise of 1838; and a large number, headed by a preacher named Van Raalte, in order to obtain freedom of worship, emigrated to Michigan to form the nucleus of a flourishing Dutch colony.

The accession of William II coincided with a period of political unrest, not only in Holland but throughout Europe. A strong reaction had set in against the system of autocratic rule, which had been the marked feature of the period which followed 1815. Liberal and progressive ideas had during the later years been making headway in Holland under the inspiring leadership of Johan Rudolf Thorbecke, at that time a professor of jurisprudence at Leyden. He had many followers; and the cause he championed had the support of the brilliant writers and publicists, Donker-Curtius, Luzac, Potgieter, Bakhuizen van der Brink and others. A strong demand arose for a thorough revision of the constitution. In 1844 a body of nine members of the Second Chamber, chief amongst them Thorbecke, drew up a definite proposal for a revision; but the king expressed his dislike to it, and it was rejected. The Van Hall ministry had meanwhile been carrying out those excellent financial measures which had saved the credit of the State, and was now endeavouring to conduct the government on opportunist lines. But the potato famine in 1845-46 caused great distress among the labouring classes, and gave added force to the spirit of discontent in the country. The king himself grew nervous in the presence of the revolutionary ferment spreading throughout Europe, and was more especially alarmed (February, 1848) by the sudden overthrow of the monarchy of Louis Philippe and the proclamation of a republic at Paris. He now resolved himself to take the initiative. He saw that the proposals hitherto made for revision did not satisfy public opinion; and on March 8, without consulting his ministers, he took the unusual step of sending for the President of the Second Chamber, Boreel van Hogelanden. He asked him to ascertain the opinions and wishes of the Chamber on the matter of revision and to report to him. The ministry on this resigned and a new liberal ministry was formed, at the head of which was Count Schimmelpenninck, formerly minister in London.

On March 17 a special Commission was appointed to draw up a draft scheme of revision. It consisted of five members, four of whom, Thorbecke, Luzac, Donker-Curtius and Kempenaer, were prominent liberals and the fifth a Catholic from North Brabant. Their work was completed by April 11 and the report presented to the king. Schimmelpenninck, not agreeing with the proposals of the Commission, resigned; and on May 11 a new ministry under the leadership of Donker-Curtius was formed for the express purpose of carrying out the proposed revision. A periodical election of the Second Chamber took place in July, and difficulties at first confronted the new scheme. These were, however, overcome; and on October 14 the revised constitution received the king's assent. It was solemnly proclaimed on November 3.

The Constitution of 1848 left in the hands of the king the executive power, i.e. the conduct of foreign affairs, the right of declaring war and making peace, the supreme command of the military and naval forces, the administration of the overseas possessions, and the right of dissolving the Chambers; but these prerogatives were modified by the introduction of the principle of ministerial responsibility. The ministers were responsible for all acts of the government, and the king could legally do no wrong. The king was president of the Council of State (15 members), whose duty it was to consider all proposals made to or by the States-General. The king shared the legislative power with the States-General, but the Second Chamber had the right of initiative, amendment and investigation; and annual budgets were henceforth to be presented for its approval. All members of the States-General were to be at least 30 years of age. The First Chamber of 39 members was elected by the Provincial Estates from those most highly assessed to direct taxation; the members sat for nine years, but one-third vacated their seats every third year. All citizens of full age paying a certain sum to direct taxation had the right of voting for members of the Second Chamber, the country for this purpose being divided into districts containing 45,000 inhabitants. The members held their seats for four years, but half the Chamber retired every second year. Freedom of worship to all denominations, liberty of the press and the right of public meeting were guaranteed. Primary education in public schools was placed under State control, but private schools were not interfered with. The provincial and communal administration was likewise reformed and made dependent on the direct popular vote.

The ministry of Donker-Curtius at once took steps for holding fresh elections, as soon as the new constitution became the fundamental law of the country. A large majority of liberals was returned to the Second Chamber. The king in person opened the States-General on February 13, 1849, and expressed his intention of accepting loyally the changes to which he had given his assent. He was, however, suffering and weak from illness, and a month later (March 17) he died at Tilburg. His gracious and kindly personality had endeared him to his subjects, who deeply regretted that at this moment of constitutional change the States should lose his experienced guidance. He was succeeded by his son, William III.

# CHAPTER XXXIII

# REIGN OF WILLIAM III TO THE DEATH OF THORBECKE, 1849-1872

William III succeeded to the throne at a moment of transition. He was thirty-two years of age, and his natural leanings were autocratic; but he accepted loyally the principle of ministerial responsibility, and throughout his long reign endeavoured honestly and impartially to fulfil his duties as a constitutional sovereign. There were at this time in Holland four political parties: (1) the old conservative party, which after 1849 gradually dwindled in numbers and soon ceased to be a power in the State; (2) the liberals, under the leadership of Thorbecke; (3) the anti-revolutionary or orthodox Protestant party, ably led by G. Groen van Prinsterer, better known perhaps as a distinguished historian, but at the same time a good debater and resourceful parliamentarian; (4) the Catholic party. The Catholics for the first time obtained in 1849 the full privileges of citizenship. They owed this to the liberals, and for some years they gave their support to that party, though differing from them fundamentally on many points. The anti-revolutionaries placed in the foreground the upholding of the Reformed (orthodox Calvinistic) faith in the State, and of religious teaching in the schools. In this last article of their political creed they were at one with the Catholics, and in its defence the two parties were destined to become allies.

The liberal majority in the newly elected States-General was considerable; and it was the general expectation that Thorbecke would become head of the government. The king however suspected the aims of the liberal leader, and personally disliked him. He therefore kept in office the Donker-Curtius-De Kempenaer cabinet; but, after a vain struggle against the hostile majority, it was compelled to resign, and Thorbecke was called upon to form a ministry.

Thorbecke was thus the first constitutional prime-minister of Holland. His answer to his opponents, who asked for his programme, was contained in words which he was speedily to justify: "Wait for our deeds." A law was passed which added 55,000 votes to the electorate; and by two other laws the provincial and communal assemblies were placed upon a popular representative basis. The system of finance was reformed by the gradual substitution of direct for indirect taxation. By the Navigation Laws all differential and transit dues upon shipping were reduced; tolls on through-cargoes on the rivers were abolished, and the tariff on raw materials lowered. It was a considerable step forward in the direction of free-trade. Various changes were made to lighten the incidence of taxation on the poorer classes. Among the public works carried to completion at this time (1852) was the empoldering of the Haarlem lake, which converted a large expanse of water into good pasture land.

It was not on political grounds that the Thorbecke ministry was to be wrecked, but by their action in matters which aroused religious passions and prejudices. The prime-minister wished to bring all charitable institutions and agencies under State supervision. Their number was more than 3500; and a large proportion of these were connected with and supported by religious bodies. It is needless to say the proposal aroused strong opposition. More serious was the introduction of a Catholic episcopate into Holland. By the Fundamental Law of 1848 complete freedom of worship and of organisation had been guaranteed to every form of religious belief. It was the wish of the Catholics that the system which had endured ever since the 16th century of a "Dutch mission" under the direction of an Italian prelate (generally the internuncio) should come to an end, and that they should have bishops of their own. The proposal was quite constitutional and, far from giving the papal curia more power in the Netherlands, it decreased it. A petition to Pius IX in 1847 met with little favour at Rome; but in 1851 another petition, much more widely signed, urged the Pope to seize the favourable opportunity for establishing a native hierarchy. Negotiations were accordingly opened by the papal see with the Dutch government, which ended (October, 1852) in a recognition of the right of the Catholic Church in Holland to have freedom of organisation. It was stipulated, however, that a previous communication should be made to the government of the papal intentions and plans, before they were carried out. The only communication that was made was not official, but confidential; and it merely stated that Utrecht was to be erected into an archbishopric with Haarlem, Breda, Hertogenbosch and Roeremonde, as suffragans. The ministry regarded the choice of such Protestant centres as Utrecht and Haarlem with resentment, but were faced with the *fait accompli*. This strong-handed action of the Roman authorities was made still more offensive by the issuing of a papal allocution, again without any consultation with the Dutch government, in which Pius IX described the establishment of the new hierarchy as a means of counteracting in the Netherlands the heresy of Calvin.

A wave of fierce indignation swept over Protestant Holland, which united in one camp orthodox Calvinists (anti-revolutionaries), conservatives and anti-papal liberals. The preachers everywhere inveighed against a ministry which had permitted such an act of aggression on the part of a foreign potentate against the Protestantism of the nation. Utrecht took the lead in drawing up an address to the king and to the States-General (which obtained two hundred thousand signatures), asking them not to recognise the proposed hierarchy. At the meeting of the Second Chamber of the States-General on April 12, Thorbecke had little difficulty in convincing the majority that the Pope had proceeded without Consultation with the ministry, and that under the Constitution the Catholics had acted within their rights in re-modelling their Church organisation. But his arguments were far from satisfying outside public opinion. On the occasion of a visit of the king to Amsterdam the ministry took the step of advising him not to receive any address hostile to the establishment of the hierarchy, on the ground that this did not require the royal approval. William, who had never been friendly to Thorbecke, was annoyed at being thus instructed in the discharge of his duties; and he not only received an address containing 51,000 signatures but expressed his great pleasure in being thus approached (April 15). At the same time he summoned Van Hall, the leader of the opposition, to Amsterdam for a private consultation. The ministry, on hearing of what had taken place, sent its resignation, which was accepted on April 19. Thus fell the Thorbecke ministry, not by a parliamentary defeat, but because the king associated himself with the uprising of hostile public opinion, known as the "April Movement."

A new ministry was formed under the joint leadership of Van Hall and Donker-Curtius; and an appeal to the electors resulted in the defeat of the liberals. The majority was a coalition of conservatives and anti-revolutionaries. The followers of Groen van Prinsterer were small in number, but of importance through the strong religious convictions and debating ability of the leader. The presence of Donker-Curtius was a guarantee for moderation; and, as Van Hall was an adept in political opportunism, the new ministry differed from its liberal predecessor chiefly in its more cautious attitude towards the reforms which both were ready to adopt. As it had been carried into office by the April Movement, a Church Association Bill was passed into law making it illegal for a foreigner to hold any Church office without the royal assent, and forbidding the wearing of a distinctive religious dress outside closed buildings. Various measures were introduced dealing with ministerial responsibility, poor-law administration and other matters, such as the abolition of the excise on meat and of barbarous punishments on the scaffold.

The question of primary education was to prove for the next half-century a source of continuous political and religious strife, dividing the people of Holland into hostile camps. The question was whether the State schools should be "mixed" i.e. neutral schools, where only those simple truths which were common to all denominations should be taught; or should be "separate" i.e. denominational schools, in which religious instruction should be given in accordance with the wishes of the parents. A bill was brought in by the government (September, 1854) which was intended to be a compromise. It affirmed the general principle that the State schools should be "neutral," but allowed "separate" schools to be built and maintained. This proposal was fiercely opposed by Groen and gave rise to a violent agitation. The ministry struggled on, but its existence was precarious and internal dissensions at length led to its resignation (July, 1856). The elections of 1856 had effected but little change in the constitution of the Second Chamber, and the anti-revolutionary J.J.L. van der Brugghen was called upon to form a ministry. Groen himself declined office, Van der Brugghen made an effort to conciliate opposition; and a bill for primary education was introduced (1857) upholding the principle of the "mixed" schools, but with the proviso that the aim of the teaching was to be the instruction of the children "in Christian and social virtues"; at the same time "separate" schools were permitted and under certain conditions would be subsidised by the State. Groen again did his utmost to defeat this bill, but he was not successful; and after stormy debates it became law (July, 1857). The liberals obtained a majority at the elections of 1858, and Van der Brugghen resigned. But the king would not send for Thorbecke; and J.J. Rochussen, a former governor-general of the Dutch East Indies, was asked to form a "fusion" ministry. During his tenure of office (1858-60) slavery was abolished in the East Indies, though not the cultivation-system, which was but a kind of disguised slavery. The way in which the Javanese suffered by this system of compulsory labour for the profit of the home country—the amount received by the Dutch treasury being not less than 250 million florins in thirty years—was now scathingly exposed by the brilliant writer Douwes Dekker. He had been an official in Java, and his novel *Max Havelaar*, published in 1860 under the pseudonym "Multatuli," was widely read, and brought to the knowledge of the Dutch public the character of the system which was being enforced.

Holland was at this time far behind Belgium in the construction of a system of railroads, to the great hindrance of trade. A bill, however, proposed by the ministry to remedy this want was rejected by the First Chamber, and Rochussen resigned. The king again declined to send for Thorbecke; and Van Hall was summoned for the third time to form a ministry. He succeeded in securing the passage of a proposal to spend not less than 10 million florins annually in the building of State railways. All Van Hall's parliamentary adroitness and practised opportunism could not, however, long maintain in office a ministry supported cordially by no party. Van Hall gave up the unthankful task (February, 1861), but still it was not Thorbecke, but Baron S. van Heemstra that was called upon to take his place. For a few months only was the ministry able to struggle on in the face of a liberal majority. There was now no alternative but to offer the post of first minister to Thorbecke, who accepted the office (January 31, 1862).

The second ministry of Thorbecke lasted for four years, and was actively engaged during that period in domestic, trade and colonial reforms. Thorbecke, as a free-trader, at once took in hand the policy of lowering all duties except for revenue purposes. The communal dues were extinguished. A law for secondary and technical education was passed in 1863; and in the same year slavery was abolished in Surinam and the West Indies. Other bills were passed for the canalising of the Hook of Holland, and the reclaiming of the estuary of the Y. This last project included the construction of a canal, the Canal of Holland, with the artificial harbour of Ymuiden at its entrance, deep enough for ocean liners to reach Amsterdam. With the advent of Fransen van de Putte, as colonial minister in 1863, began a series of far-reaching reforms in the East Indies, including the lowering of the differential duties. His views, however, concerning the scandal of the cultivation-system in Java did not meet with the approval of some of his colleagues; and Thorbecke himself supported the dissentients. The ministry resigned, and Van de Putte became head of the government. He held office for four months only. His bill for the abolition of the cultivation-system and the conversion of the native cultivators into possessors of their farms was thrown out by a small majority, Thorbecke with a few liberals and some Catholics voting with the conservatives against it. This was the beginning of a definite liberal split, which was to continue for years.

A coalition-ministry followed under the presidency of J. van Heemskerk (Interior) and Baron van Zuylen van Nyevelt (Foreign Affairs). The colonial minister Mijer shortly afterwards resigned in order to take the post of governor-general of the East Indies. This appointment did not meet with the approval of the Second Chamber; and the government suffered a defeat. On this they persuaded the king not only to dissolve the Chamber, but to issue a proclamation impressing upon the electors the need of the country for a more stable administration. The result was the return of a majority for the Heemskerk-Van Zuylen combination. It is needless to say that Thorbecke and his followers protested strongly against the dragging of the king's name into a political contest, as gravely unconstitutional. The ministry had a troubled existence.

The results of the victory of Prussia over Austria at Sadowa, and the formation of the North German Confederation under

Prussian leadership, rendered the conduct of foreign relations a difficult and delicate task, especially as regards Luxemburg and Limburg, both of which were under the personal sovereignty of William III, and at the same time formed part of the old German Confederation. The rapid success of Prussia had seriously perturbed public opinion in France; and Napoleon III, anxious to obtain some territorial compensation which would satisfy French *amour-propre,* entered into negotiations with William III for the sale of the Grand Duchy of Luxemburg. The king was himself alarmed at the Prussian annexations, and Queen Sophie and the Prince of Orange had decided French leanings; and, as Bismarck had given the king reason to believe that no objection would be raised, the negotiations for the sale were seriously undertaken. On March 26, 1867, the Prince of Orange actually left the Hague, bearing the document containing the Grand Duke's consent; and on April 1 the cession was to be finally completed. On that very day the Prussian ambassadors at Paris and the Hague were instructed to say that any cession of Luxemburg to France would mean war with Prussia. It was a difficult situation; and a conference of the Great Powers met at London on May 11 to deal with it. Its decision was that Luxemburg should remain as an independent state, whose neutrality was guaranteed collectively by the Powers, under the sovereignty of the House of Nassau; that the town of Luxemburg should be evacuated by its Prussian garrison; and that Limburg should henceforth be an integral part of the kingdom of the Netherlands.

Van Zuylen was assailed in the Second Chamber for his exposing the country to danger and humiliation in this matter; and the Foreign Office vote was rejected by a small majority. The ministry resigned; but, rather than address himself to Thorbecke, the king sanctioned a dissolution, with the result of a small gain of seats to the liberals. Heemskerk and Van Zuylen retained office for a short time in the face of adverse votes, but finally resigned; and the king had no alternative but to ask Thorbecke to form a ministry. He himself declined office, but he chose a cabinet of young liberals who had taken no part in the recent political struggles, P.P. van Bosse becoming first minister.

From this time forward there was no further attempt on the part of the royal authority to interfere in the constitutional course of parliamentary government. Van Bosse's ministry, scoffingly called by their opponents "Thorbecke's marionettes," maintained themselves in office for two years(1868-70), passing several useful measures, but are chiefly remembered for the abolition of capital punishment. The outbreak of the Franco-German war in 1870 found, however, the Dutch army and fortresses ill-prepared for an emergency, when the maintenance of strict neutrality demanded an efficient defence of the frontiers. The ministry was not strong enough to resist the attacks made upon it; and at last the real leader of the liberal party, the veteran Thorbecke, formed his third ministry (January, 1871). But Thorbecke was now in ill-health, and the only noteworthy achievement of his last premiership was an agreement with Great Britain by which the Dutch possessions on the coast of Guinea were ceded to that country in exchange for a free hand being given to the Dutch in Surinam. The ministry, having suffered a defeat on the subject of the cost of the proposed army re-organisation, was on the point of resigning, when Thorbecke suddenly died (June 5, 1872). His death brought forth striking expressions of sympathy and appreciation from men and journals representing all parties in the State. For five-and-twenty years, in or out of office, his had been the dominating influence in Dutch politics; and it was felt on all sides that the country was the poorer for the loss of a man of outstanding ability and genuine patriotism.

# CHAPTER XXXIV

# THE LATER REIGN OF WILLIAM III, AND THE REGENCY OF QUEEN EMMA, 1872-1898

The death of Thorbecke was the signal for a growing cleavage between the old *doctrinaire* school of liberals, who adhered to the principles of 1848, and the advanced liberalism of many of the younger progressive type. To Gerrit de Vries was entrusted the duty of forming a ministry, and he had the assistance of the former first minister, F. van de Putte. His position was weakened by the opposition of the Catholic party, who became alienated from the liberals, partly on the religious education question, but more especially because their former allies refused to protest against the Italian occupation of Rome. The election of 1873 did not improve matters, for it left the divided liberals to face an opposition of equal strength, whenever the conservatives, anti-revolutionaries and Catholics acted together. This same year saw the first phase of the war with the piratical state of Achin. An expedition of 3600 men under General Köhler was sent out against the defiant sultan in April, 1873, but suffered disaster, the General himself dying of disease. A second stronger expedition under General van Swieten was then dispatched, which was successful; and the sultan was deposed in January, 1874. This involved heavy charges on the treasury; and the ministry, after suffering two reverses in the Second Chamber, resigned (June, 1874), being succeeded by a Heemskerk coalition ministry.

Heemskerk in his former premiership had shown himself to be a clever tactician, and for three years he managed to maintain himself in office against the combined opposition of the advanced liberals, the anti-revolutionaries and the Catholics. Groen van Prinsterer died in May, 1876; and with his death the hitherto aristocratic and exclusive party, which he had so long led, became transformed. Under its new leader, Abraham Kuyper, it became democratised, and, by combining its support of the religious principle in education with that of progressive reform, was able to exercise a far wider influence in the political sphere. Kuyper, for many years a Calvinist pastor, undertook in 1872 the editorship of the anti-revolutionary paper, *De Standdard*. In 1874 he was elected member for Gouda, but resigned in order to give his whole time to journalism in the interest of the political principles to which he now devoted his great abilities.

The Heemskerk ministry had the support of no party, but by the opportunist skill of its chief it continued in office for three years; no party was prepared to take its place, and "the government of the king must be carried on." The measures that were passed in this time were useful rather than important. An attempt to deal with primary instruction led to the downfall of the ministry. The elections of 1877 strengthened the liberals; and, an amendment to the speech from the throne being carried, Heemskerk resigned. His place was taken by Joannes Kappeyne, leader of the progressive liberals. A new department of State was now created, that of Waterways and Commerce, whose duties in a country like Holland, covered with a net-work of dykes and canals, was of great importance. A measure which denied State support to the "private" schools was bitterly resisted by the anti-revolutionaries and the Catholics, whose union in defence of religious education was from this time forward to become closer. The outlay in connection with the costly Achin war, which had broken out afresh, led to a considerable deficit in the budget. In consequence of this a proposal for the construction of some new canals was rejected by a majority of one. The financial difficulties, which had necessitated the imposing of unpopular taxes, had once more led to divisions in the liberal ranks; and Kappeyne, finding that the king would not support his proposals for a revision of the Fundamental Law, saw no course open to him but resignation.

In these circumstances the king decided to ask an anti-revolutionary, Count van Lynden van Sandenburg, to form a

"Ministry of Affairs," composed of moderate men of various parties. Van Lynden had a difficult task, but with the strong support of the king his policy of conciliation carried him safely through four disquieting and anxious years. The revolt of the Boers in the Transvaal against British rule caused great excitement in Holland, and aroused much sympathy. Van Lynden was careful to avoid any steps which might give umbrage to England, and he was successful in his efforts. The Achin trouble was, however, still a cause of much embarrassment. Worst of all was the series of bereavements which at this time befell the House of Orange-Nassau. In 1877 Queen Sophie died, affectionately remembered for her interest in art and science, and her exemplary life. The king's brother, Henry, for thirty years Stadholder of Luxemburg, died childless early in 1879; and shortly afterwards in June the Prince of Orange, who had never married, passed away suddenly at Paris. The two sons of William III's uncle Frederick predeceased their father, whose death took place in 1881. Alexander, the younger son of the king, was sickly and feeble-minded; and with his decease in 1884, the male line of the House of Orange-Nassau became extinct. Foreseeing such a possibility in January, 1879, the already aged king took in second wedlock the youthful Princess Emma of Waldeck-Pyrmont. Great was the joy of the Dutch people, when, on August 31, 1880, she gave birth to a princess, Wilhelmina, who became from this time forth the hope of a dynasty, whose history for three centuries had been bound up with that of the nation.

The Van Lynden administration, having steered its way through many parliamentary crises for four years, was at last beaten upon a proposal to enlarge the franchise, and resigned (February 26, 1883). To Heemskerk was confided the formation of a coalition ministry of a neutral character; and this experienced statesman became for the third time first minister of the crown. The dissensions in the liberal party converted the Second Chamber into a meeting-place of hostile factions; and Heemskerk was better fitted than any other politician to be the head of a government which, having no majority to support it, had to rely upon tactful management and expediency. The rise of a socialist party under the enthusiastic leadership of a former Lutheran pastor, Domela Nieuwenhuis, added to the perplexities of the position. It soon became evident that a revision of the Fundamental Law and an extension of the franchise, which the king no longer opposed, was inevitable. Meanwhile the death of Prince Alexander and the king's growing infirmities made it necessary to provide, by a bill passed on August 2,1884, that Queen Emma should become regent during her daughter's minority.

Everything conspired to beset the path of the Heemskerk ministry with hindrances to administrative or legislative action. The bad state of the finances (chiefly owing to the calls for the Achin war) the subdivision of all parties into groups, the socialist agitation and the weak health of the king, created something like a parliamentary deadlock. A revision of the constitution became more and more pressing as the only remedy, though no party was keenly in its favour. Certain proposals for revision were made by the government (March, 1885), but the anti-revolutionaries, the Catholics and the conservatives were united in opposition, unless concessions were made in the matter of religious education. Such concessions as were finally offered were rejected (April, 1886), and Heemskerk offered his resignation. Baron Mackay (anti-revolutionary) declining office, a dissolution followed. The result of the elections, however, was inconclusive, the liberals of all shades having a bare majority of four; but there was no change of ministry. A more conciliatory spirit fortunately prevailed under stress of circumstances in the new Chamber; and at last, after many debates, the law revising the constitution was passed through both Chambers, and approved by the king (November 30, 1887). It was a compromise measure, and no violent changes were made. The First Chamber was to consist of 50 members, appointed by the Provincial Councils; the Second Chamber of 100 members, chosen by an electorate of male persons of not less than 25 years of age with a residential qualification and possessing "signs of fitness and social well-being"—a vague phrase requiring future definition. The number of electors was increased from (in round numbers) 100,000 to 350,000, but universal male suffrage, the demand of the socialists and more advanced liberals, was not conceded.

The elections of 1888 were fought on the question of religious education in the primary schools. The two "Christian" parties, the Calvinist anti-revolutionaries under the leadership of Dr Kuyper, and the Catholics, who had found a leader of eloquence and power in Dr Schaepman, a Catholic priest, coalesced in a common programme for a revision of Kappeyne's Education Act of 1878. The coalition obtained a majority, 27 anti-revolutionaries and 25 Catholics being returned as against 46 liberals of various groups. For the first time a socialist, Domela Nieuwenhuis, was elected. The conservative party was reduced to one member. In the First Chamber the liberals still commanded a majority. In April, 1888, Baron Mackay, an anti-revolutionary of moderate views, became first minister. The coalition made the revision of the Education Act of 1878 their first business; and they obtained the support of some liberals who were anxious to see the school question out of the way. The so-called "Mackay Law" was passed in 1889. It provided that "private" schools should receive State support on condition that they conformed to the official regulations; that the number of scholars should be not less than twenty-five; and that they should be under the management of some body, religious or otherwise, recognised by the State. This settlement was a compromise, but it offered the solution of an acute controversy and was found to work satisfactorily.

The death of King William on November 23, 1890, was much mourned by his people. He was a man of strong and somewhat narrow views, but during his reign of 41 years his sincere love for his country was never in doubt, nor did he lose popularity by his anti-liberal attitude on many occasions, for it was known to arise from honest conviction; and it was amidst general regret that the last male representative of the House of Orange-Nassau was laid in his grave.

A proposal by the Catholic minister Borgesius for the introduction of universal personal military service was displeasing however to many of his own party, and it was defeated with the help of Catholic dissidents. An election followed, and the liberals regained a majority. A new government was formed of a moderate progressive character, the premier being Cornelis van Tienhoven. It was a ministry of talents, Tak van Poortvliet (interior) and N.G. Pierson (finance) being men of marked ability. Pierson had more success than any of his predecessors in bringing to an end the recurring deficits in the annual balance sheet. He imposed an income tax on all incomes above 650 florins derived from salaries or commerce. All other sources of income were capitalised (funds, investments, farming, etc.); and a tax was placed on all capital above

13,000 florins. Various duties and customs were lowered, to the advantage of trade. There was, however, a growing demand for a still further extension of the franchise, and for an official interpretation of that puzzling qualification of the Revision of 1889—"signs of fitness and social well-being." Tak van Poortvliet brought in a measure which would practically have introduced universal male suffrage, for he interpreted the words as including all who could write and did not receive doles from charity. This proposal, brought forward in 1893, again split up the liberal party. The moderates under the leadership of Samuel van Houten vigorously opposed such an increase of the electorate; and they had the support of the more conservative anti-revolutionaries and a large part of the Catholics. The more democratic followers of Kuyper and Schaepman and the progressive radicals ranged themselves on the side of Tak van Poortvliet. All parties were thus broken up into hostile groups. The election of 1894 was contested no longer on party lines, but between Takkians and anti-Takkians. The result was adverse to Tak, his following only mustering 46 votes against 54 for their opponents.

A new administration therefore came into office (May, 1894) under the presidency of Jonkheer Johan Roëll with Van Houten as minister of the interior. On Van Houten's shoulders fell the task of preparing a new electoral law. His proposals were finally approved in 1896. Before this took place the minister of finance, Spenger van Eyk, had succeeded in relieving the treasury by the conversion of the public debt from a 3-1/2 to a 3 per cent, security. The Van Houten reform of the franchise was very complicated, as there were six different categories of persons entitled to exercise the suffrage: (1) payers of at least one guilder in direct taxation; (2) householders or lodgers paying a certain minimum rent and having a residential qualification; (3) proprietors or hirers of vessels of 24 tons at least; (4) earners of a certain specified wage or salary; (5) investors of 100 guilders in the public funds or of 50 guilders in a savings bank; (6) persons holding certain educational diplomas. This very wide and comprehensive franchise raised the number of electors to about 700,000.

The election of 1897, after first promising a victory to the more conservative groups, ended by giving a small majority to the liberals, the progressive section winning a number of seats, and the socialists increasing their representation in the Chamber. A liberal-concentration cabinet took the place of the Roell-Van Houten ministry, its leading members being Pierson (finance) and Goeman-Borgesius (interior). For a right understanding of the parliamentary situation at this time and during the years that follow, a brief account of the groups and sections of groups into which political parties in Holland were divided, must here interrupt the narrative of events.

It has already been told that the deaths of Thorbecke and Groen van Prinsterer led to a breaking up of the old parties and the formation of new groups. The Education Act of 1878 brought about an alliance of the two parties, who made the question of religious education in the primary schools the first article of their political programme—the anti-revolutionaries led by the ex-Calvinist pastor Dr Abraham Kuyper and the Catholics by Dr Schaepman, a Catholic priest. Kuyper and Schaepman were alike able journalists, and used the press with conspicuous success for the propagation of their views, both being advocates of social reform on democratic lines. The anti-revolutionaries, however, did not, as a body, follow the lead of Kuyper. An aristocratic section, whose principles were those of Groen van Prinsterer, "orthodox" and "conservative," under the appellation of "Historical Christians," were opposed to the democratic ideas of Kuyper, and were by tradition anti-Catholic. Their leader was Jonkheer Savornin Lohman. For some years there was a separate Frisian group of "Historical Christians," but these finally amalgamated with the larger body. The liberals meanwhile had split up into three groups: (1) the Old Independent *(vrij)* Liberals; (2) the Liberal Progressive Union *(Unie van vooruitstrevende Liberalen)*; (3) Liberal-Democrats *(vrijzinnig-democratischen Bond)*. The socialist party was a development of the *Algemeene Nederlandsche Werklieden Verbond* founded in 1871. Ten years later, by the activities of the fiery agitator, Domela Nieuwenhuis, the Social-Democratic Bond was formed; and the socialists became a political party. The loss of Nieuwenhuis' seat in 1891 had the effect of making him abandon constitutional methods for a revolutionary and anti-religious crusade. The result of this was a split in the socialist party and the formation, under the leadership of Troelstra, Van Kol and Van der Goes, of the "Social-Democratic Workmen's Party," which aimed at promoting the welfare of the proletariat on socialistic lines, but by parliamentary means. The followers of Domela Nieuwenhuis, whose openly avowed principles were "the destruction of actual social conditions by all means legal and illegal," were after 1894 known as "the Socialist Bond." This anarchical party, who took as their motto "neither God nor master," rapidly decreased in number; their leader, discouraged by his lack of success in 1898, withdrew finally from the political arena; and the Socialist Bond was dissolved. This gave an accession of strength to the "Social-Democratic Workmen's Party," which has since the beginning of the present century gradually acquired an increasing hold upon the electorate.

# CHAPTER XXXV

# THE REIGN OF QUEEN WILHELMINA, 1898-1917

THE Pierson-Borgesius ministry had not been long in office when Queen Wilhelmina attained her majority (August 31, 1898) amidst public enthusiasm. At the same time the Queen-Mother received many expressions of high appreciation for the admirable manner in which for eight years she had discharged her constitutional duties. The measures passed by this administration dealt with many subjects of importance. Personal military service was at last, after years of controversy, enforced by law, ecclesiastics and students alone being excepted. Attendance at school up to the age of 13 was made obligatory, and the subsidies for the upkeep of the schools and the payment of teachers were substantially increased. The year 1899 was memorable for the meeting of the first Peace Congress (on the initiative of the Tsar Nicholas II) at the *Huis in't Bosch*. The deliberations and discussions began on May 18 and lasted until June 29. By the irony of events, a few months later (October 10) a war broke out, in which the Dutch people felt a great and sympathetic interest, between the two Boer republics of South Africa and Great Britain. Bitter feelings were aroused, and the queen did but reflect the national sentiment when she personally received in the most friendly manner President Krüger, who arrived in Holland as a fugitive on board a Dutch man-of-war in the summer of 1900. The official attitude of the government was however perfectly correct, and there was never any breach in the relations between Great Britain and the Netherlands.

The marriage of Queen Wilhelmina, on February 7, 1901, with Prince Henry of Mecklenburg-Schwerin was welcomed by the people, as affording hopes, for some years to be disappointed, of the birth of an heir to the throne.

The elections of 1901 found the liberal ministry out of favour through the laws enforcing military service and obligatory attendance at school. Against them the indefatigable Dr Kuyper, who had returned to active politics in 1897, had succeeded in uniting the three "Church" groups—the democratic anti-revolutionaries, the aristocratic Historical Christians (both orthodox Calvinists) and the Catholics of all sections—into a "Christian Coalition" in support of religious teaching in the schools. The victory lay with the coalition, and Dr Kuyper became first minister. The new administration introduced a measure on Higher Education, which was rejected by the First Chamber. A dissolution of this Chamber led to the majority being reversed, and the measure was passed. Another measure revised the Mackay Law and conferred a larger subsidy on "private" schools. The socialist party under the able leadership of Troelstra had won several seats at the election; and in 1903 a general strike was threatened unless the government conceded the demands of the socialist labour party. The threat was met with firmness; an anti-strike law was quickly passed; the military was called out; and the strike collapsed. The costly war in Achin, which had been smouldering for some years, burst out again with violence in the years 1902-3, and led to sanguinary reprisals on the part of the Dutch soldiery, the report of which excited indignation against the responsible authorities. Various attempts had been made in 1895 and 1899 to introduce protectionist duties, but unsuccessfully.

The quadrennial elections of 1905 found all the liberal groups united in a combined assault upon the Christian Coalition. A severe electoral struggle ensued, with the result that 45 liberals and 7 socialists were returned against 48 coalitionists. Dr Kuyper resigned; and a new ministry, under the leadership of the moderate liberal, De Meester, took its place. The De Meester government was however dependent upon the socialist vote, and possessed no independent majority in either Chamber. For the first time a ministry of agriculture, industry and trade was created. Such an administration could only lead a precarious existence, and in 1907 an adverse vote upon the military estimates led to its resignation. Th. Heemskerk undertook the task of forming a new cabinet from the anti-revolutionary and Catholic groups, and at the next general election of 1909 he won a conclusive victory at the polls. This victory was obtained by wholesale promises of social reforms, including old age pensions and poor and sick relief. As so often happens, such a programme could not be carried into effect without heavy expenditure; and the means were not forthcoming. To meet the demand a bill was introduced in August, 1911, by the finance minister, Dr Kolkmar, to increase considerably the existing duties, and to extend largely the list of dutiable imports. This bill led to a widespread agitation in the country, and many petitions were presented against it, with the result that it was withdrawn. A proposal made by this ministry in 1910 to spend 38,000,000 florins on the fortification of Flushing excited much adverse criticism in the press of Belgium, England and France, on the ground that it had been done at the suggestion of the German government, the object being to prevent the British fleet from seizing Flushing in the event of the outbreak of an Anglo-German war. The press agitation met, however, with no countenance on the part of responsible statesmen in any of the countries named; it led nevertheless to the abandonment of the original proposal and the passing of a bill in 1912 for the improvement of the defences of the Dutch sea-ports generally.

The election of 1913 reversed the verdict of 1909. Probably in no country has the principle of the "swing of the pendulum" been so systematically verified as it has in Holland in recent times. The returns were in 1913: Church parties, 41; liberals of all groups, 39; socialists, 15. The most striking change was the increase in the socialist vote, their representation being more than doubled; and, as in 1905, they held the balance of parties in their hands. With some difficulty Dr Cort van den Linden succeeded in forming a liberal ministry. The outbreak of the Great War in August, 1914, prevented them from turning their attention to any other matters than those arising from the maintenance of a strict neutrality in a conflict which placed them in a most difficult and dangerous position. One of the first questions on which they had to take a critical decision was the closing of the Scheldt. As soon as Great Britain declared war on Germany (August 4), Holland refused to allow any belligerent vessels to pass over its territorial waters. The events of the six years that have since passed are too near for comment here. The liberal ministry at least deserves credit for having steered the country safely through perilous waters. Nevertheless, at the quadrennial election of 1917 there was the customary swing of the pendulum; and an anti-liberal ministry (September 6) was formed, with a Catholic, M. Ruys de Beerenbronck, as first minister.

# EPILOGUE

The dynastic connection of Luxemburg with Holland ceased with the accession of Queen Wilhelmina. The conditions under which the Belgian province of Luxemburg was created, by the Treaty of Vienna in 1815, a grand-duchy under the sovereignty of the head of the House of Orange-Nassau with succession in default of heirs-male by the family compact, known as the *Nassauischer Erbverein*, to the nearest male agnate of the elder branch of the Nassau family, have already been related. With the death of William III the male line of the House of Orange-Nassau became extinct; and the succession passed to Adolphus, Duke of Nassau-Weilburg. How unfortunate and ill-advised was the action of the Congress of Vienna in the creation of the Grand-Duchy of Luxemburg was abundantly shown by the difficulties and passions which it aroused in the course of the negotiations for the erection of Belgium into an independent state (1830-39). By the treaty of April 19, 1839, the Walloon portion of Luxemburg became part of the kingdom of Belgium, but in exchange for this cession the grand-duke obtained the sovereignty of a strip of the Belgian province of Limburg. This caused a fresh complication.

Luxemburg in 1815 was not merely severed from the Netherlands; it, as a sovereign grand-duchy, was made a state of the Germanic confederation. By virtue of the exchange sanctioned by the treaty of 1839, the ceded portion of Limburg became a state of the confederation. But with the revision of the Dutch constitution, which in 1840 followed the final separation of Holland and Belgium, by the wish of the king his duchy of Limburg was included in the new Fundamental Law, and thus became practically a Dutch province. The Limburgers had thus a strange and ambiguous position. They had to pay taxes, to furnish military contingents and to send deputies to two different sovereign authorities. This state of things continued with more or less friction, until the victory of Prussia over Austria in 1866 led to the dissolution of the Germanic confederation. At the conference of London, 1867, Luxemburg was declared to be an independent state, whose neutrality was guaranteed by the Great Powers, while Limburg became an integral portion of the kingdom of the Netherlands.

Since the middle of the last century the financial position of Holland has been continuously improving. The heavy indebtedness of the country, in the period which followed the separation from Belgium, was gradually diminished. This was effected for a number of years by the doubtful expedient of the profits derived from the exploitation of the East Indian colonies through the "Cultivation System." With the passing of the revised Fundamental Law of 1848 the control of colonial affairs and of the colonial budget was placed in the hands of the States-General; and a considerable section of the Liberal party began henceforth to agitate for the abolition of a system which was very oppressive to the Javanese population. It was not, however, until 1871 that the reform was carried out. Meanwhile, chiefly by the efforts of Thorbecke, the methods of home finance had been greatly improved by the removal, so far as possible, of indirect imposts, and the introduction of a free trade policy, which since his days has been steadily maintained. Such a policy is admirably suitable to a country which possesses neither minerals nor coal[15], and whose wealth is mainly due to sea-or river-borne trade, to dairy farming and to horticulture. For its supply of corn and many other necessary commodities Holland has to look to other countries. The fisheries still form one of the staple industries of the land, and furnish a hardy sea-faring population for the considerable mercantile marine, which is needed for constant intercourse with a colonial empire (the third in importance at the present time) consisting chiefly of islands in a far-distant ocean.

Between 1850 and 1914, 375,430,000 fl. have been devoted to the reduction of debt; and the Sinking Fund in 1915 was 6,346,000 fl. Since that date Holland has suffered from the consequences of the Great War, but, having successfully maintained her neutrality, she has suffered relatively far less than any of her neighbours. Taxation in Holland has always been high. It is to a large extent an artificial country; and vast sums have been expended and must always be expended in the upkeep of the elaborate system of dykes and canals, by which the waters of the ocean and the rivers are controlled and prevented from flooding large areas of land lying below sea level.

Culture in Holland is widely diffused. The well-to-do classes usually read and speak two or three languages beside their own; and the Dutch language is a finished literary tongue of great flexibility and copiousness. The system of education is excellent. Since 1900 attendance at the primary schools between the ages of six and thirteen is compulsory. Between the primary schools intermediate education (*middelbaaronderwijs*) is represented by "burgher night-schools" and "higher burgher schools." The night-schools are intended for those engaged in agricultural or industrial work; the "higher schools" for technical instruction, and much attention is paid to the study of the *vier talen*—French, English, German and Dutch. In connection with these there is an admirable School of Agriculture, Horticulture and Forestry at Wageningen in Gelderland. To the teaching at Wageningen is largely due the acknowledged supremacy of Holland in scientific horticulture. There is a branch establishment at Groningen for agricultural training, and another at Deventer for instruction in subjects connected with colonial life. The *gymnasia*, which are to be found in every town, are preparatory to the universities. The course lasts six years; and the study of Latin and Greek in addition to modern languages is compulsory. There are four universities, Leyden, Utrecht, Groningen and Amsterdam. The possession of a doctor's degree at one of these universities is necessary for magistrates, physicians, advocates, and for teachers in the *gymnasia* and higher burgher schools.

In so small a country the literary output is remarkable, and, marked as it is by scientific and intellectual distinction, deserves to be more widely read. The Dutch are justly proud of the great part their forefathers played during the War of Independence, and in the days of John de Witt and William III. For scientific historical research in the national archives, and in the publication of documents bearing upon and illustrating the national annals, Dutch historians can compare favourably with those of any other country. Special mention should be made of the labours of Robert Fruin, who may be described as the founder of a school with many disciples, and whose collected works are a veritable treasure-house of brilliant historical studies, combining careful research with acute criticism. Among his many disciples the names of Dr P.J. Blok and Dr H.T. Colenbrander are perhaps the best known.

In the department of Biblical criticism there have been in Holland several writers of European repute, foremost among whom stands the name of Abraham Kuenen.

Dutch writers of fiction have been and are far more numerous than could have been expected from the limited number of those able to read their works. In the second half of the 19th century, J. van Lennep and Mevrouw Bosboom-Toussaint were the most prolific writers. Both of these were followers of the Walter Scott tradition, their novels being mainly patriotic romances based upon episodes illustrating the past history of the Dutch people. Van Lennep's contributions to literature were, however, by no means confined to the writing of fiction, as his great critical edition of Vondel's poetical works testifies. Mevrouw Bosboom-Toussaint's novels were not only excellent from the literary point of view, but as reproductions of historical events were most conscientiously written. Her pictures, for instance, of the difficult and involved period of Leicester's governor-generalship are admirable. The writings of Douwes Dekker (under the pseudonym Multatuli) are noteworthy from the fact that his novel *Max Havelaar*, dealing with life in Java and setting forth the sufferings of the natives through the "cultivation system," had a large share in bringing about its abolition.

The 20th century school of Dutch novelists is of a different type from their predecessors and deals with life and life's problems in every form. Among the present-day authors of fiction, the foremost place belongs to Louis Conperus, an idealist and mystic, who as a stylist is unapproached by any of his contemporaries.

No account of modern Holland would be complete without a notice of the great revival of Dutch painting, which has taken place in the past half century. Without exaggeration it may indeed be said that this modern renascence of painting in Holland is not unworthy to be compared with that of the days of Rembrandt. The names of Joseph Israels, Hendrik Mesdag, Vincent van Gogh, Anton Maure, and, not least, of the three talented brothers Maris, have attained a wide and well-deserved reputation. And to these must be added others of high merit: Bilders, Scheffer, Bosboom, Rochussen, Bakhuysen, Du Chattel, De Haas and Haverman. The traditional representation of the Dutchman as stolid, unemotional, wholly absorbed in trade and material interests, is a caricature. These latter-day artists, like those of the 17th century, conclusively prove that the Dutch race is singularly sensitive to the poetry of form and colour, and that it possesses an inherited capacity and power for excelling in the technical qualities of the painter's art.

# FOOTNOTES

1. Hollandais, Holländer, Olandesi, Olandeses, etc.
2. In French books and documents, Jacqueline.
3. Bois-le-duc.
4. By English and French writers generally translated Grand Pensionary.
5. It must be remembered that the States-General and the Holland Estates sat in the same building.
6. Adam Smith, *Wealth of Nations*, I, 101.
7. Busken Huet, *Land van Rembrant*, III, 175.
8. *Acte van Seclusie.*
9. Nassauischer Erbverein.
10. Charles White, *The Belgic Revolution*, 1835, vol. 1, p. 106.
11. *Correspondence sécrète des Pays-Bas.* Julian received his report of the conversation direct from Count Bylandt by permission of the king.
12. From Van Maanen's private papers. See Colenbrander's *Belgische Omwenteling*, p. 139.
13. The ratification by the Powers took place on the following dates:—France and Great Britain, January 31; Austria and Prussia, April 18; Russia, May 4, 1832.
14. The Prince of Orange had married Anna Paulovna, sister of Alexander I, in 1816.
15. The Belgian coal field extends into Dutch Limburg.

# BIBLIOGRAPHY

## GENERAL

### (a) ARCHIVALIA. BOOKS OF REFERENCE

AA, A.J. VAN DER. Biographisch woordenboek d. Nederlanden bevatt. levensbeschrijvingen der personen, die zich in ons vaderland hebben vermaard gemacht, voortgezet door K.J.R. v. Harderwijk en G.D.J. Schotel. 27 vols. Haarlem. 1851-70.

BERGH, L. PH.C. VAN DEN. Over MSS betr. onze geschiedenis in het Britsch Museum bewaard. Arnhem. 1858.

BLOK, P.J. Onze archieven. Amsterdam. 1891.

Verslag aangaande een onderzoek in Duitschland naar Archivalia, belangrijk voor de geschiedenis van Nederland. 2 vols. The Hague. 1888-9.

Verslag aangaande een voorloopig onderzoek in Engelandt naar Archivalia, belangrijk voor de gesch. v.N. The Hague. 1891.

Verslag aangaande een voorloopig onderzoek in Parijs naar Archivalia, belangrijk voor de gesch. v.N. The Hague. 1897.

BRINK, R.C. BAKHUIZEN VAN DEN. Overzigt van het Nederl. Rijk's Archief. The Hague. 1854.

KNUTTEL, W.P.C. Nederlandsche bibliographic voor kerkgeschiedenis. Amsterdam. 1889.Catalogus van de pamfletten-verzameling berustende in de koninklijke biblioteek. 6 vols. The Hague. 1899, 1900, 1902.

KOK, J. Vaderlandsch Woordenboek. 35 vols. Amsterdam. 1735-99.

PETIT, LOUIS D. Repertorium der verhandelingen en bijdragen betreff. de geschied. des Vaterlands in tijdschriften en mengelwerken tot op 1900 verschenen. Leyden. 1905.

RIEMSDIJK, TH.V. Het Rijk's Archief te 's Gravenhage. The Hague. 1889.

SCHELTEMA, P. Inventaris van het Amsterdamsch Archief. 3 vols. Amsterdam. 1866-74.

UHLENBEEK, C.C. Verslag aangaande een onderzoek in de archieven van Rusland ten bate der Nederl. Geschiedenis. The Hague. 1891.

### (b) GENERAL HISTORY OF THE NETHERLANDS

AREND, J.P. Algemeene Geschiedenis des Vaderlands van de vroegste tijden tot op heden, voortgezet . . . 13 vols. Amsterdam. 1840-83.

BILDERDIJK, W. Geschiedenis des Vaderlands. 14 vols. Amsterdam. 1832-53.

BLOK, P.J. Geschiedenis des Vaderlands. 9 vols. Groningen. 1892-1908.

English translation in five parts. London and New York.

DAVIES, C.M. History of Holland and of the Dutch. 5 vols. London. 1851.

FRUIN, R. Geschiedenis der Staat-Instellingen in Nederland tot den Val der Republiek. The Hague. 1893.

GROEN v. PRINSTERER, G. Handboek der Geschied. des Vaterlands. 2 vols. Leyden. 1846.

JONGE, J.C. DE. Geschiedenis v. het Nederlandsche Zee-Wesen. 6 vols. The Hague. 1833-45.

NIJHOFF, I.A. Staatkundige Geschiedenis van Nederland. 2 vols. Zutphen. 1891-3.

RIJSENS, F. Geschiedenis van ons Vaderland. Groningen. 1904.

ROGERS, J.E. THOROLD. History of Holland. London. 1888.

VOS, J.M. Geschiedenis van ons Vaderland van oude tijden tot heden. Groningen. 1915.

VREEDE, G.W. Inleiding tot eene Geschiedenis der Nederlandsche diplomatie. 6 vols. Utrecht. 1856-65.

WAGENAAR, J. Vaderlandsche Historie. 21 vols. Amsterdam. 1749-59.

WENZELBERGER, K. TH. Geschichte der Niederlande. 2 vols. Gotha. 1879-86.

WIJNE, J.A. Geschiedenis van het Vaderland. Groningen. 1870.

# XVITH CENTURY

## (a) CONTEMPORARY WORKS AND COLLECTIONS OF ORIGINAL DOCUMENTS

BOR, P. Oorspronck, begin en ende aenvang der Nederlandsche oorlogen, beroerten ende borgelijcke oneenicheyden. 6 vols. Amsterdam and Leyden. 1621.

BRUCE, J. Correspondence of Leicester during his Government in the Low Countries. London. 1844.

CARNERO, A. Historia de las guerras civiles que han avido en los estados de Flandes des del anno 1559 hasta el de 1609, y las causas de la rebelion de dichos estados. Brussels. 1625.

COLOMA, C. Las guerras de los Estados Baxos, desde el anno de 1588 hasta el de 1599. Antwerp. 1625.

GACHARD, P.L. Correspondance de Philippe II sur les affaires des Pays-Bas. 5 vols. Brussels. 1867-87.

—Correspondance de Guillaume le Taciturne. 6 vols. Brussels. 1847-57

—Correspondance d'Alexandre Farnese, Prince de Parma, gouv.-gen. des Pays-Bas avec Philippe II, 1578-9. Brussels. 1850.

GROEN v. PRINSTERER, G. Archives ou Correspondance inédite de la Maison d'Orange-Nassau. I^e série. 9 vols. Leyden. 2^e série. 5 vols. Utrecht. 1841-61.

GROTIUS, HUGO. Annales et historiae de rebus belgicis. Amsterdam. 1637.

HOOFT, P.C. Nederlandsche Historien, 1555-87. Amsterdam. 1656.

JUSTE, TH. Charles Quint et Marguerite d'Autriche. Brussels. 1858.

LE GLAY, A. Maximilian I et Marguerite d'Autriche. Paris. 1855.

LETTENHOVE, J.M. KERVYN DE. Relations politiques des Pays-Bas et de l'Angleterre sous le règne de Philippe II. 5 vols. Brussels. 1882-6.

METEREN, E. VAN. Belgische ofte Nederlandsche historien van onzen tijden tot 1598. Delft. 1605.

PETIT, J. F. LE. Grande Chronique de Hollande, Zelande, etc. jusqu'à la fin de 1600. 2 vols. Dordrecht. 1601.

REYD, E. VAN. Vornaemste gheschiedennissen in de Nederlanden, 1566-1601. Arnhem. 1626.

WEISS, C. Papiers d'État de Cardinal Granvelle. 9 vols. Paris. 1841-52.

## (b) LATER WORKS

BRINK, J. TEN. De eerste Jaren der Nederlandsche Revolutie, 1555-68. Rotterdam. 1882.

BRUGMANS, H. Engeland en de Nederlanden in de eerste jaren van Elizabeth's regeering, 1558-67. Groningen. 1892.

FRUIN, R. Tien jaren uit den tachtigjarigen oorlog, 1588-98. Amsterdam. 1861.

Het voorspel van den tachtigjarigen oorlog. Amsterdam. 1866.

JUSTE, TH. Histoire de la Revolution des Pays-Bas sous Philippe II, 1555-71. 2 vols. Brussels. 1855.

Continuation, 1572-7. 2 vols. The Hague. 1863-7.

LETTENHOVE, J. M. KERVYN DE. Les Huguenots et les Gueux, 1560-85., 6 vols. Bruges. 1883-5.

MOTLEY, J. L. Rise of the Dutch Republic, 1555-84. 3 vols. London. 1856.

History of the United Netherlands, 1584-1609. 4 vols. The Hague, 1860-7.

TREMAYNE, E. E. The first Governors of the Netherlands. London. 1908.

## (c) BIOGRAPHICAL

BLOK, P. J. Lodewijk van Nassau, 1536-1674. The Hague. 1889.

BURGON, J. W. Life and times of Thomas Gresham, compiled chiefly from his correspondence. 2 vols. London. 1839.

HARRISON, F. William the Silent. London. 1897.

HUME, M. Philip II of Spain. London. 1902.

MONTPLEINCHAMP, B. DE. L'histoire d'Alexandre Farnese, duc de Parma, gouverneur de la Belgique. Amsterdam. 1692.

PIETRO, FRA. Alessandro Farnese, duca di Parma. Rome. 1836.

PUTNAM, R. William the Silent, prince of Orange. 2 vols. New York. 1895.

RACHFELD, F. Margaretha von Parma, Statthalterin der Niederlande, 1559-67. Munich. 1895.

## XVIITH CENTURY

### (a) CONTEMPORARY WORKS AND COLLECTIONS OF ORIGINAL DOCUMENTS

AITZEMA, L. v. Saken van Staet en Oorlog in ende omtrent de Vereen. Nederlanden, 1621-69. 7 vols. The Hague. 1669-71.

Verhael van de Nederlandsche Vredehandel, 1621-49. 2 vols. The Hague. 1650.

Herstelde Leeuw of discours over 't gepassert in de Vereen. Nederlanden, 1650-1. The Hague. 1652.

ALBUQUERQUE, DUARTE DE. Memorias Diarias della guerra del Brasil per discurso de nueve años desde el de 1630. Madrid. 1654.

Archief v. den Raadpensionaris Antonie Heinsius, 1683-97. 3 vols. The Hague. 1867-80.

AVAUX, COMTE D' (JEAN ANTOINE DE MESNIER). Negotiations en Hollande, 1679-88. 6 vols. Paris. 1750-4.

BARLAEUS, C. Rerum per octennium in Brasilia et alibi nuper gestarum sub praefectura Com. J. Mauritii Nassoviae historia. Amsterdam. 1647.

Epistolarum liber. 2 vols. Amsterdam. 1667.

BURNET, G. (Bishop of Salisbury). History of my own times. 2 vols. London. 1724-34.

CAPELLEN, ALEX. VAN DER. Gedenkschriften, 1621-54, uitg. d. R. J. v. d. Capellen. 2 vols. Utrecht. 1777-8.

D'ESTRADES, COMTE G. Lettres, memoires, negotiations depuis 1637. 9 vols. London. 1743.

GARDINER, S. R. Letters and Papers rel. to the First Dutch War, 1652-4. 2 vols. London. 1899-1900.

GROEN v. PRINSTERER, G. Archives ou Correspondance de la Maison d'Orange. 2e série. 3 vols. Utrecht. 1841-61.

GROTIUS, HUGO. Epistolae ad Gallos. Leyden. 1650.

HOOFT, P. C. Brieven (1600-47) met toelichtingen door v. Vloten. 4 vols. Leyden. 1655-7.

HUYGHENS, CONSTANTIJN. Dagboek, 1606-85. Ed. J. H. Unger. Amsterdam. 1885.

Mémoires. Ed. T. Jorissen. The Hague. 1873.

HUYGHENS, CONSTANTIJN DE ZOON. Journael gedurende de veldtochten der Jaren 1673, 1675, 1676, 1677 en 1678. Utrecht. 1831.

LAET, J. DE. Historic ofte jaerlijck verhael van de verrichtingen der West Indische Compagnie, sedert 1636. Leyden. 1644.

Marie, Reine d'Angleterre, é'pouse de Guillaume III, Lettres et Mémoires de Collection de doc. authent. inédits publ. par Mad. Comtesse Bentinck. The Hague. 1880.

Mary, Queen of England, Memoirs of. Ed. E. Doelmer. Leipzig. 1886.

TEMPLE, SIR W. Letters written by W. Temple and other ministers of State containing an account of the most important transactions that passed from 1665-72. 3 vols. London. 1702-3.

Letters written during his being ambassador at the Hague to the Earl of Arlington and John Trevor, Secretaries of State, by D. Jones. London. 1699.

THURLOE, J. Collection of State Papers, etc. 7 vols. London. 1702-3.

WICQUEFORT, ABRAHAM DE. Histoire des Provinces Unies des Pays-Bas depuis la paix de Munster, 1648-58. Edd. Lenting and Van Buren. 4 vols. Amsterdam. 1861-74.

WITT, J. DE. Brieven ... gewisselt tusschen den Heer Johann De Witt ... ende de gevolmagtigden v. d. Staet d. Vereen. Nederlanden, so in Vrankryck, Engelandt, Zweden, Denemarken, Poolen enz. 1652-69.

6 vols. The Hague. 1723-5.

### (*b*)LATER WORKS

BEINS, L. Jean de Witt en zijne buitenlandsche politick, 1653-60. Groningen. 1871.

BRILL, W. C. Cromwell's strijving naar eene coalitie tusschen de Nederlanden en de Britsche republiek. Amsterdam. 1891.

EDMUNDSON, GEORGE. Anglo-Dutch Rivalry in the first half of the 17th century. Oxford. 1911.

FRUIN, R. De oorlogsplannen van Prins Willem II na zijn aanslag op Amsterdam in 1650. The Hague. 1895.

Het process van Buat, 1666. The Hague. 1881.

GEDDES, J. History of the administration of John De Witt. The Hague. 1879.

JAPIKSE, N. De verwikkelingen tusschen de Republiek en Engeland, 1660-5. London. 1900.

LEFEVRE-PONTALIS, A. Vingt années de République parlementaire au xvii^e siècle. Jean de Witt, Grand Pensionaris de Hollande. 2 vols. Paris. 1884.

MULLER, P. L. Wilhelm III von Oranien und Georg Friedrich van Waldeck. Ein Beitrag zur Geschichte des Kampfes um das Euro-paische Gleichgewicht, 1679-92. 2 vols. The Hague. 1872-80.

Nederland en de Groote Keurvorst. The Hague. 1879.

MUTZUKURI, G. Englisch-Niederländische Unionsstrebungen im Zeit-alter Cromwell's. Tubingen. 1891.

SIRTEMA DE GROVESTINS. Guillaume III et Louis XIV. 8 vols. Paris. 1868.

TREITSCHKE, H. VON. Die Republik der Vereinigten Niederlande. Historische und politische Aufsatze. 4 vols. Leipzig. 1870.

## (c) BIOGRAPHICAL

BAUMGÄRTNER, ALEXANDER. Joost van den Vondel, zijn leven en zijne werken. (Trs. from German.) Amsterdam. 1886.

BRANDT, C. Leven en bedrijf van Michiel De Ruyter. Amsterdam. 1687.

DALTON, C. Life and times of Sir Edward Cecil, Viscount Wimbledon, Colonel of an English Regiment in the Dutch Service, 1605-31.

2 vols. London. 1885.

EDMUNDSON, G. Frederick Henry, Prince of Orange. (Eng. Hist. Rev. 41, 264—1890.)

Louis de Geer. (Eng. Hist. Rev. 685—1891.)

Pieter Cornelisz. Hooft. (Eng. Hist. Rev. 77—1894.)

GEER, J. L. W. DE. Lodewijk de Geer van Finspong en Leufsta, 1593-1652.

Utrecht. 1882.

KEMP, C. M. v.d. Maurits van Nassau, prins v. Oranje, in zijn leven en verdiensten. 4 vols. Rotterdam. 1843.

LE CLERCQ, P. Het leven van Frederick Hendrick. 2 vols. The Hague. 1737.

MARKHAM, C.B. The fighting Veres. Lives of Sir Francis Vere and Sir Horace Vere, successively generals of the Queen's forces in the Low Countries. Boston. 1888.

MICHEL, E. Rembrandt, sa vie, son oeuvre et son temps. Paris. 1893.

MOTLEY, J. L. Life and death of John of Barneveldt. 2 vols. The Hague. 1874.

OOSTKAMP, J. A. Leven en daden van Marten Harpzn. Tromp en Jacob van Wassenaar van Obdam. Deventer. 1825.

SCHOTEL, G. D. J. Anna Maria van Schuurman. 'sHertogenbosch. 1853.

SIMONS, P. Johan De Witt en zijn tijd. 3 vols. Amsterdam. 1832-48.

TRAILL, H. D. William III. London. 1888.

TREVOR, A. Life and times of William III, 1650-1702. 2 vols. London. 1835-6.

VLOTEN, J. VAN. Tesselschade Roemers en hare vrienden, 1632-49.

Leyden. 1652.

## (d) COLONIZATION, COMMERCE, VOYAGES

DEVENTER, M. L. v. Geschiedenis der Nederlanders op Java. 2 vols. Haarlem. 1886-7.

DIJK, L. C. D. Nederland's vroegste betrekkingen met Borneo, den Solo Archipels, Cambodja, Siam en Cochin China. Amsterdam. 1862.

EDMUNDSON, G. The Dutch Power in Brazil (1) The struggle for Bahia, 1624-7. (2) The First Conquests.

(Eng. Hist. Rev. 261—1896;676—1899.)

—The Dutch in Western Guiana. (Eng. Hist. Rev. 640—1901.)

—The Dutch on the Amazon and Negro in the 17th century.

(Eng. Hist. Rev. 642—1903; 1—1904.)

—The Swedish Legend in Guiana. (Eng. Hist. Rev. 71—1899.)

HUET, P. D. Mémoires sur le commerce des Hollandais dans tous les etats et empires du monde. Amsterdam. 1717.

JONGE, J. K. J. DE. De Opkomst van het Nederl. gezag in Oost Indie. 13 vols. The Hague. 1862-89.

KAMPEN, N. G. VAN. Geschiedenis der Nederlanders buiten Europa. 4 vols. Haarlem. 1831-3.

LAUTS, G. Geschiedenis van de vestiging, uitbreiding ... van de magt der

Nederlanders in Indie. 7 vols. Groningen and Amsterdam. 1853-66.

LEUPE, P. A. Reisen der Nederlanders naar het Zuidland of Nieuw Holland in de 17e en 18e eeuw. Amsterdam. 1868.

LUZAC, E. Holland's Rijkdom, behoudende den oorsprong van der koophandel en de magt van dezer Staat. 4 vols. Leyden. 1781.

NETSCHER, P. M. Les Hollandais au Bresil. The Hague. 1853.

NETSCHER, P. M. Geschiedenis van de Kolonien Essequibo, Demerary en Berbice van de vestiging der Nederlanders tot op onzen tijd. The Hague. 1888.

REES, O. VAN. Geschiedenis der Nederl. Volkplantingen in Noord America. Tiel. 1855.

—Geschiedenis der koloniale politiek. Utrecht. 1868.

VALENTIJN, F. Oud-en Nieuw-Oost-Indien, vervatt. eene verhandelinge v. Nederlands mogentheyd in die gewesten, also eene verhandelinge over ... Kaap der Goede Hoop. 5 vols. Dort. 1724.

## (e) LITERATURE, CULTURE, FINE ARTS

BRINK, J. TEN. Geschiedenis der Nederlandsche Letterkunde. Amsterdam. 1897.

BUSKEN HUËT, C. Het land van Rembrandt. Studien over de Noord Nederlandsche beschaving in de VXII'e eeuw. 5 vols. Haarlem. 1890.

COLLOT D'ESCURY, H. Holland's roem in kunsten en wetenschappen. 10 vols. The Hague. 1824-44.

EDMUNDSON, G. Milton and Vondel. London. 1885.

HAAR, B. TER. Holland's bloei in schoone kunsten en wetenschappen by het sluiten van de Munstersche vrede. Leyden. 1849.

HARTING, P. Leven en Werken van Christiaan Huyghens. Amsterdam. 1868.

HAVARD, HENRI. L'art et les artistes hollandais. Paris. 1879.

HELLWALD, F. VON. Geschichte des holländischen Theaters. Rotterdam. 1874.

JONCKBLOET, W. J. A. Geschiedenis des Nederlandsche Letterkunde in de zeventiende eeuw. 2 vols. Groningen. 1881.

KONING, J. Geschiedenis van het Slot te Muiden en Hooft's leven op hetselve. Amsterdam. 1827.

KORTEWEG, D. J. Het bloeitijdperk der wiskundige wetenschappen in Nederland. Amsterdam. 1893-4.

MÜLLER, LUCIAN. Geschichte der klassischen Philologie in den Niederlanden. Leipzig. 1869.

SIEGENBEEK, M. Geschiedenis van der Leidsche Hooge School. Leyden. 1829-32.

STRAETEN, E. VAN DER. La musique aux Pays-Bas avant le 19'e siècle. Brussels. 1872.

VLOTEN, J. VAN. Het Nederlandsche Kluctspel van de 14'e tot de 18'e eeuw. 3 vols. Haarlem. 1878-80.

VONDEL, J. VAN DEN. Werken in verband gebracht met zijn leven en voorzien van verldaring en aanteekeningen d. J. v. Lennep. 12 vols. Amsterdam. 1855-68.

WILLEMS, A. Les Elzevier. Histoire et annales typographiques. The Hague. 1880.

WITSEN GEYSBEEK, P. G. Biographisch, anthologisch, en critisch woordenboek der Nederlandsche dicters. 6 vols. Amsterdam. 1821-7.

WYBRANTS, C. E. Het Amsterdamsch tooneel. Amsterdam. 1875.

### (f) RELIGIOUS AND ECCLESIASTICAL

BRANDT, G. Historic der reformatie en andere kerkelijke geschiedennissen in en omtrent de Nederlanden tot 1600. 4 vols. Amsterdam. 1677-1704.

CHATELAIN, N. Histoire du Synode de Dordrecht dès 1609 à 1619. Amsterdam. 1841.

FRUIN, R. De wederopluiking van het Katholicisme in Noord-Nederland omtrent den aanvang der 17'e eeuw. Amsterdam. 1894.

KNUTTEL, W.P.C. De toestand der Nederl. Katholieken ten tijde der Republiek. 2 vols. The Hague. 1892-4.

MONTANUS, A. Kerkelijke historic van Nederland. Amsterdam. 1675.

MONTIJN, G.G. Geschiedenis der Hervorming in de Nederlanden. 5 vols. Arnhem. 1858-64.

NUIJENS, W.J.F. Geschiedenis der kerkelijke en politieke geschillen in de Republiek der Zeven Vereen. Prov., 1598-1625. 2 vols. Amsterdam. 1886.

REGENBORG, J. Historic der Remonstranten. 2 vols. Amsterdam. 1774.

VEEN, A.J. V.D. Remonstranten en Contra-Remonstranten. 2 vols. Sneek. 1858.

## XVIIITH CENTURY

### (a) ORIGINAL AUTHORITIES AND COLLECTIONS OF DOCUMENTS Actes, Mémoires et autres pièces authentiques concernant la paix d'Utrecht. 6 vols. Utrecht. 1714-15.

BOWDLER, T. Letters written in Holland in the months of September and October, 1787, to which is added a Collection of letters and other papers relating to the journey of the Princess of Orange on June 29, 1787. London. 1788.

Brieven en negotiatien van L.L. van de Spiegel. Amsterdam. 1803.

Brieven van Prins Willem V aan Baron v. Leynden. The Hague. 1893.

DE JONGE, J.K.J. Documents politiques et diplomatiques sur les revolutions de 1787 et 1795 dans la republique des Provinces Unies. (Ned. Rijk's Archief.) The Hague. 1859.

Lettres et mémoires sur la conduite de la présente guerre et sur les negotiations de paix, jusqu'à la fin des conferences de Geertruidenbergh. 2 vols. The Hague. 1711-12.

LINGUET, S.N.H. Lettres au Comte de Trauttmansdorf, ministre plenipotentiaire par Empereur [Joseph II] aux Pays-Bas, 1788 et 1789. Brussels. 1790.

MAGUETTE, F. Joseph II et la liberté de l'Escaut. Mémoires couronnés et autres Mémoires publiés par l'Académie Royale des Sciences de Belgique. Vol. xv. Brussels. 1898.

Malmesbury, Diaries and Correspondence of James Harris, Earl of. 4 vols. London. 1844.

MANDRILLON, J.H. Mémoires pour servir à l'histoire de la Révolution des Provinces Unies en 1787. Paris. 1791.

Marlborough, Despatches of John, Duke of. Ed. Sir G. Murray. 5 vols. London. 1845.

TORCY, MARQUIS DE. Mémoires pour servir a l'histoire des négotiations depuis le traité de Rijswijck jusqu'a la paix d'Utrecht. Paris. 1850.

VREEDE, C.G. Correspondance diplomatique et militaire du duc de Marlborough, du grand-pensionaris Heinsius, et du trésorier-général J. Hop. Amsterdam. 1850.

## (b) HISTORICAL NARRATIVES

BOSSCHE, E. VAN DER. Le traité de la Barrière. Bruges. 1880.

COLENBRANDER, H.T. De Patrioten Tijd, 1776-87. 3 vols. The Hague. 1897-99.

—De Bataafsche Republiek. The Hague. 1908.

ELLIS, GEORGE. History of the late Revolution in the Dutch Republic. London. 1789.

History of the internal affairs of the United Provinces, from the year 1780 to the commencement of hostilities in June, 1787. London. 1787.

JORISSEN, T. De Patriotten te Amsterdam in 1791. Amsterdam. 1793.

KANE, RICHARD. Campaigns of King William and of the Duke of Marlborough. 2nd ed. London. 1747.

KLUIT, A. Historic der Hollandsche Staatsregering tot 1795. 5 vols. Amsterdam. 1802-5.

LEGRAND, L. La révolution française en Hollande; la république batave. Paris. 1894.

LOON, H.W.v. The Fall of the Dutch Republic. London. 1913.

MEULEN, A.J.v.D. Studies over de ministrie van Van de Spiegel. Leyden. 1906.

ONDAATJE, Q. Bijdragen tot de geschiedenis der omwenteling van 1787. Dunkirk. 1791.

SCHIMMELPENNICK, RUTGER. J.S. en eenige gebeurtenissen van zijn tijd. Amsterdam. 1845.

VERENET, G. Pierre le Grand en Hollande, 1697 et 1717. Utrecht. 1865.

WEBER, O. Die Quadrupel-Allianz vom Jahre 1718. Vienna. 1887.

WREEDE, G.W. Geschiedenis der diplomatic van de bataafsche republiek. 3 vols. Utrecht. 1863.

## (*c*) BIOGRAPHICAL

ARNETH, A., RITTER VON. Prinz Eugen van Savoyen. 3 vols. Vienna. 1856.

KOLLEWIJN, B. Bilderdijk. 2 vols. Amsterdam. 1891.

MENDELS, M.H.W. Daendels, 1762-1818. 2 vols. The Hague. 1890.

NIJHOFF, I.A. De Hertog van Brunswijk. The Hague. 1849.

SCHENK, W.G.F. Wilhelm der Fünfte. Stuttgart. 1884.

SILLEM, J.A. Gogel. Amsterdam. 1864.

—Dirk van Hogendorp. Amsterdam. 1890.

## XIXTH CENTURY AND AFTER

## (*a*) ORIGINAL AUTHORITIES AND COLLECTIONS OF DOCUMENTS

BARTHELS, A. Documents historiques sur la Révolution belge. Brussels. 1836.

BONAPARTE, LOUIS (COMTE DE ST LEU). Documents historiques et réflexions sur le gouvernement de la Hollande. 3 vols. London. 1820.

FALCK, A.R. Brieven 1796-1845 met levensberigt d.O.W. Hora Siccama. The Hague. 1860.

—Amtsbrieven, 1802-42. The Hague. 1878.

Handelingen van de Staten General (1'e en 2'e Kamer), 1815-47. 51 vols. The Hague. 1863-97.

Histoire parlementaire du traité de paix du 19 Avril, 1839, entre la Belgique et la Hollande, contenant tous les discours. 2 vols. Brussels. 1839.

KRAYENHOFF, C.R.T. Bijdragen tot de vaderlandsche geschiedenis van de belangrijke jaren 1809-10. Nimwegen. 1844.

LIPMAN, S.P. Nederlandsch constitutioneel archief van alle koninklijke aanspraken en parlementaire addressen, 1813-63. 2 vols. Amsterdam. 1846—64.

ROCQUAIS, F. Napoléon et le roi Louis d'après les documents conservés aux archives nationales. Paris. 1875.

SOELEN, VERSTOLK VAN. Recueil de pièces diplomatiques relatives aux affaires de la Hollande et de la Belgique, 1830-2. 3 vols. The Hague. 1831-3.

THORBECKE, J.R. Brieven aan Groen v. Prinsterer, 1830-2. Amsterdam. 1873.

—Parlementaire redevoeringen. 6 vols. Deventer. 1856-70.

## (b) HISTORICAL NARRATIVES

BEAUFORT, W.H.DE. De eerste regierings jaren van Koning Willem I. Amsterdam. 1886.

BOSCH KEMPER, J. DE. Staatkundige geschiedenis van Nederland na 1830. 5 vols. Amsterdam. 1873-82.

BRUYNE, J.A. Geschiedenis van Nederland in onzen tijd. 5 vols. Schiedam. 1889-1906.

COLENBRANDER, H.T. De Belgische Omwenteling. The Hague. 1905.

GERLACHE, E.C.DE. Histoire du royaume des Pays-Bas depuis 1814 jusqu'en 1830. 3 vols. Brussels. 1842.

HOUTEN, S. VAN. Vijf en twintig jaar in de Kamer, 1869-94. Haarlem. 1905.

KEPPERS, G.L. De regeering van Koning Willem III. Groningen. 1887.

—Het Regentschap van Koningin Emma. The Hague. 1895.

LASTDRAGER, A.J. Nieuwste geschiedenis v. Nederland in jaarlijksche overzigten (1815-30). 9 vols. Amsterdam. 1839-48.

NOTHOMB, BARON J.B. Essai historique et politique sur la révolution belge. 3 vols. 4th ed. Brussels. 1876.

NUYENS, W.J.F. Geschiedenis van het Nederlandsche Volk van 1815 tot op onze dagen. 4 vols. Amsterdam. 1883-6.

RENGERS, W.J. VAN WALDEREN. Schets eener parlementaire geschiedenis van Nederland sedert 1849. 2 vols. The Hague. 1889.

WITKAMP EN CRAANDIJK. Vereeniging en Scheiding. Geschiedenis van Noord-Nederland en Belgie van 1813-80. Doesburgh. 1881.

WOLF, N.H. De regeering van Koningin Wilhelmina. Rotterdam. 1901.

WÜPPERMAN, W.E.A. Geschiedenis van den Tiendagschen Veldtocht. Amsterdam. 1880.

### (c) BIOGRAPHICAL

ABBINK, J.J. Leven van Koning Willem II. Amsterdam. 1849.

ARNOLDI, J. VAN. Leven en Karakter-Schets van Koning Willem I. Zutphen. 1818.

BOS, F. DE. Prins Frederik der Nederlanden. 4 vols. Schiedam. 1857-99.

BOSSCHA, J. Het leven van Willem II, koning der Nederlanden, 1793-1849. Amsterdam. 1852.

BRINK, J. TEN. Prins Frederik der Nederlanden. The Hague. 1881.

DESCHAMPS, P. La reine Wilhelmina. Paris. 1901.

MEES Az, G. Levenschets van G.K. Hogendorp. Amsterdam. 1864.

PIERSON, ALLARD. Onze tijdgenooten. Amsterdam. 1896.

THIJM, J.A. Alberdingk, door A.J. Amsterdam. 1893.

VOS, A.J. DE. Groen van Prinsterer en zijn tijd. Dordrecht. 1886.

### (d) COLONIAL

BOYS, H. SCOTT. Some notes on Java and its administration by the Dutch. Allahabad. 1892.

DAY, C. The policy and administration of the Dutch in Java. New York. 1904.

PERSELAER, M.T.H. Nederlandsche Indië. 4 vols. Leyden. 1891-3.

PIERSON, N.G. Koloniale Politiek. Amsterdam. 1877.

Staatsblad voor Nederl. Indië 1816-80. 46 vols. The Hague and Batavia. 1839-81.

Verslag van het beheer en der staat der Nederlandsche bezittingen in Oost-en West-Indië en ter kust van Guinea. 44 vols. The Hague. 1840-96.

### (e) GENERAL

BOISSEVAIN, J.H.G. De Limburgsche Questie. Tiel. 1848.

BRINK, J. TEN. Geschiedenis der Noord-Nederlandsche letteren in de XIX^e eeuw.

EENDEGEEST, G. VAN. Over de droogmaking van het Haarlemmer meer. Vol. I. Leyden. 1842.

Vol. II. The Hague. 1853.

Vol. III. Amsterdam. 1860.

FRUIN, J.A. De Nederlandsche Wetboeken tot 1876. Utrecht. 1881.

HERINGA, DR A. Free Trade and Protection in Holland. London. 1914.

LOHMAN, A.F. DE SAVORNIN. Onze Constitutie. Utrecht. 1907.

MARIUS, G. HERMINE. Dutch painting in the 19th century. (Trans. by De Mattos.) London. 1908.

NIPPOLD, F. Die Römische Katholische Kirche im Königreich der Niederlände. Leipzig. 1877.

Painting, Modern Dutch. Edinburgh Review. July, 1909.

ROBERTSON SCOTT, J.W. War-time and Peace in Holland. London. 1914.

ROOT, E.W. DE. Geschiedenis van den Nederlandsche Handel. Amsterdam. 1856.

SECKENGA, F.W. Geschiedenis der Nederlandsche Belastingen sedert 1810. The Hague. 1883.

VERSCHAVE, P. La Hollande politique. The Hague. 1910.

THE NETHERLANDS, *about* 1550


[Note: The Map is not available]
THE NETHERLANDS *after* 1648

# BIBLIOBAZAAR

## The essential book market!

Did you know that you can get any of our titles in large print?

Did you know that we have an ever-growing collection of books in many languages?

**Order online:**
www.bibliobazaar.com

Find all of your favorite classic books!

Stay up to date with the latest government reports!

At BiblioBazaar, we aim to make knowledge more accessible by making thousands of titles available to you- *quickly and affordably*.

Contact us:
BiblioBazaar
PO Box 21206
Charleston, SC 29413